To Steve, 11th February 2016, with many thanks and every Best Wish.

# A STORM OF RAVENS

## Richard de Methley

**Fourth Impression: April 2015**

**www.richarddemethley.co.uk**

Copyright © Richard de Methley
Richard de Methley has asserted his right under the Copyright, Designs and Patents Act 1988 to be identified as the author of this book.
A CIP record for this book is available from the British Library.
**ISBN: 978-0-9557480-7-3**
Cover design by Ingrid Freeman: **ingridfreeman@me.com**
Prepared and Printed by:
4edge Limited, Hockley, Essex.

# Dedication

*T*his book is dedicated to all those who have helped put it together, not least to Michael and Rosie Craig…and to my dearest love, Diana Mary Stirling. Michael, who has worked with enormous skill and goodwill on the new covers and has advised stalwartly on presentation; Rosie, for her unbounded enthusiasm for the project, her critical eye, her sharp intellect and her editorial skills…and Diana for putting up with me, especially when it was not going well, or the damned computer 'stole' vital bits! Outstanding…and gleaming, all of them!

Especial thanks go also to Diana Lyne-Pirkis who helped create the original story-board when it was known as *Sica*, and typed every word of the manuscript from which *A Storm of Ravens* has finally flown free.

Thank you all *so* much.

Richard de Methley:

September 30th 2014

# OTHER BOOKS BY RICHARD DE METHLEY

### THE WHITE ROSE SERIES, a Medieval tale of love, murder, treachery and adventure in the days of Richard Lionheart.

THE LION AND THE WHITE ROSE

THE WHITE ROSE AND THE LADY

THE WHITE ROSE BETRAYED

THE LION AND THE WHITE ROSE TRIUMPHANT

All these books are viewable, and purchasable, from my website, which I hope you will visit: **www.richarddemethely.co.uk.** You can pay by PayPal, or directly to me through the website. Just follow the instructions. R de M.

# Historical Note

The period of Alfred's wars against the Danes in the ninth century was surely the most important time in our early history, for without Alfred, 'England' could never have happened. At the time this story starts, the Danes had seized all of Saxon Britain except Wessex. 'England', as a real entity, still did not exist, it was only a dream in Alfred's eye...and to make it real he had first to defeat the Danes, and then rebuild everything they had destroyed. In January 878, driven into the wilderness with his family, that looked even more impossible than it had done when he'd become king seven years before.

This is, essentially, a love story, the tale of a young noblewoman, the Lady Brioni of Foxley, near Malmesbury, who got caught up in that terrible struggle. Whose life is smashed apart, and then rebuilt with the man she falls in love with. It tells of the outright brutality of the enemies who destroyed her home and family, of the horrors that she and her friends witnessed, and how she set out to be revenged on her enemies with the help of Leofric Iron Hand. A dispossessed Saxon Thane she meets with in the forests near her shattered home. It is also a tale of how the Saxon people of Wessex, rich and poor alike, despite the crippling odds, stood by their king in his time of direst need.

But not all did. Many Saxon leaders gave in and paid tribute to Guthrum, the Danish king. Many fled overseas, taking their families with them, and one of them, notably Wulfhere, the Ealdorman of Wiltshire, the one man responsible for the defence of that whole county, colluded with the enemy. He betrayed Wessex to such an extent that Guthrum's astonishing thrust to seize Alfred in Chippenham, in the worst winter for years, very nearly succeeded: The Anglo Saxon Chronicle (ASC)...**878**: *"...In this year the host went secretly in midwinter after twelfth night to Chippenham, and rode over Wessex and occupied it, and drove a greater part of the inhabitants oversea, and reduced the greater part of the rest, except Alfred the King; and he with a small company moved under difficulties through the woods and into inaccessible places in the marshes..."* Luck, and careful planning, alone defeated Guthrum at that desperate time, and Alfred escaped.

Alfred, his wife Ealhswitha and her daughter Aelfthryth, and the events surrounding them, are all real. So is the Danish King, Guthrum; as is Aethelwold, Alfred's nephew, who proved himself to be a nasty, treacherous piece of work. And my chief villain, the warlord Oscytel, the Black Jarl of Helsing, is also real.

The ASC says this:  **875**: *"...In this year went the host from Repton, and Halfdan went with a part of the host to Northumbria, and took winter quarters on the river Tyne; and the host overran that land...and Guthrum, **Oscytel** and Anund, the three Kings, went from Repton to Cambridge with a great host and remained there a year..."*

The Jomsvikings are part legendary, and were fiercely pagan but really active a hundred years after Guthrum assaulted Chippenham.  That attack, at dawn on January 6[th,] 878, was planned to result in the capture, or death, of the Anglo Saxon King.  But as the Danes burst in through the defences, across the river bridge...so Alfred and his family escaped out the back of the town into the bitter wilderness beyond, and then vanished southwards to the Somerset marshes.  To this day no-one really knows how he got out.  But my story tells of how that might have happened, and how the King lay low for a while on the island of Athelney, turned the place into a fortress and then sallied out and attacked the Danes wherever he could find them.

The ASC says:*...**878**: *"...And the Easter after, King Alfred, with a small company built a fortress at Athelney, and from that fortification, with the men of Somerset nearest to it, he continued fighting against the host..."*...  His biographer, Bishop Asser, writing ten years later, says: *"...In the same year, after Easter [23rd March], King Alfred, with a few men, made a fortress at a place called Athelney, and from it with the thegns of Somerset [and his household troops] he struck out tirelessly against the Vikings..."*  Brave, loyal Saxon warriors who risked their lives to keep faith with their King, attacked the Danish garrisons wherever they could be found, and in desperate hit and run raids degraded and infuriated the enemy.  They so kept the flame of freedom burning all through the early months and spring of that terrible year, that when the muster was called at Ecberht's Stone after Easter, Wessex did not fail its King...but that is a story for the next book in this series.

But that is what Leofric and Brioni were doing from Ford, a tiny settlement five miles from Chippenham, supporting Alfred's struggle for freedom.  Helped by all their men, and by Hugo the Bearmaster, Maritia, Godric the Cobbler and Grimnir Grimmersson the Skald...and by Heardred, with Alfred, on Athelney itself, they strove to keep faith with their King.

All those are my invention, but a vibrant resistance movement surely operated all across Wessex without which Alfred could never have raised an army to fight Guthrum later that spring.  That is the basis of my story.

So...the history is real, and so are the places for which, for the sake of ease and comfort, I have used the names by which they are known today, not their Saxon ones.

The Fosseway, built by the legions, ran from Lincoln to Exeter, and was still a useable highway in Alfred's day, though very battered and without its original stone surface. And Foxley, just outside Malmesbury which Brioni, Trausti and their men so successfully assaulted, can be visited. Though I have moved the manor from where it is today to a fine spa hotel close by, called Whatley Manor, that gives excellent cream teas and commanding views over the Avon which rushes past its feet. Here is where I have placed Wulfstan's hall where Brioni grew up. The bridge that crossed the river between the manor and the village was only recently swept away, but where the great ditches and earth-banks would have been, with their palisade, can clearly be seen, along with the gateway that Oscytel would have assaulted with his army that awful January morning.

In the story I have referred often to Ealhswitha as being 'Queen' of Wessex. But, in Alfred's day, there were no 'queens'. There had been, and Judith, his step-mother, was certainly known as 'Queen of Wessex'…and there were queens afterwards. But, forty years before Alfred was born, there had been an infamous queen of Wessex, Queen Eadburgh, daughter of King Offa of Mercia, who built the dyke. She behaved outrageously and poisoned her husband, King Beorhtric, before fleeing to France. She died penniless many years later in Pavia. So after that it was decided that the King's wife would just be known as 'The Lady of Wessex', not the queen. But I wanted a 'queen' in my story, so have given Ealhswitha that title.

We know absolutely nothing about her. Bishop Asser, Alfred's biographer, makes no mention of her in his 'Life of Alfred', and she is not mentioned in the ASC, nor any of Alfred's charters, only in his will where she was given estates at Lambourn, Wantage and Edington. But the marriage appears to have worked, and I have done my best to honour her with a fine personality and a warm spirit of love and affection for those around her.

Old Chippenham, where the river curls round on three sides, is much as Alfred left it. Up a short, steepish hill from the river his hall is on the right, now an excellent museum, exactly where he would have expected to find it, with the church almost opposite. Stand there and you can easily imagine the huddled buildings below you ringed by Chippenham's great earthen defences. The bridge is where it always has been, and how Alfred got out in one piece, with his family, is still amazing.

At Ford, below Biddestone, just a few miles from Chippenham is a wonderful hostelry called the White Hart which offers a warm welcome and a vibrant menu. Here is where Leofric and Brioni made their home for those few weeks when they were making such war against Guthrum and Oscytel's forces. In their day there was no bridge, but you can stand in the middle of that today

7

and imagine Brioni and Eadberht crossing the ford that lay below it to take the road to Slaughterford…while Gytha, and her escort took the other road to Biddestone and her fateful meeting with Godric the Cobbler.

Apples. I have had a dreadful problem with apples. You would have thought that apples and cider would have been common in Saxon England. Not so. The Romans had eating and cooking apples. The legions brought them with them. But apple trees need constant care, and if neglected for long enough will die away…so by the time you reach Alfred, four hundred years after the Eagles left these islands, there appear to have been no 'real' apples. Just crab apples. In fact apple trees were so special that they are mentioned as landmarks, and boundary markers, and only one orchard is noted in Domesday Book…which comes twenty years after Hastings. So apples and cider, as we know them, appear not to have reached Saxon Britain until the Norman Conquest, and the oldest cultivated apple in England, a variety known as *pearmain*, was only recorded in 1204. But I needed apples and cider in my story, so I have put them in…definite artistic licence!

And there were no fir trees in Alfred's Wessex. Only the Scots pine existed in Britain, and that largely north of the border as its name shows. All the pine trees we know so well today did not exist, nor did the horse chestnut. Saxon children, as well as not being able to crunch sweet apples, could not play conkers either! All pine wood for ships and building came from Scandinavia.

The Vikings themselves were a very real fact of life; brutal, terrifying and every bit as violent as I have shown them. They may have been great farmers and traders and good husbands…but they were also fearsome warriors, dedicated to Odin, whose only wish was to die in battle with a sword or axe in their hands. Ragnar, Halfdan, Ubbi and Ivar the Boneless were all real people. Ragnar was murdered in a snake pit in Northumbria by King Aelle…and Ivar did carve the Blood Eagle out of that king's living body. It is a real torture, not an invention of our Victorian ancestors, nor of Hollywood. Later Ivar also arranged the murder of King Edmund of East Anglia by tying him to a tree and shooting him to death with arrows…and that made the poor man into a saint.

Do not listen to the revisionists. The Vikings were not good people, nor were they trustworthy. They tore Saxon Britain apart in an orgy of killing and pillage. The damage they did was horrendous, and they destroyed almost all learning. Alfred writes in his Preface to his translation of Pope Gregory's 'Pastoral Care'…*"There were so few men of learning that I cannot recall even one of them south of the Thames when I succeeded to the kingdom."* And he himself could not read or write before he was twelve.

The great Iron Age fortress of Battlesbury Rings near Warminster is also very real and quite awesome, with its huge banks and ditches and long chariot ramp up to the main entrance. It is well worth a visit. Remarkably no cisterns or wells have ever been found in any of the hill fortresses that the ancients built, so the cisterns that Leofric and his men found up there are very much my invention, and there is no record of Battlesbury having been re-occupied before the great Battle of Edington. But I needed to give Leofric and his men a safe refuge, and Battlesbury, towering above the river Wylie, made an ideal choice.

So, the days of Leofric Iron Hand and of Brioni of Foxley, of Heardred, Alfred, Guthrum and the Danes were full of danger and excitement, battle, death and terror. Mine is a story of survival and bloody revenge; of valour, loyalty and battle…and of hope, belief and earthly love.

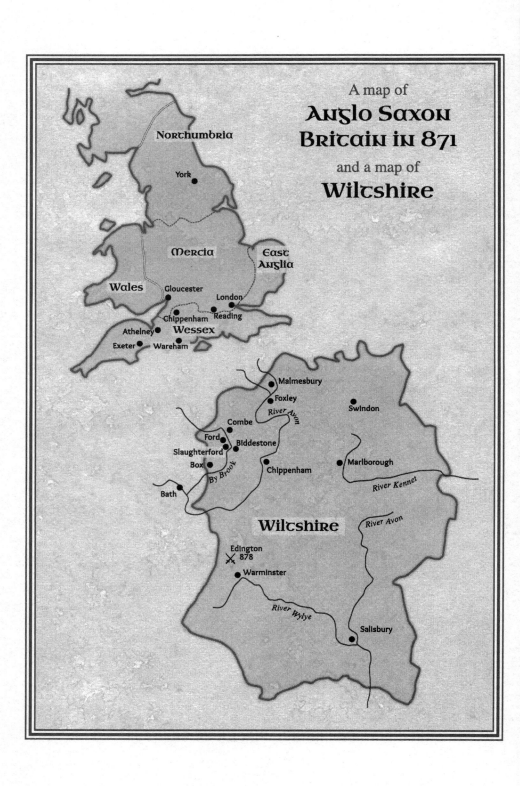

A map of
**Aɴglo Saxoɴ
Briꞇaiɴ iɴ 871**
and a map of
**Wilꞇshire**

Northumbria

York

Mercia

East
Anglia

Wales

Gloucester

London

Chippenham        Reading

Athelney        **Wessex**

Exeter        Wareham

Malmesbury

Foxley

River Avon

Swindon

Combe

Ford

Biddestone

Slaughterford

Box

Chippenham

Marlborough

River Kennet

Bath

By Brook

**Wilꞇshire**

River Avon

Edington
✕ 878

Warminster

River Wylye

Salisbury

# GLOSSARY

| | |
|---|---|
| Aidan | One of the greatest of Saxon saints, who brought Christianity back to the North of England. |
| Cuthbert | Another great Saxon saint, and much loved in his day. |
| Bothy | A small house, often with a turf roof. |
| Byrnie | Chain mail jacket, riveted iron links, or scales, stitched on leather. Worn by both sides and very expensive. |
| Churl | Peasant farmer with village rights, and land to farm. |
| Cruck House | A house with a wooden frame, like an upside down boat. |
| Ealdorman | One of the most powerful noblemen in the kingdom. Ruled over whole counties. Our word 'Earl' comes directly from it. |
| Fyrd/Fyrdsmen | The largely untrained Saxon peasant army of England. All males, fourteen years and over, could be expected to serve in the fyrd. |
| Gebur | A farm labourer without land, but rights of common. |
| Halidom | The sacred relics, often in beautiful golden caskets, and the altar vessels and ornaments, held by a Saxon Lord. |
| Huscarles | Highly trained and well equipped professional fighting men who took oaths of their lord to fight to the death. |
| Knarr | A Viking cargo ship, wider and slower than a warship. |
| Moot | A meeting for discussion and decisions on all aspects of life. |
| Odin | The Viking king of the gods, closely associated with ravens, the Viking bird of war and death. |
| Rhynes | Narrow waterways within the Somerset marshlands around Athelney |
| Seaxe | The long-bladed stabbing knife that defined the Saxon warrior, not unlike the old Roman gladius but with a finer blade. |
| Sommerseatas | The people of Somerset. |
| Swithun | St Swithun. Still remembered today. 15th July. If it rains on St Swithun's day it will rain for forty days! |
| Thane/Thegn | A lord. The Saxon equivalent of the Norman knight. |
| Thrall | The meanest form of Saxon society…other than slaves. |
| Twelfth Night | Epiphany, January 6th; then and now. |
| Witan | The Council of wise men who advised the king…all the most important men in the land, including all leading churchmen. |
| Wolfsheads | Outlaws |
| Yule | Originally the pagan equivalent of Christmas. |

# Winter, 877: Wessex, the ravaged lands of King Alfred.

## Chapter One

All afternoon the wind had blown sharply from the north-east out of a leaden sky, moaning through the empty woods that cloaked the sterile land, the sun only a memory after weeks of driving snow and a searing frost, so hard, that lakes stood thickly frozen and small birds dropped dead in flight.

A group of armoured riders, shields on their backs, swords and axes by their sides, many with spears in hand, forced their way through wind-blown drifts, the frost-spume burning their faces as they rushed by. In the frigid air their horses steamed as they thrust for the dense woodlands up ahead. Ice rimmed the furs that wrapped each warrior's face, silver agonies of breath swift frozen by their passage, the wind bitter, with teeth of glass, while the iron hooves of their horses pounded the empty trackway that wound amongst the trees.

It was five days past Christmas and all Wessex lay gripped fast in winter's iron hand. In the stark forestland that surrounded them, the trees stood like naked sentinels, their bark black and sheened with ice. Only the rose hips and scarlet berries of sharp leaved holly, shining like drops of blood, gave colour in all that bleak wilderness. The rutted ground was frozen, solid, and ice floated on the swirling dark waters of even the greatest rivers in the land; the smaller ones silent, their constant chatter stilled by ice.

Behind them the sky was deepening still further.

The clouds, heaped up like dark mountains, loured overhead, rolling down upon them like an avalanche, the steel-grey light turning ochre as a fresh snow storm swept down upon the deserted lands that lay around them. Even as they breasted the final rise that would lead them into great stands of elm and oak, amidst broad thickets of beech and holly, the wind was already beginning to back and gather itself for one more fierce assault.

To the small party toiling through that frozen wilderness, the approaching storm was all the spur they needed to press forward hard. Heads down, their thick wolf-skin cloaks drawn closely round them, they pushed their shaggy beasts with all the force they dared along the ancient trackway that led from the royal manor of Chippenham to the ancient village of Foxley, near Malmesbury town. There stood Thane Wulfstan's palisaded hall above the river Avon, a bare half mile beyond the vill, that swiftly flowed along its southern boundary; for he was their Lord...and they were sworn to carry out his will.

All but one were armed and fully geared for war, with tough iron byrnies of ringed mail on stout leather, heavy round shields slung across their shoulders, iron rimmed and leather covered, their legs cross-gartered, and heavy boots with steel insteps on their feet. And despite the difficulties of the ground that they were crossing, they rode closed up around the slight, fur-wrapped figure in their centre. For these were troubled times and no-one moved abroad except in armoured groups for fear of Viking pirates on some sudden wild attack.

For all the lands around them were held by heathen Danes; those bloody ravens, blown across the North Sea in their dragon boats years before, who had attacked England and were determined on murder, rape and conquest. And mighty had been the fighting; raging, fierce and bloody.

Nine battles in one year alone, the year of battles, the year Alfred had become King...and three bitter sieges. At Reading first in '71, then Wareham in '75 and last at Exeter, less than one year before, from where the raven Danes, that very autumn, had settled in Mercian Gloucester around Guthrum their king. They had promised peace...but were really just biding their time before storming into Wessex once again. Now, in these short days after Christmas, to move across the land required speed and courage, and none but the hardiest were like to try.

In fact they were eight of their Lord's most trusted war-companions, veterans who had fought beside their war-lord, and their king. Men who had been with the Saxon army when it had gone up against the Danish palisade at Wareham two summers back, and made a simple truce which the heathen men had broken, murdering their hostages and slipping, like dappled adders, to Exeter where King Alfred fiercely had pursued them.

So a new treaty had been made, oaths sworn on the golden arm-rings of the Danish King, Guthrum, and on their pagan gods, to leave Wessex never to return. And they had given up hostages, and gone that autumn to Gloucester in ruined Mercia, and there had settled, watched by Alfred's forces to ensure they kept their word.

Today these Saxon warriors of their lord were led by Osric, skilled in war and the best swordsman of all their lord's hearth-companions. Tall and wiry, he had joined Thane Wulfstan's war-band when his own home had been destroyed, and since had proved his worth. He too had been at Exeter and, like his noble master, had fought beside the King.

Ah...there was a wise one and no mistake, despite his twenty eight years!

The Heathen were beginning to rue the day that ever they had set their feet on Wessex soil. By God's Grace they might yet be rid of the whole pagan lot of them! Let them pillage wretched Mercia, or the ravaged lands of Northumbria, or the miserable East Angles, those that were left alive...anywhere rather than the rich, fat lands of Wessex; though God knew there was not much else to plunder in all Albion. With pirate raiders hovering on their borders, and lurking off their shores in their dragon boats and knarrs, there was always the danger of some sudden fierce attack; and Guthrum their king, cunning and treacherous as ever, would be seeking his revenge for their defeat. The loss of Wareham rankled and treaties like that at Exeter could always be broken if the gods demanded it...and no heathen pirate was to be trusted further than a West Saxon could see him.

So that winter many of the King's good men and true stood guard round Gloucester.

*

Still, it was Christmas time, and though the Heathen did not keep the feast-days of the Christ Child, they had their Yuletide celebrations just the same, and a drunken pirate was no different to a drunken fyrdsman when it came to a killing.

Come Twelfth Night, and Guthrum's army would be in no better case than Alfred's, and weather this awful would surely keep everyone pinned down, probably for weeks the way that things were looking. No-one would consider campaigning in such terrible conditions. From where would the food come to sustain a combat army on the move when all around was frozen? Or fodder for the horses on a winter march? Spring would be the time of greatest danger, when armies could move freely and the sea-lanes were re-opened to Viking reinforcements. Deep winter was the time for wassail and feasting, and harping round the hearth-fire, when the flames leapt high and the mead and beer jugs went round; when the songs of kings and heroes were shouted loud, the girls were at their prettiest and the men prepared to hunt boar and deer in the forests with horn and hound...not heathen Danes!

Osric, chuckling to himself at the thought of pirates struggling through the snow, turned in his saddle to look over his small command and check that their precious charge was still in good heart despite the awful weather, before

14

casting his eyes around the darkening countryside, more desolate and threatening with every stride their horses took.

There were still a fair few miles to cover before they reached the safety of Thane Wulfstan's hall above the Avon river at Foxley, and already the first frosted flakes were beginning to fly. He was becoming seriously alarmed for the safe completion of his mission. Just one horse to go lame now, or a rider to have a bad fall and they would find themselves in trouble, for the deeply rutted ground was iron-hard after weeks of the most bitter frost in years. Yet if they slackened pace, and the coming storm caught them, particularly when they were crossing some of the wilder, more desolate heaths and moorlands still ahead...they might all be dead by morning! The frost was now so hard and bitter, not even the steaming, gutted bellies of their horses would keep the cold out of their bodies.

He shuddered.

It might be better to walk now for a while, once they had reached the trees, and let the beasts get their second wind, than find their horses failing just when they might need them most. With the heathen men locked tight in Gloucester, as far as all men knew, they should be safe enough; but with such a precious charge placed on him by his thane, and by his Lord King, and a fierce storm now close upon them, Osric was loath to order any slackening of the pace.

*

*T*hey had been sent by their Lord Wulfstan, Thane of Foxley, and close to the King's grace, to Alfred's hall at Chippenham to escort his only daughter, the Lady Brioni, home for the after-Christmas feasting...and for her betrothal. With the whole royal court come up from Winchester for the festivities, and for the hunting in the vast forest that almost surrounded the town, the Queen, Ealhswitha, had given permission for the youngest, and most favoured, of her handmaidens to go to her father's manor for the remainder of the festival. There to enjoy the love of her family at Christmas, and for her betrothal to the Lord Heardred of the Sommerseatas...and the King himself had come to see them safely off.

"Give my good wishes to that great bear of a man, your father, young Brioni, and to your Lady mother also," Alfred had said while standing by her horse's head in the wide square before his hall. "I've missed his rugged common sense and good humour these past few months. Tell him I shall look for his banner of the fox's head come the spring muster."

15

Then, turning to her escort leader he had said: "Guard this little lady well, Osric, for she is quite the Queen's favourite, and also mine!" Adding with a smile: "Still, you should be quite safe enough here in our heartland. That pirate, Guthrum, is locked-in at Gloucester, and my scouts report no movement from either him or his followers. He gave his word on his own sacred arm ring, and has shown no sign of breaking it. But there is the smell of snow in the air, and the hard scent of ice in its wings, so do not linger on the journey. The days are even shorter now, and if a storm comes up you could find yourselves in trouble. So clap to your spurs and keep your horses moving." Then, turning to Brioni, he said: "You, my Lady Brioni, we will see again after Twelfth Night after your hand fasting with your new betrothed, the Lord Heardred, and all his men. 'Til then, God speed and our love go with you."

And with that he had stepped back, a slender figure, not heavily built like his hearth-companions, but with strong shoulders from wielding a sword since boyhood, and fine hands with long fingers. He had a curling blond beard and thick locks to his shoulders, piercing blue eyes and a firm mouth; his face was marked with pain that he carried with him always from a griping bowel that could strike him down overnight, but lightened with a swift smile and ringing laugh to warm the coldest heart.

Close-by, Queen Ealhswitha was also standing, muffled to the eyes in thick furs. Slender like her husband, despite giving birth just months before, she stood straight as a spear, but with a mother's heart for all who needed her. Brave in the face of adversity and firm with her hand-maidens and her children, she ran the King's household with skill and foresight. She was a true Queen of Wessex and all men treated her with kindness and respect.

Now she stood beside the King to wave young Brioni on her way, fearful for the girl's safety but trusting in her escort to guard her well. She would miss the child's laughter and her cheerful willingness to serve, looking forward to when she would be returned to her royal care, laughing with her husband. With raised fists and a final shout, Osric and his men clapped heels to their mounts, and in a spray of snow and slushy ice, sped towards the great gates that guarded Royal Chippenham from any wild attack.

Down the hill on which the town was built they went, past the banked defences topped with their palisades they clattered; through the heavy wooden gates that guarded the entrance to the little town, rattling over the river bridge beyond…and then through the ramshackle buildings that made up Chippenham beyond the walls, past the Stag inn and away north to Foxley along the frozen trackway, taking the Lady Brioni home for Yuletide and her betrothal.

# Chapter Two

At eighteen she had blossomed into a true Saxon beauty, long-legged, slim and richly curved, with thick golden hair that at normal times hung in two great plaits below her shoulders. Today, braided with ribbons of scarlet and blue they were coiled on either side of her head beneath a simple wimple of white sarsenet beaded with pearls, a gift from the Queen herself, the whole ensemble held in place with golden pins and a broad fillet of red Irish gold.

Her eyes were the colour of the sky in high summer, her teeth were white and even and she had a warm, attractive voice that matched her bubbling laughter. Yet despite her fresh complexion and generous ways, she had a clear-thinking, practical mind that belied her age, and the Queen had come to rely on her greatly, especially since the birth of her daughter, Aelfthryth, a few months earlier. Much Brioni had learned from her lady mother, the Lady Aethelflaeda, a woman of shrewd wit and gentle warm affection...yet could be as fiery as her Lord Wulfstan whenever the occasion demanded it. And at those times she had a tongue that could flay the skin from the toughest hide of her husband's shield-companions, sending the luckless warrior scurrying for cover amidst the ribald laughter and comments of his fellows.

Heavily wrapped in a fleece-lined fur of red fox and marten, Brioni rode her barrel-chested mount with strength and determination, her supple body moving easily to the hurrying beat of his iron hooves. This was the last Christmas she would have on her own with her parents and her tall warrior brother Gyrth, for by summer she would be married with a household of her own to manage, late at eighteen, but soon enough for her. Now she meant to visit every one of the haunts she had known as a little girl, to greet her friends and say farewell to her youth.

After the rigours and sophistication of Court life, the endless incense, prayers and priests of Alfred's entourage, the homely clutter and rattle of her father's hearth, with its rustic fare and simple tales of ancient heroes, would be a breath of fresh air. And with a bright chuckle at the knowledge of the welcome they would all be sure to give her, she dug in her heels to drive her shaggy beast forwards.

Now their horses were visibly tiring as they were forced along the track, and she was just beginning to wonder whether she really would have the strength to carry on much longer, when they reached the tree-line they had been striving for. And as they passed the first outriders of the forest, the sharp green

17

boughs of juniper and yew weighed down with snow, Osric suddenly turned in his saddle, thrust up his hand and with a great bellow that reached right to the farthest man, brought them all to a stumbling walk, reining-in his own sturdy beast to a snorting stand, pulling it off the trackway as he did so.

With a sigh of relief Brioni sank back in her saddle, allowing her tired horse to amble forward to where Osric was waiting some fifty paces further up the track.

"How are you faring, my Lady?" he called out as he watched Brioni's weary gelding stumble over the rutted, frozen ground; while she held him up expertly and bent forward over his withers to pat his neck in encouragement.

"I'm alright, Osric," she replied with a grimace as she reached him. "You get used to all this when you travel with the king. But this little fellow is almost at the end of his strength. The wind and the cold are sapping him. How much farther by your reckoning? This stretch of road is unknown to me, and my bones are aching with the cold."

Osric, who had been waiting for Brioni to fall in beside him, now turned his horse back onto the track and urged him on to lengthen his walking stride, anxious that he should not stiffen-up in the intense cold after such a hard earlier passage, but talking all the while as he did so.

"We left the old road some miles back. It was swept away in last winter's floods, but we rejoin it by the old blasted oak at the edge of your father's lands. About four leagues farther on, and from there we should be alright, for that's not more than a half hour's ride from Foxley.

"Why have we been pushing on so hard then, Osric? We should be safely home within two hours!"

"You're forgetting the wide open stretch across Kington Heath. If we get caught in a blizzard while going across that, and we may, then we may never get you home at all. These few flakes are just the beginning. Look behind you, my Lady. There is a great storm coming. These trees around us will end soon, and then there will be no shelter until we reach the blasted oak. Within the half hour you won't be able to see fifty paces…less time even than that probably. But if we can make the oak we will be alright. There we will find shelter, relief horses and riders and hot wine from hay-boxes. Your mother arranged all that with me before we left yesterday. Your father was concerned about the weather."

She smiled at her father's forethought. He always had been weather-wise; took after the old Thane Foxley, her grandfather.

"Will he be there to greet us, Osric?"

"No, my Lady. He's been bidden to stay at home by your mother. He has been coughing badly again this winter, and rage as he might, she wouldn't

18

let him go. She didn't want him to ruin your last stay at home with us through illness; especially as the Lord Heardred will be coming in on Twelfth Night to celebrate your betrothal. And anyway," he added with a pause and smile, "there are others to do that service for him!"

Brioni looked quizzically at him for a moment, as try as he might he could not keep the twinkle from his eyes, and with a sudden '*whoop!*' that made her horse dance, her face suddenly lit up. "You mean my brother, Gyrth, is home already? I had not expected to see him back so soon."

"Yes, my Lady," Osric replied, now smiling broadly. "He came from keeping the watch-guard around Gloucester just three days ago. A 'present from the king', he called it. Your Lady Mother was delighted."

"Did he come alone?"

"No…he brought his whole war-band with him!"

"All of them?" she asked aghast.

"Yes, my Lady, and a great store of supplies. And a real pleasure it is to see so many warriors around the hearth-place in these dangerous times. He even brought his own harper with him!"

Brioni smiled at that for she knew that Osric had yearned to go with her brother when he had left last spring, but had stayed at Foxley for her father's sake. He was the Thane's right-hand man, and 'though he might have liked to have gone flying after the young Lord's heels, he knew where his loyalty lay. But so many extra mouths to feed, and so late in the year, despite the extra supplies, would be a severe burden on the vill's resources…especially with the Lord Heardred expected in January for their hand-clasping. And moving closer to her escort leader so that it was easier to talk over the wind's scouring whine, she asked him how their food supplies were holding up, especially now with her brother's whole war-band to support, as well as her father's men and all the household servants.

"Well enough, my Lady. In fact, better than might be expected." Then, after turning once more to check that his men were still following them closely he added, grinning hugely: "The meal arcs are still well-filled throughout the vill, and we have had plenty of hunting parties!"

"The boar from Helm's Wood?" she asked eagerly, brushing the snow-dust away from her mouth.

"Yes! And deer and partridge too, even the odd pheasant!" The old warrior replied with a quick glance. "We've not eaten so well since the autumn slaughter!"

Brioni looked across at him and smiled.

The autumn slaughter was the time of greatest plenty in the whole year, when there was more fresh meat than most men could handle. Then did the ground run red with blood as the beasts were throat-cut, hacked apart and jointed ready for the salting barrels; hauled up amongst the rafters of the hall-place for smoking or cut into strips for drying in preparation for the winter. Then the hearth-fire would be banked high and the beer and ale casks dragged in for the feasting that always followed, with mead for the high table. For this was Harvest Home, when a whole ox was roasted on a massive spit and the villagers would pour in for food and wassail. When the hall-harp would go round from man to man, and the pipes and drums and tabors would play for the dancing that would go on until everyone dropped, ale-shot or simply too exhausted to put one more foot before another.

Peering through the thickening snowflakes now whirling at them ahead of the storm, at the harsh, bleak wilderness around her, she could wish herself at home right now, her travel clothes set aside to dry, and crab apples, cored and freshly baked with hazel nuts and spices, swimming in hot melted honey, sizzling merrily before her with thick fresh cream to go with them. It was a warm thought to relish as the fresh storm wind began once more to explore her face with cutting, brisk efficiency.

\*

All this time they had been slowly approaching the edge of Kington Heath, a huge open area of desolate wasteland many miles across that finally broke up into the thick woods that marked the boundary of her father's lands. As Osric had said, if the storm fell upon them in all its fury as they were crossing it, they could be swallowed up and lost in moments. As it was, the snow was already beginning to thicken up, the fine powdery dust of the few past minutes giving way to fat, white, goose-feather flakes that swirled wildly around their heads, filling the sky with every passing moment. Soon everyone had a fine white covering, and the trackway began to look like a smooth satin ribbon as it wound its way between the last silent black outposts of the ancient forest through which they had been travelling.

And so the storm fell upon them at last, the wind buffering around their heads, hammering at their mounts in gusts of wild fury, creating a sudden white-out through which, at times, it was almost impossible to see much beyond the tail of the nearest pony. Trees and bushes along the way, opaque shapes, ethereal in the frosted mist that now surrounded them, appeared and vanished again like wraiths, as the snow swooped and eddied in great waves about their heads.

But, with the horses more rested, and their riders desperate to move on, this was no place to stop, and Osric decided that the time had come to pick up the pace again, and signalling his men to close up around the Lady Brioni, he detailed one of them, a great swordsman named Rorsthan, to scout on ahead. Then, with a wave of his mittened hand, he dug in his heels and the whole party jingled out of the trees and onto the ribboned trackway that led across the heath, their horses snorting and shaking their heads against the swirling snow as it whirled about them, their riders hunched into their saddles, peering through slitted eyes as it whipped past their reddened faces.

\*

They had not been going for more than five or ten minutes when the scout whom Osric had sent ahead of them came dashing back in alarm. Instantly the whole troop came to a plunging halt with a slap and jingle of leather and stirrup irons, all the men edging their horses closer around Brioni as they pulled their shields round to cover their flanks, shook their swords free of their cloaks and steadied their stamping, snorting horses.

By the time Rorsthan reached the place they had halted with tossing manes beneath a small stand of beech and yew. Absolute silence had settled on them all, save for the wild curlew-cry of the wind through the trees and the sharp hissing sigh of the snow as it swirled in tossing chaos all around them.

"Riders, Osric! Just ahead of us!"

"How many?"

"About a dozen…maybe more. It's hard to see in this foul murk, with the snow falling so strongly."

"How far off?"

"Close…less than eighty paces from where we stand and riding hard. Bunched-up tight and travelling north-east across our path. Dear God! I might never have seen them if they hadn't broken the skyline just at that moment. A few minutes earlier and they must have seen me!"

"Ours…or theirs?" Brioni asked sharply, shivering beneath her cloak.

"What do you think, Rorsthan?" Osric questioned swiftly, turning to his man, his face reddened by the wind and driven snow.

"They were too far off to tell clearly in all this filth…but I'd say they must be Danes. There are none of the king's men hereabouts as far as I know, save our Thane's. Anyway," he added darkly, "this is weather for heathens not Christian men!"

"I didn't think there were any pirates in this area," one of his men queried. "This is Wessex heartland, and all Guthrum's men are safely gathered in at Gloucester, thirty miles away."

"Aye, Ulric. So we have been told…and being watched for movement too!" another replied with biting sarcasm.

"Be silent, all of you!" Osric snapped at them, his voice harsh against the wind. "Who can tell what the Heathen might get up to? Nor how good the watch has been; but the King, and the Witan, obviously feel that things are safe or he never would have brought his family to Chippenham with so small an escort."

"What now anyway, Osric?" Brioni asked urgently.

"We must move on again, my Lady," he shouted against the wind. "This weather is as bad as I can remember and we can't stay here. Rorsthan, get back up the track. Ulric, go with him. The rest of you close up tight around Lady Brioni and follow me, but slowly. They are cunning warriors, these men of the Great Army who follow the raven banner; so no noise and keep together."

With that they kicked their heels in again and moved off. But though they found the others' tracks, so much snow had fallen that they were almost obliterated and it was impossible to tell anything from them beyond that a fair body of mounted men had passed by riding hard.

Yet it was a dangerous hint that things were not as secure in Wessex as many had chosen to believe, including the king, and everyone remained tensely alert until they reached the distant tree-line. Here they were able to push forward to the small clearing where the old blasted oak stood proud amongst deep thickets of holly, beech and hazel. Here, secure in a hollow crowned thickly with yew and laurel, Brioni's brother waited with their relief as her father had ordered.

# Chapter Three

*I*n fact their arrival had been anxiously awaited for some time, and as the weather had worsened with the breaking of the storm, so Gyrth had sent a party of his own men, well-mounted on fresh horses, through the snow and up the rapidly disappearing track to look for them.

Now, as he stood watching his sister and Osric sipping at the hot drink his men had swiftly re-heated for them, he breathed a huge sigh of relief. Banging his hands together from beneath the rough tarpaulin they'd rigged off the side of the tilt cart they'd brought with them, he looked around his command, huddled for shelter around the cart and its busy fire, and peered through the whistling murk…for the flying snow and scurrying wind had not been their only problem.

\*

*T*hey had been steadily pushing up towards the little clearing where the old oak had been lightning-struck many summers back, when Aelric, one of his two leading scouts, had sent a man flying back to him with urgent news. Signalling his men to follow him as silently as possible, Gyrth, reins in hand, had trotted up beside his horse to where Aelric was standing motionless, shielding his body as best he could behind a massive elm tree that towered up into the bleakness of the weather, beside a steep slope just before him.

Here the track dipped and rose again, creating a sort of hollow, before dropping sharply down to where a second pathway crossed it just before the ford that marked the furthest western boundary of Thane Wulfstan's lands. Along this track, moving silently from right to left, thirty paces below the slope where they'd been standing, the head of a large column of cloaked and armoured riders was slowly pushing its way forward, faces muffled against the weather, with two outriders ahead of them already across the half-frozen black waters of the ford. In their black armour and masked helmets it only required one look to know who they were.

"*Danes!*" Aelric had whispered.

"Jomsvikings by their armour…axe-Danes, the sworn followers of Odin!"

"*Jomsvikings!*" he exclaimed, shocked. "What are such raiders doing here so far from Guthrum's main encampment?"

"I've no idea. But it cannot be good...Holy Cross! How have the King's watchers let this lot through their guard?" But it was Christmas, and he cursed the weather and the carelessness of those whose job it was to see no heathen men broke free without a warning.

"Do we leave them Lord? The peace is still in place!"

"No, Aelric! We cannot let them go any further along that way or they may bump straight into Osric and the others. I cannot risk my sister's life by allowing that to happen," he'd said, adding tersely: "We must attack them now and drive them off the track, no matter what. They are mercenaries violating the treaty anyway just by being here at all. They are muffled up to their eyeballs against this wind, and clearly not expecting an ambush. Carnfrith, take your men and head them off so you can take them from the front, like deer fleeing the beaters. We will assault them shortly, while they are still crossing the water. They'll never know what hit them!"

So then there had been a pause, while Carnfrith the Archer and three of his men moved swiftly away from them to the left, to head off the Danes below, two arrows each clenched between their teeth and another already drawn to their bows. Then, minutes later, leaping to his horse he had flung back his cloak, settled his shield firmly on his left arm and drawn his sword, the sound of hissing steel rippling around his command as those of his men not carrying spears had followed suit, and next moment he had led his warriors in a crashing, roaring charge. Down the slope they had rushed to fall like an avalanche of steel upon their unsuspecting enemies below, just as the first fine flurries of snow had begun to wheel about their heads.

Branches whipping at their faces, their horses fighting for a foothold on the frozen ground and shouting their war cries as they came, they dropped upon the Danes out of nowhere. Their cloaks billowing out behind them they were like winged demons from the Pit, and they laid about their enemies with spear and sword and iron hammer with all the hatred and venom at their command.

The fighting was visceral, and in those first vital moments, two Danes had been cut down before they had even managed to draw their swords. Terrific, scything blows that had sliced through their cloaks and mail like paper and split their hapless owners open in a spray of blood and mucus. Both horses had bolted, bearing their butchered riders with them, hanging from their saddles like broken marionettes whose strings have been cut through. The one man killed outright, the other screaming in agony before he fell off, his shoulder hanging from his body in bloody ruin.

But with the men of the Great Army the element of surprise could not last long, and though taken in the flank as if from nowhere, they had quickly re-grouped around their leader who had stood out as much by virtue of his glittering link-steel byrnie and his beautiful enamelled shield-boss, as by the loudly shouted orders he had given and the swift way in which his men had obeyed them.

With a single wave of his sword Gyrth, too, had rallied his men, grateful to see that he still had not lost one rider as he had drawn them all slightly back to await their enemy's swift response.

But it had not come!

Giving one loud, final yell their leader had taken off down the track, crashing through the shallow ford of half frozen water in a wild spray of ice and freezing slush, their horses jostling and bumping one another in their eagerness to get away…and without a word of command he and his men had followed him.

Down the rutted path and careering through the trees the heathen men had fled, into the very teeth of the storm that even then had rushed upon them. A raging wind, and wild blizzard, of snow and spicules of blasted ice; a desperate white-out that had closed around them, so that trees and bushes, men and horses, became indistinct, weird figures in the mist of flakes and ice-frost that now surrounded them. On around the first bend they had fled, and the next, until with a terrific crash the leading rider's horse had been felled to the ground. Legs flailing the air, blood spurting from its throat it had dropped as if poleaxed, as the first of Carnfrith's arrows, and those of his companions, had come whistling out of the storm. And as the whole enemy command had come to a rearing halt around it, so Carnfrith had shot down their leader with his second arrow, tearing out the man's throat with its iron barbs in a violent spray of blood, while his men took out the next two men who had run to offer him assistance. It was a howling chaos of fear and desperation as they had fought and struggled on the torn and bloody ground, thrusting into their enemies with spear and sword, gutting bellies and hacking into their bodies with rage and battle-fury, the stench of blood and faeces filling the bitter wind.

With the Danes unable to move and in plunging, stamping disorder, Gyrth and his small party had chopped and stabbed at them ferociously, their faces twisted with feral rage, wheeling and pirouetting on their horses as they flensed at their hemmed-in foes: swords ringing and clattering on steel and leather; shouts and cries and all the howling fury of close-quarter battle. Blood in great crimson gouts stained the snowy ground as their blades had sheared through flesh and tendons, bone and gristle, until finally their enemies had broken free again and without hesitation had driven their terrified beasts away from the track and into the very teeth of the storm, leaving three more of their number spread-eagled in death upon the torn trackway.

Tired and bloody, Gyrth's men had dragged the corpses back with ropes to where they had arranged to wait for Osric and his party. There they had stripped them of all their gear, stowing it in the tilt cart they had brought with them from Foxley. Then they had flung the stiffening naked bodies, wounds gaping, looped intestines hanging out, in a twisted heap upon the frozen ground, where fox and wolf could rend them.

Then had come an agonising wait while the snow fell harder and harder, hissing down, driven almost horizontal by the scything wind, while he and his small command had sheltered in the small clearing beneath thick stands of yew and holly, crouched over the fire they had built beneath the stout awning stretched out in the lee of the tilt cart.

*

"You're looking very pensive, brother mine?" Brioni said after a while, breaking into his reverie. "Where's the big welcome for your little sister? You've hardly said a word since we got here, but bundled us down this bank and thrust these warm horns into our hands almost before we have had a chance to breathe. There's a great pile of rank bodies over there, too. Danes, of that I am certain. And everyone seems taut and nervous!"

With a shake of his head, Gyrth turned and looked down at his sister, smiling broadly. Then, drawing both Brioni and Osric further out of the wind and flying snow, he told them what had happened.

"We've had a close brush with the old enemy while we were coming up here."

"How many, my Lord?" Osric asked quickly, stamping his feet as he sipped from a large horn of spiced wine from the covered cauldron that Gyrth's mother had sent out to them packed in a deep hay-box.

"A party of some twenty or so, I'd say at a rough guess…about a couple of hours ago possibly, maybe even less. We caught them just as they were crossing the stream lower down; coming along the lower trackway. I am not sure who were more surprised, us for finding a band of heathen pirates on the move where no pirates should have been, or they for being discovered!"

"A successful meeting, my Lord!" Osric replied, signalling towards the snow-covered bodies heaped up on the edge of the clearing.

"Yes! Very successful, as you can see," Gyrth replied. "At least we are still all in one piece, given a few cuts and bruises. And that's almost the most puzzling thing of all, for they showed no Viking spirit…no determination to kill us in return. Far more concerned with breaking clear than trying to fight it

26

out. It's so unlike them. Normally they fight like demons. We were lucky not to have lost half our number. Especially as from their war gear these were Jomsvikings, reputed to be the fiercest of them all!"

"*Jomsvikings!*" Osric exclaimed, shocked. "There is only one man in the whole Great Army who leads them…"

"Yes…Oscytel. The Black Jarl of Helsing, their most hellish leader, a named King of his people, and Guthrum's right-hand man. Now what were they doing out here on a day like this? And why not stay and fight?"

"Perhaps they are turning soft in their old age?" Brioni chipped in lightly. "You didn't manage to take any of them?"

"Bones of Aidan! No, they weren't that careless. And these were Jomsvikings! Paid killers who dedicate their lives to Odin; they slay their own wounded rather than leave them on a battlefield.

"We had a running skirmish with them for a short distance before we drove them off the track and finally lost them to the wilderness and the storm, tightly bunched together and going as fast as their beasts could carry them. But not before we had done for five of them with sword and spear, and Carnfrith and his men knocked over three more with their arrows. No survivors. The only one who might have been of use was throat-cut by Aelric before I could stop him."

"Information lost, you mean?" his sister queried sharply.

"You are shrewd, my little one."

"Comes from being around the King," she replied with a grin. "Alfred's always making the point that accurate information is vital if we are going to win this war. '*Knowledge is power*', Alfred says. '*One man's true voice is worth a whole company of the slain!*'

"Alfred is right of course, but I have never known a pirate to talk. It is part of their code never to do so."

"That's right, my Lord," Osric added. "Makes no difference what you do to them. They'll die before they break!"

"No matter," Gyrth replied, wiping his mouth as he lowered his horn. "The man had the mark of death on him anyway. His shoulder was hanging off his body and he was bleeding like a stuck pig. Too far gone along the swan's path to speak to anyone. Aelric's seaxe did the man a favour."

"What about their leader?" Brioni asked.

There was a pause then while her brother thought carefully, a look of intense concentration stilling his mobile features. It was a look that made his two companions glance curiously at one another.

"He was killed," Gyrth said at last, slowly. "His horse was shot out from under him as he rallied his men, and then he was throat shot before anyone

27

could help him. Drowned in his own blood. But I have seen him somewhere before. I am sure of it. There cannot be more than one of his kind so richly armed. His war-gear is the best I have seen amongst the heathen men for some time. And it is bothering me greatly, because I am sure it is important. I know about him…I am sure I do!"

"Why so much concern over one heathen pirate, Gyrth?" his sister chided him, cupping her long horn in her hand, as the snow whirled about them. "After all, one Viking is very much like another, and the best of all are those who are dead!"

"Because these are Jomsvikings. Because Oscytel is involved in all this somehow. This man was something special. Finest black link-steel byrnie, not iron; gold and silver inlays on his sword with a blade of Damascus steel and his great shield-boss rich with enamel. I have not seen its like since Exeter. This warrior was a man of power. One of their Jarls maybe?"

"And they left him?" Osric exclaimed in amazement. "Made no effort to recover him?" he continued, drawing in his breath sharply. "Their mission must have been desperate indeed, for usually they fight like the very hounds of Hell themselves over the bodies of their leaders. They hate to leave anyone of value behind."

"That's what bothers me so, Osric," Gyrth replied, drinking deeply. It is so unlike them to behave like that. And what were they doing out here anyway, so far from Gloucester? It is all of thirty miles or more…and in weather fit only for snow-bears."

"They must have been the same group we nearly bumped into as we approached the heath. If it hadn't been for this awful weather, and Rorsthan's quick reactions they must have seen us. As it was I was never so glad to see your men in my life!"

"Where were they headed?"

"North-west, Lord, and travelling fast. Across the old Fosse Way and then on to Gloucester I expect. With any luck they'll get lost in this white-out and freeze to death before they get there. The frost is bitter, this wind cuts like a knife, and the snow won't help any either. It'll be a very chilled band of heathen cut-throats if they ever make their palisade."

"Never mind them, Osric. What about me?" Brioni shouted at him above the wind, now rising again, as she stamped her feet up and down. "I am freezing to death here, despite my mother's spiced wine, and we've still a pace or two to go before we even reach the vill, let alone my father's hall. My feet are numb and my brain's not much better. Come on both of you. We can discuss all this with father when we get home. But unless we go now we'll

28

never reach Foxley before darkness falls...and then we really will be in trouble!"

Just at that moment one of Gyrth's men came across to say all was packed up again; the tarpaulin taken down, the fire doused and the tilt cart ready to move. Flinging his great arm around his sister's slight shoulders, Gyrth forced his way back up the bank and whisked her up onto a fresh horse. Then, with a great shout, he ordered his own escort to mount, each man leading a spare horse on a long rein. And so with two men moving ahead, and Osric and his party bringing up the rear, they all moved clear of the sparse shelter of the trees and out along the frozen trackway into a swirling white wilderness.

Within minutes there was little to show that anyone had been there, save for the few shapeless lumps that had been men. Their twisted limbs rapidly stiffening in the intense cold, they lay abandoned; just a single arm thrusting out from the white enveloping blanket, in mute appeal to the violent gods who had deserted them.

# Chapter Four

*I*n fact their journey took even longer than expected.
Twice they lost the path and had to back-track to find it again, for everything looked so different in the growing darkness and the drifts which had gathered around the trees and across the trackway in great smoking prows and dunes could not often be skirted. Forced then to push their weary mounts forwards in ungainly leaps and bounds, they struggled to forge a way through the deep snow, their horses scrabbling for purchase on the frozen ground beneath their iron feet.

So, by the time they reached the edge of the vill, they were all chilled to the marrow, wet and exhausted, horses and riders both. All more than pleased to see the horn lanterns swinging in the hands of those villagers, under his reeve, Wulfnoth, whom Thane Wulfstan had sent out to watch for their arrival.

Through the village and past the little church they had pushed their weary mounts, escorted by Wulfnoth and half a dozen of his men, across the half-mile or so that separated the village from the river, and the ancient steading above it where Thane Wulfstan's father had made his home, looking out across the countryside. Over the wooden bridge they clumped, now clouded with snow, the black waters beneath still flowing in the centre, the edges thick with ice, and on up the slope beyond it to the deep ditch, ramparts and stout gateway that guarded the southern entrance to Foxley Manor itself.

And so Brioni of Foxley came home at last, snow-dusted and weary, yet wreathed in smiles as her parents spilled out of the great house-place her grandfather had built to greet her. The warmth from within gusted out around them as her father whisked her off her feet to welcome her with bear hugs and rough kisses until her mother bore her off to change her clothes and pet her in her own special way, with Agatha, her tire-maiden and Brioni's abigail, in close and fluttering attendance.

So it was a bright and cheerful party that settled down that night around the long oaken table that stood on the top dais of the great hall, and round the trestles set up within it. All were dressed in their brightest clothes of wool and softest leather, Aethelflaeda and Brioni in long gowns stitched over with gold and silver thread with fur-lined collars; and all wore brightly embroidered fur lined cloaks in blue, saffron, green and scarlet around their shoulders, all to welcome Brioni and Gyrth home. This was not the great gathering there would be to mark the end of Yule, but a close family party with only her father's hearth companions and Gyrth's own war-band present.

The great feast of Yule-end would be a quite different affair.

Then all the villagers would crowd the place to the doors and the air would become thick with smoke and the heady fumes of ale, beer, mead and cider, carried in great casks on tough wooden stretchers to stand around the walls. The boar's head would be carried in to shouts and war horns and the cooking pits opened, that baked deer and hog's meat could be distributed to all who came there. And there would be fresh bannocks and honey cakes, spiced apples with raisins from Lady Aethelflaeda's special stores, and fresh clotted cream from her dairy. Then would the hall-harp go round for all the ancient lays and sagas; acrobats would do their turns, and to the wild music of pipes and horns and drums there would be dancing and merry-making until the dawn. There might even be a dancing bear stepping out to crumhorn and tabor. It would be such an evening that all would remember it for days and weeks afterwards.

But today it was just 'family'...all those who owed the Thane of Foxley special service and honour...and as the last scraps were swept off the tables onto the freshly strewn rushes on the floor for the dogs to gurn and worry over, so Brioni leaned back on her padded, high backed stool and stared up at the rafters. Soaring up into the blue haze of smoke from the great fire that blazed in the centre of the hall, the flames leaping and twisting in gold and scarlet splendour, they seemed like the very framework of her life.

Her family had lived at Foxley since the days of the great King Ine, a hundred and eighty years ago...a time so far away she could barely imagine it. He had been one of the greatest Kings of Wessex, pagan at first then baptised and helped Wessex to accept Christianity. Finally he had left his kingdom to die in Rome full of honour...unlike poor King Burghred of Mercia who had given up fighting the men of the Great Army and fled there, leaving his kingdom in ignominy, and his wretched people to the mercy of the Heathen.

They had promptly ravaged all for which they had not been paid ransom, or tribute, and then taken what they pleased from everyone else; murdering and pillaging at will and enslaving the people. She shivered, appalled...King or not, Burghred was 'Nithing!' No true Wessex man would ever do as he had done, let alone their king, and all Mercians were tainted by it.

This great building, with its massive beams and towering roof trees, had been built by her grandfather, Cenred the Strong. A mighty warrior, if even half the family stories were anything to go by, now long gone west of the sunset. He had filled the country with his by-blows; could drink the hardest headed warrior under the table; and chased every pretty girl he ever laid eyes on. His life had become a glorious scandal, even the bishop had failed to make

31

him mend his ways. He had lived a wild half-pagan life that had become a legend.

But, when the war-horns blew and the Saxon host assembled, then he'd become like Tiw and Thunnor, the old Saxon gods of war and thunder themselves. No man could stand against him, and wherever the fighting was hardest or most bloody...there would the great Thane of Foxley stand beneath his snarling fox-head banner, war-axe in hand, surrounded by his own stout hearth-companions, and the blood-boltered legions of the dead! He had been as true to his King as the Archangel Michael was to God Himself, and all men knew it.

The tales of his courage and loyalty were legion, and she felt a thrill of pride rush through her that she should have sprung from the line of such a strong and powerful man. And though he had been dead for years now, his spirit still lived on in her father, her brother Gyrth...and in herself.

She looked across at them both and smiled: her father, with his head thrown back in laughter, and his shoulders still straight despite his age, beneath his great cloak of brown bear skin he always wore in the winter time. Fair and wise with his people when they came together at the Moot Place and before his court, and wise and cunning in war. The fox-head symbol that he carried on his banner, and in two beautifully wrought brooches of thick gold with flashing garnets for eyes, and rich with enamel, that he always wore on his shoulders, said it all. It was the sign of their house, and he never went anywhere without them. A great bear of a man, even as the King had said, with a twinkle in his eye that her mother had always to beware of...and a fierce, raging temper that was worse than any storm at harvest time, but always swiftly over.

And then there was her brother, Gyrth.

Tall and straight, with long blond hair to his shoulders and a thick moustache to match, he was an even bigger man than her father, and he was not small. He had the strength of three men and treated her with gentle, heedless affection, much as he would any of the great hunting dogs of which he was so fond...and she adored him.

Still unmarried, despite the combined efforts of her mother and herself, he preferred the company of his fighting men and the rough pleasures of the chase to the more settled life of running a great estate, of giving dooms and attending the Shire Moot with their father.

He was not indifferent to women by any means, and attracted them wherever he went, like moths to a lantern in the dark, but he was a careless lover. Not unlike her grandfather, and she smiled to herself, doubting whether the county could stand another such as he. One tushing boar in the family was quite enough, without adding to the problems of half a dozen by-blow cousins all claiming recognition!

Then there was herself...and her thoughts spiralled around her head, like the smoke swirling upwards from the fire, weaving impossible cloud-pictures in her mind, filled with childhood memories and fierce youthful dreams of dragon-boats, fighting men and running horses. She would far rather be a shield-maiden out of ancient times, like Freyja the goddess of love and war, than the dutiful daughter of a great house of warriors destined for her embroidery frame, her distaff and the nursery!

She sighed with sadness and nostalgia for the past, for the little girl growing up in a time of great danger and uncertainty, now having to move forward into a future that was as clouded as the smoke patterns eddying among the rafters.

This was the last time that she would have the family all to herself.

On Twelfth Night, just seven days from now, the Lord Heardred would come in with a fine party of friends and warriors, all ripe for fun and mischief she had no doubt, but not until after they had plighted their troths, and exchanged gifts before the altar in her father's chapel. Old father Anselm who had baptised her, and confirmed her with the Bishop in her Christian faith, would hear their vows, and all her family would be there to honour her and see it done. Such Christian recognition was not required by law, but it would please her mother, and what pleased the Lady Aethelflaeda also pleased her Lord, Wulfstan, so it would be done...and Heardred would stand bound by it, as his parents would have wished. But Heardred was alone now, a thane in his own right with a great holding in the land of the Sommerseatas near the ancient town of Taunton. His parents had both been slain in a bloody raid some four years back while on the King's business along the River Stour, up which the heathen men had sailed to ravage all the lands. He had been sixteen then, and had served the King loyally ever since.

That was how they had met.

He, a King's thane carrying his sword amongst Alfred's loyal companions...she a young handmaiden to the queen, just sixteen and feeling a little lost amidst the strange surroundings of Alfred's bustling court. There messengers came and went at all times of the day and night; embassies arrived from all parts of the kingdom and from abroad; Ealdormen came seeking advice and were also called to give it; thanes and armed men thronged the corridors; priests and bishops, abbots, nuns and deacons of the church were everywhere; and there was the issue of Moots and the giving of dooms. The whole panoply of running a kingdom under constant threat of Viking attack was enough to dizzy the head of any girl, especially a country-bred maiden new to all the wild hurly-burly of royal life.

So it had been a strange courtship.

Brief moments snatched between campaigns, when there was little time to do more than hold hands in a frisson of excitement, and steal delicious kisses rich with earthy promise. Then he'd be away again to carry his King's messages or to rejoin the King's war-band as it trailed, panting in body and in mind behind their master's peerless spirit. They weren't called the 'King's hounds' for nothing. For where Alfred led they followed, convinced of the King's determination to fight and fight and fight again...to make the Heathen rue the day that ever they had braved the fighting men of Wessex, and dared to breach her borders.

*

*B*ut that had all been before the Peace of Exeter a year ago, and in the long hot summer that had followed, amidst the thick scent of hay meadows, whose tall grasses made a verdant couch beneath a sun-drenched sky, where the butterflies rioted and swallows filled the air, they had explored their wakening bodies with trembling hands and wildly beating hearts.

Wreaths of corn marigolds and cornflowers woven tight with scarlet campion and purple loosestrife; the soft summer airs sighing through the long meadows as they gentled one another with soft kisses and warm caressing fingers. Love offered...love exchanged, until by harvest-home, with the stubble white beneath a cloud–blown sky, and the great ox-teams turning the rich brown earth beneath the iron coulter and the wooden ploughs, they had won the approval of her parents, and of the King himself, Queen Ealhswitha acting as chaperone for her most favoured handmaiden. And a delightful rush of desire ran through her at all her memories, the heat from the great hearth hot, like Heardred's kisses on her softly parted lips...and she arched her back and closed her eyes as the memory took fire in her soul and body.

Until suddenly she became aware of her father calling her, the real world rushing in on her behind his voice, and her eyes flicked open to record her brother's look of curious enquiry and her mother's raised eyebrows.

34

# Chapter Five

"*H*ey, little one, have you nothing to say to your father who's fretted these past long months for just a glimpse of his only girl?"

"Leave her be, father," Gyrth replied, grinning broadly. "She's been dreaming of that young spearshaft, Heardred, and her marriage night to come. I'll warrant there'll be a fine 'running' between them when they meet again!"

"Don't be so coarse!" his mother replied sharply, striking his arm as Brioni visibly coloured. "She knows better than to behave so in her father's hall...and so does he! Beside it's right for a maid to dream of her betrothal day. He's a young man with much land to his name...and he carries the King's favour," she continued after a moment. "He brings much honour to your sister, who loves him greatly. At least she's doing something for this family...and that's more than can be said for you, you great lump!" she added with biting vigour. "No bride, no babies and no birthright for you to pass on! Honestly, Wulfstan," she went on, turning urgently to her large husband, lolling idly in his great chair, with a smile on his face. "Oh...I despair of the both of you!"

"At least no babies that we know of, my Lady," her husband replied with a sly grin, leaning across to his son and giving him a hearty dig in the ribs. "I am not without my own spies amongst the royal companions, you know!" he added, turning back towards Brioni with a broad wink as he did so. And she watched in amazement as her brother coloured slightly and shuffled uncomfortably on his seat, clearly unsettled by his father's comment delivered with a sideways glance from beneath his bushy eyebrows, before giving a rueful grin and a shake of his big head.

"So...you've heard then?" he questioned, turning towards his father.

"Heard what?" Brioni broke in excitedly.

"About my..my.." he muttered uncertainly.

"Well, go on," his father urged him heartily. "You couldn't possibly have thought I wouldn't find out. Not with my connections with the King and the royal army."

"Find out what?" The Lady Aethelflaeda shouted in exasperation. "For pity's sake, Wulfstan, what are you and the boy talking about? Will no-one tell me?" she ended, stamping her foot on the wooden floor of the dais. "I tell you, my Lord. Living with you, and that great lump of a son of yours, would sometimes test the patience of a saint!"

"Peace, my angel," Wulfstan replied soothingly, capturing her hands as she waved them about in frustration, and kissing them, "all will be revealed, I promise you."

"Come on, Gyrth," his sister coaxed her brother, tugging at his sleeve. "What is it that father has discovered that we don't know about and is making you blush?"

"Well?" his father queried wickedly. "Do you tell them or shall I?" And there was a further pause then until, with an unusually meek demeanour, Gyrth said quietly: "I've met someone I really care about. Met her when the King took up quarters near Southampton in the summer," he added. Then, with a bold glance at his father he said: "I intend to ask her father for her hand in the spring. I am well of age now and it will be a good match, I promise you," he said to his mother as she gasped for breath, her hand to her throat. "She is the sweetest, most gentle girl. Surely you will love her too, if only for my sake and, if my suit is accepted, this hand-clasping will bring great honour to this house. And anyway," he ended with a firm shake of his head, "I love her greatly and will not be turned from my purpose!"

"Love her?" His mother queried incredulously, breaking the sudden silence that had fallen around the table. "*Love her?*" she repeated scathingly. "Since when has that meant anything? You great ox!" she added, glaring at her big son as she spoke. "We've had enough trouble round here with your grandfather's by-blows without the need for more! And as for talk of 'honour' for the family, I am sure I've no idea what you can mean. I know the kind of girls you favour, my son," she said knowingly. "Big smiles, ripe bodies and empty pockets! They are the kind that follow any army, and ours is no exception. Oh Gyrth," she groaned, burying her head in her hands. "How could you be so..so *hopeless?*"

Thane Wulfstan chortled involuntarily, hugely entertained by his wife's sudden anger and despair so misplaced, yet so deeply rooted, that the truth almost throttled him.

"Wulfstan!" she said suddenly, rounding on her large husband like a sharp-set hound to a large bone. "Stop leering like that. It makes you look foolish. How dare you laugh at me! And tell that goat of a son of yours what's due his family. Love indeed! The idea of it in a family such as ours is preposterous. Since when has love had anything to do with life?"

"Since I met and married you, my bantam. Since I carried you off before me on Foxfire in the face of your family's anger, with a smile and wave of our hands!" Thane Wulfstan boomed heartily with a great guffaw of laughter. "Your mother had hysterics and your father threatened war! No, no my love," he added more gently, recapturing her small hands in his enormous paws.

36

"Give the boy a chance to speak for himself. He may yet surprise you. Aye, and pleasantly at that! Both of you," he added, turning to Brioni as he spoke, who was looking askance at her big brother, whose taste for loose women was well-known in his family. "Go on, Gyrth," he said then to his son, giving him a friendly nod. "Put your mother out of her misery, and your sister, before they both die of curiosity."

"Well, mother," he said briskly. "My lady couldn't be further from the kind of camp-wench you have envisaged if she tried!" And he paused then, smiling broadly for the first time. "She is the Lady Judith. The only daughter of Thane Ecbert of Southampton."

"The son of Earl Brihtnoth?" his mother questioned faintly, the blood draining from her face. "The King's own Reeve?"

"Yes, mother," Gyrth replied quietly. "And a sweeter, more kind and loving girl no man could hope to find...except for you, of course, my most loving and dearest Lady Mother," he ended with a wide grin.

"There, Aethelflaeda," Thane Wulfstan said, the laughter bubbling out of him. "I told you the boy might yet surprise you! No, my love. This is not the time for anger. Yes, we both tricked you a little," he added, as his sister leapt off her stool and rushed to throw her arms around her brother, "but there has been no harm done...except perhaps to your dignity. So, come, let us drink to his health and his fortune, which will be considerable. Then," he added, turning back to his son, "once these ale-horns and bowls have been re-charged, we'd better go over what happened this afternoon, and see what sense we can make of it!"

So saying he stood up and raised his great drinking horn, rimmed with gold, and holding it up he roared: "Wassail, my son! *Wassail!*" banging his fist down on the table-top as he did so, while the whole hall erupted in wild shouted acclaim with stamping feet and hammering on the tables.

*

Brioni, who had sat and watched the little drama unfold almost like an outsider, smiled and reached for her brother's hand, drawing him down beside her. All around the hall his men were jostling and laughing as they picked up the stools and benches they had knocked over in their excitement. Pleased that the old thane had delighted in the news their leader had brought home, and happy to sink their faces into the freshly foaming horns and bowls that the hall-servants were busily re-filling, while calling for a song from Gyrth's harper whom he had brought with him to Foxley.

"Really, Gyrth," she said as she watched her parents busily talking together, her mother now laughing at the way her son had tricked her. "You couldn't have given mother and me a bigger surprise if you had tried! You big ruffian," she added, grabbing his massive hand with both her own. "It would have served you right if mother had taken her broom to your broad sides. Nothing would have made father laugh louder! My, my, but this Judith of yours must be really special."

Her brother smiled ruefully as he acknowledged the truth of her statement, for their mother's wild use of her birch-broom was well known around Foxley. She had even chased her husband on one occasion, until he had picked her up and put her on a massive tree-stump too tall for her easily to jump down from, laughing heartily at her helpless fury.

"Yes, she is special. Very."

"Do you really love her, Gyrth? You have been here before, you know."

"Yes, I do...oh I know about the past, Brioni. But this is different."

"Hmmm...I've heard 'different' before, brother mine," she went on looking at him out of the corner of her eye. "You said Arlena was 'different'...and Bronwyn out of West Wales? And that red haired Sylvia! Are you sure it's not the land she brings with her?"

"No...though that's not to be ignored. No, I really care about her."

"Judith? That's a Frankish name, isn't it, Gyrth?" she asked him then, looking down the hall. "Like the Judith whom Alfred's father married years ago, when she was thirteen and he was returning from Rome...and then who scandalised everyone by marrying the son when the father died soon after."

"Yes! Yes it is. Her father married a Frank called Berthe and they named her Judith after her grandmother. I met the lass last spring when Alfred was near Southampton, before the Danes burned it out again. She's the fairest, sweetest thing I have ever met. Quite beyond the crude jests that father sometimes makes...and that I have deserved in the past," he added ruefully.

"So, you really intend a bridal then?" she asked softly.

"Yes, Brioni, if her father will formally accept me," he replied instantly. "But we who follow the King so closely have always been footloose. That's the way it has to be; we are not the king's 'hounds' for nothing. But if I take a wife I shall have to settle somewhere permanently. At least for as long as father is alive...for the two of us together here would never do. I am so pleased that he is willing to agree to all this. I didn't want a row with him over it, not just because it always creates such an uproar, but because I need him to stand up for me with her father, Ecbert...who is not wholly a good man, being more likely to appease the Danes than fight them...and pay her bride-price."

"You silly man!" his sister threw back at him with a broad smile. "Do you imagine the Thane of Foxley will not see his eldest child, and only son, provided for in as royal a manner as possible? Aye, and mother too. They both adore you, Gyrth. As I do. Oh, I hope I shall like your Judith, for I am as fiercely protective of my big, handsome brother as any maid could be!" And she hugged him to her fiercely.

Then, turning briefly away from Gyrth, who was now sitting more relaxed, with his ale-horn in his hands, she paused to look back down the hall at the score or more of warriors sitting there drinking with new-found relish, many of them already the worse for wear; at the racks of weapons along the walls and at the huge embroideries that had hung there from the elder days, hung on poles from great brass wall-hooks all around them, still bright with colour of every hue, and enriched with gold and silver thread; at the house-thralls weaving their busy way amongst the tables; at the women and children sitting at the far end of the great building...and at her father's hounds, wolf, mastiff and boar, softly pad-padding amongst the now soiled rushes on the hard earthen floor as they hunted about for scraps, tussling noisily amongst each other for the choicest bits.

Although this was her home, the cosy relaxed days of her childhood were long gone. The presence of Guthrum's army on Wessex's borders; their close brush with the enemy earlier on; the nearness of her own betrothal, and Gyrth's decision over Judith all made her even more aware of the dangers of their situation.

At any moment they might all be fighting, or fleeing, for their lives! Separated from their men-folk, slain, captured, or worse. And suddenly the whole situation seemed to crystallise her own deeper thoughts and feelings as she turned back towards her brother, grasping him tightly around his arms in the swift urgency of her mood.

"Oh, Gyrth, be kind to her, your Judith, and guard her well. In these troubled times there is so little guarantee of safety. You know I dream of the time when all England will be free of these heathen men for ever. Not just Wessex...but all of England. It is Alfred's dream, and mine too. So we can have our babes around us safe in the sure knowledge that no ravening pirate will tear them, and us, limb from limb, nor spit them on a pole in bloody sacrifice to their thirsty gods. Dear God, how I *hate* them and all they stand for!"

"Yet God is ever merciful, my child," old Father Anselm, her father's chaplain, gently reproved her, sitting quietly nearby. "And sometime the killing has to stop and we must learn to live in peace, or life will lose all meaning. And when that happens, then you will see that the power of the

39

Word is greater than that of the sword. How else otherwise were our own people saved? They were no different in the old days of King Ine, when your family was founded, than these heathen Vikings are today!"

"That is pap for priests, not warriors, Father!" Gyrth replied angrily. "Your trouble is that you are too good for this world we live in. It may be even as you say one day...but that day is not yet with us. And for now the finest things I have seen this day were the naked, stiffening corpses of those heathen devils we slew earlier on, and the sight of their comrades fleeing into the storm as fast as their poor beasts could carry them. *That* is the reality of our life, Father. And until we can kill enough of the bastards to keep the rest from ever coming near...then I for one can see no end to it!"

"Well said, young Gyrth!" his father added forcefully, standing up, his massive gnarled fists resting on the broad table top, while all around were suddenly stilled. *"Well said, boy!* Those are my feelings also, 'though my old friend Anselm sees things differently. He sees our salvation in the conversion of these bloody pirates, but I say we have to crush them first on the battlefield. For not until they have been smashed by the King's forces under God's Holy banner will the Heathen see sense. And until that day comes we must do as Alfred says and kill them wherever and whenever we can. For every one of our settlements they destroy, and for every single Saxon they butcher, rape or sacrifice...the lives of ten of their people will be forfeit. Blood will get blood; the law of claw and talon will prevail in Wessex until every one of their accursed breed has been banished from our land!"

And there was uproar as he finished, for this was the kind of fighting talk that every Saxon warrior understood, and as Wulfstan stopped talking, his thick hair flung over his shoulders and his broad chest heaving with emotion, the whole hall responded, the men leaping to their feet, shouting and roaring like red stags at rutting, banging on the tables and thumping their feet on the floor.

\*

As the hall settled again and Thane Wulfstan sat down beside his wife to talk some more with his war-band leaders, the old priest sat back sadly and smiled. He could not remain unmoved by what his Thane had said; after all he was a Saxon too and many of his monkish brothers had paid a martyr's price for their beliefs. Everywhere the Danes brought death and destruction: monasteries ripped apart and the monks butchered or dragged into slavery; precious manuscripts destroyed, churches burned and looted; nuns raped and murdered. Whole communities slaughtered.

Yet, inside, he was sure that he was right. That in the end the two sides must sit down and talk if any lasting peace was ever to come out of it all...and on that day Christ's message would prevail. Until then he would bide his time and pray that the heathen men would continue to leave Foxley alone; that Mercia's problems would not spill over into Wessex with the border so close at Tetbury; that the King would be victorious, and that they all might learn to live at peace with one another once again.

Watching the old man from the corner of his eye, Wulfstan knew what Anselm was thinking. Perhaps his son was right and the old priest was just too good for this world after all? But then maybe there was something in what he had said. After all, the King was always keen to convert the Heathen when he could, and had done so too, only to have them treacherously break their word, take the rich baptismal presents for themselves and return to their wicked reiving ways!

It was all very strange to an old warrior like himself.

Truly, the best thing was to hack the bastards down first and let God worry about their immortal souls afterwards! He was a simple fighting man, and much else only made his head ache. That's what made young Alfred so remarkable. He seemed able to think beyond the next battle better than anyone else. He had a dream that no-one else could see of a free Wessex with laws that everyone could understand, and a system of government that would enable him to keep an army available to fight the Heathen at all times of the year. And that was something that no other King of Wessex had ever managed to achieve before.

Well, good luck to him.

Thank God he did not have to negotiate with pirates; he would not know where to start. But young Gyrth now, he had been around the King long enough to have learned a little sense. He had been at Exeter in '76 when the last truce had been made...and at Wareham the year before that, in the very thick of the fighting. And something he had seen there had some bearing on what had happened up by the old ford that afternoon. There had been too much to do earlier on to give the situation the thought it deserved but now, with everyone fed and watered...now was the time to call his leaders together and see what they could make of it all.

# Chapter Six

With a last few words and a smile, Thane Wulfstan patted Aethelflaeda's hand and stood up again to his full height, a massive golden figure in the leaping firelight and smoky air. Cloak of brown bear edged with scarlet leather pinned to his shoulders by his two great foxhead brooches, broad golden arm bands above his elbows and the golden torque of his house around his powerful neck...he was a truly impressive figure, and all men fell silent to hear his words.

"Osric, Rorsthan, Ulric...come up here to the high table. It is time we made some decision about that skirmish today up by the old ford." Then turning to his son he added: "Gyrth, I'll have your two chief men up here as well, and let us see if we can't make some sense out of all this! As for the rest of you drunken oafs, enjoy all this while you have the time. I have a feeling that after tonight we are all going to be too busy to do this for some while...at least not until the feast of Yule-end when the Lord Heardred will come in for the Lady Brioni's betrothal!"

"Patrols, Lord?" Several of them called out with groans of dismay as the wind swooped round and buffeted the hall with wings of iron, making the wood-smoke swirl and eddy in the draughts.

Wulfstan laughed uproariously, feet planted wide and great arms akimbo. "Yes, you idle loafers. Patrols and a constant guard, snow-clearing and defence building as well, just to make your unhappy lives more miserable! So, *wassail* my friends," he roared out, raising his great ox drinking-horn edged in gold. *Drinkhail!* I give you all of the best I have. Better it go down Saxon throats than Danish ones!" With which the hall erupted at his rough jest, while Wulfstan sat down again to a grunt of satisfaction. He might not know how to negotiate with pirates...but he knew how to deal with Saxon warriors!

And he settled himself comfortably in his great chair with its carved arms like snarling bears, as Aelric, Carnfrith the Archer and the other men that he had called for began to pick their way steadily towards the dais from amongst their friends amidst ribald comments and idle, jesting banter.

"What about Brioni, father?" Gyrth questioned him as soon as the old Thane was seated comfortably. "Women do not usually attend the war council I know," he said, holding onto Brioni's hand as she made to rise from her stool. "But she has spent months now closer to the King than any of us. She may have some observation vital to whatever plans we may decide on. And Foxley is her home."

"Agreed, Gyrth," Wulfstan rumbled deeply, with a nod of his head, "and likewise you too, Aethelflaeda," he added turning to his wife. "It has always been your job to organise the homestead when we have had to go away, thralls, women, villagers, the lot. And I see no reason to exclude you now when we are talking about the defence of Foxley itself!" Then, turning back again to Gyrth, who was making room for his own men around the table, he added: "Bring out the armour and weapons you took off this young Dane you are so bothered about, and let's all have a proper look at them. You never know, they just might jog your memory."

And within minutes their council had begun, broken only by the arrival of all the war-gear that Gyrth's men had stripped from the young Viking they had slain that morning.

*

Ever after, Brioni would remember that meeting in her father's great hall: the leaping flames from the huge firepit in the middle, twisting scarlet and orange as the fire crackled and burned; the whistle and thump of the wind as it battered at the great building; the snarl and tussle from the great hounds that lounged everywhere; the buzz of sound, from voices and from soft harp music, that came up from the ranks of trestles at which their men sat and drank and roistered the night away...and the intense talk and thinking that went on around the high table that night as they came to grips with the situation in which they all found themselves, as her parents, Gyrth, and the men her father had called up around him wrestled with the difficulties with which they suddenly were faced.

"Well, clearly these are the arms of some great man," Wulfstan said after a while, his great hand caressing the dead man's magnificent helmet, with its side-plates of steel, deeply inlaid with twisting gold, its fine boar's head crest and enamelled face-mask. "In richness of enamel and precious metals this lot eclipses anything I have ever seen. Even the King himself does not possess such finely wrought armour. Yet he was a young man you say, Gyrth. The son of one of their leaders perhaps?...And a powerful one at that!

"This stuff here," he added, flicking it with his hand, "has come from Byzantium; from Miklagard itself. Look at the workmanship, the fine suppleness of the steel links on this byrnie. And those enamel colours on this shield never came out of Frankland. They do not have the trick of it over there.

43

And this sword alone," he added, drawing it from its fine sheepskin lined sheath with a whisper of sharpened metal, "has a blade of Damascus steel. Look at the fine blue lines that are woven into it. This blade alone is worth an earl's ransom. So, Gyrth, where have you seen this gear before...or its owner if you'd rather?"

"Well, father. All those we killed today were Jomsvikings, and the only man who employs them is Oscytel, the Black Jarl of Helsing. He is their King. So, like it or not, that hell's spawn is involved here in some way, 'though they did not carry his symbol of the ragged knife on their armour. Just give me a moment to sort things out in my mind and I will know who this young warrior is, for I am certain that I have seen him before." And rising from his seat beside his sister, Gyrth took his own drinking horn and moved to the very edge of the dais, the young Viking's great sword in his right hand.

And as he swung it idly from side to side, admiring its beauty and its balance, its blue-steel blade shimmering in the wavering firelight, so his mind worked its slow magic:

*Wareham*... the autumn sunshine, the great palisade that they had been unable to breach, the King in plain armour fighting at the very forefront of the battle exchanging blows with a young axe-man; the screaming, howling noise, the violent screech and clash of steel, the sickly stench of blood, the whole grinding roar of two armies at each other's throats. Then, the young axe-man down, slipping to his knees on the greasy, soiled ground...and Alfred moving swiftly forward with himself by his side, his shield held high and sword darting, weaving, sniffing for its foes.

But, just as the King was preparing to thrust the young heathen through and split his belly open like a gralloched deer, a great dark figure had appeared as if from out of the very ground itself, his shadow falling over both of them, followed immediately by the hiss and whistle of his axe-blade as he had swung at them over his left shoulder.

Alfred had just managed to leap back in time, but Gyrth's sword had been caught up in that single terrifying blow...and with the sharp brittle sound of breaking steel had been sent spinning away like a child's toy into the heart of the screaming press around the palisade.

The tall warrior had stood like a rock above the young pirate, his blade a shimmering arc of steel that no man could brave, until the fallen man had regained his feet...and then together they had fought their way back to the safety of their own lines.

*Exeter*...last summer, the negotiations of the truce, the leaders of Guthrum's army with stiff, bleak faces swearing to depart on their leader's gold arm-ring and on the names of their gods. Each filing past, one by one, beneath

44

the intense gaze of Wessex's King, Alfred, and their own Viking King, Guthrum, of the Great Army… supported by a tall, hooded faced man in black steel byrnie and heavy black leather chausses thick with mail, cross-gartered with bright saffron strips of linen. The man had a huge torque of Irish gold around his neck with heavy arm-bands above his elbows of the same precious metal, and stood beneath a black flag bearing a ragged knife in gold, edged with scarlet, across its face. Earl Oscytel, the Black Jarl of Helsing. King of the Jomsvikings.

He had been leaning on the long wooden handle of his axe whose blade was now burnished like a mirror, the sun glittering off its gold and silver inlay, and watching the whole proceedings through slitted eyes that glimmered like blue steel beneath heavy lids.

The man had exuded power, a great saturnine figure whose very silence marked him out from his King who talked with every man who passed him by. And by his side the same young man whom Alfred had nearly slain at Wareham the year before. The same bright helmet on his arm as the one his father had been exclaiming over on the table in that very hall…his sword tied down with heavy peace strings, its pommel the very same as the one he now held in his hand, a ball of steel cunningly inlaid with gold, its crest inset with a great piece of northern amber. And with that final image, Gyrth's mind cleared at last and he turned and came back to stand over the table, his face as bleak as the wilderness beyond the walls.

"It is Oscytel's whelp whom we have killed!"

"The Black Jarl?" his father, queried, appalled.

"The same. His only son. Alfred fought with him at Wareham. I was right behind the King's shoulder when the boy's father rescued him from certain death. And I saw the same warrior again at Exeter last summer when the truce was sealed. Beside his father, with this helmet on his arm," he added, picking it up. "They have the same 'look' and the same mouth. We couldn't have found a more famed hell-hound to bate if we had tried!"

"Sweet Mary aid us!" Brioni whispered, and her face drained of colour.

*

At the first mention of the great Jarl's name there'd been a sharp intake of breath from many of the men seated around the table. Even the old priest, father Anselm, had crossed himself as if the Evil One had stalked into the hall and stood before them. His gentle face was now masked by sudden fear and anguish, as he gazed into the furthermost recesses of the

45

smoke-shrouded roof, before speaking with urgency to Wulfstan who was seated near him.

"My Lord. That is the one man I know of whose death would truly benefit mankind. He is the devil's own creation. The Great Beast of whom St John wrote so many years ago," the old man went on, his voice rising. "You spoke of butchers, fiends and hell-hounds earlier on, aye and I rebuked you for in general they are but men as we are. But this one, Lord! This one is different. I tell you old friend, that even I would plunge a knife into his black heart if I could. A man so steeped in evil even the angels cry out for vengeance!" And in the stricken silence that followed, the old priest turned and stumbled away towards his sleeping place across the great hall, his hands shaking as they tried to hide the tears that now flowed freely down parchment cheeks grown suddenly more lined and careworn than Brioni could ever remember.

Watching his sister's face, Gyrth leaned across and shook her arm.

"It is always this way with him at the mention of that man's name."

"Why?" she asked, appalled.

"It was last spring, while you were away in Winchester, after the lambing. Oscytel attacked his family homestead and butchered his family...or those who were still alive after his men had finished with them. He carved the blood-eagle out of his brother's living body as Ivar did to King Aelle of Northumbria. Pulped the children's brains against the house-trees and thrust his niece through the body with a stake after his men had violated her, before burning everything in sight."

"Oh, no Gyrth! Not Eadgytha?" she cried out, her hand to her mouth. "He was so proud of her, and she was such a friendly, lovely girl."

"The same!"

"But she was only a child! What harm could she have done anyone?"

"No matter, Brioni. He set her screaming, writhing body upright in the ground as a tortured sacrifice to Odin and Thor their gods of war, while he laughed scorn on the Saxon King, his puny people and his wretched, miserable God."

"Poor, poor Anselm," she gasped, horrified. "No wonder his old heart is breaking. How could they do such an awful, terrible thing? And why did no-one tell me?"

"You were away, and these things are not uncommon now...as you know from your time at Alfred's court. Besides, Brioni, time passes and we are all so pleased to have you home."

"How do you know all this, Gyrth?" Brioni asked him at length, her eyes staring like a cat's in the chalky whiteness of her face.

46

"Anselm found them like it himself some two, three days later when he went to visit. He learned what had happened from a half-dead house thrall he found mangled beneath a heavily charred timber from the ruined hall that had been his father's home."

"And they were all killed?"

"Every one! Where that man's feet touch the ground in war he leaves a desert. I have seen his handiwork myself. He takes everything living he can find: man, woman, beast or child and butchers, or sacrifices, everything for which he has no value, takes those he fancies as slaves and then burns everything else in one great orgy of killing. The man has no heart!"

"Except, it would seem, for his son?" Brioni questioned.

"Except for his son!" her brother answered quietly, nodding his head slowly.

"And you think he will come here?" his father asked, leaning towards his son as he spoke.

"Yes, father, I do! After what we have done to him now…always assuming his men got back to Gloucester. He has no other choice but to try and destroy us too."

"Are you sure of this?"

"Yes, father, there is no doubt in my mind at all," the big Saxon warrior replied steadily, all eyes turning to where he was sitting, his big hands rubbing over his face. "I saw him at Exeter with his father when the pirates took their oaths to leave, and the peace was made. I should have realised when he and his men made no effort to attack us this morning, just fighting to get clear. I thought his face was familiar, but it was his war-gear that fixed it for me in the end."

"But why did his men leave him…his son, I mean, if he is so important?"

"Because that is Oscytel's code…and he will kill if it is not obeyed!"

"Even to leave his own son?" Brioni asked, shocked.

"Aye, Lady Brioni," Osric broke in. "We know something of him and his methods. His men are trained to stop for nothing when they are on a mission. No matter for whom. For him it is better to sacrifice one or two men, even a great war-lord, than lose everyone and their information with them. Nevertheless," he added with a dark chuckle, "I wouldn't be in their shoes when they get back to Gloucester and have to tell him what has happened to his precious son!"

"Father?" Brioni asked, raising her voice a little. "How will he know that it is us? Any Saxon war-band could have fallen in with his son today. He cannot possibly know that the men of Foxley are responsible."

"Because he is Oscytel, my little one," her brother replied quietly, his voice barely heard over the wind as it howled around the house-place, sending the smoke eddying around the huge rafters in great blue swirls. "Because he is Oscytel," he repeated grimly. "He knows everything!  He will know to the mile where his men have been, and anyway, he knows where Foxley is!"

There was a gasp of dismay at that, as all had heard what Brioni had said and had dared to hope.

"How is that, Gyrth?" his father asked, appalled.

"Do you remember Unstead, the King's victualler? Who stayed with us here at Foxley some months back?  Remember how he would never stay for the raising of the Host at Holy Mass?"

"Yes...I do," the old Thane replied slowly.

"Yes, father," his daughter broke in urgently. "He disappeared from the Court suddenly...about a week or so ago."

"Well, he was Oscytel's man, in Guthrum's pay.  A faithless Saxon betrayed by his greed.  Like many around the King I am afraid.  Only too ready to do a deal with the Danes in return for Danish gold and the lives of their families; convinced that Wessex must fall.  And a pagan it now turns out! Well, he is a dead Saxon traitor now, for Alfred's men caught him red-handed and he was cut down where he stood.  Oh, yes, my friends.  Oscytel knows all about Foxley you can be sure of it, and the state of the King's supplies in Chippenham!"  And there were several moments of stricken silence as all around the table took in what Gyrth had just said.

"This is bad news, my son," Thane Wulfstan said heavily after a brief silence had fallen on them all.  "Bad news for the King and for us.  That man is implacable by all accounts.  And I agree with Gyrth.  He will not leave one stone unturned until he has revenged himself upon us all, or been killed in the attempt, of that much I am certain.  But our palisade is strong, and this weather will make any swift movement from Gloucester impossible.  Heardred is due here in seven days with all his men, despite the greater distance he must travel to reach us.  And if I know young men," he added with a laugh and a swift nod towards Brioni, "he may well arrive here sooner than we expect!  Well before Oscytel and his wolves come hunting.  And we are in the very heart of Wessex. It will be a very bold pirate indeed to brave our might before the spring.  So do not lose heart; we will yet prevail!"

"How many men does the Lord Heardred bring with him, my Lord?" Ulric asked.

"Thirty proven fighters at the very least...and we have our own fyrdsmen from the village that we have been training all summer, and whom I have made sure carry arms of good steel, not soft iron. We are far from helpless here, I promise you."

"More, probably, father," Brioni chipped in, her face colouring delicately. "Remember it is my betrothal. Heardred's two best friends will come in too. The Lords Harold and Edwin, and their men. Especially as they are all due to join the King at Chippenham after twelfth night."

"And very glad I am to hear it!" her mother said quickly, having remained silent while the men had been talking, her face no less appalled by the news than her daughter's. "I hope this great barn of a building is more full of fighting men than there is room to put them all. For once, my Lord," she continued, turning with a smile to her large husband seated beside her. "You'll have no complaints from me, and I'll leave my brooms in their corner for a change!"

At which there was a general laugh, and a tangible lessening of the tension as she had intended, for the Lady Aethelflaeda and her brooms were well known by all visiting war-bands who had 'invaded' her home since the troubled years had come. The sight of her in hot pursuit of some brawny Saxon warrior luckless enough to cross her path when she was trying to organise her household had brought great amusement to everyone in the past, so her image of such cheerful normality was a good one for her to leave on, she knew, and rising from her place beside her husband she turned to go, bidding the others keep their seats as she did so.

"You must excuse me, Wulfstan, for clearly I have much to do if the necessary vittals are to be brought forward in time, and I must see to poor Anselm. He has not been quite the same since the murder of his family. And, Wulfstan, I know the weather is bad to say the least, but some fresh meat would be a great help with so many extra people coming in. A well-armed hunting party might make all the difference...and don't forget the village!"

"Dear my Lady! Do you believe that I would abandon my own people to that ravening beast? Then might I well be named '*Nithing*' if I left them to die just to save my own skin. And anyway I need their strong arms and bold hearts to man our palisade as we have practised all summer."

"Just so, my Lord. But I know how often the most obvious things are sometimes overlooked! I tell you one thing, Wulfstan..."

"Yes, my Lady," her Lord replied, a warm look in his eye for this woman whom he loved above all others.

"If we are going to have to fight for our lives here at Foxley, then I would rather my great ox of a husband were by my side where I can physic him properly when he is ill...than off roistering with the King where I can't get at him!" And with the laughter that followed her simple jest rippling round the tables, she turned and walked away, giving her husband's large hand an affectionate squeeze as she did so.

# Chapter Seven

With a warm smile Wulfstan watched this woman whom he loved so dearly leave the dais, picking her way past the crowded tables in the main body of the hall, her tire-maidens going with her, Bran and Utha close to her side. These two, as big as small ponies, were his most favoured wolf hounds, shaggy grey and brindled, with dark brown eyes and bristly whiskers, massive paws and feathery waving sterns. They had as much affection for their mistress as they did for their master, and for Brioni whom they had fawned over ridiculously when she had arrived late that afternoon.

With a quiet word for those of Wulfstan's hearth-companions whom she knew best, and some last instructions to the hall steward about keeping the fire well fed during the night, and the beer and ale flowing steadily until her husband had finished, she paused briefly by the entrance to her own chambers. There she looked down the whole length of the smoky hall to the raised dais at the end, where her son and daughter were already in conversation with Lord Wulfstan's war leaders, and with a rich chuckle and shake of the head at those warriors slouched insensible across the tables with their long hair draggled in their beer, and a wave of her hand to her husband who raised his own to her in response, she softly disappeared.

*

"Now, young Brioni," her father said as soon as her mother had gone, " tell us please just how the King views the situation."

"You must understand. Father, that I am not privy to his most secret councils, so I can only tell you what he tells the Queen and what Heardred has reported to me."

"I know that, but it will still be valuable nonetheless as we decide how dangerous our situation here at Foxley truly is. I haven't been to Court since the summer campaign ended, and I need to know how the King sees thing now."

"Well," she answered slowly with a frown, "he knows that Guthrum has his main army with him at Gloucester, and that Gloucester is being watched. But Gyrth is better placed to say how closely that is being done than I. The King also knows that there are still more heathen men near the coast, but he is relying on Heardred's grandfather, Earl Britnoth of the Sommerseatas, to hold them there. The King feels that Wessex is secure until the spring, when all men know the muster is to be held at Ecbert's Stone near Selwood, after Easter. The Priests have convinced him that Guthrum's oath, sworn before God and on his sacred arm ring, will hold the Danes in place. So he has sent the army to their homes for Christmas, and is himself at Chippenham with his family, with only his personal guard and hearth-companions for protection…and the usual small army of priests with whom he travels everywhere."

"So says the King," her father replied slowly, shaking his head. "Alfred always was one to listen to his priests rather than to his fighting command. But all men know the country is tired after so many years of fighting these Viking pirates. The Great Army came from Frankland in '65 and in nearly thirteen years of constant warfare has still not lost its edge. And every time we kill the bastards in their thousands, as we did at Ashdown in '71…two of their kings and five of their great Jarls no less amongst swathes of others…yet more come to join them from across the water. Look what happened at Reading. We forced them behind their palisade, and then we could not shift them; and by God we tried. We cut them down like corn before the reapers…and like rank weeds in fertile soil more seem to rise up to take their place, as many as there were before. At times it seems we will never see the end of them!"

"Yet the situation has changed, father," Gyrth broke in heatedly. "The Great Army has split up. Ivar the Boneless, who slew King Aelle and King Edmund is dead, Halfdan has settled to farming in Northumbria and Ubbi is in Wales. The Army is not what it was. It found Wessex too spiky to swallow and has gone in search of easier pickings. Only Guthrum still haunts us now."

"Nevertheless he leads more of it than Alfred can easily put in the field. And it's still the Great Army, all professional fighting men with years of experience. Like Oscytel's Jomsvikings, sworn to their Lord and paid royally for the pleasure of doing so. I wish we had troops like that whom one could rely on at any time. Furthermore he needs a victory after Wareham and Exeter. He and Oscytel both, and the Heathen are never more dangerous than when they are in a corner. Come, Brioni. What do the King's advisors say?"

His daughter paused as she thought back to the angry scene that had preceded the final decision to split the army up for the winter. Alfred had wanted to keep them all under arms, but his army commanders had told him that the men would probably desert if he tried to do so. They had been away from their families and their homesteads for many months, and with Guthrum locked in at Gloucester, and the fighting season over, now was as good a time as any to release them. So, lectured by his bishops on the truce over which Guthrum had sworn, the King had agreed to send the army home…just so long as sufficient men were on hand to keep a watch-guard on the Danes to ensure they did not suddenly break out and destroy the land.

For all men knew they were not to be trusted.

Since then, however, in deep November, with the harvest in and everything remaining quiet, even Alfred had come to believe, as his priests and bishops kept telling him, that the Danes would prove no real threat until the green-time of the year should come around again. That their oaths would mean everything to them; that God was watching over Wessex, and He would ensure that Guthrum would keep his word.

"They were the ones who told the King to send the men home. Alfred wanted to keep the army in the field, but they said it couldn't be done. That the fyrdsmen would refuse and even his thanes would be reluctant to face another winter campaign like the last one. So, reluctantly the King agreed. Since then all has been quiet. Some would say dangerously so. For like naughty children, when the Heathen are silent they are up to the greatest mischief.

"Now the King agrees with his Earldormen, and his priests, that all will be fine, the Heathen are to be trusted to keep their word, and that his heartland will be safe until the spring. That's why he is at Chippenham with his family and so few guards about him, and why he has allowed me to come home and be with Heardred here at Foxley, and not have him with the other royal companions in Chippenham."

There was a pause then while everyone took in what she had said, watching the flames in the great fire along the middle of the hall leap and splutter, casting huge flickering shadows against the embroidery covered walls, and listening to the great battering blasts of wind that curled and blathered round the building as the storm outside raged and wuthered around them.

"Well," Wulfstan said at last, "I think there are too many faint hearts about Alfred. Those murderous pirates are up to something, I am sure of it, and have lulled the King into carelessness. I think his advisers are wrong, and to trust in priests is soft-headed! He has too much faith in their words for my liking. What else were those heathen up to out here? If not on some far-flung scouting mission to clear the way for one of their sudden wild attacks.

"The King may feel himself to be safe, but I do not. Especially now that I know that Oscytel's men have been sniffing around my lands. If it weren't for this vile weather," he went on, waving his arms around him in exasperation, "I'd ride to Chippenham tomorrow with all my men and tell Alfred so. I believe the Heathen are planning an attack and soon! It would be just like Guthrum to do something wild like that in weather no sane man would be seen out in, let alone fight a battle. As I have said, they are at their most dangerous when you feel you have them trapped. And with what we have discovered today, I reckon we will be the first on their list. Is there any man here who thinks I may be wrong?"

53

To that there was nothing any man could say. Not only was their Thane's whole voice and bearing such that no-one would have dared...but they were all as sure as he was that soon the sea-wolves would be baying at their door.

"Alright, then this is what we must do. You, Gyrth, must go at first light and rouse the village. We have no idea when this attack will come...even if it comes at all despite all our beliefs. But I will not wait until it is too late. So we must act accordingly and bring everyone within our palisade as soon as possible. So, tell that plump reeve of mine, Wulfnoth, that I want everyone within the palisade by sundown: beasts, chickens, flour, meal, the lot. The old barn will hold most of them, and those that cannot fit in can throw up some shelters along the east side facing away from the walls. Remember, Gyrth, there'll be no time to collect belongings, nor any room for them either, so be prepared to be ruthless. It won't be easy, but their lives are more valuable than their miserable chattels and they'll see the sense of that if nothing else."

"What about me, lord?" Osric asked.

"You are next! I want two patrols out towards Gloucester every day to cover the north and west of the vill, for that is from where those bastards will strike us. And you'll need to organise reliefs, or when the men are needed they'll be too exhausted to do anything but sit around in glazed heaps."

"How far out?"

"Not more than two or three miles at the most. Far enough to spot them when they are still some distance away...but near enough to get back in time to give us due warning." Then, turning to Ulric, he continued: "You, Ulric, organise a hunting party as soon as maybe. Take Carnfrith here, and four of his men, and Rorsthan too and half-a-dozen of his fellows and scour Helm's Wood and as many of the brakes around and about as you can. In this weather the deer will have gone deep into the forest, the boar also, but you should surely come back with something for your pains...and the hounds need the exercise anyway. I don't want to start on the stock unless absolutely forced to do so, or we'll have nothing left from which to breed next year."

"What about me, father?" Brioni asked quickly, the prospect of action making her eyes gleam.

"Don't be so eager, my little bantam. This is not a game we play, and the Queen will be expecting you back in one piece after Twelfth Night!"

"I know that...but Heardred has taught me some usage of sword and shield, and it is at times like this that all Saxon women and girls may be expected to join in the defence."

"Wounds of Heaven!" her father exclaimed loudly. "Women in the line of battle?"

54

"It is the King's will, now, that all those who ride with the Court should have some war-training. So, Heardred showed me how."

"I care not what Alfred may say, my girl!" her father answered her briskly. "Here in Foxley, I am 'King', and I say that you will stay within the hall and help your Lady mother!"

"What? When you, Gyrth and all the rest of the village are struggling outside for your lives, you expect me to bide in here with the babes, the nursemaids and the household drabs?"

"Yes, my girl, I do indeed!" He snapped back sharply. "You'll stay with your mother, where I know that I may find you. You are no shield-maiden from the olden days, Brioni, no matter what you may think. 'Heardred has shown me how', indeed! How to get cut down more like. And nastily, too! My men will have enough to do to keep themselves alive, without having to worry about a silly chit of a girl who has more sauce than sense!"

Brioni gave her father a long, hard considering look, then dropped her eyes. He may think what he pleased, but when the horns blew and the arrows began to fly, then she would find some way to join them, she was sure of it.

"Very well, father," she replied meekly…a little too meekly her brother thought, watching her closely. "I will do as you ask and help mother with the little ones and those others who may come into the hall for safety if the Danes strike us. I am sure you are right though it cuts across the grain to say so."

Her father, still smouldering slightly, gave a sudden smile and laughed.

"Splendour of God, Brioni. You have got more spirit in you even than your dam! But your sides will smart if you defy me in this. Queen's handmaid or not, you are still my daughter and I am still head of this family, and with a gentle finger he chucked her under the chin. "Eh, come on, lass. Don't take it so hard. Give me one of your smiles and then away to your pallet. It has been a long day and you and your mother will have a lot to do in the morning…and there may not be much sleep coming anyone's way during the next few days. Oscytel may or may not attack us here at Foxley, but if he does come he will not find us unprepared."

With that she smiled at last, shrugged her shoulders in resignation and giving a deep sigh, pulled such a comic face that everyone laughed.

"Well, in that case I will leave you to put the final details together," she said rising from her stool and leaning across to give her father a kiss on his cheek. Then turning briefly to look at them all, hunched over their drinking horns and clay-fired pots, she added: "It's all very simple really. You just hold the palisades and leave the rest to us ladies!" And picking up her skirts she ran off before he father could think of a suitable reply, jumping over a set of sleeping hounds as she went until, with a swish of leather and richly

55

embroidered drapes, she disappeared behind the curtains that led to her family's own apartments within the great building.

*

"*I* wouldn't trust her an inch, father!" Gyrth said as they watched her skipping away. "She took that far too meekly for my liking."

"You think she would defy me? That she means to come out and watch us hack those bastards in pieces?"

"No! I think she means to come out and fight them with us herself! She's no fool, father. She knows that when an attack goes in like this that everybody helps to repel it, and that the village women will be out there with their menfolk manning the palisade. And the older children with them, too. Why not her?"

"She wouldn't dare!"

"Oh yes she would, my Lord," Osric replied, looking at his Thane with a steady eye. "The lass has changed since she has been away. Her time with the King; her journeying around the land; her responsibilities with the Queen and her time with the Lord Heardred have changed her. She was still really a child when she left us last spring. Now she is a woman grown…and she has her father's blood in her too!"

Thane Wulfstan laughed at that then paused while he thought deeply before replying.

"Well, we can't get her out, that's for sure. And if the Danes do attack she will be safer here than with the King who will have fewer men with him than we do here. And her mother will not go either. If the worst happens, the hall midden is not far from the west door. They can bury themselves in its depths. The crust may be frozen but below that it will be warm. Not even a ravaging pirate would search through that!"

A burst of laughter followed his statement, as the men nudged themselves and chuckled at the thought of the two principal ladies of Foxley burrowing in the hall midden like pigs after acorns.

"Enough," Wulfstan said after a moment. "It will not come to that. By the rising of the moon in seven days' time, the Lord Heardred will come in, and until then we must rely on our own hearth-companions and fyrdsmen to keep the guard."

"How are we off for weapons?" Gyrth asked, changing the subject.

"Plenty of those," Osric replied. "'Though there are more wooden helmets than iron ones, and very little mail. Boiled leather byrnies with iron plates we do have, and spears and swords in abundance. You made sure of that, my Lord, at our own spring muster last year. Enough for everyone and shields too."

"What about arrows, Lord?" Carnfrith asked. "And war-bows?" he added.

"Arrows, a certain number. Bows, fewer I'm afraid. But Aylwin the smith has plenty of iron just now and will make as many heads as you like. There are plenty of goose feathers about with Christmas just over, and arrow sticks can easily be cut from the hazel bushes and withies by the stream."

"What about the snow, father?" Gyrth asked a moment later, his mind running along a different track.

"What about the snow?"

"The palisade!" he exclaimed. "With this wind the snow is bound to drift, and unless we can keep it clear of the windward side of our outer defence it may build a ramp up which the sea-wolves might then climb over and attack us from the rear."

There was a general growl of agreement at that from all around the long table, the thought of Viking pirates breaking in behind them being instantly understood.

"A good point, young Gyrth. We'll have to check that every day. You, Aelric, can make up parties of villagers to keep it clear as best you can. Sort things out with Wulfnoth, he'll be able to help you. I know he looks like a buffoon, but he's a good man and the people trust him. He'll not let you down." He yawned widely then and rubbed his eyes. "Right. I don't think that there's much else really we can do this night. So, let's away to what rest we can get, for we must all be up betimes in the morning."

With groans of assent the men around the table stood to allow their Thane and his son to leave the dais, before seeking their own pallets around the fire where the house-thralls, under the hall-steward's eye, had laid them with coarse blankets and wool-fells to cover them. There, wrapped further in their long wolf-skin cloaks and with their weapons close beside them, they would take what rest they could.

For a short while Osric, Carnfrith and a few of the others remained at the table, talking quietly amongst themselves. But soon they too went to their rest and the whole great building fell silent, save for the wild soughing of the wind outside and the snap and crackle of the fire that would burn throughout the night.

*

Alone in her box-bed, the thick woollen mattress tight wrapped with fine linen, Brioni lay beneath fresh cotton sheeting covered with blankets and heavy wolf-skins that young Agatha, her mother's maid, had laid over her. Her body warm in its own heat, she pulled the furs up to her chin and wriggled her toes on the wool-wrapped hot brick at her feet, and stared away into the darkness around her, listening to the wind blustering around the steading and battering at the close-fitting shutters that masked the window beside her bed as the storm bayed at them from the north.

She was aware of her parents' voices nearby, softly rising and falling in a gentle rumble beyond the partition that separated their sleeping room from her own. While above her the ruddy glow from the fire in the long central hearth was reflected off the soaring roof beams and the smoke-blackened thatch as it breathed and flickered in the night, a mirror for her heart and a quiet solace for her mind.

Pray God that Oscytel did not come!

Or if he did that they could hold him off until their reinforcements could arrive. And how many Vikings would come with him? No-one had asked that question. Scores? Hundreds?...thousands even? She did not know, and better not to try and decide. That way could lead to despair. And what if they did break in...what then? To die a bloody death in the open beneath the sky would be far better than to be hunted down and captured inside, like some wild animal, to become the mewling plaything of his heathen horde. Or burned to death beneath the timbers of her father's hall.

She shivered in her long woollen shift. Not from cold, but from sudden fear, remembering what her brother had said of this man; that wherever he planted his feet in war he left a desert. She had heard all the stories and seen the results of the heathen raids all across Wessex. You could not live with the King and not know such things! And with a low moan she placed her hands over her loins as she thought of what the Black Jarl had done to poor Eadgytha.

Horrible! Appalling!

Imagining with terrifying clarity the feel of that great rough stake as they must have driven it between the child's legs, through her womb and up into her bowels. And she cried out in distress.

No! If they came to Foxley, then somehow she would break free from the great hall that could so easily become a trap, and escape out amongst the clashing steel and fury of the battle. Despite her father's comments she did have some knowledge of how to use a sword. Heardred had seen to that, and though she had found both his sword and shield too heavy for her, it had been a useful start and lighter weapons could always be found that would fit her hand better.

Oh, Heardred!

How she wished he was with her now. So kind and gentle…yet as fierce and cunning in war as any in the King's whole host. For the first time since sliding into her bed she smiled to herself, bringing her hands up over her breasts at the remembrance of those hot, balmy summer afternoons. How vibrant she had felt and how alive…and how much she had wanted him, yet had held back as much by the dictates of her situation and position in the King's household as by her desire not to dishonour herself in the eyes of her family. Now, with sudden death at the hands of the pagan Danes a terrifying possibility, she wished she had given in to her own desires and lain with Heardred as she had so wanted to…and the devil take the consequences!

And in that frame of mind she finally fell asleep, her dreams filled with red-hot desire and the flames of Foxley burning, while the storm blew itself out and the noise of attacking Danes brought her shuddering into the morning's grey light beneath the heavy furs that covered her, as Agatha shook her violently several times before she finally came awake.

"Quickly mistress! Quickly! You must get up."

"Dear God in heaven, Agatha!" she exclaimed sitting up sharply. "Is it the Danes? Are they at our gates?"

"No! No, my Lady. It's your father, Lord Wulfstan. He's been up since first light. Your lady mother also. The whole house has been astir since cock-crow. Your father has been calling for you, Mistress Brioni, and these days his temper is none so easy first thing in the morning. So hurry, please, or else I am sure I will get a whipping."

With that Brioni was instantly awake and as much aware of the appalling noise in the hall as of the cold air in her room that made her whole body shiver.

"What's going on?" she demanded, as Agatha helped her to dress, first pulling on her long, thick red woollen dress over her shift, then her woollen hose, while the young maid plumped herself down on her bed to help her on with a tough pair of leather half boots, before handing her a long fleece-lined leather over-jerkin and leaping up to pin her blue cloak to her shoulders with two large brooches of red gold decorated with pearls and garnets.

"The villagers are all coming in, my Lady," she replied, and a more raggedy, bob-tailed crew I haven't seen in a long time. The Master's roaring his head off. Fit to burst he is, Mistress Brioni. And there's children and animals everywhere. Where they're all going to go, I am sure I don't know."

"Of course, Agatha! I remember my mother reminding him about the village before I went to bed. Right," she went on, standing and shaking her shoulders to settle her clothes. "Let's go and see what we can do to help. My

59

brother never was one for the ordinary things of life. I bet he is in a rare taking!"

"Reeve Wulfnoth's done all he can to help, Mistress Brioni. But the people didn't listen."

And pausing only to have a quick look round to make sure that she had left nothing important behind in her room, Brioni and her young companion passed through the heavy curtains that closed off her sleeping place, and went past her parents' chamber, through the heavy leather curtains and on into the main body of the great hall.

# Chapter Eight

This great building lay like a vast upside down thatched boat at the top of the manor, with a log palisade atop a steep earthen bank, and a deep ditch all around that marked out the whole great compound. This was closed off with two sets of enormous double gates of laminated logs, one facing the river bridge across the Avon and the other the trackway that led up to the Malmesbury road on the north side of the steading. Each great valve hung on four huge iron pintles and were held closed with a vast squared trunk of timber that took six men to shift. On either side of each entrance were small towers for archers to shoot down on any enemy that might attack them, and there was a broad parapet walk that went all round the walls with ladders leading up to it from different places along the parados. With sufficient troops to man the walls and towers, Thane Wulfstan's homestead was indeed a fortress that few would care to attack.

Within were a host of buildings small and great: stables, sheds, hen houses, forge, brewery, a great granary built off the ground on staddle stones with mushroom heads, and another great wagon barn for general storage near the midden, and at the west end of the compound the small stone chapel of which Thane Wulfstan was so proud. Nearest the hall was a deep round well with a stone surround beneath a pointed hat, with a stone water trough beside it. And in between was the wide garth itself, now one seething mass of frightened people: thralls, geburs, churls and their families, all up from the village that lay half a mile to the south across the stream, below the hillside on which the hall of Foxley had long ago been built…all of whom seemed to be trying to push their way inside it.

\*

For a moment Brioni stood beside Agatha transfixed, and stared around her in complete amazement. Not even the periodic upheavals of the Court could really match the seething confusion and uproar that was going on.

Everywhere she looked there seemed to be children, animals and villagers milling aimlessly about, with more people coming in all the time, stamping the snow off their boots and brushing it from their clothes as they did so. Piglets, chickens, even a young bull calf bawling for its mother. The noise was horrendous.

"Dear God, Agatha! Did you ever see such a mess?" Brioni exclaimed. "I thought the villagers were to be quartered in the old barn. What on earth are they doing here?"

"You may well ask, my Lady!" Agatha replied sharply, with a little sniff of disdain. "I heard what the young Lord's orders were to that plump fool of a reeve, Wulfnoth, but these peasants have their brains in their boots. Clodpoles, every one!"

Brioni smiled at her young companion. Agatha had all the contempt of a town-bred girl for her simple country cousins.

"I thought you said that Wulfnoth had done all he could to help? From the looks of all this his brains must be as well trod as the rest of them. No wonder my father is so angry," she added pointing to where the Thane of Foxley was stamping and roaring on the dais, even his great voice almost lost in the wild hubbub going on throughout the hall.

"The fools panicked!" Agatha snorted in disgust. "As soon as Lord Gyrth said the word 'Danes' they didn't wait to hear the rest, but rushed off to gather what they could, and then came straight up here to the hall. By the time Wulfnoth had got himself together, half the village had arrived, panting and wide-eyed at our gates, and some idiot soldiers let them all in!"

"Well, Agatha," Brioni went on, laughing: "there's no point in wasting our time standing here. The sooner we can get this lot sorted out the better, before my father does someone an injury and my mother takes to her brooms! Where is the Lady Aethelflaeda?"

"Away to the kitchens to organise hot mutton broth and bannocks for all who will need feeding later."

"Well, we will go and join her shortly. For the time being her tire-women can help her. Right now my father needs us most!" And together they set off up the hall towards the dais at the far end of the building where her father was rampaging, their long skirts lifted above the soiled rushes as they quickly picked their way across the floor in their sturdy boots, avoiding the many hounds who were as interested in chasing chickens and piglets as fleet-footed deer in the forest!

Mercifully no-one had tried to bring any of the heavy working, or milking, stock into the hall with them, but despite that there still seemed to be animals all over the place mixed in with tables, trestles, benches and stools. It was all an indescribable mess and the noise was worse than a sheepfold at shearing time!

With the few windows the hall possessed tightly shuttered and barred against the weather, the only light there was came as much from the freshly banked fire as from the score or so of reed torches dipped in pine resin and placed in iron holders.  Each was hung off the mighty timbers that supported the roof and flared and flickered off the walls, and off the many shields and weapons that hung there.  And there were oil lamps all along the great table

In fact their arrival in the hall coincided with the bustling appearance of the harassed reeve who came hurrying in, with a swirl of snow, through the great oaken doors that opened onto the garth along one side of the main building.

*

*F*orcing his way through the clustering villagers, the reeve of Foxley arrived before his Thane, already fearing the worst as his lord had given a great shout of rage as soon as he realised who the newcomer was.

"*You blundering oaf, Wulfnoth!*" he roared at the man.  "You were told the old barn.  The wagon barn, you maundering idiot!" he added, waving his arms around in wild exasperation.  "What in the name of all that's holy are these..these people doing in my hall?"

"They never waited to hear the end of your instructions," his reeve replied as calmly as possible, used to his lord's occasional rages.  "They heard me say 'Danes!' and just rushed off to collect whatever they could and then came straight up here.  Then some idiots let them in!  By the time I realised what was happening it was too late!"

"Then get them out...and their blasted animals!  Sweet Heavens, Wulfnoth, how my people elected you for yet another year I have no idea.  They must be all about in their heads.  But if you don't do something about this..this *midden*," he continued gesturing at the crowd of animals and milling peasants in the hall around the dais, "then I shall probably go berserk and kill someone...starting with you!"

By that time Brioni and Agatha had made their way to where the two men were standing, arriving at much the same moment as her mother, who had come from behind the kitchens just in time to hear her husband's last words.

"My Lord!  Wulfnoth has been our reeve for the last seven years, thank God and all His angels.  And the reason he has remained so is because he is the only one of them down there, with the courage to stand up to you...and the only one with the skills and determination to get the jobs needed around the estate properly completed.  Without Wulfnoth, I don't know how I would have coped every time you had to go off on the King's business. So just you stop bullying him!"

"Thank you, my Lady. I do my best."

"Aethelflaeda," her husband said with a sigh, "the man's an idiot! Always has been..always will be, and this..this *bearpit*, is his doing!"

"Nonsense, Wulfstan!" His wife replied briskly, her hands on her hips. "The people panicked and came up here because you are their Lord, pledged to protect them, and some of your men let them in! Anyway, this is your hearth place, where else do you expect them to go?"

"To the barn, my Lady," Wulfstan replied quietly through gritted teeth. "To the barn, as was agreed yesterday."

"Very well, my Lord," she replied sweetly. "To the barn they shall go…eventually. That is after the men have made it more habitable. It is full of wagons, carts, and all sorts of assorted stuff. That all must be moved and stalls put up for the animals wherever they can be, and then simple sheep hurdles to mark out a space for each family, with a hearth in the middle…so someone will have to go up onto the roof and make a smoke-hole. Wulfnoth, can you organise that?" she asked, turning to the ruffled figure beside her with a smile.

"Yes, my Lady."

"Very well, then see to it, please. The women and children must stay here for the time being, and I am organising broth and bannocks for the little ones and the feeding mothers, as well as everyone else. The men in particular will need their strength this day, that's for certain. But Wulfnoth, my Lord is right in one thing. We must get these animals out of here as soon as possible."

"Very well, my Lady, I will see to all of that. And, my Lord…"

"Yes, Wulfnoth," his Thane growled at him darkly.

"I am sorry the people came up here. They weren't meant to. They just didn't wait to hear the rest of your instructions."

Then, before her husband could respond further, his wife's eyes fell on Brioni and Agatha, and she turned towards them quickly. "Ah, there you are my child, and Agatha with you too. Good. You can come with me and give me a hand with all these little ones. We'll leave your father to fume over his morning ale and moan about the proper place for women in his household. But in the meantime we have work to do!" And giving her large husband a brilliant smile and a swift kiss, she swept off towards the kitchens at the back of the hall, taking her daughter and her handmaid with her, leaving the two men standing.

"Well, my Lord?" the reeve said after a while, as he watched Wulfstan's colour subsiding slowly, and saw Aelric come in with a handful of his men.

"Well, indeed, Wulfnoth!" the Thane of Foxley said, sitting down in his tall backed chair. "We need five men to hold every four and half yards of wall, if the job's to be done properly. That's what Alfred has worked out for a complete defence of any palisade. And we don't have one half of that number. The sooner the Lord Heardred can reach us the better! If the Danes came right now, that lot," he gestured towards the milling crowd of villagers, now being organised by Aelric and his men, "would be off like frightened rabbits fleeing from a hawk! But once they are all settled and organised, with their wives and children around them, they will give as good an account of themselves as anyone."

"The women too, my Lord."

"Yes, I know...the women too. They have more to lose than any of us!" And standing up once more, he banged on the broad table top and roared for silence.

*

By the time the Lady Aethelflaeda had returned to the hall with her daughter, and a bevy of hall servants following, carrying a great cauldron and baskets full of bannocks and drinking bowls, the job of tidying had almost been completed, and Wulfstan was able to observe to his wife, albeit a little slyly: "You see, my dearest, all it needed was simple organisation. I have always said, 'tell the people clearly what they have to do...and there is never any problem!'

And giving a great, booming laugh, he swept her up into his arms and gave her a mighty squeeze. Then, before she could find a suitable reply to such outrageous drollery, he was gone from her side, flinging his heavy bearskin cloak around his broad shoulders, and calling to Bran and Utha as he went. With a swinging stride he was away down the hall, gathering Wulfnoth up as he went, until with a final skirl of snow the two men were gone, the heavy hall doors slamming closed behind them.

# Chapter Nine

Outside, though the ferocious wind of yesterday had gone, the snow was still falling heavily.

A vast pillow-storm of snow-feathers just tumbling down in an almost silent world through which a steady file of men and beasts were plodding, their feet completely lost in the smooth ermine counterpane that now cloaked the land. A world without colour where the wind sighed and whined in bitter gusts, whirling the snow around in billowing clouds; piling the drifts up against the windward side of the huddled buildings that stood within the compound and against the palisade. In the little orchard that stood beside the old wagon barn the trees, their branches laden with snow, stood stark against the tumbling landscape, and the bee skeps had cones of snow atop each one.

With a shout of recognition, Gyrth came across towards them from the southern gated entrance where he had been sitting his horse, encouraging the villagers as they struggled with various heavy burdens. Most particularly with the creaking ox-carts, piled high with as many bags of grain, meal, flour and oats as it had been possible to gather in the short time since they had been told to move up to the manor. All were wrapped up closely against the wind which swirled in gusts around them hungrily, tugging at their heavy, ungainly burdens.

"How are things going?" his father asked as soon as Gyrth had flung himself off his horse.

"Fairly well, father, given the circumstances. Some of the older ones would rather have stayed where they were than move up here; after all it is a fair step from the village to up here on the ridge. I see that Wulfnoth found you, then," he added, turning towards the bundled-up figure of the reeve who was bouncing his feet in the snow, his hands thrust into his armpits.

"Yes, he did at last. I only wish it could have been sooner. Those silly 'sheep' of his were in a fair way to turning the hall into a market place. Pigs, chickens, goats everywhere. Even Selwyn's bull calf, for God's sake!"

"I thought that mother, Brioni and the house-thralls were supposed to be organising everyone?" Gyrth threw back, before pausing to shout across at some of his own men who were helping to force a heavily laden wagon through the thick snow. "Sweet Jesus, what a mess!"

"Thank God for small mercies, my son," his father said, brushing the snow out of his eyes. "If the Danes had attacked us this morning, by now all these people would have been killed or captured."

66

Then, with a grunt he was on the move again, his son following on his horse, barrelling through the snow as they went towards the huge gates, tightly closed and barred, that guarded the northern entrance that faced Gloucester a distant thirty miles away, from whence any attack would surely come. There two of their men, heavily cloaked and armed, with sword, shield and long spears stood looking out across the bleak, snow-swept landscape from the left-hand gatehouse tower, the rope from the great alarum bell that hung there close to hand. Stamping their feet and banging their hands together against the cold, they were pleased to see they had not been forgotten. Throwing his cloak behind him, Thane Wulfstan busily climbed the nearest wooden ladder to reach them in a huffing-puff of effort, his breath streaming away like fine smoke as he climbed. Gyrth, meanwhile, stayed by his horse, its head tossing against the snow as the myriad flakes blurred its eyes and hung on its long eyelashes.

Beyond the towers that butted onto the first timbers of the palisade the countryside was silent. The immense fastnesses of Helms Wood, a distant panorama of black, lay like a massive fleet of gaunt masts against a sea of white that stretched away beyond the blurred horizon, while the river that ran behind the steading moved silently past the twisted willows that lined its banks. Here the black water still flowed in the middle, all else lying frozen stiff along its edges, the reeds and rushes thrusting up out of the ice along its banks. No ducks or moorhens called from amongst them, only the curlew-wind crying from the wilderness, was there to mark its passing.

"Anything moving out there, Olaf?" Wulfstan asked the older of the two men standing there, a great hefty spearman, as they stood in the sparse shelter of the shooting turret.

"No, my Lord. Rorsthan and Carnfrith went out at first light with an armed hunting party led by Ulric, followed by the first of Aelric's patrols. But they quickly vanished in the murk. And apart from a distant *taroo-taroo* of a hunting horn, I've not heard nor seen anyone. Wind's in the wrong direction."

"Well…that's a blessing in its way. Rather nothing than angry Danes! Anything else?"

"Nothing, Lord…save the villagers themselves, of course. They've been on the move all morning."

"Have you seen Father Anselm?" he then called down to his reeve who had stumped across to the gates to join them.

"No, my Lord, I haven't."

Wulfstan grunted at that: "I expected him to come to you when Gyrth went down to talk with the people. He is such a little fellow, are you sure you haven't seen him, and that rickety old horse he is so fond of?" he asked Olaf, turning back to the big soldier.

67

"No, Lord, and Ricberht and I have been here since the first hour."

"No matter then. Wulfnoth and Lord Gyrth will find him soon enough. There cannot be many places that he and Cygnet can be hiding. As for you two, I'll tell Aelric to arrange an immediate relief, you've been here long enough. There's hot broth and bannocks waiting for you in the hall. Well done, the both of you. I know it's freezing up here, but keep a sharp look out and ring that bell if you see anything suspicious!" And clapping each man on his shoulder he turned and climbed back down again.

"Now, Wulfnoth," he said a moment later as he stamped his feet on the frozen ground, a handful of villagers shuffling out of the way as he did so. "Grab Olaf's horse, he'll not be needing it for a while, and go with Gyrth and check round all the houses in the village. We must be certain that everyone's out, and that nothing valuable to an enemy has been left behind. But go to the chapel first. It may be that Anselm has gone there anyway. It is still snowing hard," he added, batting the swirling flakes away from his face as he spoke, "and with all these people coming and going he may easily have been missed."

"It is possible, father," his son replied, an edge of doubt in his voice. "There surely have been a lot of people and animals through here since first light, and it's not good seeing weather. But Olaf has sharp eyes, and Anselm is such a distinctive little figure in his purple cloak and furry leggings, and on that old nag of his, that small as he is I am sure those boys up there would not have missed him. Why all the concern?"

"I have been worried about him ever since all that talk about Oscytel last night. You know how he is about that man since his family was butchered."

"Very well, my so noble Lord," his son replied with a grin and a mock bow before swinging himself back onto his horse. "Wulfnoth and I will visit the chapel and then drop down and scour the village, as much for missed meal and hay bags as for a small lost priest. There can't be many places where he'd go, so I am sure we'll find him swiftly enough."

"You do that. I'll be away back to the hall presently, after I have made certain that things are going on well in the old barn. Good hunting to you. Send Osric to me the moment he returns, and Gyrth…"

"Yes, father?"

"Make sure those reliefs go out in time. For the patrols…and the watchers on the walls and towers. Those two boys up there are half frozen and that won't do. I don't expect anything to happen for a while yet, but you can never be too careful. With this bastard weather the way it is at the moment, there could be three hundred men out there by the whins beyond Foxley Wood, or in amongst the thickets…and you'd never know it!"

68

"We'll be careful, father," his son replied with a grin. But with Wulfnoth with me we are bound to be alright. I never knew a man with better eyesight. Anyone who can spot a meat pasty from a plateful of scones at a hundred paces won't be caught napping by anything so large and ugly as a heathen pirate!" And with a laugh, he dug in his heels and cantered away to the chapel on the far side of the garth, swiftly followed by the plump reeve on his borrowed horse.

With a final glance around him, Thane Wulfstan turned and trudged off towards the old wagon barn, head down against the whirling snow and shoulders hunched up as he ran through his mind all the things that still needed to be done. And he grunted in satisfaction as he cast his eyes around him as he went, his ears filled with the sound of frenzied hammers, loud barnyard noises and the shouts and cries of his people as they swarmed around the massive old building his grandfather had built as a home before his father built the hall.

*

Once all was finished they could be armed.

Nothing fanciful, plain swords and long spears, and helmets and shields for all. But they would be steel weapons not iron, he had seen to that last spring. And for the better fighters, whom Osric and he had been training all summer, there would be better equipment, the mail armour and helmets they had taken off the heathen they had slaughtered the other day. The rest of his fyrdsmen would have boiled leather byrnies strengthened with iron plates. It was not much, but it was better than nothing, and there were always the great boar spears that the men had gone out with that morning...and the spare weapons on the walls of the great hall itself. He snorted in satisfaction. Let that bastard come, he would not find Foxley so ripe a plum for picking as he might imagine. We might even win! And he laughed aloud.

His fyrdsmen might not make impressive warriors. Not like the professionals of the Great Army, and peasants usually left the battlefield after an hour of fighting, no matter who was winning. But here they had nowhere else to run. Their women and children were here beside them. Foxley was their home, there were battle hardened warriors to stiffen their resistance, with more to come in, God willing, and they would fight like tigers to defend it. It should be enough, and he looked up at the whirling snow and shook his head. By God and Saint Swithun, it would have to be!

And with that shake of his head Wulfstan reached the barn and stepped in out of the snow, now just beginning to slacken as the wind faltered, and looked around him.

Already there was a good fire blazing in an improvised hearth-pit in the centre of the building, freshly dug and lined with stones. It was good to feel the warmth, and to see a couple of great cooking pots already seething with a thick broth of oats and coarse vegetables, with bannocks freshly baking on a long iron plate. Looking up in the flickering firelight, through the curling smoke, he could see where some of the men had hacked out a square hole in the crumbling thatch-work of the roof to let the blue wood-smoke funnel out. There were also a number of crude torches in simple iron brackets hanging off the largest roof trees, and tallow lamps in niches along the walls where already many families had created home spaces for themselves and their dogs with the wicker sheep hurdles that were normally stacked in heaps at the back of the huge building.

All around him were the dumped stores that had been brought up from the village, and there were chickens and small animals everywhere, either escaped from holding pens or still loose about the place and scuttling in all directions. Already some of the women were shepherding their children into the building from the hall, their anxiety showing in their glances as they hurried past him.

He understood their fears, but had no time to give them more than a brief smile of encouragement before turning briskly away to stride back through the tall barn doors, Bran and Utha stalking close beside him as he went. Then he was off again through the snow until, rounding the far end of the building, he bumped into Aelric coming from the opposite direction.

"Ah, there you are, my Lord. I have been casting round for you everywhere. The Lady Aethelflaeda has been calling for you any time this past hour or more, your daughter also, and I need a pick and shovel team to have a go at the snow slopes lying across the ditch against the outer palisade."

"How bad is the drifting?"

"Right across the ditch and halfway up the palisade on the windward side, and the same within the compound. It'll take several gangs working in relays to clear it. And if this wind picks up again, we'll have it all to do again in the morning!"

"Send a runner to my Lady and tell her where I am; then pick two dozen men and get started on those ramps. Gyrth and Wulfnoth have gone down to the vill to check that everyone's clear, and all the foodstuffs have come up to the hall...and to try and find Anselm who seems to have disappeared. When they get back, tell Wulfnoth to select a relief party and to keep the work going until the snow is cleared. Oh, and Aelric, send some fresh guards out to the north gate. Those boys have been out there too long already, and keep rotating them. I don't want frozen look-outs missing vital signs. If those bastards

70

come, that is where they will attack first. Then I am going across to see Aylwin in the smithy and see that he has all he needs, and from there I will be off to check the stables. If anyone has anything to report, then that's where I'll be."

"Very well, my Lord. No news from Osric then?"

"None as yet, and his relief should be going out soon. The moment he is sighted I am to be informed immediately."

"What about Ulric and his hunting party?"

"The same, Aelric. They left at sun-up, making for Helms Wood, but it's too far to see anything clearly. And in this weather, with the wind blowing down from the north, no sound to carry up to us either. The whole countryside seems deserted. Nothing moving at all."

"At least the wind has dropped and it's almost stopped snowing," his war-leader said, beating his hands together as he did so.

"If the weather clears from the north before this freshening wind, with a hard frost to follow, I wouldn't be alone in that wilderness, not for the Emperor of the Greeks and all the wealth of Miklagard!"

"That bad, Lord?" his man asked, with a chuckle.

"Aye, Aelric, that bad, and like to get worse. There's still more snow to come. Far off as yet, but I can smell it. So, the sooner you get started on what's fallen already the better!" And with that Thane Wulfstan swung away from him towards the great, ruddy glow of Aylwin's forge where it stood near the stables. There the powerful figure of the smith was bent over his bellows as, hammer in hand, he worked the glowing iron he was holding in a pair of pincers.

Half an hour's discussion over arrow-heads and helmet strengthening, with so many wooden helmets needing it, and Wulfstan was on the move again. This time to the broad stable-block for a word and a quiet hand on Foxhead, the great black stallion of whom he was so fond, whose fine head with its white diamond-shaped blaze was already looking for him, his silky black ears pricked forward at his master's footsteps on the ground and the sound of his voice calling his name. He was a magnificent beast. The largest horse in all the King's Wiltshire forces, trained to fight and fierce in battle, he was fleet of foot and the bravest of the brave; as ferocious a warrior as his master and he knew it.

A few moments only to stroke his long nose and pat his withers, and feed him an apple taken from his wife's stores, and Wulfstan was away again for a talk with his horse-master and a careful check of tack and saddlery. Then out again into the cold air and on to the next series of seemingly unending questions and problems that set the pattern for the day as everyone slowly sorted themselves out, and a rough and ready routine was gradually established.

# Chapter Ten

At midmorning Osric returned with his two war-groups, chilled to the marrow and worn from struggling through the heavy drifts that cloaked the land. But apart from their reliefs to whom they had handed over an hour or so before they came in, they had seen nothing.

The snow seemed to have deadened everything, and though they had passed the tracks of deer, boar and hare, the animals seemed loath to show themselves. Only the dismal howling of a lone wolf from the far edges of Broken Wood had served to show that anything was actually alive out there.

Never crossing wide open spaces if they could be avoided, sticking to the tree-line wherever possible and never showing more of themselves than they were forced to do, they had carried on. Muffled up against the weather, it had been a numbing experience made worse by the constant swishing crash of branches either breaking under the weight of snow that lay along them, or springing free as the wind moaned through them, suddenly releasing them of their loads.

It never failed to startle.

Heart-stopping moments as they slithered to a halt questing for the sound, standing motionless in the swirling snow, their horses blowing noisily and tossing their heads until Osric was certain that nothing was amiss, then on again until the next time, always looking, always listening, never free from watchfulness. And when they had to stop to check the frogs of their mounts were not packed with snow sufficient to lame them, there were always watchers front and rear to make sure they were not suddenly attacked and overwhelmed.

The cold had been biting, gnawing at their hands and faces while the snow had fallen all around them, swirling about their heads and those of their horses, who travelled with heads down and tails between their legs against the bitter weather. So it had been an almost unutterable relief when they had rendezvoused at the old blasted oak with Ceolwyth and his men, the bodies of their slain enemies already torn and ravaged by beasts.

\*

Hard on Osric's heels came Gyrth up from the village, the old priest beside him on his own horse, Wulfnoth riding by his side.

"So, you found him after all?" Wulfstan said, as he and Osric strode over to greet them.

"Yes, father. Wulfnoth found him on his hands and knees in a hole he had dug in the floor of Old Mald's house."

"What? Old Mald One-Eye, the ale-wife? What in God's name were you doing Anselm?" Wulfstan asked him incredulously, as they walked towards the hall. "And you are filthy!" he added, looking at the little priest who was covered in soot, half burned twigs and ash.

"Burying your precious Halidom, my old friend," the little priest replied with a quiet smile, brushing himself down as best he could. "Took everything on the back of old Cygnet here," he went on, patting the withers of his dappled mare as he spoke. "If Oscytel comes and this place falls…or at the very least we are forced to clear out for a while; then they'll make straight for the chapel and strip the place bare. Dig up the graves most likely if they have the time. Experience tells them that valuable grave-goods are often buried with the bodies. And they have been. Jewellery, arm-bands, neck torques. And stupid as they may be, they know that Christians worship their God with fine ornaments of gold and silver…and they also know the difference between a chapel and a peasant's hovel. That building they will search, the hovel they will simply burn."

"So, burying my relics?"

"And that great store of gold and silver coins that I have been holding for you," the old man interrupted him with a grin. "Safe for the future, my Lord," and on that their eyes met; the moment broken by Wulfstan: "That was well done indeed, to try and save something at least if those barbarians come. Truly they are like ravening beasts. They burn and destroy everything."

"Precisely, Wulfstan! And very hard work it was too, I may add, for I am not the man I used to be. First I had to move the fire…for I have buried it all beneath the hearth, hence all this mess, and then try and dig into earth as hard as rock. And the place stank of stale beer and urine. I broke one spade and cracked a mattock handle as it was before I was able to make any impression. But the job's done now, thanks to my two rescuers…and the fire put back on top to hide the digging. Everything else has been brushed around with birch besom. So with luck and a fair wind, if anything does go awry, it will all still be there for us to find later."

"That was well thought of, Father," Gyrth threw in, brushing the little man down. "But if you must hie off on your own again, please tell someone first. With an attack possible at any moment, we must know where everyone is."

"The boy speaks good sense, Anselm," Thane Wulfstan added urgently. "If Foxley had come under serious threat during your absence, then not only

74

might you have found yourself on the wrong side of the gates, but Aethelflaeda would have forced me to send men out to look for you before it was too late. We have few enough trained warriors to fight the palisade as it is, without having to send good men out to look for a knock-kneed old ancient like you!"

The old priest bowed his head in rueful acknowledgment.

"You're right, of course, Wulfstan; and I am sorry for the concern that I have caused everyone. But I have now done what I set out to do. Not even Oscytel, God rot his black soul, would ever think of looking in a peasant's hovel for priceless treasure." And turning away from them all, he walked off towards the stables, the old mare plodding happily by his side, ears pricked and nudging him as she went, the two of them in perfect harmony.

Wulfstan watched them go with a sigh, then, clapping his arms round Gyrth and Osric's shoulders, he pushed them in through the hall's entrance before him. It had been a busy morning, and all were more than ready for some of the thick vegetable and oat broth, strengthened with mutton, that his Lady, with her daughter's help, had been busily preparing against their coming; while Wulfnoth went across to join his family and his people in the old barn.

*

All that day, and the next three, the business of sorting out and preparation carried on apace.

The New Year came, with little fanfare or excitement, everyone too focused on the present to give much thought to the future, and save a later evening around the fire with heather beer and some of the Lady Aethelflaeda's mead, there was no great party as would normally have been the case.

Weapons and armour were checked, loose rivets tightened, helmets strengthened with iron straps, arrow heads forged in their dozens, and blades honed to a razor's edge on the great whet-stone that stood in one corner of Aylwin's forge. Sparks flew everywhere while the men took it in turns to crank the heavy wheel, the screeling noise setting everyone's nerves on edge. Then shields and weapons were handed out and those villagers not trained as fyrdsmen were split into compact armed packets and shown where to go if they were attacked, who their leaders were, and how to take a charge, spear butts firmly grounded, points held high and shields low. The women also were given spears and swords to use, and lighter shields of inter-woven osiers backed with leather, that the boys used in training.

Those fyrdsmen whom Osric and Thane Wulfstan had been practising with all summer, some forty men or so, were given tough byrnies of boiled leather strengthened all across the back and chest with plates of iron; their leaders the chain jackets and steel helmets of the Danes whom Gyrth's men had slain by the old ford. Gyrth himself took their leader's fine chain coat, helmet and sword in place of his own, which he gave to Osric, while he kept his own shield, the enamelled one taken from the young Dane remaining hung from the wall behind the dais. All else went to the fyrd.

Then they practised.

The fyrdsmen with full armour and heavy shields, their feet wrapped in sacking to keep them as dry as possible, their sword blades wrapped in leather to save the edges from chipping and from seriously harming each other. Up and down the frozen garth they went in lines. Shields locked around each other. Right hand edge to left hand edge, each iron rim tucked in behind the other to make the shield wall, and held up high, with spears or swords thrust out to make a hedge of steel. All the other villagers doing their best to follow suit. While every evening after the light had gone the men made arrows to which the women glued white goose feathers, with one brightly coloured as the cock feather to guide the archers as they aimed. Bows were freshly strung, and shields and weapons given new binding where the old had frayed or been worn smooth through usage.

And every day the work gangs not practising for war slaved on snow clearance, and sweated and swore as they moved from one solid drift to another under Aelric and Wulfnoth's direction, until both men felt their voices cracking under the strain of constantly encouraging their stolid workers.

Meanwhile the patrols went in and out, morning and afternoon, with either Osric or Aelric in command, as the weather moderated and the snow ceased to fall except in occasional flurries; while Ulric took his hunting parties further out into the woods and forests round about, each day bringing back deer and boar, the men in good spirits the dead game strung on long poles or slung over the backs of sturdy ponies.

In the manor garth, the snow was beaten flat and smeared brown and black with mud from the constant battle practice that their thane insisted was carried out each day, and ash from the fire scattered across it to give them better grip. Shouts and rage and stamping feet could be heard as they practised a flying wedge attack, with all those with chain armour, heavy shields and great boar spears at the very point of impact; the fyrdsmen in boiled leather along the sides with spear and swords, and everyone else packed in behind them...as if the whole village and manor were one giant arrow head aimed at the very heart of the enemy. If ever the Vikings attacked and broke in this was how Foxley would defend itself against a Danish shield wall. Punch right through it and then break out and slaughter the enemy to their ultimate destruction.

76

*B*y mid-afternoon on the fifth day since that meeting in the hall, the weather had cleared before a stiff, blustery wind still blowing chill from the north, that had harried the heavy snow clouds south towards the distant sea. And as the sun slowly began to sink towards the far horizon, cloud multitudes on fire across the heavens, great rollers of crimson and gold, fringed with purple as the hot ball of the sun finally touched the distant hills, so Ulric and his huntsmen returned to Foxley after a whole day in the saddle.

One by one they came up through the now deserted village beneath a blazing sky, their figures black against the snow, the fierce winter sunset turning midnight blue above them. A long line of bone-weary men and tired beasts, even the hounds quiet as they ran in beside their masters. The pack-horses in the rear weighed down with the carcases of gralloched deer and gutted wild pig. That night both men and women dropped to their rest in clothes they were too weary to change out of and too worn down to care.

Outside, beyond the fragile warmth of barn and hall, the frost was cruel. A hard searing cold that turned the breath to ice, cutting into the bodies of those men on watch until their bones ached. Beyond the palisaded manor, the wolves came from the forest and stalked on stiff legs around the walls, their grey fur on edge, and howled for the warm meat they could smell inside. Balked by the deep ditch and tall palisade, they bayed their anger and frustration to the moon, as it sailed clear in the midnight sky, the men's breath freezing around their mouths as they gripped both spear and shield and watched from the parapet walk and prayed no great beast would try and reach them. Below in barn and straw-lined stable the herd beasts lowed and shuffled in their makeshift stalls, Foxhead screamed his fury, and the hounds howled their own rage into the frozen air at the scent and sound of their ancient enemy so close.

Alone in her bed, Brioni lay snugly beneath the heaped-up furs and wriggled her feet against the hot brick in its woollen jacket that Agatha had placed there earlier, and longed for the morning. Above her the firelight from the hall-hearth gleamed and flickered as she listened to the soughing wind outside, and the cry of the wolves out hunting in the starlight beyond the garth.

In two days' time it would be Twelfth Night, and Heardred would come in bringing his war-band with him and his closest friends with their hearth-companions...and she could not wait to greet him. The Yule-end feast and her betrothal would take place and her life would change for ever, and she hugged herself in anticipation.

She could hear the sound of restless sleepers in the hall tossing and turning on their straw pallets, and then the bang and clatter of the great doors as one set of guards was replaced by another throughout the night, their weapons ringing softly against one another as they laid them down.

Beyond the partition beside her bed she could hear her parents' voices rising and falling in the cold darkness as they talked with each other, and the rattle as her father used the covered bucket in the corner of their room. And her mind spun dreams of Heardred arriving with all his men, the thrill and excitement of being hand-fast at last and of beating Oscytel and his men into ploughshares!

But in the end she slept…only in sleep her dreams were filled with dark shadows. The shapes of weird half-human monsters running through the snow with black stone talons poised to tear out her heart, and she awoke in the semi darkness, sweat-stained and crying out with fear, still desperately trying to escape…and for some moments she lay still, her heart pounding.

All around her she could hear the sounds of people stirring: her father's voice calling for Osric from the back of the hall; her mother chivvying the house-thralls as they turned the rushes over all across the building, clearing away the dung from the hounds as they did so; the clack and rattle of the soil buckets being taken up to empty on the midden; the raucous crowing of the steading cockerels and those brought in by the village; the lowing of the oxen and the calling of calves to mothers from the barn, the bleat of the village sheep…and with a sudden sigh of relief she sat up.

Almost immediately Agatha came in with an armful of clothes, freshly warmed before the hall fire, pressed tightly to her to preserve their warmth…and a look of concern on her pretty face: "Is all well, my Lady?" She asked anxiously. "I thought I heard you cry out!"

"It was just a bad dream, Agatha. Too much of my mother's cheese, I expect," she ended with a laugh. "Are these for me?"

"Yes, my Lady. Taken from before the fire this very minute. I thought that you could do with a warm after such a freezing night. So throw them on now before the heat dies in them."

"Was it very bitter then last night?" she asked the girl as she quickly started to pull on her clothes.

"The frost was almost thicker than the snow itself, my Lady," Agatha replied excitedly, as she handed Brioni a thick woollen gown to wear over stout hose and leather trousers. "And the river has frozen right the way across. Barnaby had to use a heavy hammer to break the ice over the well at first light, and the wood-cart was frozen to the ground. It took four men to break it free!"

All the time her maid had been talking, so Brioni had continued to dress, as anxious as her companion was to be up and doing on so exciting a morning that it had taken four men to break free the wood-cart! And with a final twitch

78

to her cloak and girdle, she followed the girl out, across the hall and through the big double doors that led outside to a stunning morning.

Even at that early hour the fresh sunlight glistened off the hard surface of everything. Everywhere sparkled in the harsh sunshine; the roofs, the icicles that hung from them, the carts and wagons rimed with frost, the distant countryside...all dazzled in the sun's piercing rays. And the frost stood inches thick, turning to shimmering powder as soon as hands were brushed amongst it. Snowballs became handfuls of freezing white dust; a hard ice-crust glittered on the surface of everything, and unmarked snow could even then be walked on, its ice-hard surface coruscating like a million diamonds.

Overhead the sky was as blue as a jay-bird's wing, from which the sun blazed down with a cold heat that made men and beasts steam in the frigid air. Air that seared the throat and nostrils as it was breathed and made the eyes water; while the glare of the brilliant sunshine filled the sight with star-bursts.

Yet, as the day wore on, so the weather began to change. A cat's-paw wind that fluttered around the compound, playfully at first, strengthened after the noon meal and the temperature rose, so that boots that first had flustered through the snow at first light, now crunched heavily instead, and by the late afternoon the sky was filled once more with great pyramids of cloud that cast a strange yellow glare across the naked countryside.

The old thane had said there would be snow, and with a fresh blizzard now about to close them in again, and with nothing seen to move in that whole deserted wilderness, there was no point in risking men or beasts on further searches until the weather changed again.

With the last man safely accounted for, the heavy gates across both entrances were slammed shut and barred, the massive timbers that locked them down taking six men to drop safely into place. And so, as another day came to a close, the snow began to fall again in sharp hissing chaos that filled the night sky with whirling snow feathers. Around the palisade, and in the gate towers, the night-guards huddled below their parapet and cursed their tardy reliefs still drinking their hot spiced ale within the hall place, while the bitter wind drifted the snow into fresh smoking dunes and prows around them.

*

By the time the new day broke and the sky began to lighten in the east, the snow had finally stopped, though the clouds remained thick and heavy overhead, and the daylight was tinged with ochre. Beyond the walls the countryside was shrouded in a thick frosted mist, everything opaque, ethereal; and as the morning dragged itself into sulky life, so the men on guard

79

began to come alive again, rubbing their tired eyes with wind-chaffed fingers, their minds alert only to the promise of hot food and warmth that now awaited them.

It was Twelfth Night, the feast of Yule-end. Today, unless the weather held him off, the Lord Heardred should come in for his betrothal to the Lady Brioni. Even now the Lady Aethelflaeda was preparing the meats and pasties that would be needed later on. Battle-proven reinforcements would come in with him and all would be ten times better! There'd be dancing and feasting, the hall-harp would go round and their favourite songs would raise the roof of the great hall. It would be a night to remember, perhaps even acrobats and a dancing bear, if all they had heard was true. A circus was coming through to Chippenham to entertain the King, and their thane had sent Wulfnoth out to barter with its leader, so all were hoping they would come and do some turns for them as well. And laughing at those thoughts, the men in the watch towers turned to greet their reliefs with heart-felt cheers as they came across to change places with them at last.

Surely today would be a great day.

# Chapter Eleven

So, when they all turned back and saw the mass of figures on horseback, and on foot, coming to them from the Malmesbury road with strange seeming Christian banners to the fore, they were not instantly alarmed; just excited that the Lord Heardred had finally arrived...or the circus was coming to join them. But it was Olaf, once more up in the left-hand watch tower, who saw that it was no Christian flag beneath which the coming warriors hurried, but a bloody horse's head...and every man was wearing blackened armour with closed face-plates.

This was not Saxon armour...this was the armour of heathen men, coming from the north, from where distant Gloucester lay, where Guthrum lurked with the Great Army, and reaching for the rope beside him he shouted: "Danes! *The Danes!*" Beating a desperate tocsin with the great alarum bell that sent its wild clang ringing out across the garth, while beside him Rorsthan blew on his horn: '*Hoooooom! Hoooooom! Hoooooom!*' The deep sound going on and on and on to call the whole compound suddenly to arms.

In minutes the men of Foxley responded, those along the distant sides of the palisade rushing to the northern entrance, while from the hall place came Carnfrith and his body of archers, armed with their great war-bows to man the shooting turrets either side of the gate, arrows in their quivers, and held clamped between their teeth as they raced up the ladders and took up their positions.

From wagon-barn and great hall, the men and women of Foxley also responded to the alarum's desperate call, pouring in a wild rush from their cots and home spaces, to muster in the garth and await the orders of their war-leaders. Gyrth, Aelric, Osric, Wulfstan and all their hearth-companions rushed to take their places along the walls and to them ran their armoured fyrdsmen, armed with shields, swords and gavelock, the older children with slings and bags of sling-stones and fresh quivers of arrows; and the women with spears and light shields to strengthen the defence.

And so the first arrows came whiffling out of the freezing mist with the north wind behind them, wound-bees fired with extreme prejudice by a violent enemy, the heavy barbs smashing through chest and back armour of those they struck as though they were made of paper, dropping the men coughing and spitting blood into the quiet snow. And with the arrows came the noise, the harsh roar of countless voices, the crash of swords on shields in the usual wild

Viking taunt, the sharp '*tock-tock-tock*' of more arrows as they buried themselves in the wood of palisade and tower alike.

Down the trackway from the Malmesbury road, and out from the brakes and woodlands nearby rushed their enemies, many with great rolls of faggots and long stretchers of wicker hurdles in their hundreds to fill up the ditch and attack the palisade with grapnels, ropes and axes. While others brought with them a great ram, a vast tree trunk laid on a set of heavy wheels.

Within moments the whole homestead was in an uproar, with men rushing to the walls and up the towers, many struggling with clothes and armour as they ran, while flights of arrows flew over the walls to pierce any unfortunate caught out in the open without a shield. And as the alarum bell ceased its shouting, so the chapel bell started to peel out its own sharp voice as Anselm pulled on the rope again and again to call the company to arms. And even as the bell was beating, the first pounding blow of the makeshift ram shuddered the gates, accompanied by fresh howls of rage and defiance, and more showers of arrows as Carnfrith and his archers fired relentlessly into the mass of Danes below them at the gates, bursting heads and bodies open and hurling their enemies to the bloody ground in droves.

Made from a fallen tree, the thicker branches trimmed short as handles, the ram was wielded by a score or more of heathen men in link-steel byrnies and nasal helmets, shields on their backs; each massive stroke shaking the gates from top to bottom. Running backwards and forwards on its solid wheels across the bridge that faced the gates, it was a formidable weapon, and though the Foxley archers mauled those who ran with it, for every Dane that fell there was another rushed to take his place.

And the roar and scream of battle was constant, the wounded being brought down from the walls, the dead pitched over them to clear the way; while the women did what they could to ease those in pain and bind up their wounds, as more defenders rushed to join those already in action.

Racing up the wooden stairways to the parapet above them, they hurled their spears down upon the Danes struggling in the ditch and at those Danish axe-men now hacking furiously at the very base of the palisade. Their wounded, writhing in torment at the bottom of the snow-filled dyke, were left to struggle back to join their friends who bayed and howled their rage at the Saxon defenders above them whom they had come to slay. Sword Danes and Spear Danes in their hundreds, the whole front of Foxley manor was black with armed men, while their archers fired over their heads and their leaders, mounted on great horses, hallooed them forwards, calling for them to shed their blood in revenge for the deaths of their own hearth-companions already slain, and for those warriors these same Saxon had slaughtered in the snow just one week before.

Foremost of these was the great Jarl of Helsing, the Lord Oscytel, superbly mounted on a coal black stallion. A King to his men, in linked, riveted mail that covered him from to head to toe in blackened armour, his face hidden behind a mask of steel chased with gold through which his eyes glittered with feral rage as he called his men forward. Armed with a great axe, whose blade shimmered in the harsh light as he waved it above his head, and with a jewelled sword by his side, he carried a mighty shield across his left arm, iron rimmed and emblazoned with his symbol of a ragged knife, painted gold and rimmed in scarlet, like a lightning bolt across its front. He was a terrifying sight that no arrow fired seemed to hit, and everywhere he went his men seemed to re-double their efforts to break in...even as those around Thane Wulfstan struggled to keep them out.

*

Brioni, waking slowly, was aware at first of only a muffled roaring, the thickness of the timber walls of the great hall and the many rooms within, shielding her from the wild fury going on outside. But the frantic tocsin of the alarum bell brought her instantly alert.

*Danes!*

Oscytel, the Black Jarl of Helsing, had come for them at last...and with that she was instantly on the move.

Flinging off her thick coverings she reached for her clothes in a single bound. Not the soft, richly spun woollens that she usually wore, but her tough brown leather travelling gear, much like a man's, with well-worn leather chausses, cross-gartered to the knee beneath a thick leather jacket over a rough yellow cotton chemise. In her little room, fumbling desperately with their stout fastenings, she cursed her clumsy fingers as she struggled with the laces, the noise all around her growing in intensity with every passing moment.

No sooner had she bent to force her feet into her heavy riding boots, than Agatha came rushing in to find her, dressed herself in travelling gear, her voice and body shaking with fear.

"They're here, my Lady! *They're here!* The Danes! They've come...what shall we do? *What shall we do?*"

"Calm yourself, Agatha!" Brioni said sharply. "If you panic now you're lost. Where's my father?"

"Gone! All gone, my Lady!" the girl replied, giving a little sob. "There's only your mother and the house-thralls...and her tire-maidens left."

83

"Where's Father Anselm?"

"I don't know! *I don't know!* Ringing the chapel bell," Agatha wailed, sinking down onto her mistress's bed. And covering her face with her hands she began to rock herself backwards and forwards, keening as she did so. "They'll kill us all, I know they will! Oh, God, what shall we do? *What shall we do?*"

Stepping up to her, Brioni tore her hands away from her face and slapped her hard.

"By all the Saints, Agatha," she went on quietly, giving the weeping girl a firm shake as she did so. "You must calm down! Here," she added, turning swiftly round, as she pulled on a pair of red, fleece-lined leather gloves "take my good cloak and come with me. We must find my mother and Father Anselm, for they will know what we must do!"

Moments later they were in the main body of the hall, now tightly barred against attack, doors and windows both, the tables and benches in disarray all about them. Up on the dais her mother and the old priest were both standing, the house-thralls bunched around them, all armed with whatever weapons they had managed to lay their hands on off the walls, her mother's tire-maidens in a small group close by and clearly too terrified to move.

Outside the storm and clamour of the assault rose and fell with each resounding crash of the ram, still being hurled against the gates with unrelenting vigour despite all that the Foxley defenders could do. The Vikings hammering at gates and palisade howled like demons with every smashing blow, while the defenders bayed at them from behind their defences, driving down at their enemies with spears and lances, and shooting arrows from every possible vantage. The air was also filled with sling-stones that flayed their enemies with terrifying force, felling many with broken heads and dented armour as they clattered furiously amongst them.

As soon as Brioni and Agatha arrived, the Lady Aethelflaeda turned and spoke urgently to the little priest by her side, her handsome face as calm as if she were in a bustling market place, and not on the edge of a maelstrom of disaster.

"Anselm, you must get these two out, as Wulfstan suggested."

"What about you, my Lady?"

"My place is here, where Wulfstan can find me; you know that. But my daughter and young Agatha have no part in this now."

"How, my Lady? By the sounds of it the enemy are all around us!"

"Not quite, Anselm. They haven't broken into the compound yet. You could slip out through the half-doors at the back of the kitchens. Ecgfrith!" she called, turning to one of her serving men. "You must go with them and re-bar

84

the door once they are safely outside." Then turning back swiftly to the old priest standing forlornly by her side she added gently: "Anselm, old friend, do this for me, and please don't look so stricken. We will be alright here, just as we always have been in the past. This is not the first time Foxley has been attacked, remember? But do not linger here. Get to the chapel and then slip out over the west wall. The parados is lower there this side of the palisade and the snow in the great ditch will break your fall on the other side. Don't argue with me, please. Go, now, as quickly as you can!"

"Now, my Lady?"

"Yes, Anselm, now...before it is too late. Come, quickly, the both of you," she continued, turning towards the two girls and holding out her hands. "Go with Anselm , and do as he says. No, Agatha; don't cry. You must be brave for all our sakes. Come, Brioni, kiss me my pet, my darling," and taking her daughter in her arms she held her tightly for a few brief moments, her eyes closed in the agony of parting, the tears welling up as she did so. She felt her heart would break knowing, as she held the girl's slender body to her, that she was probably holding her beautiful daughter in her arms for the last time.

Brioni, her arms squeezed round her mother's waist, her head pressed into the soft hollow of her neck, had a sudden, terrible sense of loss as she felt her mother's hand gently caress her hair the way she had done so often when she was a child, and cuddled herself in even closer for just one tiny moment longer. Then, with a final squeeze she stepped back and gently kissed her mother on both cheeks, dashing her own tears away with the back of her hand as she did so.

"Oh, mother, I do love you so!" she said hoarsely, reaching out softly to touch her mother's face once more.

"Sa, sa, my beauty," her mother whispered in reply. "And I love you too." Then, taking a deep breath, she went on firmly: "Now, go, all of you, quickly! For you haven't a moment to lose. And the quicker you slip away...the sooner you will be back again!"

The spell was broken, and with one last tortured glance at his Lady, Father Anselm swiftly knelt and kissed her hand, then, rising and turning rapidly, he led the two girls across the dais and out to the rough kitchen area that lay behind it. Within moments they were before the thick half-doors that led outside, where Anselm paused briefly for them to gather round him.

"Are you ready, Ecgfrith?"

"Yes, Father."

"Then, we'll do it now!"

Standing to one side of the closed entrance, Ecgfrith reached for the heavy draw-bar that lay in iron hoops across the doors, and as he pulled it free,

Agatha and Brioni hauled on the two pairs of iron bolts at top and bottom that latched into the stone uprights to which the doors were fixed.

Pushing his shoulder against the rough timbers, Anselm heaved the valves open and slipped outside, beckoning immediately for the girls to join him. As soon as they were together again they leaned back and crashed the doors shut, the snap and bang of the bolts and locking-bar being slammed behind them, sounding horribly final.

*

*T*hey found themselves in the small, square kitchen yard not far from the great midden, beyond which lay the chapel. Here the dry stone walls that surrounded them stood some three or four feet high all round, and running from the doors they took shelter behind them, crouching down against the hard stones and peering cautiously out across the snow-covered garth.

All around the walls in front of them the struggle raged with deafening violence as Wulfstan and his men, with the villagers' help, fought to keep the Danes clear of the palisade. The fighting was at its very fiercest by the northern gates, now beginning to sag dangerously as the Vikings continued to batter at them with their ram, and also by a section of the palisade that the Danish axe-men were strenuously attacking.

Here, where the enemy had managed to fill the ditch with piles of faggots and hurdles, the fighting was equally ferocious. Here the Danes, having part-hacked through some of the tree trunks that made up the palisade, were attempting with grapples and heavy cable to pull the giant palings out of the ground like rotted teeth by main-force, and horses hauling back, and the struggle was epic: Spears and javelins flew in both directions, with swarms of arrows and sprays of sling-stones accompanied by howls of rage and pain as the fyrd, under Aelric, Rorsthan and the old Thane himself, fought like demons to keep the enemy out.

Time and again it seemed that the heathen men must break through…only to have their assault wither away before the hail of missiles the Saxon defenders hurled down at them and by their vicious defence by sword, seaxe and battle axe, the snow stained scarlet all around the fighting.

From her shelter, Brioni could see where her father was leading the defence against the Vikings' constant attempts to scale the walls, roaring on his men as he thrust down fiercely with his great fighting spear at the enemy hordes struggling below him in the ditch and on the palisade.

Closely supported by Aelric and his hearth-companions, who guarded their Thane's back with their shields, he fought as a leader should do, from the forefront and with tireless courage, his armour sheeted with the blood of those whom he had slain. While his fyrdsmen, some armoured and others not, fought furiously beside him, continuously risking both life and limb to heave rocks or part-worked tree trunks down upon the heads of their hated foe toiling in the ditch and on the narrow causeway they had made across it.

"Fire…bring me fire! These faggots they are using, and the hurdles, will burn if we can get fire to them. Hurry! Bring oil and fire. We can yet drive them off with frightening loss!"

Hearing her father's shout, and before they could say a word, Brioni leapt away from Anselm and Agatha and ran to the main doorway and hammered on it with a stone she had seized up on her way.

"Open, mother! Open! In the name of Christ, open! Father needs oil and fire from the hearth to burn out the enemy at the walls. Quickly! *Oh, quickly!*" And after an agonising pause, while Brioni hammered again and again with her stone; with a great, graunching of timbers the main hall-place doors swung open at last, and her mother stood there, sword in hand to usher Brioni in, while the house-thralls rushed to gather oil from the kitchens and flaming brands from the hearth at their Thane's commands.

"How goes it?" her mother gasped.

"*Desperate!* Father needs oil and fire."

"He shall have them immediately. We should have thought of it before! Go swiftly and choose two brands from the fire. Others will follow you!"

And within minutes they all ran from the hall across the garth amidst a hail of enemy arrows fired at will into the compound from beyond the walls, that dropped two of the hall servants in writhing heaps, but left the others free, and moments later Brioni arrived at her father's side, two brands held in her leather covered hands, their ends bright with flame.

"Here, father!" she shouted above the wall of noise around the parados. "The oil comes immediately in clay-fired beakers."

"*What do you here?*" he roared at her, snatching up the brands as he spoke.

"What I can! *This is my home too!*" And she leapt behind him, beneath Aelric's shield, as a spear came whistling up towards them from below, clattering off its curved surface. "The village women are here beside their men. Why not me?"

"Because I ordered you elsewhere! Where's that oil, before we lose the chance?"

"Here, my Lord!" the first of the house-thralls shouted, thrusting his clay beaker of oil at Wulfstan's face. "And more to come."

"Aelric, clear a space," he bellowed. "Then down with it onto those hurdles, and the rest. Then we shall see what these bastards think of our firedrake!"

And as he spoke Aelric, having swiftly sheathed his sword, hurled the first of the clay oil pots, now arriving in a steady stream from the hall, down amongst the enemy below them. Pot after pot shattered amongst them showering men, faggots and hurdles with dripping oil so that all slithered and slipped as they struggled to pull down the great palings above them, horses slipping in the snow as they tried to pull them out, men shouting and beating the horses with straps to make them pull harder, flung stones and arrows felling the enemy on every side. The noise continuous and deafening: roaring voices, full of rage and hate; the screech of steel and crash of blades on shields; the howling of the wounded, the screams of wounded horses and the groans of the dying, both Dane and Saxon.

Then pandemonium as Wulfstan hurled the first of the flaming brands down upon them, spluttering amidst the snow and soiled straw, and among the crushed faggots and broken hurdles with which the Danes had filled the ditch. Until, as more brands were heaved down upon them, and more oil followed, the whole mass suddenly caught fire with a sullen roar, the flames leaping and twisting up, scarlet, yellow and orange amidst a pyre of roiling black smoke, thick and oily, that engulfed the enemy who were struggling there. Some were merely singed, and some were scorched, but others were completely enveloped in flames and ran screaming amongst the rest, spreading fire and terror everywhere they rushed, until the whole ditch was one mass of writhing, oily flame and thick black smoke…and with howls of rage and pain the cables burned, the horses pulling them were run off and the attack there was foiled.

# Chapter Twelve

Away by the gates her brother was in sole command, Carnfrith the Archer and his men by his side; and in the other shooting turret more of their fellows, their stock of arrows now rapidly dwindling, as they shot continuously into the milling, heaving press that were mustered there against them. Yet no matter how many of the heathen warriors were put down, there were always more to take their place, while those Saxon defenders slain with arrow, spear or rock could not be replaced so readily, and already there were many women now amongst them, all screaming defiance and hate at the Danish Vikings fighting below them at the gates. Yet despite all that Carnfrith and those still with him could do, the enemy had managed to keep their ram going, each successive blow threatening to be the one, finally, to tear the gates apart and wrench them from their pintles.

Ordered back down to join Agatha and Anselm by the chapel, Brioni found herself alert and unafraid, untouched by the fear that had held the others paralysed, quite different from what she had been expecting. For she had been filled with excitement that flushed her face and coursed through her body like fire, the battle fury she had heard the men talk of so many times, that came upon them when the horns blew and the clash of steel rang through the air, and she exulted in it. Then, suddenly, there were figures running past her, armoured axe-men in iron helmets with brass nasals and black face plates.

*Danes!*

Spinning round with a gasp of dismay, she realised what had happened. An unmanned section of the parados, the very section her mother had told Anselm of, was now firmly in enemy hands, one pirate after another leaping down off the wall walk to dash across the garth and take the defenders in the rear.

With the fierce struggle around the gates now reaching a climax, and the north-wall defenders now trying to put out the flames they had started, no-one had noticed the small party of Danes who had slipped away from the main body of the attackers and made their way to the very back of the stockade, where, finding an uncleared ramp of fresh snow, they had clambered up, dropped down and were even now in the heart of the defence and moving fast.

"Look! They have broken through behind!" Brioni shouted wildly. "The heathen men are in amongst us. We must do something or we are lost," she cried out, swinging back to Agatha and Anselm. "There is a fallen sword over there, we must fight!"

"No, my Lady!" Anselm answered her, desperately, holding onto her leather jacket. "You must not! You will be killed!"

"No, mistress! *No!*" Agatha cried out in an agony of terror, clasping her arm. "You cannot leave us now!"

But she ignored them both, and with a fierce, wild cry she broke from them, leapt the low wall behind which her companions were still crouching, and sweeping the fallen sword up into her hand, she dashed across the compound, abandoning poor Agatha and Anselm before they could do anything more to stop her.

Hearing her soaring cry, even above the violent press of figures all around him, Wulfstan turned and roared an order through the smoke and flame of the palisade, and even before she had reached them, Brioni saw Aelric, Rorsthan, and a dozen of Osric's crudely trained fyrdsmen, rush from their positions on the wall-walk to meet this sudden new attack.

Shouting as they ran, they fell upon their enemies before they had gone a hundred paces, and a vicious, stabbing, hacking skirmish began as both parties hewed at one another across the war-linden.

But the damage had been done.

Even as the last of the incomers were slain, the Danes made a final concerted attack. Those with Oscytel up by the gates and those by the walls against the palisade they had been attacking, now severely burned through, felt the sudden slackening in their enemy's defence, and hearing Danish shouts and cries from their fellows now fighting fiercely within the walls, they redoubled their efforts.

Rushing back to the half-burned palisade, they hurled fresh grapnels up onto it, running the new cables to the horses still standing by. And with a huge roar of effort, spurring the horses forward again, that section of the palisade hacked through and teetering on the very edge of ruin now suddenly crashed outwards in a shower of smashed and burned timbers and torn lashings, spilling many of the defenders into the ditch as it fell, making a perfect bridge into the compound as it did so.

Hearing the crash and the great bellow that followed it, Gyrth immediately abandoned the defence of the gates, now staggering against their ruined posts, the massive draw-bar itself visibly splitting at every thunderous stroke of the Vikings' ram...and drew back towards the hall-place where it had long been decided to make a last and final stand.

No sooner had his men begun to move than, with a monstrous *crack!* the northern gates finally burst apart, and giving a wild howl of triumph the Danes poured in, hurtling forward on their own momentum, heads down and yelling fit to burst. But for this Carnfrith and those men beside him with arrows still to fire had been waiting, and many Danes in that first wild rush were slain, tumbling to the icy ground like shot hares, falling and spinning in their death throes as a sleet of arrows fell upon them.

Hearing the gates go, Wulfstan began at once to pull his men back, calling in Aelric and Rorsthan as he retired, and those of his hearth-companions still alive, and his fyrdsmen, now grouped round him together with all who had survived the palisade's collapse, not knowing that his daughter was anywhere nearby.

\*

*U*p by the breach Brioni had flung herself into the fray beside the screaming peasants still fighting ferociously to keep their enemies at bay, thrusting forward with her sword as Heardred had taught her long ago, desperately hampered by the lack of a shield with which to protect her open side.

*Stab! Lunge! Parry!* The heavy sword growing more leaden by the moment as she fought to keep her feet moving and her arm up. *Duck! Bob! Weave!*...bare flesh! No armour, no tunic, it had to be an enemy, a baresarker. And seeing her opening she drove at it, thrusting her blade forward with all her strength into the hard, naked belly that had suddenly appeared before her, and with a twist of her arm, as Heardred had shown her, she forced the blade over and round. And, as she had been told, the flesh split open like a ripe peach, the foetid air from the man's punctured bowels flowing hotly over her hand in the frigid air. With a terrible, high-pitched wail he began to fall, tearing the sword out of her grasp as he did so, the muscles around his punctured belly gripping the blade like a vice, too tightly for her to pull it free.

With her weapon gone, and her hands and face sticky with blood, she ran back from the crushing mêlèe to find another, just in time to see the gates fly backwards and the first wave of Danish pirates flood in, followed immediately by a second group, wearing black steel byrnies, closed up and moving rapidly. Jomsvikings, their black shields with the ragged gold knife motif edged in scarlet across the centre held close against them as they ran in around and behind their leader.

Oscytel had come at last.

The Black Jarl of Helsing in person, and despite herself, Brioni froze beside the ruined parados, the sickly stench of blood all around her.

He was a huge figure on his great black horse, his features masked by the gilded eye loops and nasal that covered the front of his face, further obscured by the side plates that protected his cheeks from stray arrows, sling-stones and sword cuts. Only the sharp glitter of eyes showed he was even human. In flowing black steel coat and broad gold arm-bands, with his fighting axe swinging from a steel chain by his side and jewelled sword now in hand, he was a stark contrast to the trampled, blood-stained snow all around him.

And with his arrival the defence of Foxley finally broke apart in howling confusion. Some remembered what their thane had tried to teach them and ran to where he was standing beneath his great house-flag of the snarling foxhead, while others dropped their weapons and tried to flee. Brioni, conscious of her father's orders, and now freed from the strange spell that had held her fast a moment earlier, desperately searched the compound for any kind of safe place in which to hide.

Everywhere she looked in the strengthening light there were the bodies of men and women slain in the fighting, and those who had been hideously wounded, both Dane and Saxon: men thrust through the throat and body with spears and javelins, their intestines bulging out upon the trampled snow; necks burst open by ripping steel, swords and arrows both; some skewered like spatch-cock fowls, the arrows thrust right through arms and thighs and throats; women hacked down beside their men, lying in whimpering bundles as they clutched at their wounds, eyes glazed in pain and shock as their blood drained remorselessly away. And then there were the grotesque: the stumbling wounded, men and women both, so badly gashed and torn that many were beyond care or recognition, shambling aimlessly in shocked abandonment, arms missing, hands gone, blood spurting from their broken bodies, some even cradling their own offal in their hands, stunned beyond pain until death claimed them.

Pressed back against a fallen timber, Brioni stood and watched in numbed horror as the final killing began. She saw old Anselm run out screaming towards the towering figure of his nightmares, a fallen spear gripped tightly in his hands, young Agatha running blindly behind him, holding her hands out and weeping, Brioni's rich cloak rippling from her slender shoulders.

With a single fluid movement Oscytel swayed his horse to one side to avoid the clumsily spearman and hacked down at the screaming, maddened old priest with his sword, his great blade splitting the old man's skull in two, spraying both horse and rider with bloody gruel. And with the same nonchalant skill he turned and butchered poor Agatha, a great scything, back-handed blow that sliced her face to her backbone, cleaving her lower jaw apart from her mandible, felling her with a single piercing scream to the bloody ground where he trampled her furiously with his horse's sharpened hooves until her poor body was pulped beyond recognition.

92

Crying out, and with angry tears pouring down her face, Brioni now ran towards the hall midden where it festered in a great sprawl, some distance from the small stone chapel where she had left Agatha and Anselm such a short time before. The one place she remembered her father saying that a Viking pirate would never think to search.

A small unseen figure scrabbling amongst the piled-up filth and ordure of the steading, the mixed dung of man and beast both, much of it snow-covered and frozen to a solid mass, but mostly only a thick crust through which she thrust her booted feet into the warm stinking ooze beneath. The stench of rotting food and animal waste made her cough and retch violently as she scraped what straw fragments she could find over her head and chest, until only the tear-filled flitter of her blue eyes were visible. And even then you would have had to know where to look.

*

All around her was a scene of utter madness: people and animals together mixed in the steel tempest that was now raging everywhere, for the stock beasts had broken free and were running, bawling, around the seething compound, only the horses having the sense to rush for the safety of the open countryside. And from her hiding place she watched the final, terrible destruction of her home, the cries of the maimed and dying mingling with those of the Saxon women whom Oscytel's men now seized, tearing at their clothes to get at the soft meat underneath, while others held their twisting bodies, all eager for their turn. Then a swift flash of steel across the throat, and on to the next, leaving each poor wretched creature to leap and flop helplessly in her own blood.

Away up by the old barn the horrors continued, for there the Danes were pillaging with a vengeance, intent only on taking with them those things for which they had a use. The old and the very young they slaughtered, dragging their wailing captives into the light and splitting their throats and bellies open until it was like the autumn slaughter, the ground running with blood and slick with offal. And those too young to walk they picked up by the heels and swung them with brutal force against the gnarled and ancient timbers of the barn, crushing their skulls like eggshells, while they laughed to see each sudden spray of blood and bone splatter the walls and bloodied floor.

Appalled and stricken as she was, still Brioni could not look away, but watched every terrible deed as it was done. Each dreadful act imprinted on her mind, and seared into her soul, for when, in God's time, she would make

Oscytel pay in blood for every deed he and his men were wreaking on her home and family.

Meanwhile the fighting round the hall-place had finally reached a climax. Wulfstan's men, together with the remains of his fyrdsmen and those villagers who had stayed with him, now drawn back in a rough semi-circle round the double entrance doors, were ready to make one last attempt to break free. All around them the Danes were shouting, their shields locked in one to another in their famous shield wall and baying for their blood, one man taking another's place as he grew weary, the smash and clatter of swords on shields and axes ringing continuously.

Then, almost imperceptively at first, as their thane shouted out his orders, the outer wings of her father's line began to wedge together as had been practised so many times in the days before the Danes had attacked them. Gyrth and himself in the very front, with all their men packed in around and behind them, now joined by her mother and the house-thralls, all armed with whatever weapons they could find. All together for this final attack. And holding her breath in an agony of expectation, Brioni waited for the break-out she knew must follow a deployment so carefully prepared.

She had seen the King practise this very manoeuvre with his royal companions on more than one occasion, just as she had watched her father across the frozen garth in the days before the attack. And she looked for some means of joining them, spotting more than one horse beyond the shattered gateway that she felt sure she could reach in the confusion that would follow her father's escape from Foxley.

Suddenly, with a great roar of defiance, spear points and swords thrusting out in every direction they all began to move, driving a wedge of sharpened, pointed steel right into the very heart of Oscytel's defence, as they rushed towards the torn breach in the palisade, swords flailing and spears thrust out all round like a hedgehog's spines.

Taken by surprise, their enemies gave way with howls and shrieks of rage and pain as Wulfstan's flying wedge attack cut through their ranks like a red hot knife through butter, scattering their enemies in blood-boltered swathes. Even Oscytel's presence could not stem her father's swift advance, as with shouts of fury Gyrth and Wulfstan, the great snarling foxhead flag above them, led their men towards the safety of the open breach and the countryside beyond.

Now struggling desperately to get out and join them, Brioni did not see the small group of shaggy stirks that suddenly cantered across her father's path, bellowing in their terror at all the noise and fighting, before it was too late. And closing her eyes in horrified dismay she heard the ragged thump and

94

crash as flying wedge and solid running beasts collided in the very moment of their victory, and her father's last attack just fell apart.

Slumped back, into the mire of the great midden, weeping with frustration and utter dismay, she watched through a haze of tears as with howls of fury Oscytel and his Danes rushed down upon her friends and family. One by one she watched them fall: Gyrth first, his body hacked and broken by a dozen thrusts of spear and sword; next Osric, Rorsthan, Aelric and all the rest as wild Danish blood-lust gathered them all in.

She saw her father turn and clasp her mother in his arms, the tears running down his cheeks as, with his own seaxe, he thrust her through the heart, her head suddenly falling against his chest as he held her to him for one moment before dropping her gently to the ground.

And then suddenly it was all over.

Oscytel held up his hands and shouted…and his men rushed in upon her father, still fighting with all his old vigour, and overwhelmed him in a body; and he was flung to the ground and swiftly disarmed before he could fall on his own sword. But what followed next was so terrible that in after years she still awoke trembling in the night and crying out.

Beckoning some of his men to him, Oscytel ordered them to search the hall and chapel, forcing Brioni to sink herself further into the foul mire around her as two of them ran past the midden and searched the small religious building not a stone's throw from where she was hiding. And all the while four of his men held the Thane of Foxley pinioned in their hands, his wounds oozing blood steadily as he stood swaying by their side, his mind dulled by the bitter events of the past few moments.

Within minutes, Oscytel's men were back, those from the chapel empty handed, but others from the hall bearing the rich war shield of Oscytel's son that had been placed on the wall…while others of his men, stooping over Gyrth's body, returned with the helmet and great sword that he had taken for his own and placed it in Oscytel's hands. Just for a moment the tall war leader stood and stared down at the weapon in silence, then, with a swift gesture and shout of rage, the Black Jarl ordered those holding her father to strip and fling him face down upon the torn ground, his blood flowing out from his wounds as he cried out in pain and sudden fear.

Then, with practised ease, the big Danish leader reached down to his waist and drew out a strange green-bladed knife from a concealed sheath and pausing briefly to hold it up in reverence before his blood-stained followers, he knelt down and with one, slow, terrible stroke he thrust it into her father's body, and dragged it down his spine.

95

With one terrible shriek her father's body leapt against the hands that held him and writhed in tortured, agony while he thrashed his head from side to side, as one by one Oscytel, with a twist of his knife broke Wulfstan's ribs free of his spine and splayed them outwards in the semblance of a great bird's wings, while his victim howled in pain and his whole body shuddered, his blood gushing out across the beaten snow-field that was his home. Then, to complete the horror, Oscytel thrust his hands into his body and lifted out his lungs amidst the bony feathers of the cage that held his heart.

Her spirit weeping, her body shaking with the horror of it all, Brioni was forced to endure each dreadful moment of the vile butchery that was going on before her, and heard her father's tortured scream as each rib was broken from his body, for this was the Blood-Eagle, the dreadful pagan ritual that would not cease until each rib had been broken out of his back and splayed like wings. As Ivar the Boneless, son of Ragnar Lodbrok, had done to King Aelle of Northumbria for the death of his father…so the Lord Oscytel did to Thane Wulfstan for the death of his son.

Unable to cry out, his blood welling in a rich flood onto the frozen, snow-covered ground, Wulfstan was beyond pain and already dying when Oscytel's completed the ritual in a final act of vile desecration as his hand closed around Wulfstan's heart and ripped it out. The blood spraying the faces of his men and of himself as he did so, with a great shout he flung it down upon the mired snow and stamped it to a bloody mush.

Dazed with horror, Brioni watched as Oscytel stalked away to gather his men together, some to strip the dead, hunting over the soggy corpses for whatever precious things that they could find; others to run from building to building with great flaming torches of straw and strangled sheaves of wattle and broken osiers, casting them inside one upon another until each shack and lean-to was one great oily mass of angry flame.

Her home was the last to go, fired by the Black Jarl himself after every one of his own dead had been dragged inside it. The flames, licking hungrily across the ancient thatch and round the knotted timbers that had stood proud through all her father's lifetime, would make a suitable pyre for all those Danes who had been killed in the fighting. Hot scarlet tongues that danced and leapt round every precious wooden limb, until the whole great building was one writhing mass of flame, ablaze from end to end.

Then, with a detail driving those captured animals the Danes most wanted, horses and good herd beasts, they all fell in before the river gateway, opposite to where they had broken in. Now hauled open against its stops, it led down a simple causeway to the bridge and then through the village, now ripped apart and pillaged, and so towards Chippenham which Guthrum's Danes had assaulted at daybreak. With spoil carts laden with goods taken from both barn and hall, others piled with their wounded, and a line of wretched prisoners, both men and women, bringing up the rear in utter, trudging misery, the Danes all turned and marched away, singing as they went, their harsh guttural voices lingering in the thick smoky air.

Leaving their dead in one huge burning pyre, and their Saxon enemies for the birds and beasts of the woods and forests, Oscytel and his men left the shattered steading of Foxley. Now wreathed in flames, like so much of the countryside round them, they left it to join King Guthrum's army as it swept across Wessex from Gloucester, already attacking King Alfred in his Royal hall at Chippenham.

# Chapter Thirteen

She was alive, and alone amongst a legion of the dead.

The sun, the sky, the distant snowscape still unchanged...when everything else around her was so horribly deformed.

Wherever she looked the carnage seemed complete; the litter of bodies that were strewn like torn rags amongst the shattered wreckage of her home showed no signs of life. There were no wounded Saxons anywhere, all had been throat-cut or simply axed to death, and their bodies left where they had been dragged from the walls, or slumped where they had fallen. And where the fighting had been fiercest they lay in heaps; the only movement that of their clothing where the bitter wind ruffled through it with spiny fingers.

Opening her mouth she howled like an animal in torment, a desperate keening that sent the crows and ravens that had gathered to feast upon the dead, wheeling into the sky with startled cries. Then, with a great roar and blast of heat, the roof of the hall collapsed, sending blazing fragments spinning in smoky arcs through the air, and clouds of sparks, like fireflies, shot high into the morning sky. And with the crash her head began to clear and, closing her mouth. the desperate keening was mercifully stilled.

She was alive!

With the recognition of survival came the sobbing tears, and at once she began to struggle from the miry hole in which she had lain concealed. Drawing her feet free at last, she staggered from the midden's stinking crest. Uncertainly at first, then faster and faster, stumbling through the scattered debris and the butchered corpses she ran weeping to where the bodies of her family lay broken in the blood-stained snow.

Twice she fell, and twice she rose again until at last she stood amongst them, a silent figure in a frozen landscape, bathed in the fierce glow of the burning hall behind her and the harsh light from a pale sun overhead.

How small her brother looked in death, his naked body horribly gashed and torn with the many sword and spear thrusts that had cut him down, and where the Danes had mutilated his body when they had discovered that he still held the sword that their leader's son had once been used to wield. His eyes still bulged with the agony of his death.

Here Osric the wiry swordsman lay, bloodied wrist stumps where his hands should be. Here too lay Rorsthan, his shoulder cleaved through to his spine, with Ulric, Carnfrith, Aelric and all the others whom she had known so well, in hacked and splintered fragments by his side. And here was her darling mother also. At the very heart of the storm-wind that had scythed them to the ground she lay, strangely untouched amongst the carnage, even as her father had laid her down despite the battle-fury all around him.

Kneeling on the bloodied ground she gathered her up in her arms and wept, closing the empty eyes with trembling fingers, crooning the lullaby that as a child she had so loved to hear. And rocking her against her breast, Brioni buried her face against her mother's cheek, so cold in death, despairing in her grief and loneliness.

At last, with shaking hands, she laid her mother down, folding her hands across her breast, pillowing her head against some scattered clothing that she swiftly gathered up, and standing once again, she turned to where her father's tortured body lay spread out, half naked, on the frozen ground.

In silence the girl stood swaying in the harsh breeze above him, and with a groan of pain, she sank down in the snow and bowed her head upon his up-turned hand, the white flesh stiffening as he lay there on the soiled and bloodied garth. It was his ring hand, and taking it within her own she raised the cold palm to her lips, sealing her hot kisses into the palm with his lifeless fingers as she did so, while her tears flooded out across their mingled fingers. And with a sense of wonderment she realised that his great ring was still there, miraculously left when all else had been stripped and torn away: his sword, his boar crested helmet, the two great foxhead brooches of gold and garnets that pinned his great fur mantle to his shoulders, his jewelled belt. Somehow his ring alone had been left behind.

On trembling knees she knelt and gently drew it free, the gold and jewelled foxhead glinting in the sun, the intricately carved and decorated mask still snarling out in grim defiance from her open palm, and with a sudden, firm deliberation she closed her fingers tightly around it, the sharp coldness of the heavy metal burning against her skin.

Suddenly she felt comforted…elated, and at one with her father as if he had in some strange way reached out to her from the spirit-world he now inhabited, across the aeons that divided them, and touched her heart. It was almost as if she could hear his deep voice telling her to be calm. She felt it was an omen, a presage of the future, a challenge for her house that only she could now fulfil. It was as if the spirits of all her forefathers were gathered there around her…right to the great God Woden from whose loins her family had sprung. And with an iron resolve now flooding through her, she lifted her arm above her head and held her clenched fist towards the sun, towards her pagan heritage…and suddenly she knew what must be done.

Beset by images from deep within her, some culled from the whispered stories of her great grandsire whose semi-pagan life had so scandalised his peers; yet others from the tales of the Ancients, harp-sung and declaimed around the fire, and with which she had been brought up as a child, she knew from whom else beside her Christian God, to seek the help she needed for her task.

She felt a new warmth and strength flow through her, for now she had the understanding, the sure certainty of knowing that the Old Ones were not the simple myths and stories of her childhood, derided by the priests and overcome by the Christ child and the teachings of His life...but living entities whose ancient power could, even now, be tapped and channelled through her soul. So with the Words of Power now forming unbidden on her tongue, drawn to her from the elder days when the fierce spirits of the gods were wooed with blood and fire, she turned and spoke to them with all the fervour of her raging heart.

"O, Tiw and Thunnor, come now to my aid as I call out for vengeance on the head and body of my enemy. O Woden, from whose loins my family are sprung, I call upon you now to hear my cry against this man, Oscytel, the Black Jarl of Helsing, who has stained our Mother Erce with the blood of my family, and only I am left to carry on their name.

"By this my father's ring and ancient symbol of our House, and by his blood, I swear that I will never rest until my sword has bathed its keen edge in his body and torn out his life as he has torn out the life from all those whom I hold most dear. Until his black heart also lies ripped and bleeding on the ground as does my father's."

And taking off her gloves, with swift, nimble fingers, unhesitating and never once letting go of her father's ring, Brioni hastily untied the stout leather fastenings on her dress and slipped it off her arms and shoulders. In one movement she pulled off her chemise so that her firm breasts sprung free. Then, with slow reverence she straddled her father's broken body, and bending forward on her hands and knees she gently pressed her naked breasts against his mutilated carcase, dragging their jutted crests against his broken ribs and ruined lungs until they were dark with his congealing blood. And settling herself down again upon the bloodied snow she lifted her head and arched her back, holding her breasts up to the sun's harsh light, cradling them with her hands in simple offer to the ancient gods of war and thunder, a willing gift of her young body to their ancient lust for blood and sacrifice.

Finally, in completion of her rite, she took her father's ring and daubed it in the blood from where Oscytel had torn out his beating heart, and with it firmly clutched between her fingers drew upon her breasts in lines of blood, the antlers of the mystic hunter Herne...the ancient man-god of her people, his horned head cradling her breasts amongst their pointed tines. Then down towards her loins she thrust the ring to paint the hard and bloody outline of a hunter's seaxe, the potent stabbing knife that long had been her people's fame…and in an agony of passion she cried out: "Through fire and water I will follow him, and over moor and mountain, forest, plain and hill until I am revenged. This on my life, great Tiw, great Woden, now I swear, or never shall I be Freya's naked handmaiden before the Beltane fires!"

Now, with the offering of her body to the gods, and with the ritual painting of the secret signs of her people upon her naked flesh, the special signs of power and protection, she stood up and raised her hands, palm upwards to the sky, her loosened dress falling in thick folds about her feet.

Naked, her pale body a fine sliver of life amidst the frozen stillness of the slain, she cried out once more to the murmuring spirits of her murdered family and friends, who with her ancestors she knew had gathered, whispering, about her.

"O, Spirits, I feel your presence round me, 'though I see you not. The oath is taken and my body bears the holy marks of death and worship. Now before my God, whose son died for me on the cross, and before all the powers of Light and Darkness, sworn beneath the morning glow of the all-seeing sun, and upon the bodies of the slain, I will avenge you all that you may be at peace, not left to wander crying through the wilderness." And she ended with the ancient oath of her forebears that had bound her people together in the days of ancient Rome: "If I break faith with you, may the green earth gape and swallow me, may the grey seas roll in and overwhelm me, may the sky of stars fall on me and crush me out of life for ever."

Then, lifting up her voice for the last time she cried out: "Hear this, Oscytel, wherever you may be and tremble. I, Brioni of Foxley, curse you above all creatures on this earth. Know that I am seeking your soul. Beware, for nothing shall stand before my vengeance. The gods of my family and the God of my heart have heard my witness and my vow. Before the coming summertime is ended, you too shall die and pour your life-blood out upon the ground in fitting harvest to the seeds of war that you have planted here!"

Slowly lowering her arms, she bent down and pulled on her chemise and pulled up her dress, pausing briefly once more to trace her fingers over the hidden patterns of blood across her breasts before she dropped her hands to the leather tie-strings, rapidly re-fastened them and then pulled on her fleece lined gloves.

She looked around her then and shook her head.

The time for tears and sadness was past. The common dead would have to care for themselves for there was nothing she could do about them. They were just too many, and the ground too hard for burial. But for her own family there was something she could do, and quickly before the carrion birds had

101

time to settle to their task. With the weather so bitter it would not be long before some questing wolf, hungry for easy pickings, should discover the bodies and call his lean, grey brothers to the feast. After all, last night they had howled all around the palisade, sensing the warm meat that safely lay inside it.

With that thought she shook her limbs to rid them of their stiffness from kneeling in the snow, and running to the nearest pile of fallen timbers and shattered walling, she began to drag what she could handle to cover the fallen bodies where they lay. Then on top of each she piled stones and rubble so that none but the most determined scavenger would bother to unearth them. It was hard physical work that tore her clothes and scuffed her gloves, a job made even more unpleasant by the need to move some of the bodies, now considerably stiffened, making them unwieldy and obstinate as she struggled to turn or roll them out of the way. Thus it was nearly midday before she felt that she had accomplished what she had set out to do, each precious member of her family now lying hidden beneath a crude cairn built from the gutted ruins of her home.

About her father's hearth-companions, and her brother's, she had been able to do nothing; she simply had not the strength or time. But for dear Anselm and for Agatha she had done her best. He at least had been recognisable, but poor Agatha had been so hacked about and trampled that had she not been wearing the ornate blue cloak that she had given her earlier in the day, Brioni doubted whether even she would have known who she was!

Poor child!

How much she had loved that cloak, fingering its softness and luxuriating in its warmth. She smiled. More than once she had caught Agatha wearing it, pretending to be her. A sudden tearful laughter caught in her throat, never again…and in a quick gesture she drew off the bracelet she was wearing, a present from Heardred when first they had pledged their hearts, and that never left her, and drawing it off her wrist she placed it lovingly upon the dead girl's arm.

"From me, my love," she said softly. "You so wanted to be a fine lady. Enjoy in death, my sweet friend, that which was denied you during life. Thus may the old Brioni die with you," and with a deep sigh she began the final task of covering her as well.

Then it too was finished, and with a groan of exhaustion she sat down at last on a fragment of the broken palisade to study her surroundings.

*

All about her now was an eerie stillness broken only by the soughing wind and the harsh caarking of the crows and ravens as they haggled with one another amongst the spoils, the chatter of magpies, the scream of a jay, while the towering plumes of smoke all about the shattered steading veered and wavered in the wind, a sure pointer for any heathen warband who might be passing through the district.

She rubbed her face wearily with her hands. Plainly to stay where she was would be dangerous. Clearly the Danes were out, and out in force, and the gods only knew who else may have seen the smoke from the destruction of Foxley. And whatever the King may have thought of Guthrum being safely 'locked-in' at Gloucester he plainly wasn't so! Far from it. If Oscytel, one of Guthrum's closest advisors, was here in Foxley; his lord king would be after even richer 'game'...the King himself, and Chippenham was less than a day's riding from Foxley. Pray God they did not catch him or Wessex would be doomed. If Alfred were lost there would be nothing left to fight for!

But what of Heardred?

He was supposed to have been here this very day. She snorted at that, and hunched her shoulders. Today was to have been her betrothal day! Some chance of that now, if ever. And she shuddered. Oscytel's destruction of her home and family had changed everything. Her dreams were as shattered as the steading and just as burned to ashes.

She sighed and rubbed her face.

Should she stay and hope, somehow that Heardred would still manage to reach her, across Guthrum's whole army? And remain a prey to whatever ruthless band of Danish wolves should happen by in the meantime? Or get out now with what she could salvage and take to the woods and forests?

There was a charcoal burner's bothy away in Helm's Wood that she knew, beyond Foxley Grove, where there should be both shelter and fuel for burning, where she could lie up and plan her next move. A place only known to a few, and far off any marauding band's track; tucked into the edge of a small clearing in the depth of the forest. She just wished she had some sort of beast to ride! Even a donkey would be better than being on foot...and anything was better than staying here and hoping for rescue. With the whole Danish host broken out of Gloucester, Heardred might never have got anywhere near Chippenham anyway, let alone Foxley.

He might even be dead!

The smoke from the burning steading would have been seen for miles, and scavengers, both human and four-footed, would soon be sniffing round the place, and by then she needed to be gone; long gone...so no waiting for Heardred now.

He was rapidly becoming something from her past, not something to savour for the future. So, the decision was made, she would leave, and soon, and she sighed again and straightened her shoulders. But leave with what, and she threw her hands up in question. That was the most pressing problem: clothes, food, weapons, she'd need them all just to survive, and her father was right. The weather could be expected to worsen again before much longer. The sun was shining now, but palely through drifting clouds, and the wind was cruel. There might be a frost tonight, but snow again come morning. Her father was never wrong when it came to the weather.

By all the signs of autumn, of red berries in profusion and the yearly skeins of geese flying south before time; of acorns in abundance and squirrels burying their nuts early, the winter might be long and hard. And with so many steadings burned and derelict from the Danes, shelter too would be most difficult to find, and she had no transport of any kind. There were carts left tilted, or on their sides, but not even a donkey to pull one that she could see. Oscytel's men had been swift and thorough, and with wolves and bandits on the prowl she might fall prey to either one of them before the sun rose over her next morning.

Time to be moving, and searching.

She stood up and stamped her feet, stretching her legs as she did so. Thank God she had been with Alfred's Court these past few months. She had become used to sudden departures and ending up in strange places for the night, often having to cook meagre meals from whatever was to hand beneath the stars. The King was no stickler for his comforts. Not like some thanes who complained if the bread was not white and the porridge not sweetened with honey! But at least that had been in high summer, when the wind was kinder and there was plenty of game about. Here in the plundered shell of her own home, with the snow lying thick and a scourging wind at night, the situation could not be more different.

She grimaced and looked around her.

True, the hall was completely gone, together with the old wagon barn and the granary, and most buildings of any importance, including the little chapel...but surely something might have been saved? In fact there were sufficient fallen timbers and other bits and pieces to build a crude bothy of sorts if she had to, and who knew what else she might find once she got started? It was the silence that was so hard to bear, and the loneliness. She shivered suddenly and banged her hands together as much to make a noise as to warm herself. Then, with a brisk air of determination she began her search, and for the rest of the afternoon she hunted through the ruins of Foxley with urgent thoroughness, and even amongst the burned out and deserted houses of the village beyond the shattered gates. And always it was to the old forge that she brought each precious find she made.

That in itself was practically a miracle, for though some of the roof trees had been badly scorched by the inevitable flames, and the stone roof tiles missing or broken in places, for some reason the fires had just gone out and much of the building itself remained undamaged. The stone walls were more or less intact and the main door still on its pintles, if somewhat battered and missing a plank or two. Thankfully her father had insisted that Aylwin must replace the old thatch with stone after the last winter's storm had practically torn the roof off. With a little effort the great hearth would still bear a fire and the bellows were still useable. Best of all, she had found Aylwin's flints and steels in his pouch underneath his sleeping bench, with his tight wooden box of tinder, where had been discarded at the beginning of the battle. Altogether there was sufficient left of the place to give her good shelter for the night.

By the time she had garnered all she could it was far too late to move. Clearly she would have to stay, and taking up Aylwin's flints and steel she managed at last to start a fire. Above her the sun was beginning its slow slide towards the creeping purple shadows of the night, clouds edged with black against a western sky that blazed with gold and scarlet fire.

And with the last breath of day a chill wind sprang up from the east that whistled through the cracks of rough planks and timbers that Brioni had wedged across the broken entrance to the forge. Wrapped in a scorched blanket and huddled on a torn pack of woolfells she had found and laid out upon Aylwin's sleeping bench on top of several armfuls of hay, Brioni sat and stared into the fire she had now coaxed into life. Leaping and twisting in scarlet tongues of yellow, orange and crimson, the flames bit into the billets of wood she had dragged from the wood pile and laid up across the charcoal, crackling and pulsing with life as she puffed the bellows up and down beside her.

Above the flames, thrust on an iron spike and balanced across the fire on two pairs of tong holders, lay a chicken she had found dead beneath a pile of timbers, and she watched it crisping nicely, its fat sizzling on the wood and charcoal beneath, while she gnawed on a half-burned loaf she had rescued from one of the cottages in the vill below the gates, across the river. Holding the blanket draped around her shoulders over her cloak with one hand, she struggled up and poked some more wood onto the fire and pumped the bellows some more with the other, and after turning her crude spit, she moved across the forge to examine her finds of the afternoon.

They were more than she had hoped for when she started off: a whole collection of horn beakers, spoons and general cooking utensils found scattered

105

everywhere up by the old wagon barn; hand towels and an assortment of woollen undergarments; a surprisingly clean kirtle of finely embroidered wool, a linen chemise and scorched linen sheeting; half a dozen blankets, only two of them slightly burned; a bundle of woolfells; two empty sacks, a torn sack of oats and a full bag of meal; a pile of cured leather hides, a hefty set of saddle bags, a pair of thick fleece-lined leather chausses and blood-stained leather jacket to match, that she had found on one of the many bodies under the collapsed palisade; two more scrawny chickens and a sack of feathers...and an odd assortment of weapons.

But, most disappointing of all, she had found no money anywhere, not even a single coin. The Danes had made quite certain of that, going through the hall and the old wagon barn for anything they could find before setting fire to them. And they had searched the bodies of all those they had slain for good measure. How they had missed her father's ring was a miracle. She jabbed the fire with a stick and groaned. They seemed to have a sixth sense as far as gold and silver were concerned. What would she do without a single silver penny to her name?

Then she laughed. The sound almost shocking in the deep silence that filled the forge.

But, jumping up, she clapped her hands for suddenly she had remembered - her father's halidom! All his special religious artefacts: the jewelled gold cross and candlesticks off the altar, his chalice and the heavy silver salver that went with it, and the three jewelled reliquaries of which he was so proud and that were always stood between them...and then there was his own personal hoard of gold and silver coins, all of which father Ambrose had buried beneath the fire of Old Mald One-Eye's half-burned alehouse. And that she knew had not been touched, because she had been in there that very afternoon to see, finding three jars of honey in the process, and she gave a wild shout of glee. Though not a king's ransom, there was still a great deal of wealth beneath that old peasant's filthy, ale-soused hovel...and that meant freedom. And with that thought she moved with quick, determined steps towards the small pile of weapons and shields that she had recovered from all over the compound.

Many were of cheap iron, but some were worth the keeping, including two good steel knives with heavy, finely-honed blades in plain antler-horn handles...and one sword in particular she thought a real find. It was a warrior's scramaseax, now held by many to be an outdated weapon with a shorter blade than most, but its balance was superb and it had a long, pointed blade for thrusting. To Brioni it was a thing of powerful beauty with a weighted pommel and quillons of burnished brass, a handle of ancient ivory lovingly inlaid with strips of gold, and a blade covered with delicate runes, incised with gold and silver, that glinted as she turned it in the firelight.

She hefted it in her hands, swinging it gently across her body as Heardred had shown her in the summer. It felt made for her! A few good sessions with a hacking post would make all the difference, and turning, she searched among the shields she had recovered. Most were too heavy for her to use and many so hacked about on inspection as to be worthless. But some were serviceable, and from those she chose a round wicker shield on an ash-wood frame, with a tough leather cover, a spiked iron boss and an iron rim all round its edge. Like the sword it was a balanced weapon in its own right, and the straps that held it in place on her left arm had been freshly fixed. Now, if she could just find a byrnie of good linked steel she really would be a force to reckon with…and not the green girl her father had taken her to be.

She stopped at the memory and sighed, then turned back to the fire, laying the sword down as she did so to turn her attention to the only two unbroken spears that she had managed to find. One was a magnificent boar spear with a great leaf-shaped blade and thick iron quillons jutting out either side of the heavy shaft some fifteen inches from the head. It was a fine weapon, its long pole polished black with age and usage, but reluctantly she put it on one side as far too heavy and unwieldy for her to use in battle.

The other was a thin-bladed javelin which, like the scramaseax, was a weapon from an earlier age. Its blade also was delicately runed, and diamond in cross-section, the long ridge running for nearly eight inches from point to haft. It was designed for throwing and lay balanced across the palm of her hand, the shaft weighted at the bottom end to offset the long blade. It was the perfect weapon for any warrior caught in open ground and forced to take a charge.

So, with sword and spear and sturdy shield to suit her mood, and two good steel knives to her name, she was better equipped than she could possibly have hoped for. With that she turned back to eat the chicken, now thoroughly crisped and smoking on its crude iron spit, shrugging into the wide fleecy jacket she had found as she did so, the thought of hot food making her mouth water.

# Chapter Fourteen

*H*er meal over, and the hot grease from the chicken wiped from her face, the food washed down with a beaker of cold water from the great butt Aylwin used for proving hot iron, she went outside briefly to squat down and relieve herself before she settled for the night. On her return she built up the fire on the raised hearth, and checked that the crude barricade of logs and timber she had built across the broken doorway was as secure as possible. Then wrapping herself in as many blankets and woolfells as she could find against the cold, which was already seeping in around her despite the fire, she lay down on Aylwin's sleeping bench on several great armfuls of hay she had pulled from a ruined stook behind the wagons, and tried to rest.

Above the ruined steading the moon rose into a star-spangled sky, its silvery light bathing everything in a harsh, cold glare; and as the night wore on the temperature dropped sharply, until frost rimed everything with its thick and icy fur.

For some time Brioni lay there looking through the broken roof, struggling to get warm beneath her many wrappings; while the ruddy light from the fire waned, casting flickering shadows across the walls and roof timbers of the old forge, the smoke winding its way up to the smoke-hole above the fiery hearth.

Only last night she had gone to bed with a final squeeze from her mother, and a few quick words with her father when he had dropped by later on to see she was alright. It had been that way since she could remember…and now they were all gone! Home, family, everything, alone out there beneath the frozen stars, and she shivered within her covers, the tears springing to her eyes as the memories came flooding in.

Surely it was all a nightmare?

Any moment now she would awake and everything would be alright. Agatha would come bustling in, she would hear her mother's voice, and her father banging out of the hall and get up and go through for her hot porridge and honey. But this was no dream! This was the truth, her body streaked with her father's blood, her home and family destroyed before her eyes, her friends butchered…and an oath that somehow she must make a reality.

She shivered again and brushed her eyes firmly with the side of her hand. It was no good. Weeping was not the answer to any of her problems…and anyway the fire was dying and she must not let that happen or else she would surely freeze, and with a groan she rolled over and got up.

Just as she was settling herself down again, the fire once more burning brightly amongst a stack of fresh wood and charcoal, now pumped up with the bellows into roaring life, she heard the long drawn-out howl of a lone wolf on the frosty air. In the stillness of the night, the sound could have come from anywhere, even from the distant edge of Broken Wood away beyond the river.

She sat up and listened, her heart fluttering.

Wolves often called to one another, miles apart, when they were out on nights like this; sitting back on their haunches and baying at the moon, now full overhead, the *wooo-ooo-ooooo* of their mournful cries hanging in the air. She would not be afraid. In the intense cold, the bodies having been dead for hours on ground frozen hard for days, surely there would be little or no scent of death to carry on the wind? And the still air notwithstanding, that last lifting wail had distance in it, taking time finally to die away to silence.

Brioni lay back again and pulled the woolfells closer around her face, laying back restless on her couch, and for some time listened intently...but that lone cry was not repeated. Only the *kwick-kwick* of a white owl hunting in the stark moonlight for rats up by the ruined granary broke the settled stillness. So, eventually she relaxed, waves of exhaustion washing over her until, nestling down into her covers, warm at last, she finally fell asleep...and slowly, slowly, the bright fire she had built began to fail, the flames gently dying to a great glowing carpet on the raised hearth.

*

Away beyond the river that first lone hunter had been joined by another, their lean shapes trotting back and forth along the river bank, hovering uncertainly beyond the edges of the village, their hot breath white in the bitter frost.

To them the place was strangely cold and silent, and the stench of burning was still heavy on the air. But there was a further, more tempting scent upon the breeze. Now strong, now weak as the wind eddied and swirled, it lured the first great beast forward. With slitted eyes and lolling tongue the grey pack leader, with powerful shoulders and heavy winter ruff, made up his mind at last and trotted, stiff legged, into the deserted village beyond. His senses soon telling him there was no life amongst the burned out hovels, he grew bolder, moving his great fanged mask from side to side as he quested the cold night air for that warm, elusive, tantalising smell.

Pausing briefly before the gutted church in the centre of the village, he threw back his head and howled again, *wooo-ooo-ooooo*, the mournful cry reaching up and outwards as he sat back and threw his voice up to the moon, the thick fur round his shoulders bristling as he called in his pack at last. And as he moved like a shadow over the bridge that led to the empty palisade above him, this time his call was answered. Each wailing cry soaring across the wastelands, *wooo-ooo-ooooo*, as in ones and twos the grey brothers came loping to join their leader, their thick winter coats and panting breath steaming in the frigid air. And as the last hunting cry died away, its faint echo lingering on the breeze a moment longer, Brioni came instantly awake.

*

*F*or a brief moment she lay there in the darkness, waiting. Then, when she heard the next chilling howl from just beside the broken palisade taken up immediately by others, she knew then that a full hunting pack had come out of the forest and were seeking a kill. With a low cry she threw off her blankets and woolfells and leapt to her feet, still firmly shod, and turning swiftly to the fire, now little more than a pile of glowing embers, she heaped fresh sticks and kindling onto it from the wood-box beside the hearth, and pumped the bellows.

Nothing!

Just a few sparks, but with those came hope, more kindling and renewed pumping...until at last, with a small popping rush, there were real flames. Within moments the fire had caught and soon, with more wood and charcoal heaped on top, it was burning well. And all the time the calls were coming more quickly, ululating all around her, until it was obvious the beasts were actually within the garth, for she could hear the jarring tussles as they tore and worried at the dead flesh they found there.

Thrusting the ends of several thick staves of wood into the fire as crude torches, she pumped the bellows again until the fire was now roaring and then placed herself against the wall furthest from the barricaded doorway. Now, with the old boar spear leaning point upwards against the stonework, her javelin in her hand and her sword thrust into the hard beaten earth by her right hand, she waited for the inevitable moment of discovery.

Pray the saints that they didn't find their way up onto the roof! For then she could find herself in deep trouble; the danger of one beast leaping onto her from above as she struggled with others in the door-place was all too real. The terrifying thought made her glance upwards and shift her weight nervously from foot to foot.

Now she could hear them out there in the frozen darkness, snarling as they criss-crossed past the barricaded entrance to her sanctuary searching for a way in, and with leaping heart she followed them, turning round beneath the roof as she heard their bodies and rough fur scraping past the walls outside. Then came the thud as the first of the pack tried to leap up onto the sloping roof.

Baulked by her rough defences, threatened by the fire inside and becoming increasingly frustrated the pack grew angrier by the minute, gnarling and howling as they flung themselves up towards the low eaves and against the wedged-in planks and logs that she had used to block the broken entrance. Backed against the wall Brioni watched in appalled fascination as they went, tooth and claw, at her barricade.

Light spear held out before her, ready to lunge forward at the first sight of grey or brindled fur, she began to shout and stamp her feet to keep up her courage, giving back howl for howl until the noise both inside and out was deafening. So conscious was she of an attack from the front where her barricade was already beginning to shift, that in all the noise and rumpus she did not hear the heavy thump and desperate scramble over her head as one fell hunter, lighter and more cunning than his brothers, finally landed on the broken roof. Tongue lolling and yellow eyes gleaming, he prepared to launch himself at the slim figure standing unaware below him. He could smell her fear and the warmth of her body, the scent making his lips curl...and with bared teeth he leapt silently downwards for the kill.

At the last moment some sixth sense made Brioni look upwards just as the lean, grizzled body hurtled down upon her, and with a wild cry she instinctively twisted her body round, bringing up her spear as she did so and braced herself for the crash.

With a rush of foetid breath and wild howl of agony the wolf took the spear full in the chest, the fine blade snapping his breast-bone and sinking in to the wooden shaft itself, the impact bringing Brioni tumbling to the ground; human and wolf instantly wrapped about each other. The girl screaming out in fear and rage, the wolf snarling, crying out and snapping at the wooden shaft as it scrabbled violently in its death throes, impaled to the heart by its own boldness.

Outside, hearing the wild screams of its dying brother, the whole pack howled their anger and tore with renewed fury at the crumbling wooden wall that was all that now stood between them and their living prey.

Rolling herself away and covered in blood, Brioni staggered to her feet and tried desperately to jerk the spear from the huddled body of the still twitching wolf, but the fine blade was stuck fast. Panting and crying out with fear she looked up in horror as she saw the first of her wedged door supports break free and fall to the ground. And with that the pack re-doubled its efforts as they felt the obstacle begin to give way at last , until she could see their cruel faces, slavered teeth and tearing claws.

Snatching at the fire brands she had prepared earlier on, she thrust them at every grinning mask she could see with shouts and yells of rage, the howls as the flames scorched them making her shout all the louder. But fire alone could not keep the wolf-pack out, and flinging the last of her torches aside onto the hearth, she leapt for the great boar spear that had so far lain unused against the wall.

*Swivel, twist, snatch*! But even as she turned back one great beast had almost forced his way through, his shoulders bulging with muscle, his lips curled up over yellow fangs; and growling and snarling with rage he bunched his powerful hindquarters together and went for her, just as with one great shout she lunged at him with all her strength. Thrusting the wide blade into his muscular chest below his shoulders, she leaned into him with all her weight in the way she had seen her father teach her brother Gyrth.

Blocking her ears to the screams and howls of pain and rage as she did so, she watched the sharp steel lance into him, splitting fur and sinew as it searched out his vitals. Blood rushing out over the shaft, the great beast was suddenly clear of the entrance and with demented fury fought to shake himself free, flinging his body from side to side, battering the girl against the walls of the forge every time he did so.

Brioni, with the memory of a dozen boar hunts to her credit, dropped down on one knee to level the angle as she had seen done by the men so many times, the heavy spear clamped beneath her arms, its butt against the floor, her hands gripped white on the shaft as it leaped and twisted in her grip.

Forced back and back she looked on in horror as the massive wolf leader, his yellow eyes mad with rage, struggled to get at her, forcing his body up the bucking spear-shank in his fury. Shaken from side to side by his demented rushes, she never once let go despite her growing weakness, knowing that the iron quillons designed to prevent a great boar from goring his tormentor were quite sufficient to bring even the heaviest wolf up short, if she could only hang on.

Yet it wasn't until she felt the wall at her back that she could wedge herself properly down behind the spear and begin to fight back, screaming out her own fear and anger as she met each thrust of his with one of her own. But by then the end was not far off, for the great grey and brindled body was thoroughly spitted, long tongue purpling as she fought him down. Then suddenly it was over as with one final, violent tremor, and soft whimper of unbearable pain, the great beast died at last, his eyes glazed over, and blood gushed out of his mouth and nostrils in one swift flood.

112

Bruised and spent, Brioni bent forward reaching for her sword, knowing that her own end was near too, for there were far too many of them out there all baying for her blood for her to fight free. When from outside came a wild crescendo of noise as a terrific wolf fight broke out amongst the pack. The terrifying sounds of snarling, growling beasts seemed to go on and on until, with one final howl of rage, they all rushed yelping and screaming into the night.

For one brief moment, a single heart-beat of hope, Brioni thought that she was safe. That by some miracle she might yet live to see the dawn at last. Her crude barricade was all but torn apart, her two spears bound up with their victims, and she had no real strength left with which to fight. So, when she heard the soft pad-padding of heavy feet returning in the snow her heart sank, and her whole spirit drooped.

In the moonlit darkness, the ruddy glow from the fire casting sharp shadows on the wall, she groped to her feet exhausted, fixing her shield on her left arm With chest heaving, she stood shaking and spent, her sword hanging in her hand, the sound of two heavy hunting beasts working together drawing nearer and nearer. She could hear their hard breathing, and the scuffling of their bodies round the walls as they quested for the opening, and she struggled to follow their movements, terrified in case they, too, should master the route up onto the roof.

Then, finally, they were back at the shattered entrance, their clawed feet scrabbling at the last scraps of wattle and timber as they forced their way through, sharp fangs snapping at the obstacles still in their path. Rumbling deep in their throats they could now see their quarry, drooping weak and spent against the far wall with arms hanging by her sides.

Away in the far corner, Brioni stiffened her stance and brought her shield up to cover her left flank as she made ready to take their charge, tightening her grip on her sword as, with a sharp cry, she saw the last of her protection fall away as the first huge, grey animal broke through at last, followed at once by another, deeply brindled and both leaping for the kill.

# Chapter Fifteen

**B**ut at first sight of brown eyes gleaming in the firelight, not wild yellow, and hairy faces with wiry whiskers, and brindled fur not grey-white, came instant recognition, and giving a huge shout she dropped her sword and held her arms out to greet them. For these were not two wolves after her blood, but Bran and Utha, her father's great wolf hounds, whom she had known since they were born. And crying with utter joy and relief she hugged their coarse, bushy heads and wiry whiskers as she fell to the ground under their assault for they were both enormous, bigger than any wolf they had hunted. Hounds, girl and shield in one great bundle of leather, paws and feathery tails.

Finally she staggered to her knees and, dropping her shield, she pushed them down, fondling their silken ears as she did so. Oh, it was so good to see them! Now, at least, she was no longer alone and, hounds or no, they were far better company than the frozen corpses huddled round outside. Gathering herself together she moved back to her bed-place by the fire and carefully went over them both with her hands, gentling their big faces and rubbing their massive chests as she did so.

"Oh, you beautiful boys," she said as she ruffled their heads and gently pulled their ears. "I am so glad to see you! How did you get here? Where have you been? How very brave of you to come and find me. Now, Bran, stand still and let me look at you. Utha, sit down, you great hairy beast and let me see your brother. No, go away," she went on, laughing, as she pushed the huge dog off her shoulders. "It will be your turn next. Now leave me be and go and worry at that wolf over there, and I will be with you shortly!"

And so she ministered to both of them.

There was blood everywhere, on flanks and muzzles, throats and hairy leggings, but most of it was wolf, not wolf-hound, and though both had several deep gashes on face and shoulder, their bellies were undamaged, and there was nothing that would not quickly heal.

Thank the lord for her father's foresight, she mused as she fingered the great fighting collars that both still wore round their necks, for they would have helped them against the wolves considerably...as well as against any Dane who tried to lay a heavy hand on either one of them. Five inches of long iron spikes thrust out from a thick leather collar around their necks...it was a wonder they had not damaged her themselves when they had come bursting in on her like that. Covered with blood and hair, the spikes had clearly done their job. There must be more than one of the grey brothers out there who were wishing they had not answered their leader's call that night!

Somehow they had avoided capture, or fought their way free, when they had seen their master fall, and had bided their time before returning. Perhaps the wild wolf-calls had drawn them back? And then seeing the struggle round the old forge, and hearing her desperate cries and shouts, had realised that someone was alive and needed help. She didn't care. It was just wonderful to have them with her, and taking care not to spike herself, she cuddled them to her side, rejoicing in their hairy fur and wet, black noses.

By the gods, her father had taught them well.

The biggest of all the hounds around the hall-place, and known wolf-killers both of them. She was delighted. Food might be a problem, but she felt sure that she would manage somehow. The wolves, once skinned, would provide meat for all of them. She swallowed hard. The thought was not a pleasant one, but if wolf-meat was all there was to eat, it seemed a small price to pay.

Forcing her aching bones to move once more, she got up again and threw some more wood on the fire, steadily building up a pyramid of logs that would last the rest of the night. Then, with her breath still hanging in the frosty air despite the fire, she did her best to replace her barricade across the broken doorway, before laying herself down to rest at last. Bran curled up as best he could at her feet, while Utha lay on a worn blanket beside her sleeping bench. She smiled to herself in the flickering darkness. Whatever else may happen, she was no longer alone!

*

The rest of the night passed without incident, neither of the great hounds finding the need to wake her, though both at different times left her side and went outside to scent the night for danger, quartering the deserted compound in their long loping stride. And each one, in his own time, paused beside the covered body of his master and cried to the sailing moon for lost companionship, taking it in turn to lie upon his frozen death-mound, head between paws, eyes alert and glittering in the brilliant starlight.

Awake at first dawn, Brioni was shivering with the cold, the fire long since having died away again, and it was her first task quickly to re-build it and pump it up again. Heating water from the old butt in a large pannikin she had found the day before, she first washed out the wounds that both hounds had suffered in their battle with the wolves, before washing herself also, having found a large cake of soap from behind the burned out kitchens of the hall. She held up her hands and grimaced, for they were covered with dried blood, as was her face, from the two wolves she had killed. And she pulled an even worse face as she looked at the two carcases, for they still had to be paunched and skinned and that was bound to be a foul and messy business, all the more so as they had stiffened up overnight.

Finding a length of rope tossed away in a dark corner, she tied it around the first animal's neck and, hoisting it off the ground using one of the roof beams, she set to work with her knives, placing a great bundle of hay from her bed-place underneath to catch the offal as she pulled it out with her hands.

It was hard, stinking work, and though paunching them was easier with their being strung up, like gralloching a deer, skinning them was a different matter and in the end she decided that doing it on the ground was easier. In many ways it was like skinning a giant rabbit, for the pelts were surprisingly loose, the most difficult bit being forcing the raw legs through the skin. Nevertheless it took her most of the morning, leaving her drenched in sweat, despite the fierce cold outside the forge, and covered in blood and foetid muck, the naked carcases looking obscene in the open air.

She had thought about leaving the heads on intact, but the difficulties of curing the whole skulls was just too great for her slim resources. So in the end she just simply cut them off, taking her knives and hacking off a large supply of meat before dragging each carcase outside...then boiling more water to clean herself, and her clothes, as best she could.

By then the sun, which had shone fitfully all morning, was fast becoming obscured by the first of a long line of great clouds from the north that swiftly filled the whole horizon. Probably there was a fresh storm brewing, just as her father had predicted. She had stayed long enough. It was time and more that she was gone from here, before human scavengers came to see what was left to pick over as the whole world would know by now that Foxley had been destroyed. And she turned to wrap the meat she had cut off in a length of scorched linen she had found earlier, placing it in the top of the torn sack of oats she had found yesterday.

Just as she was finishing she became aware that the hounds were baying excitedly by the gate entrance. For a moment she listened, unsure as to what it might mean. Tense in her anxiety that it might be the Danes returning, or maybe other scavengers drawn by the smoke of yesterday's destruction, she hesitated to show herself. That it might be Heardred did not even cross her mind, and snatching up her light spear, now freed from its grisly victim, she finally slipped cautiously outside.

There she stopped and stared in blank amazement.

116

Coming across the ruined compound, head up and moving with easy grace, his head tossing from side to side and trailing a length of ravaged halter was Foxhead, her father's great black stallion, still saddled. Ears twitching nervously, with both giant hounds loping along beside him, whom he knew well despite their noise, he came to her the moment she called him using the sharp two-tone whistle her father had taught her, reassuring the big horse immediately.

With enormous relief, Brioni hugged his neck and patted his midnight withers, almost more thrilled by the sight and touch of him than she had been when Bran and Utha had come to her last night. Aware that speed was safety, and that every hour on her feet would have been a nightmare, especially with so clumsy a pack to shoulder from all she had gathered about her, relief was the very least of her emotions at that moment.

"Well, boy," she said at last. "You are a real sight for sore eyes. Now let's see if you are as sound as you look." And with infinite care she went all over his whole body: lifting his great shaggy fetlocks to examine his hooves and their delicate frogs, check his iron shoes and run her hands all down his legs to check for strained tendons. Finally, taking hold of the chewed and torn halter, she led the big horse over to a sagging stook of hay from which she had pulled her mattress the day before.

"Oh, Foxhead, you beauty," she said, giving him a resounding slap on his broad shoulders. "I thought I would never see you again. Truly you are a gift from the gods! You all are," she added smiling, turning to where Bran and Utha were already worrying at one of the wolf carcases, sterns waving and great teeth well buried. "We are all that's left of Foxley now, my friends, and we have a real task to complete, God help us. But, Sweet Mary, it is so good to have you with me!" And pulling a great handful of hay out of the ruined stook, she began to rub down the black stallion that had been her father's pride and joy.

Now, if she could just find a horse collar and some sort of leather tack and chains, she could harness him to a small tilt cart she had found abandoned on its side yesterday and leave with all the things she had found. He would hate the whole idea of it…but beggars could not be choosers and if she could manage it without spooking him completely they would all be well served indeed.

Before long she had his coat gleaming again, and after pulling down some more of the hay for the horse to mumble over, she turned to search the whole compound once again. Knowing now what she was looking for, the search was much easier and more successful, as the Danes in their hurry to move on had missed many things that otherwise they might have burned in the

117

bonfire that had been her home. And so she returned to the forge where she made her final preparations for leaving the manor.

From there she took the two sacks she had found and stuffed them with hay from the stook outside until she could force no more into them. She cut holes in one of the scorched blankets to make a simple cape, and tied the other one around the collection of pans and utensils she had found yesterday. Aylwin's soft leather pouch of flints, steel and the kindling box that she had found beneath his sleeping bench that first evening, she put most carefully into one of the saddlebags wrapped around with a large woollen cloth. The two wolf skins that she had scraped as best she could of their membranes to prevent them from stiffening and cracking, she turned into two greasy bundles tied with the rope she had used to tie them up for paunching, and she thrust her two spears through the middle of the bundle for ease of carrying.

Then putting a proper bridle on Foxhead that she had found under some wattle fencing up by the old wagon barn, along with a scorched horse collar and the necessary chains to fix him up, she took him to where she had righted the small tilt cart she had found the day before. After much effort she finally managed to get the great stallion into the collar, which he hated, snorted, shook his head and shuffled his feet at, finally leading him back to the old forge from where she loaded-up all the other treasures she had found, including the three jars of honey from Old Mald one-eye's ruined bothy…and the two dead chickens.

So Brioni of Foxley made ready to leave, Foxhead hating the wagon to which he was tied, unbelieving of the indignity that a trained warhorse could be put to, yet willing to do his young mistress's bidding, contented in his own way that he was with those whom he knew and trusted. And having checked that she had loaded-up all she could take, she swung herself up onto the driver's box and picked up the reins.

Above her the sky was rapidly clouding over and a chill, biting wind had sprung-up from the north-east, while the light of the short January day was just beginning to fade. She could sense the temperature dropping and she was eager to be gone at last.

Her life here was over…at least for the time being anyway, and thoughts of Heardred and her betrothal had been driven completely from her head. Somehow she must bring justice down upon Oscytel's head. She had sworn it and the gods of her people had kept faith with her needs. Her own God had kept faith with her needs. She had been joined by her father's two favourite hounds and by his stallion, all of whom he had adored. Never an evening passed but he went and talked with Foxhead; it was a family joke. She had arms in her cart, a sword by her side, and food for her belly. Even money and

118

treasure once she had lifted her father's halidom and his personal hoard from beneath the hearth in the old alehouse.

She smiled ruefully.

Strange how close the two worlds had become: Pagan and Christian. The old world of the Ancients, whom many people still worshipped…and the new world of the Christ child sent by God to cleanse them all of sin and give them eternal life. Two all-seeing fathers; two gods of war and retribution, but only one offering true forgiveness and hope eternal. She sighed. Right now she was bent on revenge and retribution. Maybe when that was completed she could return to the life she had been preparing for?

Whatever she may have thought of the future, for the moment she knew where she was going. To the old charcoal burners' bothy away out beyond the edge of Helms Wood, the small clearing some miles beyond the forest edge, where there was a stream and a crude stable where the charcoal burners kept their mules and oxen. She had often visited there with Gyrth when she was a child, and since also with Agatha two springs ago, or maybe three? with Aylwin for his charcoal. There she would find shelter for the night. She might even stay there for a while until she could find a way of dealing with Oscytel. How she would do that she had no clear idea. But with God's aid and the aid of the gods she was sure, somehow, that she would achieve it. And she even laughed, knowing how little experience she really had! But it was a sworn aim and she would move the Archangel Michael to help her, and Hell and the Furies as well if that was what it would take!

So, calling Bran and Utha to the cart's side, Brioni drove out past the torn corpses of her friends, and the silent mounds of her family, and down towards the river gateway through which the Danes had left with their booty and their prisoners.

Intent only on the treasure she needed to recover, and the awful execution of the mission she had sworn on her life to carry out, she had no mind for anything that she had left behind.

She felt her whole life had ended with the destruction of Foxley and her family, with nothing left to savour but revenge. Pausing briefly just beyond the gates for one last look at her home in the frosted gloaming, now gutted, ruined and deserted, filled only with the dead, she turned Foxhead and the tilt cart for the last time and swiftly flicked him on…away down the hill towards the river, the village and the empty wilderness beyond.

## Chapter Sixteen

*H*eardred had been gathering his men together for some time in preparation for his ride to Foxley. Ever since his acceptance by Brioni's father at the end of the summer when they had last been altogether at Court, he had been looking forward to his betrothal day with enormous excitement.

The girl was highly thought of by the King and also by his Lady, Queen Ealhswitha, and Alfred had promised they would both be there on their actual wedding day after the Easter muster.

She was such a lovely creature: young and spirited, but gentle and loving also, with the promise of more fire in her firm body than most men had a right to hope for. He smiled and his whole body shook with a sudden frisson of desire. She was so beautiful. The King's own man and the Queen's most favoured hand-maid. Nothing could be more perfect, and they would have the rest of their lives to share together. Wonderful!

That summer had given him a tantalising glimpse of what the future held in store. How he had managed to prevent himself from taking her there and then he did not know. She had raised such a heat in him that even now the very thought of her exquisite body and soft warm lips hardened his loins and made his body quiver with suppressed excitement, and he smiled again at his good fortune. For she was no milk-sop maiden; loving fine armour and swords more than her stitchery, and tales of the wars and ancient heroes more than those of the saints. He had shown her some simple passes with sword and light shield and she had loved it. A shield-maiden from the olden days of her people…what warrior sons they would raise between them.

He couldn't wait!

For weeks now he had been driving his people to get the great hall ready in time for her arrival. For though they were not to be married until the spring, Lord Wulfstan had decided they should be betrothed, and that he would send his daughter, with her Lady mother, to stay at the old hall in the New Year. A decision that the Lady Aethelflaeda had not applauded, but her husband had decided that he wanted the two most precious women in his life safe in the land of the Sommerseatas, and not so close to Gloucester where Guthrum and his Danes had gone in the autumn after Exeter. And if the Thane of Foxley wanted his women in a safer part of Wessex, far from the ever-present danger of marauding pirates, then no-one would be more pleased than he!

This was not the usual course of action, but these were not usual times. To the spring muster would go every able-bodied man in the southern shires, and from all over England: from ruined Northumbria and the land of the East Angles whose king had been so foully murdered, and from abandoned Mercia whose king had fled to Rome and whose people were ruled over by a puppet-king, Ceolwulf II, put in place by Guthrum. Not one warrior was to be spared the duty of fighting for the Saxon King of Wessex. And with Wulfstan of Foxley gone with his whole war-band, and his fyrdsmen, to join in the muster there would be none but the aged and the house-thralls left to defend the hall, and the manor would become a more dangerous place in which to stay.

Malmesbury, the nearest town to Foxley, was more filled with monks and priests than with fighting men. Most of the folk who lived there were shiftless merchants in his opinion, or callow serving men and shop-keepers with their families, and the simple borel folk of the farms and villages were useless without their thanes to lead them. And with Mercian Tetbury so close to hand, there were too many Mercians amongst the West Saxons for his liking anyway…and everyone knew about Mercians!

If King Burghred could desert his people when they had most needed him, then it didn't say much for any one of them. The Old Thane, his father, felt that he was right not to trust a Mercian, ever, if he could avoid it…and that despite the King himself having married one. Had The Lady Brioni been of Mercian stock his father would never have accepted her within his walls. Heardred sighed. It was a strange topsy-turvy kind of life that all were living these days. Pray God King Alfred would drive the Danes out of Wessex once and for all, and then everything would be alright again.

\*

And so the preparations had gone on apace: new tunics for the hall servants; refurbishment of his old apartments; the embroideries on the walls removed, lovingly cleaned and then replaced; fresh linen napery, cotton sheeting and furs. He had poured out the money from his bound oak coffers in a gold and silver stream to provide his new bride with a home of which she, and her mother, could be proud. And very hard it had been at times for his comrades-in-arms and his house–steward, who had borne the brunt of his anger and frustration when things had not gone quite as he had wanted them.

As a young man with no real responsibilities beyond those of his Thanehood, he was used to leading a very free and easy life. The drinking parties that the old hall had seen from time to time had been quite riotous, and warriors had come from far and wide to join the board. But he was also the King's man through and through and whenever Alfred had needed to send a man he could trust, it was often Heardred who had gone. He was cool-headed in a crisis, could be relied on not to panic, had better sense of what the King was trying to achieve than most, and his sword arm was one of the strongest in the Saxon host.

At twenty five, some four years or so younger than the King, he had grown into a tall, well-muscled Saxon warrior with more knowledge of field warfare than ever his father had. He towered over most men, rode a horse as if he and the beast were one and was quietly courageous rather than boastful as Saxon warriors often were. The most different thing about Heardred from many others of his race was his hair. Not blond in the classic Saxon style…but russet brown, the colour of the deer in the King's forests which, together with a fine pair of steady blue eyes, made him a striking figure wherever he went.

His father, the Old Thane, had married a girl from the lands of the Corn-Welsh, dark and slight with graceful ways and a lovely lilting voice. To Heardred his mother had been the adored Lady of his heart, always ready to give her strapping son a hug when things went wrong, shielding him as best she could from her husband's wrath at the boy's misdeeds, and always keeping open home for his friends and boon companions in his later years. All the more so as he was the only bud on her branch. He had been a big baby and in birthing him she had nearly died, such that no more little ones had followed.

Then had come the shattering of his life at the vicious hands of stray Viking pirates: heathen men who had sailed their dragon boats up the River Stour, when his father had been carrying out an inspection of defences for the King, and had taken his mother with him. A stray Viking horde had swept up the river and then ridden out across the land on stolen horses like a whirlwind, catching his father with only a light escort in his train. Those men they had all cut down, but only after a terrific struggle that had seen many pirates slain. His beautiful mother they had used like a common whore, stripped naked and brutally raped before her husband's eyes by everyone who had survived the skirmish, and only freed from her utter torment with a knife, throat-cut, when the last of them had finished with her.

His father they had gralloched like a common herd beast, like a deer, strung-up by his arms upon a tree, his belly cut open with a slicing axe blow and his entrails dragged out upon the ground and burned before his face, his brave heart torn out with his offal, still beating, and all flung to the dogs to snarl and worry over. So they had been found hours later.

But that had all been before Wareham.

Before meeting with Brioni that afternoon in the King's Court where she was a new arrival, and finding it strange and difficult so far from her family. Surrounded by priests and monks and fighting men, and at the constant behest of the Lady Ealhswitha, Queen of all Wessex, now big with child, she had seemed fragile and alone. He had been stunned, and captivated, by her beauty...and by her gentleness and bright gaiety that had swiftly driven the spectres of the past back to the pit from whence they had first risen up to torture him. She was a sparkling bright spirit in a dark world; daring convention with her love of swords and armour, and her belief in Alfred's vision for a Wessex free of Danes, and not Wessex alone but all of Saxon England. She had offered him life...and he had taken seizen of it gladly with both hands.

Thus falling in love had been easy, glorious, the most exciting and delicious thing that had ever happened to him. And now he only had to catch a glimpse of her in a crowd, or watch her working, playing with the royal children or just being anywhere near him for his heart to turn over and a great rush of emotion wash over him: fierce pride, protectiveness, gratitude, sheer awe that she should even look at him, and outright desire! It made him want to run over and pick her up in his arms and hold her tight against his heart and never let her go.

She was his mother and his would-be lover rolled in one, and when he lay with his head in her lap and her cool hands on his forehead, he just wanted to turn and smother her with a hundred kisses, to wrap her in his arms; or nuzzle in her neck like a child, as he had done with his own mother when he was little and afraid. It was that final step, from child to master, that he had yet to take, but which the urge to do so was fast becoming more than he could bear.

So, now he was about to take a wife, and was turning his whole life upside down, shaking out the cobwebs as much from his home as from his mind.

As Edric the Axe-man, his father's old war-leader, had once loudly said to one of his cronies, when Heardred had been having a good shout at his hall-steward over the filthy state of everything: "It'll be a good thing for everyone when this young cockerel can get his wench truly bedded and treaded, for until he's furrowed her to the full he'll continue to plough roughshod over everyone else, and no-one will get any peace!" And chuckling heartily over his piece of nonsense, the two of them had gone off like a couple of scruffy schoolboys to finish their drinking behind the old barn where they couldn't be got at so easily, leaving Heardred feeling flushed and foolish in the middle of the floor.

But all that cosiness had changed with the arrival of Guthrum's army into Wessex. First Wareham, then Exeter and now locked in to Mercian

Gloucester. And from then on Heardred had been almost constantly in the saddle, for while the King carried out all the usual business of government surrounded by priests and scribes, his household warriors had kept watch over the Danish host, guarding against one of their lightning marches for which their old enemy had become famous.

The Queen meanwhile had been brought to bed of a daughter, Aelfthryth, and young Brioni had been continuously at her side. For though Ealhswitha may not have been the most political of wives, she did love and care for her children greatly, and was always seeking ways of making her little ones comfortable in the draughty old palaces and hunting lodges that her handsome Wessex husband continuously dropped them in. So it was no surprise when she decided to suckle this one herself, as she had all the others. Whereas often many great ladies would have refused outright, and quickly have found a wet-nurse for the child amongst their entourage, the Queen had no such scruples. She had always had plenty of milk, loved to see and feel her babes pulling at her breast, and was determined to show her fine Wessex ladies that whatever else they might choose to say of her countrymen, and women, *this* Mercian mother knew exactly what her breasts were for!

Anyway it pleased the King to watch his wife nurse their child. In the life they led, often continuously on the move, with danger at almost every turn of the way, there was something eternally right and everlasting about a nursing mother and her child that made Alfred feel at peace with the world around him. A warm feeling of home and family in a dislocated world. And it was at those moments that the Queen felt almost closer to her warrior Lord and husband than when they were in bed together…which given the current situation in the land of the West Saxons was not that often!

Thus it was natural that she should turn to her children for occupation and amusement, and that meant Brioni as well, for she was indeed the Queen's most favoured maiden. Her cheerfulness and happy knack of being able to organise something out of nothing made her invaluable. For whenever the older children became too much for their mother, or the whole situation seemed just too awful for words, with settlements in so many places being put to the fire and the sword, it was always Brioni's ingenuity, native common sense and humour that managed to save the day. And because she met every difficulty with a smile and outright cheerfulness and never put on airs and graces, nor assumed a better place for herself than she deserved, she managed to remain on good terms with almost everyone.

Even the haughtiest of Alfred's Wessex ladies about the Court were pleased to remark on what a happy, unassuming child Brioni was; not least because she herself had no illusions about her situation as the youngest, least accomplished hand-maiden in the royal entourage. She just did the best she could, with unfailing determination and good humour, as her mother had taught her. With the result that everyone loved her for it...save those with the most jaundiced view of life, or those whom she showed up for their bad humour and unwillingness to serve. And they, in the Court of Alfred the King in those days, were mercifully few in number.

So when the King returned from whatever shanty camp he had been visiting, whether above the old Mercian city of Gloucester, or elsewhere in the harried kingdom of Wessex, there was always a fire burning, hot water in which to wash, something cooking over the fire and fresh, clean clothes to put on. Little wonder that young Brioni of Foxley was so well thought of by the Wessex King and his Mercian Lady Queen.

*

*F*or Heardred, Brioni's involvement with the royal family was both a blessing and a curse. For though she was plainly safer under the royal wing than she might have been at home at Foxley, she was also a conscientious girl who took her many duties most seriously, so until after Exeter he had never managed to have long enough alone with her to steal more than the briefest of sweet kisses. Which was just as well, he had often mused, for her rich curves and sensuous nature would otherwise have made it impossible to have kept his hands off her.

Even with the army largely sent home for Christmas, their situation had not greatly improved, for until well into Advent the family had been in royal Winchester, only moving up to Chippenham for the Christmas festival itself, when he'd then had to return to his own home near Taunton.

There were many things that, as a Thane, he simply could not put off any longer. Not only were there the final preparations for his coming betrothal to see to, and the arrival of Brioni and her mother afterwards...but the Christmas tithes had to be gathered in, and the men told off for the spring muster had to have their names written down and their gear checked for battle readiness. There were also a rash of moots to attend, and the whole celebration of the season amongst his own people to be enjoyed for the last time as a single man. They expected that of their Lord, who was absent so much of the year, and he was happy to provide them with the traditional Yuletide cheer...and to return home with his hearth-companions and re-unite his fyrdsmen with their families. He was young, alive and in love, soon to be married to the most beautiful girl in all Wessex, so why not relax, be happy and let his people have their fun?

125

Yet all through the festival period he had fretted to be off, counting the days until finally he could bear the waiting no longer, and accompanied by his hearth-companions and his own war-band, and by his two greatest friends, Edwin and Harold, together with their own armed escorts, he had set out for Foxley at last. It may have been a full two days before he had any real need to do so; but his friends, exasperated by his sighs and mooning glances had been only too pleased to leave. Almost anything was better than Heardred in love, they decided, even if it did mean the end of their comfort and easy living for a while.

# Chapter Seventeen

*T*hey left with the land snow-covered and heavily frosted, the sun bright overhead and the air fresh and dry on their faces, the sky, blue as a cornflower in high summer and freckled with cloud, and a hustling breeze soughing round them. But within hours the weather changed. Great banks of cloud blew down on them from the north and the wind turned hard and bitter. The frozen trackways, already rutted nightmares, now swiftly vanished beneath the snow that came swirling down around them, and despite all that could be endured wrapped tightly in their fleece-lined fur cloaks, they were swiftly forced to seek early shelter or be lost in the storm that suddenly swept over them.

For two days they had to lie up with their unexpected hosts while the wind howled and battered around the ancient hall place in which they found themselves, piling up the snow in great powdery drifts that threatened to close them in completely.

The hospitality was unstinted, though they could tell that their host was becoming concerned for his own welfare and that of his own people. Everything pointed to a hard winter, and the sudden arrival of so many extra mouths to feed was clearly a burden on the vill's resources. So, as soon as the weather had moderated a little, they all pushed on despite the man's loud protests, knowing from the look of scant disguised relief on his lady's face that she was pleased to see them leave...and that not just because of the food situation either.

In truth Heardred was only too pleased to do so.

There had been one moment over the table on their second day when he had felt that the thane who was sheltering them was not fully of Alfred's thinking. Their host did not think that fighting the Danes was the only way to be rid of them, considering whether paying them a tribute, as so many others had done in the past, was not better than putting on his battle-harness, raising his fyrdsmen and riding out to fight the old enemy once again. He felt that some kind of peace with Guthrum and the Great Army would have got him home to his fireside in time for a proper harvest...not the sketchy one that had left the meal arks half-filled and the haylofts half-empty.

It had been a small instant of tension that had been quickly eased by the man's sudden burst of brittle laughter and swift dismissal of his fears, with his wife's eyes up to heaven and her mouth a bitter line of dismay. Words Heardred thought full of sullen platitudes: that of course Alfred was a splendid

127

King; all men knew that. Look how the country had grown fat despite the troubles all around them…and that doubtless his advisors knew what they were doing…"Ho! Ho! Ho!" Followed by a swift call for fresh ale for his weary guests to divert their thoughts from any disloyal intentions he might be harbouring.

But Heardred was not fooled, and he wondered how the conversation might have gone if there had not been quite so many of them gathered there, all grim faced and geared for war…and he a known 'King's man' amongst them as their leader. It all smacked of insincerity and a rifted lute between him and his lady, who had plainly been horrified by her husband's dangerous words before them all.

As his friend Edwin had said the following morning: "That man came as near to having his head split down the middle as any I have met with…"

"And his wife knew it! Did you see her face?"

"Green with terror. I would not have been in his shoes that night! But there are too many cravens like him in the Host for my liking, Heardred. And if anything went wrong with Alfred, then I pity poor Wessex. For if milk-worms like that one ever get a voice in the Council, then we'd be no better off than ravaged Mercia is today. A puppet king and everyone paying a heavy ransom to Guthrum for the very air they breathe and the paltry land he has left them! God help me, but it made my gorge rise!"

"Aye my friend, and he knew it, as did his whey-faced wife. Did you see her cat's eyes on me afterwards?"

"I wouldn't have her in my bed for a gift. She'd scratch you soon as look at you. You mark my words, Heardred, you'll not see him come the spring muster after Easter. He'll be too 'ill' to attend. I can hear his message now. The man's a *Nithing* and should be dispossessed!"

"Not so bold, Edwin. He may have problems that we know nothing of, and he has housed us well when we most needed it…and poured out his store upon us when so many extra mouths to feed must have been a real burden. As for his wife? Yes, I wouldn't trust her either. But her man is all that stands between her and destruction. The land is filled with fear and disquiet, and troubles seem to grow about us like tares in a wheat field. And remember that not everyone in the Council believes in what Alfred is trying to do. Indeed many believe it cannot be done and would strike a bargain with Guthrum if they dared. So why shouldn't she seek to protect her man from death if she thinks it worthwhile?"

"You are too fair, Heardred!" his friend had replied roundly, shaking his head. "Her job is to put fire in her husband's belly and send him to the Host feeling like a king himself, as if his very presence on the battlefield will be

128

enough to make any Dane up-stakes and run away! Instead of which she feeds his craven fears and aids him to skulk at home. A plague upon them both, say I. It is people like that who don't deserve a king like Alfred. They are happy enough for us to sally forth and risk our miserable lives for their well-being and safety...just so long as they are never asked to play their part. They make me vomit!"

"Ha! ha! Edwin, you are in a fiery mood this morning!" Heardred had replied laughing. "My, but you are an ungrateful dog. Here you are, being fed and watered with traditional Saxon hospitality...albeit a little grudgingly maybe, and all you can do is swear damnation on your hosts.

"Come on now. A quick gallop will drive the fidgets from your mind and put your senses back together again. If you had spent as much time as I have done travelling up and down the land on Alfred's business, you'd quickly realise there are more like him than you, my friend. Though some, I admit, are considerably worse than others!"

"Like Aethelwold!"

"Our good king's rotten nephew, who spends more time desiring his uncle's throne until it almost makes him sick, egged on by his supporters, than in learning to be a good ruler of his own estates!" Harold chipped in.

"That's the one," Heardred replied sharply. "He's one Alfred needs to watch, despite his being only twelve, or thereabouts. There are those who like an easy life who fawn on him, and would have Aethelwold as king instead of Alfred. After all he is his elder brother's child. Already they turn his head; indeed, were it not for his youth when his father died he would have been named king instead of his uncle. And he keeps company with too many Danes for my liking...but Alfred will not move against him, excusing him for his youth. He needs to change his advisors! Instead he does his best to keep the boy out of the way on his estates, while he gets on with the job of ruling Wessex. I tell you, Aethelwold needs watching!"

And with that he had brought the conversation to an abrupt end, thrusting the rowels into his beast's shaggy flanks and jingling away up the snow-bound track, his breath hanging in the air and his horse's fat behind bouncing along as his powerful hindquarters drove him forwards.

*

*I*t had started as a brilliant day, with the sun shining warm on their armoured backs and the air deliciously cold and crisp beneath an ice-blue sky. Robins sang by the wayside, and there was a flitter of tits amongst the trees and bushes now heavy with the snow that had fallen since they had been forced to halt their journey, and blackbirds with yellow beaks and feet swooped across the trackway. Everywhere there were many drifts where the wind had blown the snow across the trackway, humping it into great dunes and wild shapes against the ancient hedgerows. The ground was pockmarked with the tracks of birds and animals that had earlier crossed their path, the slotted marks of deer most prominent, but of horse and rider there was no sign. Everything glittered and sparkled in the clean air, and it was good to be alive and on your way to meet the one true lady of your life.

But by midday the weather had changed again, steadily worsening from the north-east, the sun hidden behind fresh banks of clouds and the light turning from steel grey to pale ochre. By mid-afternoon it was snowing hard, the wind turning it into a howling blizzard, driving the snow stinging in their faces and blowing it in great smoking streamers from the high banks on either side, like the spume from tumultuous waves in a raging storm.

This time there was nowhere for them to shelter, and they were forced to drive their tired horses deep into a nearby wood, floundering through the drifts amongst the trees until they were far enough in to escape the very worst of the wind's great roaring anger. And there in a dense thicket of yew, beneath a steep bank thickly overhung with laurel, they had stabled their beasts as best they could and built crude shelters of cut branches from the surrounding trees and bushes before a towering fire. Then, wrapping themselves in their heavy cloaks of wolf, bear and fox, they did their best to catch some sleep while all around them the whole world creaked and groaned to the swaying fury of the storm, that sent the snow swirling about their heads and blew it sizzling into the fire.

By the time the wind had blown itself out the dawn was breaking pink across a pale saffron sky, the sun a crimson ball in a sea of gold, they were soon on their way again, a simple broth of vegetables and oats sufficient to take the edge off their hunger, their faces reddened by the stinging glare and their hands and feet numbed by the penetrating chill.

*

All that long day, and the next, camping that second night in the ruins of a burned-out steading, they had pushed on as hard as the conditions would allow, stopping now and again to clear their horses' hoofs of hard-packed snow that could lame a beast as easily as any stone. But despite the brilliant sunshine it was hard, tiresome work, the horses fretting and steaming in the frosty air as the men cursed and struggled with each shaggy fetlock, checking hoofs and shoes, digging the packed snow out as rapidly as possible without damaging the frog inside; while taking the opportunity to eat their meagre rations of tough smoked meat and crinkled apples from Heardred's stores. Then it was up and away again until the next time, the pack animals with their supplies bringing up the rear, bouncing along as best they could, their lead riders waiting eagerly for their reliefs, and a welcome chance to warm their hands and ease their aching necks and shoulders.

*

*I*t was as they had neared Chippenham at last, the very day of twelfth night when they should have been safely gathered in at Foxley, delayed by the vile weather, that they began to realise that something terrible had happened. Still determined to reach Foxley that very day, as expected, Heardred had driven his men hard to make up lost time and was quite prepared to push across country to get there all the sooner, when they had met with the first terrified refugees already fleeing from before Guthrum's sudden, fierce advance.

Sometimes in ones and twos, sometimes whole family groups, and all with whatever they had managed to snatch up in their wild dash for freedom, tied up in loose bundles and strapped clumsily to their backs. Here a tilt cart, with old and young all crammed on to it pulled by a tired pony; there a clumsy sledge pulled by a mother and father in harness, granny holding a babe in arms amidst what food they had managed to salvage, the family dog running by its side; some on mules, othes on donkeys, more on foot. And many were terribly wounded, some dragged on a travois behind a plodding sumpter, others stumbling as best they could along the snow-bound track, all fleeing in fear of their lives. And all had the same look of fear and horror stamped across them: white, strained faces; dark haunted eyes; palsied limbs and incoherent tales of death and utter destruction, many looking behind them as they fled.

"The Danes are coming! *The Danes are coming!*"

"Flee for your lives!"

"Chippenham has fallen and the king is slain!"

"They attacked out of nowhere. All his family is lost."

"They have killed everyone and burned the town!"

"No-one is safe. All is lost."

"Wessex is lost! The Danes have conquered."

And with more desperate glances over their shoulders they had hurried on, like blind moles striving for the all-enveloping darkness and safety of the earth, not stopping for one moment longer than to cry out their terrible news: "*The Danes are coming! The Danes are coming!*"

131

Trying to get any sense out of them was pointless.

They were too frightened and too appalled by what had happened for them to know anything of any real value. For them it was enough that the Danes had attacked out of the morning darkness, suddenly and with overwhelming force. One moment all was well...the next the alarum bell was tolling, everyone was screaming and running in panic, while the enemy had rammed the gates and burst over the walls, howling their battle-fury. On horse and foot they had stormed up the hill to attack the King's hall; then all who were left alive, and were still able, had fled howling into the wilderness...or been seized.

It had been a disaster.

Alfred had been too trusting of Guthrum's sworn oath at Exeter. He had let down his guard and this was the result. Chippenham had fallen and been sacked by the Danes. But had they seized the King? Was Alfred dead, or a prisoner? Or had he and his family got out at the last moment?

"Where is the King?" Heardred demanded of one terrified group, Edwin and Harold clustered around their leader, while his men kept guard. "*What has happened to Alfred and his family?*" Heardred had roared at their leader.

"I don't know, Lord. I don't know. There were people running everywhere. The Danes were in amongst us before we were aware..."

"What of the guards? The warriors on the walls?"

"Killed? Run off? I don't know. I was too busy getting my family away through the causeway gates. Bodies everywhere. We fled along with everyone else."

"But the King? Alfred?"

"Killed with all the rest...fled with the family...captured ? I don't know, Lord. Now leave me be, for those bastards are coming, and I have my family to care for. Wessex is finished!" And violently shrugging out of Heardred's grasp he spat on the frozen ground and went back to his family, to join all the others trudging south, their few belongings in bundles on a ragged donkey cart.

"Sweet Jesus, Chippenham has fallen! Now what?" Harold asked, stamping his feet on the ground in fury. "I always thought the King was too trusting of those bastards. They lie in their teeth. Swore a binding oath and then broke it! Like Wareham, like Exeter. The only good Danes are dead ones! *Bastards!*"

"All we can do now is to press on for Foxley with as much speed as possible, and before the weather changes again," Heardred said, looking up at the sky and out across the bleak, empty countryside. "And with infinite caution. If the Danes really are out in force we will know it soon enough, for we will see the smoke of their burnings before we see them. And we would do well to get off this trackway, for those bastards will spread out like rats in a granary seeking the best they can find."

"But what of the King?" Edwin broke in urgently. "And what can have happened to allow Guthrum to have got so close without being spotted and the King warned in time? What of the watchers around Gloucester?"

"What indeed?" Heardred agreed grimly, looking his two war-leaders in the face. "I will not believe the King is lost to us unless I see his body or hear of his death, or capture, from someone I know and trust. But the watchers? Dead or fled? Or worse they abandoned their duty and went home for the Christmas feasting trusting in Guthrum's word, as Alfred did! Either way, Guthrum has lived up to his reputation and stooped like a falcon out of the blue upon Chippenham. Pray God he did not seize our royal heron in his stoop; then Wessex would be lost indeed!"

"Where now, Heardred?" Harold asked him, urgently holding his horse's head by its bridle.

"To Foxley and as hard as we can ride. It lies between Gloucester and Chippenham, and Wulfstan will fight and fight hard to defend his family. But even he will not be able to fend off the entire Danish army. So, mount up my friends and let's be on our way. We have tarried long enough, and will learn nothing from these poor fellows," he added, gesturing to the terrified groups of people hurrying along the trackway.

"One thing is for certain though, Chippenham will not have been burned. Sacked for sure, but not burned. Even Guthrum is not fool enough to do that in the midst of the worst winter for years. He has been supremely cunning. Swapping one set of winter quarters for another with even better supplies than his own! The last thing he will want is to set fire to it all. The King's advisors need their backsides kicking. They were all blind to Guthrum's skill...and so was Alfred, and so I will tell him when next I catch up with him!" And swinging himself back onto Swiftfire, his big bay stallion, he called his men forward once more in a spray of trampled snow and broken ice.

Then, hauling their beasts off the trackway, clogged as it was becoming with fleeing peasants and broken townsfolk, they drove them hard across the desolate snowy wastelands, sticking to the thickly wooded areas wherever possible and avoiding whatever distant villages and steadings that they spotted on the way, unsure whether they harboured enemies, for with Chippenham fallen and half Wessex in Danish hands the enemy could be anywhere.

If the Heathen had indeed swept down on Chippenham and seized it for themselves as all were saying, then they would be looking for easy pickings amongst the scattered manors and villages all about, and though they were all well-armed and mounted, there was no point in deliberately seeking out their

133

enemies. If there was trouble coming then it would find them soon enough, and with the need to reach Foxley now paramount in all their hearts, the only thing that they could do now was to press on as quickly as possible and hope for the best.

# Chapter Eighteen

*I*t was as they were quartering the edges of Melksham forest, a vast tract of land that stretched right to the walls of Chippenham itself, that they came upon the first piece of hard news that they had hit upon since meeting up with those fleeing earlier in the day.

The sun was just setting in a blaze of scarlet glory, the sky purpling-up for the night as the first stars sparkled into life, when one of his forward scouts had called them all to a halt, their horses stamping their feet on the frozen trackway and tossing their heads, their breath and bodies steaming in the frigid air, now colder as evening pressed down upon them.

In the deepening gloom, away across a small clearing on the edge of the great forest, a small fire could be seen flickering brightly amongst the trees. The flames made the distant tree trunks stand out starkly against the harsh whiteness all around them, their massive shadows dancing and weaving as the fire flared up and died away again. An owl called mournfully from behind them and from the forest's edge a vixen screamed.

"Danes, Heardred?" Edwin asked quietly, moving his horse up beside him as he spoke.

No...I don't think so," his friend replied softly, bending towards him as he spoke. "Whoever has lit that fire has done their best to keep themselves secret. The forest is thick and bushy hereabouts, and 'though we can see it here from the south, anyone coming from the other direction would be fortunate to see even a stray spark.

"Besides, you know what those bastards are like for fires. If that was a Danish encampment then there would be fires everywhere. Not that miserable little watch-fire!"

"Who then?"

"God alone knows, Edwin. But whoever they are knows what they are about, so we might learn something useful."

"How do you want to do this?" Harold queried, pushing up to Heardred's other side.

"With great care, my friend," he replied with a quiet chuckle. "With great care! I have no wish to be ambushed now when we are so close to our goal, so we will send four men up ahead. You pick them out, Edwin, and go with them. Harold and I will stay here and back you up in case there is trouble."

"Orders!" Harold said tersely.

"Well, if trouble breaks," Heardred said, turning quickly to his other side. "We'll go in two waves. I'll lead and you take the second group, five horse lengths between."

"No, Heardred, that won't do. If you go down then all will be lost. I will lead and you follow. Then if I go down we will still not be foiled, for you won't stop for anything, but drive straight through as if the devil and all his demons were on your tail."

"Are you sure?"

"Certain!" his friend said, grasping his hand.

"Right, let's be about it then before someone over there gets the feeling they are being watched and all clear off into the forest!"

With quietly spoken instructions and urgent gestures, Edwin mustered his scouts and pushed towards the place from where the fire was burning brightly. Not bunched together, as might have been expected, but in a single-file line so that if they were fired on they could swiftly wheel away without the danger of fouling one another.

From the thick belt of timber where they were sheltering well out of sight, Heardred had watched their steady advance, holding his breath in anticipation of the sudden rush of noise and the quick flitter of arrows across the snow that would herald a sudden violent attack...but nothing happened. One by one his men silently disappeared amongst the trees on the far side of the clearing, the small snowfield that they had just crossed suddenly bathed in pale silvery light as the moon slowly rose above the tree tops, casting great twisting, craggy shadows across the frozen ground.

Minutes passed that seemed like hours, as their tired horses stamped their feet and brumbled through their noses. Then, as if by magic, a mounted rider suddenly appeared on the far side of the clearing, merged into his horse like some ancient centaur, his figure black and menacing against the snow and the deeper shadows of the forest cast by the moon's bright silver light. A silent, motionless sentinel who after a brief pause slowly waved his arms above his head, beckoning them towards him before vanishing again amongst the trees.

Digging his heels into his horse, Harold broke from the forest edge and led his men forward through the frosted snow, Heardred following, their breath smoking in the freezing air, their weapons and armour chiming softly as they moved, their saddles creaking. Shaggy feet throwing the snow, now powdery from the bitter cold, in dandelion puffs of sparkling silver in the harsh moonlight, their patient mounts plodded forwards, ears flicking uneasily and tails switching briskly back and forth.

136

Then they were across and plunged in amongst the gnarled and knotted trunks of the great trees that edged the deep woodlands, bending their heads to avoid the lower branches, and forcing a passage through the thick tangled undergrowth of hazel, sloe and birch bound in with ivy and old man's beard. Just ahead was the ruddy glow of the fire they had spotted earlier and all around them the trees softly sighed and rattled as the night breezes hustled through their iron skeletons, the star-packed sky overhead almost hidden by their bony fingers.

Some twenty paces from the fire-source Heardred had been halted by two of the men Edwin had chosen, their bodies rising up from the ground as if from nowhere.

"It's best to dismount here, Lord. The camp itself is very small, and there is little space for the men let alone the horses."

"How many of them are there, Alfgar?" he asked, recognising the voice and swinging down from his horse as he spoke.

"Just three, my Lord, and one of them is sorely wounded. In truth I don't know how he is still alive. The other two are common townsfolk, serving men from the look and sound of them, but the third is a warrior."

"Where from?"

"Chippenham, Lord," the man replied shortly, taking Heardred's horse by the bridle and rubbing its nose. "And a rare time they seem to have had as well!"

"Guthrum, Alfgar?" he asked sharply.

"Aye, my Lord. Guthrum himself, breathing fire like a true Danish war dragon, and the whole of Denmark with him if they are to be believed... slaughtered all who got in their way. Seems the Great Army has moved again."

"Seems so, indeed," he replied tersely, flipping his reins over his horse's head and handing them to Alfgar with a grim smile. Then, giving a soft call to the war troop following behind him, with a clink of steel, he moved through the thick bushes that shielded the little encampment and into the firelight.

It was indeed a very poor resting place for the man who lay gasping for breath beneath a crude shelter of boughs and scraped brushwood on a rough bed of springy yew and sodden blankets. His left shoulder was swathed in blood-soaked bandages, black and glistening in the harsh moonlight shining down on him, and his chest wheezed and bubbled black froth from the deep spear thrust that had split his ribs apart and pierced his lungs.

How he had managed to last so long, or get so far, with such terrible injuries Heardred had no idea, but he recognised him immediately as one of Alfred's personal bodyguards, a Royal Companion who would never willingly leave his Lord unless death had claimed him first.

"Sweet Jesus! It's Sturrold!...I'd know that one-eyed old villain anywhere!" And striding towards him he swiftly knelt down in the snow by his side, reddened in the firelight, wincing at the sight of the terrible wounds in his chest and shoulder as he gently lifted his hand and chafed the cold fingers between his palms.

"Don't move, old friend. It's me...Heardred. Just lie still and we'll see what we can do to make you more comfortable." And turning to his men who were beginning to cluster round them he called out quietly: "Stand back, don't crowd him. Build up the fire and fetch me fresh blankets. Edwin, warm some ale and bring it here as soon as possible. Harold, post guards; Alfgar see to the horses, then get some sort of broth going, we all need hot food inside us. He's failing now, I know, but I must find out what has happened to the King...and only he can tell me."

Within moments the gathering had broken up as the men moved to their accustomed tasks, long months of field warfare having taught them what to do, while Heardred coaxed the dying man to talk.

"Come on you old pirate, you are with friends now." Then looking up to the stars above his head he added: "Dear Lord, don't take him yet, I need him! I need his information more than you need his soul, the old lecher! For he has had more maidenheads than I have coins with which to count them!"

"And much good they've done me too!" came the sudden weak reply as the patched head slowly turned towards him and grinned, the one good eye blinking open as he added: "Who would have thought to hear you say a prayer over me at this time of my life?" Then he gasped as pain lanced through his body and a thin spume of bloody water trickled from his mouth and nostrils, suddenly spraying out as he coughed and spluttered desperately for air.

"Easy there, Sturrold, easy. Don't strain yourself, or you'll never live to see the dawn."

"Heardred? Is that really you?" the man replied hoarsely, gripping his friend's arm as he spoke.

"Aye, you old poacher! And not a moment too soon either!" he went on in as cheerful a voice as he could muster. "I'll have some hot ale for you in no time, and fresh blankets too. You'll be just fine now, you'll see."

"Don't try to fool me, old friend," came the weak reply. "I'm for the swan's path now. West of the sunset. I've known it all along...oh God it hurts, Heardred!" he gasped, gripping his arm fiercely. If you had only been with the King it might never have happened!"

"The King, Sturrold?" Heardred asked him urgently. "Did they get him? Does he live?"

138

"Aye, he lives! He and his family just got away in time. Dear God, but it was close. As Guthrum, God rot his soul, was breaking in across the river we got Alfred and his family out the other side of the town. It was terrible! The bells tolling the alarm, everyone running about in panic, screaming, shouting. Dreadful."

"Did the plan work?"

"*Yes!* As the bells rang, we rushed Alfred and his family out through the back gates. Grabbed all that we could, then ran to where the horses were already waiting. Thank God, you had insisted we practise for just such an emergency. I know the King thought it was foolish, but at least he listened."

"Did the King get away, old friend?" Heardred asked him gently, desperately. "Did Alfred break free?"

"Yes! The gates were cleared, and those bastards could not get that far round the town. The river protected us from direct attack. He and the family got out with a small escort. But, by St Michael it was a near run thing! That's where I got these," he growled, shifting his wounded shoulder as he spoke. "Keeping them back from the gates, so the King could get away. Dear God, Heardred, but I made them pay for these wounds!"

"What happened? How did they get so close?"

"Drunken gate guards! Christmas, Yuletide...you know the kind of thing! Stupid bastards...dead bastards now!" he growled, coughing, his body shaking. "And the enemy seemed to come from nowhere. One moment the dawn was softly breaking, the next it was a scene from Hell itself. Clashing their shields and screaming like demons, wooden ladders, battering ram on wheels, the whole howling lot! They were through the gates, up over the walls and into the town almost before we could arm ourselves," he gasped, trying to sit up, blood trickling from his mouth. "They had Saxon banners at their front. Those drunken fools saw what they expected to see...a Saxon war-band coming in for twelfth night. Then it was too late. They were the first to die, gut-rotting foolish bastards. At least they managed to ring the bells, or else we might never have got the King away in time. Then everyone scattered. Ran for their lives, like sheep before the wolves! Women, children, animals...young and old...you never saw such a mess. Took what they could lay their hands on and fled off into the wilderness. God knows where they have gone!"

"Who went with the King?"

"Most of the Companions got out with him, but many rode for their steadings as you and Alfred had arranged if ever such a thing should happen. You always were a one for seeing into the future..."

"Don't waste your strength on such foolishness, old friend," Heardred replied swiftly, bending close to catch his whispered words, now becoming more gasped and laboured as the waves of pain and bouts of coughing came and went. "Where has he gone to, Sturrold?...Where is Alfred now?...Sturrold?...Sturrold?" he asked desperately, shaking him in his anguish, the man's head rolling helplessly as he did so. "Where is the King now?"

"Fled to Athelney, as he always intended," Sturrold gasped and whispered. "Into the deepest marshes where they can't get at him! He means to lay up there until the spring. Harry the bastards wherever and whenever he can. 'Keep the flame burning', he said. You know what he is like. Then have another go at them after the Easter Festival. God, but it is dark, Heardred...I can't see you my friend," he gasped, turning his face towards the fire, now burning brightly.

Turning away from him briefly, Heardred shouted sharply to one of his men standing nearby: "Quick, Aedgar, bring a torch bundle, the man is fading fast. Dear God, where is Edwin with that ale? If poor Sturrold dies before he gets here I'll stuff his own bloody seaxe up his arse!"

"Not so swiftly, my friend!" came the soft reply from the fireside. Don't be so anxious. I have it with me now...you hold him up a little and I'll see whether I can get some down him."

Coming carefully towards where Heardred was still kneeling beside his old comrade-in-arms, Edwin gently placed the drinking horn he'd brought with him on the ground. Then together they bent forward and lifted up Sturrold's shoulders moving him, oh so gently, so that he was propped up against one of the trees that had been used for his shelter, while another of their men placed some rolled-up blankets behind him to ease his back as they did so.

Now, with his face towards the fire and the dancing flames playing across his ravaged shoulder and bloody, torn chest, they tried to coax some of the heated ale down him. But he was too weak now to drink, the nut-brown liquid spilling out of his slack mouth and running through his beard. And in despair the two men knelt helplessly by his side, each chafing a hand, knowing that there was nothing more they could do for him.

"He's fading fast," Heardred said gently, after a pause. "He'll not live out the hour."

"Did he manage to speak?"

"Yes...but it cost him all he had left. Another few hours and he would have been meat for the wolves and foxes. Thank God we saw fit to come this way, or we never would have found him."

The two men got stiffly to their feet, and stood briefly looking down at the wreckage of their friend before moving quietly away, while Alfgar and another of their men did their best to make the dying warrior more comfortable.

"Is Alfred dead?" Edwin asked urgently.

"No!" Heardred breathed out, banging his hands together. "No! Alive and kicking. At least he was before Sturrold was struck down defending the back gateway from Guthrum's attack. He's fled to Athelney, deep in the marshes of the Sommerseatas. A secret place he knows of from the monks of Glastonbury. An island in the watery mire and lakes, full of rhynes and half-drowned trackways where Guthrum cannot reach him. Pray God he gets there, for it is no short journey and he has his wife and children with him and Aelfthryth is still just a babe in arms. For God's sake the Queen is still feeding her and this weather is bitter. In very truth I fear for them greatly. And with the Danes in full cry after him, anything could happen."

"They will need help."

"Yes...and as we have discovered not every thane is of Alfred's mind. There are those who may betray him. Guthrum would pay a King's ransom to get his hands on Alfred; for as long as the King lives he cannot control Wessex!"

"What now?"

"We leave before first light and drive straight for Foxley. Collect Brioni, and whoever else wishes to come with us, and then make straight for Athelney and the King."

"What? Wulfstan, Gyrth, Aethelflaeda, everyone?"

"Everyone who can, and who wants to."

"Can it be done, Heardred? Such a large party as we will be then is bound to attract attention."

"Now who's being craven?" he snapped back suddenly.

"Don't be so bloody offensive!" Edwin replied, astonished. "You know perfectly well what I mean. I just wonder whether we wouldn't stand a better chance if we split up and made our way to Athelney by different routes."

"Forgive me, Edwin," Heardred said at once. "That was truly uncalled for. Of course I don't doubt your courage. It's just I am so anxious about Brioni and her family, and what may have happened at Foxley. And you may be right about splitting up. We'll just have to cross that bridge when we come to it. See what Thane Wulfstan has to say. He is of the King's Council. In the meantime you and Harold between you must ready the men for a brisk start tomorrow. By the way," he went on turning round. "Where is that idle loafer?"

"Seeing to the horses and cheering up the men I expect," Edwin replied with a laugh. "By God, but this is a miserable place in which to spend the night!"

"We've known worse, you and I. If we build a really good fire, and get some hot food down us, it will not seem so bad."

"What about prowling enemies?"

141

"Let them prowl," Heardred chuckled drily. "No Dane I ever heard of would move around after dark if he could avoid it, for fear of evil spirits that might seize him once the sun has set and drag him down to Hel, where all dead Norsemen go who do not get to Valhalla. They know the King has fled, that he has no army to succour or protect him and that everyone else has scattered. As far as they are concerned Wessex has fallen. They'll feel secure this night, believe me. I would in their place. Warmly bedded down in Chippenham, on a night like this after a bellyful of feasting, with Saxon whores to console them...who wants to prowl?"

# Chapter Nineteen

All night they kept the fire going, throwing whatever they could find onto the blaze and listening to the singing, sizzling wood as the damp was driven out by the heat and the sap boiled and bubbled underneath the bark and from the torn ends. While many of the men stood or sat before it, with freezing backs and roasting faces, others made shallow scrapes for themselves and lay down and wrapped themselves in their cloaks and blankets, swords thrust into the ground beside them for ease of reach, shields close by and their saddles behind their heads.

Sometime towards the early hours poor Sturrold died as a true Saxon of the Old Religion should, with his face towards the rising sun and his sword in his hand. Fever bright in his head, his one eye blazing fiercely, he had called out for his King and cursed his enemies, struggling to raise his sword above his head for one more blow, Heardred by his side.

It was his last.

That final effort killed him. His lungs collapsed, blood gushed from his mouth and from his chest, and with that last great shout he was gone, flying on the wings of the morning as the sun's new light just tinged the day with duck egg blue and tangerine...while his friends who had rallied to his cry stood and bowed their heads in sorrow for his passing.

He had been a wild, rumbustious man, a doughty fighter and a trusted, loyal companion, and they had all loved him for it. Without a doubt Alfred's army was the worse for his loss, and the King would mourn him greatly.

With that they had broken camp at last, doused the fire by scattering the smoking branches in the snow and, while most of his men busied themselves with readying their horses, others toiled with trenching pick and shovel in the frozen ground to dig the man a grave.

Eventually the job was done, and wrapped in his torn cloak and broken armour, his body was laid to rest with his sword at his side and his shield across his chest. Many would have said it was a cruel waste of good war gear in hard times to place such fine steel and enamel underground. But Heardred would have none of it, and while they all bent their heads, he prayed for Sturrold's soul to find the peace and rest he had never found on earth.

Finally the soil was thrown back in and hammered down, cut branches thrown on top and his spear thrust in to mark his grave, and everyone mounted up. Then there was a brief pause while Heardred and his two commanders checked that nothing had been left behind, before, with a single violent motion of his hand, he led them out from the trees and away across the deserted countryside. With the sky now brightening from the east, where the first faint streamers of gold and crimson were beginning to edge the far horizon, it was a brisk start to a long day in the saddle.

\*

*B*y sun-up they were swinging west around Chippenham, the little town that had been a favourite haunt of Alfred's ever since he had been King, and his father before him. The hunting in the great forests of the area was always good, and the sons of Cerdic all loved hunting! And the lodge built for them had always been considered a safe place at any time, especially for the King; for the river Avon protected the town on three sides, wide, deep and swift flowing, quite apart from the steep earth banks and palisaded walls that surrounded it, with their heavy gates and towers. It was a well-founded burgh, and the enemy should never have got in, let alone so easily. How had Alfred allowed himself to be so gulled by Guthrum into believing the oath sworn at Exeter?

Heardred ground his teeth with frustrated rage. The priests Alfred was always surrounded by had much to answer for with their simplistic belief that sworn oaths in God's name would hold the enemy at bay. Foolishness! The only thing the pirates had ever respected was cold, hard steel and a will to match. Prayers and oaths they just laughed at. An oath sworn amongst friends was for life. That sworn with an enemy was good only until you deemed it of no further value!

Now Chippenham's defences were in the hands of the Heathen, Viking warriors who would not give it up so easily. Time and again the Saxon Host had driven their enemies behind stout walls and then not managed to break in and finally destroy them. Reading had proven that in '71. With all Chippenham's stocks of winter food, for man and beast, and all its hoard of weapons, it would be an ideal base from which to ride out and devastate the land. Right in the heart of Wessex. It was not a blow to be borne lightly! And with the Danish Host in Chippenham, the danger of meeting up with marauding bands of Viking pirates was now a very real one.

But the hour was early, and leaving the town well to the east they slipped by unnoticed, came down through Colerne and crossed the By Brook at Slaughterford and then drove hard for Malmesbury high upon its ridge, along the old Fosseway beneath a brilliant sun. The sky was azure blue, the snow melting in the sudden heat, while flocks of starlings, field fares and bramblings harried the desolate countryside, and crows flew caarking overhead.

144

At midday they were checked and forced to stand motionless in a spruce copse thick with yew, juniper and holly, while a large party of axe Danes coming down from the north went by them. In the distance great plumes of black smoke showed what they had been doing and Heardred's men had to be fiercely restrained from attacking them outright and wiping out their wickedness in their own blood. Bunched all together and wrapped in thick fur mantles, they were clearly in no hurry, laughing as they rode along, their shields on their backs and their fighting axes dangling from heavy leather straps by their sides. It could have been a Sunday morning spree for all the care that they were taking, supremely confident that they could do what they liked in conquered Wessex, and with no idea that nearly a hundred pairs of bitterly hostile eyes now watched their every move.

From where Heardred and his men were standing motionless amongst the trees and shielding bushes, their horses' heads held tight against their chests to stop them whinnying to the beasts now moving slowly past not a hundred paces away, the harsh Danish voices came clearly to them. There was a flash of gold and silver about them too, as they held up the various trophies that they had seized and were now showing off to their friends. It made the watching Saxons grit their teeth with rage.

Then, without warning, the whole group came to a sudden jolting halt, their horses stamping and blowing, their fine bardings jingling brightly in the still, frosty air as they tossed their heads. There was some kind of altercation, a hand pointing in their direction, wild gesticulations, raised voices and then, wild hooting laughter as one man turned from his fellows and rode steadily towards them.

Heardred watched the approaching rider through slitted eyes, his hand reaching for his sword, ready to give the signal to attack. Bunched together as they were, they would have little time in which to spread apart before his men hit them, and the Danes were not such good fighters on horseback as the Saxons were. But these were men of the Great Army, professionals, and would sell their lives dearly…and that he simply could not afford, any more than the fierce hue and cry that would follow such a bold and violent attack. For they would have to kill every Dane before them. Not one could be allowed to escape, and they could not carry any prisoners.

So it was with a real sense of relief when the man drew his horse to a halt some forty yards from the dense cover behind which his men were

145

sheltering, right by a small hollow shielded from his friends by a large holly bush, its scarlet berries brilliant in the harsh sunlight against the snow.

Flinging himself off his horse, the thick-set Danish axeman wrenched down his breeks and squatted in the snow to defecate noisily, the heavy stench wafting across the Saxons just yards away, while his friends jeered him loudly with coarse ribald comments, and a plethora of eyes watched hungrily from the trees and bushes just behind him, noting the solid set of his shoulders and the fine quality of his equipment. Marking him down if ever they should meet with him again upon the battlefield.

Then the man was finished at last and having used the snow to clean himself and wipe his hands, he pulled up his thick hose and his leather chausses, flung himself back onto his horse, now standing prick-eared towards them. But ignoring that, he wheeled round and cantered back to join his friends as they roared with laughter and slapped their backs at his antics. And with that they all moved off again, without a backward glance, rapidly quickening their horses as they bounced along the trackway they were following and disappeared from view, only the man's dung steaming in the trampled snow to show what had just gone on there.

Heardred let out his breath with a sudden relief, then turned rapidly to where Edwin and some of his men were convulsed with laughter.

"What's so funny?" he snarled at them. "We very nearly came badly unstuck there. Another twenty paces and he must have seen us. And with nearly a hundred yards between us and them, we would never have caught and killed them all. Then what would have become of us?"

"Didn't you hear what they called him?" Harold asked, still laughing.

"Who?"

"That idiot messing up the snow, of course."

"No! I didn't! I don't speak Danish and I was too busy working out how to save our miserable hides if that bastard came any closer to be aware of his name!" Heardred replied, bitterly. "Why?"

"His friends called him 'Sigursvein Clean Arse'! Edwin chipped in. "And apparently no matter where he is, if he needs a clear-out he always goes outside to do it, or behind the nearest tree!"

"They reckon that one day he'll be cleaning his arse behind some friendly bush when a hulking great Saxon warrior will come up behind and really clean him out...with a sharp iron spear head!" Harold finished off, almost rolling about with mirth. "If they only knew!" he went on, wiping the tears from his eyes. "I could have spitted him from where I was standing as easily as knocking a hare over with a stick!"

146

For a moment Heardred stood there dumbfounded, stunned by their apparent heedlessness for the situation in which they found themselves: the King fled; the country over-run by Danes who were pillaging everywhere; Brioni probably in mortal danger; disaster staring them in the face...and all his most trusted companions could do was fall about and make silly jokes about a Viking pirate's clotted arsehole while the rest of his men stood around and sniggered like foolish schoolboys!

Then finally his mask cracked, and he too laughed outrageously, as much from sheer relief as from anything else. Of course they were right. The whole world might be going to Hell in a tilt cart, but if you could laugh about life at a time like this then anything was possible.

"'Sigursvein Clean Arse', eh? His friends are right. Give me a chance like that again and I'll clean him out myself!" And to the accompanying ripple of laughter that ran round his troop, and with much brandishing of spears, they all mounted up and pushed on with their journey, scouts ahead and behind to check they were not being followed. But this time they stayed well clear of the trackway up which they had been moving, and cut across country again instead. Clearly it was no longer safe to travel so boldly, and for the rest of their journey they wood-hopped, going from one dense coppice to another, crossing the open spaces that lay between as quickly as they could, eyes and ears alert for any hint of danger.

*

As they drew closer to Foxley, so the signs of enemy activity became more numerous: burned out buildings and ravaged steadings, the smell of smoke and burning heavy on the air; cattle roaming masterless in the wastelands crying to be milked; sheep in scattered flocks a prey to every wolf for miles, and bodies everywhere...animals needlessly slaughtered and pathetic human bundles lying split open and lifeless in the soiled snow.

Women and children also, caught up while fleeing from their homes, had not been spared the biting edge of Danish steel either. Hacked down and spitted as they ran, their bodies rifled of whatever simple valuables they might have had, they had simply been left abandoned to the pitiless carrion feeders of the forest and the skies. They passed more than one babe left alive after its mother had been slain, now lying lifeless with bloodied eye sockets where the crows and ravens had plucked out the eyes as easily as from a new-born lamb.

147

Grim-faced now, and silent, the revelry of the morning long since forgotten, they pushed on for Foxley as hard as their tiring beasts could carry them.

Overhead the sun was fast disappearing behind fresh racks of cloud, all hurrying before a rising wind that gnawed at the hastening riders with teeth of glass. Rising and falling in whining cadence, it brought tears to their reddened faces...and carried with it the thick stench of charred timbers and burned-out thatch borne in the smoke that could be seen swirling across the countryside in a fine haze, accompanied by distant scurrying figures fleeing into the wilderness to escape the butchery that always followed a brutal raid.

Knowing that Foxley was both strongly built and well-defended, there was every reason to believe that all might still be well with them, as the vill was not his primary aim, though it was close to his line of march from Gloucester. So despite the obvious destruction that they had witnessed as they had cut across the Vikings' storm-path as they had swept on Chippenham, they were simply not prepared for the sight that met their eyes as they finally breasted the long ridge from Sherston that carried the Malmesbury road, and led down to the Foxley steading above the river Avon that bounded it along its southern side, some half a mile from the village itself.

To say that the place had fallen was such an understatement as to be utterly meaningless, and for several minutes Heardred and his men just sat their horses in appalled silence.

# Chapter Twenty

Wherever they looked, all they could see were blackened buildings and the pale litter of the slain, those still clothed lying like black pawns scattered heedlessly from a giant chessboard, with the occasional animal wandering aimlessly amidst the carnage. What was quite frighteningly apparent was that the place had not just been the victim of a casual raid which the defenders could successfully have dealt with. No...this had clearly been a carefully planned and ferocious assault by veteran troops of the Great Army, and driven forward without regard to cost under one of its most experienced commanders. No-one else could have defeated Wulfstan and Gyrth's combined forces, and their fyrdsmen, so completely.

The progress of a two-pronged attack was clearly visible from their position above the shattered steading, simply from the heaped bodies of all those who had been slain there, both by the shattered gateway, where the enemy ram still lay abandoned, and by a huge breach in the defences along the western wall.

Finally, and saddest of all, were the piled bodies of a last desperate stand before the burned-out shell of the great hall. They had come so close to freedom, just yards from the great gap in the palisade when their charge, assailed on every side, had clearly failed.

For the first time since he had learned of his parents' deaths Heardred felt despair in his heart. Despair that he had not reached Foxley in time to bring them aid, and that the girl he so loved might still be down there somewhere; hurt, ravaged and crying out for help with piteous tears...or dead.

"No!" He breathed out fiercely standing up in his stirrups. "No!" Then, his voice growing louder, he shouted: "No!...*I won't believe it!*" And before anyone could stop him, he had sat down firmly in his saddle, thrust his long spurs into his fretting horse and catapulted himself towards the ruined and desolate steading below them without thought, or any heed of danger that might yet be lurking amongst the burned and shattered buildings.

"Brioni! *Brioni!*" he shouted as he rode, his voice sounding thin and lonely in the ruffling airs that blew up to his men, like the desperate cry of the stone curlew mourning for its young, new stolen from the nest by ravens.

"Quick! After him!" Edwin shouted, still sitting his horse motionless with shock on the empty ridge, now suddenly stirred to life. "God knows what may be down there. You Edric, Alfgar, Baldred, you stay up here with your group and guard our backs. Harold, make for the main entrance with your men, and see what you can find. The rest of you follow me. Harrow away! *Harrow away!*" And with a rasp of drawn steel, clinging on over the bumps and hollows, all doing their best not to fall off their careering horses, they plunged after their stricken leader.

In front of them now by almost a hundred paces, Heardred was bruising the ground in his feverish haste to reach the compound, urging his tired beast over the frozen commons with flailing hands and feet, and with no sense of caution for either obstacle or danger. Long before the rest of his men could catch up with him he had reached the broken gateway and disappeared inside, his voice crying out Brioni's name to the wind as he frantically searched for her amongst the ruins, with desperation in his heart and a growing certainty that he would never see her alive again.

\*

Drawing rein as he approached the broken timbers of the stockade, Edwin first checked his men and then urged his horse forward again, stepping over and around the Saxon slain that lay heaped there until he came to the great ditch itself.

This no horse could possibly climb in nor out of, nor could it be jumped, but the huge section of burned wall that the Danes had managed to pull out had fallen far enough across it to form a crude ramp and Edwin now urged his nervous horse down and up it again, with prancing steps, to leap through the jagged breach and so into the compound itself. Behind him his troopers followed, at first cautiously and then with greater confidence, as one after another they followed Edwin into the ruined steading of Foxley.

Once inside the huge garth, Edwin came to an abrupt halt as his eyes took in the scene of utter devastation that now surrounded him for there were bodies scattered everywhere. Men, women, children...no-one seemed to have been spared, and every building he could see had been torched.

"My God, would you look at this place, Siward?" he said with awe, turning round in his saddle to talk with his big sergeant. "They've hardly left one building standing. The place looks like a charnel house!"

"Look, Lord!" the man called out suddenly, pointing with his hand over Edwin's shoulder. "Over there, by the hall place. Cairns!"

"Sa, sa," his troop leader replied softly. "So someone at least survived the slaughter. Where's the Lord Heardred?"

"I can't see him, Lord, but Swiftfire is standing near what's left of a granary. Where those staddle stones are, Lord. And there is another great

150

building up there also. A barn maybe? It's hard to tell with all this destruction. God, how I hate those bastards, Lord!"

"Me too, Siward," Edwin replied grimly, straightening in his saddle. "Me too! No matter, my friend, split the men up into pairs and search every corner. Find the stables, or the ruins of one anyway, and fix a good horse line wherever you can find a place to do so, and then go over this place with a fine toothcomb. I want it turned upside down, though God knows there is not much left to turn. But any signs of life and you are to call me immediately."

"What about Lord Heardred?"

"Leave him to me, Siward," Edwin answered him gently. "This place was his Lady's home and he is taking it hard. He'll be up with Swiftfire somewhere. I'll find him, never fear. Now, get on with it, sergeant. We have much to do and little time in which to do it."

And digging in his heels slightly he walked his horse away from the rest of his men as they began their search and went to where his friend's horse had been halted and was even then wandering loosely, reins trailing, seemingly abandoned. As he drew level with it, however, Edwin saw Heardred sitting some short distance away on a pile of smashed and half-burned timbers, his hands hanging limply by his side, his eyes staring blankly into space. Swinging himself out of his saddle, leaving his horse to forage, he went across and joined him. Laying his arm across his friend's shoulder, he sat down beside him, and the two men just sat and gazed out across the ruined steading in silence.

"No sign of her then?" he said eventually, with a sigh, watching as his men picked their way amidst the devastation.

For a few moments Heardred made no reply, but continued to sit where he was, unmoving, as if he wasn't even aware of Edwin's presence by his side. But, finally, with almost a groan, he turned and looked into his friend's troubled eyes.

"No, Edwin, nothing! There's only one thing left that we can do...search those crude mounds."

"Have you looked everywhere else?"

"For pity's sake, Edwin! Look at this place!" he cried out in anguish. "This is in a worse state of devastation than any I have come across since I was a King's man, and we have seen a few over the years, you and I. Usually they leave something standing, but this place," he said gesturing all around him, "this place hasn't just been captured...it's been stamped on!"

"Well someone obviously survived, and Saxon too without a doubt. No Dane would bother to cover the dead in that fashion. Their own are nowhere to be found. They must have burned their dead in the fire that destroyed the hall,

151

or the barn and granary. But our dead? They lie everywhere, poor souls. And from the looks of all the tracks that are scattered about everywhere, and from the state of some of the bodies, those cairns were built just in time. Wolves have been at their work here, that's for certain. But why cover some and not others?"

"Perhaps they were disturbed, and had to run off before they could finish their task properly?" Harold threw at them, suddenly coming quietly up behind where his two friends were sitting.

"So...there you are," Heardred replied, looking up at Harold's face. "I was wondering what had happened to you."

"Came up to the gate entrance and then down here in search of you. Siward said you would be around here somewhere."

"Anything your end, Harold?" Heardred asked the wiry war-leader quickly, the hint of eagerness and hope still not finally extinguished by the awful reality all around them.

"No. I'm sorry, Heardred, truly I am. Nothing but bodies, my friend. My men are still searching, but honestly there isn't that much to search."

Heardred sighed deeply and looked around him: at the strained faces of his friends; at his men wandering hopelessly from place to place about the compound; at their jaded beasts, all needing food and rest, and at the deepening gloom as the light began to fade and merge with the rapidly blackening sky.

They were right of course. There was only one thing left to do now, and that thing he had been putting off in the hopes that by some miracle they might have found her still alive amongst the ruins, somewhere. He hid his face in his hands for a few moments and turned his back on the others as the tears trickled from between his fingers. Dear God in Heaven, but he had loved her so much. It just didn't seem possible that she was dead....that they were all dead.

She had been so lovely. So warm and caring and alive, that never to see her again, to hear her laughter and the sweetness of her voice gave him such pain that at that he felt quite numb. He took a deep breath and swallowed hard, brushed his face with his palms and turned back towards his friends.

"Well..well, so then, the mounds it must be. I suppose whoever was left could only manage to cover those who were of the most importance."

"You mean the family?" Edwin asked quietly, coming back to lay his arm across Heardred's shoulders.

"Yes, Edwin. The family."

"Dear God, the family!" Harold breathed the words huskily. "Of course that would explain why..." he stopped speaking suddenly as the enormity of what he was saying struck him.

152

"It's alright, my friend," Heardred said slowly. "I have long worked that out too, though I have been so hoping not to have had to do so," he continued, turning towards them both. "Look at us all. Men and horses both, all exhausted. It is time to make an end to this business, and the sooner the better before the weather closes down again or the Danes return. It is just that I don't want to do this on my own. For one thing it would take me forever, the light is already beginning to go. For another," he said pausing briefly, "for another I'd rather one at least of you was with me."

"Edwin," Harold replied after a brief pause, "you go with Heardred. I'll go to the river gateway and start again down there. There is something I want to check over. You never know, she might have escaped. People often do in the confusion of a raid. Look at all those people we met fleeing from Chippenham. Or Alfred and his family at Chippenham, just breaking out as the Danes burst in! There's always a chance." And turning away from them he threw his leg over his horse, pulled its head round and made off towards the river gateway, its gates open but still in one piece, the river bridge below him, calling up his men as he did so.

Heardred watched him leave, heard his voice shouting to his men, his arms in motion as he gestured to them. But with his mind only half working it all seemed strangely meaningless, like watching a troop of dancers through a glass of water, all their movements exaggerated and deformed.

Could she have escaped? Or been captured and carried away with the Danes for their amusement? His face blenched. Sweet Mary! His Brioni in those bastards' hands? The very thought was more terrible than if she had been slain. He knew how the Danes treated their female prisoners, and he groaned aloud in an agony of mind and spirit. Stripped naked and forced to 'service' every one of them, while their friends drank and laid bets on her performance, bawling out lewd advice to whoever was attempting her. Then, if she was lucky, throat cut and left to bleed-out…or sold on and whored by whoever had bought her, until she was dead.

Oh, yes, he knew just what could happen in a Danish war camp when the warriors were flushed with victory and hot with wine and boasting. That's what the fairest slaves were kept for, and all men knew it. He had seen it in Saxon war-camps too, despite Alfred's orders, and Danish ones were no different. Yet this was his own sweet lady and his whole heart and soul cried out against it.

"*Oh, God, not Brioni!*" he suddenly shouted out. "I would rather she were dead than that should happen to her!" And filled with a sudden desperate madness he leapt up and ran past Edwin's startled face, past his men standing around them and raced to the nearest mound he could see, flinging himself at it and burrowing amongst the debris like a giant badger, while Edwin rushed to join him, his own men standing open-mouthed, like stone gargoyles, while the wild despair burned itself out.

When Edwin reached him Heardred was almost sobbing with exhaustion, the sweat running down his face to mingle with his tears, his mailed gloves ripped and torn from his desperate, frenzied digging, leaving him slumped on the torn ground, limp and exhausted.

"Come, my friend," he said gently, pulling him away.

"Leave me alone! I must find her...*I must find her!*"

"Of course you must. But this is not the way. Come, Heardred, you have done enough. And remember, you were not the only one to love her. One way or another we will find her, I promise you. Dead or alive, we will find her, even if we have to search through every last mound to do so. Come with me a little space, and let the men do this work. They, too, honoured her you know. You have shown what must be done, now leave us to do the rest."

Now unresisting, Heardred followed his friend a few paces, then turned to watch his men as they bent to the task of clearing the rubble and loose timber that had been so painstakingly piled up over whatever lay hidden beneath.

"Do you really wish she were dead?" Edwin asked at last, as he handed his friend a flask of strong mead he always had about him, watching his friend steadily regain control over his emotions. "Is that what you truly want for your Lady Brioni?"

Heardred, now sat down on an up turned bucket, groaned and rubbed his eyes as he did so, then sat unblinking in the fading light of the late afternoon, as he gazed at the litter of death and destruction that lay strewn all around them, while the men continued to uncover the rough cairn he had started on.

Time passed and his friend waited.

"No, Edwin," he said at last. "Not really, for if whoever led this raid really has her then there is always the chance of a ransom to get her back. The Danes are not completely stupid. Whoever it is will know she would be a valuable hostage. And if they do have her, then I may still find her and rescue her despite the dangers. Where there is hope there is life; that is what Alfred believes, and so must I."

"Well then, pull yourself together and fix a smile on your ugly features. There has to be the chance that she might even have got clean away, as Alfred did. Just cling to that and let fate do the rest."

"Pray God, you may be right, Edwin. For if she is gone, then there will be little left for me but revenge and death on all who took her from me. I swear it Edwin, on my life!" he went on, his eyes blazing in the intensity of his emotions. "If her love is lost to me, then I shall spend the rest of my days

154

killing those who stole it from me. One day Wessex shall be free of these vermin for ever, and until that day comes my sword shall never slake its thirst for Danish blood, this, on my life, I promise you!"

It was a doom-filled oath, and one that would return to haunt him, for one by one each grave revealed a body of her family.

First her mother and her brother, Gyrth, lying close to one another. The one spear thrust and hacked to death with multiple wounds that even now gaped open like hungry mouths; the other with a single wound to the heart, her eyes closed as if in sleep, her hands beautifully folded across her breasts. And all surrounded by the flower of their household warriors, many of whom Heardred recognised from their weapons and their armour, though some had their faces so badly torn by birds and wolves that not even their own mothers would have recognised them.

Then there came a shout from either end of the garth. The men standing next to a double cairn being the nearest to them, and Edwin and Heardred went at once towards them, aware that those furthest away from the shattered gateway, near the great hall, were equally insistent on their immediate presence.

# Chapter Twenty One

*T*here were two bodies lying close together.

One, with head hideously smashed, was that of an old priest, the simple wooden cross of his office twisted around his neck, his clothes soaked in blood and his parchment hands looking even more frail and white in death than one would have supposed.

The other was a girl.

Once she might have been pretty, even beautiful with long golden hair in ribboned plaits and a rich figure on long slender legs. But her face had been cloven in two and brutally trampled, as had her body. Horribly mutilated by the iron hooves of some great horse, ripped and torn as was the fine blue cloak she had been wearing, that someone had done their best to lay across her...it was a truly awful sight to gaze upon. On one straight, folded arm she wore a finely wrought bracelet of silver, inlaid with gold and richly edged with garnets, like drops of blood against the snow-bound debris of the cairn. A gift of great beauty worn only by the fair and well beloved.

For a moment Heardred felt as if the world itself was spinning, and he had to cling fiercely to his friend to stop himself from falling over, so violent was the shock of seeing her so horribly destroyed. His breath came in gasps and he felt his stomach heave in his acute distress, while tears, hot and heavy like drops of blood, fell from his eyes. With a strangled cry he fell to his knees beside the grave, his mind and soul in utter turmoil.

Edwin said nothing.

What could he say? How can you ever begin to assuage a grief so vast and terrible as that which his poor friend was now enduring? In silent homage he knelt beside Heardred and put his arm about his shoulders, while their men turned aside to tend to other things, themselves overwhelmed by what they had discovered beneath the cairn.

"Is it her?"

"Yes, Edwin," his friend whispered at length, the words almost gasped out as he strove to control his breathing. "It's her."

"My friend, are you truly certain? She has been so..so.." he could not bring himself to say it.

"So mutilated!" Heardred finished for him. "Trampled on, desecrated, hacked apart. Oh, Edwin," he cried out in his agony. "It is her cloak she wears, her golden hair that lies there drabbled in her blood...and my mother's bracelet on her arm that I gave her scant weeks ago as my betrothal gift that she would never have put off.  It is the Lady Brioni for certain.  Oh God, how could they have done it?  She was so young and beautiful.  Like a warm summer's morning.  So alive and wonderful!" and he bent his head and wept, as Edwin turned him and held him in his arms like a child.

"I am so sorry, old friend.  So terribly, terribly sorry," and motioning the men standing there to move yet further away, he held him closely for a while, conscious only of his friend's grief and utter despair...and feeling totally inadequate to offer him any other comfort.

Finally Heardred lifted his head and pushed himself away, putting his hands on Edwin's shoulders, and looking him in the eyes as he did so.

"Thank you, my friend," he said softly, "for being there when I needed you most.  It is over.  I will not let those bastards pull me any lower than I am now!  She was my life, and now she is gone.  Only their destruction can bring me any hope of peace, and that Edwin, before God, I will give my life to!"

"What do you want us to do now?  We can't stay here...and we can't leave her family to rot outside either."

"We must bury them properly, Edwin.  I know the chapel is ruined and the roof burned off, but we must lay them before the altar, where her father always intended his family to be buried.  He told me that last year when our betrothal was agreed on, and I must see his wishes carried out.  After that?  I am not sure.  I have the glimmer of an idea, but I will tell you all about that later, when I have had more time to work it out."

He turned slowly away, still holding onto his friend's shoulder, to look down once more on the poor, tattered body half wrapped in its soiled blue cloak that his men had uncovered.  "That's not my Brioni," he said firmly, for the last time.  "That is but the cracked and crumpled shell.  It is her spirit that has flown free, and when I raise my head and call her name upon the wind, I will hear her laughter come back to me on the breeze and know that she is well.  Oh, Edwin.  I shall miss her so very much!"  And wiping his eyes once more with the back of his hand, he turned then, and taking his horse's reins back from the man who had been holding them, he walked stiffly across the garth to where Harold was again beckoning him urgently from the river gateway, his horse patiently following, head down like his master's.

\*

"Now, what's all the excitement?"  Heardred asked softly as he reached where his friend was standing, his voice flat, devoid of all emotion.

"Heardred, I am so sorry.  I just heard..."

157

"Thank you for that, Harold," he replied grimly, clasping him by the arm. "It's what we have seen so many times with others. You never think it will ever happen to you. It's just devastating. But I cannot mourn her now. What goes on here?"

Harold looked at his friend, at his determined face and stiff shoulders, and nodded: "Very well, Heardred. Very well...I told you I wanted to check on something down here. Well, look," he said pointing to the trampled ground around the gateway. See these cart tracks? They lie on top of those left by the Danes when they pulled out. There has been fresh snow since then, and these lines are almost fresh, and heavy. Leading away from here down to the village below. My men have followed them to a peasant's hovel, local ale-house I would think from the smell of it. Someone stopped there and dug up the hearth, before leaving again. Just one person with a light cart and two dogs, Cynric thinks..."

"Your best tracker, if I remember rightly."

"Indeed! Can follow a deer through water. He thinks it may be a youngster, or a woman, the footfall is so slight."

"Where do the tracks lead?"

"Down through the village then away across country. There is something moving right up against the forest edge now. Too far to see anything clearly. Maybe the person who made the cairns?"

"Poor bastard! So someone survived, or came across the ruined vill after the Danes had left."

"Should we try and catch them up?"

"At this time of the day? With so much to do here? No, whoever it is I hope they find shelter before night falls. It is already growing dark now. You would never catch up with them before night, and I won't risk you wandering across this ruined countryside with lanterns to search for a will-o'-the-wisp in the forests. Let them be and God's blessings on them. I wouldn't be alone out there tonight for all the gold in Miklagard!" And turning away with his hand on Harold's shoulder, he was about to mount up when there was a loud hail from a group of men not far away around a further mound they had just finished opening.

"Now what?" he growled, stopping in his tracks as his friend pushed past him to join his men. "What have they found now?" And he moved back towards the burned-out ruins of the hall, where his friend was now standing, his face clearly shocked by what he had seen.

"What is it, Harold?"

"Look...I was so sorry about Brioni. But this? This is not going to be good either."

158

"What is this? What have they found?"

"It is Thane Wulfstan, Heardred," he said quietly pointing to where his men had uncovered another body. "But," he hesitated, looking stricken, "he has been hacked about in a manner I have only heard of before. And never in Wessex."

"What do you mean?" he questioned urgently, taking a step forwards.

"The Blood Eagle!"

"No, by God! Surely that is not possible," Heardred replied, putting his hand on Harold's shoulder as he turned towards his men. "Guthrum banned that filthy practice after Wareham. I understood he had greater respect now for a bold enemy than to tear his body apart."

"That may well be so, my friend," Harold went on grimly, his head on one side. "But you and I know of one black-hearted hell-hound who uses it whenever it pleases..."

"Sweet Jesus, the Lord Oscytel!" he exclaimed, stamping his feet with sudden rage. "That bastard is worthy of every foul name that a man can lay tongue to. He is a pitiless enemy, Harold. A man with no heart," he continued heavily. "He is considered a King amongst his own people. Guthrum's most trusted advisor and his most successful army commander.

"I thought this whole attack was too determined," he added, now walking across to where Harold's men were standing. "Too ruthless and well organised for a casual raid. That ram proves it. They brought the wheels with them, that much is clear. Dear God, what did they do to raise his anger, for this whole wretched business reeks of vengeance. Thank God Brioni was slain in the fighting. God knows what wickedness he would have subjected her too if she had fallen prisoner!"

Then they were standing above where the butchered carcase lay.

"Poor Wulfstan!" he said, looking down on the tortured features; the obscene wings made from his ribs; his lungs flobbed on top of them; his torn and battered heart, trodden and smashed almost to a pulp; the huge pool of frozen blood that surrounded him, and he sighed deeply. "You poor bastard. You never stood a chance. Even with all Gyrth's men you would still have needed more. If only you knew how hard I tried to get here...and even we might not have been enough. But I promise you this," he went on, kneeling amidst the debris of the cairn, and taking the dead man's hand in his, "on the body of your daughter whom I loved above all others, I will hunt this man down and kill him. You and your family will not go unavenged! *I promise you!*"...he breathed out fiercely one more time. Then lifting his face once more, his mouth a tight line, he gave the necessary instructions for the safe removal of the plundered corpse to the old ruined chapel. There his men were

159

already busy with pick and shovel culled from the ruins as they dug deep into the hard earth beneath the stone flags. Great square stones that old Anselm the priest had laid with his own hands long ago when all was calm and Wessex still at peace.

Turning away from everybody, Heardred left his horse in Alfgar's hands and walked up with slumbering steps to the smashed and battered gateway. Stepping over the bodies of warrior and peasant alike that now lay frozen to the ground, he leaned against the splintered gateposts, his hands buried in his cloak, as he looked out across the snowy countryside, his eyes following the distant cart tracks that Harold had earlier pointed out to him.

The wind had picked up a little over the past hour or so, curling round the deserted palisade and moaning across the open entrance to the steading, shivering the stiff grasses where they poked their heads above the snow, and tumbling the rooks about the darkening sky as they sought their nests in the woodlands all about. Black, caarking acrobats that peeled across the steely clouds that had shuttered down the thin sunshine of the early afternoon. Below him the village lay broken and empty, the timbers of the burned-out buildings thrusting up towards him like Wulfstan's shattered ribs, the cruck-house ends standing up like bishops' mitres, stark against the empty background.

He shivered.

Who had it been who had built the cairns and then slipped away into the desolate wilderness beyond the steading? Orphan youth, or woman, by the tracks that Cynric had followed in the snow? Down to the ale-house, then away to seek a place of safety from the horror of Oscytel's brutal, swift assault.

Beyond the steading nothing moved in all that bleak wilderness. In the distance there were dark columns of smoke where Danish raiders had been at their usual work of murder and destruction, and overhead the carrion birds were flighting to their nests in the distant forest lands. Behind him in the hedgerows nearby a blackbird pinked its alarm call at a stray cat, like a brindled tiger, stalking in the bottom as it paused, tail swishing before pouncing on its prey, a wayward mouse that squeaked once before it died. And he smiled as it leapt away with its mouse-moustache to seek some hidey-hole amongst the ruined bothies of some villagers around the bridge that crossed the river below the steading, the water black and swirling between the ice that rimmed its banks.

160

# Chapter Twenty Two

**D**rawing his heavy wolf-skin cloak around him, Heardred watched the stripey form, tail flying, as it paused, one paw up to stare at him with unblinking yellow eyes before whisking itself away; then turning he stared, bleak-eyed, about him and then into the frozen distance.

Lucky cat!

At least it knew what it was doing; didn't have to wrestle with the rights and wrongs of daily life; of sudden slaughter and mindless destruction. He sighed in the smoky air, the bitter smell of burning still heavy all around him. It was all so meaningless...so pointless a destruction of a place and people whose only crime seemed to have been that of being alive.

And Saxon!

What possible hope could there be of anything so long as such brutal acts were accepted as the normal course of war? Violence just seemed to beget more of the same. They raid and butcher our people...so we go out of our way to raid and butcher theirs. Destroy as many of them as possible, and then give thanks to God for our victory over their darkness.

And am I any better?

He grunted at the thought, and grimaced. He had vowed revenge on Oscytel; sworn it on the bodies of Brioni and of her father. So, what did that make of him? Where was Christian mercy and forgiveness now? He grunted again. Gone to Hell in a tilt cart until the fighting was over.

Yet pirates are human beings too, just as Saxons are, with the exception of a few who were more devil than human! Like Oscytel...while the wretched peasants simply become pawns on a giant chess-board, to be sacrificed where necessary; where the only beneficiaries are the war-lords who organise the game, and then re-invent the rules to suit themselves. Like Guthrum at Exeter, who had broken his word again, slain the hostages and fled to Gloucester! *Bastards!* So we slew his!

And he chuckled, full of sardonic humour. At the rate we are going there will soon be no people left to rule over and no rules worth living for either, and he growled deep in his throat.

Dear God, but it all seemed so hopeless. Perhaps old King Burghred of Mercia had the right idea after all. You could never beat the Great Army; everybody said so, so why go on trying and make everyone's lives unbearable? It was so much easier to give in, to flee maybe, or pay up a ransom...wasn't it?

Better to clear out while the going is good, with what little you have managed to save, than stay behind and suffer annihilation along with all the rest. Like Foxley, he thought, looking around him at the bodies and all the desolation. Save what you can and the devil take the hindmost...or come to some arrangement with Guthrum to preserve your estates by paying Danegeld. A silver ransom to save your land...and then keep paying it until you're broken on the wheel of Danish greed for land, and get driven off anyway!

He levered himself away from the torn timbers and kicked fiercely at the snow heaps that the wind had blown there, and shook his head with disgust.

That way leads to dishonour and despair. But what does a peasant care for honour when despair stares him in the face every day, and hunger gnaws his children's bones at night? What price honour then? When his wife cries herself to sleep and their home goes up in smoke and flames to satisfy an absent king's demands.

He looked up then and stared across the darkening garth, at Harold and Edwin talking earnestly together while their men finished their work in the ruined chapel, and set about finding fodder for their horses, and somewhere to sleep that night.

He remembered the thane whose hospitality they had enjoyed while on their way to Foxley. Doing a deal with Guthrum, or one of his leaders, was what that man, and his wife, clearly had in mind, and he snorted with derision.

Wrong! *Wrong!* That is *not* the way to gain peace.

*Alfred is right!*

You have to fight the bastards...and there are plenty of good caring people left in Wessex to help him. Aye and good fighters too, with men to lead them if ever they are given the chance. And not even the poorest of the borel folk would rather trust a Danish pirate than their own anointed King, be he no better housed than one of themselves, just now, nor any richer either. Just so long as he continues to fight, and graunch the bastards wherever he can find them, until he has driven them from the land for good!

England was such a beautiful country.

So rich and fair, no wonder the bastards wanted it all for themselves. Better by far than the blasted heaths of their own lands across the seas. And England was aching to be free. Now that was something worth fighting for...aye, and worth dying for also if the need arose.

The freedom to be safe in your own home at night; to rise in the morning and tend your sheep and cattle and know that no bloody pirate is going to row a dragon boat up your river and steal them from you; that never again, so long as the king should live, will you wake to the roar of flames and the screams of the

162

maimed, of the women and the children, as the enemy run, howling their battle-fury, to put your village to the fire and the sword.

The King!

In the end it all hung upon the King, and Heardred stretched his arms out and breathed deeply.

Now, there *is* a man to follow.

Alfred has the ideas, the vision and the determination...and, God willing, the strength to carry them out too, as long as he is not struck down too often with illness. For he is wracked with bowel pains at times that leave him weak as a kitten, I have seen it happen. Fight the bastard Danes! Fight them and fight them again! Never give in so long as the people remain true and follow his example. Me too! I must also remain true to the promises I have made to my King when I became a royal companion, a 'Hound of the King'. If I desert him now, then Brioni and her family will all have died in vain. My oath will fail and I will be claimed *'Nithing'*, accursed by all. Their agony and terror will count for nothing and Oscytel, and those dark-souled bastards like him will have won.

Guthrum will have won.

It was unthinkable!

There was only one route he could follow, and though that might lead him and his friends through utter darkness to the place of slaughter, then so be it for only then, on the battlefield, could the light shine through again bright and clear. And it would, he was sure of it. Bring the bastards to battle in a place of Alfred's choosing and the Saxon war-host would destroy them. It was not just something that he dreamed of; it was the truth. He knew it...a victory like a trumpet blast across the land that would be heard by the whole of Frankland. Wessex has crushed the Great Army! The Danes can be beaten!

He stood up straight then and smiled.

There *was* a way forward after all, despite the destruction of Foxley and the loss of all he held most dear in his heart. Now he knew what he must do and where he must go. To Alfred on Athelney, and with the King fight the enemy to destruction...and if that meant to his death, then so be it. He had nothing left to live for. He smiled again, and suddenly became aware that someone was speaking to him, and turning quickly round he found Edwin almost by his side.

"Are you alright, Heardred? Harold has been calling for you. We are all ready now and the men have found sufficient food and shelter for this night anyway. You seemed miles away, my friend. Was it Brioni?"

Heardred turned away then to gesture out across the darkening countryside.

163

"Yes, Edwin, I was thinking of her. Of course I was, she will be a part of me always. But there were other things on my mind also."

"What things?"

"Oh, Alfred, Wessex, England. What to do next...a hunting cat! Those sort of things."

"I don't understand."

"Nor do I really. It's just the thought of all this waste, and the endless killing. It all seems so bloody pointless! The real tragedy is that the only way to free ourselves of this canker that is eating up our land is to wade through more rivers of blood. I sometimes wonder whether it is all really worth it in the end.

"Then I think of my parents, and now of Brioni and her family...not to mention all the others we have known who have taken the swan's path these thirteen years past, like Sturrold, and then I know that I just have to go on. Do you realise," he said stopping suddenly, "that none of us has known anything other than war against the Danes our whole lives? Wessex has been fighting since '65 when the Great Army first came from Frankland. And in that time three Wessex kings have died. Of all the sons of Cerdic, Alfred is the last. Oh, God, Edwin, but it wearies me. How Alfred copes with it all I simply have no idea. And now even he has been driven into the wilderness!"

"Your problem, my friend, is that you think too much!" Edwin replied with a grin, patting Heardred's shoulder as they walked, Swiftfire following behind, his head nodding, his ears pricked. "You always were a bit of a dreamer. You and the King both. You make a good pair. No wonder Alfred likes you so much; you understand one another. But don't give up on us now, for Saint Swithun's sake, or we'll all be lost."

"What do you mean?"

"You're the only man among us who can get us out of this mess we have stumbled into. Harold and I have brawn in plenty, my friend, but you have brains as well. Show us a place to hold, or a battle-line to storm, and we know just what to do. We are good at that...but not the whys and wherefores. That is subtle work for men with thoughtful minds. Come on now," he continued, pushing Heardred along as he spoke. "We need a plan, and you are going to have to give us one. And if you have thought one up while you have been mooning about up there by the gateway this hour or so, the sooner we know what it is the better. That's why you are the leader of our jolly band...and the rest of us just do as we are told without argument!"

Heardred groaned, and then laughed, the first time since Brioni's body had been found that he had done so, for that statement was so outrageous as to beggar belief, and Edwin laughed with him.

"You two? Not argue with me? Now I know I am going mad. There is as much chance of that ever happening as there is of Hell freezing over, or a fox giving birth to a hare! Which reminds me that we haven't eaten since sun-up, and I am starving!"

"That sounds much better," Edwin answered with a broad grin. "Probably half your trouble stems from the fact that you are hungry. Come, put some food in your belly and you'll soon see things in a warmer light. I never knew a man who didn't feel better for a good meat pasty and a jug of ale. Though not even our lot could find that in this place, more's the pity."

"What about the graves?" Heardred asked, breaking into his comments. "I saw the lads at work while I was up by the gateway."

"All finished, and the bodies lying in them. No, don't fret. They are well shrouded, I promise you. And I took your mother's bracelet off Brioni's arm…"

He stopped then and turned to look at his friend, his dark brows drawing together like storm clouds: "No! I meant to leave it on her."

Edwin stopped too, and smiled gently, laying his hand on Heardred's arm as he spoke: "And have the grave dug over by Danish pirates at the first opportunity? You know what those bastards are like. They can smell gold and silver at a hundred paces. It is a miracle her body was not robbed before it was cold. Better far for you to hold the bracelet safe, than a rieving pirate should lay his heathen hands all over it. Here it is. I give it over to your safe keeping."

There was a small pause then, while Heardred looked into Edwin's eyes, then down at the beautifully worked piece of jewellery he was holding out to him, and which, with a sigh and a nod of his head he finally took into his own hands.

"That was well thought of, Edwin. You are right. Far better for me to hold it safe; I can always bequeath it to a monastery when the times are better."

"Good, that is well done. Now, though, the time has come to make an end of this business. The night is fast upon us, and there is still much to do. Are you ready now?"

"Yes! Yes, of course. Lead on, old friend, I shall be right behind you. The sooner we can say our farewells, the sooner we can rest, eat and make some plans." And with Swiftfire steadily following, his ears flicking and his head nodding to every step, Heardred and Edwin turned back towards the old chapel where Harold and their men were closely gathered, heads together and eyes everywhere as they talked earnestly between one another while waiting for their leader to return.

165

*I*t was a simple service beneath a leaden sky, made darker by the swift approach of night as Heardred, through gritted teeth and swift, deep breathing, saw his belovèd Brioni buried. Determined to shed no further tears before his men, though his blue eyes were blurred with them, he fooled no-one with his efforts, for his men stood all around to share his grief, even as they shared his prayers for all those who had died that awful day.

Later, when it was all over, and the ground beaten flat as best they could, with the stones carefully replaced, they marked each grave with a raised flag at its head. Then everyone filed out of the ruined building and made their way across the garth, now cleared of bodies, to where the old forge stood, door gaping open, with great holes in its tiled roof and half-burned timbers lying all around.

With luck they could come back again someday and have a proper ceremony, with a bishop to say the prayers, even the king himself as Wulfstan had been one of the foremost of his Council. Then the stones would be marked with the names of the dead and lovingly re-laid. But right now they needed warmth and food and shelter, for the night was upon them and the wind was hard and cruel.

# Chapter Twenty Three

"Well," Heardred asked, as they led their horses from the chapel. "What, apart from the graves, have you two managed in my absence?"

"The stables will be useable with a little ingenuity and a lot of hard labour," Edwin replied with a grin, and a hand on Heardred's shoulder, "and that is well in hand, so Swiftfire will not be stabled in the open yard after all, though many of the horses will have to be. And there is fodder for all tonight, and enough to take with us in the morning. The men found some small stooks up beyond what's left of the barn, behind the granary, also a couple of bags of oats the bastards missed hidden beneath it. And there is some kind of mutton stew that Baldred's cooking on the great hearth in the old forge."

"That all sounds good. So what are you looking so bothered for?" he asked turning to Harold.

"The forge still had a fire smouldering in it when we got there, and there was also a desperate fight there recently. No, no!" Harold said urgently, as Heardred gestured at the destruction all around them. "Nothing to do with all that. Afterwards I should say, judging by the body."

"What body?" Heardred cut in urgently.

"There's a huge wolf carcase outside, behind the forge in the snow, crudely skinned and much of its meat cut off. Blood all over the place inside, on the floor and up the walls, but mostly by the doorway, even more in the snow, and there are wolf prints everywhere."

"So then, whoever survived this savage shambles...and we know now that someone did because of the cairns, the wheel tracks and the footprints that your man found earlier...holed up here for the night, and was then pounced on by a full hunting pack of the grey brothers. He must have put up some fight. The death of only one pack member would normally not deter the rest."

"Two, my Lords!" came a gruff voice beyond them.

"Two, Cynric?" Edwin threw back at the tall figure lounging on his axe in the background.

"Yes, Lord, for we found the heads of two beasts not far away."

"Tell us," Heardred said beckoning Harold's tracker forward as they reached the forge entrance. "How do you read this?"

"Well, I have looked at all of the tracks here, Lord, before we gathered at the chapel for the burying. When we found that there was still a fire in the hearth. Before the light went. One person fought two wolves, and killed both.

One underneath a hole in the roof. A clean kill I would say, by the blood sign. The other by the doorway was quite different. A really fierce struggle. It was this battle that threw the blood everywhere. See these marks by the back of the forge?" Cynric went on, beckoning Heardred forward into the forge's light. "This is where the hunter braced himself against the wall, to make a better angle to fight the wolf."

"Hunter?"

"Hunter, fighter? Make your choice, my Lord. But you can see where his spear butt dug into the floor. This was a terrible struggle for a youngster. See these scuff marks? And the blood up the wall? He was tossed everywhere. That wolf was a big brute, Lord, enormous. The lad must have had him on a boar spear. Maybe the pack leader."

"Why a boar spear?" Edwin asked the man astonished.

"Because of the gap between the blood on the walls and the scuff marks in the floor. Only a boar spear with quillons could have held such a brute at bay. The carcase outside shows where the blade struck, just below the shoulder."

"So what happened?"

"The wolf was killed, and then the pack fled. The marks outside show that they ran in all directions. Even I cannot tell you why, too many people have passed over them since yesterday, so everything is a mess. But two wolves were skinned, in the forge, and their heads removed. The intestines are in a pile behind the building, and there are signs of scrapings, the membranes from the pelts, and there is too much blood smeared around the floor…"

"And the carcase here has lost its furry coat, and much of its meat too," Harold broke in, with a grin. "But the other carcase is missing, and there is no offal. Why that should be so I have no idea."

"Wolf meat makes fair eating, Lord," Cynric said, with a grin in his gravelly voice. "Tastes like gamey chicken!"

"Sweet Mary! Gamey chicken?" Edwin said, disgusted.

"So, someone is now roaming about with two prime wolf pelts and a sack of jointings…"

"And two dogs, Lord Heardred!" Cynric added. "Great hounds by the size of their feet. Remember the tracks I saw around the river gateway and down by the ruined ale-house? That is probably why this carcase is so chewed about. Whoever slew the two wolves needed to feed two hounds as well."

"Well, whoever survived all this, and a wolf attack into the bargain, has done his Lord and his family a great service. I wish him well. Perhaps one day I will find out who it was and be able to reward him."

168

"Perhaps, Heardred," Edwin replied, banging his friend on the shoulder. "But right now my belly is sticking to my backbone!  God alone knows what Baldred has done with that poor sheep I saw him butchering some while back, but by the saints it smells good!  Gamey chicken…God help us all, give me honest mutton any day!"

*

*H*eardred looked at the ring of faces that had clustered closer as they had been speaking, their cheeks lit by the ruddy glow from the forge fire inside, the leaping flames casting shifting patterns of light across them that made their eyes glitter fiercely, and sparkled off their steel byrnies and their burnished weapons.

"Very well, my friends, and well done too.  Come forward with your bowls and take your fill.  You have more than earned it.  Bed down here and up by the stables amongst the horses for warmth, and get what rest you can.  Your Commanders and I will be with you.  Siward, Alfgar, post guards.  I do not expect trouble, but we must be prepared for anything this night.  Then, in the morning we must be away about our business, and I will tell your Commanders what that is shortly.

"Lord Edwin, Harold, you two come with me," Heardred said, picking up a shepherd's lantern someone had found up by the old barn, "and let's have a look at these horses.  They've come a long way already.  I hope, for Jesus and St Swithun's sake that they will be sufficient to get us back again!"

With that there was a cheer and an instant buzz of lively conversation as the men moved off to collect their eating irons and feeding bowls, some running to be first in the queue that was quickly forming before the burly cook, whose skill had never failed to provide them with something…though it was sometimes better not to enquire too closely as to what he had found to cook with!

*

*U*p by the old stables Heardred and his two friends went from beast to beast, picking their way amongst the debris and rubble as they did so, the lantern's light throwing everything into sharp relief, stumbling over the numerous charred timbers that lay strewn about, discarded by the men as they had struggled to rebuild what they could of the stables before night had closed them in.

169

Mercifully the bodies that had lain there from the attack had all been dragged away and dumped in a stiff pile beneath the northern wall, there being nothing else they could do with them. Only the corpses of those they had been able to recognise had the men found the time and energy to bury, raising up a great mound of stones and fallen timber on top of them in a single giant cairn as a memorial to their bravery and courage.

"So, the men will sleep up here?" Edwin asked after a while.

"Yes, some of them. There is plenty of hay in those stooks."

"At least those bastards did not destroy everything!"

"No, in too much of a hurry to get to Chippenham later."

"In amongst the horses for extra warmth," Harold said, running his hands down the legs of his own beast. "Not much chance of a fire up here though."

"No," Heardred answered him, standing in front of Swiftfire, and rubbing his hands together as he spoke. "If they get too chilled they can always go down to the forge for a warm."

"They will grumble horribly," Edwin replied with a sigh. "Still, better that than have half the Danish Host fall on us during the night! This whole area must be stiff with them. We've been exceptionally lucky so far."

"Yes," Heardred replied, leaning back against a roof post. "And I wouldn't be surprised if we don't have Oscytel to thank for that either."

"*Oscytel?*" The two men queried, astonished.

"Yes, the Black Jarl of Helsing himself. Remember, he and his men did all this," Heardred went on, sweeping his hands all about him. "And I expect everyone in Guthrum's army will know that too, and regard this little bit of Saxon England as his 'meat', and are staying well clear for fear of his anger."

"I hadn't thought of that," Edwin replied, looking into his friend's eyes.

"Neither had I actually, until a moment ago," Heardred replied, levering himself upright and moving away. "Let's hope I am right. I don't want to have to fight clear of here and then have the bastards on our tails all the way to the river Parrett and its tidal marshes."

"So, that's where we're going," Harold said sharply, standing up from grooming his own mount with a handful of hay.

"Yes, away to join the King in Athelney, near the river Tone, where the rivers and the sea are one. Miles of empty marshlands known only to the people who live there. Alfred means to continue the fight from there, I am sure of it. Guthrum may have driven him out of Chippenham, but he does not control all Wessex, it is too great a land, even for him, with the men he has at his command right now...and as long as Alfred is alive and fighting he never will!"

170

"All of us, Heardred?" Edwin questioned him then, his eyes on his commander, as he now paced up and down, the lantern's pale light casting weird shadows on the walls.

"Well, most of us," he replied softly, pausing to look at them both.

"What do you mean, 'most of us'?" Harold asked him sharply.

"So...now we come to it," Edwin said, his voice flat. "The plan you hatched for us all while you were up by the gateway this afternoon. Before the burials in the chapel."

"Hmmm, yes. I suppose so. It is something Alfred talked with me about once, oh ages ago now, about the importance of keeping things going if anything was to go badly wrong here in Wessex. So that if he was forced to take to the hills..."

"Or the marshes," Edwin chipped in

"Yes, or the marshes," he agreed, looking at him with a smile. "Then there would still be loyal support, fighting support, that he could rely on behind enemy lines."

"Go on," Harold urged him. "You have not reached the nub of it yet, but I think I can see where you are going with this."

"Well, he will need people to carry messages and organise selected raids. People he knows where to contact. People to let everyone know that the King is alive and active, and has not abandoned his people to the Viking pirates."

"Like Burghred of Mercia?" Edwin questioned him quietly, his eyes firmly on Heardred's face.

"Exactly, like Burghred of Mercia. What do you think?"

"So, that's it," Harold said, with a grunt. "You want Edwin and me to stay on our own steadings, with a handful of chosen warriors, to carry out hit and run raids against the enemy, and spread the word of hope and encouragement that Alfred is alive and kicking Guthrum's Danish arse!"

"Yes! And kicking it good and hard!"

"What?" Edwin exclaimed appalled. "Me and that boneheaded friend of mine, staying here without your guidance? You must have barn owls in your roof trees!"

"No, I haven't, you donkey," Heardred replied laughing at his friend's mock concern. "You underrate yourselves. I think the two of you will do the job extremely well. You are both loyal to me and the King, and Wessex and England really mean something to you. And you can't fool me that there is anything wrong with your competence either! You both have your own war-bands with you, who are used to your orders and know you well. As do I."

"This is hard, Heardred," Edwin replied quietly. "You and I have been together ever since my family, like yours, was destroyed. I have been your

171

shield against Danish axemen and stray spears in more skirmishes than I care to think of. Who will be your Saxon shield man now?"

"I know, my friend. And I shall miss you both mightily too. Standing in the shield-wall is well known to all of us. It is what we have trained for all our lives. Skulking in bushes and lying low in an ambush is not a role to which any of us are well used. But it is one we have all got to come to terms with now.

"Guthrum may think he has done well to drive Alfred into the wilderness, but, as I said, his forces are not limitless and Wessex is a large country. He cannot control all of it...and therein lies his weakness; at least for now, until the sea-lanes open in the spring and he can get more reinforcements from Frankland.

"If, in the meantime, Alfred can harry his outposts, seize his messengers, cut off his foragers and generally make his life, and that of his men, utterly miserable...and make sure that all men know that he is doing so, then come the Easter muster Wessex *will* respond to him. Then we can bring the whole stinking mass of them to battle and defeat them in the open field once and for all. And by saying 'Alfred', I mean us as well. You both from your own lands, and me from Athelney. We can do this, my friends. *We can!*" he said urgently, coming to both of them and putting his arms across their shoulders.

"I don't like this any more than you do. To have to play the weasel in my own country, while a parcel of filthy, heathen Northmen lord it over everyone is very hard to take. But if that's what's necessary to win in the end, then that's what we must do, no matter how hard it is to take! Agreed?"

"Agreed!" the two men on either side of him said, repeating gruffly: "*Agreed!*" And clapping both men on their shoulders as he turned away Heardred stalked back to the old forge, his hands clasped behind his back, and his head bent forward in thought.

From the front of the wrecked stables Harold and Edwin watched him leave, then with a sigh and shiver, picking up the lantern, they followed him back to where the others were all eating, taking it in turns to warm themselves before the fire that Baldred and Cynric had kept burning on the raised hearth.

*

Though heavily overcast the night was bitter, for the wind never let up once as it sighed and moaned around the ruined buildings while the men did their best to keep warm, wrapped in their capes and mantles huddled up to their horses on a bed of hay, or squeezed in around the fire in the old forge.

172

Up on the desolate ramparts that ran all round behind the palisade, the guards Siward and Alfgar had posted stamped their feet and cursed their reliefs, shields and spears gripped firmly in their hands, eyes alert for any movement in the empty wilderness that lay about them.

In the forge the fire was kept alive throughout the night.

The guards coming across from their wall-duty for a swift warm before going to their rest, replenished the fire with wood and charcoal, pumping up the fire as they did so, pleased for a drink of hot spiced ale in the horn beakers that each man carried. Amidst them Heardred, Edwin and Harold lay cocooned in their fur cloaks, struggling up to relieve themselves in the night and check the guards themselves, only too pleased to return to the warmth of the forge and exchange brief talk with those men coming in off the ramparts, and share in a reviving drink at the same time.

*

*T*owards morning the wind changed direction and the temperature rose, a thick mist blowing in from the south-west, masking the wastelands beyond the steading so that the forests and woodlands lost all definition.

Daybreak found the whole command up and moving about.

Their horses, nose-bagged at first light with a few handfuls of oats from the great sacks found beneath the old granary, were now stamping the fidgets out of themselves and throwing their heads up and down in their eagerness to be on their way again, their bits ringing and jingling in the damp air.

Above them the sky still loured heavily over the countryside, and there was no sign of the sun, but the white snow and thick forests were now merged into a fine grey mist that had swept up to cloak the countryside. Where icicles had hung and frost had rimed the woodwork, now water ran in fine fingers along the burned and charred timbers that thrust out from the ruined buildings on every side, and hung in sullen tears from the torn eaves of the derelict forge.

In ones and twos the men led their horses down from the stables, and horse-lines nearby, to assemble before their leaders who were standing waiting for them with their shields on their backs and their weapons ready to hand should they be needed. And when Heardred was certain that all were present he carefully explained what was going to happen next, and parcelled off each man to the leader whom he had chosen to serve.

Then it was done and the time to leave had finally arrived.

Clasping their arms together Heardred bade his companions farewell, holding each man in a bear-like embrace and banging their shaggy shoulders with his armoured fists. With damp furs drawn around them against the chill, they finally separated and threw themselves up onto their waiting mounts ready to move away.

Pausing before them all, Swiftfire tossing his head and pawing at the wet icy ground, Heardred looked around at them and loved them all: for their courage, their loyalty and their dogged Saxon spirit; and with a rasp of steel he drew his sword.

"*For Alfred and Wessex!*" he roared out, thrusting his blade upwards into the misted morning.

"*For Alfred and Wessex!*" they bellowed back at him, the sound echoing dully round the compound, thrown back by the enveloping mists that soaked up their challenge like a sponge. And thumping his blade back into its scabbard he pulled Swiftfire's head round to face the northern entrance and stabbed in his heels so that the stallion suddenly took off in a wild slush of torn ice and snow towards the upper gateway, where the ram still lay abandoned. Following his lead his command swiftly pulled in behind him, while Edwin and Harold kicked their beasts into motion towards the river gateway, their own Commands following.

Across the desolate steading they hustled, past the chapel, the piled bodies and away through the river gateway, its great valves wide open to them, the wind plucking at their heels and ruffling their hair where it jagged out beneath their iron helmets, the mists eddying around them in ghostly swirls.

Then, having crossed the small river that ran blackly below the shattered ramparts, they split up into the two armed companies that had been arranged earlier. And with a final wave of their hands Lords Edwin and Harold drew away from each other for the long, dangerous ride to their own homes, while Heardred passed through the upper gate and on towards Sherston and the Fosse Way that would take them south-west towards the distant lands of the Sommerseatas, and the wild marshes of Athelney, where Alfred was laired up planning his guerrilla war against the Danes.

\*

Rising bog-eyed from his smoky pallet in distant Chippenham, with his Saxon whores beside him, Guthrum may have thought he had the King of Wessex on the run, and that he now held his land in the palms of his bloodied hands...but he was mistaken. As Heardred paused to take one final look round at the deserted, blackened homestead that had been Foxley Manor, while his men filed past him, he knew that it was only the beginning. He knew that one day, as soon as the spring was upon them, their enemy would

174

wish that they had never left their long turf houses for the dragon boats, the steep grey rollers of the northern seas and the glories of plundering the fertile lands of the Saxon peoples.

For here in Wessex they would be destroyed. The Danes had bitten off more than they could chew. Wessex was just too big for Guthrum's forces to control…and with Alfred still free, and fighting hard, if all Wessex rose to support its king, the Danes were surely doomed.

He knew it. Felt it in his very bones.

It didn't matter that Alfred, its King, was living like a hunted criminal in his own kingdom, nor that his enemies now roamed at large in a way they never had succeeded in thirteen years of fighting. With God's will they were going to be defeated.

It was simply a question of time before it happened!

# Chapter Twenty Four

That first night on her own in the wilderness was something that remained in Brioni's memory as almost the most miserable and terrifying experience of her life...almost as terrible as the butchery of her family by Oscytel's raiders. Then there had been the fury of action to carry her along, to dominate her thoughts, and the fight for her own life the previous night had not given her the time for cool reflection. Now, despite the presence of the two hounds whom she could see quartering the ground ahead and to one side of her, the situation was very different.

Alone amongst the great trees of Helms Wood, with a black wind blowing from the north-east, creaking and wailing through their twisted branches, and with little prospect of food or warmth at her journey's end, or even of shelter if the old bothy was no longer habitable, her spirits had sunk very low.

All around her the trees thrust up stark and menacing out of the white frozen ground, the snow that lay along their arms continuously falling on her as she moved beneath them until she was wet through and shivering. And driving the tilt cart was hard work, not least because Foxhead hated the whole process and made her life as difficult as he could do, jibbing at the reins and tossing his head. Several times he stopped completely in a stubborn fury from which he had to be coaxed, even led sometimes, so her feet were soon wet through as well, and she almost wept with frustration and the cold.

And with the onset of the early winter darkness came a chilling sense of being watched by hidden eyes...a sense that crawled over her spine and into her very bowels. The deeper she pressed into the giant, empty woodlands, mixed with birch, hawthorn and vast patches of briar, the greater the feeling of unease and menace that rose up to shake her. Now, from time to time she drew Foxhead to a halt and listened, peering anxiously about her as the gloom thickened and the darkness crept out across the path from amongst the gnarled trees of that ancient forest.

God alone knew what creatures lurked in the dark fastnesses of such a fearsome place as this great woodland, that stretched for miles around her... what fell beasts, and men as well. The wild, human cast-offs, sick in mind, who had been driven from their villages and now were forced to prey on lonely travellers; the robbers, sneak-thieves and murderers. More than once she had thought she had caught the glint of veiled eyes, and the sharp flurry of movement from amongst the trees and tangled undergrowth. But the dogs had not given tongue, nor raised their hackles; neither had Foxhead shown any interest. His ears had not flickered, nor had he whickered, and she had dismissed each little incident as the product of a tired mind.

Yet the sense of danger and the gnawing fear remained, for the lawless times in which Wessex now found itself had produced their own crop of desperate, masterless men who had been declared 'wolfshead'. Outlaws, who were both armed and dangerous, and had their lairs in these secret, desolate places where no sane man would ever think to go on his own, unarmoured, let alone a girl!

She shuddered violently and called the hounds closer in towards her, tightening her grip on the reins, ready for instant flight and wishing that her weapons were not so securely stowed in the cart as to be beyond swift and easy reach. No sword and no shield closeby. It was something she should have learned from watching her father's men, and the king's companions, as they were on the point of setting out: always make sure that your sword is loose in its scabbard, that your shield straps aren't caught-up and twisted and that your spear is ready to hand; and she cursed herself for being a fool. After so many years of war, of sudden upheaval and unheralded journeys, sometimes at the dead of night, she should have known better and not for the first time she felt crushed by the utter misery and desolation of her loss.

Her home destroyed, her family hacked down before her eyes, with few provisions worth the name and ill clad for the conditions in which she found herself, her position seemed hopeless. How could she, a mere slip of a girl with less fighting ability than most fyrdsmen, ever succeed in bringing down a great warrior and famous war-lord like Oscytel? The very notion was absurd, ridiculous! Swearing an oath of vengeance when the blood was hot, and anger and hatred were running fiercely through one's veins was one thing...to consider the prospect in the cold light of day was quite another!

She looked around her, at the trees in all their stark grandeur sighing and rattling above her, and at the narrow, frozen trackway that wound its way like a soiled satin ribbon amongst them and shivered, as much from the cold as from sudden fear.

She must have been mad!

Oscytel, Jomsvikings, the Heathen in all their fury...and she a lone Saxon maiden with no support, no armour, no-one to help her. Hopeless! She would be better off married, or working in some kindly household.

She grimaced suddenly, wincing at the lowly pattern of her thoughts, and at her own weakness. What was she thinking of? And she laughed at her temerity. She was Brioni of Foxley, a shield-maiden, the goddess Freyja reborn, who had dedicated herself to the Old Ones, sworn a blood-oath over the dead body of her Lord that would not be denied.  No, not if St Michael and all his angels begged her to.  She was committed, and until her oath had been purged from her soul she was not free to follow any other course.

Marriage?  She had just discarded that completely.  And a kindly household when all Wessex was now in such turmoil?  She gritted her teeth.  Not to be considered for one moment!

Not for her the awful shame and dishonour of being declared '*Nithing*'!

It didn't matter that no-one but herself knew of the oath that she had made.  *She knew of it*, and to betray her father would be to betray herself.  That was not the way a Foxley behaved.  Love and honour before the world, that was the thing that counted most.  She had a star to follow, and even if it led to her death beneath the frenzied steel of the heathen pirates, so be it.  At least she would have tried...would have kept faith with herself, and in so doing with all those who had given their lives that she might have the chance to live her own.

She laughed again at her simplicity.

Today she was on her own...tomorrow she might find a host of warriors to help her.  You never knew what lay around the corner.  That was what gave life its savour.  The priests might say it was all up to God...she was not so sure.  But right now the main problem was not what to do about Oscytel, but whether she would even survive the night!  The beasts of the forest were not used to encroaching on land habitually worked by men.  That pack of wolves had been driven by extreme cold and hunger to seek prey amidst the shattered ruins of the steading.

Here in their heartland was a very different matter.

Normally in winter time there was plenty of game for them to hunt, but this was not a normal winter.  Game was scarce, the deer and wild pig had left their usual haunts to seek food and shelter in the very depths of the forest.  So, now the grey brothers had grown bolder, and a lone traveller would be easy meat.  If the old bothy was now a ruin and she was forced to build herself a crude lean-to out in the open then she could find herself in serious trouble.  For if they caught her scent on the wind then they would overwhelm her and tear her limb from limb, and Foxhead with her.  Even if he fled they would still hunt him down and kill him.

The thought appalled her, yet without a doubt this was not a time for feeling sorry for oneself.  Her mother would have had no patience with her on that score.  Loving though she had always been. she was also very practical and would soon have chased her daughter's megrims out of her head.

There was but one thing to do...and that was to give her mind a swift kick and push on harder in the hopes of reaching the isolated clearing where surely the old charcoal burners' bothy still stood, with its stable, as it had two springs past when she and Agatha had visited with Aylwin for his charcoal. And do so before the light completely failed her.

She could hear her mother's voice in her head, and her father's laugh. So, flicking Foxhead on with the reins and calling his name loudly she urged him into a canter, for here, where the trees leaned closely over the old trackway the snow was not so deep, and though there were places where the going was suddenly treacherous and the whole equipage lurched and bounced across the track, she was able to make up some valuable time.

\*

*Y*et all the time the feeling of being watched and followed remained with her.

Maybe it was all her imagination, but the great forest felt closed in, secret, and with the winter darkness now closing in, both deeply chilled and drear; no birds called. All around her the trees seemed to be listening and whispering together, for though the wind cried and moaned through their swaying tops, down on the forest floor its wild turbulence was not so easily felt. The rattling of their lower boughs as she passed was like sharp, bony voices, and the thick bushes and tangled briars that often choked the wayside where the forest canopy had been broken, snatched at the tilt cart as Foxhead pushed his way forward, grabbing at her with whipping fingers making her cry out in sudden pain and shock.

And still the sense of being followed by some dark, invisible presence remained with her, the silence of the woodlands pressing down on her as she guided Foxhead along the twisted pathway. So it was with a deep sigh, and a murmured '*at last!*' that she burst from amongst the trees and came into the small clearing that she had been making for.

Then, reining in hard she brought the cart to a sudden slithering halt that threw up the snow in a brief swirling shower, and a jay-bird screamed his warning as she cursed herself for a fool.

For all she knew there could be a full enemy war-band camped down about the old bothy, wolfsheads, branded serfs, anybody! She should have realised she was near a clearing by the strengthening of the light along the trackway and kept the dogs by her side, while she walked Foxhead up slowly and had a careful look around. Instead of which she had come flying out from the forest edge for all the world like a maiden on a lover's chase.

She grimaced, and then shrugged with relief.

179

As it was, she seemed to be completely alone, the whole area utterly bleak and empty, her own steamy breath and that of her animals the only sign of life around her. And from the distant bothy, still there as she had remembered it, there was no smoke, and the stable closeby to it seemed deserted. Her breath, silvered in the cold damp air, shivered around her while Foxhead steamed...and nothing else moved.

\*

*T*he clearing was not huge, but it was well defined and seemed larger than when she had last been there. Clearly the charcoal burners who used the place had further cut back the forest in all directions, not just for the timber they needed for their craft, but to push back the wilderness from their home so there was less danger of their being surprised by unwelcome visitors.

The bothy itself was also larger than Brioni had remembered, and the stable beside it had been enlarged with a second storey for the hay and straw needed for the oxen the burners used for haulage, and for their mules and donkeys. From what she could remember there were usually four men working here throughout the spring and summer. Thank God she had such a fine memory for directions for she couldn't ever have been so far south of Foxley more than once or twice, and that not for some years now. She grinned. She had done well for herself, and casting the hounds out in a wide circle she flicked Foxhead forward again towards the simple dwelling that she had so hoped to find.

This was built in an ancient style, without a heavy frame of large timber crucks filled in with lath and plaster, but round and fat, with a tall thatched roof laid on a ring of posts, latched in together at the top, and laid on top of a dozen courses of thick stone walling, the chinks and hollows inside filled in with moss and clay to keep out any draughts. In the centre was a circle of great stones to keep in the fire that over the years had baked the walls and floor hard, and there was a small domed oven close by. But there was no smoke hole, as that would have caused an updraft that could set the whole building on fire. The smoke simply filled the apex of the roof and then trickled out of the thatch so that outside the roof often seemed mazed with smoke, almost as if it truly was on fire. And though the crude plank doorway looked none too secure, the uprights that carried its pintles had not rotted in any way and the latch seemed firm enough when Brioni tried it.

Thatched with tough reeds in the usual way, now dark with age, the roof was still secure. Bowed-up over the entrance porch, it reached almost to the ground everywhere else and was held down with a criss-cross of ropes tied to heavy stones that no storm could easily blow away. When Brioni peered inside she could see no snow on the beaten earth floor, and once she could get a fire going she thought she might actually be warm again for the first time since leaving Foxley.

She stood back from the threshold and sniffed the cold, dank air that came up to meet her thick with the rank scent of fox and the heavy smell of damp earth. The place had clearly been deserted for months, though she was sure that Aylwin was still used to ordering charcoal from these workings for his forge at Foxley, as he had been doing since ever she and Agatha had visited some years before. And not for the first time she thanked God for His providence in providing her with an effective shelter when she most needed it!

The old stable when she got to it, though somewhat rickety with age, had nevertheless been stoutly built, and a second storey had been added since she had been there last. This was to provide a large hay loft, with a strong ladder to get up to it, where there was a goodly store of hay and straw at either end and several large sacks of meal and oats on the elm wood flooring that covered it. The main posts were still firmly embedded in the ground and the double doors that closed off the square end of the building gave onto a row of good stalls for oxen, mules and donkeys alike…and Foxhead of course. Simple elm guttering ran round the outside leading to a great oak water butt, currently sealed with a good thickness of ice, but once broken was filled with sweet water that would do both for herself and Foxhead. There was even a large shepherd's lantern hanging from a nail, with a supply of oil nearby in what was clearly a tack room, and at the other end of the building, beneath a thatched lean-to, was a sizeable log store stuffed with the billets of wood that the burners would need when they returned in the spring.

She clapped her hands together and smiled.

With a good fire burning and the floor covered with fresh straw from the stable loft, well fresh enough anyway, and some hay to bed herself down on she should be as snug as any of the poorer geburs on her father's lands. She had Bran and Utha to keep her company and Foxhead could bed down warmly in one of the stalls that the oxen had been accustomed to using when their work was done.

All in all she was far better off than she had a right to be, given the way things were in Wessex just now. The place was far too isolated for any lengthy stay, but for the time being it was ideal, and without wasting any more of the little daylight that was left, Brioni set about the collection of enough timber from the store she had discovered at the rear of the stable to see her through the coming night.

181

*

*I*t was hard, miserable camp labour that left her back aching and her hands raw with the damp and cold as she readied herself for the night, carrying armfuls of hay and straw for herself and Foxhead alike, who had to be both fed and rubbed down as well before she could begin to think of herself. By which time her hands were scuffed and her finger nails thick with grime. Yet by the time she had finished collecting kindling, the handful of spiky twigs and sticks she needed to start the fire had grown to a fair sized pile to add to that which she had brought with her, not to mention the added stack of billets she had taken from their store against the far wall of the old stable.

Finally with a lot of muffled groans and outright oaths that her brother would have been proud of - and not a few tears of sheer frustration - she managed to strike a spark with Aylwin's flints and steel amongst the fine shavings she had brought from Foxley in his wooden box. And with much huffing and puffing she at last succeeded in breathing enough life into it all to bring the smouldering flames properly to life. Trembling little blue and orange flickers that danced sullenly amongst the pyramid of sticks that she had built to cage them in, but which grew steadily stronger as she worked on them until the dry billets from the log store caught light and she could sit back, with grimy face and scorched eyebrows, in admiration of the real blaze that she had created.

By God and Saint Swithun it was hard work, and the smoke made her cough and her eyes run in a way that had never happened at Foxley.

She had no idea that fire lighting was such an art. No wonder the hall-steward had always been so insistent on keeping the great hearth fire well fed throughout the night. If that wretched business had to be gone through every day before anybody could eat, then they would all have starved to death long ago.

She must be learning. Live or let die; kill or be killed…it was all the same in the end. The strongest survived to be free, the weak were either slain or became slaves of the Heathen. Sweet Lord, but she wished to survive, to live and be free, and the devil take any who stood in her way!

She turned then to talk to the two great hounds who were lying nearby, both worrying at hunks of wolf-meat, the blood staining their muzzles and their great shaggy fore paws with which both were holding down their food.

"Well, you two, how is this then? Not bad for a first attempt, eh? Even 'though I say so myself," she added, leaning against Foxhead's saddle, holding her hands out to the flames now leaping cheerfully in their grate. But we need a set of bellows from somewhere. This blowing and huffing is just too much like hard work. I think your new mistress is beginning to learn something about herself that she had never suspected!"

Bran put his head on one side as she spoke and gruffed at her, banging his feathery stern as he did so, and looking so quizzical, his black eyes glistening in the firelight, that she laughed. Just like some hairy old man who had heard the voice but not understood the words. And she leaned forward and ruffled the great hound's head, a liberty that he would have afforded to few others in her family.

"You just don't know how pleased I am to have you both with me, and dear old Foxhead. Without you all my life just wouldn't be worth a horseshoe nail, and in this day and age that is a very great deal, my friends. So, eat your fill tonight. We still have a long way to go before my quest is ended, and full bellies are like to be a rarity!" And pausing just to throw some more wood on the fire, Brioni turned her attention to her own bundles, and laying out her woolfells on top of a large armful of hay for a mattress, beside her blankets and her weapons, she addressed herself to cooking up some of the raw meat she had hacked from the wolf carcasses earlier in the day.

She groaned inwardly. Everything was so foul and messy.

She stank to the heavens, far worse she suspected than the meanest peasant. Her fine leather clothes were black with blood and mucus from the skinning, not to mention the filth that was still stuck to her from the midden, and though she had done her best to clean herself at Foxley, her hair was now matted with sweat, snow water and wisps of hay. She felt like old Cedda, the wild woman of Foxley, half-witch, half-wise, of whom the villagers had always been so terrified, as much for her taggled appearance as for her eldritch shrieks.

She shrugged her shoulders helplessly.

There was little she could do about her clothes, but her hands and face at least she could wash, as she had done before, with the soap she had found and some more hot water. But oh, how good it would be to be clean all over with freshly aired clothes and soft cotton undergarments, instead of the blood-caked swinking raiment that she was currently wearing.

She sighed and turned back to the task in hand, poking with a wooden spoon the wolf meat stew she was preparing in a battered pannikin, before spreading one of the uncured pelts upside down across her knees. Needing to scrape it clean with one of her knives, she was frustrated that she had none of the salts or unguents she needed to do a proper job, and prevent the drying skin from cracking.

This was a job she continued to work at for some time while her meal, now thickened with several handfuls of crushed oats from the sack she had rescued at Foxley, spat and simmered on the fire. And all the time the blue haze from its burning swept up and curled round her head, spreading out amongst the simple rafters from where it leaked out of the ancient thatch above her.

Finally she drew the pan away from the flames, and giving it some time to cool she began to eat, chewing methodically through the strange tasting meaty lumps, like strong gamey chicken, spitting the toughest fibres into the fire.

Mixed with rough oats, and with no salt or spices, it was a foul, glutinous mass that stuck in her throat. But it was better than an empty belly, at least she hoped so anyway, and with her feeding now over, washed down with a beaker of sweet water from the butt by the old stable, she lay the pelt she had been working on over her saddle for a pillow, and prepared to settle down for the night.

Pausing only to listen to the silence outside, and the snap and crackle from her fire, with Utha beside her and Bran lying before the latched door, she stretched herself out on her crude woolfell bed, drew her blankets up to her chin and fell into an exhausted sleep.

# Chapter Twenty Five

Outside the bothy the wind steadily veered into the south-west, bringing with it a fine swirling mist and the first hint of rain; a real break in the weather after weeks of biting frosts and blurring snowfalls. A change that turned the crisp snow of days to a heavy mush, and melted the ice that rimed the doors and ancient thatch.

Alone in his stable-stall the great stallion sniffed the damp air and pawed with iron feet at the straw that Brioni had laid down for him. Rubbed down with handfuls of hay and straw that she had found in the loft above, he should have been relaxed and eager to be about his mistress's business. With water, an armful of hay from above, and a double handful of oats that she had also found, he was surely as well fed as the conditions made possible. Yet he was strangely restless.

For now, along with the smell of his mistress, and of Bran and Utha, of fresh hay and damp straw, and the smell of rain, there was another scent on the air, one that wrinkled his sensitive nose, not hound or fox or wolf, he knew those. This was a deeper, more rankling stench that he had not come across before. A stench that reeked of danger, and stretching wide his nostrils he began to kick his stall with all his might and shout out a warning across the clearing, jerking his head violently up and down as he did so.

\*

Drugged with sleep Brioni did not hear the banging hooves and Foxhead's muffled calls at first, but when Utha shook himself awake, his neck bristling, and Bran began to pace the floor, both great hounds rumbling deep in their throats, she was alert and on her feet in a moment, and then she heard the stallion clearly.

She had no idea what was wrong, though his neighing shouts were now louder, and she had no idea of the hour either as there was no smoke hole through which the light might shine. The fire had died down to dull curling embers, and the first thing she did was to stir it back to life. Seizing the light javelin from where she had left it leaning against the wall behind her, she raked the fire violently, throwing on more kindling and small billets of wood as she did so, until she had a leaping blaze that thrust back the smoky darkness to give her sufficient light to see by.

185

Now that she could clearly hear Foxhead's screams of rage and fear, her next instinct was to throw open the door and rush out to see what was troubling so bold-hearted a charger. But the dogs would not let her pass.

Hackles up and bristling all along their backs, with lips drawn back over their teeth in terrifying, rasping snarls, both Bran and Utha barred her path, and she did not dare to try and pass them. Bigger than wolves, they were not to be trifled with even at the best of times; now, with their fur almost on end, they seemed twice as large. Never had she seen either of them in such a dangerous state of controlled frenzy, and she was forced to stand by the fire-hearth, spear in hand, while Bran stalked stiff-legged round her, his whole body explosive with suppressed rage, while Utha guarded the doorway. In the close confines of the bothy the noise was simply petrifying in its sheer intensity, and it took Brioni some time to pluck up the courage to lay hands on him.

Finally she did so, realising that unless she brought him under control there was no knowing where it might end. So, grasping him firmly under his fighting collar to avoid spiking her hand, and with all her strength, she pulled him sharply back, bidding him: "Stand and be still, Bran! *Stand and be still!*" as she did so.

Just for a moment she felt that he was not going to respond, that his boiling anger and alarm had gone beyond the point where he was even able to hear her, for at the first touch of her hand he had made to lunge away from her. But tightening her grip and hauling back on him again with all her strength as once more she shouted for him to be still, finally worked and, very reluctantly, he settled back beside her, his throat still continuing to gnarl and rumble with his furious displeasure.

"Utha! *Stay!*" she ordered the other hound who was preparing to join her from his place beside the door. "Stay there, I tell you! Good boys, *Good boys!* Now, be still, both of you and wait for my command!" And turning from where both animals were now bristling, stiff legged and motionless, with only their sterns lashing to and fro, Brioni stood and listened to Foxhead's challenge, desperate to pick up the direction from which the danger could be coming.

*

T hen, just for a moment, Foxhead fell silent; the two hounds ceased their terrible growling, and suddenly there was almost an eerie calm, the only sound to be heard over the moaning of the wind, the sharp pop and crackle of the fire.

Yet she knew there was something out there.

186

She had known since yesterday that there was some unknown danger lurking amongst the great trees of the forest, or the dense undergrowth that covered the ground in the wilder, more open places. That some fell creature was stalking her she was certain...and now it was here, in the clearing. Foxhead had heard it, sensed it...and so had Bran and Utha. Only she had been unable to see anything strange, nor did she know what it was. And putting down her javelin she reached instead for the great boar spear she had used against the wolves. Only this was no wolf, nor grunting boar, of that she was sure!

Sweet Mary, aid her, but she was afraid.

The gods send her their protection now for she was frightened half to death. Her horse could sense the nearness of some great beast from the forest and the hounds were quivering with pent up violence. She alone could neither pick up its movement nor its sound, though she could truly feel its presence.

Then at last, she heard it too.

A muffled, stuttering moan; the hesitant shuffle of heavy feet; a terrifying groaning, coughing rumble that grew louder as whatever ghastly menace from amongst the trees began to approach her hideaway. And with it, borne on the damp misty air of the grey dawning, came a rank stench so powerful that her heart almost quailed with fear. There was nothing in her experience to which she could match it. No animal she had come across gave off so foul and dark a scent, not even a boar in rut and, God knew, they were rank enough. No, nor that blood-curdling coughing growl either...and the most terrifying thing of all was that there was nothing she could do about it but wait, with the fire to her face and her long spear in her hand.

For a moment she thought that it might somehow pass her by, that the smoke from her fire and the scent of man might perhaps deter whatever was out there from pressing its advantage. And indeed that might have been so for she heard the creature pause in its advance and its threat sounds die away to a puzzled grumble. Even from her position in the centre of the bothy Brioni could sense the creature's uncertainty as a strange, unnatural silence settled once more upon the clearing.

But at that moment Bran and Utha growled and then bayed furiously, the sound violent in the extreme and with even greater fear than before she felt the sudden pounding of heavy feet towards them, the sound of heavy, stertorous breathing and was appalled by a monstrous bellow of sound as the creature gave a huge, coughing roar and heaved against the deep thatch of the roof as it sought a way in, the whole bothy groaning and creaking as it did so.

Twice it went round the outside and back again, quartering the ground, several times pausing to test the strength of the barrier that still foiled it.

187

Roaring and coughing, it shook the whole building and tore at the sides with its hands and feet, making the bothy sway and stagger like a ship in a storm and the roof shower bits of reed and debris down upon her, terrifying Brioni every time it did so such that she cried out and panted with fear, and cold beads of sweat broke out upon her forehead.

But in the end it was the dogs that brought on the next fierce assault, for driven wild with rage they leaped to attack at every point the creature pushed against the roof and sides, baying and snarling as they did so with teeth bared and wild staring eyes of fury. And with that the whole bothy practically collapsed, for with one vast muffled roar the whole door shattered and half the roof over it was smashed to fragments by two massive blows, like those of a monstrous boxer, left and right, that burst the thatch apart as if it were paper, scattering it in the air like autumn leaves, the rafters a mass of falling twigs, the dry stone walling a giant's game of marbles.

Leaping back from the sudden cascade of wooden poles, torn thatching and flying stonework through which daylight lanced through at last, Brioni shouted the dogs on for all she was worth, unable for several minutes to see what on earth was going on. Blinded by the dust and showering fragments, she fought desperately to free herself from the flying debris while clinging on to her great boar spear as if she were the grim reaper and it her scythe.

Finally, with a last frantic heave she was clear, and in the grey misty light of early morning able to see her adversary at last, the shock of which meeting completely bereft her of the power of speech or movement. It was a sight so appalling that never in her wildest dreams could she have rivalled it; for there, not more than a dozen feet from where she was standing, was the biggest animal she had ever set eyes on in her life. Nearly ten feet tall as it stood swaying on its broad hind legs, its great forepaws armed with a terrifying fistful of claws and grunting and roaring with anger…was a huge bear.

\*

For a moment longer Brioni stood petrified with fear, her arms dangling by her side, the weapon she held in her hand so puny beside the awesome strength and sheer power of her massive opponent; his mouth a red cavern filled with enormous teeth, his body vast and bristling with rage, his immense forepaws, with their rows of huge black claws, already raised to strike again. In any other circumstances her being there so close to sudden, sweeping death would have been insane. And it was those few moments of pure terror that probably saved her life, for during that time she noticed two things: the

188

great brute had an iron muzzle across its face from which was dangling a fair length of heavy chain…and someone was shouting at her!

"It's the dogs! *For pity's sake, call off your dogs!* He's maddened by them!"

Still stupefied by what was going on, the two hounds baying and snarling as they bounced and leapt at their enemy, the huge bear swaying from side to side as he confronted them, it took Brioni a few seconds for the words to sink in, but when they did she reacted immediately. Leaping forwards she reversed her spear and began the dangerous job of forcing her two hounds to back down, shouting: "Back, Bran! Back Utha! *Back, boys!*" as she did so, and striking at them with the long butt of her boar spear.

All the same it took some little while to separate them, for the bear was in a towering rage, and both hounds were reluctant to leave go of such a violent, unusual quarry. But with the help of the other voice shouting at the bear and waving its arms before it, the job was eventually done, and Brioni's two hounds slunk back with hackles raised and fierce snarling faces to lick their wounds. While the giant bear first sank back onto its four feet and then shuffled backwards to sit down in the snow while the voice that had been calling to it and soothing its temper finally materialised out of the misty gloom of the new day.

To Brioni's total amazement the voice turned out to be a girl!

Tall, slender, black-haired and wearing scuffed leather chausses beneath a tough leather jacket, fleece lined and edged in wolf fur, under a long well-worn black fur cape, she was an arresting sight. Astonishing in that bleak, wild place with the ruins of the old bothy scattered wildly all around them, as stepping forward on light feet encased in long knee length boots of scarred red leather, fleece-lined and with thick soles, a deep red leather bag over her left side, she went right up to where the enormous beast was now sitting, wrapped in the steam of his anger, grumbling and shuffling and swaying his head from side to side.

And as she approached the rage just went out of him.

His head ceased to sway and in moments he looked more like a crumpled giant in a wrinkled fur coat than the ravening monster of a few minutes earlier. Now sitting slumped, head down, he looked forlorn and miserable, his long muzzle chain draggled in a heap on the still frozen ground. Pausing briefly before him, the girl called his name and suddenly ran up and flung her arms around its neck, pressing her face into his shoulder as she did so, and gave the massive beast a huge squeeze.

"Oh, Oswald! You naughty boy; what did you run off for like that?" she said in a cooing voice, for all the world as if she were talking to a child. "I

189

thought I had lost you! Poor old bear, did those horrid dogs frighten you? There, there, you silly old thing! Come on now, cheer up, there's no harm done," she added, stepping back and looking him over carefully, burrowing her hands into his thick fur as she did so. "You are not hurt and I have some lovely apples for you in my bag. They are your favourites!"

Sitting exhausted in the damp snow, the wet mist swirling round her, her body still trembling, the old bothy smashed and smouldering behind her and her two hounds nursing the gashes that same 'silly old bear' had given them, Brioni could hardly believe her ears!

"*Oswald?* Poor old bear? Horrid dogs?" she gasped incredulously, watching her nightmare crunch apples, real anger in her voice. "*What in the name of all that's holy are you talking about?*" she questioned violently, dragging herself up onto her feet. "That filthy brute of yours nearly killed me, and probably would have done given more of a chance!"

"Don't be ridiculous!" The other girl flashed back at her sharply. "He's no 'filthy brute' and he's never killed anyone on his life, and I should know for my father and I have brought him up since he was a six week old cub! He broke free yesterday when some stray dogs baited him and Poppy and I have been following him ever since..."

"*Poppy?*"

"My mare. Anyway, Oswald likes people, was cold and hungry and picked up your scent. Bears are very good like that. He came looking for help. If those two hounds of yours had not gone for him you'd have been perfectly alright!"

"*Perfectly alright?* Are you mad? Look at my place," Brioni demanded, sweeping her arms towards the ruined bothy, now swathed in smoke and bursting into flame from her fire. "And listen to my horse! If he hasn't damaged his feet banging his stall like that it will be a miracle. That brute of yours would have torn us limb from limb if you hadn't been nearby..."

"He's not a 'brute'! I told you, he is named 'Oswald'...and he's muzzled!"

"*He's still got claws!*" Brioni shouted back, exasperated. "Look at them! Muzzle or no muzzle, he could have smashed my hounds in pieces with those alone. Those two of mine couldn't have held him for long and no weapon I have would have done anything to him except make him even more angry and dangerous than he already was anyway!" And there was a pause while both girls glared at one another, both furiously angry at what had happened, both equally determined not to be brow-beaten by the other.

"Oswald was alone and afraid!" the other girl countered swiftly, her eyes still smouldering. "His mother was slain by a pack of dogs in a vile bear-

190

baiting, with her chained to a post. We rescued him from the baiters. He was small, terrified, and has hated dogs ever since. He meant you no harm."

"How were Bran and Utha to know that? Or me either, for that matter? And what are you doing with a bear out here in the first place?" Brioni countered the other's smouldering look. "And how have you managed to avoid capture by the Danes?" she went on, dashing to recover what she could from the ruined bothy now burning brightly. "Their patrols must be everywhere by now. Surely you know that much about Wessex at least?" she added at the girl's sudden look of uncertainty as she moved to help her, both girls throwing burning thatch and roof poles out of the way as they burrowed frantically amongst the wreckage for Brioni's possessions. "For pity's sake, what do you imagine I am doing here in this filthy state, lurking in some mean bothy like a common drab?"

"What do you mean, Danes?" The girl threw back at her urgently as she bent down to gather up Brioni's wolf pelts and saddle.

"The pirates, you little fool! Those foul-mouthed, heathen bastards who came from Frankland and have been ravaging our lands for the past thirteen years…"

"I am not a fool! How dare you say so," she snarled back at her, dumping her burdens on the snowy ground. "And the Danes are still beyond Wessex's borders. All men know that," she added dismissively, stepping back to gather up Oswald's chain. "The King came up to Chippenham for Christmas with his whole family and will stay until after Twelfth Night. That's what we are doing here, Oswald and I, my father too, poor love, if only his shoulder would get better. We are to entertain the King of Wessex!"

"Entertain the King?" Brioni questioned, amazed, rubbing her face with her arm, as the fire really took hold. "Alfred? Look, if you think all that then you *are* a fool! You had better come over her and sit down while I tell you the facts of life. For if you attempt to go into Chippenham, bear or no bear, then Guthrum and his gang of thieves will eat you alive."

"But he's in Gloucester!" She replied shocked, standing stock-still, Oswald's broken chain hanging loosely from her hands.

"Not any more he's not! The Danes are out! Guthrum's army must have attacked Chippenham at first light two nights ago; when that black-hearted swine, Oscytel, his right-hand war-lord, assaulted my home. That man…that fiend in human shape," she added, as the memory of what had happened at Foxley rose up suddenly to choke her, "destroyed my home and massacred my family! He carved the Blood Eagle from my father's living body while I was forced to watch, unable to move or cry out from where I was hidden.

191

"I have sworn to kill him! Sworn it to the Old Ones of my people, and to God Himself also, and I alone am left to carry out the vow. But, oh God it was so awful, so terrible...so pitiless! The memory will haunt me forever. And now...this," she cried out in anguish, sweeping her hands around her, her face lit by the great bonfire the bothy had become. "This was the only home I had left. It is too much! I cannot bear it!" And bowing her head, she covered her face with her hands and wept, falling forward to her knees in the snow as her legs suddenly gave way beneath her, and rocking backwards and forwards she keened her loss in broken-hearted agony.

The other girl was appalled.

Leaving Oswald temporarily to fend for himself, she dropped his chain in the snow and swiftly ran across to where Brioni was slumped to the ground, and pulling her up she put her arms around her heaving shoulders, and holding her closely she tried to comfort the sobbing maid whose hounds had fought so bravely to protect her, and were even now close by her side as the leaping flames, with a roar and crackle of fierce energy, consumed the bothy and lit up the clearing.

*

S he felt so helpless and so mean to have attacked her for what that great oaf of a bear had done. She might love Oswald dearly, but she could hardly expect anyone else to do so! It was bad enough that the girl's family had been wiped out in such a terrible raid, but that the Fates should have sent Oswald down upon her was doubly cruel. And all she had done was rail at her for the screaming rage and fear her dogs had brought out of him.

Sweet Benedict, what a mess.

The Danes roaming at will through all Wessex, her father badly injured with a fall and half the troupe already wanting to get back to their homes in Frankland. If that happened all she would have left would be her father, Julio and Oswald...and perhaps one or two of the others closest to them.

She smiled.

Silly old bear. He had been with them for nearly five years now, ever since her father had bought him from the baiters in Neustria after his mother had been killed. He had only been a cubbling then, and in such an appalling state that he was like to die at any moment. And cubs stick close to their mothers for a long time, nearly two years, so he was in acute distress when they had rescued him. But they had hand fed him, weaned him, coddled him and generally loved and nursed him back to health and happiness until he had become like one of the family. Even more so after her own mother had died.

Now he could dance and do simple tricks that had made him a favourite at all the fairs and markets they visited. Not least because he was huge and obviously liked people; the biggest brown bear she had ever seen, and when he got up on his hind feet he was simply enormous. The trouble was, he didn't much like dogs! And unless she was close to him at all times there could be trouble. Usually they left him alone as he was so huge, and as long as that was the case then there was never a problem. But people were stupid, hunters particularly so, and sometimes egged their dogs on and then there was always a terrific fight with dust, dogs and whatever else got in the way flying in all directions.

And of course Oswald was muzzled so he could not fight back as fiercely as he would otherwise have been able to. Nevertheless, no fight ever lasted for long because he was too strong and thickly furred for that, and despite his enormous size he was quick on his feet and his massive forepaws and claws were lethal. One blow could disembowel a dog with ease or break its back. The hunters and common folk soon learned to leave him alone, but it always ruined their display and generally left poor Oswald too jangled and distressed to perform properly for several days.

She sighed deeply, and rubbed Brioni's back and held her close as she watched the flames devour the ancient bothy, while a great column of smoke swept up into the misty air.

No wonder this girl had been so frightened.

If this was all she had in the world, she thought, looking at her possessions scattered around them, and her animals her only companions, then it was no wonder she had been so angry as well. God alone knew how she herself would react to the sights this girl must have witnessed. It was a miracle she was still sane at all. She had known others who had been broken by their experiences with the Great Army in Frankland, before coming across to England. Broken both in mind and spirit...but not this one!

This one must be made of forged steel and saddle leather! Probably hadn't allowed herself the luxury of the tears and grief that were now pouring out of her. At times like these tears were a greater healer of wounded souls than anything else. Let her cry herself out and then they could both sit back and put the pieces back together again. And she had a good flask of fruit spirit with her pack on the back of Poppy, whom she had left tethered just inside the tree line, that would help put some warmth back into both of them.

God help them all. But if the Danes had broken free of all constraint then getting away from England would not be easy, for their war-boats would be everywhere. She would have to see what her father had to say when she got back to their main encampment. It might be better to remain there until the summer anyway. It was a lovely country, and a good act could always make a living, despite the presence of the bloody heathen. They liked good entertainment the same as anyone else. But first she would have to get this girl back on her feet. She owed her that at least, considering what Oswald had done. After that they would just have to wait and see.

# Chapter Twenty Six

For some while the two girls remained close together, until Brioni had cried herself out, but eventually she sat back and dashed away her tears with the back of her hand in a series of quick, angry movements, wiping her face along the sleeves of her dress as she did so; and looking across at her new companion she made a big effort to smile.

"I am sorry about that, I am not usually such a cry-baby, but after all that has happened to me in the last few days it all got suddenly too much to bear. What's your name?"

"Maritia...though my family have always called me Mari. What about you?"

"Brioni. Brioni of Foxley."

"Foxley?" The dark-haired girl queried, astonished. "Is that near here?"

"Just a few miles. Why? You seem to have heard of the place?"

"Yes! My father was in conversation with someone from there not long ago. Wulfnoth?"

"He was my father's Reeve," Brioni replied excitedly. "My father is..was..Thane Wulfstan of Foxley. That was my home." And there was a long pause then while both women took in what was being said.

"Well, Brioni of Foxley, then we were fated to meet no matter what. For we were to have performed at Foxley this very week. To celebrate a betrothal."

"*No!*"

"Yes...it was all arranged. Whose betrothal?"

"Mine!" Brioni replied in a small voice. "Mine, to a worthy man I thought I loved beyond all others. The Lord Heardred of the Sommerseatas, one of King Alfred's companions and hearth-warriors. Sweet Mary, Maritia," she added after a pause. "There was some talk of a dancing bear when I got home from Chippenham a week ago, my brother said so...Oswald?"

"Yes...poor old Oswald!" she said, looking across to where the great bear was sitting all disconsolate upon the snowy ground.

"But now all that has changed," Brioni went on vehemently. "My home has been destroyed and my family wiped out. Marriage is not for me. I have sworn a vow of vengeance against the man who destroyed my family, the Black Jarl of Helsing, the Lord Oscytel. And until that has been completed my life cannot go forward."

"And how do you think you will fulfil this vow?" Maritia asked her quietly, black eyes looking into blue ones. "You are on your own, with no-one to help or support you."

"The gods alone know, Maritia. But something will turn up!" Brioni answered fiercely. And there was another pause while both girls looked at the fire now consuming the bothy completely, at the great column of smoke that marked its grave, and at each other, each one gauging the other's temperament and intentions. Then, suddenly, Brioni laughed, the sound seeming strangely unreal in the situation in which they now found themselves, but it was enough to lighten the atmosphere, grown suddenly grim and dark as she had been talking of her family's destruction and her blood-oath.

"Who would have thought that any animal called 'Oswald' could create such a desperate mess of everything? And he really does look very sorry for himself sitting there so miserably in the snow. It's just that he is so big and I was so frightened. It's not everyone who meets up with an angry bear first thing in the morning!"

Mari smiled back and visibly relaxed, adding quickly: "And it's not everyone who would face a brown mountain bear in full fury with nothing more than a pair of hounds and a boar spear either! I tell you, Brioni, my heart was in my mouth to say the least. I thought you would never hear me."

Brioni looked into the girl's dark eyes and liked the frank honesty and good humour that she saw there, and smiled in return. Here was someone she felt she could really trust, with her life if need be. She had the grace and suppleness of a dancer, yet the square shoulders and finely muscled arms of a fighter. There was strength and calmness in her also, and Brioni suddenly had the strangest feeling that they were destined to go far with one another. If not together exactly, then certainly in constant contact.

And how strange that her father had planned to use Maritia and Oswald's skills for her betrothal party at Foxley! If not on the day, then clearly soon afterwards, and Maritia was right...surely they had been fated to meet. Just not at home, but here in the depths of Helm's Wood. The beginning of a friendship that would last them all their lives, she was sure of it.

So, when Maritia suggested moments later that they should collect Foxhead from the stables and load up the tilt cart with all her scattered belongings, she was more than willing to do so. Any ally was better than none when you were on your own in a hostile world. And with the two of them working together it was not long before they had rescued all the most important items from the shattered bothy, especially her sword and shield.

Meanwhile Brioni brought Foxhead down from the stables, struggling to lead him quietly as they approached Oswald, the stallion showing the whites of his eyes and tittuping violently at the sight and smell of so strange and dangerous a beast. Trained war-horse though he was, even the bravest could be excused his first encounter with a bear! Once more harnessed to the hated tilt cart, which Brioni swiftly loaded while Maritia collected Oswald, together they set off back to where Maritia had left Poppy, and the promised fruit spirit in her leather-covered flask, Bran and Utha questing ahead of them as they went.

Swiftly leaving the clearing behind them in the thick mists that had now closed all around them, they were anxious to move on. Anything suspicious might bring a Danish patrol down on their heads, so before anyone came to see what it was that had caused so great a column of smoke, they pushed on hard along the twisted trackways that criss-crossed the forest in all directions.

\*

*I*t was a typically raw, damp January morning with the mist clinging to the ground in soggy streamers and the snow now wet and heavy underfoot. All around them the trees were dropping their burdens with a sullen flump, and everything seemed to be running with water as a mild south-west wind came soughing through the great woodlands. The trees loomed out of the murk like strange phantoms in a dismal underworld where no birds sing, and the sun was but a shallow memory. Yet despite the difficulties of following a practically non-existent trail through the chill, opaque greyness, Maritia never faltered.

With Oswald roaming free, and Bran and Utha now close to Brioni's side, she guided her shaggy mare with unerring decision along a multitude of diverging tracks, taking every twist and turn as if she was following a set of hidden markers. Brioni, driving a reluctant Foxhead, did her best to follow, despite her cart's wheels slewing around as the stallion struggled to keep up.

But before long Maritia felt they were far enough away from the place to slow their beasts down to a steady walk, as much for Foxhead's sake as anything else. And with no sense of being followed, they ambled through the silent dripping forest for all the world as if they were on a gentle summer's hack, and not two girls alone in a bleak countryside where every bush and boulder might conceal an enemy who was desperate for their blood, be that Dane or Saxon wolfshead.

In fact, with the relaxing of tension, Brioni was eager to learn more about this strange girl with her forthright manner and almost feline suppleness who had come so suddenly into her life.

\*

"W"here's your camp, Mari?" she asked her, as she flicked Foxhead on with the reins. "For I could see no sign of anyone in this area when I came here yesterday."

"About three miles in a straight line from your clearing. But it is a good deal further east than you were, and further still across the ground, for the trail is tortuous as you can see," she said, turning to speak to Brioni on the driving box of the old tilt cart. "But I have been to that clearing before…"

"Before?" Brioni questioned her, astonished, jabbing at Foxhead's reins in surprise.

"Yes! Several times, for charcoal. Oswald and me. That's how he knew where to come…and I to find him. The burners always keep a store of apples in a great barrel when they are there. And Oswald loves apples!"

"So I noticed," Brioni said, looking at where Oswald was just then lolloping through the undergrowth in a spray of snow and slushy leaves. "And that's how you know your way through these lands so well."

"Yes. We have a small tilt cart that father uses especially for simple carrying tasks. He uses the charcoal in a hand-forge he has for mending the things we need in our acts, and for our braziers when it is cold."

"What about the wolfsheads, outlaws, who are supposed to abound in the deeper parts of the old forest?"

"We see them sometimes…small bands of armed men. The villagers seem to think them harmless."

"What villagers are those?" Brioni questioned her sharply. "I don't know of any village this side of my father's lands."

Maritia looked at her out of the side of her face, her eyes concerned, her voice hesitant. "Well, not villagers at all really, I suppose. Just a handful of simple people living in a crude collection of huts and bothies in a big clearing," she said vaguely. "Foresters, farmers and their families; a shepherd, a potter, a woodsman with a lathe, a jobbing farrier…just people."

Brioni returned her look steadily. "You mean masterless men, with no reeve to organise them and no Lord to give them protection? That's one of the things Alfred believes in most. That everyone should have a Lord to give them justice and protection. The wolfsheads will eat them alive!"

"Normally I am sure that would be right, but the wolfsheads don't seem to bother them greatly, though clearly they pass through here from time to time. Some may even have those amongst the villagers they know well…"

"You mean sleep with? Families?" Brioni asked swiftly, surprise in her voice.

"Perhaps," Maritia replied vaguely, looking at her again out of the corner of her eyes. "Maybe. But they don't bother us and we don't bother them. God knows we have little enough to interest them. Besides, Oswald is a fine obstacle to any sudden attack, for we always leave him on a long chain at night linked to his wagon..."

"His wagon?" Brioni interrupted her, intrigued.

"Yes, he has a heavy travelling wagon that he sleeps in at night. Iron bars all round and a solid timber frame. We cover it with thick canvas against the rain, or snow. He is chained to that, with his muzzle off I may add, and if you don't know him he's a frightening enough sight to keep most people away."

"Well, I can certainly vouch for that!" Brioni replied, smiling, as she watched Oswald's lumbering progress through the close undergrowth. "I was terrified for my life! By the way, where did you learn to speak such perfect Saxon? From what you have mentioned already you've obviously spent much time in Frankland, and your name isn't Saxon either."

Maritia smiled across at Brioni's earnest face and then laughed. "I was born not far from Paris, but my mother was a Saxon girl whom my father rescued from the Danish riever who had seized her."

"A slave you mean?" she asked, shocked.

"Yes! She was captured in some raid or other on your south coast, near the great marshes of Pevensey I think, so mother said; and had not been well-used when my father came across her. Anyway he bought her freedom, they fell in love and here I am. There were other children, but they died young. And when I grew up she taught me her own tongue, and very fierce she was about it too, I can tell you," she said with a chuckle at the warm memory, before turning in her saddle to look for Oswald.

"But that was years ago," she continued, turning back again. "Before the Great army came to Frankland and ravaged Neustria. Mother's dead now, died three summers ago, poor love. She got caught out in a storm and came back soaked, got a cold, became feverish and was dead in six days. We did all we could, but she had the lung sickness, couldn't breathe, and there was nothing we could do.

"So you came here?"

"Yes. Father, Oswald and I came across to Wessex with our troupe of jugglers and acrobats and have been here ever since despite the troubles. We are the 'Circus Maximus'...means 'great' in Latin."

"I know. Our old priest, Anselm, hammered it into me when I was younger."

199

"My mother also. Not personally, of course. She hired me a tutor. Wanted her only child to be literate, and Latin is still used a lot in Frankland. All contracts are in Latin. Hugo the Bearmaster and his troupe are well known across all of Frankland. Mother had a huge hand in all that we did."

"Do you miss her?"

"Oh yes, Brioni. Almost every day for something. She was a lovely lady and father adored her, we all did. She was the heart of the *Circus Maximus*; father was lost without her for ages. She was always so warm and cheerful, with a good word for everyone, and she loved Oswald dearly. He always looked out for her when he was in his travelling cage, and she always had a sweetmeat for him, or an apple. He loves apples..."

"Yes, I saw that this morning."

"Silly old bear!" And they both laughed

"He must have missed her after she died."

Maritia sighed and briefly bowed her head. "We all did. I wept for days, and father still mourns her. That's partly why we came across the narrow sea. Still," she said more cheerfully, "There's no point in moping about it. She'd never thank me for it, and her memory is too precious and loving to shed tears over. Mother's life was ruled by laughter. Unhappiness hurt her deeply, so I'll not be a party to it myself."

"Why did they call you 'Maritia'? Brioni asked a moment later. "I'd have thought they would have named you after her."

Maritia laughed again before replying: "That would have been terrible! Poor mama, she had one of the 'Aethel' names that your people are so fond of, Aethelwuffa, as it so happens. Father just called her 'Wuffa'. She had always loathed her name and had no wish to saddle her daughter with the same awful handicap. So I was named after my grandmother, my father's mother."

"But that's not a Frankish name either, is it?"

"No. My father's family came from Bavaria, near Lorch as a matter of fact. But when the Emperor Charlemagne died the family moved to Neustria, and have been there ever since. What about you?"

Oh, nothing nearly so colourful. Our people came across with some of the first settlers. When Vortigern was High King of Britain, with Hengist and Horsa, just after Rome fell for the second time. We are true Woden born, or so I have always been told, and came here to Foxley in the time of King Ine of Wessex and have been there ever since. My father's very close to the king...or was, until those heathen swine butchered him!" she added after a pause. "And I was Queen Ealhswitha's favourite handmaiden before all this happened, part of the royal household. That's how I met with the Lord Heardred. We were to have been betrothed this Yuletide end. The party your father was going to come to? And now I don't know whether any of them are alive or dead. King Alfred, his family, Heardred...none of them. And though I have no wish now to be betrothed to anyone, I would not want harm to come to him. That's the worst thing of all, Mari, not knowing. The one thing I am certain of however is that the man responsible for the destruction of my family will pay with his life, if it is the last thing that I do on earth!"

*

*M*aritia looked at her companion's set face and sighed. So young, yet so determined. She couldn't be more than eighteen, if even that, and she had her whole life ahead of her – if she got the chance to live it! At twenty-two it made her feel suddenly old to be faced with such a fiery spirit. So untamed and free. Well, she would not be able to hold her long, that was obvious. But a few days of rest, warmth and good food would give her a better start if nothing else. To fight the Black Jarl Oscytel on her own was just madness. She would need an army for that. Or at least a good war-band to rely on, and its leader...and she had someone in mind who just might change everything for her.

And with all the treasure she had in the old tilt cart anything was possible, for good men cost money and that was one thing of which Brioni had plenty. She just had not realised how important her father's halidom was going to be in her quest to put down the Black Jarl of Helsing.

Reaching across Poppy's withers, she tapped the edge of the cart and gave Brioni a brilliant smile, wicked in its anticipation. "When we get home, you can be certain of a hot bath for both of us. There's nothing like being clean all over. I love it!" And digging in her heels she urged her mount along the still snowy trackway, now turning to slush in the seeping mists, their breath steaming in the dank, chilly air as Brioni and her hounds followed close behind her.

*

*I*ndeed it was a very damp and weary group that finally draggled into camp hours later, just as the light was really fading into night, the sun having been absent from their sight all day.

Checking Poppy just before she reached the clearing's edge, Maritia jumped lightly from her back and called Oswald to her. Eager for an apple he came at once, and drawing his leash chain from a small saddle pack beside her she slipped it through the heavy iron hoop that had been riveted firmly onto his

201

broad leather collar, its flanges bound over with stout cord, sliding it through until it was held in place with a broad steel bar.

"I can't risk him running off again into the night. Next time I might not be so lucky in finding him. Those two hounds of yours must have been well trained to have left him alone all this time. You are to be congratulated."

"That's my father's doing, Mari, not mine. They were his hounds long before they were mine. But I have been a favourite with them since they were puppies. Funny to use that word about them now they are so huge!"

"No matter, Brioni, they have been beautifully trained," Maritia replied with another brilliant smile. "So has Foxhead. Any horse, particularly a stallion, that can cope with being close to a bear is remarkable. You are most fortunate. With companions like that around, you should do well in any situation that might confront you. Bears or otherwise, if I may say so!"

And giving her new friend a quick grin she led the way forward to where her father's tents had been carefully erected, their heavy canvas sides spread out above the ground like swooping wings, just waiting to enfold them in their ready warmth and closeness.

# Chapter Twenty Seven

*T*he clearing they now reached was much larger than the charcoal burners' in the further forest, though the heavy mists that swirled around it made its true extent difficult to establish.

Nearest to where they had entered it a sizeable tented encampment had been thrown up: one great pavilion of faded canvas in blue and red stripes, like the great sails of dragon ships stitched close together, with quite a number of smaller ones thrown up around it. There were also a collection of heavy wains, several still covered over and roped down securely against the weather, and a heavy travelling cage on solid wooden wheels with its thick canvas hood drawn back to let in the air, its barred front swung open and propped up with two great forked timbers.

In front of those a huge fire was burning brightly, the leaping flames driving back the foggy air to send rolling waves of heat quivering out to greet them. And while there were no stables as such, there was an extensive horse line, with a rough lean-to built to cover it that had been crudely thatched. Thick straw had been thrown down to cover the ground from which the snow had been largely cleared, and there was a sizeable midden not far from the stable area, wreathed in steam from the hot dung, both beast and human, cast out upon it every day.

Finally, away across this great opening in the trees, a small collection of bothies and lath and plaster houses could dimly be seen against the far forest edge. Not more than a dozen of them, they had been built near a broad stream that flowed down from the north and cut them off from the rest of the clearing. Usually it would have been running bright and free but now, due to the heavy frosts and bitter weather, it was mostly choked with ice, only a fine black line coursing through the middle to show that there was any life in it.

And while there was a rough track running right across the clearing, from tents to houses, there was no bridge, so there must be a ford instead, Brioni reasoned to herself, peering across to the crude shelters beyond it. The wonder was that there was anyone living there at all for they were in one of the remotest corners of the great forest, far from any real habitation. A part of her father's lands that she had never visited. Yet, though she could not see anyone moving about, there was a blurry skein of smoke above the snow-covered roofs where a handful of ponies were loosely tethered, and a few distant hogs scratched about hopefully to find themselves something to eat. Rooting at the ground with their fat snouts, and squealing at one another over every scrap and morsel they discovered.

Brioni shivered, and shook her shoulders.

It was all very strange, and there was an air of watchfulness about the whole clearing, a sense of unusual stillness and false calm that was amply borne out by a shrill whistle from nowhere that now greeted their arrival, and almost at once it seemed to Brioni, some half a dozen men came bounding into sight.

For a moment she thought they were being attacked, as with wild whoops and shouts they rushed towards them, and instinctively she drew back hard on Foxhead's reins, cursing once more that she had no weapon to hand and no shield. But within moments her would-be attackers, all dressed in garish clothes, with gay bandannas around their heads and broad sashes round their waists, began to leap, spin and cartwheel in front of them, while others with pipes and tabor, oliphant, lute and crumhorn, ran out to join them, much to Foxhead's dislike who shook his head and stamped his feet in disgust. Some ran up to where Oswald had plumped himself down in the snow again to give him the warmest of welcomes, while others plucked Maritia out of her saddle and carried her, laughing gaily, in mock triumph round her large, furry companion now standing on his enormous hind feet and turning slowly round in a stately shuffle to the music, waving his massive forepaws about as he did so.

It was a strange, madcap scene lit by the blazing light from the great fire nearby that cast their shadows in weird, swooping shadows across the grey-white snowy ground.

"Put me down, you fools!" Maritia cried out laughing. "I've brought a young guest with me who's in sore need of warmth, food and clean raiment!"

But her friends clearly had other ideas and, whisking off her cape, they tossed her lightly from one to another for several minutes, catching her expertly every time, while Maritia herself tumbled and flew through the air with the simple grace and easy fluid motion of a bird, until with a final twist and turn she landed on her toes beside a startled Foxhead who leapt sideways in alarm, almost turning the tilt cart over in his sudden distress.

"Well that's warmed me up for certain," she said breathlessly to Brioni who had watched the whole performance with open-eyed admiration and clapping hands. "Now, come on," she added, as her friends ran back towards the striped pavilion ahead of them, Oswald following. "Let's get you out of those filthy rags. A bath, some hot broth and a fresh set of garments, and you'll be a different person from the foul creature who came bursting out of that bothy covered in the filth and dirt of ages this morning to face my Oswald."

Swinging down from the tilt cart Brioni laughed, her voice sounding light and silvery on the misty air: "You're probably right! Certainly I smell like a privy and these clothes are fit only for the fire. As for my stomach, broth would do me very well indeed, for I don't know that the wolf stew I had last night has done me a great deal of good!"

"Wolf's meat stew?" Maritia said, with a deep grimace and a hand to her mouth. "Sweet heavens, Brioni. You are made of even sterner stuff than I am. The very thought of it makes my belly turn."

"Well," she replied, smiling ruefully, leading Foxhead forward, "that was my reaction too! But when you are starving hungry, as I was, then anything is better than nothing. As it is, Bran and Utha can have the rest of the meat I hacked off those carcasses. They don't seem to mind what they eat!"

And linking arms with the older girl, now leading Poppy by her reins, Brioni with Foxhead, and the wretched tilt cart stepping out behind him, she allowed herself to be led away to the large tent that was clearly the family dwelling in this desolate place, Bran and Utha loping closely at her heels.

"Will my baggage be safe?" she asked a moment later, stopping to watch as a camp ostler came to lead Foxhead away to the rude stable area for unharnessing, a good grooming and a warm meal of mashed oats and malted water.

"Your father's treasury, you mean?"

"Yes, Maritia. There's more wealth there than most people could even dream of, and my weapons are no less precious either. Without them I would be no better off than the meanest kitchen maid. That sword of mine is a true craftsman's masterpiece, worthy of Wayland himself."

"Wayland?" Maritia asked, puzzled.

"A sword smith of magical, mythical quality. He is the man who made Beowulf's sword, and his coat of mail, when he slew Grendel and his mother. Do you know the tale of Beowulf?"

"Even in Frankland we have heard the story of Beowulf. The warriors of my people love to hear that story, especially after a good feast!"

"Always after a good feast," Brioni replied laughing. "Well, my sword is as special to me as Hrunting was to Beowulf."

"Well, that's clear enough, anyway," Maritia said, stopping and turning to face her new friend, putting her hands on Brioni's shoulders as she did so. The tension and uncertainty that were running through the girl felt clearly through her fingertips, yet she was determined to allay her fears before she brought her forward to meet her father.

205

"Look, Brioni, these people have been with us longer than I care to remember," she said, gesturing around her at those she could see moving about. "Most of them are family of one sort or another, and for even one of them to steal from a guest under my father's roof would be as unthinkable as if they were to steal from one of themselves...and that they never would!

"Relax, you are among friends. By the time you have greeted my father, and bathed yourself, you will find that everything special will have been brought to your bedside in my own pavilion. There are no enemies here you know, Brioni. No thieving bandits who are out to strip you of your inheritance. So, come now, sweetheart, let's have a smile and less concern, for right at this moment you are carrying a look that would curdle the freshest cream!"

Brioni looked into Maritia's still, dark eyes and grinned shamefacedly: "I am sorry, Maritia. I didn't mean to question anybody's worthiness. But when you have witnessed as much raiding as I have, and seen the turmoil that Wessex has had to endure for all these years, and the killing and the destruction, then you would understand my caution. I am not used to trusting so completely people whom I have only just met. But somehow you are different. So," she went on after a brief hesitation, "this time I will do as you suggest," and she bowed her head in simple acceptance. "Now, lead me forward to your father's 'hall', and into his capable hands, for the bath and the broth are calling to me. And if I have to spend another night in the company of this rancid dress then I shall foreswear arms, and my mission, and give myself to Thunnor's vengeance!"

And holding her nose in mock disgust at her own reeking person, she and Maritia swept through the entrance flaps and on into the interior of the huge tent on a gale of laughter.

*

*T*his was far more comfortable and complex an area than Brioni had expected. Apart from a main living space which was extensive, there were a number of partitioned alcoves around the sides that took the place of sleeping compartments, together with a covered opening at the far side that led to separate tented enclosures for Maritia and her father's personal use, Maritia's already being adapted for Brioni's unexpected arrival.

The ground at the entrance was thickly strewn with straw to control the mess of entering and leaving, but everywhere else it was covered with thick woven matting of plaited rushes in bright colours. Upon this a large wooden dais had been placed at the far end for a long table, benches and several armed chairs on which bright woolfells had been cast for added comfort. There were

206

eight charcoal burners, great iron baskets on heavy tripods, around the edges, and a quantity of oil lamps on small wooden stands that gave off a warm, mellow light sufficient to entice any casual visitor to relax.

But the most arresting sight of all was the great bearded figure hunched into a monstrous bearskin cloak of shining black fur, with his left arm and shoulder heavily strapped against any unguarded movement, who hauled himself out of his tall-backed chair to come across and greet them.

Brioni gasped.

He was enormous...even larger than her father, and the Thane of Foxley had not been a small man! His hair was as black as a raven's wing, like his daughter's, only with a white streak in it that ran across the back of his head and down into his forehead where an axe-blade had cut him down many years before. His face was seamed and craggy, full of rude health, and he had a pair of shrewd periwinkle eyes that twinkled at his daughter merrily as he swept her up in his one good arm, as though she were no more than a bunch of flowers, and gave her an almighty squeeze.

"Well, my pretty, so you have come safely back to your poor old father, after slipping out at almost dead of night in pursuit of that great hairy monster. *Ho!*" he roared giving a mighty shout, "But you gave us all a nasty fright, my beauty. I ought to take my stick to your sides for that," he challenged her with a twinkle. "And me no more than a broken down warrior who is full of coughs and wheezes; shame on you for taking such advantage of my infirmity!"

"Pooh, father," Maritia replied, laughing, as she whisked herself away from his embrace. "I did nothing that you would not have done yourself, if you hadn't hurt yourself in that fall. Mother would never have forgiven us if I had not done so, for surely Oswald meant as much to her as I do to you. She adored him...as you do.

"And as for your coughs and wheezes, there's nothing wrong with you that fresh air and a little exercise won't cure. Get away, you old fraud, you are fitter than most of the men in the troop...and well you know it! Besides, if I hadn't gone out after our furry friend, I would never have met Brioni, and that would have been a terrible shame, for she is younger than me and twice as pretty. Come Brioni, meet my father. He's the biggest rogue this side of Paris, and has the softest heart of any man I know."

Brioni, who had been watching the quick exchange of words and glances that had flown between the two of them, was quick to respond, recognising instantly the close bond that existed between father and daughter, and was only too pleased to join in such a warm and loving closeness. So like her own relationship with her father.

207

# Chapter Twenty Eighth

"SO, you are the Saxon beauty my bear almost plucked out of the ground," he rumbled gently, coming up to her and putting his great hands on her slim shoulders, forcing her to look up at him, as he towered over her. "My people did not do you justice," he continued, smiling at her look of amazement. "You are as lovely as a summer's morning...though right at this moment you look more like a rose after a sudden thunderstorm! Come, smile my child. Here you are among friends, and I, Hugo the Bearmaster, the most famous circus leader in all Frankland, bid you welcome to my house, such as it is, and offer you whatever hospitality and kindness you could possibly desire!" And pulling her quickly towards him, before she could protest, he gave her as big a squeeze as he had just given his daughter, only releasing her when she was almost breathless.

"See, Brioni," Maritia said, smiling, after he had put the gasping girl down again, "the biggest rogue this side of the Seine river, not to mention flatterer as well! Now, come with me, before he has a chance to say anything more, for, believe me, once he has a pretty girl anywhere near him he becomes just insufferable, and then I'd never be able to prise you loose!"

"You see what I have to put up with, Brioni of Foxley?" Hugo replied mournfully. "No kindness at all. No charity...ah but she has a hard heart, my daughter. Who would have thought that anyone so beautiful could be quite so unfeeling?" And he dropped his head into his huge hands, just leaving a gap between his fingers for his eyes to twinkle down at her.

"You talk a greater lot of nonsense than the silly geese at Christmas time," Maritia replied, pulling his hands open to drop a kiss on his forehead. "Now, father, you stay here and order that idle goat, Gilbert, whom I can see skittering about in the shadows, to prepare us all something warm to eat...and I'll take Brioni away and give her the bath I promised her this morning when we met. Then when she is properly dressed again we might just come through and join you."

Hugo the Bearmaster looked down at Brioni, in her filthy clothes and tattered hair and smiled: "Would you like that, my little one?" he rumbled, in his deep voice.

Looking up at him, deep velvet blue into twinkling periwinkle, she smiled back at him brilliantly. "Yes please. I'd like that very much," and curtseying as if it were to the King himself she added: "And I thank you for your kindness, and your generosity in inviting such a disreputable stranger into your house."

Throwing back his head, he roared with delighted laughter, relishing the quick wit of the girl standing so straight before him, who, despite her situation and her appearance, which were both dire, could yet make subtle jokes about it.

"Go on, away with you both," he replied with a bang of his hand on the table. "I will see you later, my Lady Brioni, when you are properly rested and re-clothed. We are well met indeed, for your name is known to us. And though I never met your father, his reeve was full of praise for his master, and the *Circus Maximus* would have given you all great entertainment.

"Go now with my daughter, and we will talk of everything later. Maritia will see to all your needs, she is an expert in such things; takes after her dear mama. Then we will see what can be done to help you." And turning away, he banged his hands again on the table to call for Gilbert his cook-steward, for his own body servants and camp varlets, while Maritia took Brioni by the hand and led her towards her own private section that lay just beyond the huge tented pavilion that was her home.

*

*T*he rest of the evening passed in a welter of conversation and light-hearted banter; all the how, why, and where of Brioni's experiences at Foxley; of her time with the king and of her planned betrothal to Heardred. How Thane Wulfstan had come to engage the *Circus Maximus* for her betrothal day, and of how her family's destruction and her blood-oath had changed everything for her...and how Hugo and his people might help her.

It was an exhilarating evening, with laughter and sadness in equal measure, and Brioni had loved the quick and easy repartee that passed between Maritia and her father, and admired their grasp of the situation that Wessex found herself in. All the more surprising that the latest Danish attack should have caught them so unprepared. For a family so well informed, she would have thought they would have known what had happened immediately, and planned accordingly. But then her own family had been caught equally unprepared and they had been connected directly to the King...and where was he now? Dead, captured, driven into the wilderness? And the Queen and her little ones? No-one seemed to know. It just went to show how little trust one could put into anything these days.

The meal was simple but sufficient: a hearty meat broth with onions, purple carrots, parsnips and barleycorns; fresh bread from a simple bell-shaped *clibanus* baked on a charcoal burner, the whole washed down with new beer, and finished with some of the stored apples that Oswald loved so dearly, and slices of hard cheese from Hugo's stores. She sighed with pleasure and wiped her mouth with the hand cloth one of the camp varlets had given her at the start. This was not home as she had always known it…but infinitely better than the burned out bothy she had left that morning!

Foxhead had been groomed and fed, as had Bran and Utha who had soon rejoined her, and were even now lying not far from her feet, their heads on their massive forepaws, their sterns gently waving. She had found warmth and sudden friendship where she had least expected it, and shook her head at it all in amazement.

Maritia, somewhat awed by the bloody marks she had seen smeared on her body when they had bathed, had recognised the antler symbols immediately. And, bobbing her head in acceptance of the blood-oath they represented, she had traced them across her breasts and loins with her fingers, while Brioni told her again of how her oath had come about.

Now, as she looked across the table at where the dark-haired girl was leaning animatedly towards her father, she shook her head again. The girl seemed to believe that, somehow, her oath could be fulfilled, despite all the difficulties that faced her, but was being very coy about it at the same time. Her father, Hugo the Bearmaster, was also hinting that things might quickly change for their sudden Saxon guest, but was refusing to elaborate. Just smiling and laughing at her questions. All of which did nothing to still the little quirk of uncertainty that continued to unsettle her, and that despite all that Hugo and Maritia had said and done since she had arrived to make her feel safe and welcome.

Certainly she was better fed, clothed and housed than she could possibly have expected when she had left Foxley Manor yesterday. As Maritia had promised, her shield and weapons had been placed by her bed, and her father's whole halidom, and his treasure, were now in two great sealed boxes that Hugo had found for her. The two wolf skins had been taken over for proper curing, and she had been given new leather clothes to replace those ruined ones in which she had arrived.

Yet there were still many questions in her own mind that made her uneasy. Principally about the events that Maritia and her father had hinted at for the morrow; the strange presence of the bothies and frame houses across the clearing where none, as far as she knew, had ever stood before; and especially the casual mention of wolfsheads in the area as if they were the most usual people in the world.

But then these were unquiet times for everybody.

210

The Danes had smashed so much of the fabric of the country, and not just Wessex but elsewhere too, from monasteries to whole communities, that maintaining any form of law and order was supremely difficult. Masterless men roamed free everywhere that local thanes had been killed, dispossessed or fled. *'Every man should have a Lord'* was what Alfred believed in. *'Justice and protection for every man under the law'* And in the absence of that it was not surprising that people gathered together where they could, so some sort of normal life could still be followed. Was that what had happened here? Or was this a haunt of wolfsheads? Was that why Maritia had been so coy about her friends? Yet she had assured her that her treasure would be as safe in her father's care as if it were in Thane Wulfstan's own iron-bound chests at Foxley.

She felt confused.

Not least because she had a heightened sense of impending action, a deep-seated need to be on the move again that made her restless, and a strong feeling that her meeting with Maritia and her father would bring her the help she had the sense to realise she now so desperately needed. If she were to have any hope at all of fulfilling the vow she had made over her father's body, she would need a proven warrior to help her...and that she did not have!

She did not know how the help she needed would arrive...she was just sure that it would. It was such a strong feeling that it filled her heart with warmth, and it was with just that glow of confidence in the future that she fell asleep.

\*

*T*hat night the wind swung further round into the south-west, and by morning was battering noisily at their sprawling encampment. With the warmer air came the rain, rattling like a hail of sharp pebbles on the heavy canvas above her head, and turning the already softened snow into a slushy mess.

Snuggled down beneath the thick furs that covered her, Brioni listened to it beating down on them and could clearly imagine the grey curtains that would be sweeping across the clearing. Shrouding the iron gauntness of the naked trees with a hissing cloak of wet misery, they would turn the ground outside into a soggy quagmire of half melted snow, sodden straw and grasses and churned-up mud.

Brioni shivered and pulled the heavy coverlets up to her chin, grimacing at the thought of how she would have had to cope with it all on her own if she had still been at the old charcoal burners' camp. Instead of which here she was

211

deliciously clean and warm, safely in the dry, and mercifully in the company of good-hearted people. Let the world outside wait on its own a little longer.

Though destiny may await her she was in no mood just yet to leap up and meet it. The Fates could keep spinning their threads a while yet. Her meeting with Maritia yesterday was as much a part of her life as the doom that had fallen on her family at Oscytel's hands three days before…and just as fixed as her oath to the ancient gods of her people that had flooded into her head from nowhere. And if it was her fate to fulfil her oath, then the gods had better bestir themselves in her favour or she would never get beyond Hugo's fireside.

It was all too large a picture for her mind to cope with and she lay on her back, her eyes unfocused on the canvas ceiling of Maritia's chamber, grey in the morning light, listening to the rain sweeping in rattling waves across it, while the glowing warmth of the charcoal brazier that a thoughtful Gilbert had placed there flared and winked at her with fiery eyes.

*

She had not lain there long in that delightfully dreamy state, halfway between sleep and wakefulness, when she heard the desperate, wild beat of approaching hooves being ridden like the wind.

Then sudden pandemonium: shouts, cries and the crash of steel. Oswald roaring; men's voices bellowing and horns blowing, the Frankland burr of Hugo's voice halloaing, clearly mingled with the harsh guttural sound of Norse voices she had come to know so well and hate so deeply, and the clatter of steel on shield rim.

*Danes!*

They were attacking the camp, roaring and braying as only they could. They had arrived at last in a dawn raid to wreak their vengeance, as they had at Foxley. Flinging off her coverings, she snatched up her sword that she had unwrapped and placed beside her bed, and with Bran and Utha bristling by her side, she leapt across to where Mari was still lying as if she had not a care in the world.

"Danes, Mari! *The Danes are here!*" she shouted at her, violently shaking her by the shoulder. "Quick! Throw some clothes on and come with me. Come on Mari! We must get out before it is too late! *Wake up!*"

"What is it, Brioni?" Maritia cried out in alarm, springing up in startled nakedness. "For God's sake, what is going on?"

"*The Danes!* A mounted party have just arrived!" And turning away, she began to fling on the fresh set of black leathers over her shift that Maritia had given her the night before: trousers, tunic top, thick striding boots, swirling cloak. Outside all was shouting and the clash of weapons; inside, fear and determination, as Brioni dressed herself and settled her weapons about her. Yet after her first alarm, Maritia still had not really stirred, until finally, in desperation, Brioni tore off the furs that covered the girl and flung her clothes on top of her.

"Get up, Maritia! *Get up!* Before they are upon us!"

"Sweet Mary, aid us! Are you sure?"

"I heard their voices and the clash of steel. Don't lie there arguing, you idiot, unless you wish to be raped where you lie. Come on, I know Danish voices when I hear them. Sweet Jesus, I ought to after Foxley! Now, move yourself!"

Maritia, sitting there half naked, her clothes around her, listened to the clash and clatter of shield and sharpened steel, and the shouts and cries that could now be clearly heard above the fierce patter of rain on canvas, and was unmoved, while Brioni became increasingly frantic.

"*Get dressed!*" she screamed at her, desperate at the lazy manner in which the other girl was behaving. "Dear God, they will be on us in moments. *Do you wish to die?*"

"Did you hear any names?" Maritia asked her, slowly beginning to pull on her clothes.

"Names? *Are you mad?*"

"Trausti, Hannes, Finnar?"

"*What?*"

"Names, Brioni!"

"Yes, *yes!*...Danish names...Now, for pity's sake, *come on!*"

But they had delayed too long, for with a sudden clatter of canvas being flung back and the ringing sound of steel on chain mail, they both heard a number of men come bursting into the main pavilion.

By this time, of course, Bran and Utha were on their feet too. Backs bristling and snarling deep in their throats, they stood on either side of their mistress, a terrifying spectacle for anyone rushing in on them. She, having jabbed her sword through the matting into the ground, had turned and snatched up her javelin and was now stood, with feet braced well apart, blade thrust out before her, a pace or two back from the entrance to what had now become their lair.

Now, finally, Maritia too was dressed and ready; but far from joining her friend in some sort of escape, she just sat on her bed as if nothing was wrong at all. As if the whole Danish war host could break in upon them and she not care whatsoever. Her whole attitude infuriated Brioni, who felt completely betrayed by her new friend. There must be half a dozen of the heathen bastards out there

213

already by the sound of it…yet the stupid woman continued to behave with complete indifference.

"Don't you care about your life?" Brioni snarled at her over her shoulder. "About your father and your friends?"

"Yes, passionately, Brioni," she replied urgently. "But, don't you see? Those names out there *are* my friends!"

"*What?* Danish pirates are your friends?"

"Not pirates, silly. Just 'Danes'…" But before she could finish they both heard a fresh voice raised above the rest, a deep Saxon voice that came ringing clear over the sounds of clashing steel and mingled oaths, a voice of command: "By God and Saint Michael, Hugo, where have you got to, man? Here am I, my hungry heroes and myself no less, with bellies slack and tongues hanging out like limp rags, and now you are hiding from us! Come on you fat Frank, you were here a moment ago, I heard you. Now, come and give us some of your best.

"And, Maritia, my lass, where are you hiding, too?" the large voice bellowed with a booming laugh. "We have come ten leagues already since the moon went down, two of my men are injured and we are all soaked to the bone." Then there was a pause while the men around him could be heard pushing their way into the great tent, before the voice came to them again: "Dear God, Trausti, sometimes I think I'd be better off like Oswald! At least he gets fed and watered twice a day. Here am I come all this way to greet an old friend for breakfast and all I get is fresh air!"

There was then a further pause, the sound of furniture being shifted and the bang and clatter of hard boots on the dais; the coarse unexpected laugh of a girl, rude guffaws and the sound of someone hawking noisily. But despite Maritia's comment and her calm acceptance of all that was going on, Brioni stood her ground unflinching, unwilling to lower her weapon until she was certain that all was truly safe.

Then suddenly both girls heard a quick, heavy step advance towards Maritia's chamber, the sound of chiming mail and of rough hands on canvas, and with a shout of laughter the unfastened screen flaps were rudely thrust back. A huge shadow leapt across Brioni that made her dig her feet into the matting for firmer purchase and grip her spear shaft ever more tightly in her hands, while the two great hounds beside her bayed with sudden violence, straining towards the massive figure that had just appeared before them all.

214

# Chapter Twenty Nine

*T*he man who stood there towered over her, and was also a clear head and shoulders taller than any of the others she could see crowded together just behind him. Yet, big though he was, there was a supple lightness in his movements as he took a pace towards her that belied his great size; there was grace there also, and a certain flexibility in the broad spread of his shoulders that proclaimed the axe-man. A thought confirmed by the thick muscles that bulged around his neck and pushed against the linked chain mail armour that encased his whole upper body. This hung down over his leather chausses that were cross-gartered to his knees with thick scarlet tapes, and over which his baldric of scarlet leather edged with gold was firmly cinched.

That he was a born warrior went without saying, for his armour was of prime quality, for each ring was of steel, not iron, and individually riveted, and he had sheathed weapons by his side. A long sword with wide quillons, incised with gold, and an ivory handle with a silver cross embedded in its broad pommel against his left leg, and a warrior's seaxe, like a shortened sword, with long, pointed blade against his right, and over his right shoulder jutted the covered blade of a brutal Danish war axe. But his hair, matted with rain, was blond and hung to his shoulders as a Saxon would have it, his moustache was in the classic style of King Alfred's court, and his short beard was neatly clipped.

But it was his eyes that really drew Brioni's gaze, more so than his immensely powerful physique, for they were large and unusually bright, like great polished emeralds with flecks of gold in them that made them seem to dance and sparkle in the brazier's fiery light. Were he to smile she was sure they would dazzle any on whom he looked; as it was they were cautious, watchful and alert to her every move, the intelligence of the man shining through them like a beacon in the night.

These were not the hard, furtive eyes of a killer, nor the blank, glazed look of a brutish follower who would cut her down without thought. They were open, clear and well-spaced in a pleasant, rather craggy face that was cruelly marked with a long white scar that ran across his right cheek from jaw to hairline, the whole more seared by weather than the cares of command. That this man was the leader of the band of warriors that stood, or lounged about beyond her room, Brioni had absolutely no doubts whatever. Nevertheless she was determined to make a stand, and barring his entrance she shouted: "Take

215

one more step towards me and if my dogs do not tear out your throat, I will! You may be the friends of the people in this place, or you may not," she added in her bright, clear voice, never taking her eyes from his, the shining steel of her javelin marking his every move. "But you have Danes at your back, and no Dane is a friend to me. Now, speak, Saxon. Tell me who you are and what your business is!"

At the sound of her words, so boldly uttered, and the clipped tone of her voice, a frozen hush had fallen over everybody, as many watching the unwavering steel held firmly in her hands as were gazing in some awe at Bran and Utha. Both huge hounds filled the space with their bristling bodies and the snarling rage of their voices, their lips pulled back over teeth as terrifying as those of any wolf the men had seen.

The combination of brutish hounds and stalwart maiden, sword by her feet and spear in her hand, was enough to give any man pause for thought over action. And while some of the men behind him made as if to surge forward with growls of dissent and anger at such treatment of their leader, they were stilled into silence, and stillness. With a single gesture of his hand, the man filling the doorway with his massive frame and thick bearskin mantle, held them all in check.

To say that he was surprised at his reception was to put things mildly! Maritia's warm arms and her hot kisses were what he had expected…not to be faced down by this fierce-eyed girl, shapely and beautiful, who now threatened him with great hounds' teeth and shining steel, whose blue eyes were locked on his with hostile intensity and whose voice proclaimed her birth for all to hear.

He could probably take her quite easily, but it would not be without a struggle despite his size and experience, for she had placed herself just far enough back to make a quick lunge very dangerous, her spear point held perfectly balanced for just such a sudden thrust. Someone had trained her well.

And then there were her two enormous hounds!

Stood on either side of her, he had never seen such huge, vicious brutes. Bunched on their forepaws, ears back and mouths slavering, snarling and gnarling with their formidable fangs already bared, they were just waiting for her to release them. And judging from Maritia's smile, sitting demurely on her bed amidst all the hubbub, clearly he could expect no help from that quarter.

It was all very strange, for not only was Maritia undisturbed in any way…but he also instinctively liked this girl who now faced him down.

There was breeding and spirit in her voice and in her lovely face, and the way she held herself showed an unusual knowledge of arms, together with the courage and determination to use them. Without doubt she meant what she had said. If he made one careless or sudden move, she would release the two

216

hounds and try and split him with her spear. And between the three of them she just might succeed where countless Danes had tried and failed.

Holding his hands palm up towards her, he gently backed away, speaking as he moved: "My name is Leofric of Wimborne, some call me 'Iron Hand' for I am ruthless to my foes, and no man tells me nay. But my friends know my worth, and with those I always deal with justice and Christian values. I have no quarrel with you, or yours, and my men are not the bloody rievers that you think them to be. I mean no harm here."

"So, Leofric Iron Hand, of Wimborne," she threw back at him sharply, stabbing her javelin towards him as she spoke. "What do you here on my father's lands so far from your home, and with Danes at your back?"

"Your father's lands?" he quizzed her, moving his big hands to rest against his hips.

"*Don't move, you pirate!*" Brioni spat at him, her hounds baying at the snarl in her voice, the noise brutal in that small space. "Do that again," she added, threatening him with her spear again, "and it may be the last move you make. I am the Lady Brioni of Foxley, and my father, Thane Wulfstan of the King's Council, owns all that you can see here from Malmesbury tump to Corston Heath. Or did until the Black Jarl of Helsing and his Danish curs tore out his life. *Danes*, Leofric *Wolfshead*!" she raged bitterly as the full realisation of what he truly was hit her at last, her eyes blazing with sudden hatred. "*Just like the ones who stand behind your back!*"

Leofric watched her with every caution and was impressed.

This was no common wench who confronted him, but one of the best the county possessed, and close to the King. No wonder she had knowledge of arms, and held herself so bravely. He had troubles enough without tangling with anyone so close to the King…yet that very closeness might aid him in his quest.

"So…I am proclaimed 'Wolfshead' now am I?" he mocked her gently. "I, whose blood is no less pure than your own. What makes you think so?"

"I have heard of you. A little, you bandit! A word here and there in the King's royal chamber."

"So, you are close to the King also?"

"To the Queen, the Lady Ealhswitha, I am her most favoured handmaid, and thus well known to our Lord King as well. You harm me at your peril!"

"'King' now in name only," he replied harshly, "for Wessex has fallen and Alfred has gone, no man knows where. It is Guthrum who now rules in his place, King of the Danes, with the Lord Oscytel by his side…"

*"How do you know that?"* Brioni snarled at him sharply, her eyes narrowed to slits of pure venom. "What doings do you have with that..that *animal?"*

"I have Danes in my command, as you can see, and I speak their language. My nurse was a Danish girl whom my mother fostered. She taught me. My men have been into Chippenham, they know what has happened," and he dropped his hands to his side. "But Oscytel is no friend to me, of that I assure you, and his Jomsvikings are some of my most bitter enemies!"

That mention of the Black Jarl in those last few moments distracted her, and her spear point shifted from his face. Now, he could take her. And though her great hounds were still a problem, his armour should protect him long enough for his men to deal with them.

Brioni almost looked away, but Bran and Utha had not dropped their guard an instant, and suddenly growled deeply and hunched their shoulders as if they could sense what was in the mind of the big warrior who stood so nonchalantly before them, and Brioni's stance suddenly stiffened.

"Oscytel is my bitter enemy too," she said, turning swiftly back towards him, her mouth a pale slash in the sudden whiteness of her face. "He murdered my whole family and smashed my home to fragments. I have sworn a blood-oath to destroy him. How came you, a noble man given to command, to be proclaimed 'Wolfshead'?" she demanded of him, taking a pace back to maintain an even distance between them.

"Raid, counter raid and flight. It is an old story, Brioni of Foxley. A greedy noble of Prince Aethelwold's retinue, the late king's son, coveted my father's lands around Wimborne where King Aethelred, his father, is buried. He and his hirelings slew my father in a sudden night attack. I, younger and more rash in those days, killed him in return and the Prince's elders had me named 'Wolfshead', Outlaw, and I was forced to flee.

"Since then the Danes have turned Wessex upside down, and my war-band has grown, both with Danish fighters disaffected by the wars, whom I would trust with my life; as well as masterless Saxon warriors who have joined me for plunder and a fresh start under a new lord. Here, with Hugo, who is my good friend, I can find some respite from the fighting which has claimed so many lives. We go where the Danes are, and make their lives a misery wherever we can find them; that is why two of my men are injured.

"When this madness is over I intend to seek the King, wherever he may be, and have the record set straight and regain my father's rights as 'Thane'. Until then I and my men must live as best we may. Now, Brioni of Foxley, will you let me pass? I mean no harm here, as I said, and these people are my friends," he gestured broadly around him with his arms, especially to Maritia who throughout this had sat sleekly curled up on her bed with a smile on her face. Brioni looked at him more calmly and liked what she saw.

Anyone proclaimed 'Wolfshead' by Aethelwold was full worthy of consideration. That young man, though still of tender years, was a thorn in his royal uncle's side, and what her father had had to say about those around him as 'advisors' did not make pleasant listening.

Besides, clearly Maritia and her father trusted him...could she do any less? The presence of so many Danes in his war-band would warrant further talk, but for the time being she was prepared now to give him the benefit of the doubt. And, apart from anything else, she had a mission of her own to fulfil, and getting herself killed here for nothing would not further her aims.

The man had style and presence; he was a proven warrior with fighting men to back him and, with luck and some guile of her own maybe, she might even persuade him to adopt her cause. Stranger things had happened; look how she had met with Maritia. And, like with her, she felt strongly drawn to the man despite the manner of their meeting. There was that in him that called to a maid, and she was feminine enough for her to want him for herself.

It was enough!

Dropping her spear point, she stepped back, Bran and Utha following suit so that everyone relaxed, and looking up at him she gave Leofric a dazzling smile that made him blink and grin suddenly in immediate response.

Certainly she was a stunning creature, and without hesitation he stepped quickly forward before she could change her mind, and clasped her boldly to him, while his men crowded around them both with shouts of praise and hearty laughter. It had been a tense few minutes that could have gone either way; now they could all relax and enjoy the kind of boisterous hospitality for which Hugo the Bearmaster was famous.

\*

*D*elighted by the manner of their meeting, Maritia fought her way through the milling press of hounds and sweaty warriors to throw her arms around Leofric's brawny shoulders and clamour for a kiss. Her plans for him and Brioni were working far better than she had dared to hope for.

The only fly in the ointment was Velda!

Yet surely the woman could only complete Maritia's triumph? All it needed was for her to come up from her bothy across the clearing and join them...then Leofric would see what a jewel he had unwittingly laid his hands on, for there was no comparison between the two women. Not only that but

219

from what little she had seen of Brioni's mettle, there was no way that she would now stand aside and calmly stomach that woman's rude coarseness, especially if she stood in the way of her own destiny, and the blood oath she had sworn on her father's body. And once having set eyes on such pure-bred, fiery beauty there was no way, either, that Leofric would continue to put up with Velda's base lewdness.

But there was only one way that such a situation could be resolved. The custom of her people laid that down, a custom that Leofric knew well and had long accepted, and Maritia was determined that when the fight came, the Lady Brioni of Foxley would be the outright victor.

Leofric deserved a better mate than Velda would, or could ever be, and if he was to win the recognition, and the free pardon from the king that was rightly his, then he needed Brioni by his side. Her royal connections, her loving support and her natural loyalty and ancient breeding would do more for him than anything else. Loving them both as she did, even though she had only known Brioni for a few days, what more could she possibly hope for than to set them both on the road to lifelong happiness and freedom?

Long she had waited for someone like Brioni to come forward to challenge Velda for Leofric Iron Hand's place beside him. Brioni was the perfect foil for all his hopes. Somehow their fortunes were all bound in with one another, their destinies inextricably entwined...and she for one was delighted.

The future beckoned them, and it was right that they should all go on together.

## Chapter Thirty

**B**rioni felt engulfed by the man, swallowed up in his embrace, her face buried in his great bearskin, her body crushed against his armoured chest, bound into him by the power of his arms against which there was no possible hope of struggling free.

The man was like an oak, ribbed muscles everywhere, and legs like hewn timber. She felt utterly helpless...and revelled in it. She hadn't felt quite so safe since her father had last greeted her, aeons ago it seemed now, when she had returned from Chippenham. And she liked the warm feel of his breath on the nape of her neck that sent a shiver down her spine, and the pressure of his hands across her back. But, despite her immediate feelings, she was not to be won over quite so easily, and drawing back her foot she gave his shin a hefty kick with her heavy boots.

With a sharp yowl of unexpected pain he let her go and furiously rubbed his leg where she had kicked him, while the men who had gathered to his shoulder laughed heartily and thumped his shoulders.

"So, Brioni of Foxley," he said grinning ruefully, hopping on one leg and then another as he rubbed them with his hands, "that was ill-deserved, you little hellcat...but may we be friends at least, now that you have put down your arms? By the saints, you are a fierce one and no mistake. I wonder the Queen of Wessex lets you anywhere near her bower for fear of scaring her other ladies from their stitchery! I had not expected so warlike a reception in the hall of my old friend, Hugo the Bearmaster."

"And I, Leofric Iron Hand, am no hellcat, for I can purr far more than I yowl," she replied boldly, with her hands on her hips. "But I did not expect to find Danes waiting to greet me either," she added with biting sarcasm. "And Queen Ealhswitha has never seen me with weapons in my hand. I was not like this in Alfred's court. Oscytel changed all that for me, as I have told you.

"But tell me, you great Wolfshead, how come you have so many of the sea robbers in your war-band? And what are you doing here so close to the King's hall in Chippenham? How came you to meet with Maritia and her father? And why do you, too, talk of Oscytel as an enemy? There are many things you have to tell me, Saxon, before I will give you my hand in friendship."

"And so he shall, my little lady," a great voice boomed across at them. "And so he shall, just as soon as I can clear this motley collection of lazy

221

warriors and loutish horse thieves out of my daughter's chambers!" And surging through the opening to Maritia's chamber, scattering aside the men who were standing there, Hugo flung his arms round Leofric's brawny shoulders, and banged his fists against his back.

"Ho there, you big ox!" he greeted him warmly, crushing the life out of him with his good arm as he did so. "My, but it does an old man's eyes good to see you so young and strong," adding with a twinkle to his daughter, "when his own strength is leaving him behind so quickly!" Then turning his head to take note of Brioni standing quietly by Leofric's side he added: "I see you have met my little forest waif who came so helpless to my encampment last night. I hope you have been kind to her, you big lump, for she is all alone in this world now and badly needs your assistance."

"Kind to her, Hugo?" Leofric replied in mock outrage, as his men burst out laughing. "This little 'waif' of yours damn near spitted me before I had taken twenty paces past your entrance!" Adding with a broad smile: "And as for that Jezebel standing there before you, looking so meek and mild, she just sat on her bed and grinned. I might have had the whole Danish host before me for all she cared!"

"And quite rightly so too, you hound!" Maritia threw back at him swiftly, throwing her arm around Brioni's shoulder, and looking up into his face with a mocking smile. "Bursting into a maiden's chamber so unceremoniously. Just what were you hoping for, may I ask?"

"Not a spitting Valkyrie, that's for certain," Leofric replied. "Though a kiss for my pains in not wrapping a certain little lady's spear shaft round her pretty neck would go a long way to soothing my wounded pride...not to mention my throbbing shin which she so heartily kicked a moment ago," he added, rubbing his leg again.

"Give you a kiss indeed!" Brioni answered him with mock outrage. "I had rather box your ears for your impertinence. That I, Brioni of Foxley, should give such a pirate as you a kiss is unthinkable," she added haughtily. "Nevertheless, you did show some courage I suppose," she went on, now smiling up at him again. "So bend your face for me, my Lord Leofric Iron Hand of Wimborne," she said meltingly, "and I will grant your request." And with a wicked grin at Maritia, she reached her hands up to Leofric's face, caressed his cheeks with her finger tips, and then kicked him hard on his other leg.

"See there, you robber!" she said, laughing as he fell about again with a shout of pain. "You wolfshead pirate, that's what I call a maiden's kiss. Obviously the Saxon girls who live around here are not made of such stern stuff as I have become!" she went on, as Leofric hopped up and down again,

222

fiercely rubbing his leg, tears of anguish in his handsome eyes; while his men howled with mirth and slapped each other on the back at the way she had outwitted him.

Hugo threw back his head and roared aloud, slapping his thigh, doubled-up with laughter. "I can see you two will get on famously," he said, tears in his eyes also. "Now, Leofric come away out of this hell hole that my daughter is pleased to call her room, and sit down with me. You girls, too, must come and join us. There is a deal to talk about, I can assure you, and I never think well standing up. Besides, you must have as great a thirst on you as I have, hunger too I am sure. Gilbert has prepared some kind of meal against your coming so let's get to it before anyone begins to wonder from what it has been made!"

And sweeping all before him, like shooing sheep into a dipping pen, Hugo hustled Leofric, Maritia, Brioni and the four or five men who were still standing there, back through the narrow opening in the tent side, and so back to the more expansive living area beyond.

*

The food that Gilbert and the men of Hugo's troop laid before them, thick lamb steaks with roasted vegetables and coarse bread, was a sufficient breakfast for twice their number, so all ate heartily. And as no-one had eaten for some little while, there was a period of intense silence round the long table as they all gorged themselves; finishing off their meal with goats' cheese and late stored apples, all washed down with hot spiced ale and beer.

But before long the conversation was flowing again, Leofric explaining what his men were doing in the great wood, and why there were Danish warriors in his war-band.

"Not all Danes are pagans, my Lady...just as not all Saxons are Christian, as I am; as are most of those who are with me. But there are many Danes who long for peace, have been wronged as I have been, and have no love for what their fellow Danes are doing to Wessex. They will fight for peace, and see Alfred as a better provider than Guthrum; they see our Christian God as more powerful than their own. They are with me to a man! Now, my Lady," he said fixing her with a warm smile, "it is time and more that you told me what you are doing here, and why you talked so bitterly about Oscytel."

With a sigh, Brioni rubbed her eyes with the palms of her hands, then, looking round at his commanders and into his green eyes, she told him what had happened at Foxley three nights before, of the destruction of her home and

223

the foul killing of her father, his men following her every word with harsh grunts of rage and startled comments for her actions during the attack.

"So, it was the Black Jarl himself who led the assault on your home?" Leofric said when she had finished, rolling his horn beaker between his big hands.

"Yes! It was his son whom my brother slew, so the father came seeking revenge, destroyed my home, butchered my whole family and carved the Blood Eagle from my father's back. Where there had been life he left a desert."

"Aye, it would be so with that man. And only he would dare such an obscenity after Guthrum banned it at Wareham. As I said earlier," he added with grim definition, "that man and his Jomsvikings are no friends of mine!"

"Why?" Brioni asked swiftly, her eyes fixed on his.

"He attacked a homestead after Wareham, before I came here; as the Danes fled to Exeter. A place that was special to me, from my green days, before my father was slain. They were unprepared, and his men broke in with fearsome violence and in their ravaging they brutalised one who was very dear to me at that time. I had word of their doings and arrived with my men just as they were leaving. We fought his Jomsvikings with all our fury and they fled before our battle-storm...but we were too late to save the family," he ended, his voice dropping as he spoke.

"I am so sorry, Leofric," Brioni said, reaching out to clasp his hand. "And the one who was dear to you?"

"There was nothing anyone could do. I had loved her dearly, but my outlawry by Aethelwold put her beyond me. They had used her horribly. She died in my arms, poor lass." And turning towards her he said quietly: "I have not loved a maid since. Despite all my strength, I failed her. So, the Black Jarl is no friend of mine, I assure you. Like you, I am committed to his death. How was it with you at Foxley?"

"The same; they butchered everyone. It was beyond awful. Every man, woman and child, the little ones worst of all, and I was forced to watch it all from the steading's midden, buried in all that filth up to my eyes. Watched my mother fall beneath my father's seaxe, and all my family killed. My poor father last of all. Wounded, captured and disarmed, then flung down in the dirt and hacked open like a pig at the autumn slaughter. I can still hear his cries in my head," she ended, her eyes full of tears, the whole table stilled by her words.

"Was that when you made your oath?" Leofric asked her gently, turning his hand over to hold hers in his firm grasp.

"Yes. At that moment my whole life changed. All that had gone before was as nothing. I made my oath then to the ancient gods of our people. I don't

224

know from where the words came, but they flowed out of me as If I had known them all my life. And as I marked my body with my father's blood, I felt a great power surge through me. I felt as if all my ancestors were beside me giving me the strength and courage to see it through…"

"But you are only a girl," Hugo interrupted her. "Oscytel is a great Danish war-lord, Guthrum's right hand man."

"Has been so since the Vikings came from Repton in '74," Leofric added grimly. "The same year they drove the wretched Burghred out of Mercia! Oscytel was considered a king then, almost equal to Guthrum, with an army of his own at his back. An army of Jomsvikings, the most feared and determined pagan warriors of all, who have dedicated their lives to warfare and the slaughter of all who stand against them. They take an oath of death to their leader, and will die to the last man if he falls, rather than leave the battlefield.

"As my warriors do to me," Leofric said calmly, turning first to look at Brioni, seated beside him, and then at his officers all around him, each one intent on his every word. "I support them in all things; I reward them with arm rings of gold and silver and we divide all the spoils of war equally amongst us according to our standing. But, like Oscytel, I am the sole leader of my war-band, and will defy anyone who challenges me, even to the death if need be. There can be but one leader of the pack. I may seek advice, but I alone determine where we go and what we do," he added, looking firmly into her eyes. "And to whom we give our support. Once that has been decided all must follow my lead or be declared '*Nithing*' and cast out."

She looked again into his green eyes, the golden flecks within them sparkling from the braziers around the edges of the long dais, the rain still rattling on the thick canvas of the main pavilion…and her heart quailed. She knew so little of this extraordinary man. Yet instinctively she liked him, and she believed that he liked her too. But to ask for his help now, on the first day of their meeting? Was that not a step too far?

She looked from his face to those of his officers: to Trausti and Finnar, Raedwald and Beornred…and to Hugo, sitting in his great chair, a vast bear of a man whose periwinkle eyes were still, watchful, studying her with firm appraisal beneath a faintly raised eyebrow of query and intrigue. As if daring her to ask for the help she so desperately needed. And then to Maritia, seated beside her father at the opposite end of the table, whose look clearly told her it was her decision, and hers alone.

That in this matter no advice would be forthcoming.

And taking a deep breath, looking directly at the big Saxon war-leader beside her she said: "I am committed to the destruction of Oscytel by whatever means comes to my hand, as you say you are too. I was supposed to have been

225

betrothed this Twelfth Night passed, to a Saxon thane named Heardred, one of Alfred's closest men. But that never happened, and now it is all over between us. I have sworn a blood-oath to God Himself, and to the gods of my people by which I am now tightly bound. I must keep faith, I can do no other. My family have always served the Kings of Wessex since first we settled at Foxley in the days of King Ine, and I am Woden born, as is the right line of Cerdic from which King Alfred sprang, so I am the King's 'man' to the death. But I cannot fight the Black Jarl on my own. You are right in that, Hugo," she went on, glancing across to where the Bearmaster sat looking at her, as he acknowledged her words with a dip of his head and a slight smile.

"To avenge my family and cancel the oath I made, I need help. And not that of an absent king who has been forced to flee his enemies and may even be dead for all I know. I need the help of a proven warrior, and of his men. Help that I can pay for with my father's gold..." and there was a bustling stir around the table at that, for none knew of her father's treasure. "And, for those who want it, with land from my father's estates, and," she added in a final appeal, "with the help of King Alfred whom I know, freedom from outlawry once the Heathen have been defeated," and there was a wild shout at that from every fighting man around that table, even from Leofric, who then banged his hands on the table for silence.

"So, my Lady Brioni of Foxley," he said after the room had quieted, fixing her eyes with a firm stare, "it is my help you ask for, and that of my men?"

"Yes, my Lord Leofric of Wimborne," she said formally, laying her hand on his arm as she spoke. "It is your help I ask for in the king's name. Alfred may be down, but he is not 'out'! He may have been forced out of Chippenham, but I must believe that he is still alive, and free.

"It is my belief that together we can harry the Danes wherever they may be, and build an army of stout warriors that we can bring to the Spring Muster at Ecberht's Stone, east of Selwood. This I know Alfred had planned for some time after Easter, and if we then join with the king to create an army that can drive the Danes from Wessex...then who knows what good things may not come out of that?"

"That is some belief, my Lady," Leofric replied, looking down at her, a half smile on his rugged face. "And you would ride with us, I suppose?"

"It is the King's belief, my Lord Leofric," she replied sharply, her eyes fixed on his, "that only by fighting the Danes at every turn of the track; by making them pay in blood for every Saxon they slay, that we can rid our land of these," she paused then as she looked around the table, "these *pagans* that infest our homes. These wild ravens who have flocked from overseas and turn

226

our people into carrion for their feasting! And, yes!" she added, banging her fist down on the table as she had seen her father do on so many occasions, "I believe that if we make some noise in this part of Wessex that the King will be sure to hear of it, and will richly reward all those who have made it."

"If the King lives!" Hugo replied swiftly.

*"Of course the King lives!"* she answered him fiercely, her eyes flashing. "Though God knows where! All will be revealed in due course, of that I am certain. Were he dead surely all the world would know it by now!"

"And when is the muster, my Lady?" Leofric asked her then.

"I don't know. Easter is on March 23$^{rd}$, for Bishop Asser who advises the King told me so. So it will be in the spring, or maybe early summer. May perhaps? When the ground is drier and before the sea-lanes open."

"Yes," Leofric replied slowly. "Before the sea-lanes open, you are so right," he added, impressed with her comment, "when Guthrum can massively reinforce his army from Frankland, especially as he is now the overall King of all the Vikings fighting in Wessex."

"So now he outranks Oscytel?" Brioni asked him urgently. "They are no longer joint Kings of the Great Army?"

"Oh no. Oscytel may be the leader of the Jomsvikings, their 'King'. But Guthrum wields the greater force by far, so he commands the greater respect. He is truly King over all, especially since he forced Alfred into the wilderness and seized Wessex. Now others will flock to his standard. So, you would be right; Alfred must bring his enemies to battle before that can happen. You are a good tactician, my Lady. The King would be proud of you."

"Not just the King. My father was a member of his war-council for many years, and I am a good listener."

"But what of you, my Lady?" Leofric said, repeating his earlier question. "Would you ride with us?"

"Where you go, there go I also! I am no milksop maiden. I can wield a sword and hold my place in the battle-line as I did at Foxley, and camp under the stars as I have with the King's grace on occasions; I can stitch a wound as easily as I can sew a fine seam and blood does not make me faint. You will not find me lacking in spirit, nor in humour, and campfire talk does not make me blush. And if you will neither aid me, nor take me with you, then I shall have to pursue my quest as best I may on my own, for I will not have any man say me 'nay!', any more than you would, my Lord," she ended, her eyes as fiercely set upon his own as ever eagle fixed its eyes upon its prey. Then, turning, she looked back down the table at Hugo with a swift tilt of her head and a smile, while all around her Leofric's men broke into wild discourse:

"Impossible!"

227

"No woman can hope to hold her place in the shield wall."

"She would slow us down!"

"But she is friend to the King, and has treasure to share with us…"

"And land for farming!"

"We could all be freemen again…"

"And honourable!"

"What about Velda?" Beornred said, bringing his hand down with a sharp bang on the table top. "This is all fine talk, Leofric…but what about Velda?" And there was sudden silence around the table.

# Chapter Thirty Oneg

"Who is this Velda?" Brioni asked sharply, looking at the men's faces. "And what has she to say about this? Lord Leofric is your leader. Surely it is his word that carries the day? Not even my Lady mother would interfere with what my father said. Thane Wulfstan's word was law at Foxley. Surely it must be so with you also?"

"Velda Gaerwulf is the Headwoman of the outlaw village you saw when you arrived yesterday,"

"So!" Brioni said, bitterly, turning to Maritia. "I was right! Those cotts and bothies I spied as you and I arrived last night are a nest of outlaws that has hidden itself in this clearing. There is no real village. I thought as much when I came through yesterday. They are all Wolfsheads...and you just talked to me of masterless men!"

"No!" Maritia said sharply, breaking into the conversation and laying her hand on Brioni's arm. "They are not all outlaws...but they are masterless men, those who have fled from the Danes and from absent lords who have no care for their people. Men who have put their families before their rents, and have been declared Wolfsheads by the Shire Moots. Velda's husband was one such, Thatcher Gaerwulf. He made himself their leader, but he was killed fighting the Shire Reeve's men in a squalid brawl, and she took on the responsibility from him. Now she wields great power over the villagers, on whom Leofric relies for many things. And some of his men have taken women to themselves from amongst her people."

"So, this Velda runs an illegal village on my father's land, on my land now that he and my brother have been slain, and she holds the people in the hollow of her hand. What has this to do with me and Leofric riding out together to fight Oscytel?" And she looked around the table with fierce eyes, while the men shuffled themselves awkwardly in their seats and Hugo smiled at Leofric with his head on one side.

"Do I tell her, my brave Saxon war-lord...or do you?"

"Tell me what?"

"About Leofric and Velda," Maritia said quietly.

"Well?" Brioni asked penetratingly, looking up at Leofric's face.

"Oh, very well, my Lady of Foxley," he said heavily, his green eyes troubled. "It is a well-known tale enough, I suppose," and he sighed. Then, looking down at her, he said: "After Emma died..."

"...The one who was very dear to you?" Brioni interrupted him, quietly.

"Yes. I loved her with all my heart, and afterwards I had no interest in anyone special; took things as they came. Fought the Danes because I hated them for what they had done to Emma and her family, without really thinking about Wessex, or its King whose nephew had dispossessed me. And I enjoyed the fighting. Killing Danes and taking booty was good for me...and for the men who gathered around me. A successful war-lord soon collects men to him like bees to a rose in bloom, and my hoard is good."

"Then he met me," Hugo broke in with a smile, "and came here, and settled with his men...and so he met Velda. She is a force to be reckoned with, and rules her people fiercely. So her good will was important, and Leofric was 'convenient' to her, and she to him. Some of his men took women from her village, and her people have been good to them."

"And so you took her to your bed," she said bitingly to Leofric, with a look of disdain.

"That may have been so...but I am not bound to her in any formal way," he added swiftly, "and she does not fight by my side. I and my men go where we will. She does not attend our war-council. Trausti here," he said, turning to the big Dane beside him, "Finnar, Raedwald and Beornred are my closest advisors. But my word is always final, and they have learned to trust my judgement."

"So, this Velda is in some sort your 'consort'," Brioni said then with a sneer, snatching her hand away from him. "But she neither fights by your side nor takes her place in your councils. She is nothing but a 'bedspread'," she added dismissively, "and you, my Lord Leofric are no different from my brother, Gyrth, in that you use women for your gratification...not for the care and wisdom they bring with them.

"My father never treated my Lady mother so. He respected her advice which he always sought. He may not always have taken it, but he knew better than to ignore her...and all men deferred to her. She was honest, true and deeply loved by all at Foxley. Is that so with this Velda Gaerwulf?" she asked contemptuously, looking at Maritia and Hugo, and then on around the table, her eyes diamond bright. "Or does she rule with fear and loathing? Threatening with banishment those she takes against, or will not do her bidding. Driving them out from even this poor safety," she added, gesturing towards the village beyond the pavilion in which they were seated, still rattled by the wind and rain outside.

"With fear and loathing, Brioni!" Maritia said sharply, before any other could speak. "And an intemperance that gets worse with every passing day. She is lewd and coarse and her language is vile like her behaviour. She is no consort for the rightful Lord of Wimborne. She is no better than a common

230

trull, a doxy of the worst sort," she said fiercely, "and my heart writhes that Leofric ever bent his eyes to her. And so I have told him!"

"True, her people help Leofric and his war-band. But there are many I am sure who would do no less in return for the protection of his strong right arm, and those of his men, without the need for Velda. But until now there has been nothing to fight for beyond Danish scalps and booty."

"Now," Hugo broke in once more, leaning to where Brioni sat opposite him. "God willing you can give him a purpose that before has been entirely lacking. Now, if my good friend will accept your challenge and join with you to fight for Alfred, and against Oscytel, then he will have a goal to aim for. And all his men will benefit, for the badge of outlawry, of being Wolfsheads, with every man's hand against them until death, can then be lifted by the King himself. And *nothing* beats that!"

"Least of all Velda, my Lord," Trausti said, leaning across the table towards the big Saxon war-leader, now sitting back in his high-backed chair while the conversation flowed around him, his face turning this way and that. "We who fight by your side have watched you these past months and know that you desire better. That what before might have been convenient, even amusing, has now long palled. I have seen you wince at her speech, and her manners, in a way you did not when first you met with her."

"Aye," Beornred rumbled in his deep voice, speaking for the first time. "I, too, have watched you, my friend. This Velda has been but a distraction. Amusing at times, it is true, but lately she has taken to abusing your name amongst us, and amongst her people. She forgets who you truly are, Leofric. It is time for a change, and it seems to me that the coming of the Lady Brioni amongst us is a sign from the gods that you must move on. And be assured, my friend, that we will follow you. We are your 'hounds' and will bay for the blood of your enemies. Be the huntsman we know you to be, Leofric. Let the Lady Brioni be your whipper-in, and we will hunt that wild boar, Oscytel, to his lair and there destroy him!"

"Then why is Velda a problem?" Brioni asked sitting forward once more. "I do not seek your body, my Lord Leofric, though God knows there is enough of it," she added as she and the men around her laughed. "That is not my need. It is your men I need and your fighting arm and bold courage. If no man tells you 'nay!'...then how may any one woman do so?"

"It is not that, Brioni," Maritia said then, holding her hands out to her new friend. "It has become accepted that the Headwoman and the War-leader should be together, as one. She may not fight beside him, but he cannot leave with you beside him either!"

"*What?*" she cried out, enraged. "He cannot take me with him without his doxy's say-so? I, who am true Woden born and favoured by the king, and on whose land she and her people squat? When my father's halidom, and his treasure, will have been used to make this new 'war' possible? No! and *No!*" she shouted then, leaping up, pushing her stool over as she did so. "What manner of woman is this to whom I must be so beholden?"

"She is a coarse bully, of little virtue and no wit!" Hugo snarled then from his place at the far end of the dais. "And all men know it," he added, looking around the table fiercely, and at Leofric who had not spoken since Brioni had leaped up. "I have said so myself to Leofric, and to Finnar and Beornred also. Trausti here has had more than one run-in with her, Raedwald also. Her language is foul and her manners loathsome. For all that she is a handsome woman, and strong. She almost slew the last challenger for her place, for that is the only way that things can change."

"Someone must challenge Velda for her place beside the war-leader," Beornred growled deeply, drinking from his ale horn, "and no-one has dared to do so since she took her chains to young Sylvia's flesh at the time of the autumn slaughter. Her she marked for life, mauling her so badly that it was a miracle she lived. Since then none has dared, and everyone suffers because of it!"

"What? And you men allowed it?"

"That is the custom," Hugo replied dryly. "The women must fight it out!"

"*Faugh!* I never heard so much nonsense," Brioni snarled. "That degrades all who are involved. Bringing cool decision-making down to the level of a common cat-fight; an unseemly brawl between slatterns that can be witnessed in any alehouse after a hard night's drinking! A spectacle for men to ogle, and decent women to avoid like the plague itself. And you would have me engage in such a wild bout to secure the help I need? Help that you all agree would be right, and fruitful, just to satisfy some strange custom that I have never heard of? Is that how it must be?"

"If you were Velda," Raedwald asked gruffly, "and like to lose your man to another, be she the daughter of a thane or a common herdsman, wouldn't you fight?"

"This is different," Brioni replied angrily, banging her hand on the table again before reaching for her stool and sitting down. "This is not for the love and body of the war-leader. To that she is welcome! This is about Wessex, and the death of Oscytel. About Alfred and the return of honour and the lands of Leofric's fathers."

232

"All that may be true, my Lady," Hugo said quietly. "But what do lands and honour mean to one such as Velda Gaerwulf? She will see that her man is going off to war in the company of another, and another younger, more beautiful and infinitely more wealthy than she can ever hope to be. What does she have beyond the walls of those poor cotts and bothies beside the stream? She may not rule wisely, or even well, but she does rule...and to lose Leofric will destroy her in the eyes of all those who tremble before her. And many do. So, yes, she will fight."

"Dear God, what have I got myself into?" Brioni groaned, dropping her head into her hands. "I thought I was come amongst friends. Now I am being pressed into a fight that is not of my choosing, nor of my desiring. Oscytel has much to answer for beyond the deaths of my family. Now I must fight again just to have the right to claim a place by your side," she added, turning to Leofric who had been silent throughout the flow of talk. "What if I should lose?"

"Then you will have been judged unworthy," he replied calmly, looking at her beside him.

"Unworthy?" Brioni gasped. *"Unworthy?"*

"Yes, unworthy. You made an oath to the gods of your people, and to God, yes?"

"Yes."

"Then this struggle with Velda is part of that oath. You cannot fight Oscytel without help, you want...no, *need*...my help," he answered harshly. "My men to stand beside you in that fight, that all men know must cause the deaths of many. Are they to stand forth for an untried girl? Be she the Lady Brioni of Foxley or no. They have heard how bravely you fought with Oscytel's men. How you witnessed the deaths of your family and swore a blood-oath in your father's blood.

"That they know. Now is the time to prove your courage and the rightness of your cause. You fight...and I *will* pledge my men and their courage to your cause, and together we will go out and destroy Oscytel, and do our best to keep Alfred on the throne of Wessex. And trust that in so doing he will give us the pardons we shall have earned. *Do you acclaim that?*" he shouted to his leaders around the table.

*"Aye, we acclaim that!"* they all shouted in return, standing as they did so, and raising their drinking horns in sudden wild assent.

"So be it, then," Brioni agreed, standing up and lifting her own horn beaker to the men around her. "What my Lady mother would think of my behaviour I dread to think. She would think me wanton in the extreme, though

233

my father would never have me back down from a challenge. That is not what a Foxley does! My brother also would acclaim my decision.

"So, my Lord Leofric of Wimborne, I take up the challenge," she said, turning towards Leofric, her blue eyes blazing into his green ones. "If Velda shall stand against my journeying with you, or challenge my place in your warband by your side, then I shall take up arms to defend my right!"

And standing she raised her horn high and shouted: " *Drink hael!*" And to the banging of his men's hands on the table, and their returned shouts of "*Drink hael! Drink hael!*" and the beating of their feet on the dais, she drank deeply and sat down again beside Leofric, looking up to smile back at Maritia who clapped her riotously.

\*

*T*hroughout all of this Leofric had taken the time to study the girl beside him. There was no denying that he was fast becoming quite captivated by her. Not only was she undeniably beautiful, but she had more fighting spirit in her than many thanes that he could think of. Noble men who were more concerned with their estates and welfare than fighting the Danes who threatened to swallow up all Wessex. Certainly she had more raw courage than any woman he had ever come across, especially his Emma who would have been appalled by the very thought of fighting in a battle. Something that with this girl simply made her eyes sparkle. Besides, there was a graceful, almost regal quality about the way she moved and held herself that proclaimed her breeding, and in her eyes there was a bright flame that drew him like a moth to a candle.

She was as different from Velda as a wolf was to a badger!

Passion, desire, a quick, hungry mind and a sense of destiny that made her irresistible to him; it seemed almost as if time and space had conspired to draw the two of them together. There was a strange 'rightness' about their meeting that seemed to defy all the usual conventions that governed their society. How strange that Oscytel's destruction of Foxley should have drawn them together, and he thought at once of Emma, and what that man had caused to be done to her. Now, here was another maiden needing his help and protection and this time he would not arrive too late, and reaching down he took her hand and squeezed it, her fingers wrapping around his instinctively as he did so, while he said quietly: "I will not fail you!"

\*

234

*M*aritia, watching them from the corners of her eyes as she listened to her father and Beornred talking with Trausti and Raedwald about the sudden push into Wessex that Guthrum's army had just carried out, smiled as she saw his hand take Brioni's in a firm grasp. Amazed though she was by the turn events had taken in so short a space of time since they had met she, too, realised that there were forces at work in both of them of which she had but little understanding. Brought up in Neustria she had never, for herself, experienced the horror of a Viking raid. Though she had witnessed the destruction they could wreak, by God's Grace she had not herself been touched by them in the way that both Leofric and Brioni had been.

Clearly this was the beginning of something for which the Fates alone were responsible, and where they were concerned anything might happen. That Velda would fight was beyond doubt. She had too much to lose not to do so, as her father had said! The question was not 'if', but 'when', it all depended on how soon Velda found out about it, and though she could see that in many ways she was responsible for bringing Leofric and Brioni together, what happened next was largely beyond her control.

The gods would decide.

# Chapter Thirty Two

*I*n fact Maritia was wholly correct, for word had already been swiftly brought to Velda of where Leofric was, and that he was closely engrossed with another girl, though not whom that other girl was.

According to her informant, she was nothing but a cheap hussy who had come in from beyond to serve Maritia, had taken one look at Leofric and since that moment had not been able to keep her cow's eyes off him. Nor her hands either. Pressing her firm young body against him, so she had been told with much excitement, and encouraging him to fondle her as intimately as it was possible to do so without tearing off her clothes. A succulent little piece, by all accounts, with long legs, a tight little arse and tits enough to make a strong man's eyes water.

Well, the little besom would soon learn who was the most important she-wolf in *this* forest! Aye, and she would let Leofric know just what she thought of him too! Just one more swallow of the ale she had poured out for herself, or maybe two or three, and she would be ready to leave this miserable cottage that Leofric called a home when he was not with Hugo in his great pavilion.

By all the gods, but they would wonder what had blown in amongst them or her name was not Velda Gaerwulf. She would tear the tits off the one and mash the balls of the other if she had her way. Oh yes! By St Swithun, they would all soon know how she felt about the situation. Leofric, Hugo, Beornred, Trausti and all his fine friends. They would soon know!

And being of a bitterly jealous cast of mind, with a tongue of verjuice and a coarse manner to go with it, she was shortly on her way across from her wattle and plaster home on the other side of the clearing to confront them all, sloshing through the ford as she went, so the heavy leather chausses she had on were soon running with water and her boots thick with slushy mud and snow.

There had been other challenges to her position as the War-Leader's woman in the past, that trull, Sylvia, last autumn for one, and she had never had any problem in dealing with them before. Hers was a basic, earthy nature that had always matched a chord in Leofric's make-up, until recently. Since Sylvia the bond had seemed to be weakening, he not being so eager to bed her as before, and away from her side more often. This time she felt that whoever the unknown girl was with whom her man was sitting, so obviously enthralled, she was a greater threat to her domination of this area, and of the wolfshead leader who had found her there, than any other female who had crossed her path before.

And that was not to be tolerated.

So, by the time she reached the two guards whom Leofric had placed by the entrance of Hugo's great tent, she had succeeded in working herself up into such a frenzy of jealous rage, made fiercer by the quantity of strong beer that she had been drinking since first light, that nothing would have stopped her spilling her bile over everyone. There was something about that nut-brown froth that made everything seem so clear and simple, and easier to express herself in difficult situations like the one she now faced. So she had no hesitation as she approached the two burly warriors who now stood, with crossed spears and shields held high, barring the entrance against her.

"Where's the little bitch who thinks she can just walk in and steal my man from underneath my nose?" she shouted at them, infuriated beyond measure by their blank stares and seeming ignorance. "Out of my way, Cadoc, you stupid Welshman! And you, Ricberht, let me through I say, or your doxies will pay a bitter price when next you leave the village! No cheap hussy out of the wild lands is going to take the place of Velda Gaerwulf!"

"No, Mistress Velda. You may not pass!" the dark haired Welshman said firmly, blocking her way with his spear and shield locked together, Ricberht beside him. "Lord Leofric has said none are to pass without his say so."

" 'No, Mistress Velda!' " she lampooned his Welshness cruelly, tossing her head as she spoke. " 'You may not pass!' Idiot!" she shouted at him. "I am the Lord Leofric's woman, *of course I may pass!*" and throwing her arms upwards she forced her way past both men, confused by her determination and unwilling to injure her, and so forced her way to where everyone was now standing.

So the first sight Brioni had of her rival was of a wild-haired woman of some thirty years of age, dark locks straggling beneath a fleece-lined hood, strong of body, with a broad face and dark brown eyes, almost black, and flushed with rage. Her loose-limbed frame was heavy of flesh and bone and her handsome features were marred by coarseness and constant drinking, the skin of her face blotched, and there were two hectic fever spots on either cheek.

Dressed in scuffed leather trousers, cross-gartered to the knee, with a partially unlaced tunic of green linen beneath which her heavy breasts swagged down freely, she was nevertheless an arresting figure. Her long cloak of fleece-lined leather ran with water at every step, as she lurched across to confront Leofric, his two hapless guards following behind her.

Hearing the furious bustle of her arrival Leofric had at once risen, as had all the others around the table, except Hugo who had remained massively in his great chair, and with a gentle gesture he moved Brioni carefully to one side, where Maritia was swift to come across and join her.

"So, my fine Saxon war lord," the woman snarled up at him, throwing off her hood, eyes staring with jealous rage, hands thrust onto her broad hips. "Where's the 'fair maiden' whose hot, stinking hands have doubtless been reaching for your fat prick? Don't you glower at me, you whoremaster! I hear she offered you a feel of her wet hole and you couldn't wait to plumb it!" she leered at him, her eyes wide. "Or was it her tight little arse you fancied, my noble Lord of Wimborne?" she sneered, wagging her fingers at him. "You have taken mine often enough, you bastard!" And flinging off her cloak she turned away from him briefly, bending over to waggle her hips provocatively at the men around her, now seated in cold, embarrassed silence, while she fondled herself lewdly before them, unaware of the smouldering anger and disgust that was burgeoning in all those who were present.

"That's enough, Velda!" Leofric snapped at her fiercely, stepping off the dais and seizing her by the arm to pull her upright. "*Enough!* Leave your body alone, and still your foul clacking. We are all guests here, and you vilely dishonour Hugo's hospitality with such coarse behaviour."

"Leave me alone, you *Nithing!*" she shouted at him violently, snatching her arm out of his grip, ignoring the gasps of astonished anger that followed her wild outburst. "I thought you liked my big tits?" she shouted at him, shaking them at him lasciviously, her words slurring as she spoke. "Want to see them, my doting lord?" she continued loudly, ripping frenziedly at the remaining fastenings of her tunic. And scooping her breasts into her hands she held them out to his reddening gaze, while she preened their thickening teats with her thumb and forefinger, and the men looked on in appalled amazement.

"Aren't they more succulent than that dung-hill peasant's you've been fingering? Don't they tempt you, my Lord?" she moued at him, swaying her breasts in her hands, her tongue flicking in and out like a snake's. "D'y want to furrow me now so she can watch how it's done, the puling milk-worm? Here on the floor before your faithful followers, while they clap their hands in time to your strokes?" And flinging herself on the plaited matting she bumped and ground her hips against the floor, moaning in foul, mock ecstasy of their former mating.

Stepping forward again, Leofric grasped her hands and tore her off the ground, his face like stone, his eyes glittering dangerously as he swung her away from him and slammed her back on her feet.

"Cover yourself!" he rasped, tugging her chemise back across her open breasts, and sweeping her long cloak off the ground, flinging it around her as he spoke. "You disgust me when you behave in such a low and bestial fashion. I warned you of what would happen the next time you flung yourself about like a common whore," he snarled at her, shaking her violently. "You make me sick with your foul speech and disgusting barnyard manners. Had you been a man I would have killed you for what you have said of me this morning! But as it is I cannot.

"For one thing I do not make war on women…for another you are as close to being soused as any man I know. I wouldn't sully my hands with your silly life. But for now, Velda," he continued taking the woman firmly by her elbow and pushing her before him towards the entrance, "I cannot stand your vile contortions one moment longer. Our relationship has long been soured by your foul tempers, the bile in your mouth and your drinking. It is time to make an end. You were once warm-hearted, compassionate and loving, and I loved you for it. You have forfeited all that these many days past. There can be no further communion between us!" And turning her away, now open-mouthed and swaying on her feet before the iron faces of his commanders, and of Hugo's implacable stare, he frog-marched her to the two soldiers who had tried to prevent her entry.

"Cadoc, Ricberht, put down your weapons, and your shields, and take her out of my sight. Sober her up in the stream, that should cool her ardour! One more outburst like the last, and I shall take my horse-whip to her naked sides."

"You would not dare!" she screamed at him over Ricberht's shoulder, as the man moved her forward, her arms pinioned to her sides, her feet scrabbling on the matting. "You Saxon piss-pot! You miserable pig's turd!" she railed at him wildly. "Flog me at the common whipping post? Your sense of decency would not let you, and as for that blue-eyed jade, that low-born little whore whose weeping body you just can't wait to devour," she continued in an agonised wail of bitterness and spite, her words tumbling over themselves in her eagerness to spit them out. "I'll tear her breasts to pig's meat and shred her loins with my chains, as I did the last foul bitch you rutted with!"

And suddenly tearing herself free of Ricberht's hold, shoving Cadoc out of her way as she did so, she turned to face Leofric, her eyes fever-bright with madness, her hands clenched into fists and spittle running down her chin.

"You'd better look your fill of her, my so 'noble' Lord of Wimborne," she shouted at him with feral violence, her dark eyes evil slits of hatred in her face. "For when I have finished with her not even the dogs will lick her blood, or piss upon her grave, for I shall cast her shattered body into the Black

239

Swamp, and still alive, or dead, I care not, for she shall perish and vanish as if she had never been born!"

*

All this time Brioni, with Maritia beside her, had been watching Velda in amazement, appalled at her crudery and ashamed for Leofric, and her own maidenhood. The woman was little better than a common drab who could behave towards a man in such an appalling fashion, particularly towards someone who had given her his protection – for whatever reason. And clearly from the reactions of the men around her, this was not the first time that she had thrown such a disgusting scene.

Her blood seethed within her veins.

How could Leofric have stomached such a woman who showed him so little consideration and respect? Who seemed intent only on shaming and embarrassing him before everyone?

At first there had seemed little she could do to show her total distaste for Velda's coarse behaviour. But her last sally, coupled with Leofric's comment about 'not making war on women', gave her the opening she had been looking for, and it didn't need Maritia's whispered encouragement to step forward and take the lead.

She had no fear of the woman's threats.

Surely the power of the Old Ones flowed through her veins. She could feel it as a vital force, flooding upwards from the ground, and surrounding her with an invisible aura that no harsh words, or biting steel, could shatter. She felt inviolable, as if she was treading a pre-ordained path from which all obstacles would be removed.

If Velda really wanted a fight to the death then so be it.

She, Brioni of Foxley, had no doubts whatsoever as to the outcome. She had a blood-oath to fulfil; she had a place to confirm beside Leofric's war-band, to prove herself worthy of their regard...to be worthy of their blood in her quest to put down Oscytel. Leofric was right. To accept Velda's challenge *was* part of her oath to her father, for only across the woman's fallen body could she reach the spears she needed to fight Oscytel. And stepping forward towards Leofric, who was standing with arms crossed, and body frozen like a marble statue, she touched his arm and said in an icy voice, laced with contempt: "He may not care to lay leather to your tarnished flesh, you doxy, but I have no such scruples! What kind of creature are you to behave in such a low manner to one of noble birth who has stooped to aid you?" she continued as she moved, gracefully, to where Velda now stood, staggered at Brioni's

240

words, slack-mouthed beside the two men whom Leofric had ordered to remove her.

"You look, and sound, more like a sick cow in heat than any woman I know. *Faugh!* You cheap baggage," she threw at her in disgust. "I am no common whore, as you have chosen to believe, I am the Lady Brioni of Foxley, Woden born and favoured of the King. I own every foot of soil you stand on, and since the death of my father, and of my brother, my word is law across the whole of his estates. Do you think I fear you?" She threw at her, as Velda flinched away, whey-faced, as she realised who Brioni truly was, and understood her lineage. "I, who have faced a baresark Viking charge, aye and killed my man as well.

"You common trull! No leader of men warrants a slattern like you by his side. The meanest thrall on my father's land was more honoured than you are here, aye, and more honourable too! I declare you '*Nithing!*'" she said with utter finality, and stepping forward she struck her, open-handed, across her face, the blow crumpling the woman backwards into Cadoc's arms, before turning contemptuously away.

Behind her Velda was shocked to the core by what had happened. No-one had ever spoken to her with so dismissive a sneer, nor struck her with such power, and she was beside herself with rage, as a boiling fury at Brioni's words and actions totally consumed her.

Seeing the look of shock, and rage, that crossed Velda's part-glazed face, and the looks of expectation, and consent, that now ran around the faces of the men who had moved aside to give her room, Brioni knew that she had got her timing, words and actions just right. But she also knew that she was now going to have to fight this woman for her place beside Leofric, and those of his men, as he had suggested...be that as shield maiden or bed mate, and she was surprised to discover that she was as excited by the one as by the other, and she blushed to realise that either way she was looking forward to it.

There was a magic quality about Leofric that she had sensed the moment he had put his arms around her, and that had thrilled her to the very centre of her being. A power, and kindness, that she had felt when he had clasped her hand at the table and promised he would not fail her. But more than that, she recognised a kindred spirit in him of freedom, and the desire for righteous dealing. Above all things he wanted his good name back! Here was no simple robber war-lord feathering his nest at the expense of others, while all Wessex bled and cried out for succour against the Danish ravens who now tore the land apart.

Here was a man whom any woman should be proud to serve and stand beside. Loyal homage and fealty need not be the drudge that many women found it. Her mother had not discovered it to be so with her husband, a man whom she had loved all her life, moreover a man of enormous personality and determination. Like Leofric in many ways...maybe that was why she was so drawn to him? And given the right man, such duty could become not only a fierce pleasure but a shared one also, and things shared must strengthen any relationship. Her parents had always discussed everything. She had heard them talking together every night in their bed. And while her mother may not always have agreed with Wulfstan's decisions, she never failed to support him in open Council.

Clearly, too, they needed each other, she and Leofric Iron Hand.

First, however, she must win the right to claim his favour, and the due recognition of his men, by defeating Velda, now beside herself with rage, who had almost hurled Cadoc and Ricberht out of her way to get at her.

"You sow's bladder!" The woman shouted at her violently, the spittle from her words flicking everywhere. "You bitch-whore! You pathetic Woden-born doxy! You dare to challenge me to combat? Here before all these men, for the right of bedding with their Lord?"

"*No*, Velda!" Brioni replied sharply, taking a pace towards the woman, now restrained again by Leofric's two burly soldiers. "Not for 'bedding'!" she snarled contemptuously at her, her face a picture of disgust. "That is neither my need, nor my way...but for the right to call myself his 'Companion-in-Arms', *yes!* Though that, clearly, is a thing beyond your understanding. And know this also," she continued crisply, "I do not need to fight you. Not now, or ever. Your village squats without right, or order, on Foxley land. *My* land, Velda Gaerwulf!" she said with crystal definition, staring fiercely into Velda's shocked black eyes. "I do not need the Shire Reeve's authority to clap you in irons, and have the whole village razed to the ground. *I* could so order that...and I have no doubt that the Lord Leofric would be delighted to carry out such an instruction, especially after the foul manner in which you have abused him.

"But I have some consideration for those who have chosen to follow you," she continued, waving her arms towards the great clearing, "so that is not my intention. But for the right to stand beside the Lord of Wimborne, whose title I fully recognise, for that I *will* fight you...and to the death if need be. You see him only as a safe protector and provider of all your wants and needs, gross as some of them may be. But I see him as a man, and a warrior for Wessex and the King, wherever he may be. And for the rest? I also see him as a man who has a right to the warmth and loving respect of any woman with whom he may choose to share his bed. He is a true Saxon warrior.

242

"A man whom my father would have been proud to stand beside in the battle-line, and lock his shield. And my father, the Thane of Foxley, was a man whom the King trusted above all others.

"Today, you have forfeited all rights to this man's care, or protection," she added, pointing to where Leofric still stood in marble silence. "I am not the 'doxy' here, Velda Gaerwulf, *you are*, and you are the '*Nithing*' here also, not the Lord Leofric. So, yes, you wilted flower, I will fight you, and, what's more, I will win!"

And turning her shoulder to the other woman she stepped back to Maritia's side, while Leofric's men dragged Velda off, still struggling fiercely and shouting out, away from the great pavilion and back to the stream as Leofric had so ordered them to do.

# Chapter Thirty Three

"Sweet Mary, Brioni, I so hoped you would do that," Maritia said to her when she got back to her side. "But I never dreamed that it would come so soon. She has been riding for a fall any time these past three months. But there's been no-one up to now whom Leofric has been remotely interested in, nor anyone with the strength and courage to take her on."

"What about that Sylvia, last autumn?"

"Poor child. Pretty, but a dreamer. Velda just swept her away. Almost killed her. She never really had Leofric's interest. With him it was just a passing fancy that Velda snuffed out before it even got started."

"To tell you the truth," Brioni replied, seating herself again at the table, "I doubted it myself until I saw the vile way in which she behaved, and the clear disgust that Leofric, and his men, felt towards her lewd behaviour. Hugo was appalled!"

"He always has been. He has never cared for Velda."

"Well, after that, my love, there was no way that I could prevent myself from interfering. I felt that Leofric and his men expected it of me, seeing they were helpless to deal with it in a way they would have liked. So, it was up to me to make the difference. Besides, I feel that in some way I do not understand, Leofric and I are destined for one another. He draws me in a manner that no man, not even Heardred, has ever done before."

"That is lust, my sweet," Maritia replied with a smile, looking at her over the rim of her drinking beaker, a quirk of amusement twisting her pretty mouth. "And there are far worse things that can befall a maid than lying with the man she wants above all others."

"Bed with Leofric?" Brioni asked, shocked. "Such has not been in my mind one moment!" and she blushed.

"And that reveals all, my love," Maritia replied laughing, holding her hands to 'warm' them on her cheeks. "Yet with an oath of blood to perform, surely such things are mere figments of the imagination?"

"Don't tease me so unfairly," Brioni replied, blushing again. "I feel so drawn to him, Maritia. There is something really warm and special about him. He took my hand and promised not to fail me. It made my heart jump. I want him to take me in his arms and possess me. I know it sounds wildly abandoned, but that's the way I feel. Not even Heardred made me feel that way.  He always sought to protect me.  Leofric is quite different.  He makes me feel that I will always be a part of his schemes.  No matter how hazardous…and I want that!  I want to be as important to him in his life as I possibly can be.  Near him, of him, round him.  I can't explain it Mari…it's just something I can't resist!"

"Surely you cannot mean that you are falling in love with your bold Saxon war-lord, Brioni?  Loving isn't possible after so short a time, is it?"

"Oh yes it is," her friend replied with a slow smile.  "A week ago I would have agreed with you whole-heartedly.  Now, however, I know differently!  But enough of that for the time being," she went on seriously.  "What happens now?"

"You and I must wait here while Leofric and my father sort things out.  This is no ordinary fight, my sweet.  You two have challenged one another to death or submission and banishment, and for that all Leofric's men, and the people from the village, must be present to see fair play.  Believe me when I say that you carry all their hopes on your slender shoulders, for few have any love for Velda.  Leofric's men especially have long felt that it was high time that Leofric changed his mate.  Be patient, Brioni, I assure you that their arrangements will not take too long."

\*

*I*n fact, however, it was not until afternoon that Hugo and Leofric were satisfied that all was as it should be for so important an event.  This was no bar-room brawl, but a blood-meeting that could change everything for all those involved, both in the outlaw village and amongst the Wolfsheads, and for Hugo and the *Circus Maximus*.  So, during this time no-one approached either combatant.

Beyond the stream, in her bothy, Velda Gaerwulf prepared herself with the help of one of her people more bound to her than most others.  Furious at the manner in which she had been dragged out and doused in the freezing waters of the stream like a common trollop, she swore constantly as she stripped off her soaking clothes and was rubbed down with a rough towel.

Then, before the fire in her small cottage, stripped down to the laced tunic top and heavy chausses allowed for such a trial-by-combat, that form of dress having long been established, she pulled on the heavy boots she always wore.  Choice of weapons being left to each fighter, Velda always fought with fine, hand-forged iron chains that hung from her wrists off thick leather cuffs, padded for comfort, and with which she was an expert.

Then, dressed and ready, with her long fleece-lined cloak over her shoulders, she sat by the fire in her lath and plaster cott, drinking warmed ale, while she waited for the soldier whom Leofric had placed outside her door to call her forward.

*

Brioni, meanwhile, was with Maritia in her room, where she stripped her of her tunic and undergarments and then began to rub her upper body with a thick, greasy oil that she poured over her shoulders from a heavy flask standing near her bedside. Rubbing it in with long firm strokes down her arms to her wrists and back again, especially across her belly, breasts and lower back, she grunted with the effort until Brioni's flesh glistened in the flickering light from the brazier that had burned there all night.

"What are you doing, Mari?" she had questioned her at the start.

"Velda will fight with chains, Brioni. Long lengths of finely forged iron that hang down from each wrist. They are her favourite weapon and she is good with them. Against bare skin they can be lethal, causing horrible tears and deep bruises. This oil will help you, my love," she went on, rubbing her down thoroughly. "It will soak up the blows and make the iron slide across you, and not bite in so badly. And if she should try and grapple with you, then it will be like trying to seize hold of a piece of wet soap, and you will be able to slip away."

"What about her? Will she not do the same?"

"No! Velda will fight you as she is. She has no idea of the quality that will face her today. She will rush at you like a tigress, and try and finish you off in the first swift moments. That is her style. Keep her at arm's length and twinkle around her, and she will swiftly tire. She will also wear heavy boots so she can kick the life out of you, and that will slow her down. But you, my sweet, will wear the boots I do when I am working, my acrobat boots. Tough, but light-weight. You will dance rings round her!"

"So, she fights with chains. I will use my sword, it fits my hand well and is finely balanced. If I can close the distance and attack within the swing of them, then I can hurt her. Weaken her, until she is forced to drop her arms..."

"Then kill her!" Maritia said fiercely.

"No, Mari. I don't want to kill her. She is no Dane for whom Blood Drinker was made to slay..."

"...Blood-Drinker?" Maritia asked her, shocked.

"Yes! I have named my sword as my people used to do years ago. As the Danes do today. Blood-Drinker! It seemed appropriate."

246

"You, a good Christian girl, giving a pagan name to her sword?  Seems barbaric in the extreme."

"Even so, it pleases me," Brioni said smiling, as Maritia slipped her boots over the other girl's feet.  "I like my sword to have a brutal name...and if Leofric has not chosen one for his axe I will insist on it!" and both girls laughed as Maritia turned then first to bind Brioni's breasts tightly with broad strips of cotton, before lacing her firmly into the short-sleeved tunic required; binding her wrists with further strips of cotton towelling to stop any oil from dripping onto her hands.  Then, finally she plaited up her hair, binding it to the top of her head with fine strips of scarlet cotton tied in amongst it and fastened under a tight headband so nothing could shake it loose.

"There, finished!  And my boots fit you perfectly.  I thought they would. Now, see how that all feels?  Take up your sword, and be sure that you can breathe easily beneath my binding."  And taking a pace backwards she paused to view her handiwork, while Brioni turned and moved across the room, shaking her head to test the bindings of her hair, and pick up the great scramaseaxe that she had found at Foxley, and with which she had fought against Oscytel's Jomsvikings across the palisade.

Watching her move, her skin glistening in the warm lamplight from the oil and grease that now sheened her upper body, Maritia was reminded of a great spotted fighting cat she had once seen in Paris, a leopard; soft-footed, sleek and deadly.  Whatever else Velda might have been expecting it was not this finely muscled beauty who crouched before her, flexing her arms and shoulders, her feet firmly planted and correctly spaced, both for balance and swift movement.  Her sword sweeping in broad cuts and swirls, her whole body driving to the lunge as she thrust forward and leapt back again, practising the movements that Heardred had taught her so long ago, and that she had seen Gyrth hammer into his men so many times.

Fully clothed she was beautiful...stripped for fighting, her toned body gleaming with the oil rubbed all over her, she was stunning.

Maritia wasn't sure who was in for the greater shock.  Velda, who was expecting an untutored girl with more breeding than either sense or ability...or Leofric who was probably expecting his new lady-love to be cut down and mangled to a bloody pulp, as Sylvia had been, within minutes of the fight's commencement.  Either way the faces of all those gathered there today would be pictures of
 amazement and appreciation...and the betting would redouble, the moment she stepped out into the arena!

"Well, love, are you ready for this?"  Maritia asked her friend quietly as Brioni bent and stretched her legs and tendons.  "It will not be easy for you to

247

walk out like this," she added gesturing to her sleeveless jerkin, tight laced across her breasts. "Nor to fight beneath the avid gaze of so many men, many of whom will have laid money down on the outcome…and many will shout for your opponent!"

Brioni looked across at her and smiled, amused by her friend's concern for her modesty when it was her fighting ability that really mattered.

"Truly, one woman is much like another. We all have the same body, and thanks to your binding they will see less than they might have hoped for. What none of them will have seen is a woman who can fight as well as many men; aye, and with the same weapons too."

And coming up to her she leaned forward and kissed Maritia on the mouth. "That is in thanks for you and Oswald, without whom I would not be about to become so unlawfully attached to the finest man, next to the King himself, whom I have ever met. But mostly for you, dearest," she added giving her a warm embrace, "whose warmth and kindness to a lonely soul in torment was more welcome than a hot meal to a starving man.

"Now, come on, Maritia, for I can hear your father's voice calling us forward. The time is come, the place is set, and I can see no useful purpose in prolonging the agony of waiting one moment longer. Tie Bran and Utha up firmly," she added, fondling the two hounds' great heads. "They will hate it and will fight to get free, but I cannot leave them loose because they will savage Velda the moment she attacks me."

But, before she could swing the flaps open that closed them off from the main pavilion, Maritia called her back.

"Wait! Wait, Brioni!" Maritia cried out to her, laying a firm hand on her arm. "There is something I must tell you. Yes, Velda fights with chains, like twin flails, but she has a weakness in her right arm that prevents its full usage. An old break that never mended properly. However she has made up for it with added strength in her left, and a vicious trick of flicking her iron links like an ox whip. Watch out for it, I beg you, for I have been told of more than one poor wretch with her face torn open to the bone and her eyes pulped to jelly!"

"Thanks for the warning, that is truly worth the knowing, Mari! But, quickly now for your father is calling to us again, does she signal it in any way? Is there any means of telling when it is coming?"

"Watch her right arm. When that drops to her side and the left continues to swing round her head, then you will know it is on the way. Three times round, Brioni, then the flick. Remember, three times round…" But she was talking to thin air for her friend had gone through the flaps, and to roars of acclaim was striding boldly forward to meet her challenger.

248

With the steady swish of the rain falling out of a leaden sky onto the dark canvas that reared above her head, she might have expected that they would have to fight inside. But that was not to be. With all Leofric's men called in from their duties, together with Hugo's people and those from the outlaw village across the clearing, equally keen to witness this sudden fight for control of their lives, there would have been no room inside the tall pavilion. Besides, no-one can fight to the best of their ability when cramped into the tiny space that would have been available had that course been followed. So it was with chill water, and a damp wind blowing across her body, that Brioni finally approached the crowd of people who had assembled round a crudely cleared circle of slushy mud, trampled straw and hay, to see that justice was served.

Beneath the trees, and in many corners, the snow of the previous weeks still lay in pockmarked heaps, and the ground was treacherous beneath the slushy surface, still frozen after the bitter frosts of just days past. To her left as she walked out, now escorted by a troop of Leofric's men who towered over her as they cheered her appearance, lay the horse-lines and wagons that Hugo needed to move his circus, now deserted, except for poor Oswald alone in his travelling cage and calling for attention in his special, growling voice. Overhead the rain continued to fall, now slowing to a patter as the weather changed at last, a corner of blue sky showing in a brief gap between the clouds.

And as she walked, she felt no fear, only a heightened sense of awareness, as if each drop of rain was a single teardrop, repeated again and again. And though her naked flesh had puckered to the cold water that ran across it, her mind was quite still and clear, unclouded by the stares and shouts of appreciation that had greeted her appearance. Not just because of her graceful, swaying carriage...but also because of her choice of weapon, its heavy blade gleaming in the grey light, more like an extension to her arm than a separate fighting blade, the runes it bore stark in their simplicity.

# Chapter Thirty Four

Velda was already there, heavy, thick-soled leather boots on her feet, her scuffed trousers bound round with scarlet plaited cord, two lengths of fine iron chain strapped round her wrists and dangling to the ground in simple coils, her dark hair a wild chaos about her head and down her back. Around her, on that side of the circle stood her supporters, and all the men and women from the outlaw village, many baying and hallooing like hounds before the chase, and hooting in derision at Brioni's appearance, pointing and laughing with obscene gestures at every move she made.

Behind Brioni stood Leofric's men, and those of the *Circus Maximus*, who had danced and spun around her when she had first arrived at their encampment. All now shouting and whistling their appreciation for her, whom they saw as their own champion, as she stepped into the cleared circle that had so swiftly been prepared.

Before her, opposite the stream end of the clearing, Leofric and Hugo were seated on high-backed wooden chairs on a section of the dais, especially brought out for the purpose of raising them up above the soiled ground. Over their heads had been raised a simple canvas canopy to shield them from the worst of the weather. Both men wore their heavy fur mantles drawn over their necks and shoulders, their faces masks of studious indifference to the fate of the two women, who with Brioni's arrival, now stood defiant before them and who would soon be at each other's throats until the death, or craven submission, of one of them brought their contest to an end.

With Brioni's arrival, Hugo hauled himself to his feet, his shoulder still heavily strapped, and drawing himself to his full height began to speak. His voice, sounding like thick gravel underfoot, was a sudden rasp of sound, the stark gravity of his face masking his anxiety for the slender girl whose pale body shimmered like a candle in the all-enveloping murk. Beside him Leofric Iron Hand sat like a figure carved in stone; only his eyes moved restlessly in his head, as his heart churned with fear for the lovely creature standing so still and silent, sword in her right hand, with the rain pattering over her naked shoulders. 'God aid her! Saint Michael stand by her side,' he prayed with all the fervour of his being. But if she survived this day, win or lose, he would love her until he died. A sudden deep realisation that shook him to his core.

"You both know why you are here," Hugo's words cut into his thoughts with brutal force. "And that this miserable business must end in the death, or banishment, of one of you. Do either of you wish, even now, to withdraw from this contest?" And everyone waited with baited breath to hear the response to Hugo the Bearmaster's considered words.

"No! I will not withdraw!" Velda spat back at him violently, whistling her chains around her head as she spoke. "This noble strumpet will rue the day she ever challenged Velda Gaerwulf to a fight!" And her supporters screamed their approval.

"Nor I, Hugo the Bearmaster!" Brioni called back, her voice crisp and clear. "May God give me the right!" And a great roar went up from all those around the circle who supported her.

"So be it! You have both chosen, and there can be no other conclusion once you have taken your places at either side of this circle, from which neither of you may leave until this conflict has been resolved. Are you agreed?"

"Yes, my Lord Hugo. We are agreed!" The words jerked from them in startled unison, their bodies already poised for movement, their minds beginning to plot and formulate the steps that would bring them both to victory or defeat.

"You have set your course, now you must run the race," Hugo finished heavily, beginning to sit down, his hand gripping Leofric's shoulder to encourage him. "And may God defend the right!"

Without looking up at the big Saxon war-leader again, or searching for Maritia's face in the packed crowd, Brioni swung away to the edge of the circle where her place had been marked by a spear, and turning there she swung her sword round her head and back again, her body automatically adopting the wide-spaced fighter's stance that Heardred had taught her, and Gyrth had made his men adopt every time they faced each other off in practice. A stance that would give her the ability to lunge rapidly in whichever direction she chose. And in the pause that followed she had the time to appraise her opponent, now beckoning the crowd to support her.

Certainly the woman was much more heavily built. Her breasts, unbound beneath her tunic top, and her shoulders, were fuller, and her arms were much meatier than her own…and she had a belly on her that would not have disgraced several innkeepers that she knew of! And though she was moving easily at the moment, Brioni decided that there was more soft flesh on her body than hard muscle; that she was a stranger to exercise and perhaps loved dark ale more than was good for her. With hard, swift movement she would probably swiftly tire; at least she hoped so, for, dear Lord, those chains were wicked weapons. If she once gave her the chance really to use them on her they would punish her severely. Clearly the thing to do was to rush in and cut her where she could. If she could damage her sufficiently, make her vulnerable, then surely it would only be a question of time before she had her at her mercy.

*

*L*ooking across at each other across the wide circle, they both shook their weapons and gave a great shout, stamping their feet as they did so…and so the fight began.

Slowly the two women crabbed round one another, eyes fixed, both watching for an opportunity to rush forward and strike a swift blow before retiring again. Both moving on the balls of their feet, both watching for the slightest hint of an attack, bobbing and feinting as they circled one another warily.

Then suddenly Velda moved.

Darting her feet forward, her chains whistling round her head in perfect unison, the big woman rushed in on Brioni, almost taking her unawares. *Left! Right! Left!* The wild iron curtain whirred round her head as Brioni dodged and weaved violently, swaying her body this way and that, fending off with her sword, the sound of steel on iron brittle in the damp air as the people crowded round the circle bayed and roared at every strike.

Smashing into the ground beside her feet, Velda's chains showered her legs with mud and water. Yet while Brioni parried her blows, her back and shoulders were caught in the sudden onslaught; the smack of each blow making her wish time and again that she had her light shield to cover her left side, as she skipped and slithered out of Velda's reach at last.

Sweet Mary, that was close!

The woman had moved more rapidly than she had expected. Heavy of flesh Velda might be, but she could still move like lightning. Too many of those and she must really catch her eventually. She must dash in beneath those chains, risking some damage, and cut her across her chest, or left arm. If the right one was already damaged, then it was the left she needed to cripple if she could. The loss of blood would weaken her still more, and if she could pierce her shoulder, the sweeping power of those fearful chains would be broken. She was turning out to be a much more dangerous opponent than she had thought.

One mistake now and it might well be her last.

Following up her advantage, Velda continued to press forward while Brioni managed to keep just out of range, flicking her sword in and out towards her, *Stab! Stab! Stab!* feinting right and left as she did so to draw her anger, while she watched Velda like a hawk, and waited for her to make a mistake.

Then, mercifully, there was a pause, the chains slowing but still turning and whistling through the air as the rain returned, falling steadily and running off the oil that cased Brioni's body, giving her some respite. Her feet braced for movement, her breath scant, her heart pounding, her sword heavy in her hand…she waited.

Eyes wary, she constantly watched Velda whose chest was deeply panting; her heavy breasts, unbound, swagged in her tunic as she bent over to ease her breathing, her chains almost falling around her as she did so, and around them the crowd itself seemed to pause for breath. And there was a sudden stillness into which stray sounds burst: the scream of a jay in the forest, Oswald bawling from his cage, a crying child, Bran and Utha howling…and Velda straightening, her right arm dropping to her side, her left beginning again to speed up its swing.

*MOVE, NOW!*

With violent energy, heart pumping madly, Brioni leapt forward beneath the glittering arc of iron now whirling round Velda's head again and, sword across her front, she slashed the other woman expertly across the top of her breasts. Twisting her blade she sliced down across the lacings that held them in place, the flesh opening beneath her razor sharp blade in one long scarlet line. The laces on her tunic flying apart as she finished her attack, Velda's heavy breasts spilled out before her, hindering her, the blood spurting out to sheet her stomach with scarlet, mixing with the water that was now running freely over them, to flow pinkly down to the sodden ground.

Velda screamed, high pitched, and unearthly, and the crowd roared, "First blood*! First blood!*" as Brioni ran out away from her, her body low to avoid a counterstroke. But, clutching her ruined tunic with one hand, Velda brought her left arm down and violently flensed Brioni with the chain it held.

Striking her back with sufficient force to hurl her off balance, Brioni suddenly teetered in her flight, and before she could right herself her feet slipped in the miry surface of the fighting circle and she crashed face down onto the icy ground, her sword flying from her hand as she fell. And again the crowd roared, while Hugo and Leofric leaped to their feet, shouting for Brioni to: "Get up! *Get up!*"

With wild rage suffusing her face, and her breasts covered in blood as they swung free of her slashed tunic top, the older woman went for Brioni like a tigress after a tethered goat. Flailing at her as she lay on the bitter ground, the chains tangled with one another in her fury to fall like small iron clubs on Brioni's back and shoulders, the crowd roaring out at every strike.

Flinging and rolling her lissom body to left and right Brioni struggled desperately to get back onto her feet. But every time she almost

253

succeeded...she was struck down again by Velda's iron links so punishment was unavoidable, inevitable, and every time the older woman struck home, pain lanced through Brioni making her cry out in agony, until from neck to thigh she felt her flesh to be on fire.

So Velda hunted her unmercifully as she struggled in the slush and mud to get free, and every time she cried out, the crowd howled their opinions, some calling on her to get up and fight, some for her to give in; some for Velda, some for the Lady Brioni...but all roared something.

Yet, try as she might, Velda had not yet managed to strike her enemy in any vital part. Brioni's face and loins were still untouched, and though her chest and belly were marred with the trampled straw and hay that now mired the ground, the thick greasy oil that Maritia had rubbed into her skin still protected her from the worst effects of the cold, and the woman's wicked chains, that otherwise would have brought the struggle to a swift and bloody end.

Again and again, spinning, rolling and stumbling on her hands and knees she just managed to evade the full weight of Velda's fury, the woman panting from her efforts and plainly tiring, blood from her chest wound running down across her body like a crimson sheet. And all the time the crowd standing round bayed and howled their excitement, egging both women on to ever greater heights of rage and fury, hooting every time Velda caught her lighter opponent a smashing blow across her back and shoulders.

Suddenly, from her position on her knees on the torn ground, Brioni once more saw Velda's right arm drop as she prepared to use her chains like a monstrous flicking whip and flog Brioni to a bloody pulp. Only this time she had forgotten the calibre of the girl whom she was fighting and had moved in for the kill. It was just the error that Brioni had been hoping for, and springing forward like the great cat she was, she launched herself at the long length of chain that now hung motionless from Velda's right hand to the ground. It was a single fluid motion that caught everyone by surprise, even Leofric who was standing on his feet shouting to her to go for her sword.

One moment it appeared to be all over...the next she seemed to fly up off her knees, and seizing hold of the loose chain, pulled her heavier adversary face down in the vile muck. Twisting her weak right arm mercilessly up her back, while covering Velda's body with her own, Brioni struggled to wrench the loose chain over the woman's left shoulder, twisting her damaged right arm up her back and hold her there, the woman's blood flowing freely over both of them as she did so, both women shouting out in rage as they fought one another with mindless fury.

254

Rolling over and over on the filthy ground, mud and slush flying everywhere, they tore at one another, tooth and claw, like two wild cats, while Brioni fought to hold the heavier woman down and prevent her free left arm, with its flailing length of iron chain, from doing her any further injury. Time and again Velda tried to grip Brioni's arms and shoulders to free herself from her grasp, but each time her hands slid off the younger woman's oiled flesh, made slicker by the blood that now covered both of them.

Finally Brioni brought her to a stop, the woman panting furiously and struggling like an eel in a trap, her back upon the ground; and humping up her body to straddle it, Brioni raised herself up and stabbed her knees down with all her force into the slack muscles in Velda's upper arms, making her scream out in agony and thrash her legs impotently on the ground, water spraying up everywhere. Then, with the older woman bucking and twisting to try and throw her enemy off, Brioni slid down to her waist and viciously plunged her hands onto Velda's naked breasts, clenching into them like steel talons. Gripping each bloody fruit with a strength burgeoning on madness, she squeezed them so fiercely that the sharp wounds they already bore from her sword cut spurted her life out like bloody milk upon the wet and torn ground. And the crowd roared: "Second blood! *Second blood!*"

Pain bursting behind her eyes like exploding stars, Velda screamed out in torment, her whole body leaping and flacking beneath Brioni who was now clamped to her like riding a wild mare fresh from the herding, slushy mud and ice cold debris flying everywhere. And all the while she used Velda's savaged breasts like soggy handles to lift the wretched woman's back and shoulders off the ground and slam them down again, her victim's sobbing cries rising in anguished crescendo, her legs drumming a desperate tattoo into the churned earth as she writhed about like a spitted snake.

But she could not dislodge her ferocious enemy, and just for one moment their eyes met. Brioni's blue ones fierce with the lust of battle-fever...Velda's dark and glazed with pain, dulling with exhaustion as Brioni steadily crushed and battered the strength out of her, fighting to break her will, if not her body.

Badged with blood and mucus, the crowd, baying and shouting like hounds at the kill, and almost pushed right up to where they were struggling, the two women could not go on much longer.

"*Submit!*" Brioni gasped out, as with one more terrible cry Velda's tortured body hit the semi-frozen ground again, the force jerking her head up and down wildly so it banged into the ground too. "Submit, Velda! You are finished. Your body can't take any more. *Give in now!*" she shouted at her, violently banging her down again, the blood spurting out freshly from her wounds, "or I'll kill you where you lie!"

But the woman was too far gone even to reply, her head flopping from side to side, her eyes turned up, her mouth slack and fish-like. And releasing her hold on the woman's slumped body, Brioni staggered to her feet, too exhausted herself even to walk properly. And with pain, spurting through her she lurched clumsily across to where her sword gleamed in the dirt.

Bending slowly forward she reached down for its hilt and picked it up, and as she did so she felt new life suddenly flowing through her aching limbs. It was as if someone had given her a draught of heavenly elixir, and with renewed vigour she turned and walked back to where her fallen enemy lay sprawled out on the ground, her arms, now freed at last, stretched out as if upon a crucifix.

It was time to make an end, and kneeling above Velda's splayed out body, she raised her sword high above her head, the magic runes it bore sparkling like living flame in the pale light of the sun, now just breaking through the clouds that all morning had rained on them so wretchedly. And giving one victorious shout, she drove the great blade down with all the strength and power at her command towards the outspread arms.

Once, twice, she struck, first one wrist then the other, the blood spurting as she cut down, and each time the crowd, now packed around her, swayed and groaned, her supporters roaring out: "Last blood! *Last blood!*" every time the unconscious woman's body leapt and jerked disjointedly, like a broken marionette, as each massive blow struck home.

Then it was done, and stooping over Velda's prostrate body, Brioni reached for her bloody trophies and held them up for all the crowd to see, and they howled their assent, while parting for her to walk back to the little dais where both Hugo and Leofric were now standing, wreathed in smiles.

"Is it enough, my Lords?" she shouted out unsteadily, holding up her hands.

"Yes, my Lady Brioni of Foxley," Hugo roared out to her above the wild hubbub going on around them, bowing as he did so. "It is enough. Now bring those bloody things to us here, and let's have done. You have given us a fierce thirst and all are hungry...and you need warmth and clothing!"

But before he could say anything further, nor Maritia reach her as she was struggling through the crush, nor Leofric take her in his arms as he had sprung forward to do so, the whole business caught up with her. And without even a sigh, all her energy rushed out of her and she simply collapsed onto the cold and slushy ground, the chains she had hacked off Velda's wrists falling from her unconscious hands as she did so.

256

# Chapter Thirty Five

Around them all a cold wind hustled, despite the pale sunlight now flooding over the whole clearing, as the rain clouds finally blew away and high overhead the sky turned blue.

Leaping off the dais, Leofric raced across to where Brioni was lying collapsed on the ground, and flinging his great bearskin cloak over her he scooped her up into his arms. Then, holding her against his chest, he forced his way through the milling press of admirers that had surged forwards with him, and the huddled crowd of gamblers shouting out and striving for their money, and strode back towards Hugo's pavilion.

In fact Maritia was there before him, bawling for Gilbert to bring hot water and fresh towels and linens to her room; while her father was busy waving his arms and shouting for new-filled braziers, for food to be prepared against the arrival of Leofric's chief advisors, and his own right hand men, and for someone to do something, "with these two damned hounds before they drive me mad!" For Bran and Utha, freed from the chains with which they had been tied, bounced and leapt on everyone in their eagerness to be with their mistress again.

*

Meanwhile Raedwald and Trausti, who both had women in the outlaw village, had rushed over to Velda, their women with them, to where her body still lay sprawled out where Brioni had left her. Her breasts horribly bruised and torn, the blood still sluggishly flowing from all the wounds Brioni had given her, especially her wrists where Brioni's great blade had deeply scored them, she looked in the last stages of life, ashen-faced and breathing so softly that for one moment they really thought that she was dead.

But even as they knelt down beside her, Trausti covering her with a coarse blanket that his woman had brought with her for the purpose, her eyelids flickered, and she groaned briefly before stretching her neck and vomiting her misery onto the bloodied ground again and again. Too weak even to flop over onto her hands and knees, she could do nothing to help herself, crying out with pain every time they tried to move her. But, as there was no way they could all just leave her, they simply had to grit their teeth against her frantic yells and get

257

on with moving her, placing her on a sheep hurdle covered with the blanket, her body by her long cloak, and carried back by four men whom Raedwald seized on for that labour.

One thing was certain, it would be a long time before Velda Gaerwulf would be in any condition to fight anyone again. And by then she would no longer be in the village, for though she was alive, she would now be banished from the clearing and would have to start all over again with a new life somewhere else: Chippenham, Melksham or further afield in distant Trowbridge…anywhere other than Helm's Wood near Foxley. But first she would need Old Anna, the village wise woman, to care for her; to stitch up the vicious slash across her breasts, bind up her wrists and do her best to physic her back to health.

So, gently as they could, they carried her across the stream to the shabby cottage that served her as a home; those who had once owned her as a friend now taking care to distance themselves from her in defeat. Never really popular with any of them, less so since her temper and behaviour had slipped so badly, she would soon discover what true loneliness could mean.

\*

With the fight over, and the two combatants borne back to their respective homes, those who had been left hanging round the now deserted arena slowly wandered away, drifting off in ones and twos and in small groups. Those who had backed Brioni jubilant with their winnings…those who had failed her resigned in defeat, but full of praise for the Lady of Foxley's amazing victory over so accomplished an enemy. Their conversation was dominated by all they had witnessed, and there was fierce discussion over the way the two girls had looked, the weapons they had used and the fierceness of the fight. While above them the sky continued to clear, the great wracks of cloud that had loured over them now blown apart by a fresh wind from the south, the sunshine strengthening until it was warm on their backs, making the men smile and want to kick their heels.

Still carrying his precious burden, Beornred following close behind him with Brioni's sword resting across his arms, Leofric burst through the entrance to Maritia's chamber. Shouting to the people crowded there to clear his way, he gently laid her down, face upwards on her bed, still unconscious, and quietly stepped back.

"Will she be alright?" he questioned Maritia urgently, as she ran towards her friend. "She looks so still and pale. Dear God, I should never have let them fight! You know how vicious Velda can be when roused to fever pitch.

258

Just what would have happened had Brioni not been so well trained and fit, and confident, does not bear thinking of!"

"You dolt, Leofric! How dare you think so poorly of this girl lying here who has cleared the way for you to build a better life. She would never have forgiven you, had you done such a foolish thing as prevent her from fighting Velda!" Maritia exclaimed, fluttering her hands violently over Brioni's face as she spoke.

"What do you mean?"

"Oh, God help me, Leofric, but I sometimes wonder whether you men have any brains at all for anything other than fighting, drinking and hunting!"

"I don't understand?"

"No, you big ox," she replied exasperated, as she turned back to her charge, now moaning softly as she began to come round. "I don't suppose you do. *She fought for you*, you big lunk! For her own honour, and to prove herself worthy of you…and that crowd of meat-heads you have gathered around you and, God aid us, for the King, for Wessex and for her own self-worth. But mostly she fought for your approval of her in your war-band…*and for you!*"

"For me?" he queried her with a puzzled frown on his big face, as he continued to hover over Maritia's shoulder, she bending over to twitch his great furry mantle from Brioni's exhausted body, he hampering her movements and getting in her way.

"Yes! For you. Now, for pity's sake, Leofric, go away! Your lady will be fine, I promise you. Bruised and sore she may be, but the oily grease with which I doused her, and rubbed into her skin, will have taken up most of the graunching punishment that Velda meted out. She should come out of this unmarked. The rest will be up to you. Now, don't start with more questions, please," she sighed with a smile. "Just clear off for a while and ease your mind with a drink at my father's table. You have much to talk about, the two of you. Anything more would probably exhaust you. Go on! *Go on!*" she added, exasperated, flicking him away with her fingertips. "When she is ready to see you, I'll give you a call…but it will not be soon and she will not be up and about again for some while. She is badly hurt and exhausted. In the meantime, for my sake, if not for hers, leave us alone!"

And with a sharp flounce of her shoulders she hurried back to where Brioni was lying, eyes now wide open, and her body on fire from head to heels. Leofric, feeling helpless and rejected, had nothing left to do except leave and stamp his way across to the wider room beyond, where Hugo and his men patiently sat waiting for him, his mind filled with all that Maritia had said.

And thinking of it a while later he, too, smiled.

Behind him Maritia began to work gently on Brioni's body, cutting away the rest of her clothes with a fine-bladed knife she had to hand and carefully, carefully, feeling for any breaks or fractures that she might have been given in those places on her arms, back and legs where Velda's chains had struck her. And with Brioni's body now laid bare, and mottling up with bruises everywhere, she began to bathe her all over with hot water and her own most fragrant soap from Castile, brought back by her father from Paris, and only ever used on special occasions, such as now. So, with the hot water that Gilbert continued to bring to her screened doorway whenever she called out, she used a great sponge from the Greek islands to squeeze it over her, as well as for gently washing her; soothing her battered body, and cleansing her face as she did so.

Poor love; she had certainly taken a dreadful beating before managing to turn the tables on her powerful adversary. For when she finally managed to turn her over onto her chest, with some help from Brioni who had at last recovered her senses, she was appalled by what she found there.

All across her back, despite her leather jerkin, there were cruel purple-black welts that ran down over her buttocks and round her thighs. Her arms and shoulders were also deeply scored in places where she had used them to protect her breasts, with the bruising she would carry for weeks already blackening her skin. The frightening thing for Maritia was that she was dealing with the winner. If this was the condition that Brioni was in, then Velda must look like a raddled beetroot after a herd of stirks had trampled over it! Almost too horrible to contemplate, and she had that long gash right across her chest from Brioni's sword that would have to be stitched, and her wrists had been deeply scored as well. Whereas Brioni was marked not gored, Velda had been scarred for life.

Without more ado she began to massage some life back into her friend's body, using arnica oil and witch hazel from her own private store, doing her best to ignore the groans of pain that came to her with increasing frequency. At the same time she ordered Gilbert to get her fresh ice from the stream, and soft cotton pads with which to wrap it in. As her mother had long ago told her, something cold on a bad bruise would help it heal more quickly, and crushed ice laid to Brioni's bruises would help her now to recover more swiftly.

"Oh God, I hurt, Maritia," Brioni called out weakly. "It feels as if every bone in my body is broken. *Ouch!* Be careful, you brute, I am not made of oak you know, just feeble flesh and blood. *Ow!* Sweet Mary, be gentle with me," she continued, as Maritia's hands worked their way over her shoulders and down her spine. "*Gently!* Sweet Mary, much more of this and I shall be wondering whether I wouldn't rather still be out there!"

Maritia laughed and patted the round globes of her backside as she did so, reaching for her fat, soapy sponge to cleanse her still further, and then from there she worked her way up the long column of her back and across her shoulders, both horribly marked by Velda's chains.

"If that's the way you feel, I am sure it could easily be arranged. But I must warn you that despite the sunshine, the wind has an edge to it that was not there a while ago, shifting from south to north-east again; however, if you are that determined?

"No! No!" her battered friend replied quickly, with a laugh stifled by pain, "I am really quite comfortable here upon my chest. It is just that I feel like a roll of dough beneath your kneading fingers, and in my present state everything you touch hurts so badly."

Maritia laughed again as she probed the knotted muscles round Brioni's neck and shoulders, making her groan. But after she had finally removed the last vestiges of the thick, greasy oil that had done so much to minimise the damage done to Brioni's body, she could feel her body relax. And as Maritia then began to massage her again with some of her delicately perfumed preparations, she finally discovered that she could move her limbs with more ease, and a truly delicious sense of languorous well-being began to flow through her. All she wanted to do now was rest. Leofric, Alfred, Oscytel...all could wait until she felt really better.

The struggle with Velda had been more terrible than she had thought possible, and the knowledge of what those chains could have done to her had she been less well-prepared made her shudder. She must find some way of rewarding Maritia for her advice and all her care, for without it Velda, who was larger and heavier, might well have pulverised her to a mumbling jelly as she had threatened to do.

*Mmmm!* Maritia's hands felt so good on her back and shoulders. Too much of that and her legs would never support her when she tried to stand...and stand she must, for she had yet to present herself to the men whose approbation and support she so badly needed. She had put herself through Hell to prove her worth, not just for Leofric and the others of his warband who followed him, but also for herself. Velda had been her own personal firedrake. She had needed to know how she could cope on even terms with a ferocious enemy, with the pain and fear that went with such a struggle. Now she knew, and so did they.

And if in the doing she had won the heart of the man she felt she loved, then so much the better, for she needed that as much as she needed his hands and warm mouth on her body…though not yet! Not until she was truly recovered. She so wanted to get up and show herself to them all…but did not trust herself to be able to do so, and she groaned aloud her whole body suddenly shivering with delayed shock.

"Where's Leofric?" she asked weakly. "I must go to him. Show myself to everyone. Prove myself worthy."

"Not for a while, my love," Maritia said firmly, covering her body with a cool cotton sheet, followed by a thick fur blanket. "Not for a while. You have taken a real beating and your body will take days to recover its bounce. Some of those bruises will take weeks to disappear. I have arranged for ice to be brought from the river for the worst of them. My mother taught me years ago that an ice compress, as she called it, was the best thing for a deep bruise. That, and the arnica oil and witch hazel I have been using today will return your body to true health, and then fitness can follow. But present yourself to that lunk-head, and my father, who is little better? No, my love! I utterly forbid it! You will lie here in my chamber until you are truly better. Then we will see. Then, you may do all the 'presenting' you like, but not today!"

"But I must!" Brioni protested, bursting into tears of frustration, her whole body shaking to her sobs.

"No, honeyone. Look at you," Maritia said gently, squatting by her head, her arms across her tormented shoulders. "These tears tell me all I need to know of your condition. No-one doubts your courage, Brioni, nor your determination to fight. Cry this one out, sweetheart; you are not strong enough to defy it anymore. You have fought a bitter battle this day…and won! No one could have done more. Let that be enough for now; the men can wait. When you can stand tall again, and move without wincing, then will be the time to show yourself and claim the right for which you fought today. Until then, you must rest."

"What will happen to Velda now?" Brioni asked, turning her head on the pillow Maritia had placed beneath it.

"She has to leave as soon as she is able," Maritia said, drawing up a chair to sit beside her. "That is the custom, 'law' one might almost say as far as these matters are concerned. Why do you ask? She would not be concerned about you."

"Because, despite all, she fought well, and must feel very alone and frightened just now. I feel like a lump of battered meat…and I won! What must she be like? And I cut her with Blood-Drinker, right across her chest and scored her wrists when I hacked off her chains. These people are all she has since her husband was killed," she went on, raising herself up on her arms.

"She has lost Leofric, and to be cast out now, with all Wessex in turmoil, and the King dead for all we know, would hardly be an act of Christian charity."

"My, but you are a strange one, Brioni; all fire and battle-fever one moment, and the milk of human kindness the next. I assure you Velda would not be thinking of you in such terms had she won. You heard what she said? About the Black Swamp? Though I doubt whether Leofric would have allowed that. It has been done before."

"Well, Mari, that's where I am different. I had Christian charity hammered into me from an early age," she said, thinking of Father Anselm when she was growing up; and of her mother's innate kindness. "She is not me, and I am concerned for her. Look, Mari," she said, shifting her body with a groan to hold a hand out to her. "I know she won't take anything from me after all that has happened. But I have all my father's hoard with me here, and a handful of silver pennies would not go amiss, and might give her the chance to start again somewhere else. Now, don't look at me like that," she added, as Maritia snorted and her dark brows drew together in anger. "I know how you feel, but I am as responsible for what has happened to her as she is. And just because she's a foul-mouthed baggage who has deserved all she has got, that is still not a valid reason for not doing something to help her. Alfred is always doing that to the Danes!

"So, please Maritia, will you find some way of getting the money to her, and of making sure she takes it too? She has her pride I am sure. Call it guilt money if you like. But having spared her life in battle, I see no reason to rob her of it now. Besides it would please Leofric to know that the lass he saw out there today has more than just good looks and fighting spirit to recommend her!"

"Very well, Sweetheart, I will do as you ask," and with a smile and final nod of agreement, Maritia bent forward and kissed Brioni's forehead as she now lay slumped back down on her chest, her face turned to one side on her pillow. And laying her hand on her shoulders, she got up and moved to leave.

Pausing for a moment at the doorway of her chamber, she looked over Brioni's supine figure and smiled. She had known her for such a short time, yet so much had happened. From pampered handmaid of a Queen, the much loved daughter of a noble Saxon thane, to the bruised and battered lady of a Wolfshead warlord...that was some journey in anyone's account. How much further would she travel before safety wrapped her round again? And what did it all mean for her father, and for her herself, for the whole of the *Circus Maximus,* including dear Oswald who had started it all? She did not know, the Fates had all their lives in their hands. And with a shake of her head she left

263

the chamber to rejoin her father and tell him, and Leofric, that Brioni was not to be disturbed.

# Chapter Thirty Six

*I*n fact it was a week after her fight with Velda before Brioni was in any fit state to present herself to Hugo and Leofric in a formal manner, though she had been up and about, limping and groaning, within hours...only to be put back to bed very firmly by Leofric and Maritia and strictly ordered to rest.

Every day that second week in January, the wind remained bitter despite the sunshine and clear skies overhead, the snow of Christmas and the New Year still lingering beneath the trees, with hard frosts at night when the sky was clear and filled with stars. And every day she managed to move more easily, the deep black bruises that criss-crossed her back and shoulders finally fading to blue and yellow. And though her legs had quickly firmed up, still Maritia would not let her onto the practice ground that Leofric had established for his men. There, armed with lead-covered practice-blades, as the Roman army had done centuries before, his men swung and cut at tall hacking posts buried deeply in the ground, and practised with locked shields the moves needed when facing a fierce enemy across the shield wall.

Then, on the second day of her convalescence, came the news that all had been waiting for so anxiously since Brioni had first joined them. The news that Alfred lived!

\*

*L*eofric and his commanders had been seated with Hugo in the great pavilion round the long table one late afternoon, their men at trestles scattered round them, the first day that Maritia had allowed her fully up, when an exhausted rider had ridden into the encampment. Galloping into the clearing in a spray of mud and slush, as the sun went down in a blaze of gold and crimson, he had flung himself off his exhausted gelding and come rushing in amongst them. Brioni, gingerly seated on a large cushion with another at her back, Bran and Utha closeby, was on her feet in moments, all discomfort banished, as were many around them, Leofric leaping up beside her to greet his messenger, his drinking horn swiftly cast aside.

"What news, Sigweald?" he called out as the man staggered through the flaps and flung himself to his knees before him. His face and armour splattered with mire, his shield on his back, he was panting with exertion and the importance of his news, and seeing the state he was in Leofric called out to Hugo's steward: "Ho, Gilbert! Give this man some spiced ale, his mouth must be dry from travel."

"Thank you, my Lord," Sigweald gasped out, seizing the deep horn swiftly thrust at him and drinking deeply.

"Now, soldier," Leofric demanded of him moments later, as the man wiped his mouth with the back of his hand, "your news!"

"My Lord... The King lives! Alfred is alive, and fled to the land of the Sommerseatas."

"Where?" Leofric shot back at him as everyone around the table gasped.

"To Athelney, Lord. Right in the centre of all the marshes."

"How do you know this, Sigweald?"

"Grimnir Grimmersson the Skald told me. He is in Chippenham now, amongst Guthrum's men, he came to me at our trysting place this noontime, at the ale house at Biddestone. Where you told me to wait. That is why I am so late in reaching you."

"When did Guthrum know?"

"Not until yesterday, when news came in from some treacherous Saxon thane that the King had passed through his steading on his way there."

"Was the Queen with him when he fled, and the family?" Brioni asked swiftly, leaning forward across the table, hungry for news.

"Aye, Mistress," Sigweald said, rising from his knees and turning towards her. "The children were with her, and she had a babe at her breast. They were all in a great hurry."

"How did they get out?" Leofric asked him amazed. "By all the gods it must have been a close run thing!"

"It was, Lord. As the Danes broke in across the river, Alfred escaped from the back of the town. He had horses waiting there in case just such a thing happened. One of the King's men had planned for it. Others gave their lives for him and the family to escape. Fought by the rearward gates like demons while the King rode off into the wilderness with no more than could be carried, and his halidom and treasure strapped to the backs of two mules."

"Sweet Jesus, that must have been terrible!" Hugo chipped in brusquely in his deep voice. "Thank God he had a plan."

"Heardred's plan," Brioni said quietly, looking up at Leofric. "The man to whom I was to have been betrothed. He and the King both are long-headed planners. It is why Alfred likes him so."

"Seems like the King chose well, my Lady," and he gripped her hand tightly and smiled down into her blue eyes. Then, turning back to his messenger he asked tersely: "How many in the King's party, Sigweald?"

266

"A dozen proven warriors, my Lord; four priests, two serving women and an altar boy."

"He always has liked priests, the King," Trausti sneered. "Fat lot of good they will be against Oscytel's Jomsvikings...and an altar boy? They'll relish him that's for certain!" And a light ripple of laughter flowed round the table.

"Who leads the King's men?" Brioni asked, her face pinched with concern.

"Hereward the Strong."

"God and his angels be thanked for that," she said then, briefly covering her face with her hands. "The family are running free, and Hereward is well-named, Sword Guardian! He is a good man and a fearsome warrior; he will keep them safe. But God rot the man who betrayed the King," she added looking up fiercely, banging the table with her fist. "Alfred deserves better than that from his people!" And her eyes sparkled with anger.

"That is as maybe, my Lady," Leofric replied calmly. "But at least we know the King is alive and where he is. I know all that land down there. Amongst those rhynes and rivers Alfred is almost as safe from his enemies as he would be behind the grey walls of Winchester, safer even. Fish and waterfowl are plentiful, and there is water everywhere, great lakes and bays of it, miles of it, and only the local people know their way amongst the secret paths and ridgeways. Every village is an island. You have to use punts and boats for everything, even for moving horses! Guthrum must be spitting blood and splinters that he did not catch the King in Chippenham. Without black treachery he will never get him now!"

"What will the people do?" Hugo rumbled at Brioni.

"The Sommerseatans?"

"No! The people of Wessex. Will they support their King?"

"That will depend on what the King does," she answered thoughtfully. "If he gathers men to him as he promised should such a disaster ever happen, and makes war on the Danes wherever he can, really sticks his saexe into them wherever possible...then..then they will fight!

"As long as the King is alive and active, Guthrum will never control Wessex. He may claim to be King of Wessex, but as long as Alfred makes him bleed, he can only ever be king in name! Heardred and the King had long discussed it, and laid plans for armed resistance everywhere. Wessex is too great a land for the Danes to control it all, from Kent in the east to Cornwall in the west. At least that is so now. But come the spring, when the sea-lanes open and Guthrum can be massively reinforced from the Danes in Frankland? That is a question no man can answer, Hugo."

267

"So, the time has come to make a move, and sooner than we had planned...before the spring. We can do no good skulking here in Helms Wood, miles from the Danish base at Chippenham. We need to move much closer where we can do some good. Maybe even get into the town itself and make some mischief!"

"Into Chippenham? Right in amongst the Danes? Where Guthrum and Oscytel have their greatest power?" Brioni asked aghast, her eyes wide with shock. "Surely that is madness?"

"It is certainly risky," Hugo replied slowly. "But maybe not impossible. I might be able to help you there. I and the *Circus Maximus*."

"Us, father?" Maritia asked, no less shocked than Brioni had been.

"Yes, Mari. The Danes like entertainment no less than Saxons. And we are the best. Guthrum and his leaders are beset with problems, what could be a better distraction for their problems than the arrival of a circus in their midst? And no-one will have seen a bear like Oswald. We can arrive outside the walls of Chippenham with drums and trumpets, pipes and cymbals and they will beg us to come in. Grimnir can help..."

"Grimnir?" Brioni chipped in suddenly. "Who is he?"

"Grimnir Grimmersson the Skald, you heard his name a few moments ago," Leofric replied with a smile, "from Sigweald. He is a Skald...a Norse harper, and a teller of tales and singer of sagas, like the tale of Beowulf and Grendel. He is a good one too; knows all their songs. He is a true Norseman, but follows me. His wife and child were slain in a vicious skirmish by rogue Danes three years ago, after Wareham. Guthrum knew who the leader was, but made no move against him."

"Oscytel!" Brioni said, bitterly. "Sounds just like Oscytel!"

"Yes! It was the Black Jarl," Beornred answered her in his gruff voice. "From that moment Grimnir sought revenge, and when he met up with Leofric later, he became our man from then on."

"And Cadoc can help," Trausti added, rubbing his hands together. "He has a woman in the town who works in the King's Hall. The bastards spared her when they broke in because she was the only one who knew how to brew the beer they like. But her old parents were not so lucky. They were butchered when the town was captured, along with so many others. Too slow to run away!"

"But where will you lie up?" Maritia asked, astonished at the way the talk was going. "Surely the Danes will never allow any warrior group such as yours to get near them without a bitter fight, which you must lose for there are so many of them, and only a handful of you!"

268

"First who's going to tell them? And second, what do you think we have been doing all these past days, while the Lady Brioni has been so laid up?" Raedwald replied briskly. "Playing flash the fingers? A few of us have been scouting far and wide, and have found the perfect place to lie up, not far from Biddestone, where Sigweald was waiting for news from Grimnir. Leofric knows the place, and the people there. Has known them of old, Trausti and I have both been over the ground before."

"It is a strong place for a well-disciplined war-band to lurk," Trausti said with a grin, picking up the tale. "Far enough from Chippenham not to be swiftly thought of, but near enough to nip out and attack the Danish outposts, kill their messengers and disrupt their affairs. We will not be able to stay there long. But it will do nicely for the time being...and will enable us to make the Danes wretched, unhappy lives more miserable!"

"And where is this place?" Brioni asked, sitting forward on her stool.

"At Ford," Leofric said. "A tiny settlement along the By-Brook, where the stream can easily be crossed. It is a deep, narrow valley, with steep banks all round down which no Dane could ride, nor easily attack on foot without falling on his face. There is a trackway that runs above the stream to another place where the river can be crossed, at Slaughterford. Hold both ends and no-one can easily get at you. There are trackways to Biddestone, and to Colerne and over the top from Ford to Combe. And there is also a simple trackway from there to the coast."

"Yes, I know of those places," Brioni said thoughtfully. "And the ground around them is steep and not well used. But all those settlements along the river are tiny. Just a handful of houses, and sheltered farmland."

"It is perfect for our needs, and there are good people there who will help us," Leofric said then, looking around the table. "There are barns at both ends we can use, stacked with fodder, and simple granaries on stone staddles beside the river. From there we can raid all across Wiltshire until we need to move ourselves again. Hit and run, hit and run, until we drive the Danes into a frenzy. Then, one day, we will just disappear as we first arrived, taking everyone with us, like the mists off the river on a summer's morning; only to start up again somewhere else."

"And if the Danes are canny enough to find you, and send in a flying column to attack?" Hugo questioned him.

"Then we scatter up the different trackways that abound and re-group at Battlesbury Rings, near Warminster."

"But that's miles away, my Lord Leofric," Raedwald, said. "Near my old home at Sutton Veney."

269

"That's right, my old friend," the big war-leader said, leaning across to grasp his arm as he spoke, "and on the line from Athelney where Alfred is hiding out. A line that he must take if he is to attack the Danes at Chippenham with an army. If the King is to bring Guthrum to battle in the spring, before Guthrum can be reinforced, then he must come near Warminster to do so. That old fortress is also close to Ecberht's Stone where the muster will be. We can join him there in the spring."

"You seem to have thought it all out," Hugo said, with a gruff burst of laughter. "So after we have done what we can in Chippenham, if we survive that long, we must come then and find you at Battlesbury Rings, wherever that may be in this wet, soggy country of yours. Yes, yes! Near Warminster. I heard you say. But where is that, my fine Saxon war-lord? You will have to show me before we split up.

"Now, Sigweald," he bellowed at the weary messenger, standing close by still spreckled with mud. "Come and get some food inside you, and when you have eaten, get a wash, you need it!" And everyone laughed. "And as for you two young ladies, away with you too. In particular, my Lady, it is time you rested," he said sternly to Brioni. "First proper day up, and full of excitement. If you are to leave with the Lord Leofric at the week's end then you must be fit to do so. And you yet have to make a formal presentation to both him and me following your defeat of Velda two days ago. Since you have inherited all the Foxley estates, including all the land on which they live, the fate of the outlaw village, and all its people, now rests in your hands. Deal wisely, my Lady Brioni, for much depends on what you do and say."

Rising from her stool, she dropped the huge circus leader a swift curtsey: "Hugo the Bearmaster," she said formally, "you have given me much to think on, and I have much to live up to also, so I will do as you say." And smiling at all the men seated there, and especially at Leofric, who briefly held out his hand to her as she passed by, she left the wide chamber, with both cushions clasped against her chest, Maritia following.

# Chapter Thirty Seven

*T*he next five days were days of intense activity as Leofric and his men prepared to leave: weapons and armour were checked and rechecked, stores of food and fodder for the horses gathered together, horses' hoofs and iron shoes closely examined by Arnwulf the farrier who always travelled with them. His charcoal and field forge safely packed in a small tilt cart with all his tools and spare blades, spear and arrow heads, bags of rivets, bundles of leather and pigs of iron for repairs. He was one of Leofric's most valued men, and he had a strong sword arm when needed.

Bandages, liniments, healing oils and herbs were also safely bagged and packed in wicker panniers, made for the purpose, and placed under Brioni's especial care...and all on the understanding that she would be travelling with the war-band, her formal presentation to Hugo and Leofric still not having yet been carried out.

\*

*A*nd all that time Brioni forced herself to exercise with sword and shield on the practice ground, Bran and Utha by her side, Maritia no longer able to restrain her further. Beneath a jigsaw sky of fractured blue and grey, with the mid-January sun breaking through to lighten the mood, she drove and hacked at the hated posts that Leofric had ordered thrust into the ground. With lead covered practice blade and light shield, as Leofric's men did, she swung her arm and bounced on her toes and heels.

Thrust, return, *thrust!* Hack left, right and *overhead!*...again and again until her body and her mind screamed out for rest, and her arms felt like the lead with which her blunted blade was covered. Stamp forward, block and parry; sword level as Heardred had taught her, and shield held high, while Trausti yelled out the orders and hers, and the men's, feet beat out the time. While Finnar whacked those whose arms dropped, or bodies drooped, with a gnarled length of tough vine stick before he bawled "*Rest!*" Stamping forward to the 'advance'...and lurching backwards to the 'retreat', horns blowing and everyone shouting until the big clearing rang to the sounds of battle.

If she could bear the extra weight of metal on the practice ground...the weight of her own scramaseaxe would be as feathers when she held it in her hand to fight. But not for her the battle-line as Leofric's men would hold it, with their heavy shields of linden wood, covered with leather and reinforced with stout metal rims and iron bosses, all locked in with one another. Right-rim inside left, in a long unbroken line that made the shield wall. That would have been too much for her, she did not have the strength. No maid would have done, no matter how brave or well-intentioned.

The battle-line was a place of men, and men with iron thews and the fighting spirit of heroes. Men who could stand and take a Viking charge and not retreat; be drenched in blood and soaked with urine without flinching; who could stand the stench of blood and fear and faeces all around them, the ground slippery with blood and offal, and roar out their battle cries without turning tail to run, screaming out in terror, from the horror that was the shield-wall when Saxon fought Viking to the last gasp of life, and the last drop of blood.

One step behind the main shield-line was her place, where she could strike past the close-linked shields and pierce the flesh and gizzards of her enemies. Thrust and recover, thrust and recover, until the whole battle-line could stamp forward to victory, faster and faster until the horses were brought up and the enemy were routed.

But when the fighting was over, she had the knowledge, skills and neatness of hand to stitch and physic her comrades back to health...and keep their war-leader balanced and happy. As long as she could bring her steel to bite a Danish pirate somewhere, or put a Saxon warrior back into the fray to do so, she would be pleased.

Every day she returned to Maritia's care exhausted, her body dripping with sweat, bruised from the knocks she had received and chafed from the armour that Leofric had found for her to wear: a thick jerkin over-stitched with iron scales that hung below her waist, stout leather chausses with riveted chain to her ankles, and tough leather boots with shaped steel over her insteps and her toes. And every day she returned more determined than ever to be worthy of Leofric and his whole command, and not droop like a wilted flower before them. She was Woden born, the daughter of a noble thane belovèd of the King, and she would not let him down before his men.

*

*T*hen, finally, on a day heavy with clouds underscored by veils of white before a hustling wind, all the preparations were over, everything packed and ready to leave, and it was time to present herself to Leofric and Hugo before they left. And for her to determine what was to happen to all the people of the outlaw village, who would be coming together that evening for her declaration.

Not just because leadership had changed since her fight with Velda Gaerwulf...but because she was the Lady Brioni of Foxley on whose land they lived and breathed and had their being. Since her father's death, and that of her brother, Gyrth, she was the sole holder of all that great estate, despite being unconfirmed by the King, and as such was responsible for all those who lived on it. And, if she was to leave with Leofric, all those left behind must know what was expected of them.

So she sat in Maritia's chamber, naked except for the rough cotton sheeting that Maritia had given her, her muscles toned with Maritia's oils and perfumed unguents, old bruises now yellow and purple across her back and shoulders as they faded more and more each day...new ones freshly rubbed with arnica oil and witch hazel. While her friend ferreted about through her clothes baskets and chests for something really special for her to wear, on this their last evening together before leaving for Ford in the morning, she warmed herself before the glowing brazier, filled with charcoal and fruit-wood logs, that stood in Maritia's room. Breathing in the wood incense as it wafted around her, she luxuriated in the heat that flowed out across her body making her whole torso glow and prickle with its fiery touch; her eyes partially closed in the joyousness of feeling truly well again, while all the time she waited for her friend to find what she was looking for.

All her exertions on the practice grounds were as nothing to the beating that Velda had given her, and it had taken some time for her body to recover. But now, more soothed by Maritia's studied handling than she could have believed possible, her body felt supple and at ease. The welts and thick weals that had hurt her so badly at first were now little more than a minor irritant, driven into the background by the remorseless exercise she had been taking, and the ice-cold compresses that her friend had insisted on laying on her every day she had returned from battle-practice.

Then, just as she was beginning to wonder whether she shouldn't move before she actually roasted herself, Maritia gave a soft cry of satisfaction and came quickly over to where Brioni was still gently toasting herself.

"Here you are, my love, the very thing! My father brought it back from Cologne when he was there a year or so back. Come, try it on. I know your body has richer curves than mine, but it should still be alright. At the very worst it will only serve to enhance them!" And pulling Brioni onto her feet, she held out the garment for which she had been so desperately searching.

Of the finest Egyptian cotton, and dyed a most delicate shade of blue that complemented her friend's eyes, it was intricately embroidered with summer flowers and grasses in brilliant colours, with tiny birds fluttering around them,

273

that wound up from the hem to the bust. It was a thing of such supple, flowing beauty that all Brioni could do at first was stare open-mouthed.

"Don't you like it?" Maritia questioned anxiously as Brioni remained silent. "I grant you that the woollen threads are rather bright perhaps, but it is the finest Saxon needle work, and I did so hope you would be pleased."

"*Pleased?* Oh, Mari, it's beautiful!" she exclaimed. "The loveliest thing I have seen since leaving Court. Oh, sweetheart you are such a good friend to me. I did so want to look my best this evening, with my presentation before Hugo and Leofric, and all the people from the outlaw village coming for my decision on their future. But this," she gestured to the dress that Maritia was still holding up, "this is just exquisite. Won't your father be disappointed that I am wearing it and not you?"

"Don't be such a big silly. Father will be delighted. Now, you can slip it on in just a moment, but let me braid up your hair now that it has dried out at last. Tonight you are the Lady Brioni of Foxley, in all her glory...not the tousled, blood-streaked shield-maiden the villagers last saw grovelling on the ground with a sword in her hands; nor the fighting virago the boys have been seeing these past few days on the practice ground!

"Somewhere amongst the wreckage you can see strewn about, there are some soft leather shoes that should fit you, with wedge heels, and I have some silken under garments too. They are some of the few things, along with my soaps, sponges and perfumes, with which I indulge myself. Father moans bitterly about the expense, but when a girl spends the better half of her life living like a humble camp follower in the train of an invading army, with a great brown bear for a companion, then she has to have something to remind her that she is a woman and not a performing boy!"

\*

*T*hat day Hugo, Gilbert, and all their helpers from the village excelled themselves despite the weather, and by evening the great pavilion was dressed as for Yule Night.

Branches of yew and holly had been bound in around the great tent poles with yellow gorse and pink milkweed, and more hung in cheerful swags around the dais. Extra braziers had been brought in and loaded with fruit-wood to provide sweet incense, as well as charcoal for raw heat, and there were large wrought iron stands of oil lamps in brass brackets in every corner, with more lamps along the middle of the long table on the dais.

Elsewhere crude trestles had been set up for Leofric's men with long benches for them to sit on, simple oil lamps on each table, and everywhere the plaited matting had been brushed and strewn with herbs, and fresh straw laid down at the main entrance, itself guarded by two of Leofric's men on a strict rota so no man would be left out from the celebrations. Great barrels of ale and beer had also been brought in, and laid on broad cradles for the feasting that was expected to go on until there were no men standing except the guards!

Into this joyous arena poured all Leofric's war-band, together with the performers of the *Circus Maximus*, even Oswald had been brought from his cage on his chain. Massive, and wearing a great knitted scarf of scarlet and blue around his huge furry neck, he swayed his head from side to side with small grunts of pleasure that made everyone smile. And all the villagers from the clearing had come in too, as much to enjoy a good drink as to hear the judgment that the Lady of Foxley had prepared for them.

So it was that some while later, with a noisy *Hoo-Hoo-Hooom!* on a war-horn, Leofric, Hugo, and all the others who had gathered to Hugo's great pavilion were startled into silence as Brioni and Maritia, with a rustle of their dresses and the scent of high summer clinging to them, their hair dressed high on their heads and covered with silk coifs threaded with jewels, came quietly through and bowed their heads before their two leaders. Bran and Utha, pacing in beside them, seated themselves upright on either side of their mistress, groomed and brushed until their fur glowed, their fighting collars gleaming in the evening lamplight and the flickering braziers on the wide dais.

"So," Hugo rumbled at Brioni stern-faced, heaving himself up to greet her, the whole pavilion before him packed with people, "you have come at last to this meeting, as was agreed many days ago, to present yourself as is required after such a fight as you and Velda Gaerwulf fought last week."

"Yes, Hugo the Bearmaster, and my Lord Leofric of Wimborne," she replied in her crystal voice and a brief nod of her head to the big Saxon war-leader now also standing beside the Bearmaster. "I am come before you as victor to claim my right, as expressed on the day that Velda and I fought with one another, to the death or banishment. The right to claim your help in my quest to destroy my enemies…a promise that was witnessed, and acclaimed, by all present on that day. And to lay my doom on those who live on Foxley land at the edge of this clearing."

"That is your right, my Lady Brioni of Foxley," Hugo replied with a similar bob of his head. "All who were here that day gave their assent in ringing tones."

"And that assent will be upheld," Leofric declaimed loudly, with a smile. "I hold you to be worthy in every way, my Lady Brioni. Worthy to rule all in Velda's stead…and more than worthy to join with me and my men as we move to fight Oscytel, and the whole Great Army as well if necessary; as I promised you." And turning to face his men around the long table, and then all those gathered in the hall from the village across the clearing, he roared out: "*Do you assent?*"

"Yea...we assent!" came the shouted response, everyone raising their arms in the air and stamping on the plaited matting that covered the floor, Leofric's men thundering on the dais with their boots, "*We assent!*" And Brioni beamed at them all, her smile lighting up her face, and she felt sudden power race through her body, leaving her very finger ends tingling. And turning from Leofric, himself beaming across his rugged features, she then addressed all those who had come across the stream, the clarity of her voice cutting into every corner of the great tent into which they had gathered.

"By all the customs you hold here, and have done for some time, I take up the challenge of ruling you as my father would have done had he not been butchered by the enemy and all his people slain," and she looked all round the huge tent, and into every face. "This then is the doom I lay on you all," she said, straightening to her full height, her voice suddenly becoming harsh in its delivery. "This village is to be abandoned! Razed to the ground and the land returned to the forest. It is illegal and cannot be allowed to remain."

At which there was a terrible groan from the people standing there, many crying out in anger and dismay, and there was a sudden surge towards her, stilled immediately by Bran and Utha who leapt to their feet and bayed their anger, their teeth, huge and frightening as they stood their ground beside their mistress, their fur bristling all along their backs.

Leofric also was appalled by such a harsh judgement, as were all those of his war-band who had women and children in the village, so many of his men also cried out against her, as he did himself. "You cannot do this, my Lady," he remonstrated with her bitterly. "This is not worthy of you. Unsay it, I order you!"

But Brioni stood there unmoved, her face like stone before the shouted anger of the people, and Leofric's furious intervention. And she raised her hands for silence, standing there alone, her great hounds by her side, until slowly some measure of calm returned to the pavilion.

"Oh, ye of little faith," she declaimed loudly, her eyes flashing, her voice clipped and hard. "You have not heard me out! Would I, Brioni of Foxley, behave so basely towards so many of you who have aided me and the Lord of Wimborne? Be silent and listen to all I have to say before you dare to judge me. My home, Foxley manor, was destroyed by the Viking war-lord, Oscytel, the same day that his King, Guthrum, assaulted Chippenham and drove our own belovèd King, Alfred, into hiding.

276

"And when that barbarian destroyed Foxley he slew every man, woman and child who lived there. I saw this with my own eyes. Yes, this village, here, must be destroyed," she said, waving her arms around her. "It is illegal, you *all* know that, and when things return to normal, and they will, then the Shire Reeve will raze it to the ground and all who live here will be turned off and abandoned. That is the law and the law must be obeyed. Every man must have a Lord...that is Alfred's law, I know, for I know our King. So...*I will be your Lord!*" she cried out holding her arms out to them all as they gaped in astonishment. "And to you I will give the lands of Foxley that my father's people lived and worked on," at which there was a great gasp and stir amongst the people, and much noisy murmuring with broad smiles and many open mouths.

"But not as common geburs, bound to the land with few rights, but as churls paying rent, and for those of you who may have money, the right to buy the land outright and become Freemen. *But I will still be your Lord!*" At which there was a huge cheer that went on and on, and turning she gave Leofric a wide grin and raised her eyebrows, admonishing him with her fingers as she did so, before turning back and raising her arms once more for silence which, this time, fell swiftly amongst them all.

"Foxley is a ruin. All was burned to ashes by our Viking enemies on Epiphany. Today I give you the right to cut down what trees you need to re-build it as it was. Hall, barns and storehouses; chapel, houses and palisade, until the job is done. Foxley will rise again. I have sworn it many times, and now with new life to fill the spaces left by all whom the Vikings slew that day, it can happen. Now," she demanded of them all in ringing tones, "*do you assent?*"

"Aye, my Lady, we assent!" they roared out to her, with waving arms and stamping feet. "*We assent!*"

And with that she turned away, her eyes filled with tears.

# Chapter Thirty Eight

"Well, that was bravely done, my Lady of Foxley," Hugo said to her, as she cleared her face with the back of her hand, his voice warm with approval, while he conducted her to a tall-backed chair beside Leofric's when the wild hubbub had eased, and all the villagers had left chattering volubly amongst themselves.

"I did not know you were such a showman. I have a place for just such as you in the *Circus Maximus*. You held them in the palm of your hand!"

"But not me, you little fiend!" Leofric snarled at her. "You made a complete fool out of me! You might have let me know that was what you intended."

"And you, my Lord, might have trusted me better!" she shot back at him, her eyes sparkling with swift rage. "You do not know me, Leofric Iron Hand. As if I would do such a wicked thing? Especially after I had suggested to your men that I would give them land on my estates? And what about all those of them who have women in that village, and children?" she went on, her eyes flashing. "How could I raze their village to the ground and cast them out without giving something in return? And you, my fine Lord of Wimborne, must have known all along that the village was illegal and would have to be destroyed. Or did you blind yourself to all that while you were rutting with Velda? 'Unsay it, I order you' indeed!" she mimicked him, enraged. "Who do you think you are to give me orders, my fine Saxon war-lord?"

"Then? When I called out at you? No right at all, but you angered me greatly," he said seizing her hand and holding it close in his own. "It sounded so brutal. So unlike the 'you' I have come to know…and no, I don't know you as well as I would like to. But you could have told me what you intended," he added looking fierce. "After all we have talked often and long these past few days, and of many things, while you have been recovering from the battering that woman gave you. I thought you might have learned to like me…to trust me!"

"Like you? Of course I like you," she said, kissing his hand, "more and more each day. But trust you? When you seem to treat women no better than my brother Gyrth?"

"You told me he had changed. That the new lady in his life, the Lady Judith, had changed him. That until her he had been uncaring; spreading himself too easily. Like me with Velda. And as with Gyrth and Judith, so it has been for me with you. You have changed me, Brioni. And not because of your sweetness alone, but because of your courage and determination; your simple honesty...and you have been incredibly brave," he said then, stroking her hand and bringing it up to his lips. "And Trausti tells me that you have been unrelenting on the practice ground. The best recruit he has had for months. He tells me that if every man he worked with had your determination and vigour that he would clear the Danes out of Wessex in a six month!"

"Did he so?" she asked, suddenly diverted, her eyes sparkling at his praise. "For I tell you that he is the hardest man to please I ever met. He has really made my body droop with exhaustion, and he has given me many more bruises!"

"But why did you not tell me about the outlaw village?" he persisted, "I could have supported you better had I known. And you are right. I didn't think much about what would happen if the Danes were driven out. Alfred was then far from my thoughts. I was much too concentrated on killing Danes and building my hoard. I knew the village was illegal, but as there was nothing I could do about it I simply ignored the fact. And Velda did have a part to play there. She was not all bad to start with...the badness came later."

"What has happened to her?"

"She has left the village. Old Anna patched her up. Stitched the slash you gave her and bound up her wrists; physicked her, gave her an elixir to take when she felt ill, and sent her on her way. Almaric the Smith gave her a set of panniers to go on her horse, and helped her pack. He also made sure she had the silver you gave her through Maritia. You should make him your Reeve when you leave with me tomorrow. He is a good man, Brioni, and will do you well. But as for Velda? She has gone from our lives for good."

"No regrets?" she asked him quietly, head on one side, blue eyes on green.

"No! How could there be? There is no comparison between you. You are everything that poor Velda could never be. 'Rutting' was about right," he added shame-faced, looking down as he spoke. "That's what she was good at, and it was all I needed at the start. But I need more than that now," he went on, looking into her eyes and taking her hand to his lips, "knew it months ago, long before I met you, and had already started to distance myself from her. She could never have been 'My Lady of Wimborne', no matter how much she may have wanted to be. You saw what she was like. Our relationship was deeply strained long before you fell in on us from nowhere."

"Well that's alright then," she said with a smile, turning his big hand over and planting a kiss in the centre of his palm, closing his fingers over it as

279

she did so. "That is one for you to keep safe. To enjoy when I am not beside you."

"That will not happen any more times than are necessary," he assured her with a grin. "You are in my command now," he said firmly, capturing both her hands and looking into her face, "and I demand complete obedience from all who fight with me."

"So that's what you meant by 'then'," she said, rubbing her fingers over the back of his hand with a quiet smile.

"You remembered?" he chuckled. "Yes. You are now in my command, soldier, and I am an exacting war-leader. There can be no room for dissent when we are in the field. As I said a week ago, when you were newly come amongst us, no-one says me 'Nay'. After discussion my word is final, and all men...and women now, must accept that."

"I do! You will have no complaints from me on that score," she said, looking at him deeply, her blue eyes shining in the lamplight, her mind a jumble of emotions.

"You look ravishing, my Lady," he said, unable to keep his eyes off her; staggered at the change that had been wrought in her by Maritia's expert care. The difference between the deadly, spitting virago he had witnessed the week before, fighting in the slush and snow; the determined armoured warrior he had watched since on the practice ground, with sword and shield, shouting and stamping under Trausti...and the most elegant and beautiful creature he had seen speaking with the villagers with such command, was just too amazing for words.

"And you, my Lord," she replied with a brilliant smile, "have bold eyes and a dangerous smile for one so unpractised as I. I swear upon my honour that you look ready to devour me!" And the men sat around the table nearby laughed.

"More than likely, you little lynx!" he threw back at her, joining in the laughter that had run round the group of burly warriors gathered around the long table. "What did you expect of a Saxon warrior about to enter into a fierce war, when seated beside a maid of such sauce and beauty? For I am no monk, my Lady...and by Saint Michael, you are no nun either!"

"Beware Bran and Utha, my Lord Leofric Iron Hand," she said with a swift gesture of her hands, and a wicked grin, as her two great hounds came instantly to her side. "Remember, these are wolfhounds, and wolfhounds are trained to hunt wolves...and you, my Lord, are still a Wolfshead! One false move and they will surely devour you!"

And everyone laughed at her swift wit, while Gilbert and his house thralls brought out the food that all had been waiting for, and with great relish

280

were swift to get their knives and teeth into. Meanwhile great jugs of beer and ale went round and horns and drinking bowls were raised and quaffed with wild shouts of *'Wassail!'* and *'Drink Hael!'* as all those gathered there at crude trestles on the floor, and the long table on the dais, embraced the feast that Hugo had provided, and gave another great roar of approval as a vast hogshead of wine was trundled in on a small cart by four of Gilbert's helpers.

*

For the first time in months their leader was relaxed and happy. They were safe from enemies for the time being, there was food and drink in plenty and, for many, their women were now waiting for them across the clearing. What more could a good Saxon warrior and hearth-companion need than that? They had money to come to them from the Lady Brioni's hoard...that would remain under Hugo's care and control when they left...and there was the promise of action to look forward to, with still more booty to claim.

Every dead Dane had money on him somewhere and many had arm rings of gold or silver to be stripped from their bodies. And some had armour even the King would be proud to wear. So, with much laughter and warm-hearted rivalry, Leofric's command settled down to a raucous evening of heavy drinking and good cheer.

Tomorrow they might all be fighting for their lives against a great company of Danish Vikings...tonight they were free to indulge themselves to the full, the drinkers standing to shout their toasts, ale and wine slopping everywhere, Leofric acknowledging every call with a wave of his hand when he was not wholly engrossed with his lovely Saxon lady.

*

For Brioni and Leofric that evening in Hugo's company, with Maritia and his troupe to entertain them, Oswald to perform his tricks to riotous applause, music from harp, crumhorn and tabor, and all Leofric's commanders around them, was an evening that, long afterwards, Brioni remembered as one of the best times in her life. An evening of laughter and excitement...of subtle magic, music, soft words and loving gestures despite the noise going on around them. So much so that she and Leofric were swiftly lost in the warm mystery of their own hearts, each giving to the other some measure of the deeper feelings that had stirred them when they had first met, and they sat, with hands deeply curled together, as they touched and stroked each other's fingers.

There was affection and loving warmth between them that hardly seemed possible after so short a time of knowing one another, a closeness from Leofric especially that soothed Brioni's uncertainties. Each of them sharing the other's feelings as if they had known one another all their lives, and with that special depth of understanding that often only lovers have.

And as the evening progressed they were soon totally engrossed in one another to the exclusion of everyone else. Their eyes shone with the sure knowledge of the feeling each shared with the other, and of knowing that another human being, that you care about so deeply, really cares for you, and in the same way. Someone who is not simply paying lip-service to calm a fluttering heart before pouncing like a leopard on a tethered lamb!

And there was the wonder, and the inner glow, of simply '*being*'...of being valued, and needed...of being loved and cherished; with the bitter-sweet agony of desire that cannot immediately be fulfilled, but must be waited for.

They were both in heaven, and in hell.

Both wanting more but forced to be satisfied with less. Each touch and glance that passed between them a sensuous, erotic promise of the love they meant to share once they were finally alone. A knowledge that broke every convention with which Brioni had been brought up by her mother and her church; a convention that had held her back from Heardred...but which with Leofric she was prepared to break in every way. So much so that she blushed and turned her face away from Leofric's hot gaze, while her heart fluttered wildly in her breast.

He smiled, and held her hand closely in his own.

"You know, I was really afraid for you out there with Velda," he said quietly after she had turned back to him again. "I really thought she was going to kill you, that you would never find your feet, or your sword. That she would do to you what she did to Sylvia..."

"Shh," Brioni whispered to him, gently putting her finger up to his mouth. "You must learn to trust me, even as I must learn to trust you," she added, thinking of what had passed between them earlier. "I told you I was no milk-sop maiden, remember? She was tiring all the time and I knew I was the better fighter, carried less weight and was more fiercely determined. You fret over me too much, my love," she said, hesitating slightly over the words. "See, I am here beside you, before all your friends in a way my mother never would have allowed before a formal hand-clasping, nor the Queen! And I am not ashamed. I fought for the right to be a part of your war-band...and to be by your side."

282

"Always?" he asked, huskily, the gold flecks in his green eyes sparkling.

"Always!" she whispered back at him, holding his hand fiercely. *"Always!"*

Without another word, Leofric took her face between his hands and looked deep into her eyes. Then, with infinite care, he kissed her brow, moving his lips to cover her eyes which he caressed with feather-soft kisses, while his heart went out to her, and all he wished to do was hold her close and love her to exhaustion. To lie beside her till the soft light of morning brought them to their senses, to hold her close to his heart and never let her go.

"I love you, my Lady Brioni of Foxley," he said then, leaning over her, his voice deep and slow. "I have never felt this way about any woman since Emma died, nor have I used those words with another. I have so armoured myself against such feelings that it frightens me a little. It makes me vulnerable; gives me a weakness that an enemy might exploit. I am used to battle, the smell of campfires, the roaring of my men, the excitement of the chase...killing Danes.

"I have so little to offer you. No proper home, the fear of death or capture ever present, carrying all we have on our backs...and no hope of real marriage until this is over. Then there is the question of my outlawry, my stolen lands and the uncertainty of earning Alfred's pardon. It is no life for a girl like you! It has never bothered me before, but now, suddenly, I am unsure. I feel I ought to leave you here with Hugo and Maritia..."

"Now, listen to me, Leofric Wolfshead," she interrupted fiercely, drawing out of his arms to face him, while all around them his men continued to feast and drink themselves to the floor; Hugo roaring and rollicking in his great chair, arm-wrestling with Beornred, Leofric's giant commander, while Maritia sat beside him and shrieked with excitement. "I have not come this far for you to draw back now! Look at me, my fine Saxon love. What are you afraid of? I am not going to change my mind just because of a parcel of silly conventions. Life is too short for that, and too precious. Nor am I made of curds and whey. Feel my heart, Leofric," she said putting his big hand over her breast. "It beats for you, my life, not for any other."

"You do me too much honour, my love," he said quietly, kissing her hands again. "I nearly stopped you from fighting..."

"I know. Maritia told me, what you said," she replied fiercely. "And she was right. I never would have forgiven you! I told you, I fought Velda to win my place by your side; to prove myself in your eyes, and in those of your men sitting round here amongst us. And to face my own firedrake! I needed to know whether I could take the pain and fear of battle, and not run from the field in terror. Don't look so puzzled, dear heart. I know what happens in the

283

battle-line. Gyrth has told me many times: the fear, the dryness of the mouth, the roaring shouts, the stink of blood and offal…the terror that opens a man's bowels, that makes a man flee when the enemy crash into the shield wall."

"Dear God and Saint Michael, protect you from that!" he said vehemently. "Before Christ, the battle-line is no place for a woman!"

"You are right, my love," she said, twining her fingers round his. "A woman's place is not in the battle-line. But when Oscytel came to Foxley all the women came out to fight; to be with their men, and the older children too, with slings and stones. And I ran out to join them. But that was a general action, not single combat. I needed to know how I would feel face to face with my enemy. If my strength, my courage, was good enough? And it was. Velda was my firedrake, and when I beat her down, I beat that down also."

"Your 'firedrake'? I did not know that good Saxon girls would know of such a thing?"

"You forget that this 'good' Saxon girl has been with the King and his 'hounds' for many months. I know all about a man's 'firedrake', the fire-breathing dragon that is his greatest fear. That he must face and beat down for him to be a man…or break in the attempt."

"And Velda was yours?"

"Yes. She was mine. More so than Oscytel at Foxley. She was a personal challenge. The barrier to all my hopes and dreams, to my blood-oath. To you!"

"And all the rest? The uncertainty of life together? Of life in the field, with few comforts and in constant danger?"

"I warrant you I have spent as many nights under the stars these past six months or so as I have done in a bed! You try to leave me here, my Lord and I will follow you on Foxhead, with Bran and Utha by my side, until the sea freezes over and the sun is nothing but a shallow memory in the dark corners of the mind!

"There is no way I am going to let you put me aside…*so do not even think it!* Now, hold me close and don't be such a goose. Sweet Mary, will this feasting never end," she murmured as Hugo and Beornred fell into a roistering heap on the ground. And snuggling into his shoulder she turned to look up at him with sparkling eyes: "I have a special gift for you, my Lord, that my whole body is yearning now to offer you…yes!" she continued in a gentle whisper, as his eyes suddenly widened as the full meaning of her words struck home. "I am still untouched. And no maid ever had a better, more loving man on whom she could bestow herself!"

Leofric looked down at her nestling in his arms and kissed her softly.

"So be it, my gentle lady," he breathed softly. "Come then with me, Hugo has had a box-bed made up for us beyond the canvas screening over there. There are even good woolfells on the floor."

"It seems you have thought of everything!" she said then, burying her face in his shoulder.

"It was Maritia's idea that Hugo embraced. Whatever you two have been talking of, you certainly convinced her that tonight would be the night for both of us!"

"What about all these others?" she asked dreamily, as Raedwald, Finnar and Trausti staggered off together, arm in arm and singing loudly, out to their bothies in the outlaw village.

"This day has run its course, my love, and so have they," he added with a laugh as two more of his men keeled over onto the floor. "Beornred will go with Hugo presently and see to Oswald, then he will sleep here with all the rest ready for the morning. Maritia will be in her room and Hugo will go to his chamber. Only Gilbert and his team will stay up a while to clear up and tend the braziers."

"Then take my hand, Leofric Iron Hand, and make me yours. My skin burns for your touch and my body melts beside you. Pain there may be, my Life, I have long known that. But pain borne out of love can still be ecstasy if gently given."

And standing up in one graceful, fluid movement she held out her hands to him, and arms wrapped closely round each other they slipped quietly away beyond the shadows of the flickering firelight, away from the men still roistering amongst the lees of wine and slopped ale, while Maritia watched them go and smiled.

# Chapter Thirty Nine

The room he led her to was both warm and cosy, despite being against the outer skin of the pavilion.

There were a number of thick fleeces on the rush matting floor, and a great box-bed, like the one her parents had used, dominated the chamber Hugo had created at Maritia's suggestion, with fresh cotton sheeting and French feather pillows on a great mattress of layers of beaten fleece-wool in thick linen ticking, with linen sheeting, furs and blankets over all. To one side was a glowing brazier, and Hugo had ordered a tall wrought-iron stand with three oil lamps sitting in brass rings to be placed in one corner.

"Oh, Heart of Christ, but I want you!" he said huskily, turning her towards him and kissing her fiercely. "You are so lovely, that I cannot bear not to touch you. I have known you so short a time, yet the thought of not always having you with me, or near me, is simply unbearable!"

"I will always be with you now, Leofric," she replied, smiling up at him, putting her hands behind his head. "I have told you that, my darling, my own true love."

"It all seems too wonderful to be true," he replied, kissing her again, more gently. "What have I done, sweetheart, to deserve your beauty and your love in my life? Make no mistake, Brioni," he continued, pulling her closely to him. "I can fight all the battles that the enemy may choose to put my way. But without your love, what do I have? All the victories in the world can never make up for that.

"You are the most precious thing in my life now, my darling" he said, putting his arms round her and holding her close. What you fear I shall conquer; what you hate I shall triumph over; what you desire I shall strive to win for you and what you love I shall try to hold precious also. Just love me and need me and all will be well for us."

"I do, Leofric," she whispered. "*I do*, my love, and I always will."

And without another word she lifted up her face and kissed him, twining her arms about his neck, mouth seeking mouth in one long timeless kiss, his darting tongue playing games of fire with her own, until she was coached to return his kisses with a wild fervour that made her whole body quiver, and her heart pound in her throat with the pure ecstasy of their passion. And as she felt his hands slide up her back she leaned in towards him, devouring him with her love until the room dissolved into a haze of warmth and light, time and place having no meaning, his tongue flicking and dancing round hers like a bright flame, while his hands caressed her up and down her spine, until she was panting with desire.

Then she tore herself free, and stepping back she loosened the tie strings of the dress that Maritia had given her to wear. Bending forward she reached for the hem and in one swift movement drew it over her head and dropped it in a soft, glowing pile by her feet, her loosened silk underclothes following it with a gentle rustle to the floor.

Like a living statue of alabaster she stood naked before him, her loins open and ready to receive him, her breasts thrust out for him, her nipples hardening with desire as she drew her hands across them.

"Oh, God, you are so beautiful," he whispered hoarsely as he drew her back towards him. So very, very beautiful." And running his hands up the long, silken smoothness of her legs, he caressed the rounded globes of her buttocks, the warm flesh springing up against his hands. And with a soft moan he pulled her forward and kissed her throat and her breasts, pressing his mouth onto each one, savouring every inch of them in turn until she could take no more, her head thrown back in blind, trembling rapture.

"Oh, God! I am all yours, my darling! *All yours!*" she cried out. "Just take me and use me any way you wish, even if you hurt me. You are my man, now and for ever. I have been a maid long enough. Make me the woman I so long to be."

And picking her up in his arms he carried her to the great bed that had been prepared for them, and tearing his clothes from his body in the soft glow of the lamps Hugo had placed in their room, he took her, and made them one for then and ever after.

\*

During the night the weather changed, the wind blowing down from the north-west in sharp gusts, and daylight crept greyly in on them with the sound of a brave cock crowing from across the clearing, and Oswald grunting from his cage; the rattle of pails from the horse lines and Gilbert's men arranging the stools and chairs on the dais with a bang and clatter. No rain that morning, but a bloom of light that flushed the tent walls, and threw shadows on the sides from the brazier and lamp stand in the corners of the room.

Naked in his arms, Brioni stirred and pushed her buttocks into his loins, nestling against him, his big hands curled round her breasts, his thighs pressed into the back of her legs. Spoons…and she relished his nearness and the strength of him as he held her in his arms.

Then she smiled, and before his body could respond properly for him to take her again, she turned in his arms and kissed him, before dragging herself up on an elbow and looking down at him.

"My ever loving Lord. I don't know where I am, what day it is, nor yet what year. I only know I love you…and with more love than I knew ever existed. Last night…this morning? I know not, neither do I care, but that was the most wonderful way that any maid could have of being made a woman by the man she loves."

"Did I hurt you?"

"Only fleetingly. Love's passion washed it all away and then the only pain I had was the pain of wanting you again, and again. Even now my body is ready for you. No peasant could rut more fervently than I, when my Lord demands it of me. You have turned me into a wild wanton. No wonder my mother smiled whenever she looked at my father. I had never thought of it before, but they must have been lovers many times over."

"Then he was a lucky man to have found a woman to love him so completely," he said leaning up to her for a kiss.

"Mmmm," she responded warmly. "Pray God that you and I will be the same after our children have grown and gone their ways. But not now, my Lord," she shrieked, as he reached for her again, clutching a fur rug to her as she leapt out of their bed.

"The cock has crowed," she grinned at him knowingly. "And your men are already stirring. I will not have it said that I have diverted their Lord's attention away from his duties! Not today of all days," she said with another shriek as Leofric leaped at her from his side of the bed. "You will get no more than a kiss from me, you pirate," she berated him with a laugh. "So put that great 'spear' of yours away for another time," she added, putting her hands around him as she spoke. "And not in me! Though God knows I would love you to take me again! But one of us must be strong, and I am up and on my feet; so it may as well be me, as I can see where your thoughts are this morning! So get dressed, my noble Lord of Wimborne," she said with a laugh, throwing his clothes at him as she spoke. "And I will go and find my gear from Maritia's chamber, have a strip wash, and come and find you in the main pavilion as soon as maybe."

"Very well, my love," Leofric agreed with a huge sigh. "But see just what you reduce me to when I am near you! No better than a rutting stag in the autumn," he added, catching her at last and wrapping his arms around her, her slender frame engulfed in his embrace, overwhelming her in just the way she

288

had felt when she had first met him. Was that only a scant week ago? It did not seem possible. Now she had given him all she had to give, and she felt ecstatic!

"Put me down, Leofric!" she laughed at him, as he swung her up into his arms, spinning as he did so. "Before you drop me! Beornred and Raedwald will be along for you shortly, and will need to find their war-lord dressed and ready for action…and not that kind of action," she said with another shriek of laughter.

"Oh very well," he said with a grin. "But it was worth a try, my darling, and you are so very tempting in every way. And, before you ask, Velda was nothing compared to you. *Nothing!*" And before she could say another word he pulled her head down and kissed her deeply. "Now, you brazen hussy," he added, smacking her bare rump heartily, "away with you to Maritia. Sort out some clothes suitable for hard travel, and make sure you are armed and warmly wrapped, it is still bitter out there. I want to be away before the sun is too high. We must move nearer to Chippenham, so we will strike out for Ford, and hope to reach there before dark."

"Very well, my Lord and Master," she said with a smile and a mock bow. "I will go now and get organised. Maritia and I have long discussed what I should wear, and what I should take with me. You will not be disappointed!" And pausing briefly, she slipped the rug she was holding off her shoulders and flashed her shapely body at him, standing for a brief moment with breasts and loins open to his gaze, her hair a golden swirl across her nakedness, her eyes a blaze of blue…and then she turned, the fur wrap was whisked back across her white waist and shoulders, and she was gone before he could say another word.

\*

Several hours later, long after sun-up, Leofric's whole command came together in the great pavilion for the last time.

Leofric, flanked by his principal commanders, Beornred, Raedwald, Trausti and Finnar, stood with all his men before him, some, like Cadoc, Hunfrith and Raynar with long bows over their shoulders others with their axes, some with their long spears, and all fully armoured-up with swords and seaxes by their sides, the long, sword-like daggers that were the mark of the Saxon warrior, and their helmets in their hands. Each man's armour had been shined and greased, each helmet with side plates and nasal protection, some inlaid with gold and silver. All carried their great shields on their backs, every shield covered with brightly painted leather with iron rims and pointed bosses, the boss as much a weapon as each man's sword.

Clad in tough leather covered with iron scales or riveted mail, leather chausses ring-mailed from waist to ankle, or cross-gartered from the knee, they were an impressive, frightening group of men, stern-faced and now waiting for orders, a group to which Brioni quietly added herself, Bran and Utha by her side as always, their fighting collars wicked in the shifting light.

Similarly dressed, throwing spear in hand, but with a light wicker shield across her back instead of the great linden-wood shields of Leofric's men, she was both proud and intensely self-conscious. The thick fur cape Maritia had fixed across her shoulders with strong plaited cord, hung heavy down her back and was warm in the confines of the big tent which sighed and billowed to the wind outside it.

With a few chosen words, Leofric outlined where they were going and in what order they were to leave: Jaenberht and Aldred the Swordsman well ahead of the column as they moved along the trackway amongst the trees of Helm's Wood; himself, Beornred his shield-man, Raedwald and Brioni at the head; Trausti and Finnar with a rear guard behind them. From the edge of the forest it was but a short step to the ancient roadway, the great Fosse Way of the legions many centuries before, and was still used by many to that day. Travelling across country, and down the old Roman road to where it crossed the By Brook on an ancient stone-slabbed ford, they would travel as swiftly as they were able; then along the distant watercourse to the Combe and so to Ford, their destination.

Difficult country, and dangerous, especially the ancient Fosse Way where Danish patrols might easily be found as Guthrum's army spread itself across Wessex in a bid to control the whole kingdom. And every man listened to his words with tight concentration, knowing that their lives might depend on the manner in which their orders were carried out.

Then it was over, and with a roar of acceptance the men dismissed to their tasks and to their horses, all tacked and ready to start on their long journey to their destination, the tiny settlement of Ford.

"So, Hugo," Leofric said, going across to where the giant Bearmaster was standing on the dais, Maritia by his side, "we go now to the gorges along the By Brook beyond Combe, below Colerne and Biddestone, south-west of Chippenham. Cadoc knows the place well, and will be our eyes and ears in Chippenham where his woman works in the King's Hall that Guthrum has taken over since he seized the town.

"You, my large friend," he added with his arm across Hugo's shoulder as they moved off the dais and towards the entrance, "must move out from here and take your people down to the town itself. Do it in easy stages, so as not to alarm the enemy. We will do all the alarming they need, and make their lives hellish in the process. That way they will be even more pleased to see you.

"We have talked this over before, as you know. But all the world likes good entertainment as you said the other night, and the Danes are no exception. Grimnir is also in Chippenham and will be a help to you. He can make the introduction to Guthrum, who is as wriggly as a sackful of ferrets, so beware. That Dane is a cunning bastard and has fooled Alfred on more than one occasion, so be certain of what you agree. But he should pay you all well. God knows the bloody man has enough in his hoard to do so easily! Whatever you discover, tell Cadoc and he will tell me. Then we can make a plan together."

Hugo looked across at his friend and smiled broadly as Leofric turned to his horse, Wotan, a great bay with a white blaze on his forehead, and threw himself up into the tall saddle with a jingle of spurs and crash of steel, Beornred handing him up his big shield before clambering up onto Warrior, his own chestnut charger. The large Saxon war-leader had proved to be a good friend, trustworthy and a born leader. They had come a long way together since he and Maritia had rescued him after he had been outlawed by Aethelwold, and his land and honour taken from him.

"You are a good man, Leofric Iron hand," he rumbled, his craggy face breaking into a smile. "You have something else now to struggle for, my friend. A real chance to restore your honour and your place amongst men...and you have someone special to help you. I have never met anyone like her," he added, turning to where Brioni was standing by Foxhead ready to mount.

Her hair brailed up beneath a tight blue woollen hood, her helmet hanging from the cantle of her saddle, she was as ready to leave as all the rest of his command. The great wolfskins she had taken for herself, now properly stripped and cleaned with the necessary oils rubbed in, were rolled in with her other belongings behind her saddle, and from her waist hung her short sword in a fleece-lined scabbard that Beornred had found for her, her armour gleaming and her light shield on her back. Only a proper long sword was missing from her equipment...then Blood Drinker would become the long bladed saexe that every warrior carried on his right side.

"You, my Lady of Foxley, have chosen to follow a fine man," Hugo said, strolling across the straw-raddled ground to join her. "Hard in war, firm of purpose and generous in love. Any father would be proud to wed his daughter to such a man...and her mother would be proud also," he added with a smile. "Serve him well, and he will love and honour you all his life. Play him false...and you will lose everything!"

291

Eyes shining brightly, Brioni laid her hand on Leofric's arm and gave him a dazzling smile, before turning back to Hugo and giving him a hug.

"Hugo, I love him with all my heart. We who come from the blood of King Ine and are Woden born follow always the path of truth and honour. That was how I was brought up. That's what my parents hammered into me. Leofric Iron Hand, has my love and holds my life in the palm of his hand. I will not ever fail him!"

Her bold reply brought a roar of acclaim from all the men assembled there, both Leofric's men and Hugo's troupe of clowns and acrobats, while from her father's side Maritia ran out to give Brioni a warm and clinging hug, the two girls, dark-haired and golden as the sun, pressed close together for just a few heartbeats of time before they kissed and Maritia ran back to Oswald who was looming hugely closeby, his furry forepaws held out in open embrace, grunting in farewell, his great head swaying from side to side as he did so.

Then the men swung themselves up onto their horses and moved away from the clearing, armour flashing in the January sunshine beneath a pale blue rain-washed sky, the clouds high and streaked with grey. Their horses snorted and tossed their heads as they moved, while the folk from the village, especially the womenfolk, led by Almaric the Smith, their newly appointed Reeve, crowded round to see them off, Brioni and Leofric the very last of all.

One by one they pushed their horses forward into a sharp canter, hoofs spraying up the water that had collected from the rain that had soused everything the day before, each mirror puddle shattering into a thousand sapphire droplets as the heavy beasts crashed through them, while the great forest breathed deeply in the chill mid-morning air.

\*

And so Brioni of Foxley went to war to avenge her family and cleanse herself of the blood-oath she had sworn on her father's body, with a smile on her face and her lover by her side. And with a final wave to the enormous fur-clad figure standing on the edge of the clearing with his daughter on his arm, and Oswald calling to her loudly, she disappeared from view; Bran and Utha ranging somewhere far ahead, and Leofric calling to her as he pushed his horse towards the head of the long, bouncing column.

So, jamming in her heels, and with a ring of bright laughter, she followed his lead, the sound of her voice floating back on the breeze as they rounded the far bend in the track and cantered off between the great trees of the forest, the faint echo of their passing finally fading away to silence.

# Chapter Forty

All that morning they rode steadily south-west before a freshening wind, the thin January sunlight filtering through the great trees in pale bars of harvest gold that made the dripping forest glisten, and the snow, still lying thick in places, sparkle in its shine.

Above them the pale blue of the early dawning hardened into azure splendour, and the air was keen and crisp. Each stinging breath made their nostrils quiver as they drew it into their lungs, only for it to vanish in white huffs of cloudy vapour past as they pushed their beasts hard along the miry ways. Together they poured out their energy as they hustled along, each snorting beast like a small dragon, as they pounded the narrow trackways.

Sticking to the simple paths that criss-crossed amongst the trees, they pushed on throughout the day until they came out upon the great highway that had once carried the legions swinging down from Lincoln to Exeter, the ancient Fosse Way.

Built of packed stones on a bed of rocks and covered with close-fitted slabs, cambered and with deep drainage channels on either side, the legions had built well, and even now, nearly five hundred years after the eagles had flown from these shores, it was still in remarkable health. The top dressing may have long been stolen for building, but the hard core still remained, so in most places the old roadway, though heavily overgrown with grass and mosses, was still firm underfoot, and once out of the trees, and on to it, they picked up the pace as they hurried south-west across a devastated countryside.

Everywhere beyond the forest showed signs of flight and destruction as the Danes had spilled out from their line of march on Chippenham, unable to keep their hands from looting and destruction. Burned houses and barns, dead cattle and sheep rotting feet up in the snowy fields were everywhere, and pathetic bundles of humanity lay cut down as they had fled. Men, women and children. Sometimes singly, sometimes whole families had been put to the sword, their poor belongings rifled through and scattered, left like their bodies, eyes pecked out by birds, to rooting boar and the tooth and claw of the wild.

It was a bleak and wretched sight.

But there was nothing that could be done for any of them, so Leofric and his command pressed on, their faces hard, their hearts filled with rage for their people and for a lush countryside torn apart by the lusts of their hated Danish foes. No wonder men gave up hope when faced by the Great Army, and Saxon thanes came in to give tribute to Guthrum rather than have their steadings destroyed and their people butchered. No European kingdom had been able to stand against so brutal an enemy, and all in Frankland had paid to be left in peace.

But that was not the way.

Leofric knew that in his heart. Knew that Alfred was right, and only by defeating the Heathen in the field, in open battle, could Wessex be saved. And looking across at where Brioni rode beside him, tears flowing down her cheeks at the sights around them, he gritted his teeth and became even more determined to help her fulfil her blood-oath and slay Oscytel. Somehow that goal must be achieved...because until it was she would never wholly be his to love. And he led his command south with a grim ferocity he had not known since Emma had died, her poor body torn apart by those who had raped her.

*

By the time the sun had tilted towards the horizon in a red ball of flame, and the mists were rising from the frigid ground, it was time to call a halt, men and horses both in need of food and rest, and it was then that Jaenberht, who had been scouting far forward of the main column, came back to tell them of a place he and Aldred had found where they could camp down for the night with some security. A shattered steading where there was a ruined cow byre for the horses and where the main hall had not been fully burned out, enough to shelter all of them for the night, with a well for fresh water that had not been spoiled with the dead.

"What of the owners?" Brioni asked Jaenberht when he had finished reporting to Leofric. "I could not rest easy with their bodies scattered round the garth. I had enough of that at Foxley!"

"And where is Aldred?" Leofric asked him.

"No sign of them, my Lady," Jaenberht replied to Brioni with a shrug of his armoured shoulders. "They must have fled, along with most of their animals. As for Aldred? He found a sheep wandering loose...dead sheep now," he added with another shrug and a grin. "No point in leaving that to be eaten by Danes when there are hungry Saxons in need of a good meal. He should be cooking it by now, left him skinning it out. He never travels without his iron cook pot, so we should have some sort of mutton stew to warm us before too long." And with a clap on the shoulders from his war-leader, he leapt back on his horse to lead them forward to where the ruined steading lay a short distance from the ancient roadway they had been following.

294

*

*T*his had once been a handsome little holding: hall, byre and stables round a wide garth, with a well close to the byre, and other small buildings for storage scattered around, even a forge. All now mostly burned out and ruined, the thatched hay stacks and straw ricks just piles of blackened rubbish, the stables wrecked, the forge destroyed and all its tools scattered. Only the cow byre, for some reason, still stood and the fires had not wholly burned the hall-place, the great wooden trusses that held it up not fully taken by the flames. Maybe the Danes who had attacked here had got bored, and left before finishing the wanton destruction that so marked their advance into Wessex.

No matter, the buildings left would suit Leofric and his command well, and no sooner had they arrived than he was busy issuing the necessary orders to his men for them to bed down their horses and then scatter and scour the steading for anything of value, or interest, they could find, before coming together in the remains of the hall-place for food and drink: Aldred's mutton stew with onions and turnips, and plenty of fresh water. Clear heads were what was needed on a field march, when every steading they came to might harbour an enemy, and the road itself be patrolled by armed and energetic Danes.

"Brrrr, but it is a raw evening," Brioni said, shivering, drawing her fur mantle closely around her in the smoky air from Aldred's fire. "Thank God Jaenberht found this place before the sun finally fell away. I wouldn't have enjoyed stumbling about in the dark trying to throw up some form of shelter, and get a fire started."

"He's a good man, Jaenberht," Leofric replied, drawing her close and throwing his mantled arms around her, nuzzling her hair as he spoke. "Found him a few summers ago when we were fighting up in Mercia, making King Ceolwulf's life miserable, the client-king whom the Vikings put in charge up there? After Burghred abandoned his people and fled to Rome?"

"I know," Brioni chipped in with a smile. "Who could forget? Never trust a Mercian! Yet Alfred married one and he adores her. Poor Ealhswitha; she never will live that down. I wonder how she is coping in Athelney, and with a baby?

God aid her, and the King!" and she sighed. "But what of Jaenberht? I interrupted you."

"Oh…caught him red-handed trying to sneak his way into our cook-pot, the idiot. He should have known better," he added with a laugh. "Snaked his way past three of my guards, before I nabbed him with our ladle in one hand

and a wooden food-bowl in the other! Liked his nerve, and his sense of humour, and he's been with us ever since."

"And he didn't like the food when he got it in the end either!" Raedwald threw in laughing. "Said he had tasted better at the King's table!"

"Not now, that's for certain," Trausti added in his deep voice, with a chuckle. "As for before, I wouldn't be surprised. That man moves like a shadow. He could slit the throats of half a dozen pirates and be gone before they were any the wiser! I'd rather have him with us than against us any day!"

The men chuckled at the memory of Jaenberht and the cook-pot while Brioni snuggled into Leofric's warmth. It was good to be in the company of such burly men with their rough good humour and their campfire memories, and she leaned back into his embrace and looked out across the darkening garth, while the fire that Aldred had lit in the old hearth place of the ruined hall flamed and sparkled behind her. From it the heat spread out to welcome the men as they began to gather about them, as well as to cook the mutton stew that Aldred was stirring for their supper.

Each man, as he came in, brought his saddle with him and a good horse blanket, having fed, watered and rubbed his beast down in the old cow byre, where a stack of unspoiled hay had been found. Then they had gone out again to gather more wood for the fire, determined to be as warm as possible on such a raw January evening.

"What next, Leofric?" Finnar broke in as his leader moved to warm himself at the fire, Brioni slipping away to attend a call of nature.

"A good question, my tall friend," he replied thoughtfully. "A good question indeed. Well, we must follow the old Fosse Way right from here, almost to where the road crosses the By Brook. I had thought to join the watercourse below the old ford, but the pathway there is very twisted and narrow, and it may be better for us to take the trackway above the ford that runs east towards Yatton, and then finally to Chippenham. Before Yatton we must drop off the ridge down to Combe, then take the track from there to Ford. The land is very steep and heavily wooded, but it will be better than having to pick our path along the river bank. And it's the only way that Arnwulf's cart can stay with us...and him we cannot do without.

"That is all very rough country," he went on, raising his voice as he realised more of his men had stopped to listen. "Deeply sloped and thickly wooded, especially once off the main trackways, and the paths beside the river are tortuous, where willows abound, thick briars and alder. That is one reason why we have stopped early. I want to get there by midday tomorrow, to make that descent to the river, and then up the trackway and down again to Ford in daylight. It is very steep in places and we will have a problem with the cart.

We will need trail ropes and a drag-beam before the wheels, or else we could be in trouble. And we need the help of the people we shall settle by at Ford. We have many Danes with us, and it will not help us to be seen as a Danish war party rather than a Saxon one. Trausti, Raedwald and I have all been there before, and I have a talisman they will recognise. So we should be alright, but I don't want these people startled. It is a small steading, with a handful of cottages, and they will be suspicious enough of strangers anyway. If we are not careful they can do us great scathe. It would only take one of them with a taste for Danish gold to go to Guthrum's hall in Chippenham for it to be all up with us in no short order! So we will make sure we arrive in as full daylight as possible."

"Who runs this steading?" Brioni asked, quietly.

"A good Saxon couple, Eadwine and Aelfrid, and their sons, Alfweald and Cuthbert. Alfweald lives in a cottage nearby, with his wife. Cuthbert and Gytha with his parents in the main steading. I believe them to be good people."

"Let's hope they will remain so after we are come amongst them," Trausti growled. "That Cuthbert has a mean face. He was not so pleased to see us there the last time, I could tell."

"He will do as his father orders him," Leofric said sharply. "He is the youngest. He knows where he stands."

"I hope he does," Trausti replied darkly. "But I wouldn't trust his wife, that Gytha. She has her husband under her thumb, and Cuthbert is weak and greedy. A bad combination!"

"You gathered an awful lot in our short stay there," Leofric commented from beneath raised eyebrows.

"I am a good listener, and know more Saxon than maybe they realised," the tough Danish warrior replied with a smile. "She needs gold to out-do the other wife, Ethelinda, who is as sweet as Gytha is sharp tongued. That one feels her husband is not so well regarded as his elder brother, Alfweald. But as he does more work and with less complaint than Cuthbert, then it is not surprising the father favours him. You may see them all as 'good people' my Lord. But there is bad blood there, and that may be a problem."

"Then make sure you do all your business with Eadwine," Brioni replied. "And if there is bad blood between the brothers, and the woman, Gytha, is involved then I will find that out from the steadman's wife, Aelfrid. She will know for certain. And then you will know whom to trust and who must be watched."

"That makes sense, Leofric," Beornred said then, in his gruff voice. "After all, the Lady Brioni will be highly regarded for who she is. They cannot have had anyone so closely connected to the King under their roof before. That alone will make a difference, believe me."

"That is so," Leofric replied thoughtfully, looking at Brioni with a half-smile and raised eyebrows as he spoke. "That is so indeed, so we will leave all to you, my Lady," he added, giving her a little shake. "But what about taking the higher road out of Combe?"

"That seems good to me," his big Danish second said then, in his deep voice. "From what I gathered from Trausti and Raedwald, that watercourse is a twisting nightmare. To take the trackway above it makes good sense, even though we may have to help Arnwulf over the worst parts of it. To attempt that in the dark, when we do not know the way, would be asking for trouble...and that may come upon us anyway. The old Fosse Way is a well-used route, the Danes would be mad not to patrol it. We must be prepared for the worst."

"That is why I want to be gone from here at first light, and keep a full watch-guard throughout the night," Leofric added, kicking a log further onto the fire in a shower of sparks, as Brioni slipped away from him to relieve herself outside. "I don't want to be caught out before we have even got started. Did anyone find anything of value out there, apart from the animal fodder in that old cow byre?"

"I found a sack of oats. Bag singed but oats alright," Ricberht said after a moment's silence, drinking from his horn beaker.

"And I found a load of tools scattered around the forge," Arnwulf threw in, "Nothing I don't already have; but I will keep a few as spares."

"But nothing else of use, my Lord," Raedwald added, "save a bundle of woolfells and that hay. Those bastards did a pretty good job of destruction."

"They even burned the carts, traces, hoes and pickaxes," Cadoc said, in his lilting Welsh voice. "Just wanton waste, I say. And they are supposed to be farmers. I hate them all!"

"Not all, I hope," Beornred said gruffly, bending to throw some more wood onto the fire. "We *are* good farmers, when we are not out there fighting. And craftsmen, and traders. That's why I and my men are with Leofric and not out butchering with Guthrum! We want peace, and to be free to farm and trade and bring up our little ones in safety, same as you. This, as Cadoc says," he added, swinging his arms out in a wide gesture of disgust, "is pure waste! Guthrum won't stop this, nor that bastard Oscytel. It is a part of them, it's what they believe in. But Alfred can stop it. He has vision, even if it is I, a Dane, who says so. Those who follow me, and Leofric Iron Hand, want peace not slaughter...even if it means we have to fight our own people to achieve it!"

"Where did all that come from?" Brioni asked quietly, stepping back into the firelight from the ruined garth as Beornred had started speaking. "I

298

have not heard you say so much in a host of meetings since first I came amongst you."

"It is why I became Leofric's shield-man. It is why I follow him and my friends also. He saved my Dana, and my two little ones, from a Jomsviking raid on the northern borders of Wessex where we had settled. They wanted war...I wanted peace, to lay my spear and sword aside, and be the farmer I once was before I went ganging in the dragon boats as a younger man.

"I found some land, and a little homestead like this one, abandoned and half ruined and brought it all back to life. Then I found a Saxon wife and had two little ones, before it all started once again. My Lord wanted me back in his war-band. I wanted to stay with my family. He sent his men to bring me to my senses, and set fire to my steading. I fought back in the only way I knew, killed four of the bastards with Fire Flame," he said in his deep voice, drawing his long sword and waving it over the fire so that its blade was the colour of blood.

"Cut them down as if they were grass before the scythe. But there were too many for one man, and I was wounded, took a deep cut to my shoulder, and because Dana was Saxon they seized her and were set to throw both her and the children into the flames when Leofric turned up with his men and slew them all. Pretty nastily I seem to remember," he said with a smile, turning to where Leofric was standing, grim-faced, his arm round Brioni. "And everything was put to right. Dana went with the children to her mother, and I stayed with Leofric and joined his war-band as his shield-man. I have been guarding his back ever since."

"Who was your Lord, then?" Brioni asked bitterly, putting her hand on the big man's arm.

"It was Oscytel! Even in those days he was considered a King in Guthrum's army; he and Anund both – he who was killed at sea fighting with Alfred in the summer of '75. And Oscytel's reputation was already fearsome.

"Now here we are, in this little place, so like my own steading, and I am gripped with anger and sadness. Until you came among us we had nothing to fight for except money and the joy of killing. Now it is different. You have given us all something extra to fight for: hope, and our freedom to be men...and not the shield slaves of Guthrum and what is left of the Great Army in Wessex. And not for that bastard Oscytel whom I hate as much as Grimnir does, or you my Lord Leofric...or you my Lady of Foxley. Slay him and the rest are a rabble. Oh, they may fight to the last man, his Jomsvikings, that is what they are sworn to do; but the heart will go out of them and the rest of the army. Out of Guthrum, too, I should not wonder.

299

"We are a superstitious people, we Vikings.  And if Oscytel can be defeated by the God people, then surely their God must be stronger than ours and we should join them or be destroyed ourselves!

# Chapter Forty One

"That is what Alfred believes," Brioni said then from under Leofric's arm. "And what his priests teach. That God rules all, and following his rules will bring victory to the righteous, and the Vikings will be defeated and driven from our land."

"What philosophy from you all tonight," Leofric said then with a smile, putting his other arm round Brioni as he spoke. "But talking will not secure us this homestead. Nor prepare us for tomorrow! So, Raedwald, Trausti, get the men fed, then post your guards; the rest of you must settle as best you can round the fire. Every man must stand his watch, and they must keep this fire burning. It took long enough to get started in the first place, and I don't want to have to go through that again in the morning. Up at first light and then away down this roadway and off across country to Ford by midday."

"And if we run into the enemy, Leofric, what then?" Raedwald asked.

"If there are too many we split up and run for it. Our horses are in better fettle than any of theirs. But if they are a small group we will try and bluff our way close enough to take them. There are many Danes with us, and I speak Norse. With luck we can trick them with false peace strings on our weapons and sweet honey voices; then out swords and at 'em!"

"What about the Lady Brioni?" Trausti asked him, nodding to where she stood against his chest.

"We must get her away to safety."

"No!" Brioni broke in heatedly, turning to look up at him. "If you stay, I stay. I have earned that right. That's why I fought Velda, for the right to be by your side. My sword arm is no more weary than yours, than any of yours," she went on gesturing at all the men clustered round the fire. "So, don't talk to me of safety!"

"What about your oath?" Leofric questioned her, holding her away from him.

"Death cancels all!" she answered him enigmatically. "You are my chosen Lord, as you are theirs, and I will not desert you in the field. That is the way of *Nithings*," she added with disgust. "Leave that to Mercians! I am true Wessex born; I am done with running, especially after Foxley. No, Leofric Iron Hand, if we have to fight, then I fight with you, and that is an end to the matter!"

"Quite a little bantam we have amongst us, Lord," Raedwald said smiling.

"Yes, isn't she? And I will make her your special responsibility, my good and loyal friend; you and Daegberht together," he said turning to a large Saxon warrior with a certain glint in his eye. "You are both big enough, and if we have to fight then I will rely on you to keep my lady safe. And you, my fine Wessex Lady, will do as I say!" he said sternly, turning to her and shaking her as he spoke. "I cannot have my men distracted from their business in worrying about you. And they will be if they think for one moment that Danish steel might threaten you. As I would be too. So, if it looks like a fight, you will stick to these men whom I trust absolutely. Do you understand, my love?" he ended fiercely. "I am the war-leader here and no one says me 'Nay'! Remember?"

"I remember, my Lord Leofric," she answered him then with a smile and a slight bow. "I am one of your soldiers now, and I know better than to defy you!"

"Just as well, my Lady, for I will not spare your hide if you disobey me!" he said, showing her the flat of his hand. "Surely I will dust your tail, armour or not, and my hand is hard!"

"You would have to catch me first, my brave Saxon war-lord," she replied with another smile, "and I am fleet of foot," she said scuttling to where the two men were standing, shuffling herself between their comforting bulk. "You would soon tire! Anyway you would then have to fight Raedwald and Daegberht into whose safety you have placed me, and they would surely defend me to their last drop of blood," she ended putting her arms through theirs as she mocked him, while all around them laughed at the swift way she had turned the tables on their commander.

"Very well," he said, grinning back at her. "Very well! Just see that you do. And you two," he added wagging his fingers at them with a raised eyebrow. "Keep her safe!"

"Yes, Lord," they both intoned together with a grin. "We will keep her safe, our lives on it!"

"Mmm...I hope not! But I take the point. But if we have to fight we must do our best to kill them all. I don't want anyone left to tell in which direction we were travelling, nor how many of us there were. So, you archers amongst us, Cadoc, Orn, Caewlin and you others with Syrian bows, Wybert, Cenhelm and Eadulf, see to your strings and your arrows. And make sure you travel at the back under Raedwald's orders

"That way while we up front face out, you can come in from the sides, and from behind, and finish them off. Now, food, drink and a good night's rest. We have a fair distance to travel tomorrow, and a sleepy warrior is more danger to his friends than a dead one!" and a ripple of laughter ran round them as the meeting broke up and the men went to their bed spaces for their wooden bowls and spoons, while Aldred stirred his meaty stew with his spear shaft.

*

*T*he meal, though simply made, was sufficient for their needs, with coarsely baked bread from the outlaw village to sop up the juices and fresh spring water with which to wash the whole down. And having posted guards both along the roadway and round the ruined steading, the whole company settled for sleep around the fire they had built, Leofric and Brioni wrapped closely together in their furs, saddles at their heads, weapons by their side and dressed for instant action.

Yet the night passed peacefully, save for a vixen's scream, chill and clear that came with a sharp frost in the early hours, and the staccato *bark! bark!* of the dog fox as he replied to her call. Above them the stars glittered, as the flames from the fire danced and flickered amongst the wood. Every fresh log that was thrown on sent a myriad bright sparks soaring and spinning upwards towards the shattered roof of the hall place as the sentries came and went throughout the night. Leofric taking his turn, the same as his men, breathed in the sharp frosted night breezes and enjoyed the wood-scented air as his lady and his command slept and the sky slowly passed from starlit blackness to pale grey as the dawn crept over the horizon.

*

*B*ut as the night passed clouds blew up from the west beneath a warmer wind, bringing a cold fog in its wings, turning starlit blackness to a grey-white blanket that covered everything, so heavy that even the cow byre across the garth was shrouded, opaque, and the ancient roadway beyond was completely hidden. It was a raw morning, everything cloaked with a fine mist and sound deadened, a pair of cackling magpies simply shadows of themselves as they swooped across the ruined farmyard with dipping tails, the horses shaking their heads as the water rimmed their ears and dripped off their long lashes in countless teardrops.

The guards came in off the road, unable to see anything clearly in the grey darkness before dawn, while all around the steading the men rose and shook themselves, ready for the long day ahead, stamping their feet and banging their hands together as they cursed the weather. In twos and threes they gathered about the fire whose glow lit up the ruined hall-place and pulsed

303

with warmth, their heavy fur capes drawn close around them, their breath white in the sharp cold that surrounded them.

"This changes nothing," Leofric said, sipping from his horn of mulled ale that Brioni pressed into his hands, scooped out of the deep pot that Aldred had warmed up at first light. "In fact it will be more of a help than a hindrance as this fog will mask all our movements. And if there are Danes out and about this morning, the last thing they will expect to bump into will be a full war-band of armoured Saxons hungry for their blood!"

"And Danes, Lord," Beornred growled at him softly.

"And Danes, indeed, my worthy shield-man," he replied, clapping the big warrior across his shoulders. "So, let's get to it. A warm drink and a bite of cheese, then up and away," he added before issuing a string of sharp orders.

"Right! You all know what to do. Sigweald, Jaenberht, I want you out ahead of us to point the way. Sigweald in command as you have travelled this route before. It's murky out there to say the least, so keep in sight of one another as best you can. At least the old Romans built in straight lines, so you should not get lost. But keep your eyes peeled and your ears long. Sound is deadened in this sort of fog, so take care you do not stumble onto an enemy patrol unawares.

"Daegberht, Raedwald, you travel at the back with the Lady Brioni, Arnwulf and our archers, though in this fog they may be of little use to us today. They are your special responsibility, so use them wisely...and guard the lady well. Raedwald, you command the rear.

"You two up front, do not miss the turning for Yatton. If you come to the old Roman ford over the stream you have gone too far. There is a steepish drop down to it, so you should know before you get there. Go back up the track and wait for us to join you. If you see anything, Sigweald, come back and warn us. Jaenberht, you shadow the enemy, if enemy they be. You are the very best for that, and we will come forward as swiftly as we may. *Brrrr!*" he added sharply, stamping his own feet. "This is a raw start indeed! Aldred, some of your mulled ale for all of us...then we must be away."

\*

*L*ong before full daybreak had lightened the fog around them to a thick, grey whiteness they had swung back onto the trackway again, with only a great pile of smouldering ashes to show that anyone had been there. The richly scented droppings from their chargers and baggage horses had been scattered wildly about to disguise their numbers from any enemy who might pass by, or come in search of them, and every man had buried his own dung.

Brioni also, so that no casual search would tell anyone how many had paused there.

Out on the shrouded trackway they were forced to walk-march their horses in pairs, Arnwulf's tilt cart at the rear, each pair keeping in sight of the men in front, their horses making almost no noise as they pushed forward, save for the occasional snort and toss of the head as the animals cleared their faces. While all around them the thick fog pressed in on the empty woodlands and countryside, lightening as the sun rose above the horizon to a soaking whiteness, the ancient trackway opening out before them just enough for each pair to see the other better. But the fog remained thick, so that those at the front could not see the rear, and those at the tail of the column could not see beyond the fourth pair of warriors ahead.

For all the world they might have been the only ones on the move that morning, as they passed no-one, and no-one came upon them from behind. Everything was still and silent, as were the men, conscious that sound can do strange things in fog, and all rode alert and with strained ears to pick up anything that could indicate an enemy was close by.

\*

*A* mile ahead of the column Sigweald and Jaenberht also rode in silence, their bodies swaying to the constant motion of their mounts as they strode out along the track. Each man within touching distance of the other, shields across their backs, swords loose in their scabbards, both ready for instant action. No peace strings across their quillons, and their axes with uncovered blades poking up above their shoulders. But they rode with their helmets loose on the pommels of their saddles, so that no sound would be deadened by the tough metal face plates that each helmet carried to protect its wearer from arrow strikes and sword cuts.

All around them the white silence pressed in upon them as they rode, turning their heads to the sides, so neither of them saw the cow trotting out of the opaque murk right ahead of them, until they were almost right on top of one another. The beast, a hefty mother with a brown mottled hide, had an impressive spread of horns...and a calf at foot with a torn rope halter hanging down from its delicate black muzzle.

"*Wooah,* Rollo!" Jaenberht sharply called out to his horse as it suddenly shied away, and kicked out his back legs, startled by the sudden appearance out of the fog of the cow and its calf. "*Wooah!* Y'big silly," he said, bending forward to pat his withers as the big horse slithered to a halt. "It's only a cow, for goodness sake, and you've seen plenty of those. Now, calm down, you big

305

lump.  Easy now…Siggi, grab that damn calf's halter and the old beast will follow you.  Now, what brings you out here, old lady?" he said to the large stray as his friend leapt off his gelding, and ran to catch up the torn halter, the big cow calling anxiously as he did so.

Soon both men were off their horses, while Sigweald drew the thick rope from his saddle bag that he always carried with him and swiftly fashioned a halter for the old cow, while its calf buried its head beneath her quarters and dunted at her udder for the milk he needed, his tail wriggling wildly as he did so.

"Well, at least someone is having a bit of warm breakfast around here," Jaenberht said, watching the calf busily at work beneath the cow's hind quarters.  "What now?"

"What now indeed?…and where has this little one, and its fat mama, come from?" Sigweald asked, puzzled, looking around him.  "This calf has obviously been much loved and cared for," he went on, fingering the calf's torn halter, "and it's a bull calf too.  This old cow has not been left in the fields to take its chance with its babe.  It's been safely in a byre.  Maybe even in the house-place itself?"

"But, Siggi, it could have wandered miles!"  Jaenberht exclaimed exasperated.

"Maybe, my friend, maybe.  But I think not.  This beast has not been out all night.  See, its feet are barely muddied.  I think she has been startled and fled out across the track.  I smell mischief," he said sniffing the wind, which was suddenly heavy with the scent of burning, and looking around him fiercely.  "And where mischief is about, then we should be doubly careful.  Something is not right!"

"No!  I can smell that too!" Jaenberht said, suddenly straightening and staring away beyond his friend's shoulder as a sudden glow in the distance burnished the fog with a tinge of orange.  "Look! Over there, a ruddy glow!  Leofric needs to know what's happening here, and fast!"

"Right.  You stay here and eel your way towards that sudden flare-up, for that's a fire or I'm a Mercian!  Leave a stripped hazel patteran on the path to show where you have turned off.  Meanwhile I'll take this beast and its little one back towards Leofric, and bring him forward as swiftly as maybe.  You, get back onto Rollo and see what you can find out.  If need be tie him to a tree, or something, and get forward on foot.  But look to yourself, y'big lummox.  I don't want to lose another friend to Guthrum's bully boys!"  And with that he flung himself back onto his own horse, and with the long rope halter he had made he tugged the cow off, mooing mournfully for its warm byre, with its little one following, and disappeared into the fog.

306

# Chapter Forty Two

Left to himself, Jaenberht shook himself up to settle his armour across his shoulders, before turning to his horse quietly cropping nearby, its outline hazy in the fog that surrounded them.

"Now then, Rollo. You and I had better see what's what before our Lord and Master has us over a barrel...and I wouldn't like that one little bit!" And flinging himself back up into the saddle he walk-trotted his horse further along the ancient roadway to where a battered track, marked with the splatter of many hoofs and cart trails, led off left between the trees. Here he paused to leave a stripped hazel patteran to show the way, before putting on his helmet and closing its face-plates around his cheeks and kicking on towards where he had spotted the fire-glow earlier, the smell of burning growing heavier in his nostrils as he went.

Two dozen paces more along the track and it was time to get down and tie Rollo up to a small sapling nearby. With his painted shield still on his back, but helmet on with face plates closed, and using both hands to make his way, he pushed forwards through the brakes of beech, yew and hazel that shielded the little steading from which a host of flames were bursting out in all directions, the smoke from the burning thatch and timber swirling up into the fog, itself driven away by the fierce heat.

It was a sight that he had seen many times, but when a raid was over...not in the very act of progress.

Now, with a dozen figures capering, shouting and running around, some with burning torches in their hands; some herding cattle, pigs squealing, chickens fluttering round the garth and sheep fleeing in panic as the enemy chased after them, it was a scene of sheer pandemonium. A scene from the very pit of Hell itself; Danes, outlined in leaping flames, stabbing and hacking down with spear and sword at their hapless victims cowering on the ground in terror, devastation all around...and in one corner a small handful of prisoners, all women, screaming and tearing their hair in utter torment as the men in their lives were stripped and tortured, and their children were killed. Speared or cut down as they ran, the smallest swung by their heels until their heads were smashed against the stone supports of hall place and cow-byre, none were spared.

Those who had been slain lay like discarded bundles of rags, their limbs askew and limp in death. But three men had been tied to the posts that held up the small cattle byre, flames flaring all around them as they struggled and howled in agony while two men cut at them with knives, flaying the skin from their living bodies…the raiders hooting and cheering every time a fresh cut was made and their wretched victims screamed and leaped in their bonds, in a wild frenzy of unbearable pain.

It was a scene of such vicious brutality that tears sprang from his eyes and he ground his teeth with impotent rage. Soon it would be the women's turn to be brutalised, stripped, raped and left with their throats cut, unless they were considered pretty enough to be spared such horror, and dragged back to Chippenham for their leader's amusement. There they would be whored by their captors or sold as slaves to Guthrum's commanders, to Oscytel or others of the Great Army who followed him.

Without support there was little that Jaenberht could do, save watch and wait, and hope that Leofric would come up before the Danes started on their women captives. As it was, he was forced to watch while they tore out the lives of the men they had already seized, while the women shrieked in anguish, their children were slaughtered and their home went up in flames around them.

*

*B*ack on the ancient roadway, Sigweald had made all haste to where Leofric was still moving forward, pushing his horse on with all possible speed in the thick fog, the old cow on its long halter behind him, the calf running beside its mother, as they hustled through the cloying murk. The cow mooing and tossing its head, Sigweald cursing and calling it on: "Cush! Cush! Come up you owd bitch! Come up now!" while striving to keep his own horse moving forward as fast as possible.

Then, suddenly, they were amongst Leofric's vanguard, the thick misty whiteness all around them, now shining with the sun rising above it, filled with vague figures that rushed forward out of the fog in a slush of sound and softened outlines. First Ricberht and Alnoth the swordsman and then Leofric himself, with Beornred at his shoulder and the whole of his command filling the roadway beyond; Brioni, her escort, with Bran and Utha by her side and Arnwulf and his tilt cart, at the rear.

Swiftly news was exchanged, the men's startled comments at the sight of Sigweald and his charges giving way to laughter as he struggled to the rear of the column. There the young calf was swiftly tied up, feet together, and heaved up onto the tilt cart where it bawled its misery to a heedless world, while his mother was tethered to the tough backboard where she was free to run after it, mooing all the time, as Leofric led his men forward at a swift canter to where Jaenberht had been left to follow his instincts.

*

At the homestead the buildings were then well alight, the flames twisting up into the fog in dense, roiling pillars of thick smoke and leaping fire, the heat creating a strange bubble of clarity around the steading, where all those involved in its violent rape and destruction stood out in stark, roaring outline…while all beyond the garth was still vague and opaque, the fog heavy with smoke in the treeline and in the brakes and coppice that surrounded it.

Jaenberht, still shielded by the dense thickets he had been hunkering behind, watched as the Danes' prisoners died horribly, the flames now towering up in great red and orange flares, now blown sideways amidst a slew of sparks and flaming debris. And while most of the raiders capered and shouted around the burning buildings, or herded the few cattle they had found, chasing the squealing piglets to spear them for amusement, there were a handful who had gathered around the women they had taken, and were in the act of dragging them to where their men had been tied up and butchered, when they were stopped.

Two men in black link-steel byrnies with round shields across their backs, their helmets in their hands, face-plates hanging open, held up their hands and the captives were released to cling together in a small group, weeping piteously and shrieking out, while the taller of the two men began to sort through them with sharp blows and harsh guttural shouts, tearing the clothes off one, roughly handling another.

*Jomsvikings!*
Oscytel's butchers.

Men who feared nothing and for whom death in battle was a sure pathway to Valhalla; men whom they were all committed to killing wherever they could be found. And Jaenberht watched them eagle-eyed, his hand on his long-bladed seaxe, as he stalked and slithered his way closer and closer to the action, the thick fog and swirling smoke shielding his movements. If Leofric came swiftly then he would have the man nearest to him. and free the wretched women who were being examined with such ruthless interest.

*

Back on the roadway Alnoth had pulled up his horse by the stripped hazel wands Jaenberht had laid down, while Leofric held up his hand to bring his men to a slithering halt, his war-band swiftly gathering around him as closely as possible, horses champing on their bits and stamping their feet in their excitement while he issued his orders.

"Sigweald said there was mischief hereabouts and he was right! We can all smell the smoke, and that glare over there to the left, beyond these trees, speaks for itself. But I don't want to rush in on something that may end in the sudden deaths of our own people.

"Trausti, Aggi, Gunnar, I want you up with me and Beornred, you too, Finnar. Your Danish voices will help us. We must try and bluff our way right in amongst them. Close up together. Full helmets with closed faceplates and leave the talking to me.

"Raedwald, Daegberht at the rear with Lady Brioni and Arnwulf. Brioni, control those hounds. The Danes see those and they will know instantly we we are not part of the Great Army. You archers with Cadoc, spread out on either side and make sure no-one gets away. If we have to fight we go in hard and no fancy stuff. Now, we must bustle about, but not too eager. We are on our way to join Guthrum at Chippenham, saw the fire and have come to see what's going on. So, lightly now, lightly. And keep an eye out for Jaenberht, you will know him by the scarlet dragon he carries on his shield...I don't want him speared in all this murk. Now...let's be about it!" And digging his heels into Wotan he jagged them all on their way; Brioni at the rear, with Raedwald and Daegberht on either side of her, Bran and Utha on tough chains by her side, followed by Arnwulf, the tilt cart and the old cow right at the back.

Along the twisting trackway, collecting Rollo as they passed him by, they pushed on right up to the edge of the steading, now wreathed in fire, and saw the usual desperate litter of the dead scattered everywhere, both human and animal, some with spears still sticking in them. And as they slowed to a strong walk, so the sun broke through at last to bathe the whole ghastly scene in a misty golden light, the trees reaching up to embrace a blue sky snagged with carrion birds all winging to the feast.

At once the two leaders, whom Jaenberht had been watching so closely, moved to intercept them, one staying near the corralled women, while their followers threw their torches into the flames and many reached for their weapons. Some snatched spears up from the bloodied ground, swordsmen shrugged their shields onto their left arms, some axemen standing loose-limbed with the fearsome Danish weapons for which the Vikings were so famous already swinging in their hands, while others just stood around and watched as the whole Viking war-band straggled into formation. Their war-leaders in front, their whole command behind, they were all clearly unsettled by the sudden appearance out of the fog of so determined and well-armed a body of men where none had been expected.

310

Meanwhile Leofric and his men continued to press forward gently...while Jaenberht flitted from bush to bush as he moved closer to where the main leader was standing in the middle of the track, a huge warrior with his hands held up in front and shouting for Leofric and his command to stop.

But, as Leofric could see from the general hesitancy of their movements, they were all uncertain of these bold newcomers' intentions, for Leofric showed no surprise in his steady approach. On the contrary, he gave open welcoming gestures as his command continued to advance, calling out in Norse to the men ahead of him, his vanguard drawing closer and closer, shouting out in Danish as they came forward, their hands waving in friendship, while the rear-guard remained shielded by the fog that still clouded the trackway behind them.

Nevertheless, the Danes would not let them come right in amongst them, making it clear with shouts and sharp banging of sword against shield rim that they were to halt.

"Who are you who come so boldly into Guthrum's territories?" the big Viking war-leader called out loudly, his black armour suddenly flashing in the sun as he moved. "Only warriors of the Black Jarl, Saxon scum and bandits should be out within this sector!"

Leofric laughed loudly at that, throwing back his head and bellowing with outrageous mirth, the men around him laughing in the same way, shouting out Norse oaths as they did so.

"Well said my worthy Huscarle," he called back in harsh Danish, edging his horse forwards as he spoke. 'Saxon scum and bandits!' I like it well, but must disappoint your men of their chance of glory. We are part of Olaf Thorhollur's war-band out of Mercia," Leofric went, on finally reining Wotan in a horse's length from where the big Danish leader was standing. "We have been sent to the King's holm-ganging at Chippenham, but missed our way in this wet filth. We came into Gloucester two weeks back, but found the army gone, and were sent on here. See, we have the golden arm-ring of Aethelwold the Fair to prove our allegiance and our worth," and he reached beneath his great bearskin cloak to show him.

"Gently, gently," the big Dane repeated, holding his hand up again. "And hold your horse!" he exclaimed sharply as Leofric edged Wotan forward a further step. "My name is Einarr Ragnarsson," he added, his right hand on his sword's hilt, his helmet still swinging from his left hand. "I know of Olaf Thorhollur, but not that he was on his way to join King Guthrum. I am of the Lord Oscytel's army. It is he who has sent us out to scour the land clear of Saxon farmers wherever we can find them, so our own men can take over the land. Here we have just burned out a nest of rebels. Men who bore arms

311

against us," he went on, pointing to a pathetic collection of crude spears, an old sword and a birding bow, with a bundle of roughly fletched arrows.

"We accept no excuses," he added as Wotan suddenly dragged his iron feet on the ground, "and we have left a reminder of what will happen to all who resist," he went on, his eyes blue and piercing, as he gestured to where the ghastly flayed figures of three men drooped in their bonds against the timber posts they had been seized against. Their blood, in black sticky pools around their feet, and their skin hanging in vile strips from their bodies like torn lace. "So, Olaf I know, but not you, my Lord," the big Dane replied, "and I don't like surprises!"

"Leofric Iron Hand," came the deep reply, with a salute across his chest, his whole body tense from what he had seen, ready for immediate action, his eyes aware that Cadoc and his men were already angling their horses sideways to mount an attack from either flank if necessary. And his eyebrows rose in surprise behind his armour as he saw Jaenberht slink up in plain sight from a tight thicket of hazel, not ten paces from where the women were being held, and Einarr Ragnarsson's other commander was standing.

"And no bad surprises, just golden ones," he added, putting his hand towards his arm, all eyes following his actions. "Come, let me show you, and we can drink a horn to Odin in payment for your direction to Guthrum's hall which I know is somewhere nearby." And he put his right hand under his left arm as if to pull off an arm ring as the big man opposite threw back his head and laughed, all men knowing that the old Saxon King's whelp had gone to the bad and was prepared to do anything to aid his royal uncle's downfall…even to making foul bargains with the Heathen pirates to do so. Reasoning that if the Danes could support Coelwulf, the puppet king of Mercia, then they could do the same for Aethelwold of Wessex, the rightful King of the West Saxons since his uncle, King Alfred, had usurped the throne!

"So…Leofric Iron hand. A good name for one of Olaf's followers," the big Dane said as he studied this 'Danish' war-leader, larger even than himself, who sat his horse before him with such ease, and nonchalance, his own eyes glittering from behind his helmet, side-plates closed…as were all those others grouped around him. "Come forward and join us," he called up to the big man on his horse, beckoning with his arm as he did so, "and we will see this golden ring that comes from Aethelwold's court. Meanwhile my friend and I were just about to examine these Saxon bitches whom we have taken. One old sow and three pretty piglets. Nothing good enough for Guthrum, nor my Lord Oscytel. But they will do for you and me, if you have a mind to a young Saxon bitch? They are well enough once you have hammered them a little. If not my men can have them for a while."

Behind him his own war-band, who moments before had been menacingly swinging their weapons and shifting their weight from side to side in readiness to fight, were now clearly relaxing. Calling out to their friends, they also gestured to the men opposite to ride in and join their fun, both sides exchanging calls and laughter, the Danes already thinking of the fine drinking they would all have later on...and the excitement of taking the women they had captured in the only way that a good Viking warrior knew!

Still a little uncertain, but willing to be lulled, the big Danish leader motioned Leofric forward again, watching him curiously, as did his men, as he tugged at a heavy golden ring that clasped his upper arm where he had thrown back his thick bearskin cloak to get at it more easily, his heavy steel-linked byrnie suddenly sparkling in the sunlight that now pierced both cloud and hazy mist as the fog shredded away before a fresh westerly breeze.

# Chapter Forty Three

**B**rioni who was still carefully sandwiched between Raedwald and Daegberht, had watched all this with steady amazement, her heart hammering in her chest as Leofric had pushed his big charger closer and closer to where the Danes were standing, noting the exchange of greetings between the two sides while not understanding the swift flow of Danish conversation, but horrified by the sight of the three men's drooping bodies by the little cow byre, while her heart went out to the four women clustered together just to the right of the ancient hall-place.

Not ten paces from where Leofric was talking with the big Danish warleader, another Dane had suddenly appeared out of the smoky murk from behind a broad thicket of hazel. A large Danish warrior with a scarlet dragon on the shield at his back! Jaenberht's shield? And she gasped, with her hand to her mouth. It must be Jaenberht!…and with that connection in her head, everything around the distant warriors broke apart in a sudden maelstrom of violent action and roaring shouts.

*

**F**or, suddenly, everything seemed to happen at once, and with mind-blurring speed.

With a flick of his wrist Leofric unclipped the solid-looking ring and hurled it, spinning sideways, full into Einarr's open face, breaking it open from cheek to jowl in a sudden burst of blood and teeth. A hideous yawn that flung him to the ground with a great shout, just as Jaenberht leapt upon the other leader from where he was standing near the huddle of terrified women.

Grabbing the man's head with one hand and driving his seaxe through his throat into his brain with the other, Jaenberht felled the man to the ground with one violent upward thrust…just as Leofric drew his sword and roared out: *"On them! On them!"*

Jagging Wotan violently with his spurs, the big horse knocked the leading Viking to the ground and then stamped down on him as he had been taught. And behind him came Leofric's whole warband, their horses trampling the man's writhing body beneath their hooves as they rushed forward to hack through the first rank of Danish warriors as if they were straw figures on the practice ground.

314

Standing transfixed by the speed and suddenness of the attack, they fell like nine pins while Leofric led his men forward, his sword rising and falling in a spray of blood and brains at every stroke.

With Leofric's sudden movement, the whole of his command seemed to be in action at the same time. Cadoc and his archers joining in the violent skirmish, some on foot with their great war bows pulled to their ears, their arrows whistling into the enemy from both sides of the garth. While those with Syrian bows shot down from the back of their horses, a devastating arrow storm that ripped the heart out of the opposition, tearing through body armour like a knife through paper, bursting hearts and throats apart in a mere instant of time, blood spraying out at every strike.

Even Brioni, who had been expecting it, was stunned by the sudden violence and the visceral nature of Leofric's assault, and was suddenly very glad of the imposing armoured bulk of the two big men between whom she was now securely wedged, while Bran and Utha leaped and bayed to join the fighting.

Left and right Leofric hewed at his enemies without mercy, standing in his saddle to give himself more power and greater ease of movement to wield his sword with unrelenting vigour, parrying with his shield one moment and hacking down with his sword the next. Great swingeing blows that jarred his arm and splattered his face with blood and splintered bone. And where he led, Beornred at his shoulder, his men followed hard on his heels, swords sweeping through their enemies' guard to hack their bodies open with bloodied steel that felled many of them before they could get themselves organised in any way, toppling them onto the rapidly torn and soiled ground in head-broken, bloody wreckage.

And while many of his men stayed on their horses, others leapt off to hunt their enemies on foot with axe, spear and sword, their faces hidden behind their helmets, their voices roaring out as they formed their own shield wall and stamped their way forward, unstoppable, treading over the dead and wounded as they came. Behind them, on foot, arrows to their great war-bows, came Cadoc and his men: Orn, Aelric and Caewlin and others shooting where they could, their arrows bursting through their enemies' armour to fling them backwards to the ground where their comrades advancing behind their shield wall ground them to the dirt with spear and violent sword thrust.

Their attack was swift, bloody and overwhelming. Only where there were axe-Danes was the opposition anywhere like effective, where the warriors stood with a wall of shields locked in front of them, their great axes swinging in a shimmering figure of eight. Up, round their heads and down again in a terrifying rhythm that drove Leofric's men backwards and slew two of their

315

horses horribly, slicing the legs off one and the head off another, taking both riders down with them in a violent spray of blood.

By then the bulk of the Danish war-band had been cut down and eviscerated, brains smashed out in bony ruins, bodies pierced with arrows and bellies ripped open. Everywhere there were men falling in a welter of twitching limbs and writhing bodies beneath the iron hoofs of Leofric's chargers, until only half a dozen Danish warriors were left.

Shouting defiance, they waved their weapons at Leofric and his command; the garth now looking like a charnel house, filled with the dead, both Saxon and Danish, a wall of which lay between Leofric and the remnants of the enemy command. Some were crouched down behind their shields, while others stood with their axes cocked over their shoulders, blood running off their armour, their helmets closed about their faces, their eyes masked by their nasal protectors and their heavy eyebrow armour. Only their eyes glittered with rage and hatred as they waved and roared abuse at their Saxon enemies.

\*

For a moment the action halted while Leofric re-organised his men and the Danes howled their defiance. Leaping and waving their axes in fury they bayed in derision, surrounded by their dead, while Leofric strengthened his shield wall with a hedge of spears, and brought up his horse archers whose short, re-curved bows, Syrian bows, were ideal for mounted warfare.

Then, now on foot, his big axe in his hands, he led a roaring, bellowing rush to assault the remaining Jomsvikings behind their big round shields with the ragged knife symbol in gold rimmed with scarlet stabbing down from them.

And while he and his men charged the Danish shield wall, so his mounted archers, led by Wybert and Cenhelm, opened fire, sending their slim shafts whistling overhead to pierce Danish faces, arms and bodies…wherever a gap appeared in their enemies' defences, until the two forces crashed together. One of Leofric's axemen to pull down the front edge of an enemy shield with his great blade, while the man behind thrust forward with long spear or sword to pierce the man's breast with his bitter steel, the noise hellish: screams, shouts and roaring voices; the shrieks of the wounded and the groans of the dying mingled with the sharp clash and clatter of steel against steel, hot sparks flying amid shards of wood as each side hewed furiously at the other across the war-linden.

\*

*I*t was a fierce and brutal skirmish, that violent struggle in the burned steading's ruined garth, but it could not last long. Outnumbered and outfought on every side, their Danish foes were swiftly overrun until, with a howl of triumph, Leofric cut down the last Danish axeman, Beornred taking the man's final desperate blow across his shield while Leofric hewed at him two-handed with all his power, cleaving his head and shoulders apart in a spray of scarlet that spattered all around him.

And, as suddenly as the attack had started, it was over.

Bodies everywhere…and a robin singing from a nearby tree, his breast as scarlet as the blood running on the ground, his song liquid, beautiful; a stray piglet wandering in the garth rooting for food; the fresh face of the sun beaming down upon the pile of shattered bodies from whom the steam, in thin tendrils, rose up into the glory of the early morning. And as the mist of battle-rage cleared from his sight, so Leofric turned to look around him at the heaped bodies of the slain, at his own wounded and finally across the garth to where Brioni had been seated on Foxhead, Bran and Utha on chains by her side…but she was gone.

*

*H*er two bodyguards on either side of her, her face white with the horror of all she had seen, she had sat stiffly upright in her saddle the whole time as if nothing of note was taking place, her two great hounds leaping and snarling to be free.

She had fought Velda for the right to be there. She was the war-leader's lady, and she would not bring shame on herself, nor on him, by wilting in the saddle now. But, Dear God, it had been awful! The frightful killing of the three men, the demented shrieks of their women and then the swift fury of the fight itself, with Leofric right in the forefront of the muck and arrows had been terrifying. Blood-spattered but whole, he was now moving amongst his men, Beornred at his side, and she bowed her head in thankfulness.

But it was not enough to give thanks to God. She was not here to sit out each bloody raid with her heart in her mouth. She was here to fulfil a blood-oath. To learn to fight as Leofric's men had fought. She could see she was not ready. Not yet. But she would be…and then all men would see just what a Saxon shield-maiden she truly was. And leaping off Foxhead she released Bran and Utha to seek their own way into the ruined garth, while she ran for her bag of bandages, tinctures, needles and ointments from the back of Arnwulf's cart.

317

The fighting might be over, but she had a task to fulfil that she had been trained for by her mother since she was a little girl. Wield a sword and shield she would do, that was her destiny, but sewing a fine seam amongst Leofric's command must come first, and no-one amidst his whole warband was better trained to do so than she was.

# Chapter Forty Four

"*H*ot work, my Lord!" Beornred said, dashing the sweat from his face as he came up to where Leofric was standing beside his horse, dipping his reddened axe blade in a wooden bucket of water. "But that was a rare blow. One of your finest; cut him right to the heart. One more for Valhalla, the bloody bastard!"

"Yes! Swift and certain execution, but not without cost, I am afraid. I saw Eadberht go down with his horse, and there were others I saw fall, too. And we cannot spare one of them! Now we must clear up this mess and be on our way as swiftly as may be before someone comes looking for them. What was the final tally?" he asked him, wiping the long blade on Wotan's mane.

"Six down altogether, Leofric. Five killed outright, and one dying even as we speak," his big second said heavily. "But Eadberht will surely live to fight another day. His arm is hacked but the blood has been stopped, the wound stitched and he will surely mend. But Ufford of Brightwell has breathed his last, poor wight. Speared through his chest and lung-froth spewing from his mouth, he won't last the morning. And poor Cedd and Eynfryth have also taken the swan's path this day, shields split through and butchered to the groin. Cedd fell in front of me and was wolf's bait within moments of hitting the ground.

"Osweald and Rayner both fell in our final assault and Thorir with them. Those axemen knew what they were doing, and breaking a shield wall held by Vikings is never an easy matter, let alone Jomsvikings," he added bitterly with a shrug of his shoulders, twirling his sword in his meaty hand. "Even though pierced with arrows they still fought like bare sarkers."

"That was bravely done, poor bastards. And all is better than I might have expected. It was good we took out their leaders at the start. Berti did an amazing thing with that seaxe of his. Where is he, by the way? And what about the Lady Brioni? I can see those two hounds of hers, rooting about amongst the dead, but what of her?"

"Jaenberht is comforting the Saxon girls we rescued, where else would he be?" his big second said with a chuckle. "And the Lady Brioni is safe and well and fit to be tied!" he finished, laughing outright. "She was not impressed with being kept out of the fight. Though she knows you were right to do so this time."

"So, those two did their duty. And Raedwald kept the rear-guard under tight control?"

"Aye, Lord, managed our archers with precision. Without them our casualties would have been much higher. Though I doubt they relished staying out of it all. And your lady is in a fume about being kept so unceremoniously clear of the fighting. Right now she is organising the women we found here into caring for the wounded, including the ripe dame who is those girls' mother.

"She's called 'Osburgh', named after Alfred's mother. It was her husband and her brother whom those bastards flayed, along with the eldest girl's betrothed, poor lassie. A bloody business to say the least, Leofric. But none of them are the equal to the Lady Brioni who has them all sorted and running about with buckets of hot water and clean bandages. She is doing her duty by us all, as she said she would. Eadberht is alive now because of her! And she has been about the rest as well, some nasty cuts that she has sewn tight and bandaged, most others with naught but bumps and scratches. She is seeing to them all, with the help of those whom Jaenberht saved right at the start.

"But you won't keep that one doing that all the time; 'though she does sew a fine seam, as she said she did, and has not keeled over yet. And when you start sticking needles into a fighting man you must expect the language to get fruity...and she hasn't blushed at that either," he laughed. "So, all in all she is doing very well, my Lord, as she said she would! Quite well enough to earn your praise and your promise to get her properly trained before she sweet-talks someone else into doing it!"

"She wouldn't dare!"

"She's the Lady Brioni of Foxley, my Lord. So of course she would dare!"

And he smiled as Leofric took off his helmet and scratched his head, rubbing his big hands over his eyes as he watched where his belovèd was moving swiftly amongst his men, two of the younger women trailing after her with bandages. The other two going to the well beside the ruined house place, there to draw up the water needed for heating and cleansing the many wounds that Leofric's war-band had collected in defeating their enemies.

"What about our dead, Lord?"

"Burn them! All of them. Ours and theirs together. I don't want anyone to know what happened here. But search the bodies of their two leaders. They may have something useful on them, and keep the best of the armour."

"The lads are already doing that, but burn them all? No burials of our own?"

"No! I want the ground cleared of all sign of us. Oh, they will guess that a terrific fight took place, we cannot hide everything. But who did the killing, and what really happened here, and how many of us there were, I want that to remain a mystery...save for one thing. We will leave them a sign, an image of a fox's head nailed to one of the timbers on the old byre where those poor bastards were cut to ribbons.

"We will leave Oscytel that, and let him make of it what he can. And every time we cut his men to pieces we will do the same thing. Let him fret over it. It is time he was made to sweat for a change. See how he likes knowing that someone out there is stalking him!"

"That is good, Leofric," the big Dane chuckled in his gruff voice. "We Danes are a superstitious lot. Many fighting groups have their own witch with them to give them courage. Cast spells and divine the guts of sheep and chickens for the omens. Do that to him and his men, and they at least will begin to see danger in everything. You will turn their hearts to water. And you will make him doubt himself!"

And throwing his arm across Leofric's shoulders, he picked up his shield, hacked and battered from the fight, and walked with his commander, Wotan following behind them, back to where their men were busy clearing up, stripping the enemy of their armour and searching the bodies for whatever gold and silver they could find.

\*

*I*t all took longer than expected, so it was past midday before Leofric's command was ready to leave. By then the whole steading had been cleansed of bodies, all cast into the fires, even the butchered remains of the three men whom the Danes had so horribly tortured, and the children they had brutally slain. Their bodies wrapped in bloodied sheeting, their remaining family gathered around them weeping, Leofric had spoken a few words over them before ordering his men to cast them into the flames.

Finally the little cow-byre was pulled down and set on fire also, one great wooden pillar left standing on which Raedwald hammered a simple representation of a Fox's head that Osburgh and her daughters had roughly fashioned, with Brioni's advice, from their own garments, their nimble fingers making light work of the design. Meanwhile Aldred prepared a simple chicken broth from the many carcases the Danes had left scattered around the garth, thickened with oats from the sack Ricberht had found the night before.

Then, while the smoke from the newest fire rose up over the countryside in a great spiralling cloud, they left with the sun over their shoulders, Jaenberht

321

and Sigweald out ahead of them as before, Leofric, Brioni and Beornred at the front with Raedwald and Trausti. At the rear was Arnwulf, the old cow still tied to his cart, on which Eadberht, his wounds freshly bandaged, had been placed beside the young bull calf. Beside him rode Osburgh and her daughters on some of the Danes' horses, all the others running behind on long leading reins, too valuable to be left behind, and with every bit of foraged armour, carcases and equipment strapped to their backs...even loose chickens caught, tied and bundled in simple rough-made crates. And right behind them the small herd of cattle the Danes had been rounding up, no more than half a dozen shaggy beasts, lowing and scampering, with three of Leofric's men to drive them. Beasts that the few people of Ford would be pleased to accept as payment for their hospitality.

*

Out onto the old roadway they went, cantering along in fine style upright in their saddles and looking keenly about them until a few miles or so later they came to the turn in the roadway that they had been making for. Leaving the old Fosse Way where it dipped down towards the broad stream known as the By Brook, they took the trackway towards Yatton, Combe and distant Chippenham, the centre of King Guthrum's Danish power in all Wessex.

Here the countryside was wild and wholly untamed, all part of the great forest that stretched from Chippenham to Melksham where the Saxon kings had hunted. Vast stands of trees, oak, elm and beech, and huge tracts of rough open land stretched everywhere, broken up with broad thickets of gorse and hazel, laced with briars, amidst jumbled stands of holly and juniper. Close to, tall banks loomed over the narrow track that ran between deep gullies like a switchback, while dense copses of birch, yew and ash pressed in on every side, so that their journey was considerably slowed, the horses forced to pick their way in single file. While the simple roadway was just wide enough for Arnulf's tilt cart their passage was further hindered by the snow that still lay deep in sheltered places, so that it was necessary for some of the men to dismount and help the cart's wheels over the most dangerous places.

And in all that journey they saw no-one!

No herder with his beasts for market, no trader with his goods on a pony, no worker with his tools on his back, no-one out hunting with his hounds and his party of friends. Just the empty countryside, bleak and deserted on that sunny morning, with the sky blue overhead, splashed with crows in black squadrons, and the wind sharp and fresh amongst the trees that thickly bordered the trackway. Tall columns of grey smoke could be seen away in the far distance, smearing the sky, where stray parties of Danes were out ravaging the land with fierce intent. But they came upon no stragglers and none cried to them for help.

Just a mile from the Fosse Way turning, Leofric came to the place where they must all turn off to the right and drop down to Combe, a steep, narrow track with high banks on every side, that snaked its way down to the river at the bottom where a small cluster of houses marked where the stream could be forded, the water flowing broad and fast across a slimy path of great stones.

Here they needed trail ropes and a roll of timber before the wheels to slow their descent down the narrow trackway that ran beside the stream before climbing out of the valley up another steep hillside thick with coppiced trees and scrub. Here Leofric had to harness another horse to help pull Arnulf's cart, now heavily laden, up the twisting, sharp incline and even then it required several men to help the cart up the steepest parts of the track, the deeply wooded hillside falling sharply away to the stream far below, and streaked with white where the snow still lay in drifts where the banks were steepest.

By the time they reached the top they were all exhausted and the sun was well over the meridian, long shadows stealing across the countryside as the short January day slid to its close...and still they had a distance to go before reaching the safety they had been striving for since first light.

"Not much further now," Leofric said as he bit into a late apple from the store that Maritia kept for Oswald. "But I don't want to leave anything to chance. Alnoth, Ceawlyn, I want you to go on ahead of us to Ford with Raedwald and Trausti, and speak with the headman there, Eadwine, and his goodwife, Aelfrid.

"They keep the steading there as I said, and are well known to me. Give them this token," he went on, handing Alnoth a silver talisman in the shape of a stag, "and tell them I will be with them shortly with my whole warband. They may be shocked, but they will not be surprised it is me. They sheltered Raedwald and Trausti when they came through here with me some weeks past. But those two are Danes while you are both Saxon, and they will understand you. Now, kick on," he said, giving Wotan a swift buffet on his quarters. "They will need some time to get themselves and their people organised. And the day is passing. Give them my warmest wishes and tell them we will be with them before the sun sets." And giving them all a hearty wave, he turned back to his command to urge them into action before muscles stiffened and the will to move on left them.

\*

*T*wo hours later, with the sun dropping behind the hills in a ball of fire that lit up the snow, grey woodpigeons flighting into the trees and thickets all around them on white-barred wings, they dropped down into Ford at last. Here the trackway fell away very steeply onto the old Bristol trail, and then further into the steading itself that lay beyond it.

So much so that Arnwulf's cart had to be held back again by extra ropes attached to two of the strongest horses in Leofric's command. Even then it still needed a roll of timber held on long ropes before the wheels, and the wooden brakes pulled hard against their iron wheels as well, to make sure the whole equipage did not run amuck and smash itself to pieces on the steep hillside. Eadberht and the bull calf, whose shouts and bellows of alarm could be heard long before the cart came into view, were equally relieved when they reached the bottom, cattle and drovers racing past the rocking tilt cart, its iron wheels smoking as they did so.

But at least they had arrived, and to a warm welcome from Eadwine, tall and rangy with a wild mop of straw-coloured hair above eyes of acorn green; and Aelfrid, his wife, tall like her husband, with broad hips and a laughing face, who came running out to greet them with half a dozen others. All carried bright lanterns on long poles to show the men where they could put the cattle in a byre nearby, including the cow and her calf, and their horses in rough lean-to stables sheltered from the prevailing wind beside the house-place.

This was a very large, cruck house building with thick lath and plaster walls, with alcoves along its sides for sleeping rooms and storage, a deeply thatched roof, and a big fire right in the centre over which a cauldron of broth was already heating; the kitchens, brick oven and brew house all close by.

Beside the hall there was a small collection of cotts and bothies with their own gardens, piggeries and chickens that straggled up the simple trackway leading to the coast twenty miles away, but was seldom used. Much like those around the clearing from where they had set out two days before, most had a large single room with a fire in the centre, a place for beasts and storage at the back, and an extra sleeping space in the rafters reached by a ladder.

Close by in the steading's garth there was a small granary on staddle stones beside the stream, a handy forge and a great midden for all the waste straw and dung that the steading produced. Beyond were two large fields, fenced with stone walls and wild bushes behind a deep ditch, across one of which the hamlet's cattle roamed at will, eating what they could find. In one corner there was a great barn for carts and shelter, and thatched hay stacks on wooden pallets. And all around the little settlement the trees pressed in on every side: towering oaks and beeches hung with ivy, huge coppices of silver birch and ash; a profusion of willows and alder along the streamside and dense thickets of holly strewn with old man's beard and thick with berries.

True, there were trackways going in all directions, but the place was as secure from prying Danish eyes as was possible so close to Chippenham, and Leofric was delighted.

"Well met again, my friend!" he said to Eadwine as he walked with the wiry Headman and the horses towards the stables, while his men bustled about and Aelfrid took Brioni, Osburgh and her daughters under her wing into the hall, Bran and Utha following. "We are come, as I said we would, and I bring others in my train. Especially the Lady Brioni of Foxley, whose home was destroyed by the enemy a few weeks ago, and with her four women whom we rescued this morning from Danish raiders."

"That's bad, my Lord. Could they find their way here?"

"Not unless Odin releases them from Valhalla, or Freya from Folkrangr!" he said with a grim snort of laughter. "We slew all the bastards after a fierce skirmish, and have burned their bodies to leave no sign...and those of the men and children they butchered at the steading."

"Guthrum's men?" the man asked, concerned.

"No! Oscytel's. The Black Jarl of Helsing. Have any been here?"

"No. We have seen no Vikings here, nor expect to see any either. We are well hidden down here, and too small and too far for them to bother with. And now you are here we shall be well defended. What do you intend?"

"To use this place as a base from which to ride out and harry the enemy wherever we can find them. No...not here, Eadwine," he said quickly, laying a hand on the man's arm as he recoiled in dismay. "Like a cunning fox, we will not hunt in our own backyard. But further afield...anywhere that bastard places his garrisons that is a distance from Chippenham. And news of what we do, and where the enemy are, we will send to Alfred at Athelney."

"So, my Lord Leofric. You are for the King, now? Not just out for plunder as you were used to be!"

"Yes! And you? Are you for Alfred still...or for Guthrum now the King has been forced to flee?"

"For Alfred. Always have been. He is of the right line of Cerdic, from whom all the great Wessex kings have sprung. I know some of our leaders have fled overseas and others are already paying tribute. But I fought for King Aethelred, his brother, at Reading in '71, and then later the same year at Ashdown. We held the place of slaughter then and chased the bastards all the way back to Reading but couldn't dig them out of their fortress. Then

325

Aethelred died and Alfred became King and still we fought them. That is the only way. Now Chippenham has fallen, I know, but Alfred is still alive…"

"You have heard?" He asked, astonished.

"Yes, we have heard. Even down here news reaches us, and as long as he remains so the fight must go on, until we can defeat those pagan bastards once and for all. So, you do what you must, my Lord. And be sure your back is safe."

"Including your son?"

"Alfweald?" Eadwine said, astonished, stepping back and looking up at Leofric. "He is as stout a follower as I am!"

"No…the other one. Cuthbert, the one named for the saint. I have heard talk."

"He may be lazier than his brother, but he knows his place. I would proclaim him '*Nithing*' myself and cast him out if I thought otherwise," he replied gruffly. "He may be his mother's favourite, the youngest often is, but I am the master in my own home and all men know it!"

"Just so, my friend," the big Saxon war-leader said, clapping the man on his shoulder with a smile. "Just so! I meant no harm, but my life, and those of all who follow me, are in your hands…mine too, so it is right to ask the difficult questions now. But be assured, Eadwine," he went on tersely, "if any action of Cuthbert's should threaten our security then my hand will fall upon him like a thunderbolt!"

"If that should happen, my Lord," the tall Headman said, standing straight before Leofric, his eyes locked on his, "my own hand will fall upon him first, I promise you."

For a moment the two men stood eye to eye, before Eadwine thrust his hand out and Leofric grasped it firmly. "So be it, my friend. *So be it!* Now, let's get back down amongst the others, there is much to discuss, and some papers we took from the Viking leaders to mull over. They are in the ancient Nordic script, and will take some pondering to make sense of them, runes were never my strong point! And then again, we are all tired and hungry, and that broth your lady has cooking smells wonderful, and so does the bread from her oven!"

# Chapter Forty Five

**S**ometime later, with the meal over, washed down with home-brewed barley beer from barrels in the brew house attached to the steading, Leofric and his command, together with Eadwine, his two sons and Brioni, were sat on benches round the fire, for there was no dais in this house place as there had been at Foxley. Scattered amongst them on the rushes that covered the floor were a pile of hounds, Bran and Utha by Brioni's side; the tables, being simple trestles, having already been removed.

Outside clouds had come up with the evening, and the weather had closed in again with a wild, blustery wind and sharp falls of icy rain that rattled on the roof, and at the plain wooden shutters that covered the windows. Blown by the wind that wuthered down the long valley in swooping gusts, the great trees creaked and groaned to the pressure, swaying in the rushing darkness and scattering twigs and small branches everywhere.

Aelfrid, having withdrawn from the big room to a smaller one of her own with Osburgh and her daughters, was seated with her stitchery around a great iron brazier filled with charcoal and fruit-wood chips, while the men, wrapped in their fur cloaks, were clustered round the fire where Leofric had pulled out the rough sheets of vellum that his men had taken off the Danish leaders that morning.

"Here, Trausti, see what you can make of these," he said handing them over to his Danish sword-master. "They have been written in old Nordic script that I never did learn to make sense of. You have spent time with Grimnir who has them off by heart."

But it was not an easy task, for the Black Jarl was superstitious and did not trust the words so belovèd of priests, so all his messages were sent in the old runic script. Those strange angular marks that could be understood by very few…and they were mostly the skalds that travelled with each Danish host, or the captains of companies whom Oscytel had chosen personally, and who alone knew and understood the writing of their ancient gods and heroes.

Leofric, close to the fire, with his arm round Brioni's shoulders, waited patiently while Trausti struggled to make sense of the fine hatchings that ran across the papers he held in his hand, smiling quietly as he watched the big Dane scratch his head and rub at his nose as he always did when he was deeply thoughtful.

"Well, old friend," he said at length, "what do you make of them?"

327

"It is not so easy, Leofric, as some may think," Trausti replied with a rueful grin. "I only wish that Grimnir Grimmersson was with us. He knows every scratch and wing of them. But as far as I can tell they are instructions from Oscytel to several of his captains who have been sent out with their companies to occupy some of the larger villages and steadings in this area."

"Are they indeed!" Leofric exclaimed, straitening, his eyes sparkling with sudden interest. "How far to the nearest of these outposts?"

"Box, it says here. Where the Romans had a big settlement."

"Where is that?"

"About seven miles from here," Eadwine broke in sharply. "South of where you are now, and seven miles from Bath."

"And how far is Bath from here?" Trausti broke in urgently. "Because that is another of the places that Oscytel has named here that he wants his men to garrison. And Bradford-on-Avon," he went on, screwing his eyes up at the document he held in his hands, as he twisted it this way and that in the fire light.

"About twelve miles, a good day's journey there and back from Bath, less from here to Box, but both are twisty and you will need a guide. Especially if you intend to leave in the dark."

"Anything else in those documents, Trausti?"

"I cannot be sure, but Melksham is indicated and Malmesbury and Marlborough. But truly, Leofric, it is not easy to be absolutely certain. I am no expert in these matters. The old runes are hard to understand and there is much magic about them anyway. I never was the best of pupils at their study either. There is much here that I cannot read, but the names at least I can recognise. And the numbers."

"Numbers?" Leofric questioned him eagerly.

"Yes! Numbers of troops to be stationed at each place."

"So...excellent news indeed. But the Black Jarl has moved fast. Clearly he means to establish himself strongly in the area, but if he is going to garrison all those places his forces will be stretched to the extreme. The Danes reckon their men in crews. A large dragon boat can carry sixty men. But most boats carry about thirty, so we put down a whole 'crew' this morning, and its leaders, and took all their accumulated booty and equipment. That will have hurt him. And if we can keep on doing that so much the better."

"But we lost seven men out of our own 'crew' this morning," Beornred said, with a grim face. "Six killed and one so wounded that he may be out of action for weeks! That way we will run out of men long before he does!"

"On the face of it that may be true," their big war-leader conceded. "But our actions will also draw men to us. They always have done. But you cannot make pancakes without breaking eggs! Here we have a list of places that Oscytel means to garrison," he went on, pointing to the documents that Trausti still held in his hand, "and I say we should attack them as soon as we are able to do so!"

"King Aethelred always said we must go on fighting them," Eadwine said, standing up to fill his horn with fresh beer. "And Alfred took up that torch after his brother died. I hung up my byrnie years ago, but my arm is still strong and my sword is sharp. My shield is hanging above the door-place and only needs new straps to be as worthy as it ever was. You lead, and my sons and I will follow you!" And there was an immediate roar of approval from all around the room, Alfweald on his feet beside his father, his eyes blazing, while his brother, Cuthbert, held back, looking to where his mother's room lay at the back of the hall, his face suddenly bleak with fear.

*

Secretly he was appalled, as his mother would be once she heard what his father had just promised!

Let his brother and his father hazard their lives in this ridiculous struggle against the Vikings. The Great Army had come to England thirteen years ago, three years after he had been born, and no-one had yet managed to drive them out completely. Even the great Alfred had been forced to pay them off after the disaster of Wilton, and defeats again at Merton and Basing, in the year of battles following the Saxon victory at Ashdown in '71.

Thousands of pounds' weight of silver.

Since then he had seen his father go out to war many times...and seen him come back again, cut and battered, his energy drained. And now Guthrum and Oscytel had seized the whole kingdom and driven that ass, Alfred, out into the wilderness. Surely now they would make a peace with Guthrum without any more blood being spilled on hopeless causes?

It was madness to continue the struggle against the Danes any further, surely all sane men could see that? And the more his father continued to support this Saxon lunatic and his warband at Ford, the sooner the Danes would find out and destroy them all! Let father and Alfweald go out and fight. He would find a way to bide at home. He would talk to Gytha. She would know what to do. And then plans could be made. He did not really want his father dead, nor his brother either. But they never had listened to him, nor valued him. So they could be the masters of their own destiny...not his!

And he watched from the shadows as Leofric and his men detailed who would go where and what was to happen next.

329

*

*B*rioni, who had watched and listened to all that had been going on, now stepped forward with another thought.

"Well, now we know where some of his garrisons are, and how large each one is to be, and that gives us a clear advantage. But my father always said that no matter how many of the bastards you killed, they always managed to reinforce themselves from overseas, like what happened after Ashdown in '71...remember? They sailed up the Thames to Reading and made good all their losses? It was as if Ashdown had never happened. And Oscytel is no different. For him to make himself secure," she went on, moving closer to the fire as the wind suddenly battered at the hall with a wild gust that made the shutters rattle, "he needs more men, and that means ready access to a good port...and the nearest and the best from here is Bristol!

"Oh, I know that right now it is little more than a fishing village, and few go there, but it sits right on the river Avon, which is navigable for miles. Papa always said that was what is so terrifying about the Vikings. You can live miles from the sea and still be in danger of waking to find the Heathen are tearing the life out of you with flames and axes! It is something the King has often talked about, the fact that these murderous swine are not just professional killers and fighters, but hard-nosed traders as well. When they have finished burning and pillaging they'll need an outlet for their rape of Wessex. Oscytel particularly if he wishes to rival Guthrum for the full crown of Wessex, and Bristol would suit him very well. It has good links with Wales and Ireland, and he'd have easy access to Frankland for reinforcement as I said earlier."

"And every Dane who was interested in land and booty would flock, like the ravens they are, to his bloody standard," Raedwald said, stirring the fire with his boots. "You have raised an issue, my Lady, that I had not thought of."

"What the Lady Brioni says sounds right to me too, my Lord," Hannes broke in, his big face wrinkling down at her with a smile. "No Viking is happy far from the sea and his dragon boats, his 'Wave Riders', his 'Ravens of the Sea'! And Oscytel is no exception, believe me. Let him but settle his men in Bristol and that's where he will move to. The place may be tiny now, but with hard work and plenty of men he could turn it into a fortress stronger than Chippenham, or Wareham, and getting our hands on him then will be next to impossible!"

Leofric smiled at their anxious faces and gave Brioni a swift squeeze.

"You all worry too much," he said calmly. "The information that Trausti has just given us is perfect for my plans," he went on, waving his own drinking

330

horn towards the lean, wiry Dane who had just sat down again. "Oscytel can't settle in Bristol, or anywhere else other than Chippenham for some time yet. Not until Alfred has been dealt with, and not if I can help it. Least of all do I want Danish war-parties clattering past here and ruining our peace and quiet," he added with a laugh, that rippled out amongst his men. "No, I mean to keep him permanently in a state of alarm.

"We'll harry his outposts, kill his messengers and burn out his steadings. We'll cut his crews to pieces. Wherever he has men posted we'll attack them. Put the fear of God into them, as well as play on their own superstitions with the foxhead symbol of the Lady Brioni's house which we will leave behind us wherever we attack them. Every skirmish will be a thorn in his side. We'll so gall and goad him that he will not know which way to look for comfort. And every bit of information we get about Guthrum and the Great Army we will send on to Alfred in Athelney."

"How long do you think we can expect to stay here before he discovers our lair?" Beornred asked him quietly. "After what we did this morning, the Earl may be scouring the land for us already."

"And what will he find? Even if he knows where his men were, and that's not certain. That captain had a wide-ranging brief. There are no bodies, we burned them, and there is too much footfall on the Fosse Way for anyone to follow them. We have covered our tracks well, my friend. And besides," he went on, looking round him, "who in their right minds would expect a full Saxon war-party to linger near where the Danes have the centre of their power? No, he will curse the mischance that brought his men into contact with the enemy and assume we were on our way to join Alfred in the marshes of the Sommerseatas."

"All the same, Lord, it is a risk," Cadoc said in his soft Welsh voice, a stark contrast to the clipped speech of his Saxon leader. "We cannot hope to remain here undiscovered for ever. No matter how well we conceal our whereabouts, or how far we have to travel to destroy the enemy."

"Much will depend on the people here," Leofric replied briskly. "And Eadwine assures me of their loyalty, and of his own, as you heard earlier. And we have a brilliant friend in Hugo the Bearmaster, and his people. They will be in Chippenham before long, and will keep us informed as best they can of all Danish movements. Grimnir will still come out to Biddestone where Sigweald can meet him at St Nicholas church on market days. He will be our immediate contact with Hugo and Maritia. And together they have never failed us!"

"There is just one thing you are forgetting, Leofric," Trausti said then, his face going pale, his voice dark with foreboding,

"What is that?" Leofric shot back at him.

"The stone knife, *Sica!*"

"But that is only a legend," Leofric replied quietly as two of his men gasped and others looked bleak. "A bloody one, I grant you, but still only a legend."

"Nevertheless, legends have a nasty habit of sometimes becoming real, and the Black Jarl never lets it out of his sight, or possession. He certainly believes it all, and his men fear it worse than the plague. It is the very symbol of his power that they all carry on their shields."

"Very well, Trausti. Tell us what you know, and we will see. For you and the Lady Brioni share something here that all should know."

# Chapter Forty Six

"What do you and I share, Trausti?" Brioni asked the big Dane swiftly, her eyes wide with curiosity.

"Well, many years ago, I was one of Oscytel's men," he said, adding to Brioni's surprised gasp: "One of his hearth companions, I thought you knew."

"No! I had no idea," she exclaimed, her eyes wide with shock, hand up to her mouth.

"Well, I was a much younger man then, with a woman of my own and a daughter whom I loved, like Beornred. He was not come to his full power then, the Black Jarl, but his men feared him even so. He had come to believe that no man of his should be weakened by having a family. Women for amusement, yes. But real attachments? No! He believed they weakened a man; distracted him from warfare, from committing himself to his fellow Huscarles and to his Lord.

"Huscarle?" Brioni queried him, head on one side.

"A warrior who takes oath of allegiance to his Lord above all things," Eadwine replied, standing up and moving to refill his drinking horn. "It is a Danish thing. It binds the warrior to his Lord until death if necessary. In return the Lord provides for him, shelters him, rewards him with arm rings of gold and silver, and pays him in money, booty and women."

"It is a fierce blood-oath," Trausti continued, as Eadwine filled his horn and sat down again. "Fiercer than that which binds us to Leofric. If his Lord falls in battle then his Huscarles will fight on, until the last man. As those axe-Danes did this morning. No quarter asked or given, and the Huscarle has no family beyond his Lord's. Others have believed the same, but not to the level of the Lord Oscytel. I would not turn my family away as I was ordered, so he took his stone knife to them both instead while I was away on a mission, *Sica*...the same he used on your father!"

"So...that is what links us!" she exclaimed softly, tears springing to her eyes as she relived her own horrors.

"Yes, my Lady," the big Dane said looking into her face, his own eyes filled with pain. "When I returned, they were both dead! He had cut their hearts out. The girl first, her mother after. And he had made all his men watch while he did so!"

"Oh no, Trausti, *no!*" Brioni cried out, bringing her hand up to cover her mouth, the rest of Leofric's men looking bleak, while Cuthbert retched into a corner, his face white with horror.

"It's alright, little one," he replied gently to her, "it was many years ago now, many years. But I broke from his service and received his curse; that is why I and my fine friends serve with that big Saxon ox of yours. We have no more love for what our wolfish brothers are doing than you do. Leofric had occasion to save my life a short time after, at great risk to himself, and I took oath of blood-friendship with him. With me went my men also. So, now you know...but it does not get us over the problem of the knife...of *Sica!*"

"What is so..so terrible about this knife? About *Sica?*" she asked bitterly.

"Tell her, Trausti," Leofric said quietly. "It is a tale worth the telling, true or not, for she has sworn on her father's body, as you know. An ancient oath before Tiw and Thunnor, when Oscytel carved the Blood Eagle from his living body. It is the only thing that stands between us and the altar, for by Christ and His Angels, I do not ever mean to let her go!"

"So, that is the way it is between you two?" Eadwine said, with a smile. "Aelfrid wondered what had wrought such a change in Leofric's life. He was wont to fight only for money and killing Danes. Now he seems to want to fight for Wessex and his King. It is quite a difference!"

"I am his until the sun freezes over," Brioni replied with a dazzling smile of her own that seemed to light up the room. "But I cannot be handfast to him before God until Oscytel is dead! So tell us what you know about this knife, this *Sica*," she said again, expressing the name like a snake's hiss, as she settled herself against Leofric's shoulder, her two great hounds close by her side, their heads on their paws and their sterns gently beating.

*

*T*rausti sighed and took a deep pull from his horn of beer, while the wind blustered around the hall, flacking the old shutters and making the fire quiver in its draught.

"Very well then," he said, as the men about him shuffled and stirred with interest, even though many had heard the tale before. "Very well, I will do so, for there are some for whom the story will be quite new. Eadwine and his sons have not heard it, I know for certain, nor the Lady Brioni of Foxley," he added with a smile into Brioni's deep blue eyes. "And she needs to know it all more than any of you others," he added, looking round the room, at the shadows from the lamps that leapt and flickered round the walls and at the people gathered there.

"It is a strange tale," he said with a shudder, "and one shot through with dark magic that does not make pretty hearing!"

And without further pause, as the wind cried and moaned through the seething darkness outside, and the flames of the great fire that had been built in the hearth leapt and flickered in the smoky air, he told them all the legend of *Sica*, the stone sacrificial knife of the ancient Egyptian gods. And all the while they listened in rapt stillness to his words, wrapped in their thick mantles, their weapons to their hands and their eyes gleaming in the twisting light like a great company of hawks still-hunting for their prey, their talons ready for the pounce, their bodies tense with the excitement of the chase.

So he told them how *Sica* had been formed and fashioned out of jade, a rare green stone of stunning beauty from the furthest bounds of the earth, polished like shining glass, sharpened to a razor's finish and placed in a golden handle by Osiris, the eldest son of the earth god, Geb, and Nut the goddess of the skies. Osiris the Beautiful he was, later murdered with great wickedness by his brother Set. He, jealous of his brother's goodness, and desiring the knife, tricked Osiris into lying in a great box that he swiftly sealed with lead and cast into the Nile...taking *Sica* for himself.

And how Isis, Osiris's lovely wife, searched for her husband everywhere, and finding the box buried in the trunk of a tamarind tree, forced it open, brought Osiris back to life, and mated with him fiercely, only to have him die again later. She buried him, and brought up the child of their mating, her son, Horus, the god with a hawk's head, the protector of all pharaohs...only for Set to find his brother's body, and using the jade knife, hacked Osiris into fourteen pieces that he cast throughout the land, the blade forever scored by Osiris's blood.

But Isis, who had adored her husband, searched out all the pieces and bandaged them together for a proper burial, except his phallus which had been eaten by a catfish and could never be recovered. All this the gods had watched, and inspired by the devotion Isis had shown, resurrected Osiris as the God of the Underworld, the Egyptian God of the Dead, with green skin and a great feathered crown.

And then he told how it was this knife, *Sica*, stained with the blood of Osiris, that was passed down from hand to dark hand through the ages, its blade never blunted, gaining in power and evil as it did so. Of how it gave strength and protection to whomsoever possessed it until it had so devoured its owner's soul that there was nothing left for it to consume save the darkness of its owner's lusts and the sour dust of broken hopes and spent ambition, when it would leave its owner's possession for ever.

335

Finally he told how Oscytel had come upon it in Miklagard, in the great city of Byzantium, where he had served with the Emperor's Varangian guard and stolen it by wilful guile from the gold-encrusted crystal case in which it was preserved. How he had fled the city, killing those who hunted him for it, and thence gained his black name and even blacker reputation. From there he had returned, become the leader of the Jomsvikings, and joined the Viking hosts of Ragnar Lodbrok's sons.

Had held Aelle down as Ivar had hacked the Blood Eagle from his spine outside York; had beaten King Edmund of the East Angles in battle, and stood while his Jomsvikings had then tied the King to a tree and murdered him with arrows, and had gone on to carve that foul emblem in the bodies of many others, like Wulfstan of Foxley...or cut out their hearts as he had done to Trausti's little family, and how the more lives the green blade tore apart in screaming agony, the greater the strength and invincibility the wielder gained.

It was a black and blood-soaked tale that he told that wild night in Ford, with the wind swooping and moaning around them and the pebble-dash of icy rain against the roof, while those who listened sat white-faced and enthralled, even those who had heard the tale before, as his words flowed over them.

"So, you see it is no easy matter that we are attempting, Leofric," he said at last, looking to where his leader stood with his arms around Brioni, impassive, his mouth a tight line. "There are many who have tried to strike the Black Jarl of Helsing down with sword, spear and arrow, or long-bladed knife in a pitch black room, and none have succeeded. The thrice cursed hell-hound is still with us...and the bones of those who have tried to slay him lie scattered from here to Miklagard itself!

"God and St Michael aid us, but you have chosen a perilous path on which to lead us. I could almost wish we had never set out!" And in heavy silence he came and stood over the fire, his eyes lost in its swirling, twisting brightness, his tall frame suddenly seeming bent and knotted with unutterable weariness.

"How do you know all of this, Trausti?" Brioni asked in the silence that had followed his tale, putting her hand on his arm.

"I was in Miklagard the same as Oscytel," he told her, looking down into her strained face. "We both served in the Varangian guard, the elite personal troops of the Emperor himself. I saw the knife in its gold and crystal box in the Imperial Palace, and learned its tale. We were all terrified of it. To hold it is to possess it, and then only death can free you from its power. Oscytel's eyes gleamed with passion the moment he learned its secret. He yearned for its power above all things. But I was bound to him then, and followed him in his flight. Became a Jomsviking. I still carry his curse, but would not hesitate to cut him down should I ever find myself able to do so."

"Are all these things true, Leofric?" Brioni asked him then, a small catch in her voice, as those around them broke the spell of Trausti's telling and began to stir and mumble amongst themselves.

"It is only a legend, my beauty," he said clasping her to him, her eyes wide, her body suddenly shaken with fear. "A dark story of black evil to frighten the faint-hearted. Green headed gods, and those with hawk's eyes and curved beaks? Really...those Egyptians will believe anything!" he said with a laugh, crossing himself swiftly.

"No less than Danes believe in Valhalla and Ragnarok," Trausti replied angrily. "Or you Christians who believe your God is a man brought back to life from death on a cross!"

"I did not mean to mock you in any way, my friend," Leofric said then as Trausti's face darkened in sudden anger. "I know how you feel about this thing, *Sica*, and about the power you believe it gives to Oscytel. But the man is only a man after all. He eats and sleeps and breathes as we do. And as he is a man he can be killed. Does the legend speak of immortality? No, it does not, old friend.

"So the man has the luck of the Devil...but I tell you that his luck is already deserting him. No-one has struck such a blow to his reputation and morale as we have today. Thirty of his men, a whole boat's crew, and two of his chosen captains dead and burned to a crisp; their equipment taken and their intelligence papers in our hands. A complete disaster for him. There will be many in Chippenham this night who will be saying his time is over. Guthrum especially, for Oscytel threatens his rule, of that I am certain.

"We do not seek his power, nor his filthy talisman. We only seek his life...and that is forfeit to my Lady here who has sworn on her father's heart-blood to wrest it from him or die in the attempt. And it is doubly forfeit to me for the love I bear her, as it is to all of you who follow Leofric Iron Hand to battle and to freedom."

Then, leaping to his feet, he seized his sword and raising his great shield he crashed the blade against its iron rim. *"Death to Oscytel, the Black Jarl of Helsing. May God aid us to victory!"*

And suddenly following his lead, his men leapt to their feet also, Bran and Utha up and baying with the rest, as his whole company banged their feet on the ground and clashed their swords in one wild burst of sound: *"Death to Oscytel! God aid us! God aid us!"* A roaring tumult that brought the women rushing from Aelfrid's bower to discover what had suddenly got into everyone, swift to add their voices to those of the men, their defiance ringing and echoing

337

amongst the rafters...all except Gytha, Cuthbert's handsome wife, who held back on the threshold of Aelfrid's room while her eyes sought out her husband, standing silent at the back of the room where his brother and father, right next to Leofric, could not see him.

She would talk with him later. Find out what had been said to keep the men so long from their own firesides, then they would make plans of their own. Plans that could deliver the whole steading into their hands, and keep the Danes from plundering Ford for all time.

Finally, with one last shout that mocked the storm stamping fiercely outside, Leofric thrust his arms into the air and peace fell upon them all as suddenly as the noise had first erupted. And with flushed faces and warm hearts they waited for his dismissal, while Brioni ducked under his raised sword, deftly slipped her arm round his waist and stood spear-straight and glowing with pride beside him. Truly he was her Lord, and she revelled in his strength and spirit.

"Come now, all of you. Rest well and be merry. In three days' time we will pay an armed visit to Box. Reconnaissance first, then we will pounce at dawn. Eadwine to provide a tracker; and all before word has time to spread that there are Saxon warriors nearby.

"So, off with you all. Tonight we will keep a light guard only, four men in all. Raedwald will post you, and there will be reliefs. The fire to be kept in as usual, and we will have a wooding party in the morning.

"Now, my Lady and I have much to discuss," he said holding her close, ignoring the gale of laughter that swept the room, "and she is probably as tired of your silly faces as I am. So clear off, the lot of you," he ended with a broad grin, "and woe betide anyone who is not up and raring to go when I am!"

With that the meeting cheerfully broke up, the men full of chatter, each going to his own bed-place along the walls, saddles to lean up against, thick furred cloaks to cover themselves, weapons by their side. While Beornred and Raedwald sorted out the guards and Eadwine conducted Leofric and Brioni to a spare chamber beyond his own, where a large box-bed had been made up, woolfells on the rush covered floor, tallow lamps on an old oak chest against the wall and a covered wooden bucket in one corner.

It was nothing like what she had been used to at Foxley, nor with Hugo in the forest, but it was dry and warm and she was with the man she loved. To Brioni right then it was perfect.

*

338

*E*adwine left with his best wishes for a good night, the leather curtain that covered the door space swished into place, and they were alone together at last. With a great sigh of pleasure he gathered her into his arms, and lifting her up he carried her to the bed, its broad leather straps creaking under their weight, the mattress of thick linen newly filled with fresh hay and lavender, the rough cotton sheets covered with great rugs of fox fur and beaver.

Revelling in her untrammelled freshness, the scented creams with which Maritia had rubbed her body still lingering in her embrace as they kissed, Leofric was overcome with a fierce desire to possess this girl who was offering the secrets of her body, swiftly shorn of its coarse coverings by his questing hands, to the hot urgency of his mouth and loins.

This was no gentle love-making but a fierce mating of hungry souls, desperate to share as much of one another as was possible before being forced apart again by the harsh dictates of war, and the dangerous times in which they found themselves. A roaring, pulsing rush of blood through their bodies that made them both cry out, and left them feeling gloriously sated and deeply aware of the need and love for each other that ran through them like fire.

She was so beautiful, so loving, he reflected later as he ran his hands over her breasts and the silky firmness of her thighs. What right had he to expect such love and loyalty from one so lovely and so gently borne? Yet he did so! Aye and received it too in greater measure than most men could ever hope for. She may not have been his first love by any means…but, by God and His Angels, she would be his last and only one from now on.

He kissed her gently, caressing her breasts again with his hard hands as he did so before drawing her close against his heart, her body pressed against his own, the fur rugs drawn up close around them in the flickering darkness from the lamps on the old chest and the fire in the hall.

"Well, my beauty, am I forgiven for this morning?" he asked quietly as he brushed her hair with his lips. "For keeping you out of the fighting? You and your hounds both?"

"I suppose you are, my Lord," she replied with the hint of a pout. "Though don't think to get away with it a second time," she added swiftly, sitting up and leaning over him. "You made me feel like a child at a banquet being led away by its nurse before the adults get too unruly. Really, Leofric, I felt quite humiliated."

"That's not what Raedwald said. He said you sat throughout as if you had seen it all before. Upright in your saddle and calm of face and voice. It was Bran and Utha who made all the fuss!"

"Did he really?" she replied eagerly. "I so did not want to let you down, Leofric, no matter what I was feeling inside."

"Well, if it's any consolation, he and Daegberht were no more pleased with my orders than you were! No, listen to me, sweetheart," he went on sharply as she tossed her head and glared at him. "It wasn't just because I love you, and because you are precious to me, though God knows you are…but because you have no experience of open warfare, and none of how my people go about their business. And you need practice in your arms. You would have been cut down in moments in that garth today. And then where would we be?"

"What about Foxley?" she replied sharply. "And Velda?"

"At Foxley you were in white heat, surrounded by your own people and fighting across a palisade…and Velda was a woman. Against a veteran of the Army? Fresh and battle-wary? You would not last three minutes. You saw what happened this morning. Six of my best men killed and one really cut about and almost maimed. "But you will get there, Brioni. By St Oswald, my darling, you will pass muster, of that I am certain. But until I deem you ready you must stay here and practise. Now hear me, Brioni," he said sternly, seeing a flash of defiance in her eyes. "It is as your commander I say this, not your lover. And you will obey me, or it will not be my hand you will feel on your stubborn Saxon hide, but Beornred's, and he will not spare your blushes I assure you, if by your actions you endanger the men with a wild escapade!.

"Life is going to be difficult enough as it is anyway, without having to risk even more by going out and having to rescue you, my lovely, from the consequences of your desire for revenge before you are truly ready. But I promise you this, my dearest Lady Brioni of Foxley," he said, looking down into her eyes. "that when you can stand up against Finnar, Beornred or Alnoth, or any of my closer hearth companions, then on that day you will take your place beside me, aye and lead your own war group also. For then you truly will have earned it…and the men will follow you for your own sake and not just for mine!"

She sighed and lay back against his arm, staring up into the flickering darkness from the lamps and distant firelight, listening to the wind as it wuthered around the steading and flung the rain against the roof with a relentless swish and patter.

He was right of course.

In her heart of hearts she knew it, remembering how safe she had felt with Raedwald and Daegberht on either side of her while Leofric and his men had ferociously assaulted the Danish war-band that very morning. From a standing start to stamping violence in a spray of blood and human debris.

Terrifying to even think that she could do the same. Yet he believed her capable.

Stifling and frustrating though it might be, nevertheless she would do as he said. She had sworn her allegiance, and she would obey her commander. But perform kitchen duties she would not. Osburgh and her daughters, Rowena, Ethelflaeda and Leola could do those, together with whatever servants Eadwine and Aelfrid had about the place. Poultices, ointments and herbs that she had done with her mother, she would do. And she would do her best to physic and restore his men when they were injured. But for the rest? Weapon skill and endurance? She would prove herself if it killed her. They would soon learn, as the King had done, just how determined she could be. Trausti had said she was his best recruit. Very well she would prove it again, and again and again until Leofric was satisfied.

She may be the Lady Brioni of Foxley…but her place was by her Lord's side, lover, husband or not, it made no difference. Until this war was over, Oscytel slain and the King returned to his rightful place on the throne of Wessex she would put off her woman's clothes and stick to the tough leather and iron of the warriors who surrounded her. And she would cut off her hair, she suddenly thought, running its long tresses through her fingers. No helmet yet made would sit securely on top of all of that!

She had an oath of which to cleanse herself, and her father's blood to wash out of her soul, before she could consider her role as a woman again, and she looked up at him with a smile and tweaked his beard.

"Very well, Leofric the 'Cruel'," she said grinning ruefully. "I agree, 'though I don't like it one little bit, and you can expect a very frustrated lady from time to time, I assure you. But, for now, dearest of men, I will bide my time because I know that you are right. I would not have lasted three minutes this morning. I need hours on the practice ground. So, will you have someone put up a hacking post for me? And my wicker shield is still too light. I could not manage a full linden war-shield, that would be too heavy. But my own will not take a full sword strike and needs strengthening, but not enough to slow me down, and I need a long sword. Blood Drinker is fine as my seaxe, but it will not do if I am truly to prove my worth before all comers. My greatest strength is my speed, so I will need steel armour, like yours. Iron is too heavy for me. You just wait and see, my noble Lord. I will surprise you yet."

"I am relying on it. I have not forgotten what Trausti said of you at Hugo's after you had fought Velda. So all shall be done as you ask, shield, sword and armour. I give you my word. Now, my Lady Fair…you can give me your lips in return, it is far too long since last I kissed you!" And taking her in his arms he did just that, gently at first and then very thoroughly, with deeper all-consuming passion that lit such a fire in them both that, like harts in the chase, they were soon left panting for cooling streams.

War and death might well come between them in the months, even years to come. But for now they were together and that was a greater boon than he had a right to. And holding her closely to him, her breathing finally as soft and gentle as a child's, he nestled her face against his neck and together they fell asleep.

# Chapter Forty Seven

And that established their pattern for the next three weeks, while January played itself out and faded into a memory of biting winds, swirling snow flurries and bloody screaming death...punctuated by periods of studied boredom, when the men cursed the weather, mended worn straps on fighting harness and saddlery and swapped tales of courage and conquest. Then tempers frayed and men and horses stamped their feet in frustrated idleness, itching to be up and away from the slushy mire of fouled horse lines and the confines of the steading.

Days of reconnaissance and careful patrols, when plans were laid and the men were put through their paces. Archery practised and sword play sharpened.

Hacking posts were hammered into the ground and the men were set to before them by Trausti and Eadberht, his arm strapped, seated on a wicker chair, who drove them on mercilessly, sometimes in one-to-one combat and other times in a long line of stamping feet, locked shields and roaring voices as they practised the shield wall. And sometimes in packets of three: shield-man, spear carrier and axe-man, fighting as a unit to give the axe-man all the protection he needed to wield his frightening weapon to perfection.

And Brioni, her long golden plaits cut off by Aelfrid and placed with love into a finely woven basket of dyed rushes, both weeping as she did so for they were the very symbol of her womanhood, worked as hard as the men. Sometimes in leather tunic and cross-gartered trousers, sometimes in iron ring-mailed byrnie to her knees – her steel armour having to come from Frankland as no Saxon smith could make it - her short hair bobbing from side to side as she jumped and drove backwards and forwards across the practice ground.

For many, her new cut was considered shameful as it left her like many of the men with hair just to her shoulders, and no girl ever cut her hair like that...not wore men's clothing either. But Brioni quite liked the shorter cut, it being easier to care for with none of the endless brushing and combing that long tresses required. Best of all, her helmet, with steel face plates, fitted her like a glove over her padded arming cap of soft fleece and leather, and that pleased her hugely.

*

*I*n the midst of all this the Box garrison was put to the sword, their command post destroyed, their wattle shelters fired; Leofric's men rushing and roaring amongst them out of the dawn darkness in a thunder of hooves, swords and swinging axes. Even so the Danish Huscarles died, hacked down as they came stumbling out of their shelters, or burned in their beds, the wretched peasants fleeing into the barren winter wild of frozen copse and scrubland that surrounded their tiny settlement.

Yet their flight left two dozen shattered Danish corpses strewn across the vill in various attitudes of violent death: arrows stuck in them like the quills of porcupines, heads struck from bodies, brain pans burst open in pools of blood and white shards of bone to show that it was not the hand of God who had struck them down. But that of some Saxon lord who still stood by his King, had managed to evade the steel net that Guthrum had tried to cast round the land, and even now was bringing death and destruction to the enemies of Wessex in a sign that all was not yet lost.

And in their leader's dead hand Leofric thrust the foxhead symbol of Brioni's family.

Made of leather, black wool and a tuft of russet fur it was a potent sign of resistance to Oscytel's grasp of power, and Leofric smiled at the thought of the fury that would consume the tall, black-eyed Viking leader every time he saw one. And, God willing there would be many of them. Enough to force him out amongst them in person, when they would combine their strength to kill him!

That night there was feasting in full as Leofric and his men celebrated the first of their victories, counting over the pile of weapons and war gear they had stripped from the dead before they had left. Collecting the booty into a goodly pile to be shared out in due course, gold and silver arm rings and a great hoard of coins from all over England, and elsewhere that Oscytel's men had served, Beornred and Raedwald were delighted.

And the money was not all that had been seized because there were many horses as well that could be sold in distant markets, used as re-mounts for their own forces, or used to mount the new warriors they knew would come in to them as the words spread that there was a Saxon command in the field killing Danes, with money, horses and war gear to spare.

Wessex might be down…but she was by no means 'out'!

\*

344

S o, raid followed raid, each one meticulously planned and reconnoitred. Two men going amongst the enemy to sniff out the lie of the land, see where guards were posted, how prepared the enemy where, how confident, where they ate and slept...and how best to bring hell bursting in amongst them with flame and fury and biting steel.

Then, with Alfweald and Eadwine to guide them, Sigweald back tracking, the attack would go in with all the rage and bloody violence that Leofric's men could manage. Shouts, screams, the thunder of hooves and the baying of great hounds as Bran and Utha joined their new master, leaping and knocking down each terrified enemy who ran from them.

Snarling and worrying their human prey, their teeth red with blood that matted their fur, they tore out the throats of their screaming enemies whom they hunted down mercilessly...and for whom each beast was like the huge wolf, Fenrir, from Ragnarok, the end of all Viking days, who bit off the right hand of the god Tyr and would devour Odin himself. From them there was no escape. Every Viking the two hounds seized they killed, leaping for the throat as they would any wolf they had been trained to hunt, then tearing at it until the wretched man was dead.

And Leofric's men brought fire with them as well as sharpened steel, blazing torches to set thatch and walls aflame, burning some enemies to death where they lay in their stupor, drunk on ale and mead, like roasting pigs and smelling much the same.

Box was followed by Bradford-on-Avon, where the river runs through the town and is crossed by a broad ford that gave the place its name. Past its church Leofric's men plunged, and in amongst the cots and bothies that made up the settlement, searing the places where the Danes had set up their barracks and toll booths with cleansing fire. The men, muffled in their heavy capes, had their faces hidden by crude animal masks of wolf, fox and badger, the furred face of each beast mounted on the men's helmets - an idea of Brioni's to bring more terror to their foes and garnered from the old spirit gods she had encountered on that bloody morning at Foxley when her father had been slain.

For, like the hunting beasts whose harsh faces they hid behind, they gave neither ruth nor quarter, and there were many heathen pirates whose last sight before they were cut down, or brutally maimed, was the pitiless glitter of hard, cruel eyes behind a stiff mask of howling fury.

And those few who escaped brought such gibbering tales of terror back with them of hideous creatures hunting them, half man half beast, accompanied by Fenrir, and by Skol his fearsome son, that even Oscytel could not easily persuade his men to garrison the towns he wanted. He had to threaten them,

345

and show them his knife. Remind them of the oaths they had taken to follow him, while every foxhead talisman that was brought to him filled him with rage...and a hint of fear in his dark heart that maybe his power, at last, was passing.

For after each shattering attack Leofric and his men would disappear into the cloaking woods and forests from whence they had come like wraiths. Like creatures of the mists, will-o'-the-wisps, with no substance, that would lure you to your death if you tried to follow them. Back-tracking and laying false trails to confuse their enemies each time they made their way back to Ford and the safety of the tiny settlement that sheltered them amongst its steep banks and empty trails.

And it wasn't only the larger Danish outposts that suffered either, for more than one of the Black Jarl's messengers fell foul of their ambushes. Sometimes a swift, barbed arrow in the back or throat that brought them down in a spray of blood; sometimes a thin wire stretched across the track that could almost take a man's head off, neatly garrotting him without a sound...and with every kill they made the knowledge they gathered added to the picture of Guthrum's movements in Wessex. Especially where his power centres were, who was paying tribute, what villages and towns had been garrisoned and where other loyal bands of Saxon fighters were operating.

It was nasty, brutish, dangerous work.

Yet every little success they had encouraged those others who were struggling to confront the Danes. And as the word of their resistance spread out, so their numbers grew as more fighters came in secretly to join them, sometimes in ones and twos, sometimes small groups, until the little settlement was bursting at the seams with fighting men...and every scrap of information they gathered was sent on by fast courier to seek out Alfred's lair in Athelney. There the exiled King received unexpected hope, and vital news of how his people were coping with the Danish attempt to take over his kingdom.

Indeed, so many men came in that Leofric was forced to split his command, sending half his men to Slaughterford, the next tiny settlement along the By Brook stream that he had already reconnoitred, separated from Ford by a narrow twisting track high above the river. To them he sent Raedwald and Jaenberht to organise them under their own chosen leaders, after first ensuring they took oaths of allegiance to himself and King Alfred.

*

Meanwhile Hugo the Bearmaster moved the *Circus Maximus* to the edge of Chippenham as he had arranged he would, arriving beyond its palisades with trumpets, cymbals and all the ballyhoo of a travelling circus. Tumblers leaping and spinning, jugglers, clowns and Oswald, dressed for the occasion in a huge scarlet jacket and Maritia's favourite muffler of blue and purple plaid, safely muzzled and dancing in slow circles to pipes, crumhorn and beating tabor, with swaying head and massive forepaws, as his mistress pranced beside him with his chain.

It was a bravura performance, and out to greet them came the whole town and most of the garrison, clapping and laughing at their antics, the girls and young people running and screaming from Oswald as he was paraded amongst them. Dogs barking and horses bucking, the noise and confusion made Hugo and Maritia smile, confident that Guthrum would invite them into his defences to entertain his hearth companions and the captains of his army.

And amongst the crowds was Grimnir Grimmersson the Skald, neat and tidy, small of stature with eyes of blue steel and a beard of silver, his harp in its green leather bag, a long cape of blue and heather plaid around his shoulders and knee length boots of scarlet leather. With him was a slender girl with dark hair and hazel eyes, a long green kirtle, brown leather boots and a dark russet cape with a hood laid back to show her face...Cadoc's lady, Rhonwen, who brewed the Danish king's beer and served at his table. And Maritia saw them and smiled, for with their help Hugo would soon be before the Danish king, and the next part of their plan could be put in operation.

*

And all the time Brioni worked with sword and scramaseaxe at the hardwood posts that Leofric had ordered to be dug into the ground and hammered down. Posts that he and Beornred insisted every man of their command should practise on.

Here she used a practice sword, not the fine long-bladed weapon that Leofric had now given her, with damascened blade and gold wire handle, the very weapon she had so hoped for, with which to fight the Danes of the Great Army. This was a sword with a blunted blade covered in lead, to toughen the sinews and build the muscles of her right arm and shoulder. Yet still she carried her scramaseaxe by her right side, the beautifully balanced short-bladed sword she had fought with at Foxley, and with Velda, her Blood-Drinker.

These were days when her shoulders felt on fire and her wrists went numb with the unaccustomed weight of her practice sword, the lead with which its blunted blade was covered making her forearms droop, and the stunning jolt of every assault she made jarring her whole body. While Eadberht from his chair, his arm heavily bandaged, and Trausti from behind her, called out the blows, encouraged her when her strength flagged and cursed her when she made foolish mistakes…or flung her weapons down in despair when it seemed she would never succeed in mastering her self-appointed task.

*Head, neck, waist…left, right and overhead*, as the legions had practiced centuries before, jumping from side to side, shield on her left arm, right swinging round to cut across each side of the hateful post, while her new shield, heavier than the one she had found at Foxley, dragged her left arm down, and her iron byrnie, that Leofric forced her to wear at these times, gnawed and rubbed her unmercifully until its edges were sorted out.

"Keep your shield arm up, Brioni!" Eadberht would shout out to her as she cut and hacked at the post in front of her, the anger in his voice making her shoulders stiffen. "And remember to angle your blows to the neck. That way you can be sure of a kill, and not glancing off some part of his helmet and striking his armoured shoulders instead. Now, once more…and put your whole body behind your blows this time, not just the weight of your arm! Come on! *Come on, my Lady!* You look more like a common trull than a warrior maid. *And keep your bloody shield up!*"

And so it had continued.

Eadberht and Trausti determined to keep Brioni working until they were truly satisfied with her progress. Demanding more of her than they would of any other of their men, continuously chafing against her natural fiery spirit that would brook no delay, but fretted against the apparent mindless, grinding toil to which they were subjecting her. Until, one clear morning in early February, with the sky midsummer blue and the woodlands full of snowdrops and early daffodils, the constant struggle finally came to a head after a particularly lively exchange of words following yet another clash with Trausti.

"That's it! You miserable tyrant…and you, you broken-down excuse for a Saxon swordsman," she had shouted at Eadberht, throwing her arms down with a crash and sinking to her knees with exhaustion. "No more! You understand? *No more today!* My shoulders are stiff and my arms feel like leaden branches," she added. "I've had enough!"

"You've had enough?" Trausti had roared back at her, blackbirds flying in all directions. "*You've had enough?* What of your oath, you pathetic creature? What of Leofric's love and the risks he takes in your honour? Not to mention the time and effort Eadberht and I have put into your training. *Get up, you doxy!*" he had gone on remorselessly, kicking her shapely backside as he spoke, tipping her forward onto her face in his burning anger. "How dare you say you have had enough as if you were no better than a limp-brained fyrdsman, a feeble serf of no breeding and less intent! Do you think a veteran warrior of the Army will just let you walk away because you are feeling tired? Well? Do you? *Do you?"*

"No! *No, I don't!"* She had yelled back at him, tears of shame, anger and humiliation sparkling in her eyes.

*"Then get up off your knees and pick up your weapons!"* He had bellowed at her, red-faced with anger. "By St Michael and his angels, I will make a warrior of you yet, my Lady, even if it kills me!" And with no little satisfaction he had leaned against a nearby tree beside Eadberht's chair and watched while Brioni, her teeth locked together in bitter fury, had hacked and slashed at the hated post with all her strength, sending thick splinters and fat chunks of wood flying wildly in all directions.

It had been a bitter lesson for her, but she had the sense, despite her hatred of the whole miserable, wretched process that she was being made to suffer, to realise the necessity of what the two men were doing to her, and the rest of Leofric's command, and that only served to re-double her determination not to fail.

Just so it went on day after day.

Shield held high and brought round to cover her open side as she moved and circled on the balls of her feet, blade flicking round to cover her imaginary adversary, she was like a leopard, her attacks lightning swift and deadly; and as she progressed, so Trausti and Eadberht found her a string of opponents to practise on. And with that her fighting instincts really took hold: *lunge, cut, parry, return*...the clash of steel, the whack of blade on shield, the now friendly and accustomed weight of her harness, the growing strength of her body, all led her to become one of the most formidable of Leofric's band of fighters. Soon there were few who could stand against her as she punished herself unmercifully in order to win Leofric's praise, at first grudging then whole-hearted, and earn herself the right to stand by his side, to lead her own fighting group as he had promised, and give herself the chance to prove herself before his people whose approval was as important to her as that of their leader.

\*

When she wasn't practice fighting, sewing up wounds and physicking Leofric's command, or preparing ointments, tinctures and liniments, she chatted to Aelfrid and Osburgh and observed Cuthbert and Gytha closely as they went about the settlement. Unsure of their loyalty, she watched and listened as Cuthbert stayed in the background and his wife gossiped with his mother, or slipped to the market at Biddestone with Osburgh and her daughters, often coming back flushed and full of good spirits.

She seemed especially interested in Rowena, whose husband had been so horribly slain by the Danes, while Eadwine and Alfweald threw themselves into supporting Leofric in every way possible.

*

"*I* am concerned about Gytha and Cuthbert's loyalty," Brioni said one Monday night as she and Leofric lay together after another hard day on the practice ground. "He does little except moan about the numbers of men we are now supporting here, and about all the disruption we have brought to the settlement."

"I know," he said, rustling his shoulders against the pillows. "He doesn't believe that we should be fighting the Danes. He keeps dropping hints that Wessex would be better off with some sort of peace with Guthrum, as I hear many thanes are already arranging."

"He says that paying tribute to have their lands spared from pillage and destruction, is better than fighting for a hopeless freedom," she said, snuggling into his shoulders. "One of these days Trausti will take his seaxe to him!"

"Talk is cheap, Brioni," Leofric countered lazily. "I have heard what he has to say, and his father has strongly rebuked him. He is a young man full of hot air, they almost came to blows; but Eadwine and Alfweald are stout supporters. None could be better, and our assault on Bradford last week could never have been so successful without them. Both men scouted, with Sigweald, and Eadwine led the second attack party with real vigour. Let Cuthbert be a bent reed. He has no authority here."

"No, he doesn't...*but he wants it!*" she said sharply, sitting upright in their bed. "He wants it badly, and doesn't feel that he is ever consulted. Just ordered to do stuff. He may be a 'bent reed', but I think he is dangerous. Not on his own, maybe," she went on urgently. "He has neither the brains nor the drive. But add in his wife, that Gytha, and he could become deadly!"

"What's her background?"

"Townie! Daughter of some sort of merchant from around here who got himself in difficulties over money. Married the girl to Cuthbert to pay off the debt and she resents it all badly. Wants gold to puff off her consequence with the other wife, Ethelinda, a really lovely lady; one who adores her husband and is mightily proud of all he is doing. Longs to be pregnant and wants a whole brood of little ones.

"But Gytha wants gold and status more than anything. Not for her a full nursery. Wants to 'lady' it beside her husband before the world. It is she who

350

is pushing Cuthbert to betray the family, I am sure of it. And he is weak enough to go along with her."

"My, you have been busy!" he exclaimed, laughing, giving her a swift cuddle.

"Just listened, chatted and watched...but what his parents make of it all is hard to tell, as he is his mother's favourite and she protects him from his father's anger."

"I am not sure they trust him either," Leofric replied, thoughtfully. "But maybe that is because he is not a fighter, like Alfweald?"

"Happier with sickle and billhook than sword and battle axe...and not too much of those either," she riposted with a snort of derision. "Swifter to give orders than to carry them out."

"And his workers don't rate him highly either," Leofric agreed with her. "No wonder he is not much listened to!"

"He is privy to too much information, Leofric!" she exclaimed, anxiously. "He knows all that we do, and that wife of his is a constant rattle. And, like me, she can write! She and that Rowena are as thick as thieves and after her experiences at the steading that girl wants peace above all else."

"Because she is pregnant?" he asked her, leaning further back on the pillows

"So...you knew then?"

"Aelfrid told me this morning. You are not the only one she chats to. She is carrying her betrothed man's child and does not want to lose another babe to Danish steel!"

"Peace at any cost," she replied, bitterly. "Rather than fight for something permanent, go for an arranged truce that those bastards will break as soon as it suits them to do so! How can people be so blind?"

"Because the alternative requires blood and steel, and for many the cost is too high. It is easier to give in than continue the struggle," he answered her, pulling her down beside him.

"No, Leofric!" she replied tersely, struggling out of his arms and turning to face him. "What about Cuthbert and Gytha? She is off to Biddestone market again tomorrow, and not for the first time, with Rowena and the younger girls. Sigweald is going with them, but I don't trust her not to slip someone a message that could destroy all of us. She goes there too often!"

"Slip someone a message? That's a bit fierce isn't it, my darling? That would put the cat amongst the pigeons and no mistake!"

"Don't talk to me about cats and pigeons, Leofric," she flashed back at him swiftly. "Hawks and rats round the hay stack...with us the rats to

351

Guthrum's hawks! No thank you! But I have a nose for trouble, and what I can smell is not good for any of us!"

"Very well," he said after a pause, looking down at her with a smile, "go as well if you are so concerned, but secretly. You have already said you need some rough cotton for bandages, and with luck Grimnir will be there also. It is the last Wednesday in the month so he should be near the church where the market is held. They can go with Jaenberht and Cadoc, and Sigweald. You take Eadberht with you, he is mending at last and needs to get out of this place too.

"A trip to the market would suit him well. Go by the longer route through Slaughterford, and dress like a working boy with his master, long brown cape and dull colours. I'll help to bind your breasts to hide your figure, and wear loose breeks...and take just Blood Drinker with you. Leave your long sword behind; it is too fine a weapon for a farm boy to carry. And don't groom your beasts, or dress them up. Let them be serviceable, not flashy, you don't want to draw attention to yourselves if you can help it. Find Gytha out...see what she does and to whom she talks. And, if you can, tip Grimnir off that there might be a problem. Don't worry about the boys, I will speak to them myself."

"Mmmm, good idea. I had not thought that far. What about his father?"

"Leave Eadwine to me. If there is a rotten apple in the family barrel then he will deal with it. He told me so himself the day we got here. He and his sons go to the big horse market at Chippenham in two weeks' time. It will be a packed-out affair and I would love to go there too, but it is too risky," he added swiftly as he saw her brows come together. "So I will send Beornred and Raedwald instead. They can blend in nicely and find Hugo, and Grimnir, and find out if there is anything going on that we should know about.

"The time may come when we need to get into the place and forewarned is forearmed! Now come here and give me a kiss," he said, throwing his arms round her and pulling her towards him. "I haven't tasted your lips all day and that's too long a time for me!"

# Chapter Forty Eight

*T*wo days later, with the February sun warm on their faces and the woods and thickets full of little birds, a woodpecker drumming madly in the distance, the market party set out for Biddestone. Osburgh, her daughters, and the two wives, Gytha and Ethelinda with Sigweald, Jaenberht and Cadoc as their escort, all in their best clothes, crossed the ford and took the steep, twisting trackway that led directly up the hillside to Biddestone and its market.

The men as gaily dressed as the women, were out of their armour to avoid too much notice, but had their swords at their sides; soft hats pulled well down across their faces with long, bright feathers in their crowns, their trousers cross-gartered in red and green, and all with sweeping cloaks in gay market colours around them, for despite the sunshine the breeze was still sharp. Chattering busily amongst themselves, like a small flock of starlings, they sloshed their horses through the By Brook, the men leading, and disappeared up the steep, narrow pathway in front of them.

A short while later, Brioni and Eadberht also left for the market, both soberly dressed in dark russet and brown.

Brioni, with her breasts bound as they had been for her fight with Velda, and her short hair, looked like a boy rather than her usual shapely self, with her leather fighting trousers loose about her rounded hips to blur them and cross-strapped to her knees with strips of dark green linen, a long brown cloak with a deep hood over her head and her scramaseaxe by her side. Eadberht was similarly dressed, but with his long sword hanging from his waist; both had feet thrust into tough workday boots and were mounted on shaggy horses, their bridles dull and no decorations on their saddle ware.

Just a stalwart countryman and his boy on their way to market, armed as so many were those days, their horses no different from many that side of the winter, unremarkable and sturdy, with no hint of the speed and toughness they really possessed. Both warned not to attract attention to themselves amongst the cheerful crowds that made up Biddestone's busy market, they were still excited to be going. Unsure of what might happen, and careful not to be spotted, they too crossed the stream but took the upper side track that led first to Slaughterford and then steeply up to Biddestone and to St Nicholas' church where they hoped to meet with Grimnir the Skald.

*

*U*p ahead of them, but on the other side of the hill they were climbing, Gytha and Rowena were busy chattering inconsequentials, Rowena's head full of plans for her coming child, Gytha's full of the meeting she was hoping to make with her father's old partner, Godric the cobbler.

He came to Biddestone for the market, but ran a busy stall and big workshop in Chippenham the remainder of the time. He was a handsome man with a roving eye and a clever way with leather, neat stitches and lovely patterns that pleased both men and women…and he had direct links with the Danish army of King Guthrum, making sturdy boots for his men and his commanders, and fancy shoes for the king and those in his court.

He was the best shoemaker for miles around, and to him came the great and good of Danish and Saxon society, at least those Saxons whose lands had not been destroyed and had the gold and silver with which to pay for his wares. And it was to Godric that she had decided to turn, Godric whom she had known before her marriage, whom she had met before and to whom she had already given herself with wild abandon, and whom she was sure would help her to get her message through to the Danish rulers of Wessex…that there was a violent Saxon warband operating out of Ford that needed to be put down!

It had taken many hours of talk with Cuthbert to perfect this way.

Not that he needed much persuasion; his dislike of his father and his brother was very strong. No, he was concerned about his mother. How to protect her, and himself, from Danish bile. The condemnation from fellow Saxons of his betrayal at Ford he could shrug off. After all, he would be on the winning side and in war truth and loyalty were often the first casualties. What was the point of being loyal to a vanquished King? No, he needed to be true to himself, and as he saw himself as the 'better' man with regard to his father and Alfweald, the rest was easy. And he would not be alone in his betrayal, for hadn't many thanes already changed their allegiance? And as for his mother, she was always telling him to be forthright and determined, to act with strength, so when he became 'Thane of Ford' under Guthrum, then surely she would be proud of him, and Eadwine's death, and that of her son, Alfweald, would soon be forgotten as of necessity, if not forgiven.

Now she had the message she needed to give, and the silver coin it would take to get Godric to pass it on to the Danish King, and a frisson of desire coursed through her body at the remembrance of their last meeting, of how he had kissed her, wrapped his arms around her and then roughly taken her, making the beast with two backs right there on the floor of his stall tent, where he slept overnight.

It had been the most exciting thing that had ever happened to her.

He was a bold lover, and she would have married him had her father not sold her to Eadwine for his son. Something to do with a failed deal her father had made. And knowing Godric was so close had been a temptation too hard to resist. Cuthbert was a weak man, as greedy as she was, but stupid. Only seeing what he wanted to and refusing advice even when it was in his best interest.

He was hopeless. But his father had much land, and with things the way they were in Wessex he might end up a thane, and if they all died she would end up with it all, for Saxon women were allowed to own land in their own right. It all depended on whose side you were on. And with Alfred fled into the wilderness of Athelney, Guthrum's men all over Wessex and so many Saxon leaders fled abroad or paying tribute, there was little doubt in her mind as to who was winning.

This nonsense of fighting the Danes on behalf of a man who was King in name only, whose only kingdom was a few thousand acres of watery wasteland of the Sommerseatas must end…and clutching her bag over her shoulder, she knew she had the means to stop it.

Looking across at Rowena she laughed delightedly, her face flushed and full of excitement so that Jaenberht, ahead of her, looked towards her and smiled.

A foolish girl that Rowena, but she was a perfect foil, she would easily be persuaded to go shopping with her for trinkets. Those three boneheads with their swords and fancy feathers would be sure to let them wander off while they went to the ale barrels for a deep wet. Then she would find Godric, and all would be well, and she laughed excitedly again.

Ahead of them Jaenberht and Cadoc exchanged glances, and shook their heads, while Sigweald pushed on ahead. They had their orders from Leofric. They knew what was in the wind, for he had briefed them in deepest secrecy, and looking back at Gytha with shaded eyes, they kicked on, determined that even when let loose they would do their best to keep both women in sight.

*

When they got there the market was in full swing. A wild medley of stalls and market tents, many with brightly coloured awnings and flags, and signs outside to show what might be found within: chickens, calves and piglets in the beast lines; local produce of many kinds; potters selling crocks, bowls and dishes; weavers with cloth and matting; drapers with a wide range of materials, exotic as well as homely, striped, plain and plaid; butchers, bakers, furriers, basket makers, even an armourer with swords, knives and ring mail byrnies…and Godric the cobbler. Wandering amongst them all were hot pie sellers, with ringing bells and trays of good fare and wandering pedlars with a host of trinkets, toys and ribbons hanging from the long poles across their shoulders. It was an amazing, bustling scene to which half the countryside had come to enjoy on that bright February morning, thronging the stalls in a kaleidoscope of movement and colour into which the small party from Ford, having left their horses in a handy compound, swiftly vanished with laughter and excited faces.

Brioni, coming later, and from the other end of the village, was dismayed as she and Eadberht swung off their horses, their eyes scanning the milling, mass of humanity who thronged the village on this, the first really warm day to celebrate the end of winter.

"Dear God, Eadberht!" Brioni exclaimed appalled. "I never thought it would be like this. Half the world and his wife must be here today. We'll never spot them in all this!"

"Don't you worry, my Lady," he replied with a quiet chuckle. "I thought it might be like this. That is why the boys are wearing bright feathers in their caps, and the girls their distinctive coloured capes. Pheasant feathers dyed scarlet and blue will stand out even in this crowd. Leofric has told them to keep the girls together, except those two, so keep your eyes peeled and we will find them, even in this crowd. Meanwhile, the church is close by, the sun is high and Grimnir should be in the porch shortly with his harp on his back. He never moves without it.

"Come on, Mistress Brioni," he chided her as she looked blankly around them, "let's be about it. There is a corral for loose horses just over there, and we have a job to do. If that lassie is playing us false as you suspect, then she must be stopped before she kills us all!"

*

*B*ut in the end it was chance that came to their aid, not their sharp eyes as finding the other party in all that crowd, despite the colours they were wearing, proved a task too far. And it was as Eadberht and Brioni were standing beside a pedlar admiring the long ribbons of blue, red and emerald green he had in his hands that Gytha, with Rowena by her side, almost walked into them.

At the last moment Brioni spotted her, and with a gasp whisked a startled Eadberht aside to admire a large set of attractive woven baskets in a stall close by. Their dark hoods pulled well over their faces, they were not spotted as the two girls passed them by in lively conversation. Next minute they had stopped in front of the broad tent of a tall cobbler with swathes of finest leather in his hands, and a powerful mastiff on a long chain by his side in a large wicker basket, not ten paces from where they had found their sudden hideout. A man whom Brioni thought she knew.

Standing beneath a wide awning that covered a number of tables on which were displayed a beautiful collection of boots and shoes in a variety of colours, some of them in finest suede, the man was almost as surprised to see the two women as Gytha was excited, giving a small screech as she rushed into his arms and kissed him. Rowena, standing close by, was covered in confusion and turned her face away, while her companion, who plainly knew the man she had come to see, patted the grizzled hound, pulled the man into the tent and dropped its flaps to shut them off from the common gaze, talking volubly all the time.

"So, that's what all this has been about!" Eadberht said disgustedly, slipping further into the shadows of the basket weaver's stall. "She is cuckolding her husband. Any minute now the walls of that tent will start to shake and that will be that. You were wrong, my Lady," he said sharply, making the sign of two horns with his fingers behind his head. "For all her finicky ways, she's just a common tart deceiving her husband with a slick lover!"

"Not so fast, Eadberht," Brioni snapped back, her hand on his arm. "She may well know that man, a cobbler by his trade," she added, sneaking a further look at his wares, and at Rowena sitting in a deep chair by one of his tables as far from the mastiff as she could get. "But I want to know what they are saying. Come swiftly behind his tent. She is talking twenty to the dozen, and loudly. Whatever else she may have come for it is not just his body she is lusting after. She is up to something I swear it…and knowing what I do of her now, none of it will be good!" And in moments they were standing right at the back of the cobbler's tent, where he had left his cart and hobbled his horse, a large bay gelding with a nosebag over his face and a bucket of water nearby.

And talking Gytha was: about her husband, whom she despised; about her life as the youngest wife, that she hated; about life away from a busy town, that she missed; about the Danes, who were clearly winning in Wessex…and about the Saxon war-band that had swept into her life and now threatened everything. And, with a chink of coins, she told him there was a message she wanted taken back to Chippenham for the new Danish authorities. For them to come to Ford and sweep the Saxon scum away who had settled there…and were making such hay out of the Lord Oscytel's soldiers!

Had he, Godric, not heard?

357

Indeed he had, and the Lord Oscytel was full of black rage about his losses, while the Danish King, Guthrum, was privately pleased, joking about the man they called 'The Fox', from all the foxhead symbols that had been left behind at every killing. And, yes, he would take the message; and, yes, he had missed her and couldn't wait to see her again. After which their voices fell into a confused mumble and moments later the tent walls began to shake, so Brioni led Eadberht away in disgust, beyond the horse and cart, to sit on a sackful of woolfells that had been left nearby, before he plunged through the tent wall with drawn sword and killed them both!

"Sweet heavens, my Lady," he gasped out in a rage. *"You were right!* The wicked little mare, she deserves a whipping at the cart's tail at the very least, and that miserable scrap of a husband, a rope's noose from the tallest tree! To think that he would sacrifice his family for gold and a thane's torque round his neck, let alone us with them! *'Nithing'* is too simple for such treachery. What do we do now?"

"Cool down and find the others. I bet Jaenberht will not be far away, nor Cadoc. Leofric told them to let her and Rowena steal off, and do their best to keep them in sight, but not to startle them. This treachery is dire, Eadberht, but it can yet be turned to good account. The person we want now is that cobbler, that Godric.

"He is the one we need to put the fear of the gods into, with steel and hot iron if necessary," she added darkly, still thinking she knew the man. "Right now, you go and find Grimnir and see what he knows of Godric the cobbler. I will try and find the others, to let them know the trap has been sprung. As for Gytha...leave her be. Let her think she has triumphed.

"You watch, she will be full of the joys of spring today. And after her little 'assignation'," she added with biting sarcasm, "even more so than she was when they all set out! If we can 'turn' Godric, then that stupid little traitor will have done us a better deed than she could possibly imagine!"

*

*T*hat afternoon, as the shadows lengthened across the market beneath a royal sunset of gold and crimson, great clouds edged with scarlet sailing up to fill the horizon; with men everywhere packing up, collapsing their stalls, collecting their horses and harnessing their carts, women and children helping; when all was bustle and yells and swearing and the market officers were ringing their bells for market end as a chill returned to the air with the setting sun, three men and a boy came across to where Godric the cobbler was loading up his tilt cart and stopped his work.

The large tent was still up, because he slept in it on market days, and Oscar, the great mastiff in his basket, was chewing on a bone from the butcher who had been busy all day, his master pausing to ruffle his enormous head as he passed by, when they came purposefully towards him.

The cobbler's hands were strong from the work he did and he had sleepy eyes that watched everything with interest. He was tall and well built, but he was not a fighter, and he watched two of the men who came across the green towards him with a grim mouth, for he could tell that these were fighting men. Men who walked with a lithe step and whose hands were on their weapons, leopards in men's clothing with scars in fine white lines that marked both their faces. And the boy who walked with them was the same. Light on his feet, his face hidden by the hood he had over his head, a long-bladed killing knife at his side. And he was thoughtful...for the third man he knew.

A small man, with a silver beard and a green harp-bag on his back, neat in apparel and scarlet boots on his feet. Grimnir Grimmersson the Skald. The gifted glee-man who played for King Guthrum in his hall and was popular with all who feasted at the royal table, especially with the tall, bleak-faced Viking war lord with black armour, whom all men knew as the Lord Oscytel, the Black Jarl of Helsing.

Seeing them coming he moved to the tables beneath the awning, now cleared of all their stock, reached into the tent for a great stone carafe of ale and a stack of bowls from which to drink it, and called up the dog to sit at his feet.

"I see you, Grimnir the Skald," he called out then, sitting down on the chair that Rowena had used earlier. "And those with you," he added with a nod to the hard faces of the two big men who slipped in with the little harper, their hands on their swords. "Is it singing you want with me...or business? My stock is packed away, but if there was something special you wanted, I am sure it could be found. Come, have a stoup of ale with me," he said pleasantly, indicating the carafe and bowls. "It has been a long day, and a good one."

"It is not your stock we are after, Godric," Grimnir said in his precise voice, the tone light, conversational. "It is something far more precious."

"I do not understand," the man replied carefully, his eyes ever watchful. "What could be more precious to me than my stock which I have spent so many hours in perfecting?"

"Your life, master cobbler," the tallest of the men, Jaenberht, growled at him, his voice full of danger. "Your life. And if you value it, and the hound by your side, that I swear I will slay the instant it moves," he threatened darkly, a heavy throwing knife suddenly in his big hand, "listen well to what we have to say, and no-one need get hurt."

"What is this about?" Godric asked him calmly, his heart beating a wild tattoo, his hand falling onto the mastiff's thick neck as it growled deeply for the first time, his eyes fixed on the speaker, his mind racing. Grimnir he knew, but what the little harper had to do with the two killers he had come with, and the boy who was with them, he had no idea.

"It's about a visit you had this afternoon from a certain young lady we know of," Eadberht replied sharply, coming under the awning, his hand on his seaxe, followed by Brioni, her face still in shadow, now sure of her suspicions, her scramaseaxe loose in its sheath. "A young lady whom you had knowledge of later," he added heavily. "Who is married, and with whom you cuckolded her husband!"

So that was it. Gytha!

Were these her husband's friends come to sort him out? It was possible. Though what part did Grimnir have to play in all this? He did not know, and those two looked like professionals, not scrub villains good with a knife. But Gytha was not worth fighting over, nor was he about to risk Oscar's life. So, with a casual smile, he rose and led the big dog away, dragging its basket with him, shortening its chain round the heavy post to which it was fastened, and coming back to the table, he picked up his own bowl of ale and laughed.

"So...this is about Gytha; married to that idiot husband of hers, that Cuthbert. If it had not been with me it would have been with another. I have known that light-skirt for years, she is not a virtuous girl," he replied casually. "I have known her before this day. Is it for that my life is in danger?" and he laughed again.

"No! You 'mender-of-shoe-leather'", Eadberht snarled, stabbing the table violently with his seaxe as he leaned forward towards the tall cobbler, making him jump. "This is not about that little tart, you may have her as often as you like for all I care. This is about the message she gave you. The one she wishes you to hand to Guthrum's officer of his guard! The one I heard you talking of."

"Think carefully, Godric, before you answer," Grimnir said then, his voice soft and dangerous as he came right up to the table and leant towards him. "I know you, where you live and where you work and I am close to the King. He listens to me, and I have the ear of the Black Jarl of Helsing. You start passing messages, to anyone, and I will make sure that it will be the last thing on God's earth that you ever do. My friends are everywhere, Godric: in the King's hall, among the houses and ginnels of the town, amongst the common soldiery who love my songs and poetry...amongst those who need money."

"Are you threatening me?" the tall cobbler said then between clenched teeth, sweat springing on his forehead as he realised the deadly nature of this sudden visit. But why Grimnir? He was the Danish King's man, wasn't he?

"Yes, Godric! I am threatening you because I will not have the safety of Alfred's men threatened for a handful of silver!"

"Alfred?" Godric questioned, astonished, his mind spinning, his eyes calculating as he looked at the big men who now crowded him. "The King of the Marshes of the Sommerseatas. That bog-wight?"

And then there was sudden violent action as the two big Saxon warriors flung themselves on him, ale and bowls flying everywhere, and scrabbling and bucking wildly they forced him down on the table, his arms spread out, his face twisted rightways against the wood, Grimnir's own stabbing knife pressed into the back of his neck.

"You forget who is the rightful King of Wessex, Godric," Grimnir said softly into the man's left ear, moving his blade to cut it off, his tone full of menace. "That 'bog-wight' is our rightful King…not Guthrum, not Oscytel, though he would like to be. *Alfred*. A man who holds my heart in the hollow of his hand, and the hearts of all those who surround you, and thousands of others throughout these lands.

"He may be 'King of the Marshes' of the Sommerseatas now, but before the end of this year he will be King of all Wessex again, where he belongs, and the Danes will be crushed! It is I who say this, Godric, with the magic of words and the promises of God. So choose wisely. I could then be best friend to you and your business…or the most dire enemy who will destroy you and take your life. The choice is yours!"

Godric tried to get up then, his body heaving against the vice-like grip that Jaenberht and Eadberht had on him, but with Grimnir's knife against his left ear he swiftly subsided, relaxing his big body and his arms as the boy with them leapt forward and laid the point of her scramaseaxe against his neck and said, in a light voice: "One more struggle like the last and I will kill you! This knife is called Blood Drinker, and with it I prefer to kill Danes…but scum like you who do deals with the enemy will be just as good. My knife will not care whose blood it drinks!"

"You have me all wrong, you bastards," he swore then from the corner of his mouth, kicking out at his captors as he spat the words out across the table, subsiding immediately as he felt the point of the boy's blade pushing into his neck, a trickle of blood falling onto the wood. "I thought you were Gytha's protectors, not Alfred's! Yes, I gave the little tart her needings…she's good at that! I've had her before, as I said. But I am not against the King, for all I called him a 'bog-wight'! Now, let me up. I cannot talk to you like this…and for pity's sake get that damned boy to take his knife out of my neck!"

# Chapter Forty Nine

M inutes later and they were all seated round the table, bowls of ale in their hands, and Oscar back with his bone beside his master whose neck had been bandaged by Brioni, her hood thrown off and her long-bladed scramaseaxe safely back in its fleece lined sheath. The two big warriors who had come with her were also seated, Eadberht opposite the tall cobbler, Jaenberht with Grimnir beside him, his harp bag on his back, their stabbing knives in their hands.

"Not very trusting are you?" Godric said, eyeing their long knives.

"That's why they are still alive and their enemies are dead," Grimnir said calmly in his precise voice. "And be certain that a stoup of ale will not save your life if we do not believe you. We are still waiting to hear your tale, Godric the Cobbler, and it had better be good!"

"Boys turning into girls, as well," the man replied, looking closely at Brioni sitting beside Eadberht, her blue eyes chips of ice as she stared back at him, a stir of recognition running through his mind. "This is turning into a remarkable day...and thank you for the bandage, that was neatly done," he added with a dip of his head towards her.

"Come now, cobbler," Jaenberht said darkly. "Enough of these niceties. I do not have Grimnir's patience. It is time you told your tale. You are not out of the woods yet, my fine leathery friend," and he tapped his knife blade significantly in the palm of his hand.

"Very well, I will do what I can," and he paused to drink, his eyes thoughtful, his mind racing as he marshalled his thoughts. "Gytha and I were sweet on each other years ago, and once I would have married her. But she was only ever after a better life, with gold to spend and fancy clothes to wear. There was nothing in her heart. She came to me here last month, and a vile day it was too until she turned up with that dark-haired friend of hers...and we re-kindled our relationship," he added with a shrug and raised eyebrows, wholly unabashed.

"Knowing I was in the market it was what she had come for. I told you, she is not a virtuous girl, our Gytha, with a shallow heart and few principles. We talked of this and that, about Chippenham, the Danes, my work, her life at Ford with her pathetic husband, his family and your lot. Drank some ale, had some fun together that left her panting for more, and parted company on good terms. She smug and self-satisfied...me with a problem on my hands.

"We'd both had what we wanted out of our meeting, and she said she would come again when she could. So I was pleasantly surprised when she and that Rowena turned up again today. But her talk was wild, and her desire to pass a message on to Bjorn Eriksson, Guthrum's guard commander, was utterly out of character unless it was of benefit to her!"

"Which it was," Eadberht snarled. It was designed to kill off half her family, the treacherous little bitch, leaving her and her feckless husband with everything, and all of us slain as well! You don't know how close you were to death this afternoon. I would have slain you both if I'd had my way. But this little lady here saved your life!" he said, indicating Brioni, sitting silently opposite him.

"I thank you for that," he said, dipping his head towards her again with a smile. "That would have been a waste of the best cobbler this side of the Thames river, and Oscar would have been lonely," and he bent down to ruffle the big dog's head again.

"And half the ladies of Chippenham as well, no doubt," Grimnir said sardonically with a raised eyebrow. "But you have not finished your tale, Godric. What about the message?"

"This, you mean?" the big cobbler asked, reaching into the breast of his tunic and pulling out a square of parchment that he handed over to Grimnir who cast his eyes over it hungrily, before handing it to Brioni who snorted with rage: *'Beware. This comes to you from a Saxon well-wisher, happy to accept Guthrum as King of Wessex. Know that your enemies are at Ford, below Biddestone. Come quickly. Cuthbert of Ford.'* The rat! Our 'Fox' will be truly grateful for this," she said carefully, folding it up and slipping it into the breast of her chemise. "He will not forget a good deed!"

"Nasty, isn't it? That would have gone into the fire this evening. I told you, you had me wrong! I am no supporter of Guthrum and his Danish takeover. Under him Wessex will be ruined, and we will never be free! My business will flourish far more under Alfred with good laws and trading rights, than the Danes who will tax us out of existence as well as demanding tribute for us to continue in business.

"They will want to protect their own traders who will flood in from all their English lands, and from overseas, as soon as they have either slain Alfred in battle, or forced him to flee to Frankland, as Burghred of Mercia did five years ago. Then Guthrum's grip on Wessex will be complete, and our freedom to trade will be snuffed out!"

"So, you are Alfred's man?" Eadberht asked him, hefting his knife in his hand as he spoke.

"Yes!" he replied definitely. "Yes, I am!"

"Then why the 'bog-wight' insult?" Jaenberht flashed at him.

"To test you!"

"*Test us?* You damned near had your throat cut, you idiot! We are not peasants afraid of spilling blood. And this 'boy' here," he added, indicating Brioni with deep sarcasm, "would have skewered your neck to your own table if I had told her to! You took a frightening risk."

"Yes, I did. But the moment I saw you I thought you were fighters."

"Why did you think that?" Grimnir asked him, his eyes fixed on the cobbler's face.

"It is a subtle thing," Godric replied looking at the two big warriors. "Plain clothes cannot hide what you are, the way you walk and handle your weapons, the way you look. No farmer looks like that, nor a merchant. The lady here has it too. And you look and sound like Saxons, so, if you were Saxon fighters, then perhaps you were part of this renegade Saxon war band that has been making a monkey of the Black Jarl's Jomsvikings. This 'Fox', as they are calling him, who has given Oscytel such a sour belly ache, and turned his men's hearts to water."

"So, they have heard of us then?" Brioni asked quietly, startling Godric who had not heard her speak before.

"All Chippenham has heard how the 'Fox' has been killing Vikings…though they do not know his name."

"That is good," Brioni said, looking at him. "Long may that be so."

"Do you know this 'Fox'?" he asked her then, his eyes looking into her so that she shrugged with discomfort.

"That is for me to know and for you to find out," she answered him enigmatically. "Maybe when we know you better," she said then, hardening her voice, "you will be told many things that right now are best kept secret."

"And yet I am sure I know you," he said thoughtfully, his eyes looking over her again. "Though I cannot say from where."

"And what if these two were of this 'Fox's' war band, Godric," Grimnir asked him softly, nudging him with his hand. "What then?"

"Then I would declare myself, as I have done. Hand over the message Gytha gave me and seek an alliance. It was clever of you to have Grimnir with you," he said to Jaenberht with a grin. "His presence confused me to start with. What was Guthrum's Danish harper doing with two Saxon fighters? A man I know to be close to the King and his right-hand commander, the Black Jarl of Helsing, whom I would rather keep at arm's length than any other man I know!"

There was a pause then as they all drank from their bowls and darkness crept cold across the market green, those tents that were remaining now

365

lighting up from within, some families building fires beneath their awnings, the usual cooking pot hanging from an iron tripod over them. While overhead the light died in the west, long streamers of golden light squeezed against the horizon beneath the weight of clouds coming in for the night.

"So, an alliance?" Grimnir questioned him intently.

"Yes...an alliance! Let Gytha come to me with her messages. That will please both of us," he added with a sly grin and a shrug of his shoulders. "She will expect it, and it never does to disappoint a lady!" and the men laughed. "Then, like today," he said turning to Eadberht, "you and the 'lad' here can come to my stall afterwards and we can share the information. That way you will know immediately what she has to say. Then the Lady Brioni can re-write them, signing herself 'Cuthbert of Wessex' to keep the Danes guessing."

"Good point!" the little Norwegian Skald said.

"Then you, Grimnir," the big cobbler said, turning towards him, "can come to my big workshop in Chippenham and we can discuss the matter further. When it suits us each message can be passed on to Bjorn Eriksson, Guthrum's guard commander, and I have lots of ways of doing that. That way we can feed him false information that will make his eyes sparkle."

"I like that," Brioni said quietly, her soft voice dropping gently into the conversation. "That will keep all suspicion off you, Grimnir. Do you know Hugo the Bearmaster?" she asked Godric, turning towards him.

"The enormous man who runs the *Circus Maximus* that arrived a few weeks ago? Yes, I know him. I have made shoes for his daughter, Maritia, to dance in."

"She is a special friend of mine, whom I dearly love. Anything you and Grimnir think that the 'Fox' needs to know, tell her...whether from Gytha or not. We need to know what the Heathen are up to. She is due to visit us at Ford shortly and can bring us all we need to know."

"What will happen to all this information?" he asked, looking round the table.

"It goes by fast courier to Alfred, the 'King of the Marshes'," Brioni answered him with a raised eyebrow and a sardonic smile.

"The 'Fox's' men are just one of a number of groups operating throughout Wessex," Grimnir said then. "A resistance movement that gives hope to all who thought Alfred had given up, and keeps the Danes on the hop. And every Danish outpost that is destroyed, or messenger whom we kill, weakens the enemy."

"You talk as if you and the King planned all this," Jaenberht said, looking at the little harper. "I thought you joined us, and settled in

Chippenham by chance. Now I am not sure whose tune we all dance to? Alfred's, yours or," he hesitated, "the 'Fox's'?"

"That's easy," the little man said, with a grin. "You dance to the 'Fox's', he dances to mine and we all dance to the King of the Marshes!"

"So, are we all agreed on how we proceed from here?" Brioni said, snuggling into her cloak. "I am getting cold, it's almost dark and we have a step to travel yet before we get home."

"Yes," Jaenberht said, putting down his bowl. "Gytha gives her messages to Godric, who shares them with Eadberht and Brioni for immediate transfer of information. She re-writes them in Gytha's hand, but signing them 'Cuthbert of Wessex' to disguise from where they are coming, while keeping the original, and they then go forward to Grimnir. Cross information of what the Heathen are up to comes to us through Maritia, and then onwards to Alfred in Athelney.

"And Godric feeds the necessary stuff through to Guthrum's guard commander whose name completely escapes me!" And they all laughed.

"And how do we know we can trust our leathery friend here?" Eadberht asked, his knife back in his big hand.

"Because he says so!" Grimnir exclaimed swiftly, looking the big cobbler straight in the eyes. "And because if I get a hint of treachery, just so much as a sniff of it, then he will be a very dead 'leathery friend' before that day's end. My word on it!

"But if he remains true to his word, then when Alfred is returned to the throne of Wessex in Winchester, the King will reward him mightily, as he will all those who have stood by him in the darkest days of his life. My word on that too!"

"Why are you here?" the big cobbler asked, turning to Brioni, as they all stood up to leave. "And why do these men confer with you so easily? That is beyond my understanding...and why do I think I know you?"

"Because I am the 'Fox's' lady," she answered him, calmly. "Because I am the Lady Brioni of Foxley, the sworn enemy of the Lord Oscytel by a fierce blood-oath I made on the butchered body of my father, Lord Wulfstan, the Thane of Foxley," she said, enjoying the flash of recognition that lit up his eyes. "A man as close to King Alfred as you are to Oscar," she said simply, adding with a smile: "And you have come a long way since you made a pair of shoes for the newest handmaiden of the Queen of Wessex!"

"*You!*" he said with a gasp. "The Maid of Foxley with the sparkling eyes! I thought there was something familiar about you, when you dropped your hood. I am astonished! And the shoes?"

"Destroyed by Oscytel's butchers when they burned Foxley. It is sturdy boots I need now, Godric, not fancy shoes."

"And you shall have them. The best that I can make, my Lady," he said earnestly, his big face wreathed in smiles, "and with steel insteps to protect you on the battlefield. Come to my workshop and I will cut them to fit you like a glove. My hand on it!"

And with a burst of laughter they all split up to collect their horses from where they had been left, and to ride back through the village leaving Godric to feed and water his horse and settle for the night.

In one day his life had been changed for ever in a way that he could not possibly have divined when he had set out for Biddestone market, and he was amazed.

*

"Well, what a day!" Jaenberht exclaimed as they walk-trotted out of the village a short while later beneath a cloud hazed sky, a single line of crimson against the trees and fields, the first stars just shining out. "Who would have thought that Grimnir was so close to King Alfred? Leofric has played that very tight to his chest. It must always have been planned that our little Norwegian Skald would make himself indispensable to Guthrum, with his music and his sagas, and base himself in Chippenham."

"And what about Godric?" Brioni exclaimed, astonished. "He turned the tables on all of us. Rabid adulterer and treacherous sympathiser one moment, with Eadberht rampant to slit him open from chin to navel…and loyal ally the next in our battle against the Danes. I am astonished!"

"And him knowing you, my Lady," Eadberht said, his voice filled with wonder. "That really settled it for me. That he had served Alfred's family while they were still in the town, and would rather live under Saxon rule than Danish was completely clear cut. These merchants have it all worked out, down to the finest piece of shoe leather!" and they all laughed again.

"Good job that dog didn't get involved," Brioni said with a shiver, jagging her horse forward. "That Oscar. He was a lovely animal, and clearly Godric loved him greatly. Could you really have taken him out so swiftly?" she asked, turning to Jaenberht. "I would have hated to see him killed."

"Seen him do it," Eadberht replied sharply. "Similar kind of beast, all deep chest and massive teeth. Threw that big knife right into its heart. Dropped like a stone, no trouble. Old Berti would have had that Oscar on his back in a moment. Not pretty, I grant you, but very effective!"

There was a pause then, as they kicked on past a row of mean bothies at the edge of the village, where pigs rooted for grubs and food refuse off the middens behind each little house. Chickens cackled from the sheds into which they had been gathered for the night, a goose hissing its alarm at being disturbed as they passed by. Ahead of them a fox crossed the trail, pausing briefly to look at them, ears pricked and brush down, before whisking himself away into the gathering night.

"The really difficult thing, for all of us, is what to do about Gytha, and her wretched husband!" Brioni said a few moments later. "Who should know of her treachery? We three, and Cadoc...and Leofric of course, we already know. And Beornred, Raedwald, Trausti and Finnar should also be told. They are Leofric's closest advisors. But what about Eadwine and Aelfrid?" she went on appalled.

"And Alfweald!" Jaenberht said with a rush. "Surely he should know of his brother's treachery too. I know the two of them don't get on, but for one to plot the death and destruction of the other, let alone his whole family, is beyond shocking, beyond being declared '*Nithing*' and cast out. It is worthy of death. Even hanging is too good. And what of the woman? Not only has she cuckolded her husband, but she has plotted to betray us all to the Vikings. She should be slain along with her man who was more than happy to go along with it!"

"But it's not just the treachery," Eadberht broke in earnestly, "though that's bad enough. It's how to benefit from it! If that wasn't an issue then both should be put to death straightaway. They are far too dangerous to be let loose. But for their treachery to be of benefit to us, they must be left totally in the dark and so must the rest of the family."

"That's right!" Jaenberht agreed swiftly as they reached the narrow trackway that led down to the settlement, the trail steep and treacherous in the extreme. "One hint that we know all that has happened today and the pair of them will be off from their sinking ship like the rats they are. Then God alone knows how it will all end. I am just glad it's not me having to make that decision. Leofric will know what to do, that's why he is a leader and I am not, thank God," he said with a chuckle. "Now, stop the chatter. This track is bad enough in daylight. Right now it is lethal, and I have no wish to be carried home on a hurdle!"

*

"So, my darling, an eventful day after all," Leofric said hours later when they were both in bed, wrapped up in rough cotton sheets, heavy fur rugs all across them, Bran and Utha stretched out on the rush covered floor. "And you were right, too," he said softly, cuddling her in. "That stupid little bitch was all ready to betray the lot of us…and half her family! I have her message safe. How she imagined the Danes would have honoured any promise they might have made to her is beyond belief."

"The thing is, Leofric," Brioni said to him as he bent down to kiss her. "What do we do about it?"

"Nothing!" he said succinctly. "We do nothing, my darling. We leave her free to wander, as she always has done, and chat to Aelfrid and Osburgh and all the others…but we watch her like a hawk! See if you cannot get one of Rowena's younger sisters to tell you what she talks about. One thing's for certain, neither she nor Cuthbert can leave the settlement without Eadwine's agreement…and on one of our horses. And that's just not going to happen without my permission and an escort."

"And Eadwine?" she asked him anxiously. "Aelfrid and Alfweard? What of them?"

"What the eye doesn't see the heart cannot grieve over!"

"So, you tell them nothing either."

"If I do, then all hell will break out," he said with a deep sigh. "And rightly so too…after Eadwine has been forced to believe it. And that won't be easy! He will cast them both out. He may even have them both hanged, which, in all truth, would be the best answer, certainly the easiest. And he will blame us for the whole of it. Especially the mother who dotes on her son, named after one of our most loved saints. It will all be an unholy mess! A good job you kept that message, as we will any others that are sent. That is the only proof we have of their wickedness."

"Were it not for the benefit we can get from knowing of their treachery I would be all for exposing them immediately," she said heavily. "But the chance to hoodwink our enemies is just too good to waste," she ran on with enthusiasm. "Just think, Leofric, we could send them all in one direction while attacking somewhere else. True, we might not be able to do that more than once, but even once would be just wonderful!" and there was a pause while both thought of the consequences of Gytha's actions, both to her family and to themselves.

"What settlement do you have in mind to attack next?" she asked him then, changing the subject somewhat.

"Bath!" he said at once. "It has been in my mind for some time, and I don't want the lads to get stale. Bath's a two day business, probably three by the time we have reconnoitred the ground and made our plans. But, before that we might test this little traitor of ours. Give her something to get her teeth into. A couple of attacks we might make on some of Guthrum's smaller garrisons at Malmesbury and Melksham."

"You mean real information, Leofric?"

"Yes, sweetheart. Let them test how good her knowledge is. Let those bastards take the bait. We will turn up as 'arranged', there'll be an exchange of arrows and our boys will melt away again as usual. Minimum casualties."

"Won't they suspect?"

"That they are being played with? I don't think so. They will see what they expect to see. Saxon warriors coming to attack them. Then we will really hoodwink them, send them all in one direction while we attack in force in another. Then we will vanish. Off to Battlesbury Rings with the whole settlement. Everyone. Let the bastards find Ford if they can, we will not be there - and at Battlesbury I will tell Eadwine and Aelfrid about their son and his wife. It will not be pleasant, but it must be done."

"So, Bath's the big one?" she asked eagerly.

"No...Chippenham!" he said casually, his eyes on hers with a smile.

"*Chippenham?*" she questioned, horrified. "Right into their greatest fortress? Darling, you must be mad!"

"No, Brioni. Not so mad as you might have thought. If we do Bath, out of the blue, with no warning of any kind, after two false starts; putting the Heathen to the fire and the sword in some order...and then they get a message that we are going to assault Swindon, where they have a small fortress and garrison, what do you think they will do?"

"Go all out to destroy us! They will be so enraged by what has already happened that they will throw caution to the winds and come for us with all they have, while we attack Chippenham, the centre of their power! Leofric, my darling man, that is brilliant!"

"Well, brilliant? Maybe! But damned worth trying certainly."

"Have you discussed any of this with Beornred, or any of the others?"

"We have been agonising on how to make such an assault on Chippenham work for a while, especially with the horse fair coming up shortly. There are so many troops in there we would be cut to pieces. Just could not see how to make it work. Now we have this treacherous pigeon come suddenly among us, I can see how we might be successful. Just a shame we cannot bring Oscytel to battle first. It is his beard we are tweaking right now, so it will be he who will lead his men off to defend Swindon leaving Guthrum behind. But Guthrum will do for me! It was Alfred's turn to be driven out on Twelfth Night...it will be Guthrum's turn at Easter!"

371

"And me?" she asked eagerly. "What of me?"

"This time, my little fighting cock," he said with a smile, "you will lead your own battle group!" And ignoring her gasp of pleasure and her shining eyes, he added "Trausti and Eadberht tell me you are as ready as you ever will be, so you can lead them on the first of our mock attacks. Malmesbury I think, my darling. It is close to Foxley, and you will know all that countryside. It's time you put all that training to the test, time you were blooded. And Malmesbury will do nicely!"

And with a little shriek of joy she flung herself upon him, wrapped her arms and legs around him and kissed as much of him as she could reach, laughter and excitement quickly turning to passion as she showed him just what a thorough harlot a good Saxon lady could become, given half a chance to be so.

# Chapter Fifty

Malmesbury,

A pretty town on a hill round which the river Avon flows in two directions, dominated by its ancient abbey church of St Mary founded by St Aldhelm when Ine was King of Wessex; a time when Brioni's family had first come to Foxley. It was a place well known to her, where old Father Anselm had been a monk before he became chaplain and priest to her father and the good people of Foxley.

That day Malmesbury basked in warm sunshine for a bright February morning, the sky blue overhead and a fitful breeze rustling the naked trees and bushes around it. And the town was already busy, full of cheerful merchants and bustling people, now gripped by Guthrum's forces who had set up toll booths at the main gateways to tax all those who came to do business there, and whose frightening presence and rough, uncouth ways threatened everyone. A town with ramparts of ancient earth that had been there since before the Romans came, greatly softened and worn by time, but now strengthened with stone and timber where the roadways breached them, but more open than closed in, where sheep and cattle grazed and the two rivers gave the place a swiftly flowing moat.

A town that Brioni must assault in two days' time with vigour and determination.

To Trausti and Eadberht who had come with her, and Bran and Utha, to view the place and plan their attack they made it seem a daunting task, and they appeared dismayed. To Brioni who knew every twist and turn of Malmesbury, and its defences, it was a challenge that she believed possible, given courage, speed and luck.

"This is hopeless, my Lady," Eadberht said, lying on his belly in a small hollow shielded with beech scrub and hazel close where the Sherston road, joined by the trackway coming in from Tetbury, entered the town. "Those walls may be softened by age, but those gateways are a nightmare and they are stopping everyone," he added, pointing to a strong party of well-armed Danes who were busy jostling a parcel of merchants and travellers with needless aggression, laughing as they pushed and shoved them about. "This is far from the 'open' town we were expecting! We might as well blow dandelion seeds amongst that lot as waste good arrows. 'Make an armed demonstration and then withdraw', Leofric said to us yesterday. That's a laugh!" he exclaimed bitterly. "They are too alert, and we don't have enough men. It's hopeless!" And turning to give Eadberht an enigmatic glance, he lay on his back and looked up at the sky, watching a pair of crows struggle past him against the wind, while Trausti picked his teeth with a hazel stick and scowled.

"There's a reason that Leofric chose me for this task, you pair of old misery guts!" Brioni said, sliding down beside them, where her two great hounds were lying head on paws, only their sterns waving. "I know this place like the back of my hand; where there are ways into it and where the defences are in such a poor state a fat sheep could push through them!

"Don't be so defeatist! Of course the Heathen are in a state of high alert. They have been told we are coming, remember? But I have been watching them closely, and they are not all as keen as you might think. Four of them are lounging against that gateway half asleep in this sunshine, with their spears propped up against the stones and their swords nowhere to be seen. Look at them and tell me they are alert! Even the three who are ruffling those merchants are only doing it half-heartedly.

"Oh they are unpleasant enough, but they are not checking everything; more larking about than doing a good job of work. Presently they will charge them for entry and let them go. See," she said urgently, jabbing Trausti on his shoulder, "they have not even attempted to check that wagoner's load. Any number of men could be hidden in the back of that cart, or weapons and they would never know it! See what I mean?" she added as the wagoner's whip cracked and his big ox cart lumbered forward. "They are sloppy and over confident, relying on their walls to keep them safe! This task is far from hopeless. But an 'armed demonstration' will not do, my friends. We need to get inside, and I know just how to do it!"

And with a shrug of their shoulders, the two men slipped away from their hollow and eeled their way with Brioni back to where they had left their horses less than a furlong away; her two hounds leading the way, loping ahead in the easy way that wolf hounds always do.

*

374

*F*ive days before, the message had gone out to Godric, carried by Gytha to Biddestone Market on one of Leofric's horses with Cadoc as her escort. Tailed as before by Brioni and Eadberht, on a day of sharp winds and squally showers, with the crowds thin and huddled under capes and hoods, they had sheltered in the church and watched her from afar before joining Godric after she had left.

'*Beware*', they had read with grim satisfaction, Gytha's writing spiky and ill-formed, rough ink spluttered from her quill amongst the letters. '*Within the week the Fox will attack Malmesbury and Melksham. He is Leofric Iron Hand, Lord of Wimborne, based at Ford. Come quickly and destroy them all. I have warned you before. Cuthbert of Ford.*'

A message that had made Brioni and Eadberht suck their breath and squint their eyes with rage as they had read it, and Godric ruffle Oscar's great head with wicked pleasure while Brioni re-wrote it in the same stuttering style, discarding all the details of Leofric's name, and where his warband were lurking so close to Guthrum's power, simply warning the Danes of a coming attack and signing it: 'Cuthbert of Wessex'.

"Clever to sign it with Cuthbert's name," Godric commented as Brioni re-wrote it. "Tried to make sure they would take it seriously. A woman's name would have thrown huge doubt on it. And then if it ever did come to light she could claim it was nothing to do with her! Nasty piece of work, that one."

"You should try being us having to live and work amongst the two of them without giving anything away," Brioni spat out, looking up from the grubby piece of parchment Godric had given her to write on. "Especially when the mother tells everyone how wonderful her son is! Bah, this whole business sickens me! This had better work, or I'll take the next message that little bitch tries to send and make her eat it!"

\*

*N*evertheless it was a message that found its way a day later to Bjorn Eriksson, the King's Guard Commander, through Rhonwen, Cadoc's woman in the town, the King's own brewer, who had '*found it, my Lord, thrust in amongst my yeast and barley*'…from an unknown hand. But who, in truth, had received it from Grimnir Grimmersson, the King's Norwegian Skald whom all men knew, and who came and went amongst the King's most trusted companions all the time.

A message, the original much folded that Leofric kept in the bag he always carried with him; a message that reached the Danish King, Guthrum, as he sat in Alfred's hall at Chippenham that very evening.

Surrounded by his army commanders at a long table, with his skald beside him, he was seated in Alfred's great armed chair on the dais that lay at the head of the long hall, and he made an impressive figure. His broad shoulders were covered with a great cloak of fur, black against the thick golden torque of his kingship, his once golden hair and beard shot through with silver, his bearskin cloak pulled back to reveal his massive forearms, each bound with broad gold rings marked with the magic runes of his people, rings of power on which his men swore their allegiance to himself and to Odin, the king of their gods.

Opposite him, on sturdy carved pillars at the far end of the hall, was a hanging gallery for priests or musicians, with a great firepit stretching down the centre of the building, the blue scented smoke spiralling upwards from the leaping flames to the wide smoke-hole in the roof high above them, with its own thatched roof cap to keep out the rain. Great round war shields decorated the walls, their leather covers garishly painted with wild Norse symbols of fantastic, writhing beasts, supported by a host of weapons: swords, spears and long-handled axes.

Behind the King, from a great bronze pole, hung a glowing screen of Viking embroidery, vibrant in its workmanship, that showed *Yggdrasil*, the mighty Norse tree of life, a deep rooted ash, with its stags, gigantic swirling dragon, *Nidhoggr*, giant eagle and the squirrel, *Ratatosk*, who carried words of wickedness and malice from top to bottom of the tree. All in brilliant colours of red, blue and shifting green, with gold and silver thread running through them, it shimmered in the firelight, lamps and flaring sconces with which the hall was lit.

And high in the rafters, fixed with long wooden pegs between the kingposts that supported the whole building, was the great dragon prow of the Viking warship that had first brought the Danish King to Britain. Ferocious, open-mouthed and threatening, still brightly painted, it seemed to breathe fire, the smoke within the building billowing around its wide nostrils and gaping jaws like living steam.

All around the hall at trestle tables, on wooden benches, sat his household troops and hearth companions, dressed in their finest clothes of linen, wool and leather, all in striking colours, many with great fur capes of wolf, fox and bear. Before them were stale bread trenchers soaked in meat juices, and in their hands deep drinking horns, some with gold or silver feet, from which they would drink their beer and mead until they fell on the floor, or

376

forwards onto the soiled tables. Music there was also, amidst the shouts and yells, from crumhorn, pipes and drums and raucous singing to the hall harp that was passed from hand to hand as the warriors seated there took their turn, or bellowed out the choruses they knew to every favourite song or saga.

Into this feasting and wild bursts of noise, a servant brought the parchment message, soiled and scrappy, on a wide silver christening dish of startling beauty that Guthrum had ravished from the ruined lands of the distant north, a message that he read with widening eyes and snorts of rage, like an angry bull, while Grimnir Grimmersson watched him with a bland face and racing mind.

A message that made the tall Danish King smack his hands and shout for peace round his table…and for the Black Jarl of Helsing to read it too, who ground his teeth with silent fury that someone whom he did not know, and could not find, was making war on them with such impunity. Making his Jomsvikings fall in pools of blood, slaying his captains and leaving the symbol of a fox's head at the scene of every killing. And not for the first time he fingered the great golden foxhead brooches on his shoulders that he had taken from the broken body of the Thane of Foxley, his right hand straying to the golden handle of the jade knife he carried next to his own heart, to *Sica*… and wondered what it meant.

"Strengthen those garrisons, Oscytel," the King ordered tersely after Brioni's message had been passed amongst his commanders. "Alert them to an imminent attack."

"Do you believe this message, Guthrum?" Oscytel questioned him urgently. "This could be a trick to get you to move our men about needlessly. Weakening your base here. I don't believe it!"

"How many men have you lost to this 'Fox', my Lord Oscytel?" the King asked the tall, dark haired Viking leader menacingly, leaning towards him, his big face glowering.

"A few, my Lord King. A few!"

"*A few?*" Guthrum snarled at him. "More than two crews, Oscytel! Not counting the crew that vanished a month ago, with both its captains and all their equipment. We found the settlement they had attacked completely burned out. Nothing left of the men save a few shards of bone, some half-burned skulls and a host of footprints that led nowhere!"

"That could have been anyone, Guthrum. There is nothing to connect their loss with our present difficulty…this bastard 'Fox'."

"And no connection with those brooches you took off that Thane you butchered either?" Guthrum glared at him darkly. "I told you, Oscytel, after Wareham, no more 'Blood Eagles'…now all this grief!"

"Coincidence, my Lord King. *Sica* has never been wrong," he said with chilling certainty, his hand on its golden handle.

"Leave that infernal weapon out of it," Guthrum growled, his blue eyes flashing. "I know its weird tale as well as you do. Take care its power does not slip away from you just when you need it most. Perhaps this 'Fox' will be your doom?" he suggested, smiling as Oscytel visibly flinched at his words.

"We will find him," the tall black-clad Viking war leader said with chilling precision. "And when we do, ban or no ban, this blade will drink deep!" And he pulled *Sica* out far enough for all to see a flash of emerald green, looking around the table with hooded eyes as he did so, knowing that no man there would dare challenge him.

"So, find him," the King replied sharply, unabashed. "*Find him!* You've had your patrols out everywhere, and not a sniff of him! And you want to know who the winner is in all this mess? *Yes?*" he shouted, red-faced, hammering the table where they were all seated. "That bastard Alfred! Sitting pretty in the rank marshes of the Sommerseatas where we cannot get at him. And every success this 'Fox' has is one more thread that Alfred can hold in his hand to draw Wessex together again. And he is not the only one, this 'Fox'! There are others like him at work throughout these lands."

"We should have caught that royal Saxon bastard in January, when we attacked this place," Oscytel said in his cold voice, his words harsh, his eyes glittering in the firelight that flamed and flickered in the long hall where they were all gathered. "Odin knows we tried hard enough! I should have been with you."

"Odin be damned, Oscytel. That bastard had his God on his side. The Christian God whom we have made such fun of all these years! Maybe it is time we changed our beliefs? And yes! You should have been with us," he snarled, shaking his big fist at the man beside him. "Not sliding off to pursue your own vengeance. We needed those extra men, you arrogant bastard!" he swore at him, his eyes flashing. "We had Alfred in our grasp...and yet somehow he managed to slip away. Complete surprise was what we had aimed at," he raged, staring round at his commanders. "Attack in the depth of winter when no-one could possibly have expected us to do so, and at their Christmas season; when they are all as drunk as Vikings in Valhalla. We should have caught him cold! But somehow, as we broke in, that bastard slipped away into the wilderness with his family and escaped!

"Impossible, we all said. *Impossible!*" he shouted, banging the table again with his fist. "Yet he managed it despite the weather, the worst in years, and with his family in tow. Priests, children, Queen with her babe at her breast for Odin's sake! No-one saw them go and no-one caught them either…and you tell me that his God had no hand in it?" he sneered. "I am not so sure.

"Thirteen years we have been fighting to seize Wessex and complete the work that Ivar, Ubbi, Halfdan started in '65," he raged, infuriated. "Northumbria, East Anglia, Mercia all are ours. And Wessex should have been too! Yet here we sit, in Alfred's hall in Chippenham, while that *bastard* cocks a snook at us from his bloody marshes. *Now this!*" he exclaimed, waving Brioni's doctored note in Oscytel's face. "This note that tells us where that Fox is going to attack us next. The first break through we have had in months of campaigning and you think it's some kind of trap?" he shouted at Oscytel, his eyes bloodshot with fury. "Well, my Lord of Helsing, trap or not we *will* strengthen our garrisons, *and* warn them to be alert.

"If nothing happens we will know this message is a hoax. But if that bastard turns up, we will know that somehow we have found a traitor in his midst that he knows nothing about, and then, with luck, we will track this 'Fox' to his earth and wipe him out!"

*

*B*ack at the camp they had made on the edge of Hyam's Wood, not far from the ruins of Foxley Manor, now being re-built by Almaric and his people from the outlaw village, Brioni gathered her war leaders together. Trausti, Cadoc and Eadberht, together with Jaenberht and Sigweald, all men whom Leofric trusted to help keep her safe; and over a deep bowl of broth that Aldred had prepared against their return, she outlined her plan. As usual Bran and Utha were beside her, one upright his head almost level with her chest, the other resting at her feet, his stern thumping the ground.

"I have had a lot of time to think this one out, and this is the best I have come up with. It is not without risk, but since when has that stopped us before?" she questioned them urgently.

"Since Leofric put you in our care, my Lady," Sigweald replied gruffly, waving his spoon at her. "He is trusting us to bring you safely home, and with no holes in you either. So that makes all this much more difficult."

"Who's in charge here?" she asked sharply, looking round her group.

"Now, that's a very good question, my Lady," Trausti answered her sternly, without a twinkle in his eyes. "You have a third of our forces with you. Fifty men, many of them veterans…and you have no experience at all. Straight off the training ground! Jaenberht, Cadoc, Eadberht, Sigweald, myself.., and many others, like Aldred and Ceawlyn, have been with Leofric for years, and have come to trust his judgement even when things have looked very risky indeed. Losses in war are a fact of life, we all know that, but we cannot afford to lose any men in this escapade if we can help it. Bath comes next and then Chippenham...and that gives me butterflies in my belly just thinking about it!

"So we need every man, my Lady. If we get back in two days' time with half our men dead or badly injured, it will be my head that's on the block, not yours, for allowing you to hazard them against orders. 'An armed demonstration and withdrawal' is what Leofric ordered for us here at Malmesbury...yet you want to assault the town from within!"

"You cannot expect us to follow you just because you order it," Eadberht chipped in. "Not in these circumstances. But tell us your plan, Mistress Brioni," he said to a chorus of grunts and nodded heads from the grizzled men around him, "and then Trausti and I will tell you who is in charge!"

Brioni looked at them, with their beards and scars and hard-bitten faces, their hands curled round the wooden bowls that each man carried with him, now filled with the broth that Aldred had cooked up, and she sighed.

Trausti was right.

She knew nothing of war, not really.

She had seen it, played at it, experienced it...but never waged it. But she did know Malmesbury and believed she could get them safely in, as safely as anything could be considered so, and get them out again. At least with an acceptable risk, and if she could achieve that then next time she would be more readily believed, and followed. These grizzled veterans of the Danish wars of Wessex, with their battered byrnies and notched shields, sipping their broth in this little clearing in Hyam's Wood, would accept her and Leofric would be proud of her.

"Very well, I accept. If I cannot persuade you to try this, then we will do as Leofric has ordered. Rush up to the walls with all the noise we can muster, fire off a host of arrows, and then rush off again before they can mount up and catch us. 'An armed demonstration and swift withdrawal'. And if we hit anything with those walls around them we will be lucky. As Eadberht said this morning, 'we might as well blow dandelion seeds amongst them!'

"But if you will follow me we can burn out their toll booths, seize their money and kill many of them as well, and if I can get us out as easily as I can get us in, then our visit here will not have been wasted and this talisman," she added, waving the foxhead symbol at them as she spoke, "will make them grind their teeth, not least because we told them we were coming, and still hit them where it hurts most, in their pockets and in their reputation!"

"So," Trausti grunted, looking at Eadberht with a secret smile that Brioni missed, both sitting back against their saddles. "How do we do this?"

380

"With skill and guile, my friend, with great skill and no little guile. As you saw, those ramparts are soft and worn by great age. Only by the entrances have the Danes made any difference with heavy timbers, stone buttresses and a wooden palisade. Beyond those the town is largely open, and on the edge of the escarpment on the north side is the abbey church of St Mary, built of stone and roofed with slate. It is a solid building with a deep undercroft supported by vaulting and pillars of stone. St Aldhelm built well and finished off with the great tower that springs upwards from the west end of the building. Beyond lie the abbey gardens that run down to the river, also on the north side, and are protected by a wall with a stout portal opposite the water, where there is a narrow pathway that runs right round the bottom of the old ramparts. I know it all so well.

"At the south end of the town there is another gateway, and a wooden bridge over the river Avon that flows past Foxley, Malmesbury and on to Chippenham. It is the only bridge for miles, and the main river is too deep and fast flowing there to cross without a boat and there are none.

"On the east side is the other gateway into Malmesbury beyond the ford that crosses the secondary river round the town, the Tetbury Avon. That gateway the Danes will also have strengthened; that leads to Cricklade and the Thames, up which the dragon boats sail from the sea, but is too far away to help the garrison that Guthrum has placed here.

"Everywhere else are the ancient ramparts that were built before the Romans came. They are double banked and steep in places, but have not been properly fortified and cannot be held by the troops that have been stationed here because there are not enough of them. The enemy hold the gateways, but not the walls, and will be concentrated in the market square in the centre of the town.

"So, my Lady," Trausti grunted, looking fierce. "You have an eye for the land, and I think I can see where you are going with this. But I am an old soldier and like my commander to spell things out so I can understand better," and he relaxed back against his saddle, a horn of mulled ale in his hand, and a sly wink at Eadberht sitting close beside him.

"In two days' time I will ride back to town on the shaggiest pony we have," she said blandly, with a half-smile on her face, "and bluff my way past those guards and get into the abbey." At which Eadberht sat bolt upright and dropped his horn, while the rest of the men seated there, spluttered into their drinks and shouted out: "No! Too risky! Leofric will have our guts for bowstrings!...This is madness!"

Only Trausti remained calm and unfussed by what their young commander had said, studying her carefully, before asking her to explain the

381

rest of her plan, while Eadberht glared at him and the rest of the men remained sitting tense and upright.

"I told you there was an element of risk. But no-one will expect a young 'boy' to be a threat. I told you this morning, those men out there are over-confident and sloppy. Despite any warning they may have been given, they are not really fully alert. And I can sound as rough as any local. I will go in unarmed with a message for Abbot Wilfred, whom the Danes will know. It will be in Latin, which I can read if I am challenged to prove my worth, and he will back me up if necessary."

"You know this Abbot Wilfred then?" Trausti growled at her.

"He is my uncle and my godfather, and has doted on me since I was a child. I know every twist and turn of that abbey, and have played with the monks in their garden. I will ask him for the key to the river gate at the foot of it, and his permission to hide you in the deep undercroft of the building."

"All of us?" Eadberht asked, astonished.

"No! Half of us," she replied swiftly. "Five of our archers, the rest general warriors with sword, spear and battle axe whom you will choose from amongst us. They will picket their horses at the back of the old ramparts and approach the abbey from the river path in the darkness of the evening. When the sun has gone, and only a rind of light remains in the west, I will let you in and hide you in the crypt until after Vespers when the monks will feed us. Be sure to bring my armour, my sword and Blood Drinker, and my shield."

"So, you mean to attack the enemy from within as you suggested this morning. What of the rest of us?" Trausti demanded, drinking deeply from his beaker.

"A violent diversion at the south gate after dark. Using fire arrows against the gates and nearby buildings; tumultuous noise, shouts, horns blowing, clashing shields - anything to create a panic. The moment we hear that we will break out of the crypt and attack the east gateway, kill the guards and set fire to the buildings, the gates and the palisade, take anything of value we can find, then dash off into the night, horse up and clear off...and rejoin you by the ruined homestead we all sheltered in after leaving Hugo's encampment last month."

"So, that's why we brought pig skins and oil with us," Ceawlyn said with a chuckle. "I wondered what we were doing with them, given Leofric's orders. Does he know about all this?"

"It was his idea too," Trausti said tersely, to Brioni's complete astonishment, standing up and moving to the centre of the clearing. "He knew the state of Malmesbury's defences. Knew that a swift arrow storm would achieve little, and briefed me on what we might do..."

382

"So, this was all a test?" Brioni interrupted angrily, shaking her fists at him.

"Yes, my Lady. Of your resolve and courage, your willingness to listen to those around you, to make up your own mind without fear or favour, to make a clear plan and persuade others to do what you believe in. A test of your fitness to lead."

"So all that 'misery guts' stuff this morning was fake? Made up to test me? To see if I had what it takes to be a leader?" she stormed at him. "And if I failed?"

"Then my orders were to step in and advise you, to encourage you and support you...unless you proved completely hopeless."

"And then?"

"Stand you down!" he replied firmly, his eyes fixed on hers. "Take over, and lead the men myself. If I had no trust in you, the men never would either and the whole assault would be a disaster."

"And now?" she asked him, sharply, her arms folded across her chest, while the men seated all around them waited for Trausti's decision.

"And now you have surpassed yourself, and proved what Leofric and I have thought for a while, that with continued support and advice you will make a damned good commander of our forces.

"You spotted, as Eadberht and I had done, how slack and idle those men were down there this morning, that was good; but to hazard yourself as you suggest is a brilliant move, my Lady, one we had not thought of...nor of using the abbey itself to shelter our men. We had thought to get over the old ramparts right at the back and attack from there tonight, while the rest of the lads made a wild diversion in front of the south gate. But your way is much better. And proves how right Leofric was to trust you...and your use of Latin to convince an ignorant enemy Huscarle is gleaming. As you said, a plan 'not without risk'. But with your courage and our luck, this attack should be a success."

He strode over to her then, and before she could say another word he seized her right hand and raising it high in the air he shouted: "I give you our war cry: *The Lady! The Lady!*" And in moments all their men were on their feet and shouting out also, with a clash of sword on shield and stamping feet: "*The Lady! The Lady!*"

Trausti threw back his head and laughed, while Brioni had the grace to blush, both knowing whom the men really followed. But it was a start; she had won his praise and his agreement, and he had not humiliated her. If tonight went well, then all men would know 'The Lady' was a bold commander whom men could trust to do her best.

383

She had won the right to lead.  The rest was up to her!

## *Chapter Fifty One*

*T*wo days' later, with the sun warm on her back and mounted on a small shaggy pony, her hounds left with Trausti, Brioni quietly hacked her way up the slope to where the Sherston trackway joined the Tetbury trail in front of the eastern gateway into Malmesbury, almost beside the abbey itself. Wearing the same long monkish brown cloak with its deep hood that she had worn to track Gytha, and clad in rough leather trousers, baggy and cross-gartered to the knee, with worn leather boots on her feet she looked like any other traveller: a youth with a deep scrip over his shoulders and a small leather purse from his waist hanging off a tattered belt made of soiled rope.

Already there were quite a few people waiting to enter the town: a tilt cart with rough crates of chickens, and a pair of geese tied in a wildly hissing bundle; a pedlar in a large felt hat with a wide drooping brim and his pole of trinkets; a trio of builders with buckets, hods and trowels in their hands; children with their mothers; a handful of washer women with baskets on their hips and at their feet; workmen with large canvas bags of tools; a pair of masons with a great block of stone in a hand cart for the abbey, part worked, with mauls and chisels in their hands, while the guards who were lounging there sorted through them all, took tolls, peered into faces and rough-housed the women.

With her heart beating a fierce tattoo, Brioni swung off her pony and joined the throng, while three of the Danes, in battered link-mail byrnies with long swords at their sides, their helmets hanging off their baldrics on thick leather chin straps, hustled through them, their voices rough, their Saxon vile and mixed with harsh Danish curses.

"What do you want here, boy?" the larger of the Danes said, in his guttural voice, grabbing Brioni by her shoulders.  "And take a look at this miserable pony," he called to his friends, shaking the poor beast's head by its bridle. "Did you ever see so wretched an animal? He would be better in the pot than carrying you!"

"I am here to see the abbot, Father Wilfred," she said calmly, her heart racing. "I bring him a message from the Bishop. And it's a her, 'Poppy'…and you are frightening her," she replied, reaching to take hold of the bridle.

"Not so fast, boy," the smaller of the three men growled, hitching his sword belt over his belly. There's still a toll to pay, and I need to see your face. We are told that a bunch of scabby fighters are on the way here and we are to examine everyone who enters. You might be one of them!" he laughed, snatching the hood off her face as he did so, cuffing her sharply in the process.

"Well, who's a pretty boy then?" he guffawed as Brioni shook her head from the blow he had given her, her short hair bouncing across her shoulders in a wave of gold, her blue eyes blurred. "Just what those monks need, you are," he added coarsely, pumping his arm at his friends. "Just ripe for fucking…shame to let the abbot take him first!" and he reached down with his big hand to feel her crotch.

But before he could touch her, Brioni swiftly danced away from him, pulling her pony round between them, her face a blaze of red, her mind racing. "Keep your ugly hands off me, you demon," she shrilled. "I am no catamite! I am dedicated to St Aldhelm who built this abbey. I have the toll, and am waited for by the abbot. Please let me pass!" And she dropped her head and took refuge in a wild burst of tears, while most stepped away from her, fearful of being drawn in.

But she was rescued by one of the women waiting to enter the town, a formidable matron with a broad back and beefy arms, and a huge basket of washing on an ample hip, who stepped up and gave the man a hearty buffet on his shoulders: "You great Danish bully, Dagmar Ragmarsson, leave that boy alone or it will be the worse for you. This is Captain Ránnulfr's washing that I have brought up straight from the stream. And if this gets in the dirt because I have to stop your little games, he will not be pleased!"

"It was only a bit of fun, Old Mother," he growled at her, turning round. "I was only teasing the boy. Here, you," he snarled at Brioni. "Hand over the toll, a silver penny, and get on your way! The gods curse your abbot, and your scrawny 'King of the Marshes'." And taking the small coin from her hand, he gave Poppy a smart whack on her shaggy rump, sending Brioni stumbling towards the open gateway and the ancient abbey church beyond it, shouting her thanks to the stout washerwoman as she went.

But it was not to be so simple because as she reached the gateway, leading Poppy by her reins, a tall Danish warrior in polished black scale armour and mail chausses, thick soled boots on his feet with metal insteps over them, suddenly appeared between the gates and stopped her. He held his helmet in his hand, its faceplates swinging open, and on his right shoulder was the jagged gold knife emblem of Oscytel. A Jomsviking, his eyes almond shaped and steel blue, who looked at her with unsmiling intensity, his mouth tight, a parchment message in his hand. The very captain the washer woman had spoken of.

"So, who are you to disturb my men?" he asked her tersely, his hand grasping for Poppy's bridle. "We have a message from our King to search all those coming in to Malmesbury," he went on, waving the parchment in her face, her eyes following his every action, supremely grateful she had no weapon on her, her long cloak safely covering her hips and rough trousers. "I have not seen you before. What are you doing here?"

"I come with a message for the abbot, Father Wilfred, from Bishop Aethelheah of Sherborne about the Easter service and the giving of alms to the poor," she said reaching into her scrip.

"From Sherborne?" he asked her sharply, studying her face with narrowed eyes, his Saxon fluent, his accent harsh. "That is more than a day's journey and you have no spare clothes with you."

"I am an acolyte on a holy mission," she invented wildly, remembering what Father Anselm had said to her about the various grades of Holy Order, her words coming out in a rush. "The Lord Christ instructs all those of my brethren to give aid to one on a mission."

"Bah! 'The Lord Christ' indeed!" he exclaimed disgustedly, cuffing her as he spoke. "If I had a silver penny for every mewling priest I have slain since coming to this country I would be a rich man. By Odin, I have no patience with the orders I have been given to respect you wretched people. *None!* If my Lord Oscytel were King you would all be put to the sword and be done with you!" And he growled deep in his throat with frustrated rage, before twisting her hair in his hand to make her squeak. "You have no tonsure, boy," he said, giving her head a fierce shake then releasing her.

"No, Captain. I have taken no vows yet," she spluttered rubbing her head, tears in her eyes.

"But you have some learning?" he questioned her, watching her closely.

"Yes, my Lord," she said then dropping her face, hoping the title would please him. "The monks have been teaching me."

"Show me this message, boy!" he demanded, holding out his hand.

And praying that he would not notice that it was not sealed with the Bishop's mark, she drew it out of her scrip and handed it over; standing inwardly shaking as he unrolled it and held it up to the light, while all the others who had been waiting to enter the town bustled past them, handing over their tolls with much grumbling as they did so, dropping them into a rough wooden bowl that his men held out to them.

"This is in Latin, boy," the tall Viking commander said accusingly, putting the parchment down. "I cannot read it."

"All such messages are written in Latin, Lord," Brioni said quietly. "But maybe I can point out to you Abbot Wilfred's name, and that of Bishop Aethelheah of Sherborne at the bottom?"

"I am no fool, boy!" he snarled at her. "I can see those for myself. I know enough for that!" And he paused again as he looked at her, before saying sharply: "This seems to be in order; now get on and complete your mission, you are free to go!" And he watched as she put the message back in her scrip, her heart bumping in her chest, her hands slightly shaking, and almost dropping him a curtsey, she bobbed her head to him just in time instead before turning to go.

But even as she reached the shadow of the gateway he stopped her again.

"Show me your hands, boy!" he ordered her, his voice harsh, reaching for them as he spoke, while his men turned to watch, alerted by his tone as he seized her hands in his grasp, forcing her to extend her fingers while he rubbed his thumb over them and felt her palms, noting the ink stains from the writing she had done...and the rough texture of her skin where constant swordplay had thickened her hands.

"So, boy, you have the face and lashes of a girl, the inky fingers of a schoolboy...and the callouses of a swordsman. You interest me. What is your name?

"They call me Oscar," she said immediately, horrified by his words, but remembering Godric's mastiff. "Oscar of Wimborne. And when I am not studying I goad the Bishop's ox at ploughing and rake the grass at haymaking," she rattled on, trying desperately to think of farming things that would account for her calloused palms. "I have never held a sword, my Lord."

"Never held a sword, eh?" he mused, running his thumbs over her palms again, while he looked her over sharply. "Maybe, Oscar of Wimborne. And maybe you lie? I am intrigued," he added, his brows drawn together. "Be certain I will be looking out for you while you are here in Malmesbury.

"Now, clear off to Father Wilfred with your precious message," he sneered, "and stay clear of my men. You are a pretty lad, pretty enough to be a girl, and some of my men would not be too bothered about the difference. They are good fighters, but rough in their ways. Be thankful you did not cause my washing to fall in the dirt for then I would have taken a stick to you!" And conscious of his eyes on her back as she walked Poppy through the gateway, her hands shaking and suddenly damp with sweat, she entered the town at last.

387

*

*B*ack on the trail Cadoc watched her disappear past the guards and through the ancient ramparts, where the tall gates stood open on their pintles, and sighed with relief. From where he stood his great war bow could have skewered the tall Viking captain to his own gateway, and slain the three Danes who were frisking the crowd an instant later, and in the confusion Brioni could have got away. But all their careful planning would have been ruined. This way his job was done. She was in, and he could return to Trausti and his companions to arrange the next part of their mission.

*

*T*wenty minutes later, her breath still panting, her hands now steady and dried on her trousers, she was in the Abbot's office at last, holding a bowl of mulled wine in her hands and pouring out her tale of Foxley, Hugo, Oswald and Leofric to her incredulous, and scandalised, uncle and godfather, the Abbot of Malmesbury. A man of middle height and finely built, his face long, framed with white hair and a neat beard, Father Wilfred's mouth was firm like his hands, and his eyes bright brown and wrinkled with laughter. Incredulous that she was alive, when he believed all her family to have been brutally slain at Foxley, he was also scandalised to see her with shortened hair and in men's clothing, totally against the rulings of God and Holy Church, and 'what would your mother say?'

"My mother would say I must do what is right...what I believe in, uncle," she said, her eyes flashing. "And my father would have me honour my vow to slay Oscytel."

"Yes, child, I am sure they would both," the old priest said with a shake of his head, fuzzing his beard with his right hand, his brown eyes twinkling at his favourite niece and goddaughter. "Wulfstan always was a fighter, and your lady mother a great believer in a girl's right to make her own choices wherever possible. She and Anselm between them have brought you up well. I can see that. Eh, child, but I shall miss them both now they are gone. And your father and brother. It was a good family into which you were born. My sister chose well!" And there was a pause then while both thought of the past, looking into the flames that flared up from the big iron burner in the abbot's rooms, the scented wood smoke spiralling up amongst the rafters, making them both blink and rub their eyes.

388

"Now, uncle, will you help me?" Brioni said briskly looking into his eyes after a brief sigh. "We fight for the 'King of the Marshes', Leofric and I. For Alfred. Our men are laid up a mile down the Sherston track, just on the edge of Hyam's Wood. As the sun falls, after the gates are closed for the night, I need to get them into the town, through the river gate at the bottom of the abbey gardens, and into the crypt between Vespers and Compline. They will need food and ale, and so will I.

"Leofric does not lead these men, Uncle, I do," she said urgently, her blue eyes intense in her face, "with the help of two of his most experienced war leaders of course," she added seeing the shock in his face at her words. "They are trusting me to get half their men into the town, while the rest make an attack on the south gate. When that starts, my men and I will sally out from the crypt and attack the east gates here. Burn them out with pig fat and oil, kill all the Danes we can find and escape."

And there was another pause then, his eyebrows raised in astonishment, while he thought of all she had said.

"So...you will need the key to the river gate," he said at last, his voice sharp, his body tense. "And the church is always open as you know," he added. "But I will leave candles burning against your arrival, and oil lamps in the crypt where the brothers will bring you food and ale as you have asked."

"Oh, you are the *best* of uncles," she said then, leaping up and throwing her arms around him. "Mother always said you were wasted on the priesthood. I only saw the sainted monk you had become, not the fighter that lurked beneath your monkish garb. She would have been so proud of you!"

"It is her memory that leads me on, young Brioni, not any desire I may have to see the Danish barbarians who have ruined Wessex pay with their lives for their wickedness. Though the Black Jarl is one man whom Christ and His Saints would all rejoice to see in Hell, of that I am certain!

"Now, come on, there is much to arrange and little time in which to do it, and they strengthened the garrison here two days ago with a captain and two dozen men. You met him this morning."

"Captain Ránnulfr?"

"Yes...a Jomsviking. One of their worst. His name means 'Plundering Wolf'. His men are terrified of him!"

"How do you know that? About his name?"

"You learn many things about these people, my Brioni. Knowledge is power. Surely the King has taught you that?

"Yes, uncle. I have learned much from being near the King, but Viking names?

"Know the name, know the man! These heathen men live their names. Knowing that helps in dealing with them. This is one bad man, my Brioni. You were lucky this morning."

"He is pledged to Oscytel. The man who butchered my father."

"As I said, my child, Christ and his saints would rejoice to see that monster in Hell. God grant you and your Leofric Iron Hand can send him there...all of them!" And getting out of his great chair he opened the door of his rooms and hustled off to get the key she needed.

*

*A*lmost dark now, a sliver of orange along the horizon, and a chill wind blowing, the purple clouded sky clearing overhead, as men and hounds gathered round the fire. Last words of warning and advice, armour covered with their cloaks, shields and bows on their backs and weapons loose around their waists, horses on short reins snorting and stamping their feet.

Then, general movement: the two leaders clasping arms, a bang on an armoured back, a burst of laughter and both parties leaving; the one to ride in then circle the town on foot, their beasts left on short picket lines with two of their men...the other to ford the river above the town and then ride to the south gate to make their assault. Bags of oil hanging from their saddles, arrows wrapped in cotton, bows across their backs atop their shields, swords, spears and axes ready to their hands, all armed to the teeth for war. Trausti leading the one group and Eadberht the other, both men alert to all the dangers, yet ready and excited by the promise of immediate action.

*

*H*orse pickets, at the back of the ancient ramparts in a great stand of trees, each man hammering in his stake with its metal cap and 'T' bar to which his reins could be attached, each looking to the other for confirmation that all was well, before handing their beasts over to the care of Waldhere and Dragmal who would guard them and keep them calm while the assault went in.

Then off in pairs on foot, shields on their backs with their bags of oil and fatty pigskins, archers with their bows in hand and quivers over their shoulders, loping in the great ditch between the earthen ramparts from the days before the Romans came. And with them went Bran and Utha, their fighting collars firm on their necks, trotting like the wolf killers they were, heads up and eager, the scent of battle in their wet, black noses.

390

To left and right the earthen walls soared up into the night, silhouetted against the dying light from the western sky, beyond which lay the town of Malmesbury: cruck houses of thatch and wattle, bothies, barns and stables, shops and store sheds, forge, brew houses, granaries and middens, chicken sheds, piggeries and byres...and the soaring tower and mass of St Mary's abbey church with the abbot's house, dormitories and work-shops for the monks who lived there. And the Danes in their palisaded gatehouses and toll booths, guard rooms, armouries and lock-ups.

On silent feet Eadberht led his men at a striding run round the earthworks, not breaking the skyline, silent save for the rattle of their breath and their armour where it struck shield rim or sword hilt. Above them that February night the stars came out, wheeling inexorably across the heavens, a million sparkles of distant light to show them where to put their feet as they ran towards the sound of water as the Tetbury Avon flurried round the north side of the town, the damp, earthy scent of it, of weed and silt and draggled leaves sharp in their nostrils.

Then came the long wall of the abbey gardens, where they slowed to a panting walk as a sharp frost settled in and a fine mist arose from the river and the land around them. Shuffling their shoulders with the weight of metal on them, scale and link-mail armour, shields coming off their backs and onto their arms, swords and axes to hand, stabbing seaxes loose in their scabbards, they pushed forward hard...until suddenly a door opened wide before them. And there was their commander to greet them with a smile, her two great hounds leaping up to fawn over her, their faces bristly with whiskers, their tongues warm and wet on her face, their dark eyes gleaming in the star light.

"Well done! I only heard a rustle on the wind, and you were here. Now, come on, this is not the place to stop!" And she stood aside as they all shovelled past her, leaving her to check that all were in and lock the door again behind them.

Up from the river through the abbey gardens they now ran, dark shadows in the night, past rows of carrots, onions, turnips and clumps of herbs: sage, rosemary and thyme; and bare against the south walls, cherries, pears and apricots; crab apples and quinces. The climb steep, breath coming in gasps, rasping in their throats after their long run, sweat running down their faces, cramps in their sides; then the great abbey church itself, towering up into the night sky, dwarfing their crouching forms. And so through a side door and into the nave at last, echoing footsteps of armoured leather on stone; and finally down the narrow steps into the crypt, warmly lit by candle light and oil lamp, with wooden benches to sit on, covered buckets in which to relieve themselves

391

and blankets to keep off the chill from the stone that surrounded them like a tomb.

"You made it then, Eadberht," she said, banging the gasping man on his back, her breath white in the chilled air. "I was never more pleased to see you in my life!"

"Well done, my Lady," he said, bending over to get his breath. "All sweet as a nut...but you took a chance this morning. Cadoc told me there was a hold up."

"Yes! I was lucky. Saved by a washer-woman, and then stopped again by their commander. Captain Ránnulfr, a Jomsviking, means 'Plundering Wolf' according to my uncle...typical for one of Oscytel's butcher boys, part of a reinforcement of two dozen that came in two days ago. Boasted of how many priests he had killed, the bastard. Wanted to examine my hands, and knew our writing. I have never been so scared since Foxley. But my disguise held and he let me go."

"And your uncle?"

"Outstanding. Shocked by my appearance, but took it all in his stride, poor love. My mother was his only sister and he adored her. He has given us all this for our comfort," she said, gesturing widely around her. "And the brothers will bring us food and ale before compline. Then we can move up to the abbey entrance and wait for Trausti to make his attack. Did you bring my armour and my shield and weapons? I feel naked without them!"

"All here," he replied, straightening up. "Ceawlyn has your armour, and Aldred your sword, shield and Blood Drinker. Come, I will show you, and help get you ready. You have done your bit, my Lady. Now it is time for me and the lads to do ours!"

\*

*T*rausti, leading his commando across the river below Hyam's Wood, waded his horse chest deep through the water, all the others following, before turning onto the trail that led from Foxley village to the town. From there he cut across country to approach Malmesbury from the south, where the only bridge took the trackway on to Wootton Bassett, Swindon and Wantage where King Alfred had been borne.

Rough country in the starlit darkness with no track to follow, and only the sound and smell of the river to guide them as it flowed westwards to Chippenham and the sea; curling round the eastern side of the town to the ancient mill with its wide pond, clanking wheel and mighty grind stones, now stilled in the blackness of the night. Owls called and deer crashed out of their way, startled by the sudden rush of iron hooves through the brakes and thickets that bordered the town. Overhead the sky had cleared, now moonless and filled with stars, the ground sharply frosted, a faint mist rising off the water as it rustled by.

Then they were there, right by the bridge with its wide wooden roadway and ancient balustrades, the great trestles that carried it across the river plunging into the water that raced by them in white streamers.

"Off here, lads," he called softly, swinging off his horse. "And picket them where you can. Hunfrith, Aggi, you stay by the horses and keep them calm. I don't want them stampeding all over the place once the fun starts.

"Now, come on. Jaenberht, Sihtric, over first with Sigweald and seize that mill. Kill any Dane you find, but spare the miller and his family. Remember what I said earlier, we do not wage war on our own people. Stick to the sides of the bridge and move swiftly.

"All the rest follow me, bowmen first, Orn, Caewlin, Aelric and all the others, and don't forget your fire pots and tinder boxes! Now...move!"

*

*I*n the town all was dark save for a few houses on the hill in front of them, where faint lights glowed, and on the southern gatehouse ramparts where two flambeaux flared and flickered, their flames never still in the light wind that blew chill around them, where two men could be seen, helmets and spear points glimmering in the fitful light that silhouetted them perfectly.

Trausti saw them and grinned in the darkness, patting Orn on the shoulder to point them out, knowing the archer could not miss such a well-lit target: "Make those the first to fall; while the horns blow, we bang our shields and the rest pour in their fire arrows. I want that whole position one mass of flames before we retire. Now go!" And he urged him forward with a firm push on his shoulders and a soft, "Good luck!"

Then they were all up and running, in short bursts, from balustrade to balustrade, the main roadway bare in the sharp starlight, crouched down with shields on their arms and weapons free, the mist masking their movements. Ahead of the main assault Jaenberht and his men scuttled to seize the mill as a command post, and stop any sort of warning from reaching the Danes manning the palisaded gateway. Behind them came the rest of Trausti's men, their hearts racing, their breath pumping from them in white clouds, the air sharp in their nostrils, their mouths dry with excitement and fear.

With a sharp rush they were over, the hollow sound of their feet replaced with the firm thump of leather on hard ground. Their breath rasping, they gathered crouched down around Trausti beside the old mill, the water rushing through its sluices, where one man lay in a pool of blood by the door, his throat slit from ear to ear, another slumped in an untidy pile with the spear that had gutted him still thrust into his belly.

"Just the two of them," Jaenberht growled at his leader from the darkness. "Never knew what hit them. I took the one by the sluices, Siggi speared the other, shook him like a pike on a gaff, while Sihtric dealt with the miller. His wife tried to shriek but Trici hit her with a bolster and she went down like a skittle. None harmed and all are calm now. The miller says that a captain in black armour came in two days ago with two dozen men. Nasty piece of work by all accounts. Has been throwing his weight around all over the place."

"Black armour...one of Oscytel's men! So the message worked!" he exclaimed briefly. "No matter, the attack goes forward as planned. How far are the gates from here?"

"A hundred yards and steeply up hill."

"Well within bowshot, despite the oily rags. Muster the men. Concentrate the archers, I want their fire to be intense. There are two Danes up there Orn and I saw earlier. He is to take them out first, then a general attack. Send a small party to nail those gates with oil bags and those pig skins we brought with us. There's nothing like pig fat to make a fire forge-fierce. We'll give them time to get in position, then when we blow our horns and bang our shields they can scamper out and nail in those bags. If they are quick they should get away with it."

"Risky, my friend," Jaenberht said shaking his head. "Risky anyway, but doubly so without a signal first to let you know the men are in place."

"Yes, but those idiots have got two lovely great flambeaux up either side of their gate-head. That is like giving Orn and Aelric a gift at Yuletide. The enemy will be finely back-lit by them and our boys will skewer anyone who tries to throw something down on them."

"Very well, my Lord...but you still need a signal! I will go, and take Siggi with me and half a dozen others. We have the nails and hammers. One good bash each should do it. I doubt those timbers have been replaced in years. I'll give one great blast on the horn when they are in place, then you can go into your routine."

"Good man! I knew I could count on you," and with a swift arm clasp they parted. Jaenberht to take his small party up the hill to the very gates of the town where the Danes had left thick cover beside them; Trausti to muster his men above the bridge, horns, bows and weapons in their hands, shields on their arms and all hidden amongst the trees and bushes that masked the roadway around the mill.

And then they waited...for the night to advance and for Jaenberht and his men to eel their way up to the gates in readiness for their assault, while all around them was silent. The town quiet, no sudden honk and gabble of geese nor Danish horns to warn of an attack, no wild shouts of men or blaze of light. And from the countryside just the wind in the rushes by the river, and through the scrub and briars beside the roadway; the eerie howl of a distant wolf from the forest, and the barking of a lone guard dog from some settlement beyond the river.

# Chapter Fifty Two

Up by the east gates, Jaenberht and his men huddled beneath the ancient ramparts that had been built of earth and stone before the Romans had arrived with their legions and their eagles. Here the growth of ages had cloaked the ditches with bushes, trees and saplings. Growth that should have been removed the moment the Danes had garrisoned the town, but had been left to prosper. In fact all the way up the slope from the bridge there was oak scrub and bushes of hazel that had made perfect cover in the darkness of the night, the mist rising all around them as they had wormed and scuttled their way up the hill until they were no more than a dozen paces from the gates themselves.

These were gnarled and ancient; once stoutly laminated and studded with iron, now the wood was cracked and clearly rotted in places from where many of the old studs had fallen out. Even in the darkness Jaenberht was sure that one good crash with a ram and they would just fall apart. They should have been long ago removed and replaced with fresh seasoned timber; as it was they were ripe for destruction. If they could get their oil bags nailed in then there was every chance that Trausti's storm of fire arrows would do for them once and for all.

Looking up, he could see the great flambeaux the Danes had placed on the edges of their wooden parapet, the flames leaping and twisting in the light breeze that was blowing across them, the mist writhing round the foot of the gates and ramparts, but not up to parapet height, and he grinned to think that he and his men would be suitably hidden by it when the time came to attack.

He looked up at the sky then, sharp and clear, and down to where the bridge lay, now almost hidden in the mist rising off the river, and at his men, and nodded his head...all was still. Much longer and the target might be obscured, and standing up to signal his bag and hammer men forward...he immediately sank down again as from round the far corner of the ramparts a Danish foot patrol suddenly appeared.

Five men, one out front and two pairs, all with round shields on their arms, two with long spears at the trail, the others with axes over their shoulders and all talking quietly amongst themselves, a chuckle, a bang on the arm, a good natured push. Just soldiers finishing their stint of duty, and all looking forward to a stoup of barley beer and a warm bannock with cheese and yellow butter, they were far from alert and quite unprepared for the silent rush of dark figures, their faces frighteningly hidden behind the masks of wolf, bear and fox, that seemed to leap right out of the ground and fall upon them with brutal ferocity.

Suddenly the silence was broken with desperate grunts and cries as Jaenberht and his men slammed into the enemy patrol. Hammers and seaxes in hand, no time to draw their swords, they stabbed and smashed their way into the armoured bodies of their enemies, the noise immediate and violent as heads were crushed and throats cut in a spray of blood and bone. In moments three were down and spread-eagled in death, their blood black in the starlight.

But these were men of the Great Army, and the other two were not willing to give up their lives so easily. Shouting out to their friends above them, they backed away to the gates themselves, and to the small sally port within them that Jaenberht had not spotted in the darkness.

And now a desperate fight took place.

Jaenberht dropping his hammer, sheathed his seaxe and drawing his sword, shield on his left arm he leapt into the attack like a tiger; Sigweald beside him, their swords flicking out in the lunge and parry, sparks flying in the darkness to the wild shriek and scream of sharpened steel. Sword on sword, sword on axe, shields clattering to blows wielded with maximum force, men panting and shuffling on their feet, the mist rising around them, their breath rasping and filling the frigid air with puffs of dragon vapour.

Above them all was chaos as the enemy suddenly realised their men were under attack, and with wild shouts and cries a flurry of spears flew down from the ramparts, thudding down into the ground and into the bodies already lying there. Two missed by a hair's breadth the men who had rushed out from their concealment, bags of oil, pig skins, long nails and hammers in hand and with lethal speed struck them into the ancient timbers, some so rotted that the nails almost disappeared from view.

And from somewhere overhead a great bell began a strident alarum that burst the night apart.

*Stab, lunge, parry, block!* Jaenberht and his opponent face to face, Dane to Saxon, eyes hard, teeth gritted, breathing fierce as both men struggled to

397

break the other's lock, then Jaenberht gave one mighty push to send his enemy stumbling back to slam up against the left hand gate, his arms suddenly flinging wide. And in that moment the big Saxon war-leader struck, a brutal right-sided cut that hewed into the joint where head met shoulders, hacking his enemy's neck apart in a fountain of blood that almost severed his head, so that it flopped sideways as the man slumped onto the ground...just as the sally port behind him opened and a rush of men began to leap out from it.

Spinning round Jaenberht lunged forward and skewered the first Viking out, thrusting his sword into him so fiercely that the man's screaming body blocked the narrow portal, just as Sigweald finished off the axeman he had been fighting with a swingeing cut to his waist that bent him sideways followed by a frightening overhead blow that took off his arm below the shoulders, dropping him screaming to the bloodied ground.

Then there was a brief pause while Jaenberht finally managed to blow his great horn, while his men raced back to cover him, Sigweald holding his arm where the Danish axemen had caught him a glancing blow, Sihtric helping a comrade whose thigh had been pierced with a spear.

*

Below by the bridge, Trausti heard wild noise break out, the bell, the shouts and wild cries and rushed his men further forward, in case the Danes broke out of the town and rushed down towards him, trapping Jaenberht between them. Swiftly they formed the shield wall across the track, each shield locked in behind the man's beside him, right overlapping left rim, and legs braced against assault, while his archers raced left and right of the line to pour in covering fire if there should be a sudden wild attack.

Then came a long blast of noise from the curve of the hill that all men had been waiting for: *Hoom-oom-oom!* and again, the noise reverberating into the very soul, cutting through all the shouts and cries on that misty night.

And as he heard it so Trausti blew his own horn: *Hoom-oom-oom!* and roared out 'Loose! *Loose!*' to his archers, while more horns in his line gave out long, winding blasts: *Hoom-oom-oom!* again and again. The deep sounds going on and on, followed by the wild shouts of his men and the ringing clash and clatter of swords on shield rims as Trausti moved his small command closer to the gated entrance of Malmesbury.

And as the violent Saxon challenge rang out, and Jaenberht's men withdrew back down the hill...so Orn's and Aelric's arrows arrived with a whistle and a thunk overhead, followed by a further flight as the first Danes on the palisade were killed, shot through the head and body in a spray of blood

398

and bone. Like half-filled sacks of meal their bodies toppled off the parapet to thump down around the Danish defenders from the sally port as they scampered round the gates, some tumbling to the ground like shot hares as the Saxon arrows bowled them over.

In the town there was wild panic as Trausti's violent assault began and the bell began its desperate call to arms, lights bursting out everywhere and shouts and screams as the people within reacted to this wild attack. Some rushed out into the narrow ginnels that ran between the houses, others flung open their doors to shout and cry out in terror, all the more so as the first arrows rattled into the yards and alleys that made up the town, or smacked into the thatch of the houses that lay beside the gateway.

Above Jaenberht the enemy reacted with cries and shouts of their own as they struggled to respond. Shooting wildly down into the mist with what bows they had, several of their arrows struck the shields now on their attackers' backs, two lodging in Jaenberht's armour, unable to pierce the thick link-mail over his shoulders, but stuck in it like two weird feathers that waved above his head every time he moved.

Now, with shrieks from the wounded and shouts of rage from the defenders, three more bodies tumbled from above to sprawl like broken marionettes on the ground, made bloody from their wounds. And as Jaenberht withdrew down towards the river with their wounded, so Trausti's men loosed the first of their fire arrows, their cotton wicks dipped in oil and set on fire by tinder box and fire pot, each a flaming ball that soared up and fell thickly upon the gatehouse thatch and on the houses on either side the Danes were barracked in…and on the gates themselves.

At first nothing happened, but as the arrows continued to fall like flaming meteors in steady arcs of fire, so the thatch caught at last. First a thin tendril of smoke, then a flicker of flame and finally, with a rushing crackle, the whole roof went up in a blaze of red and orange flame, and with it the roofs of both buildings either side, driving the defenders away, many of whom fell screaming into the very heart of the furnace that had been created and were consumed by fire.

But the gates took longer.

The timbers, ancient and cracked though they were, were thicker and it took several oil bags to burst before, with a bang and roar, they too caught at last and within minutes were a great sheet of fire, almost white-hot where the pig fat flared and sizzled. Huge leaping flames that could be seen for miles amid a vast roiling cloud of smoke that obscured everything. Flames that incinerated the bodies of the dead lying there, and drove those few who had survived the struggle before the gates to take shelter in the great ditch that still ringed the defences.

It surpassed all Trausti's expectations, and he left his men whooping and leaping in excitement to greet Jaenberht as his small force struggled back towards him with their wounded.

*

*I*n the abbey church of St Mary, Brioni and her command, having eaten and rested from their run, and relieved themselves, were already clustered around the great doorway when they heard the noise of Jaenberht's attack break out and the wildly tolling bell. Most had their shields on their arms, oil bags and pig fat over their backs; only Cadoc, Cenhelm and their archers carried no shields, but they had quivers stuffed with arrows over their shoulders, bracers on their forearms and swords and seaxes by their sides...all waiting for Jaenberht's horn to set them loose.

Outside, the town was already beginning to react to the fierce shouts and cries coming from the south gate when Jaenberht's horn was sounded, followed immediately by Trausti's fierce reply, the winding *Hoom-oom-ooms!* sounding hollow in the mist, the first of the fire arrows rising up out of it in increasing number, disembodied, like mystic fiery balls. So panic was already spreading around them when the door of the church opened and a flood of dark armoured figures raced out towards the Danes in the east gateway.

Confused by what was happening, the enemy did not at first respond to this disciplined rush until the silence was violently broken by Eadberht's men roaring out: "*The Lady! The Lady!*" as they came, a solid group of armoured figures with swords and axes, those with bows stopping in a double line to fire a first flight of arrows up at the palisaded battlements. There two great flambeaux, just as on the south gate, lit up the scene with flaring red and orange flames, back-lighting their enemies in the darkness. Three times they fired up at the Danes standing there all shouting and holding up their shields, killing many and wounding others, then rushing forward and firing again even as the first bodies were tipped over the side to fall like broken dolls onto the frosted ground beneath.

Then, with Eadberht leading half his group to the ladders rising up to the ramparts, Brioni led hers to the gates themselves, and to the buildings beside them, her long sword in her hand, her thickened wicker shield on her left arm; running to remove the long bar that held them closed and swing the great valves open, nailing their oil bags and pig-fat carcases to them as they did so.

400

Above her the battle for control raged fiercely as Saxon fought Dane across the war-linden.  Sword blow for sword blow, thrusting with spears, parrying with shields, both sides shouting and roaring at one another in feral fury, feet stamping, arms rising and falling in a whirl of blood and bony splinters, while utter pandemonium gripped the town: dogs barking, donkeys braying, the alarum bell ringing on and on and on, and people screaming and rushing about in blind terror.

Below at the gates, Brioni's men struggled with the broad cross bar that held them closed; while others raced into the buildings on either side on an intense search and kill mission.  Warped and knotted with age, for a while the bar would not be moved, but after three attempts they had it off and flung to the ground at last, and with two men on each side, backs to the gates and muscles straining, they forced them open, the ancient valves creaking and screaming on their pintles as they did so, the iron dry and rusted, little care having been taken of them for many years, as Malmesbury was an open town and her defences long unused.

Even as they paused with heaving chests, the great gates now against their backstops, a rush of Danes fell upon them and Brioni had her first taste of real battle: the stench of fear, of sweat and urine, of punctured offal and the sweet smell of blood as she fought for her life in the darkness, lit only by the flaring light from the broad flambeaux wavering and flickering above her.

Light on her feet, she danced around her enemies, kept her shield high and her sword flicking out and round, edge and point as she had been taught. Parrying with blade and shield she rushed in on the man before her, then suddenly off balance on the rutted entrance, his shield dropping, and so she lunged with all her weight behind her, sword arm locked in a straight line…and felt the gasp of breath as her blade struck home on the Dane she had been fighting, bursting through his mail with a rush of foetid air, his blood rushing out to cover her hand and arm as with a wild shriek he fell away from her.

Gasping for breath, she had no time to pause before she was confronted with another enemy, a tall Danish warrior in black scale armour, his helmet's faceplates closed around him, his heavy shield on his arm already swinging towards her, his sword coming round to hack down into her shoulder, a killing blow that would shatter her body and hew her open from chin to navel.

The Danish captain himself, Ránnulfr, and, for a moment, she was appalled.

Dancing sideways she took his shield on her own, riding the blow as Eadberht had showed her, allowing it to spin her away in a sideways wheel to land on her feet while she brought her own sword down against his with a screel of metal and bright shower of sparks.  Then she was upright again and

401

darting in with her sword, *Stab! Cut! Stab! Parry!* taking his sweeping blows on her shield, every blow jarring her through and through as they landed on the iron boss that Leofric had got Arnwulf to place in its centre, or on the flat around its iron rim.

Now all that training paid off as her sword remained tight in her grip, feeling so much lighter than the heavy practice swords she had worked with on the hacking posts, as she went through the routine that Trausti and Eadberht had hammered into her: *Lunge! Parry! Cut! Return!...Side to side and overhead!* Always doing her best to keep outside the main reach of the Danish captain's arm; rushing in to cut and thrust, dancing back to parry and take his blows on her shield arm.

Her breath rasped in her throat, tasting of blood, her heart hammered in her chest...her energy steadily failing before his violent assault, her muscles screaming as his greater strength steadily sapped hers. Beating her backwards with every step to pin her against the gates behind her, the big Dane pursued her mercilessly, determined to skewer this insolent little Saxon warrior who would not be hacked down, but seemed to slip away from his reach every time he thought he had him beaten.

Eadberht, seeing her in trouble, rushed to support her but was foiled by two Danes who got in his way, whom he was forced to cut down first, the one with a brilliant thrust to the face over the top of his shield not held high enough, in a violent spray of blood and shattered teeth. And the other with a sweeping back cut to the neck, taking the man under his helmet, a flashing blow that almost severed his head, as sweet a stroke as any he had delivered for a while, that fountained blood everywhere.

And when he looked again for Brioni her enemy was down, rolling on the ground in agony with her standing over him, her helmet in her hands as Cadoc and his men raced through the open gates, their fire pots in their hands, ready to send a wild flurry of fire arrows into the thatched houses on either side of the gates and into the thick wooden valves themselves, now standing wide open, the water skins filled with oil hanging from them like obscene fruits, targets that they could not miss.

Everywhere there were bodies, some Saxon, but mostly Danes, scattered across the torn and bloodied roadway in careless abandon like discarded toys, and now Cadoc and his men were firing again, *bend and loose, bend and loose*, their arrowheads wrapped in cotton and soaked in oil, lit by tinder box and fire pot, and arcing up in a fiery stream to set the thatch on fire, and the wattle walls of the nearby buildings that the Danish garrison had been using. Within minutes the flames had taken, the thatch crackling into life with gouts of scarlet and orange fire that soared and wavered in the light airs of that February night.

Next it was the gates' turn to feel the breath of Wessex's dragon, the Wyvern beast of their King and his people, as Cadoc, Cenhelm, Wybert and their men poured their fire arrows into them from almost point blank range, bursting the fat bags apart until the oil ran down them in dark streams and finally caught alight with a roar and fierce blaze of fiery heat that made them all stand back, stunned by the speed of the fire's spread and by the coiling, leaping flames that so swiftly devoured them, until they reached up to the sky in one great towering inferno.

"Where's the Lady?" Eadberht asked of Cadoc sharply, his wolf helmet in his hand as he tightened a rough bandage round his upper arm with his teeth. "Where's Mistress Brioni?"

"Talking to a prisoner over there," he said, stroking his long bow stave. "She was in trouble with him. Beating the hell out of her he was, driving her against the gates, when I put an arrow in him. Lovely shot it was," he said in his Welsh lilt. "Took him just below the shoulder. Knocked the stuffing out of him I can say, threw him sideways and she did the rest. God knows what she is saying, bach, but we need to get out of here! We have hammered these bastards good and proper, but it will not take them long to recover. This is the Great Army we are fighting, remember boyo. This will really put a burr under them. They will be angrier than a hornet's nest broken with a stone. We need to be gone, and fast!"

"I agree," Eadberht replied swiftly, looking around him. "Shame about Baldric and Sigbert, they were good men. Sweyn also, and Aella, and Eadric has been so gashed I doubt he will live. You go and find Brioni, I will round up the others. At least we got their coffer out before we burned the buildings," he added with a grin. "Stuffed with silver. Leofric will be delighted. And I expect the lads will have picked up some booty from the men we killed. Like rats up a pipe...they never miss a trick!"

And sheathing his sword he left, shouting out names as he went, eager to be gone before the enemy came looking for them.

*

Not far from where the gates were now groaning on their pintles, bowing outwards as the flames ate into them, Brioni was standing over the man she had been fighting, her two great hounds by her side.

Now seated on the ground, an arrow sticking right through his shoulder, the man had his helmet off and his face dragged down with pain as he looked up at her, the roaring fire perfectly silhouetting her against it.

403

"You are one lucky little foxy bastard," he growled in his rough Saxon, looking at the fox mask she had over her face and on her helmet. "I had you! One more stroke and it would be you lying here dead, not me with an arrow through my shoulder," and he gasped in sudden pain.

"That is because I fight with God on my side...and you only have Odin to protect you. It is no contest. I win...you lose!"

And with a sudden growl of rage he leapt at her, reaching for her seaxe as he did so, having been disarmed after he had been wounded. But she was too quick for him; knocking him sideways with her shield onto his wounded shoulder that made him cry out, clutch himself and roll on the ground in pain while she stepped on his other shoulder, thrusting her sword point up to his neck, Bran and Utha instantly snarling at his throat.

"One more move like that and I will let my hounds tear you apart. They are very good at it...and they are hungry! Now lie there, Captain Ránnulfr, you 'plundering wolf' and listen to me," and she smiled as much at the sudden shock of hearing his name and its meaning from her lips, as from his terrified glance at Bran and Utha's jagged mouths just inches from his throat, their teeth dripping with the blood and sinews of those they had already slain.

"Yes, you heathen pirate," she snarled at him, through her metal mask. "We have met before," and she whisked off her helmet and shook her head, her short hair glowing gold in the fierce heat and light from the burning gates.

"No! *It cannot be!*" he gasped, outraged.

"Yes! It can and is. I am that 'Oscar of Wimborne' whose hands you felt this morning, and whom I gulled so prettily!" And he ground his teeth with rage.

"I have spared your life, Jomsviking, for one reason and one reason only. You are to take this message back to your Lord, the Black Jarl of Helsing, the great Lord Oscytel," and she threw him the foxhead symbol that had been left at every attack the Vikings had suffered in the past six weeks, and smiled at the added shock she had given him, his face screwed up with fury.

"And tell him this for me. I am no 'boy', you bastard," she swore at him, bending closer as she did so, her long sword still at his throat, her hounds slavering over him and growling deep, "I am the Lady Brioni of Foxley. It is my family whom he slew last month, and my father he butchered with his 'Blood Eagle'. I was there! I saw everything! And after he had gone, I cursed him and swore an oath on my father's torn heart, on his very heart's blood, you *Nithing!* and to the ancient gods of my people, that I would have Oscytel's life before the year's end. By Tiw and Thunnor I swore it. His life is forfeit to me...and I will not be denied!" And she relished the hate in his eyes, his powerless rage, his shivering fury, and standing she picked up his sword and flung it into the fire behind her. "Your mother gave you life once, you pirate. And loved you, poor woman. Now, *I* give you life, Captain. Make sure you use it well and take my message to that demon whom you call 'Lord' and tell him that the Lady Brioni of Foxley seeks to send his soul to Hell!" Spurning him with her sword, she turned away, calling her two great hounds to her as she did so, and went to join Cadoc who was just coming to find her, her mission completed, certain that her message would be delivered...and she smiled.

*

*M*oments later and they were all gone, only the enemy dead and dying left behind, stripped of all the gold and silver they had on them and anything else of value that Brioni, Eadberht and their men needed; their own dead taken with them, and Eadric doing his best to keep up with their flight, his shoulder roughly strapped, his armour thick with blood where a Danish axe had caught him.

Back around the ancient ramparts they went, the fire seething and roaring behind them, the gates and roofs collapsing in vast towers of sparks and twisting flame that shot up to the heavens as they dashed off, the stars frosty sharp in the sky above, the mist rising up around them as they ran back to where Eadberht had left the horses. There Dragmal and Waldhere were only too pleased to see them, both eager for news and saddened by their losses, both concerned over Eadric's wound which Brioni now did her best to bind up again before mounting up and riding back the way they had come.

Down the Sherston trackway they rode at a fast canter, not wanting to push their horses too hard, their iron hooves rattling on the frosty track as they barrelled on their way. Always checking to see if there was to be some pursuit, or whether they would meet up with Trausti and his men before they reached the ancient forest of Helm's Wood, they stopped twice to listen. But each time there was no sound and they soon came to the clearing in which the outlaw village had nestled, and where Brioni had first met with Hugo, Maritia and Leofric.

Now deserted and empty they pushed on through the starlit darkness, the sky lit up behind them with the fierce fires that they had left burning furiously behind them, until with the faint light of early dawn they came to the great Fosse Way, riding down it to the small ruined steading they had come to all those weeks ago when they had all set out for Ford, and there they found Trausti and his command waiting for them, a thick meaty broth that Aldred had on the simmer, and spiced ale to drink.

*

*I*t had been a risky business as she had said right from the start, but it had been her first command and she had not been found wanting.

Jumping off her horse and reaching down to her two great hounds to ruffle their heads, thick with blood, and praise them, Brioni of Foxley laughed and with a swing to her walk she swaggered off to join Trausti and Eadberht for a well-earned stoup of ale, proud of what she had achieved, eager to return to Ford, to share her experiences with Leofric and hear how his attack on Melksham had gone forward.

# Chapter Fifty Three

*A*rrived and welcomed with shouts and laughter, they stripped their dead of all their armour and weapons, buried them in one corner of the ruined garth, the furthest from the well, and piled timber and rubble from the wrecked buildings on top of their graves, shallow in ground still frozen from the bitter winter. Eadric, weak from his wound and leaking blood, lay a small bunch of early daffodils he had found growing near the half-burned hall on top of the rough cairn, while Trausti spoke a few words of comfort for their half Christian, half pagan souls before they pressed on again.

\*

*F*ull daylight saw them pushing hard along the ancient Fosse Way, the countryside deserted save for two hares running in circles around each other in a distant field, the ground still misted under foot, the February sky now blue overhead. With two men a mile out front, the rest pressed close together, they passed the shattered steading where they had destroyed the Danes a month before, and were relieved not to have met any stray travellers as they turned onto the narrow trackway that would lead them down to Combe.

With no cart to slow them down they splashed across the By Brook in fine style and walked their horses up the steep, twisted hill track beyond where Arnwulf had had such trouble, the water running off their fetlocks.

And so down to Ford at last, with the sun pale overhead but warm on their shoulders, startling a nye of pheasants that had been feeding amongst a thick coppice of hazel, who whirred cockling wildly away from them, wings beating furiously, tails spread and necks stretched out for the sky,

Then they were clattering down off the hill, across the narrow Bristol trail, to the wide garth before the steading, close to where the By Brook crossed the ford, and suddenly the whole courtyard was filled with figures rushing forward to greet them. Horses turned heads with ears pricked, and hounds leapt and bayed, as Leofric and his men, some with bandaged wounds, ran to help them off their beasts, to support their wounded and take from them the great coffer they had liberated from Malmesbury's Danes with such fierce success.

Leofric, Beornred, Finnar and Trausti were raucous in their greeting, arms around each other, their feet beating a fierce tattoo on the wide stone flags outside the house place, shouting and roaring their heads off in delight.

"We slaughtered them!" Leofric shouted, punching the air. "Rode in on them at first light, with horns blowing and torches flaring and terrified the lives out of them." Then, breaking away, he called out: "Where's my girl? Where's the Lady Brioni of Foxley?"

"Here, you pirate!" she shouted with a ringing laugh, "*Here!*" And swinging off her horse she ran and leapt straight into his arms, Bran and Utha jumping up on either side of her. "Here I am, the Victor of Malmesbury come to claim my prize."

"And what prize would that be?" he teased her, nuzzling her hair.

"The prize of knowing that I have done all things well and have pleased you, my Lord," she replied, kissing him thoroughly, smiling broadly. "And that some of the silver we have brought in should be given to my men who risked everything for me and who fought so bravely."

"So, Trausti," he said, turning to the big Dane beside him, dropping the lovely woman in his arms down to the ground, "how did it go? Were they prepared? And did they fight hard?"

"Yes, the message worked. They were prepared, but not nearly as well as they should have been. The Lady Brioni got her men right into the town by a brilliant trick that you and I had not even discussed. And when Jaenberht and I made our attack on the south gates, she and Eadberht burst out from the abbey church and assaulted the bastards from within, forced the east gates, and looted their buildings before setting the whole lot on fire. And they did fight like demons!

"We lost four killed and several wounded, one very badly, young Eadric. But the lady has stitched and bound him so, God willing, he will recover. In the end we all got out safely and left the place with both gates wreathed in flames and their silver on the back of one of our horses."

"And how did she fight?" he asked sharply.

"Like a tiger! Slew her man with a straight edged thrust to the belly and then faced their leader. One of Oscytel's best."

"A *Jomsviking!*" he exclaimed, astonished, looking down at Brioni with pride and amazement.

"Yes, and for quite a while, Eadberht tells me, she danced rings round him."

"And he didn't mark her? Not a scratch?"

"No!" Brioni broke in hotly, standing away from him. "But he would have done if Cadoc hadn't put an arrow through him. He was beginning to press me hard, Leofric, and I could feel my strength going when he suddenly gave a desperate cry and keeled over with an arrow right through his shoulder. It was outstanding! One moment he was battering the life out of me...the next he was rolling on the ground. And the truly shocking thing was that I knew him."

*"Knew him?"* the others queried, astonished.

"Yes. He is Captain Ránnulfr. Uncle told me it means 'Plundering Wolf'!

"The good Abbot Wilfred," Leofric said in sudden recognition.

"Yes, he got us into St Mary's, but Ránnulfr literally had me under his hand at the east gate entrance as I entered the town, but I gulled him into letting me go. It was quite the most frightening part of the whole assault. He thought me a boy. But later, with him at my feet in the flaring darkness, I took off my mask and helmet, tossed him the foxhead emblem, and told him who I really was, and that I was after his leader's life for my father's murder. It quite silenced him. Did I do wrong?"

Leofric threw back his head and laughed. "Wrong, my Lady? No, let the bastard sweat. I would have given my share to have seen his face. He must have been shocked to his rotten core to realise he had been fighting a girl! He will be the laughing stock of the whole Viking army!

"Guthrum will be quietly delighted, and Oscytel will be livid! It just makes you more vulnerable on the battle field, my love," he said gathering her under his arm. "And on the next assault, because they will want your scalp so badly, they will make every effort to put you down! But, no, my dearest, you have not done wrong. You have done *brilliantly*, and I am so proud of you. So, yes, I salute you, my Lady Brioni of Foxley, and your men can indeed have a handful of Danish silver to celebrate their first victory under your command."

"You mean I keep those men?" She gasped up at him. "Trausti, Eadberht, Jaenberht, Cadoc and the rest? They are mine to command?" she asked, astonished.

"No, sweetheart. Not all of them. Just those whom you led against the east gate to start with. Make them 'yours' and I will add to them as time goes by."

"Hmmm, I thought that was all too good to be true," she said, hanging her head a little. "But what you have given me is just outstanding anyway," she said then, with shining eyes. "I will make them the best in our little army!" and in front of all his commanders she reached up and kissed him, while all around them both commands mingled and laughed and shared their experiences, consoling those who had lost friends while they led their jaded beasts to water, a nosebag full of oats and a good rub down.

*

"So, Leofric," Brioni said a little later, leading her man and his friends to a long bench against the house wall, where the late February sunlight bathed them in its warmth, "you have heard about Malmesbury; what about Melksham?" And while Osburgh and her daughters brought jugs of beer sweetened with honey to fill the great horn that each man carried in his belt, and fresh baked bannocks thick with butter, he told her what had happened.

"As I said, we slaughtered them!" he said, sitting back in the sunshine against the plastered wall of the house place, his drinking horn in his hand. "We camped out in a forest clearing that Eadwine knew of and reconnoitred the place first. Tiny, with about a dozen cruck houses and bothies, and all the usual buildings. Lot of cattle and geese, sheep and goats on both sides of the river, something of everything…and a very good ford, barricaded of course, and guarded."

"They knew you were coming then?" Trausti asked, wiping his mouth with the back of his hand.

"Oh yes, they knew we were coming. Their barricade was thick with them, and that ford is the only reason those bastards are there. It's the only one between Malmesbury and Bradford, and Bradford we did over two weeks ago. Well, they'll need to re-think their strategy after this because we didn't leave a man alive to tell the tale. Bodies everywhere, we must have killed a whole crew! The lads had a store of rings and silver coins off them, and some lovely weapons and armour. Those Danes may not have been very brave but they were beautifully equipped!"

"So, how did you go about it, Lord?" Trausti asked, reaching for the large jug of beer that Osburgh had left on a table close by.

"We attacked at first light, before the sun was more than a flush on the horizon. With horns and torches and our masks. We just needed Bran and Utha to complete the picture, and we could all have come straight from Ragnarok! We were on them and over their barricade before they could think. They'd have done better to form the shield wall fifty yards behind it and slug it out."

"That's everybody's lowest point, just before the dawn," Finnar pointed out, his mouth full of bannock. "Half asleep, waiting for your relief, dreaming

410

of beer and getting your head down. No-one's alert. That's when your under-officers need to bear down on the men most."

"Warrior and Wotan are big enough in broad daylight," Beornred chipped in with a grin. "In the grey darkness they were huge, and neither Leofric nor I are exactly small. Those poor bastards took one look at us in our masks and beast helmets thundering towards them and fled. And between a warrior on a horse and one on the ground running there is no contest. We cut them to shreds!"

"We got there the day before," Finnar said, getting up to fill all the beer horns from the great jug that Osburgh had left for them, "so we had plenty of time to spot where they were barracked, which barns, which houses they had taken over. And while we slew all those we found outside, Orn, Aelric and their men poured a stream of fire arrows into the barns and houses they were sleeping in and burned them out like rats in dry grass. Some never made it. They burned where they lay. Those that got out we slaughtered. They tried to make a fight of it, but they never got the chance. We were all over them."

"And they lost their leaders early on," Leofric said, taking up the tale with relish. "Beornred and I took out one. A giant axeman, and he was good. You should see what he did to Beornred's shield! But he never touched me, though he came close. Blade to blade he was almost as big as me, sparks flying everywhere, and his blade glancing off my helmet plates. Shook me, but did no damage, and I had him in the end, the sweetest blow. As he swiped at Beornred, I took him with a violent upswing that split him from groin to navel, guts and offal everywhere, and when he collapsed forward I took off his head with the return stroke. Bounced it yards in a fountain of blood."

"Orn skewered the other with a perfect shot that took him right below his helmet straps," Beornred said, tossing his beer down his throat in one enormous swallow. "Tore out his throat; he was dead in moments, blood spattered everyone near him. And that took the stuffing right out of them. Gleaming!" and he rubbed his hands with undisguised glee.

"Then we soothed the natives with most of the Danes' horses," Leofric said, stretching his legs out as he leaned back. "Cleared the ford of its obstacles, sorted through the bodies which we left there in a great pile. Put the axeman's head on the top with the foxhead symbol in his mouth for the enemy to find, then left. Backtracked through the forest to confuse their searchers and got back here a little after midday...not long before you arrived. Brought their toll chest with us too. There's nothing like hitting those bastard where it hurts most, in their pockets. The Danish High Command will not be happy when news of all that we have done reaches them. Crews and treasure lost in both places…despite being warned beforehand. They'll *hate* it!" and they all laughed and shouted and stamped their feet on the stone flags.

"So, that's Malmesbury and Melksham, Leofric," Beornred said, leaning forward, his big drinking horn between his hands, his head turned towards his leader. "What's next? Bath or Chippenham? Because I don't think we can do both. After this last escapade, the Danes will be like enraged hornets. They will buzz furiously everywhere…all the unlikely places as well as those they think they know of. Like looking for your lost sword in a laundry basket when you've searched everywhere else and can't think where to look next. They will come to Ford, and then we'll be finished!"

"Hmmm," the big Saxon war leader replied, looking at his second thoughtfully. "What you say makes sense. We need to give that some serious thought, but without too many pitchers with long handles nearby," he added, catching a glimpse of Gytha with her husband driving cattle up by the barn beyond the house. "Does Aelfrid know about her precious son and his wife?" he asked of Brioni, sitting upright on the bench.

"No! Not a suspicion. Eadwine and Alfweald?" she replied tersely.

"No! They don't much like him, but he is still family, and the thought that he might be trying to betray them all has not even crossed their minds. What will happen when they find out does not bear thinking of. They will be appalled and mortally ashamed as well," he said, rolling his gold-rimmed horn between his hands, as he looked across the trackway and up to the thick woods beyond. "And if Bath is to be the last we do after all, then we must lay plans to move everything, and everyone, from here to Battlesbury Rings at the same time.

"They all will need to leave here the same time we leave for Bath…be on their way before news reaches Guthrum of what has happened to his men at Bath. When the Danes get here, they must find nothing but the buildings to destroy. And destroy them they will, in some order! But houses can be replaced and barns and granaries rebuilt. The people are a different matter. We have lost enough young Saxons to those barbarians as it is. I do not intend to make them a gift of any more.

"So, one more big raid, then off to Warminster. We will need to move the people from there up to the rings, as their ancestors did long ago before the Romans came. Rebuild the fortifications, then we can really set to and gather an army for our 'King of the Marshes'."

"Is that the plan, my Lord?" Beornred asked of him, his eyes on his Lord's.

"Yes, but that is only an outline. We need a proper meeting at Slaughterford to perfect it…and a decision about our two cuckoos. If we are to

412

do Bath then it might be good for the enemy to think we are out for Swindon instead, where they have a small fortress and garrison. One more message, and wrong-foot them completely."

"Destroy Bath and slip out from under their noses at the same time," Brioni said. "If that doesn't put a burr under Oscytel's saddle after that, then nothing will. I like that!" and she clapped her hands as the men around her laughed at the thought of tricking the enemy so successfully.

"Right! We must go in and eat. Aelfrid and her ladies have laid on a real spread for us all. First light tomorrow we will ride over to Slaughterford with Raedwald and Cadoc and thrash this thing out properly. Then we can get moving. I want to be gone from here by the end of this month. Spring is coming, then Easter and the King's muster and we need to be settled in the Rings before that." And standing up, he swept them all before him into the house place, Brioni beside him at the last, her head high, her arm around his waist.

Who could not love so splendid a Lord, who held so many good men under his hand, who had such plans in his head...and the means to carry them out. How her father and brother would have liked this man, and her mother too, and her eyes suddenly sparkled with tears. They were gone, but she carried their blood in her veins, and dashing her tears away with her fingers, she smiled and walked in beside her lord as proud as any peacock.

*

*U*p by the barn and haystacks Cuthbert and Gytha were moving cattle in the late sunshine, and seeing to the little bull calf and its mother that Leofric had brought in with his men the previous month. With winter almost over and spring in the air at last they were all boisterous, the little one especially so, kicking up his heels and tossing his head, his black nose wet and his great dark eyes lustrous in the way that cattle have, with long lashes and a tufted forehead.

"I don't understand it!" Gytha said, giving one of the heifers a hearty whack on her broad hindquarters to move her on. "This is the second message I have sent in to Chippenham, yet nothing has happened. I told them what was going to happen, and where to come. I signed with your name so they would believe it all the better. And nothing! I just don't understand it!"

"Perhaps Godric was not able to deliver them?"

"Don't be so feeble, husband!" she snapped at him, hitting out at another beast that was reluctant to move. "He never said there had been a problem when I went to his stall the other week with the message about Malmesbury

413

and Melksham, and where to find Leofric and his men. Now look at them down there," she snarled, pausing to look at the big Saxon war-leader and his commanders lounging beside the house place with their drinking horns, Brioni beside them. "They are full of their success, when they should be moaning their losses. And that Brioni of Foxley? Look at her, the cheap hussy, for all she is the Lady of Foxley Manor! How dare she dress like the men, cut her hair and carry on as if she were one of them. It is wicked and shameful," she went on, filled with jealousy and spite.

"No less wicked and shameful than what we are doing, Gytha," Cuthbert replied sharply. "They at least are fighting an enemy that has ruined this country for years. We are planning the destruction of my family."

"Don't be so weak, Cuthbert," she snarled, rounding on him. "This was your idea, remember? You came to me for help as to how to make your position in Ford secure, more 'worthy' was the word you used. You have hated your father and brother for years. He's the one you so wish to supplant, that Alfweald, and your father, who never gives you the time of day.

"Your mother is the only one you really care about...and being 'Thane of Ford'. And that you cannot be as long as your father and brother are still alive. So, don't go soft on me now, not when we are about to succeed in all our dreams. Land, money and power. It's what the Danes want, and what we want also!"

"So why haven't those heathen bastards swept through here like a dose of black elder, and swept these Saxon bandits away?"

"*I don't know!*" she exclaimed, exasperated, striking out at a lazy heifer with her stick. "That's what I was asking a few minutes ago. And the only thing you could offer me was: 'perhaps he was unable to deliver them.' I wonder now whether he even tried to find that guard commander, that Bjorn Eriksson!"

"Why would he be so treacherous as to let you believe he would put such dangerous information into Viking hands, and then deliberately fail to do so?" Cuthbert rounded on her tersely. And as a sudden thought crossed his mind he looked at her from beneath his eyebrows. "Unless he was meeting with you for his own ends, Gytha. Isn't he the man you were going to marry until your father got into trouble? Our gold for your father's tanning and furs, with you as the glue, as I remember. Not Godric's shoes."

Then, as stray thought turned to swift realization, he leapt at her with upraised hand before she could reply, his eyes blazing: "By St Michael and his Angels," he swore, slapping her across her face. "You little *whore!* That's what all this is about. You are whoring yourself for that bastard's pleasure. No wonder nothing has happened!" he shouted, shaking his fists at her, as she

414

cowered away from him. "He has got you right where he wants you! Why bother with the Vikings when he has our silver in his fat pockets, and you to rut with. He must be laughing all over his rotten face" and seeing her go red at his words he shouted: "*You bitch!* You are cuckolding me with that bloody cobbler!" and he hit her again with the flat of his hand before she could protect herself, knocking her to the muddied ground, sending her stick flying, while he grabbed her hair and dragged her through the mud to the barn, kicking her feet from underneath her every time she tried to stand up; all the time shouting and roaring his anger to the wind and cattle.

"Stop, Cuthbert! *Stop!*" she shrieked at him as he hit her again, each wild blow sending her head flying. "Stop! You are wrong! *Wrong!*" she cried out, tears and bloodied mucus streaming from her eyes and nostrils. "I never did anything like that. *Never!* There has been no man in my bed save you. I swear it, upon my life," she cried out then on her knees, "*I swear it!* Please stop hitting me," she begged him. "I am no whore but a true and honest wife. As God is my witness," she implored him, grasping his ankle and putting her head on his foot, the blood from her nose streaking her face. "I have never cuckolded you, Cuthbert. No man but you has ever touched me. I swear it!" and she lifted her tear-puffed face to his, her eyes wide as a deer's, terrified for her life as she looked into Cuthbert's eyes, now harder than she had ever seen them, his mouth a grim line, his hand on his seaxe...and knew that she was only a thread away from sudden death.

"You swear it, Gytha. On pain of your immortal soul," he ground out to her, his light voice now dark, with gravel in it. "No man but I has ever touched you? This Godric is nothing to you? Nothing! You have not dishonoured me in the eyes of the world?"

"I swear it, Cuthbert," she said then, still on her knees, wiping her face with the back of her hand and looking up at him, her face smeared with blood. "On my life before God, Godric is nothing to me. You are no cuckold. No-one can make the sign of horns at you. *I promise you!*" And she gasped with relief as she saw the anger rush out of him, and rose swiftly to put her arms round him, and hold him to her breast, her face throbbing where he had hit her, her eyes wide open and tilted to the sky as she heard him say: " Sweet God, I was so angry, Gytha. I love you so much I could not bear to think of you with another man. I believe you. I believe you. Forgive me," he implored her. "I was so angry with you. Forgive me!" And he kissed her neck as he spoke, and held her close.

Her head against his, her whole body panting, she exulted that she had calmed the beast in him so easily; knowing how much he loved her, how much

415

he would 'search the forest' for her happiness. Even to sacrificing his family for her smiles.

The pathetic fool, she had his measure now.

But if he tried to beat her again she would be ready for him with a long bladed knife of her own. Then she smiled. She would not need a knife. She had the Danes to use against him instead. When they had finished with them all at Ford she, as their friend, would be the only one left. As the rightly married wife in the family, she would inherit everything. And whoever ruled in Wessex when the wars were over, Dane or Saxon, she would be wealthy two times over for her father had no sons to follow him. She was his sole heir too, and clasping her husband to her, her hands across his back, she kissed his neck too and looked askance at the sky above, now darkening as the sun passed over the hills.

But maybe Cuthbert was right? Maybe Godric's lust for her was all that this was about, and he had just thrown the messages away! It did not cross her little venal mind that Godric might be a true Saxon believer in the King of Wessex. That he might have double-crossed her for the lust he felt for her she could understand, after all that was what had drawn them together again in the first place...but that he might have used a rush of carnal desire to cloak his patriotic duty was beyond her understanding.

However, if there was one thing to come out of all of this it was that she utterly despised, and hated, her husband. Not only that but she was also no longer certain of relying on Godric either. And if that was the case, the only way of being sure of getting a message through to Guthrum was to deliver it herself. And that she could not do without Cuthbert's help, for with his father's face turned away from him the only other person with the power to authorise a visit to Chippenham was Aelfrid, Cuthbert's mother, who so doted on her youngest son that she would move heaven and earth to assist him, even if in doing so she earned her husband's wrath.

So, if Godric could dissemble to fool her...then for certain she could dissemble to fool her husband, and everyone else as well if necessary, she thought, putting her hands up to her face where Cuthbert had struck her. She must be sure to wash her face in the stream before entering the house place. No-one must know of the dreadful row they'd had. And with that firmly in her heart and mind she followed him down off the field.

Like black cock on the lecking ground, they had fought together, all furious beaks and ruffled feathers. Now with that settled, each hiding the wounds the other had inflicted, they walked back to the homestead to join the others in the victory feast that Aelfrid had provided. Cuthbert to renew his love

416

for the woman he had married, Gytha to plan his downfall and his family's utter ruin.

## Chapter Fifty Four

*L*ater that night, when all the feasting was done and Leofric's command had spilt up and gone to their billets in Slaughterford and elsewhere in Ford, Beornred staying in the hall, he and Brioni lay together in their bed chamber sated from their love making, each working out on the other the passions raised from fighting face to face with a brutal enemy. The fierce give and take of sword, spear and battle axe, the fear of death, the excitement of the kill extinguished in a similar burst of wild love-making as each gave to the other all their bodies had to give, until they climaxed together with a shout of exultation that left them both limp and drained of energy.

"Oh, God, Leofric, I do love you!" Brioni exclaimed softly as she panted in his arms, her heart fluttering in her breast, her pulse slowing as she wrapped her arms and legs around him. "The priests never tell of this when they talk of 'love' such as ours as 'sin.' If this is 'sin' then give it to me as often as you can, I adore it!" and she laughed, a ripple of sound as light as a mountain stream that he loved to hear.

"The priests know nothing of real human love, my darling. Their hearts and minds are filled with the higher things of life, of God, the Christ child and the Holy Spirit. The lives of men and women like you and me pass them by, unless they are perceived as touched by God. And you, my darling, are very much touched by God," he went on kissing her. "For I only have to see you to want you.

"I cannot keep my hands from touching you, caressing you, holding you in my arms and loving you to extinction. You put such fire in my blood that it is all I can do to stop myself taking you there and then. You are the eternal temptress, you leave me panting for more," he added, kissing her deeply..."But not now, you little devil," he said moving her hand from his manhood with a chuckle. "Later, I promise you. Right now I want to talk with you about Bath!"

"Oh, Leofric. Not now. I want you so much too. Why don't you plunder me again first and then talk about Bath!" she exclaimed softly, putting her hand back onto him, feeling him stir even as she spoke.

"No, my darling, later, if you still want to after I have told you what's in my mind."

"Oh no, my Lord," she said with a groan, letting him go. "That does not sound good," and she sat up in their bed and leaned against the pillows facing him, her breasts bare to his touch, her face suddenly concentrated on his eyes as she looked at him and waited for him to speak. "Tell me, Leofric. What about Bath?"

"I am not taking you with me."

"*What?*" she almost shrieked at him. "After all I went through at Malmesbury, I am not to go with you to Bath? What maggot has eaten into your brain, Leofric, to deny me this chance to prove myself in front of you? You take all my men and leave me behind. That is wrong, my Lord. Plain wrong!" And she stormed off the bed, to stand naked before the big iron burner that heated their room.

"Come back to bed and listen to what I have to say, before you catch your death," he said to her with a smile. "It is still cold out there, and you have given me no chance to explain my decision before you have flown up into the boughs like a screaming jay bird. Now come back, Brioni, for I have a job for you that only you can carry out that is more important to me than having you in my battle line."

"And what is that?" she queried sulkily, turning then to face him, her arms crossed beneath her breasts, still angry but interested in what job it was he had in mind for her that could possibly be more important than standing beside him and Beornred, Trausti, Cadoc and all the others. With a frown across her forehead she turned and stalked back to where he was sitting upright in their bed, the heavy fur coverings flicked back to persuade her to hop back in beside him. "So," she said, flinging herself on the bed at last, "what job is this you have for me that could possibly make up for not being with you at Bath...you pirate!"

"Did you watch those two 'cuckoos' of ours today?"

"When they came in to join in with Aelfrid's feast?" she asked, puzzled.

"Yes! Did you notice anything?"

"They had obviously had a terrible row. Gytha's face was a mess, even though she had washed it, and bruised by the look of it. Seems Cuthbert had a go at her up by the barn, where I saw them both earlier checking the cattle; while we were relaxing by the house place. That's when you mentioned pitchers with long handles. Why?" she asked him her head on one side.

"I think he may have worked out why she has been so keen to go up to Biddestone at market time."

"Godric?"

418

"Yes, sweetheart. Doing with Godric exactly what we have been doing ourselves. What you found her up to the first time you and the others met him!"

"They must both have been wondering why nothing has happened here, I suppose," she said, coming close to him again. "He has put two and two together and made three out of it! Worked out that she has been cuckolding him, and tackled her about it. No wonder she looked so battered this evening. But she was also keen to be seen holding his hand and looking lovingly at him. She really is a precious piece. Do you think that she has worked out what Godric is really all about?"

"No! I don't think her mind is subtle enough for that. It runs on gold and silver, not love of her country. She will just think that Godric is out for what he can get of her. Silver for his coffers and a lively rough and tumble on the floor of his trading tent, no questions asked. But that makes her all the more dangerous, because she will also have learned not to trust him. And she certainly has no love for her husband, despite all that she has tried to show us tonight. And that brings me back to Bath."

"Now we come to it, Leofric," she grumped beside him. "You want me to play the 'Watcher' while you and your commando ruffle it at Bath!"

"Not nearly so simple, my Lady," he replied seriously, shifting his body to look down at her, now snuggled back beside him. "I am certain that we cannot stay here much longer. We have stung that bastard Oscytel really hard. Damaged his command structure, killed his crews, taken their booty and wrecked his reputation. His men are terrified of us. Before long he *will* come here, and he must find us gone. All of us. Everyone!

"Today is Monday and I aim to attack Bath in five days from today, on Saturday. We will leave here in three days, Thursday, and, my darling, we will not be coming back. So, between now and then the whole settlement must move out," he said to her, as she looked up at him open-mouthed with shock. "Men, women, children and all that they can take with them: cattle, sheep, pigs, geese, chickens, goats, dogs, cats, *everything!* From both settlements, Slaughterford and Ford, and I want you to organise and oversee it."

"*Me and whose army, Leofric?*" she gasped in horror. "I cannot do this on my own, and that column will need protection. If not from the Danes, then from masterless men, brigands, thieves and outlaws; anyone who fancies easy pickings. Not even I can do all of that."

"Nor shall you have to, my darling. I will give you all those who fought with you at Malmesbury, and they are some of the best I have. And you will also have those who have been wounded, at least a dozen more. Some of whom can certainly wield a sword or bow in your defence. I am relying on you completely, Brioni, to bring all those people safely to Warminster, to the Battlesbury Rings above the town by Sunday when, God willing, we will return to you from Bath…and to have moved the town's people up there as well."

"The townies also, Leofric!" she exclaimed, appalled. "How in God's name do I do that? They'll *never* want to leave their comfortable homes for a godforsaken camp on the top of Battlesbury Rings. They'll simply refuse!"

"Then, if necessary, you burn them out!" he replied grimly. "Threaten them, terrify them, even kill the real protestors if necessary. After we put his Bath garrison to the fire and the sword Oscytel will know exactly where to find us, and if they don't move, then Guthrum will destroy them anyway, be certain of it; for we will have the Black Jarl on our backs within days, and he will have no mercy on any Saxon he finds wandering free in that area. I have scouted the Rings. They have triple ramparts in places and there are two entrances through them that will need to be defended, with two huge cisterns on the top that can be fed both with rainwater and by hand, from water brought up from below the ramparts."

"Still there? After all this time?" she asked, astonished.

"No, collapsed, but with hard work and determination I am sure they can be rebuilt and made useable again. And water is a must for the whole community, both people and animals. For not only will you have those you are bringing with you, sweetheart, but also those up from the town, and from the surrounding area who will flood in once it is known we are properly established up there. You will need water parties every day."

"Dear God, Leofric! You are loading me with a vast responsibility that I am ill equipped to carry. How will I do all this without you to guide me?"

"You underestimate yourself, Brioni. You have proven warriors to help you, and you will have Aelfrid, Osburgh and her daughters to support you, and the two wives. Aelfrid will manage the local people from Ford and Slaughterford, she has been doing that for years. But you have been with the King, Brioni. You know how Alfred and Queen Ealhswitha would do things. You have witnessed the Court's removal from place to place. This will be no different…they must just do your will, not their own. And you will have Eadberht, Cadoc and Cenhelm and their men to help you. And I will give you Trausti, Jaenberht and Aldred as well," and she gasped.

"*No!* Do you mean it?" she asked astonished. "Trausti alone is worth his weight in gold. Together they would be invaluable. Will they do it, Leofric? Come with me instead of going to Bath?"

"They will do as I say, my darling!" he exclaimed gruffly. "Remember, 'No man says me nay.' Not in my army! But they will do it as much for your sake as for mine, I promise you. Your actions at Malmesbury impressed everyone. And there will be as much danger attached to your task as to anyone going with me up against the Bath garrison which is already large and well constituted. Attacking Bath will be no easy matter, believe me."

"Who goes with you, Leofric?" she asked, putting her arms round him.

"Everyone who can ride a horse and wield a sword, save those going with you. And that will include Cuthbert. He goes with his father and Alfweald. I want that young man under my eye. After his bust-up with Gytha this evening I trust him even less than before, if only because he will not sanction her visiting Godric again. That is for certain. Yet it is desperately important that we get another message through to Guthrum that it is Swindon that we intend to attack. So, after tonight, no mention of Bath at any time. Let them all think it is Swindon we intend to ravage, then with all the rest that will be going on around here what we are really doing will get lost."

"But what about Gytha?"

"Watch her like a hawk! She must not be allowed to leave this area for any reason until it is time to move the whole settlement out to Warminster."

"But the message, Leofric? If you intend to leave here in three days' time, what happens with the message?"

"You must write and take it to Godric on Wednesday in the usual way. After all, it is actually your handwriting that the Danes know, not Gytha's at all. You have transcribed every message as your own. Get that to Godric on Wednesday and it will reach Guthrum in time for him to move his troops out to reinforce Swindon, leaving Bath open to our assault in five days from now, on Saturday. That is why you must watch Gytha so sharply, my darling. Any hint that we are not planning to assault Swindon and all will be lost, and we cannot have the Danes descending on Ford until both settlements have been completely abandoned.

"She must not be allowed to leave. Keep her busy, God knows there will be enough to do here in the next few days for that, and when you leave put her in a cart, not on a horse. Who knows what she might choose to do on horseback once Cuthbert has left with us, and she is on her own? But Aelfrid must not know what she and her son have been up to. Not until we are all back from Bath which, with God's love, will be a week from now."

"And if she tries to leave...to escape?"

"Stop her!"

"Permanently?" she asked, her eyes shocked wide with his words.

"If necessary," he said grimly, his own like chips of ice. "Keep Cadoc beside you, and if she flees the settlement, and there is no other way, a swift shaft may be the only solution."

"You are sure, Leofric? You want her killed?"

"If she leaves with 'Bath' on her lips, not 'Swindon', and gets to Chippenham, which is possible, then we are finished.  For not only will Guthrum strengthen Bath beyond all things, but he will descend on you here like a thunderbolt, before anyone has left.  And that simply must not happen.  Better Gytha dies than that, my darling!"

"Very well, Leofric.  We shall watch her like hawks, I promise you.  How far from here to Warminster?"

"Thirty miles by track and roadway; maybe less if you are lucky with the weather.  Twenty as the crow flies, and you will have to stop somewhere for the night; I suggest Trowbridge.  There is good pasture land there and plenty of water from the Bliss that runs through the village.  From there it is just a short step to Westbury, Warminster and Battlesbury Rings."

"Have any of the men you are leaving me, been there?" she asked anxiously.

"Trausti has.  He, Beornred and Raedwald came with me a year ago and reviewed all these places.  We were looking for safe places to hole-up against the Danish incursion at that time, so he has some knowledge of the area.  Otherwise you will need to find local guides to help you, so take all the silver from the raids with you.  You will have need of it."

"That is good, Leofric," she said more brightly, "for my father's hoard is still with Hugo, and a good handful of silver can smooth many paths."

"Also, you must leave in staggered groups, sweetheart.  Beasts on foot the soonest, sheep and cattle together.  It will take several days to drive them, and that is with experienced drovers which you do not have; 'though you will have the shepherds and their dogs who will help all they can...so give yourself as much time as possible.  All the rest must go by sun-up on Thursday at the latest, by cart and on horseback: piglets, goats, chickens, geese and children, old and young, dogs and cats, and only what they can carry in their arms..."

"So, no cumbersome furniture, Leofric; loose horses on long reins and as much food, fodder and beer as we can take with us; we can water-up on the way.  That will be hard on everyone, especially the old folk who will want to take all their treasures with them."

"No, it will not be easy.  But you must be ruthless; these people have one chance of life and that must not be bogged down with moveables, no matter how precious.  But my men are biddable and used to taking orders.  You will need to delegate as much as you can to leave yourself free to sort out problems and make sure everything is moving."

"Won't the Danes be suspicious of so many people and animals moving about?" She asked him then, looking anxiously up at him.  "We will be quite a convoy."

"I don't think so. There are still displaced folk moving all over the place, and the Danes are not thickly spread everywhere. You are more likely to be challenged by stray parties of masterless men and outlaws."

"Like you were, you pirate!" she interrupted with a grin

"Just so, but you and your men will drive them off easily. Such men do not have the stomach for a stand-up fight. One sight of Trausti, Eadberht, Jaenberht and all the rest and they will be off like the rabid wolves they are."

"Just as well, for the column will be a long one and not easy to defend. Dear God, Leofric, but you have set me a labour that even Hercules would not find easy!"

"I know I leave you a mighty task," he said, looking down at her with a certain smile, "but this is what you were born to do. This is what your mother had to do whenever your father went to the wars. Manage everything at Foxley so it was still all there when he returned. Did your mother ever fail him?"

"No, she never did! Nor shall I fail you either," she added, looking at him steadily. "It will be done as you have outlined it. With Trausti, Eadberht, Cadoc and all the rest it will be done. My mother and our Lady Queen have taught me well, and so have you. Dear God, did I ever envisage this in my life as a Wolsfhead's doxy?" she asked him then, looking up at him with a pair of sparkling eyes. "War leader, spy-mistress and now a caravan driver. What else shall I be before all this is ended?"

"My lover and the queen of my heart," he answered with a grin. "Now come here, my most beautiful temptress," he ordered. "I promised you more and now it is time to deliver; so enough of this talk. Right now Bath, Gytha and the Danes may all go to the Devil for all I care; it is you I want…and I want you now!" And with a broad smile and enormous intent writ large across his face, already fiercely aroused, he wrapped his arms around her and kissed her; and with a deep sigh of pleasure she received him in the way only a woman can, arching her body as he entered her, her legs wrapped around him and her lips crushed beneath his own.

\*

*I*n their own bower Gytha and Cuthbert lay back to back with an ocean of cold blank space in between. He, with his mind full of murderous thoughts towards Godric, and his own family, in a potent mix of jealousy, hatred and ecstasy that saw him victorious, Thane of Ford and all that implied, with the lowly Godric dead at his feet and the lovely Gytha in glowing form by his side. And turning impulsively he reached his arms out to draw her to him more closely.

She lay there in the darkness beside him, her face bathed in witch hazel to draw out the bruises he had inflicted on her by the barn, her thoughts filled with anger, despair and a fierce determination to be freed from all of them: her husband, his family, Godric who had betrayed her, and the Saxons who had come so suddenly amongst them. Her feelings made her groan with ill suppressed fury. Somehow she would escape the suffocating net they had cast over her, get to Chippenham and throw all their lives to the Danes who would reward her with the lands and gold she so desired in gratitude for her disclosure. She would find the King, Guthrum, and throw herself on his mercy in return for the certain knowledge of where their enemies were and what they were planning to do.

As she felt Cuthbert's hands on her shoulders she shivered with revulsion, then turned on her back, her mouth a tight line and her eyes open to the rafters above their heads, and the flickering light from the flames in the hearth-pit in the centre of the hall. And she stiffened as she felt his hands pawing at her body...that he might have for the taking, but her heart and mind were her own.

*

*I*n the King's hall in Chippenham, the news of what had happened at Malmesbury and Melksham arrived with the evening meal.

Brought by a trembling servant to the King on the same great silver charger that had brought Brioni's message, with Captain Ránnulfr by his side, there had been a furious outbreak of rage and condemnation from Guthrum towards the Black Jarl of Helsing, especially when the wounded Viking captain had delivered her personal message of contempt, along with the hated foxhead symbol she had thrown at him.

"*I told you to strengthen your defences, Oscytel!*" the Viking King shouted, thundering on the table with his hand, the whole room stilled by his fury. "I ordered you to reinforce your men in those places. Yet you have defied me!"

"*Not so, my Lord King,*" the tall jarl shouted back in justified anger. "I sent more men to both places, and with renowned captains to lead them. And still it was not enough! The men we are up against are demons, with the helmets and faces of wild beasts. They come with hell hounds in their train, the very brutes of Ragnarok itself. They put fear into my men's hearts that turned them to water..."

"And turned maidens and boys into warriors," Guthrum raged at him. "*Isn't that so, Ránnulfr?*" he roared, turning sharply to the wounded captain who was still standing before the dais where he had delivered Brioni's message, his shoulder heavily bound. "Maidens and boys into dauntless warriors, yes? You were beaten by a girl, you thought was a boy!" he snarled, bitterly sarcastic, his eyes fixed on the man's face, now pale before his King's anger. "One of my foremost captains and leaders; known for his heavy hand and sharp sword, beaten by a silly girl?"

"Yes, my Lord King," Ránnulfr replied through gritted teeth, ashamed before all his comrades and appalled by the King's attack on him. "But this was no 'silly girl', my Lord King. She fought like a true warrior. But I had her measure, my Lord, and would have slain her had an arrow not pierced my shoulder and felled me to the ground."

"*Bah!* No arrow would have stopped me, *Captain!*" Guthrum bellowed at him, leaping to his feet, flourishing his great war axe in his hand, his huge form dominating the whole room with his fury. "I would have split her in two, from chin to navel," he shouted at the Viking leader, as Ránnulfr took a step backwards in sudden fear of his life. "Then torn the arrow from my shoulder and stabbed her heart with it! You are no man for me, Captain," he shouted, and dismissed him with a wave of his hand that left the young Viking war-leader seething.

White-faced before all his peers, he was determined, somehow, that he would be revenged on the Lady Brioni of Foxley if it was the last thing he did. He had men he could use, trained professionals he could call on at a moment's notice; all Danes who had worked with him before. He would watch and wait. You never knew from what hole a rat might break. He would watch and wait and bide his time, then be the pouncing wolf his name recalled and drag this Saxon shield–maiden before the Danish King and thus regain his honour.

With those thoughts in mind he left the hall while Guthrum turned, enraged, to the tall war leader sitting by his side and sneered: "As for you, Oscytel, I warned you at Wareham. No more Blood Eagles, you bastard. *No more!* And now this message from this Brioni of Foxley, whose father you brutalised. I told you when that last message came. This is their God's doing. We fight both the Saxons and their God, and we are losing! *Losing, you bastard!* I will not have it.

"I want these Saxons tracked down and every one of them slain and their leaders crucified as their Christ was crucified…and we will see whose God is the strongest. *Yes?*" he roared out, shaking his weapons at them all.

"*Yes, my Lord King!*" they all shouted back, banging their fists and drinking pots on the tables.

"By Odin, no more sweetness and light towards these people. I want their priests and their bishops enslaved before me, their churches burned and their monasteries razed to the ground. *By death I swear this!* And you, Oscytel, will deal with this outrage to my warriors. Find these Saxon scum who have belittled you, and wipe them out. But not the girl, this Lady Brioni of Foxley. She is my meat, and I alone will determine her fate!

"Wessex I will have despite all that her King might do or say…their precious Alfred who lurks amongst the marshes of the Sommerseatas, who pricks my hide with his attacks and wild tactics. Come the spring, when the sea lanes open and our brothers can join us from Frankland, we will rise up and crush him once and for all. One glorious battle that will ring from end to end of the land, and we will win all that our hearts most desire."

And standing before all his men, legs apart and arms upraised with his war axe in his left hand and his sword in his right, he roared the Viking battle cry that all men knew from the magic raven banner, stitched in a single night by the daughters of Ragnar Lodbrok: *"Land Ravager! Land Ravager!"* And all his men responded, baying like wolves, roaring back and stamping their feet: *"Land Ravager! Land Ravager!"*

# Chapter Fifty Five

**R**ising at first light, with the cocks crowing the new day that again promised to be clear and warm, with a faint blush from behind the hills and the moon a pale circle of white light, Brioni and Leofric were swiftly dressed in their usual work clothes and heavy boots. Bustling into the main hall of the building they kicked fresh life into the fire and threw on more fuel from the huge wicker box near the door, while Aelfrid's hall servants, still rubbed their eyes and looked for the buckets to relieve themselves.

"*Up! Up! All of you!*" Leofric roared through the house. "Eadwine, Aelfrid, Beornred, to me, to me! Trausti, Cadoc...Swindon in five days, and not a moment to lose. *Ho the House!* Bring mulled ale and bannocks to the table, fresh cheese and cold bacon, hard eggs and smoked meat. A meeting of all leaders swiftly round the fire. The day is alive and waiting to be breathed. So, up, all of you! Before I come and throw you out of bed myself!"

It was such a summons as could not to be ignored, and before long all those he had called for were appearing, blurry-eyed and still stuffing their shirts and tops into their trousers, pulling on kirtles, long tunics and assorted footwear. Aelfrid's servants, roused to action by his shouts, scuttled feverishly about the place to find benches and erect trestles, while the kitchens, galvanised into action by his fierce energy, rushed to fulfil his orders. Striding outside, Leofric shouted for his guards to send for Raedwald, Finnar and Eadberht in Slaughterford, a swift half hour's ride away from them, and the elders from that settlement.

There was much to do, and he had no intention of wasting a moment's more time than was necessary.

*

**B**y the third hour, with the family fed and the sun flushing up crimson and gold in a sky of unbroken blue, the big room in the centre of the house was filled with Leofric's leaders. His own commanders being present, and the heads of families in both Ford and Slaughterford, Eadwine having summoned them at the same time, knowing already what was in the wind. And with the men came their women, curious, anxious, excited and afraid, headed by Aelfrid and Osburgh who had discussed between them what must happen now, and with them Osburgh's daughters and the two young wives, Ethelinda and Gytha.

The whole company was abuzz with speculation, for no such gathering had been called before. So everyone wanted to know what was happening, especially as once all those who had been called in had arrived, Leofric put a strong guard on every door out of the house place with strict orders that no-one was to be allowed out unless accompanied by one of his war leaders.

Crammed in together, most standing, the elders seated round the fire, they were a very mixed group. Dressed in muted greens and browns with a sprinkling of blue and russet amongst them, some in scuffed leathers others in rough woollens; the men with hats and hoods, the women with their long hair plaited and coiled on their heads. Some wore simple bonnets, some linen wimples and others just as they had risen, their long plaits hanging to their waists with big bows of coloured ribbons at each twisted end. All jostled for a sight of Leofric who had climbed on two benches placed side by side to address them, there being no dais in the building. Trausti and Beornred stood on one side of him and Eadwine on his other, all three men on the ground, their big hands ready to steady their Lord should he need it.

And with that the meeting started with Leofric telling all those assembled that the next planned assault on Swindon would be the very last and then, to gasps of consternation and shock, he told the people from both settlements that every man, woman and child, and all their beasts, must prepare to leave their homes and move to the ancient hillfort above Warminster, known as 'Battlesbury Rings', as without doubt Guthrum's Danes would come and destroy everything they held most dear.

For almost a month they had been kept safe from Guthrum and Oscytel's searchers, he told them, but such protection could no longer be relied on. The next raid on Swindon would see the enemy scouring all the nearest places that so far they had ignored.

"So far the enemy have been pleased to believe that no Saxon warband would dare to operate so close to the heart of Danish power in Chippenham," he told them clearly. "They have concentrated their energies to the north and east of Ford, into ruined Mercia around Tetbury and the lands around Oxford and the Thames valley. There they have been assured is where their enemies lie up and hide themselves, and around Marlborough and beyond, in the Vale of the White Horse of Uffington. Not so close to home as Biddestone and Ford, just five miles or so from Guthrum's very hall in Chippenham!" And he laughed.

"How do you know this, my Lord?" a grizzled family leader from Slaughterford called out to him from the back of the hall.

"Aye, my Lord Leofric," called out another. "How do you have such knowledge? My family have lived here for generations. Why should we move now, because you say so?"

"Because a very brave man whom I have known for many years, who is as close to Guthrum and the Lord Oscytel as Eadwine is to me now, says so. He stands in Guthrum's very shadow, and what he says has always been good. Only now does he deceive this Danish king. One false move and he is a dead man."

"And who is this mystery man?" Cuthbert shouted from his place, close to where his mother was seated by the fire. "Why should we believe you who have come amongst us from nowhere, and now seek to rule our lives?"

Eadwine, furious with his youngest son for his outburst, made to reach him and pull him down, only for Leofric to check him.

"No! Let this young rooster crow," he shouted out, pointing to where Cuthbert was standing, his face red at Leofric's words, trying to avoid his brother who had also made a fierce move towards him. "He will know soon enough, though I do not give that man's name now to anyone."

"How will I know?" Cuthbert shouted back, while all men watched, amazed at his brusque attitude before his father.

"Because you will be coming with my attack force to Swindon when we leave here in three days' time," Leofric replied sharply, his eyes fierce, his manner lethal. "And then, when we are all safe in Battlesbury Rings, I will tell you!"

"I am to go with you?" Cuthbert asked, appalled, his face white with shock.

"Yes, Cuthbert of Ford, it is time you took a stand beside your brother," Leofric replied pitilessly, signalling Eadwine to be silent with the flat of his hand. "Alfweald and your father, whose swords have been ever hot for the King, have played their part already while you have sat at home and minded the cattle and the bees. Now it is time you were blooded too, and fleshed the sword you were given last year. So, you battle-virgin," Leofric said, bending towards where the young man almost cowered beside his mother, her face pale with dismay, "it is time your apron-strings were cut...so you come with us on Thursday, along with every able-bodied man who can wield a sword and ride a horse who is not needed to help and guard the travellers."

"But why must we leave now, my Lord Leofric?" another Saxon elder asked, his wide face anxious, as Cuthbert slumped away from Leofric's fierce gaze, his mind in a turmoil at the very thought of going with Leofric on the coming raid. "My sheep are due to lamb, to move them now will be disastrous."

"Better to move them now, Cedric," Eadwine replied calmly, raising his voice so all might hear, "and save what you can, than have them all butchered by the Danes when they sweep through here four days from now."

"Why?" called out another. "We have lain here safe this past forty days or so. Why should we not be safe for longer?"

"Because, come the evening in three days' time, our man in Chippenham will tell the King about Ford," Leofric said then, to gasps of horror. "He must do that to survive so close to the Danish King and his lords..."

"Why?" interrupted another man, loudly, banging his leather hat across his knees in a rage, his large wife beside him, her face drawn and anxious. "Why must he betray us to the Danes?"

"*Because he serves our King, Alfred!*" Leofric roared at him. "Because his knowledge of what the enemy are up to is vital for the King on Athelney. He placed this man where he is, and I will not undo what my King has stitched so carefully together."

"I do not understand," the same man shouted out, shaking his hat in the air, his face red with anger. "Why must we be sacrificed to save the King? What has Alfred ever done for us?"

"You always were a cussed bastard, Ethelred," Eadwine answered him tersely from Leofric's shoulder. "Always the first to complain, always the first to demand that to which you have no right. Stay here then, when we have all gone," he shouted down at him, leaping up beside Leofric on the benches. "You are a miserable cur of a man whom no-one will miss. Stay here, proud fool, and see how much shift the Danes give you when they arrive, for we will all be gone and there will be none to defend you save yourself!"

"What of me and the bairns?" his wife shouted back, horrified by what her husband had said, turning on him with a clenched fist which was meaty to say the least as she was no small woman, thumping his shoulder so he reeled beside her, appalled by her vicious anger in so public a place, while all around them cheered and called her on.

"*You dolt!*" she raged at him, knocking him silly at every shout. "You moaner! How dare you disparage our King. I disown you. We are yours to command, my Lord Leofric," she shouted, turning towards the giant Saxon on the benches. "No matter what this *Nithing* may say to you!"

"You cannot call me that!" her husband railed at her, holding his arms up to protect himself.

"*No, Ethelred!*" Eadwine thundered down at him, from beside Leofric. "Mildrythe cannot cast you out...*but I can!* Silence, you fool, or what

430

Mildrythe has started I will finish. Though I am not Thane of Ford, I am nevertheless your given Lord. You hold your land of me. And where I go, go you also without question...or you will stay behind and face Guthrum in all his fury. And if *you* are so stupid as not to understand why the King's man must give true information to Guthrum to remain safe from suspicion, while Alfred bides his time in Athelney...be assured that *I am not!*" he exclaimed fiercely. "I can see why it is necessary for both settlements to be abandoned, and I commend the Lord Leofric's plan to all of you!" he roared out to all those assembled there.

"So all of this abandonment is about Alfred?" Another of Eadwine's men called out, tall and rangy, with powerful arms and shoulders.

"Yes! I said so when first we arrived here a month ago," Leofric replied. "Does that matter to you?"

"Yes. I am the King's man, and always have been."

"Berhtulf is right!" shouted another, raising his arms above his head. "Alfred is our King, of the right line of Cerdic. I fought with him at Ashdown in '71, when his brother was still King. That Ethelred is a dolt indeed and always was one. The Danes are welcome to him. Alfred is our rightful King, not this brigand Danish Lord, this King Guthrum, who has seized Chippenham and whose men are killing all who defy them. I stand for Alfred, as all good Saxons must," and he looked round at the packed people around him while they all cheered and stamped their feet.

"So, are you all agreed that this place must be abandoned and everyone in it long gone?

"Aye! *We are agreed!*" came the shouted reply from most people, some silent, many anxious, but all determined to see it through.

"I cannot force you to leave," Leofric said then calmly, when the noise had fallen away to a murmur. "But any of you who choose to stay, be advised that you will face the Danes alone in all their battle-fury.

"Four times we have destroyed their forces, burned their camps and barracks, stolen their silver and humiliated them. Box, Bradford on Avon, Melksham, Malmesbury...all have been attacked and their garrisons put to the fire and the sword. See," he added, throwing the lids back of two great coffers of coins that his men had brought in, "here is the wealth of Wessex that the Heathen men have stolen," and he bent and picked up a double handful of coins that he allowed to pour through his fingers in a cascade of chinking silver that glittered in the leaping flames, the people crowding forward to watch, open-mouthed at such amazing riches, the likes of which none had ever seen before. "And all who come with me shall have a share of it to help re-build what the

431

Danes will destroy and set on fire," and a collective sigh of pleasure and relief rushed round the hall.

"Anyone they find here will be butchered, flayed and split apart. These are Vikings of the Great Army, and Oscytel's Jomsvikings are the very worst of them all. Five boatloads of his sea wolves we have destroyed since we came here a month ago. Five whole crews and their leaders, if not more, for which a mere handful of my men have lost their lives. They will come here filled with bitter rage, so imagine how they will feel towards any they may find here when all else has been abandoned."

"It will be bloody murder!"

"I saw what they did in Chippenham…"

"And elsewhere!"

"And that will be nothing to what they will do here!"

"*Save us, Lord Leofric! Save us!*"

"Very well," he called out to them, as the shouting died away again. "I hear you. Is that the desire of all of you? Are you agreed now that we must move? *Everyone?*"

And with one voice they all shouted, and hammered their booted feet on the floor: "*Aye, Lord, aye! We are agreed!*"

"Then so be it, but there is much to do. All beasts must leave today, the sheep, cattle and oxen, with two carts for any lambs that may be dropped, and fodder for all, especially the dogs, and another for all the belongings of those who travel with them. Take warm clothes, for the nights are still chill, and waterproofs where possible; good footwear and no more extras than you can carry in both hands. Eadwine will appoint you. And a good company of my men will escort you. Everyone else must be gone before sun-up on Thursday."

And the tall Ford homesteader duly called out a flurry of names, and pointed to all others who flung up their hands and offered their immediate help in the matter, while Leofric looked round the room for Gytha. Already in swift conversation with Cuthbert, and his mother, she was animated about something to which Aelfrid was already nodding her head, and Leofric gritted his teeth, his frown formidable as he watched them all, before stretching his shoulders and speaking again.

"On Thursday, my men and I will leave for Swindon before cock crow…while all of you must have left from here by the third hour, before the sun is above the hills," and there was a groan of dismay because he would not be with them. "But I leave you with the Lady Brioni of Foxley and her whole war group," he shouted out, calling Brioni up beside him and Eadwine, Bran and Utha by her side. "They are some of my best men, with one of my most successful commanders in support, Trausti Longsword, whom I would trust with my life.

"And with her go all our wounded, many of whom can now fight as well as most of you. Be assured that the Lady Brioni is the light of my life," he said, putting his arm around her briefly. "She carries my word amongst you all as if I was there beside her. She has travelled with the King and Queen Ealhswitha in better times, and has their love as much for herself as for her father, the Thane of Foxley, who was one of Alfred's closest advisers. Serve her as you would serve me and you will be serving the King.

"Now, I have arranged beer for all this morning. That will be served outside, not least because it will be a fine day today and there is less space in here than a flea could find on a dog's back. So, this meeting is over. Eadwine and Alfweald will move amongst you and appoint you your jobs. But the sheep, cattle and oxen must move off today with their dogs, their shepherds and their drovers," and with a clap of his hands he shouted: *"So let's be about it!"*

And with that the whole meeting broke up, everyone flooding out of the building to fill the garth outside with their noisy chatter and concerns. Many were excited, others appalled by the task that Leofric had set them. And amongst them Aelfrid and Osburgh now moved with all their helpers, great jugs of barley beer and malted ale in their hands, every man and woman having brought their own drinking bowls and horns with them.

# Chapter Fifty Six

"**W**ell how did that go?" Leofric asked his own command group later, as everyone broke up to go about their own business, his gold-rimmed drinking horn in his hand. Behind him those whom Eadwine had noted, and who had offered their help in droving, were already in one large group, waving their hands and laughing over the job they had taken on; their wives in another circle shaking their heads over all that must be done by the time it came for their husbands to leave.

"Well enough, my Lord," Beornred said in his deep voice. "At least they seem cheerful enough," he said with a grin and nod of his head over his shoulder. "Though there was a moment when I thought there might be a riot over that Ethelred, but his wife had him well under command," he laughed, slapping his thighs. "She had him banged to rights in no time! Not even I would want a clip from her hand. Did you see the size of her? Massive! Her arm was almost as thick as your leg, Leofric. No wonder he reeled about like a drunken sailor."

"Wish you hadn't mentioned Grimnir," Brioni said quietly. "I know you didn't mention him by name, but if such information ever reached Guthrum his life could be in deadly danger, for Oscytel would leave no stone unturned to disclose such a traitor."

"I hadn't meant to. But so many were questioning my advice that I felt I had to say something," he replied, looking anxious. "I can only hope that it will have passed most by."

"And then there was that Cuthbert," Trausti growled. "His father would have struck him down if you hadn't stopped him, the treacherous little cur!"

"But I did stop him," Leofric said with a loud snort. "And it gave me great pleasure to tell the little shit, in front of everyone, that he was coming with us."

"Did his father know beforehand?" Brioni asked him, her hand on his arm.

"Yes...but not his mother. Did you see how shocked she was afterwards, poor woman? And in swift talk with that Gytha. Do you know what they were agreeing to so busily?" he asked her, looking grim-faced into her eyes.

"No, but I will find out. Ethelinda will tell me, she is no friend to Gytha but has become a bosom friend to me over the past few weeks. She's a really lovely girl. If she knows, she will tell me for certain. And since her last trip to visit Godric's stall, Rowena has not been such a good companion to Gytha either, so I am sure, one way or another, that I will find out. How about Eadwine? Is he still on side as much as before?"

"Yes, but shaken by the turn events have taken since we arrived. He wasn't expecting life to become so interesting! Moving both settlements out was not on his list of things to do. Now, however, he can see that there is no other way that his people's way of life can be preserved. We just have to make sure that Alfred wins this bloody war, and they can all move back again and re-build."

"The coffers of silver were a brilliant move, my Lord," Trausti said with a grin. "You made even me salivate when I saw you pouring all those coins through your fingers. Where did that come from?"

"From the Lady Brioni," he said, bowing towards her slightly with a broad smile. "She thought it might help to convince all our good solid Saxon homesteaders to go along with us, if they were promised a share to help them re-build what Guthrum and his merry men will tear in pieces when they get here!"

"And she was right," Eadwine said, coming up to them. "That really was the end of the reel; the last dance of the night. They could all see that whatever happened, as long as they were alive they could rebuild, and all they would have suffered would be a temporary setback. But for that to be achieved the Danes must be defeated, and if that means surrendering their homes, then they would rather do that than have their lives torn out of them for nothing.

"This way there is at least a chance of success, and your presence among them and the success you have had against the enemy has shown them that the Danes can be beaten. Even the best of them. And if that is what a few hundred men can do...then think what thousands of angry Saxons can do when properly led in battle!"

Leofric laughed and banged the rangy steader on his back. "That is music to my ears, Eadwine, truly. It is also what Alfred is trying to do for all Wessex. To show, by not giving up and continuing to fight these bastards in every way he can, that they are not invincible. That the Great Army that came here in '65, whom we thrashed in '71 and drove out of Wareham and Exeter can be beaten, despite Reading and the year of battles, and what happened at Chippenham in January. The enemy here are no longer the 'Great Army' that came across with Ivar the Boneless, Halfdan and Ubbi...just an army of weary Vikings no further forward in Wessex now than they were thirteen years ago! That is what this has all been about, wearing the bastards down. But what about you and Aelfrid?"

"That was a nasty shock you gave her in there, my friend. And I could have knocked that young idiot into next week for what he said. But she has known it was coming, and despite all the weeping she will be there to see him off on Thursday like a good Saxon mother should do when her son goes forth on his first campaign. She and I are alright, I assure you.

"As for Cuthbert, he will be fine once he is away from his mother, and his wife. I wish now I had never arranged that marriage. She unsettles everyone, that Gytha, and the two of them are barely on talking terms at the moment. God knows what has happened. But she came in looking terribly battered the other evening and not even Aelfrid can get anything out of either of them. So taking him off on Thursday will be a great boon to all of us!"

And with a cheery wave he strode away to see to the business of getting all the beasts rounded up from field and byre ready for their drovers to set them moving as soon as possible. With shouts and cries others rushed to harness up the three carts that Leofric had ordered to be prepared, two tilts and one great wain, while their wives and families went home to seek out all their men would need to take with them for such a trip: clothes, boots, tools, weapons, tinder boxes, food, waterskins and beer.

Leofric and his close command, with Brioni beside them, watched as Ford literally began to shake itself apart. It was as if a great stick had been thrust into an ant's nest and been stirred briskly round. From ordered life, where nothing much untoward happened from day to day, they had gone to frenetic activity with people rushing hither and thither in the warm February sunshine, everyone carrying something in their arms from boots and clothes to harness leather and spare horse shoes.

"So what happens when he and Aelfrid find out what their precious son has really been up to," Trausti asked Leofric, watching a reluctant horse being backed into the shafts of a large tilt cart.

"God knows!" Leofric replied with a broad shrug of his shoulders. "Maybe he will be slain in the coming attack," he added, careful not to mention Bath in his comment. "That would solve everything for them. His death fighting they could accept. Denouncing him before all the people would be just horrific. It would break the family apart.

"Eadwine would never be able to lift his head again, and Aelfrid would blame everyone for her son's treachery except the boy himself. Like murderers, they are always 'lovely boys' to their mothers who can see no evil in them even when it is open before their very eyes! And as for Gytha, whose very plot this truly is, I would hang her from the nearest tree, or sell her to a passing pirate for a handful of silver. It is what she deserves," and he sighed deeply as he watched her beneath beetling brows, his eyes hard and unforgiving, as she walked, laughing, towards the house place with Rowena and Ethelinda by her side.

"You could of course do nothing," Brioni said quietly, putting her arms around his waist. "Just wait and see how this all turns out. If the Danes are thrashed, as we all hope and believe, Oscytel is killed and Alfred regains his throne, all their plans will have been completely dashed and saying anything may have no meaning...except as a terrible warning for the future."

"The Lady Brioni is right," Beornred cut in, throwing his arm around Leofric's shoulders. "Do not be overburdened by all this, my Lord. We will take the young man off with us to tickle the Danes in our next assault, and leave the girl to be watched by your lady, Trausti, Eadberht and all the others.

"Tomorrow Cadoc and Jaenberht will escort the Lady Brioni up to Godric's stall with the next message, and the day after that everyone leaves. Next thing that Gytha will be tied down with the convoy with no horse on hand to escape on, and Cadoc watching her every move. One slip and he will plug her with a hunting arrow that will tear the very life out of her. You worry too much at times, my friend," he said with his deep laugh. "By Sunday it will all be over and we can all relax!"

*

Gytha, watching from the corner of her eye as she walked past them all standing there talking, was determined that somehow she would get out of the settlement and escape to Chippenham before everyone left. From there, with Guthrum's help, she could rejoin her father and his business in leather and furs at Cricklade, from where he had removed her to be married to Cuthbert of Ford and become part of her husband's family, whom she now heartily despised.

She laughed.

Poor Cuthbert...dragged off to fight after all! He had been terrified, and was as likely to drop his sword in fright as bolt off the field on the first horse he could get his legs over. The Lord Oscytel's Jomsvikings would kill him for certain. Utterly pathetic, all talk and no substance, despite his attack on her at the barn. How could she have been so foolish?

When this was all over, and the Danes had thrashed Alfred out of the country, she would claim the lands that were rightfully hers and rule them in her dead husband's name under the Danish King. But first she had to get away, and the best way of doing that was to borrow Aelfrid's mare, Gemma, that she was so fond of, and use her to get to Chippenham and find Bjorn Eriksson, the Danish Guard Commander. The odious woman had already given her

437

permission to take the mare to Slaughterford to have her shoes checked before leaving, as their own forge was fully taken up with Leofric's men and their weapons and horses.

She would tell Cuthbert's so doting mama that she needed to go to Godric's stall that Wednesday market to collect a special pair of boots that she had ordered for him two weeks before, and that would now be ready in time for him to leave on Thursday as ordered. A special pair of fighting boots with steel toes and insteps. His mother would be thrilled, and be certain to give her the permission she needed to leave the steading. Of course she would not go near Godric. She no longer trusted him, but from Biddestone to Chippenham's defences was only five miles.

She would be up and away before anyone could know, or find her gone. And then she would tell the Danish King all she knew about Leofric, Brioni and the nest of vicious Saxon fighters lurking so near his ramparts...about Swindon, and about the secret man they had in his camp. A man whom she did not know, but who must be close to the King and his officers to influence them so easily. She would tell them everything...and they in turn would surely reward her mightily.

She laughed again, and rubbed her hands together with glee. She was sharp, she was quick and she would beat them all!

# Chapter Fifty Seven

*M*idday, with the sun at its highest and the blue sky of the morning now mottled with cloud, and the beast convoy was ready to leave with its dogs and drovers. All the cattle in one group, young stirks and heifers and cows in milk with calves at foot, including the old cow with its handsome bull calf they had rescued from Osburgh's ruined steading a month ago.

With them went the heavy oxen that pulled the ploughs, eight great beasts on wide splayed feet and massive quarters, six yoked up to pull a great wain deep laden with supplies of many kinds: tenting material, poles, rope, stakes, cauldrons and tripods; sacks of ground meal, flour and oats; great swatches of hay and straw, buckets, charcoal, water skins and the men's personal weapons and belongings without which they could not manage.

In another group were the settlement sheep and their shepherds, their collie dogs and their two large tilt carts, two horses to each cart with space on board for any lambs that might be dropped along the way, and all the men's clothing, food, tools and personal belongings in leather carry-bags, with heaped waterskins filled to the stoppers, and their spears and shields.

Everyone came to see them off, to cheer and weep as the men and boys left their homes for ever, the noise almost indescribable: the men shouting and calling out, while the boys raced around, shrill with excitement, with hefty sticks of hazel and stout ash, and were cursed and bawled at by everyone With whips cracking, dogs barking, sheep baaing and cattle lowing it was such a cacophony as none had heard before, and chivvying them on their fast horses rode their escort, their armour glinting in the sunshine, shields on their backs, swords and spears by their sides.

Off up the Colerne trackway from Ford they flowed, half the escort going first, with the cattle sharply trotted out by the drovers with dogs and boys at their heels. Next the sheep with their black faces and grey-white woolly backs, jumping and running as sheep do when driven in a flock, ewes baaing for their lambs, the dogs racing to bring back those who were determined to go in the wrong direction, the shepherds with them whistling through their fingers, waving their arms and crooks and calling; "Coom up, ba! Coom up!"

Last came the oxen, solid and plodding, their heads swaying to their feet, their horns polished and gleaming, their massive backsides waggling at every step. The big four-wheeled wagon they hauled creaked as it moved, its great wheels rumbling, its axles squealing, while beside them walked the boys with their long pointed goads to drive the oxen on to cover the twelve miles that each great beast could travel in a day.

And with them came the remainder of the escort and the only spare pair of oxen they had, tossing their heads as they walked, their noses gripped by thick brass rings with straps attached, black muzzles wet, their huge eyes sleepy and long lashed, as patient as the earth on which they strode out. And unless something spooked them into a mindless panic, plod along they would, stolid and slow moving from dawn to dusk, with more endurance than a horse.

Brioni, Leofric and Eadwine, standing on a small knoll, watched them leave, staying there until the last great hoof had plodded on its way and the people gathered there had begun to move off and ready themselves for the complete move from there in two days' time.

"Well, that's that!" Leofric sighed, his arm around Brioni's shoulders. "They have gone and God, and Alnoth keep them safe. He is the finest swordsman in my command, and has the coolest head in a crisis. If he, Raedwald and their dozen troopers cannot keep that lot in one piece, and moving, they are not the men I think they are!

"They have five days to get there, and unless something disastrous happens they should be fine. In fact you should catch up with them before Friday is out. That way you should all arrive at Battlesbury Hill together. And that will be fine, because it is a steep climb up the ancient chariot slope to the old north-east entrance high above. A stream runs close to the bottom of the hill, so be sure to water up before you climb. And take plenty of water skins with you. You will need them until you can re-establish the old cisterns at the top…and they will have to be filled by hand."

"What's it like up there?" Brioni asked.

"Bare and windy," Leofric laughed, "and very impressive. The old ramparts are massive, with almost a sheer drop on the west and north-east side. You wouldn't want to fall off the outer ring anywhere. And attacking such a place would be hard in the extreme. You can see for miles. No Danish war party will get within sight of you without being spotted. I certainly wouldn't want to attack such a place. A real nightmare."

"So, my Lord," Eadwine said, looking at him. "No cover up there."

"No, my friend, nothing except acres of good pasture. You'll need to build stout shelters with what you can find, and what you can take with you. Start with tough tents of poles and canvas, then when we all get there on Sunday we can toil up and down with timber, wattle poles and rushes from the many streams below and from the river Wylye that runs through the valley, and throw up more substantial shelters, as well as fortify the main entrance and block off the other."

"And you expect me to harry those poor devils out from their comfortable homes by the river to the top of Battlesbury hillfort?" Brioni questioned him in dismay.

"Yes, my darling. I do. Between you and Trausti, you will put such fear in their bellies they will all leave in droves! That way they can watch the burning of their homes from a place of safety...and not as wretched corpses!" he replied tersely, looking down into her eyes. "Be certain, my darling, those bastards will spare no-one. Any they find will be killed, from babes in arms with their heads smashed against the house beams, to old gaffas and gammas with their throats cut and their bellies split open. All will die.

"It is the Viking way, unless they are taken as slaves. Impress that on the good people of Warminster, and you will have them eating out of your hand," and banging his own hands together with relish he turned to Eadwine and said: "Now, friend Eadwine, while Brioni goes off to talk with your lady wife, what do we do about the pigs and goats? For of a certainty we cannot take them all with us!" and heads pressed together in earnest talk, arms gesticulating, the two men walked away, leaving Brioni to shrug her shoulders and stalk off to find Aelfrid and Osburgh about the next stage of the evacuation of the two settlements.

*

*B*y the evening of the first day, a huge amount of organisation had been put in place, each little settlement turning to its own Headmen for advice, backed up by Leofric and his men where necessary, or by Brioni whose experience with the King of moving whole communities was greater than anyone's. When Alfred's Court moved, so did all the services on which the King relied: armouries, bakeries, cobblers, farriers, clothiers, priests...everything. And under Brioni's tutelage, aided by Aelfrid and Osburgh at Ford and by Cyneburga, the Headman's wife at Slaughterford, and two of her friends, the families were soon sorted with all that they could take with them. From favourite doll to pet cat and kittens; cooking pots and cauldrons to bee skeps, chickens in rough crates, the family goose and grandpa's chair...all had to be sorted and agreed on.

Each family had one tilt cart for all the belongings they could take with them, including children and the elderly, and Eadwine and Leofric detailed two big wagons especially for goats and piglets, it being decided to release into the wild all the mature beasts they could not take with them. That way, when they returned to re-build, some animals the Danes had not found might be discovered still alive.

Nevertheless many favourite beasts had to be either left behind or put down, blind kittens and puppies bucket-drowned to the cries and tears of the children who adored them all; some mature animals were also slain, their hides saved, their meat shared amongst the people as it was at the time of slaughter in the autumn, when there was more meat to eat than many could manage, and the ground was soaked in blood. There was plenty also for the hounds that each family possessed, and for Bran and Utha, who were always in Brioni's sight, their huge forms loping beside her wherever she went, while the steaders' dogs were chained, howling, to avoid them running off and being lost before they left.

Much favoured furniture and family treasures had also to be abandoned, sometimes forcibly by Leofric and his men among much weeping, pleading and stamping of angry feet when families were found saving things that took up too much space. In all this dreadful turmoil Aelfrid showed remarkable strength and courage in disposing of some of her own most treasured possessions…the lovely dresser that her father had made for her mother when they had married and the two great chairs they always sat in. All of which she had taken out and burned in order to show an example to the other wives in the settlements, and to ensure she was not bitterly accused of favouritism as the wife of the most influential Headman!

*

*A*nd all day, Leofric and his men, when not sorting troubles, readied themselves for the coming raid on Bath. Weapons were honed to a razor's edge and polished, as was their armour. Rust ground out with pumice stone and rough sand soaked in vinegar, and all bumps and nicks in sword or battle axe were hammered, or ground out on the treadle stone that each farrier had in his forge. The screeching sound dinned in people's ears continuously, the sparks flying in every direction but mostly into the leather apron lap of the master farrier in each settlement…and in Arnwulf's portable forge on his own wheel that was kept busy throughout the day.

The horses' hooves were looked over as were their shoes for loose nails or torn metal; loose rivets were hammered home, shield rims repaired, or even replaced, their leather covers checked for damage, and the fleece-wrapped metal bars behind the boss, by which each shield was held, were also gone over with great care. All the leather straps on shields or battle harness were checked

442

and checked again so that no fighter, in the very heat of battle, would have his life endangered by faulty equipment.

Up and down, favoured horses went to the settlement forges: Wotan, Warrior, Rollo and Foxhead and all those who belonged to the men, and those who would have to run on leading reins behind the wagons when everyone left before sun-up on Thursday. A constant stream of beasts and riders coming and going, besides the children with arms filled with goods and provisions of every kind, bustling amongst the warriors, getting underfoot, and being sworn at by fractious adults, themselves rushing to get as much done as possible before the day was spent. Especially those families whose men had already gone on ahead, and who needed more help because of it, Leofric's troopers stepping into that breach along with other friends and family. All striving to be as far forward as possible before the sun's light finally left the valley and all was still at last.

By nightfall everyone was exhausted, and most fell to their rest early, knowing that they would have it all to do again in the morning: beasts to cull, stores and furniture to sort and pack; those animals going, to be fed and watered; hens to crate up, pigs and goats to be tied, geese to be bound, bee skeps to be sorted, carts to load…and all to be done by lunchtime!

*

*I*n their bed that night, too tired to make love, Brioni and Leofric were just happy to be close cuddled each by the other, her head on his shoulder, his arms wrapped round her, their fur covers pulled well over them for the night had turn chilly with a light frost after a warm day and a cloud-free sky.

"How was it for you today, Sweetheart?" he asked her after a while. "You seemed to be everywhere at once today. Every time I looked round you were somewhere else!"

"Desperate, at times, Leofric, *desperate!* Children in tears over their pets, women weeping over their treasures and the men dour and grim-faced. Some of them have so little. Just a few sticks of furniture and a handful of precious pots and pans; some copper bottomed that must have cost a fortune, and still they cannot take them all with them.

"And have you ever loved a pig? These people have - watched it grow, nurtured it, fed it the best scraps they could find, walked it out into the woods for roots, acorns and beech mast, saving it for the autumn slaughter and all the good things you can get out of a fat pig. And there am I saying it has to go! They can't herd it from here to Battlesbury, so they can't keep it. And today I saw grown men cry over a pig. I felt like one myself. And the children and

443

their pets? Kittens and puppies drowned in buckets of water because they are too young to survive! Hateful! *Hateful!*

"And poor Aelfrid and her lovely dresser and two armed chairs; dragged out by the hall servants, broken up, and set on fire along with a whole host of clothes and embroideries. She just stood there weeping, and I could do nothing to help her. And all the time her precious son and his wife are planning such wickedness that it almost choked me! I had to walk away and leave her to it. Just awful, Leofric, *awful!*" And she promptly burst into tears on his shoulder.

"My poor darling. You have truly had a beast of a day. But think of all that has been achieved. The herd beasts have all left and are safely bedded down not ten miles away at Box. Ricberht came in to tell me just before we all went in to eat, did you not see him? I have ordered a fast messenger every day until we leave on Thursday morning. These people here need that encouragement, to know that the plan is working despite all their fears and concerns."

"No, I didn't, but it is so good to know that all is well. Everyone will have been wondering. I was in the back counting pots and pans with Ethelinda and Rowena, and wondering what to do about the ovens. The girls will have one more bake tomorrow before drawing the fire. It seems such a shame to break them up, they are beautifully built. But I am loth to leave anything for the enemy to enjoy. So I suppose they must go too!"

"Same with the animals, really," he replied with a deep sigh. "The enemy should be left with nothing to succour them, so anything we cannot take with us should be destroyed. Yet every family has its pig, the granaries are still half full and so are the meal arcs. And then there is the mill. I cannot bring myself to tear it down, or burn it. I will leave that to the Danes, they may spare it.

"But the mill stones we can take and hide in the woods. It will be a great labour, but that we can do tomorrow for they are the heart of any mill and cost a fortune. I am detailing one wagon for wheat and flour, and another for forge equipment like anvils and bellows, grind stones, proving tanks, tools and spare horse shoes. Arnwulf will have his own cart for those things he always takes with him, but the farriers here will need help with all their gear, so that is the least I can do."

"And there is only one day left in which to do everything, "she said, with a sudden shiver, "and then you will be gone and I will be left to carry on. And I know I have Trausti and all the others, but it is not the same as having you, Leofric. Any order I give they tend to look to Trausti first, they know him so much better than me. The whole thing is incredibly daunting!"

"I know, my darling," he said, giving her a great cuddle and a kiss on her forehead. "But, as I said a few minutes ago, look at what you have achieved already: Beasts gone ahead, families organised, carts allocated, goods and chattels sorted. Of course it has been a time of bitterness and hard words, but they know you are right, both the steaders and my own men," he assured her.

"Not once has Trausti questioned your decisions with me. And every time he backs you up, the men will question you less. And when you come to lead them into battle once more, they will be that much more willing to be led. Take heart, Brioni of Foxley, you are doing a grand job!"

"Well, dearest of men, I do hope so; but seeing Aelfrid weeping over her burning treasures, and the children screaming over their dying pets, so wrung my heart today, that I wept and cried with them. And the men were little better.

"Pray God tomorrow will be a happier day, though I doubt it with the mill to deal with and much favoured beasts driven into the deep woods to survive as best they can. Thank God, the weather at least is clement, if that turns as well, then everything will be twice as hard.

"Oh, Leofric," she cried, turning to bury her head in his shoulder, "this evacuation business is hell. No wonder all men hate the Danes and wish them sped, or dead. Come the spring muster surely all true Saxons will come together to beat these bastards once and for all! Alfred will get such a welcome as must surely warm his heart."

"Especially after a winter in the wilds of Somerset on Athelney, with few comforts and little cheer!" he replied, giving her a squeeze. I just hope that all the messages we have sent in will have heartened him. And we are not the only group fighting back. He has been active himself, as have others of his hearth companions.

"The flame of freedom has been kept burning throughout these past months. The Danes know it, and so do I. How they must have railed against fate, and ground their teeth with rage, that they did not catch him in Chippenham as they had planned!" and he laughed, and rubbed his face in her hair.

"When they missed their heron with that winter's stoop, they lost Wessex. With the King still alive and kicking they could not claim mastery of the whole land, and despite all their efforts they have yet to winkle him out of his hideaway. So, come Easter next month when his messages will go out all over Wessex, and to the lands beyond us, all true men will come to the muster at Ecbert's Stone in May…and then we shall see what happens!"

And wrapping her in his arms he turned and burrowed into the great pillows at their head, their fur covers pulled right up to their chins, while a chill wind chivvied the thatch and a distant wolf howled in the forest, its *woo-oo-ooo* calling in the grey brothers to a hunting, as the scent of fresh blood from all the late-day killings drifted through the empty wastelands.

\*

Gytha, lying in her bed, with Cuthbert beside her, heard the wolf call and lay there awake in the darkness listening for it to come again, and to the wind as it wuthered round the house place, praying for a change in the weather, for blurring rain in the morning instead of frost, or a thick mist which often came at this time of the year, filling the valleys and hollows with a wet, pale whiteness, so that she could make good her escape.

She would take Aelfrid's grey mare, Gemma, and amble her across to Slaughterford. They would give her an escort, of course, but with all the immense bustle going on around both settlements, and the Swindon raid being hotly prepared for, she had no doubts that she could slip her leash and escape up the steep side track that led to Biddestone on the tops where the market would be held as usual. Then away across the flat to Chippenham by a back route that she knew of and so to Guthrum's host at last, when they would soon know just what was going on beneath their fine Danish noses.

She had her message written, and would carry it hidden it in her chemise in case she could not get into Guthrum's hall to find the King in person. Aelfrid would speak with Leofric in the morning about Cuthbert's boots, and insist Gytha be allowed to go for the sake of her son. That she had agreed to, and to her taking the mare. She'd had that promise out of her at the meeting, when she had realised her precious son was going to fight in Leofric's command alongside his father and his brother.

Pulling the heavy wool blankets up to her chin that covered the coarse sheets in which she was curled, she turned for sleep, the wolf calls more insistent but still far off down the valley as the grey brothers gathered for the kill...while outside the men kept the wolf-guard with their big lanterns, long spears and their hunting dogs.

And as the night passed, and the men cursed and stamped their feet in the cold, so the weather changed in answer to Gytha's prayers, for the wind dropped and a thick mist arose, mixed with low cloud. By first light the whole valley was filled with a fine, whiteness that swiftly covered everything in an opaque blanket from which the mizzle fell in a drifting veil of penetrating wetness.

# Chapter Fifty Eight

**M**orning came and it was a shambles!
A thick mist had descended on everything, and despite all the men could do the wolves had got in amongst the herded goats at the top end of the settlement and there had been a killing. Not that the weather was so bitter that they had been forced by hunger to raid a human settlement…but that the blood from all the earlier culling had drawn them in. Opportunist hunters, January was a time of mating for wolves, like foxes, and with the lead female now heavy with pups, her mate had led the grey brothers in an easy hunt for meat with which to feed her, and in the thick mist had made a swift slaughter amongst the herded goats. Despite the spears and shouts of the wolf-guard massed against them, lanterns on poles and dogs straining beside them, the wolves had still attacked.

Huge snarling beasts with yellow-orange eyes and thick grey-white fur leaping at them out of the wet darkness of the curling mist, great ruffed bodies with bared fangs and lolling tongues, there one moment and gone the next. Terrifying in both noise and sudden sight and size, making the herd dogs bark and cry, sometimes in bravery and often in fear, while the goats bleated, screamed in death and fled in all directions so that it was impossible to see what was going on, or where to concentrate a strong defence.

Just one wolf was dead and two of the dogs, and two men had been badly bitten before the grey brothers had finally been driven off…called away by the wild *woo-oo-oooo* of the pack leader from the wood's edge beyond the settlement. But not before a dozen goats had been slain in a killing frenzy and six carried away to be noisily torn apart beyond the reach of man or dog, the remainder of the herd scattering in terror to the woods and forest that surrounded them.

"God's curses on all damned wolves!" Leofric swore when Eadwine came in to explain what had happened. "You should have called us. Bran and Utha might have been able to help. They drove off the wolves who attacked Brioni at Foxley after the Danes destroyed the steading."

"We had enough of everything, Leofric, and your men helped mightily anyway. But this was our problem and the mist so thick you could hardly see anything out there. My men might have speared the Lady Brioni's two hounds as easily as any wolf; God knows they are big enough. Those bastards came and went much as they pleased. But we got one of them, and injured others.

They will not come again. It was the blood from our culling that drew them here so strongly, and they will have the lead bitch, big with pups, to care for. With a wolf pack only one female breeds, the rest protect and leave her food; but the damned goats have scattered far and near, and it will be the Devil's own job to catch them all again!"

"You know your wolf-lore well, my friend," Leofric replied with a grin.

"Those of us who live in the wilds near the great forests need to. Or else the wilderness will break in and destroy us. You cannot hunt your enemy unless you know him well, and I know the wolves well who live around us. Only if the winter is bitter cruel, like this year's, are they ever a real danger…or when they have pups and you get too close. They will not bother us again, but they have just left us a real mess to clear up, and this mist will not help us."

"Is it bad?"

"Come and see for yourself," Eadwine said, leading him to the main door through which his own men were already moving backwards and forwards with armfuls of clothes and equipment. "But it is not clever!" And he stood aside as Leofric brushed past him into a bleak, grey-white morning.

"Damnation!" the big man cursed quietly as he looked round at an opaque world of chilly whiteness, where nothing beyond fifty paces could be clearly seen, and he banged his hands together in frustration. "I so didn't want to be hindered today of all days when there is so much to do. Where is Gytha?" he asked urgently. "I have been meaning to talk with her."

"Gone to the stables to check on my wife's mare. The beast needs her hooves tending and fresh shoes before we all set out tomorrow. It was impossible yesterday. I have agreed for her to take the horse across to Slaughterford to see Thurwold the Farrier. He's good and will deal well with her. Gemma that is," he added, laughing. "Though with Gytha you never know."

"Flighty is she?"

"Mmmm, could be. I wondered if that was what was behind their row the other night?"

"Between Cuthbert and Gytha? Brioni thought there might be something wrong. She came in looking red-faced and battered."

"Something to do with Godric the cobbler, I think," Eadwine went on, not noticing the intense look that passed across Leofric's face. "She was going to marry him until her father stepped in and stopped it. Did a deal with me instead. Maybe Cuthbert got the wrong idea about her going up to see him on some market days."

"All the better they will be separated after today for a while."

448

"Absence making the heart grow stronger, you mean?"

"Something like that," Leofric agreed with a grunt, his mind busy.

"Oh, that reminds me," Eadwine said. "Aelfrid has asked that Gytha be allowed to go up to Biddestone market today to collect a pair of special boots for Cuthbert before he leaves tomorrow.

"From this Godric the cobbler?" Leofric questioned him, astonished, his thoughts in a whirl. "He won't like that."

"Well he will just have to stomach it, especially as it is for him that she goes. His mother ordered them through Gytha several weeks ago; tough leather with steel toes and insteps, a sure protection against sword cuts and stabbed feet in the battle line. I said I would ask you, but assured her it would not be a problem," he added, seeing the look of concentration on the big Saxon's face.

"I know that you want to keep everyone close today, Leofric, and busy, but he is her youngest and she dotes on him. She was deeply shocked to learn he would be coming with us tomorrow, and she would be much easier in her mind if he had his new boots on his feet when he leaves in the morning...so would I."

Leofric paused then and looked around him, thinking of the dangers in having the girl leave the steading, how that would cross with his own plans around Godric, gauging how thick the mist would be on the tops, who should escort her...and whether to say 'no', as was his first inclination. But looking down at Eadwine beside him, completely innocent of any subterfuge around the girl, or his son, he smiled. "Of course, my friend. She must go and find this cobbler, Godric. Is he any good?" he asked, dissembling as he did so.

"The best this side of the Thames, so they say. Did work for Alfred and his family; probably doing the same for Guthrum now, sly bastard. These craftsmen will make a coin out of anyone who can afford to pay and call it 'business'!"

"So, send her to me and I will give her a pass. All the tracks away from here are guarded. She will not get past one without my say so. Now, my friend, a warm bannock first with a chunk of good cheese and pickle, and a horn of ale, and we will be about it. Brioni will be going up to Biddestone market as well, she has need of the cobbler too," he said with a wry smile. Then he laughed: "The two girls can go together. It will be company for them both while we get on and get things sorted down here," And with a bright tune on his lips, as if he had not a care in the world, he and Eadwine swung back inside, Eadwine calling for the hall servants to bring them food and ale.

*

449

*G*ytha, summoned by Aelfrid later, went with beating heart a'flutter to her bower, her mind full of concerns, if not a little fear, to be met by a smiling, gracious lady with a handful of coins ready in a small red leather purse to pay for the boots her son needed.

"Here, child, this is for you. More than you told me was needed, so any left over you may use for your own amusement. Buy something pretty or a hot pie to keep you going, it may be the last time for a while. My husband has spoken with Lord Leofric and he has assured him that all will be well. You just need to go and see him and get a pass out of the valley as all the trackways are now guarded; he will be with my husband sorting out the mill. Go there and you will find them both. Just be sure you watch your tongue well, though, especially as you will be going with the Lady Brioni and her escort."

"With the Lady Brioni?" Gytha questioned, appalled, her eyes wide in her narrow face.

"Yes, child. She will go with you to Godric the cobbler. There is some commission she has to conclude with him too, I understand. So you can go with her escort. That way you will be safe from any man who might choose to accost you." Then, after a pause, as the girl stood there beside her uncertainly, she asked: "Is anything amiss between you and my son, Gytha? You both looked in a dreadful state the other evening...and your face looks bruised," she went on, lifting her hand gently to the girl's cheek. "That was not kindly done."

"We had a difference of opinion, my Lady," she replied stiffly. "He sought to show me the error of my ways. It was but a brief interlude. I understand him better now. And he has apologised."

"That is good, my child. And I am probably to blame. He is my youngest, and my last child; so I have probably indulged him more than I should have. He can be petulant when crossed. But he is still a charming youth when all is said and done, and there is no malice in him. You will see," she went on, patting Gytha's hand, who had sucked in her breath at Aelfrid's words. "The soft word disbands anger, I always find. I am sure you will learn to manage him, and then all will be well. Remember he loves you greatly," she added with a smile. "He has told me so many times. Now, run along and find Lord Leofric. The sooner you are gone the sooner you will return and there is so much to do today before they all set out tomorrow!"

*

*N*ow, what was that bitch up to? Why did she need to see Godric? And, dear God, how can I face Lord Leofric? He will take one look at my face and know that I am full of lies today. But what can he do? Go back on his word? No, he will not do that, that is not his way. And what can he know? No-one has stopped me before from going up to Biddestone market and seeing Godric. I have done that many times, and have always been chaperoned. Not that Rowena has ever been a real chaperone, and knows why I go there I am sure, or thinks she does! And she laughed at how shocked they would all be if they really knew what she was up to. It was all so exciting!

She already had her message written, simple, urgent and to the point: about the next raid, about Ford and the money held there, and about the secret traitor who was so close to Guthrum. Then off to Lord Leofric and her father-in-law, Eadwine, for the pass.

And she would wear her white deerskin cape, over her long scarlet wool skirt and blue embroidered tunic. It was off a white hart that had been shot on the distant moors and had cost Cuthbert a fortune. She loved the look and feel of it, especially as it was lined and rimmed with wolf fur, the hood also. In the grey-whiteness outside it might even hide her from prying eyes, and anyway she felt good in it and it might impress the Danes.

Perhaps she could get Guthrum to spare the mill and the granaries. Re-building them would be such a labour. Shame about the ovens, they were the very best she had ever used. She shrugged, they could always be re-laid and a few days without fresh bread would not be a disaster. But a few handfuls of that silver would be wonderful! And with that thought in her head she hurried off to her own bower to change, her skirts shushing up around her.

*

*B*rioni, seated in her own chamber, was doing the same task with quill pen and scruffy yellow coloured parchment, a far cry from the beautiful white vellum made from calf skins, and used by the King in all his documents. '*Beware! The Fox will soon come to Swindon from Ford, below Biddestone. I have warned you before. Come swiftly and destroy them before they leave. Cuthbert of Wessex.*' She held it up and looked at it critically: sufficiently spluttered with ink and the letters poorly formed. It would do. As similar to all the other messages that had been sent to the Danes before; nothing to make them suspicious. And she sprinkled sand powder on it to dry the words swiftly, shaking it over the floor when she had finished before folding it up ready to be passed on to Godric...and so to Guthrum's hall in Chippenham.

Then, rising, she dressed herself carefully. This time she would go as herself, but mutely dressed in long skirt of dark green leather, split either side for riding, with blue chemise and russet over tunic, long boots on her feet, well scuffed and battered, and the brown hooded cape she had worn into Malmesbury. She looked longingly at the beautiful wolfskin cape, lined with fleece and edged with fur, that had been made from the two beasts she had slain at Foxley. She loved wearing it, it was so warm, just perfect for a chill, mist laden, February morning. But it was too distinctive, so she settled for a tough sheepskin jerkin with deep pockets, and wide leather belt around her waist off which Brain Biter hung from her right side. No steel linked byrnie today, nor shield on her back, or closed steel helmet on her head, but armed she would be just in case.

And she was to travel with Gytha, but without Bran and Utha. They must stay with Leofric. They were just too distinctive, and she wanted her visit to be as discreet as all her other journeys to the market had been.

That would be interesting. Godric's stall was the last place the girl would want to have been seen after her row with Cuthbert about him. The servants were full of it, they always knew everything. But here Aelfrid had approved her going for a special pair of boots for her son that had been commissioned from the big cobbler weeks ago, so Cuthbert could hardly complain! And she would explain her own connection with Godric with the truth; the one thing no-one could find a hole in. That she knew him from her time with Alfred in Chippenham; that he had made her a pair of shoes when she was handmaid to the Queen of Wessex, and had long promised her a pair of boots that would fit her like a glove. It was a perfect explanation, and would give her the time she needed to hand over her own message for Guthrum, while Gytha, having completed her purchase stayed outside, powerless, with her escort, Cadoc the Welsh bowman and Jaenberht the hard-bitten Saxon huscarle whom she would trust with her life.

She stood up and stamped her feet to settle them in her boots, and picking up her own leather purse of soft yellow suede, which she slid into her jerkin pocket along with her message, she swirled her cloak over her shoulders and swept out of her chamber to find Leofric.

*

Down by the old watermill he was struggling with Eadwine and half a dozen others to move the great grinding stones to a safe place within the forest, while all around them the people of both settlements made ready to leave before sun up the following day, their busy figures shrouded in the mist that covered everything. Horses, carts, furniture, rough crates being hammered together, animals herded into small enclosures all half-hidden in a white veil from which a fine mizzle fell depressingly on every man and beast. Not a steady rain that could have been born more easily, but a persistent dampness that seemed to get into everything.

"So, you are ready my darling," he said to her when she appeared out of the mist, as he stood up and stretched his back, the first great millstone safely on the heavy sledge that had been provided for it, the two big horses harnessed to it stamping their hooves and tossing their heads and tails against the wetness.

"Yes. And I have Blood Drinker with me just in case. But why me, Leofric, when I have a host of other jobs to do before you all leave tomorrow? Why must I play the nursemaid?" she hissed angrily.

"Because I want this little harlot closely watched...remember what we discussed last night? She knows too much and cannot be trusted. I did not seek this, but it cannot be denied without much damage to goodwill and morale. So, go she must, but with you as a close guardian. Cadoc goes with you and has his Syrian bow with him just in case. But no soldier should be left to make so ultimate a decision. That is for you, to do, my Lady," he replied harshly. "And besides, I need to be certain our own message goes out as safely as possible. We always agreed that you and Cadoc would see to that.

"But Eadwine has asked especially that Gytha should go to Godric today; check Aelfrid's mare on the way with Thurwold the farrier at Slaughterford, and then up to the market at Biddestone. As I said, my darling, this is not what I wanted, but then things don't always work out the way one wants them too," he added with cocked eyebrows. "I could just do without this damned fog everywhere!"

"It may not be so bad up on the tops," Eadwine said, coming up to them, shaking the mizzle drops off his leather hat. "Sometimes these mists are only in the valleys, and the tops are in clear sunshine. You can never tell on days like this. Ah, here is young Gytha come for her pass," he went on with a smile as the young woman swept towards them, her scarlet kirtle making a bright stab of colour beneath her long white deerskin cape. "I only wish I was coming with you. I could just do with a break from duty. Never mind," he continued blithely, while Leofric handed her the bright green ribbon pass his men would be looking for, "here is your escort, two men whom I put my trust in to keep you safe. Now, away with you, and we will see you back in time for a last meal all together. Have fun and take care."

453

And while Leofric bent to give Brioni a close hug and kiss farewell, the rangy Headman boosted Gytha up into Gemma's saddle, and then stood by while the small party clip-clopped on its way to ford the stream and take the steep track that would take them up and over to Slaughterford, and from there further up the steep hillside to Biddestone market.

# Chapter Fifty Nine

Slaughterford was a tiny settlement even smaller than Ford, with one trackway across the bustling stream that led right-handed up to Colerne on the top of the hill, and another, just before the ford itself, that led up a steep twisted trail to Biddestone village where the market was held every Wednesday.

A neat place it was, with just a handful of houses along the bottom of a steep hill that led to the ford, with granary and communal barn, and a spacious forge and brew house closeby that on such a chill, misty morning was a warm and welcoming place to be. A wide-fronted building where a cluster of men and horses were already waiting for the farrier, a large man with ruddy face, rough beard of coarse black hair and hands like boiled hams, to see to their needs.

"So, my Lady," the big smith growled pleasantly as soon as he saw Brioni, "what can I do for you this murky morning? And for you, Mistress Gytha?" he added, smoothing his heavy leather apron as he spoke, seeing her companion pushing her way amongst the hearty warriors gathered round the big forge's entrance, sneaking a warm at his great charcoal fire, happily jostling for their place and full of banter.

"We have come up to have Mistress Aelfrid's mare seen to, Thurwold," she called out, pushing back the deep hood of her brown cape. "Have her feet and shoes checked before we all leave tomorrow. She is in fine fettle, and bursting with good feeling, but she has a distance to travel and Headman Eadwine wanted her checked over by an expert," she ended with a smile, knowing her little flattery would please him.

"Well you are welcome, my Lady," he said with a small bow. "And I will be with you presently," the big man added, waving his hammer and wide nail pincers in his hand as he spoke. "Just as soon as I have finished shoeing this misbegotten son of Satan, this lazy trooper seems to set so much store by," he added in his growly voice, as the horse he was standing beside stamped his foot and shuffled his wide body against the smith, tossing his head and snorting. "He's a villain, is this Storm, and no mistake, but brave as a lion in a fight, and that gurt fool by his bridle is less than useless," he added to much laughter. "So this may take some time."

"That is no matter, Master Thurwold," Brioni answered him lightly with a smile. "We can wait."

"Leave the horses on the rail and go inside, my Lady," the big smith replied, with a slight bow. "Edita is inside sorting things out for our journey tomorrow. She will give you warmth, a fresh scone and some mulled ale. I will call you when all is done. Now, Danny Hewitt, you useless lump," he snarled at the tall, wiry trooper at the horse's head. "Hold his bridle, and talk to him, or we will never be done!"

And while Cadoc and Jaenberht swung off their own horses and joined with the other warriors milling and joking outside, the two girls, now off their own beasts, tied them to the long wooden rail along the south wall of the forge, and pushed inside to the house-place beyond.

This was a large room with a fire in its centre surrounded by great stones to keep it in, with two louvres high up in the roof space for the blue wood smoke that permeated the building to escape. There were benches to sit on, a stool and a pair of deep wooden chests with red glazed oil lamps on them, and two windows with horn plates in simple casements with painted shutters. There was a huge pile of utensils, clothes and rough towels wrapped in a great linen sheet in a corner by the door; a baby on a brown deerskin rug near the fire, and a toddler clutching onto its mother's long skirts near to a curtained opening that led further inside.

On a broad iron griddle at the edge of the fire a handful of flat cakes were baking, with butter in a neat earthenware dish and a chunk of honeycomb in a large bowl on a wooden stand nearby.

"Good day to you, Edita," Brioni said in her clear voice. "Your man bid us come through to you while he deals with Aelfrid's mare that Gytha here is riding today."

"You must be my Lady Brioni of Foxley that we have all heard about," the woman answered shyly, bobbing a curtsey at her, her long hair bound up beneath a close fitting wimple of blue dyed linen. "Come you in and sit down, my Lady. We are having griddle scones with butter and honey this day. You are welcome to join us, and there is some malted ale to wash it down."

"That is most kind of you, Mistress, and we are pleased to accept. Now, who is this fine fellow I see peeping at me?" she said, holding her arms out to the child still hanging on uncertainly to his mother's long kirtle of russet wool.

"This is Durwin, means 'Dear Friend', and so he is to us both," his mother replied with a laugh and a ruffle of the boy's head. "Always helping his Mama when he is not in the forge with his Da. He loves to watch the sparks fly when Thurwold is working the hot iron, and the sizzle and burst of steam when it is plunged in the proving tank. He is a good boy."

"Of course he is. But will he come to me? I have a kindness for children, and was handmaid to the Queen for her baby, Aelfthryth, before the latest troubles."

And while Brioni and the farrier's wife chatted and played with the children, Gytha glanced round in disgust at the whole display of chattels and furniture around her, swirling her white cape close around her as she sat down and looked: at the simple homeliness of the place, its dirt floor with tired rushes all over it, the iron utensils, the fat bacon hanging from a beam near the fire, the plain wooden chests, the painted leather screen that shielded the big box bed the family slept in, and she suddenly felt the urgent need to relieve herself, a thing she had not done since rising at first light.

"Mistress Edita," she said uncertainly, standing up and looking around her as the woman was speaking with Brioni. "Please, I need to go!"

"Of course, young Gytha," she said with a smile, and a gentle pat on the girl's shoulder. "We have an outside privy," she said proudly, as the girl slipped off her cape and hung it on a nearby hook in the wall. "My husband dug it a few months ago, with a wooden seat and everything. It is behind the forge, I will take and show you." And leaving Brioni with Durwin and the baby, she bustled through the curtain that shielded the other door, sweeping Gytha along with her to find the privy, a simple enough wooden shed over a deep hole alongside the forge, with outer door and raised seat inside, a box full of torn cloths and a bucket of water.

\*

Seated, with her skirts fluffed up around her, Gytha was impressed. The door of vertical planks had a proper latch and a long piece of cord so that in warm weather you could sit and look out as you relieved yourself, free of too many flies, yet could swiftly pull the door shut if needed. And it was decorated with a pattern of stars round a crescent moon, through which you could see if anyone was coming, in time to shout out before some great ham-fisted warrior attending the forge should reach out and shake the door open and so reveal you! Close-by also was the wood pile, so after each visit to the privy an armful of firewood could be brought into the house.

With enormous relief she emptied herself to the last drop, and was just reaching for a cloth from the box to complete her business, when three men from the forge came round the far corner to collect charcoal for the smith from his covered store opposite. Two of them she didn't know, they were based at Slaughterford, part of Raedwald's war group, but the third man she did know, for it was Cadoc the Welsh bowman, his recurved Syrian bow thrusting out

457

from above his right shoulder…his horse bow, so different from his great war bow that could shoot an arrow nearly three hundred paces.

"So, lads, are you ready for this attack?" she heard him ask in his sing-song voice, her heart thudding in her chest at the thought that they might be coming to use the privy as well, and was just about to call out when the man's reply shocked her to her very core.

"Yes! Bath won't know what has hit it," the man said with a laugh, hauling out a sack of charcoal from its covered store, "My sword is as sharp as a razor after Thurwold gave it his closest attention; we'll go through those bastards like a dose of black elder!"

"So, boyo, you know it's Bath, not Swindon, we are going for?" Cadoc asked, hitching his bow up on his shoulder more comfortably, reaching for an armful of wood from the pile beneath the deep eaves of the forge.

"Yes, Cadoc," the other man with them replied. "Landry and I picked that up quite quickly. Don't really know why Lord Leofric needed the deception. There's no-one near us to listen in to our words and no true Saxon would betray us anyway."

"You can never tell, Bach," the little Welshman said darkly. "Loose talk can cost lives, remember, not all Saxons believe in their King. There are those who would do a deal with the enemy if they thought they could profit by it."

"What? Out here in the middle of nowhere? You have been eating too many leeks!" Landry said, slapping his thigh with a big laugh.

"Don't you be so certain, my friend," Cadoc answered him seriously. "Look you, boyo, there are those amongst these settlements not sure about us at all. You heard that Cuthbert the other morning. He's one to watch. Why do you think we are taking him with us? Fight? He'd wet himself before he could lift his sword. Say 'Boo!' and he'd fall over with fright. His brother is worth ten of him, but the Iron Hand doesn't trust that Cuthbert. Good job I am going with the travellers, or my little popper here," he said patting his bow, "would knock him over before he disgraced everyone and fled!"

"And what about his wife? That Gytha?" Landry's large friend asked. "If he's soft, what about her?"

"What about her indeed?" Landry replied, with a coarse laugh. "If that Cuthbert's soft, I know one or two who are hard as bliddy iron," and he pumped his arm while the others snorted like rooting pigs that made Gytha cry out softly in distress, immediately stifling her cry with her hand, while the others laughed and jostled their way back to the forge with charcoal and arms full of wood.

All went back round the corner save Cadoc, who turned at the last moment and looked at the little privy with concentrated effort, his eyes crinkled, his ears stretched for stray sound...then, with a shrug, he shook his head and walked out of sight.

*

*P*etrified, Gytha sat there like a pheasant on its chicks when it knows a stoat is hunting them. Terrified to move, her hand still across her mouth, she waited until she was sure the men were not going to return, knowing that she must go back inside before anyone came calling for her.

*And Bath...not Swindon!*

Dear God, she could not believe it! Swindon was what all the talk had been about. Always Swindon. And it was Swindon that was in her note. Yet Bath was where Leofric's attack would fall. Unprepared, it would be another Saxon victory. Such an easy success was not to be borne, not if she could help it. And finishing with the cloth, she stood up, pulled her clothes around her and pushing the thin wooden door open, was out and away in a flurry of scarlet skirts to the back door of the house-place before anyone could see her, leaving the privy door swinging open on its long metal hinges.

*

*I*nside, Brioni and Edita happily had their teeth stuck into the fat, round griddle cakes that were now ready, eating off wide earthenware plates with a dark green glaze on them, now swimming in a lovely mixture of honey and melted butter that both girls had no hesitation in licking off the glaze and then off their fingers. And were happily laughing when Gytha came bustling in from outside, her face pale, her hands almost shaking.

"Whatever is the matter with you?" Brioni asked at once, her voice almost sharp in its interrogation. "You are shaking like a leaf in a storm."

"A rat!" the girl replied, inventing wildly. "A great big corn fed rat in the privy. Came nosing in when I was sitting there. *I hate rats!*" she exclaimed truthfully, shaking her hands wildly. "He stood up and whiffled his whiskers at me as bold as a miller's shirt. I shrieked, he scampered off and I ran back in!"

"Oh, you poor dear," Edita comforted her. "I hate rats too! I have seen that one before. Big, cheeky fellow. I will tell Thurwold, and he will have a go at it."

"Not before he is ready to leave, I trust," Brioni said then, with a smile. "I can see you have made a start," she said pointing to the piles of sheeting and utensils already gathered near the door. "But we leave before first light tomorrow, and we need you with us. I will tell that cheerful rabble outside that they must be the very last. Then Thurwold can pull his fire and dismantle his forge.

"I see you have your cart ready and your horses nearby, I saw them in the paddock as I came down to the forge. He will need his bellows, his anvil, his proving tank and as many of his tools as he can manage, and spare horse shoes and iron ingots. Then there's you and the children and what things you can take with you. I will make sure you have all the help you need from those loafers outside.

"Now, Edita, give some of those excellent pancakes to Gytha and then send her out to join us. She and I are off up to the market with Cadoc and Jaenberht, and will be back down again presently. By then you need to be loading up. I know it is miserably wet and misty out there, but you must not miss leaving at first light. I suppose you will go over the ford here and up to Colerne from this side of the hill?"

"Yes, my Lady," the woman replied, balancing her baby on her hip, young Durwin clinging on to his mother's wide skirts, a grubby thumb in his mouth. "Me and the family, with Bobby and Peterkin to pull us, and the rest of the settlement. We won't let you down."

"Excellent, Edita, I knew I could count on you," she said, reaching out to her impulsively. "Now, just let me rinse my sticky fingers in the water you have warming on the other end of this fire then I will be off. Gytha, on your horse as soon as possible. Cadoc, Jaenberht and I will be waiting for you." And giving her a searching look, she turned with a swish of her skirts and left the house place, wishing she could relieve herself in Edita's privy as easily as Gytha had done...rat or no rat!

\*

*O*utside, the dank mist still made sight uneasy, though at least the mizzle had stopped. Cadoc and Jaenberht, standing beside their horses' heads, were ready to mount up, while Thurwold brought Gemma across to join them, having checked her frogs, tightened two of her shoes and put new ones on her two back feet.

"There you are my Lady, all sorted and a proper job!" he said with a smile.

"Good, and here's the money to pay for all," she said, handing him some coins from her purse. "I have spoken with your lady, Thurwold, and told her what you need to do. Here, Landry," she called to a tall, well-built trooper with hazel eyes who came across to her at her shout. "You are finished here at the forge, yes?"

"Yes, my Lady."

"Good, then you and your team can help Thurwold here at the forge for the rest of the day. He needs to get ready to move himself and his family out at first light tomorrow.

"Then, boys, if you have time you can amuse yourselves with a rat hunt. There was a monstrous great rat in the privy round the back a short time ago. Frightened Mistress Gytha half out of her skin; made her shriek, she tells me!" And they all rolled about, the thought of a girl with her skirts up, sitting on the privy shrieking, and a great rat sniffing at her, making them double up and slap their thighs. All except Cadoc who looked extremely thoughtful, and beckoned to her urgently.

"Yes, Cadoc, what is the problem?" she said, coming across to him with a smile.

"Very serious, my Lady," he said quietly, leading her to one side, wiping the good humour from her face immediately. "Look you, Mistress Brioni, I was round by that privy just minutes ago, with Landry and another of the lads. They were talking about the coming raid, saying as how it was Bath we are going to and not Swindon," and she gasped, her mouth a tight line, her brows ferocious.

"Oh, I shut them up pretty quickly," he said, seeing her face, "and warned them about loose tongues…but not before the word was out. I thought I heard a sound from that privy just then. It's only a very short step to where we were collecting charcoal and timber for the forge, but I could not be sure. I lingered afterwards, for just a minute or two, but I heard nothing more; and certainly I saw no rat and there was no shriek. I think she knows! The boys were not quiet; they had no reason to be. But Jaenberht and I agree, if she was in there…then she knows!"

"By God and St Michael, Cadoc, that is ill news indeed! If she does then we could all be in deep trouble, Grimnir also. But keep it close to your chest, the both of you," she added, looking up at the big Saxon huscarle who had lounged over to join them with Rollo in his hands. "I do not want her to know what we suspect.

"I have to go up to find Godric. Our message must get through to Grimnir, and then to Guthrum by tomorrow, for Oscytel to move his men out, and for Guthrum to attack Ford on Friday, the day after everyone has left. The timing is critical if Leofric is to be clear to assault Bath on Saturday.

"You and Jaenberht must watch her like a pair of hunting hawks while I am with Godric, and she has completed her own bit of business. And not that

461

kind of business either," she said tersely to his arched eyebrows. "If she tries to escape, seize her!"

"And if we can't?" Cadoc asked, looking at her directly.

"Then shoot her down! That's why you have brought your Syrian bow with you, because you can use it from horseback. Now, 'ware hawk, my friend, she is upon us. All smiles, my little Welsh archer, and you, Jaenberht. She must not know that we suspect her.

\*

Gytha saw them waiting for her and gritted her teeth. What did they know? Why the subterfuge of Swindon if they knew nothing? Or was Lord Leofric so uncertain of them all at the settlements, as to suspect that loose talk might be a danger? Certainly not all were with Eadwine, like that Ethelred who made such a fuss the other morning…and her foolish husband! Was that all it was? Just being careful? She looked at the three of them, all smiles and laughter, and shivered. Not just the cold seeping into her from without, but a sudden frisson of fear that she was in deadly danger. But, surely if they suspected her they would arrest her now? Tie her up and drag her back to Ford in utter black disgrace. But look at their smiles and gestures of friendship…no-one could be like that and be sincere. Could they? But that Jaenberht looked murderous. No smiles there now, whereas before he had been all sweetness and light. Was that a sign? Or had the little Welshman said something to upset him? They were not always friends, and the big Huscarle could be prickly. She shivered again and straightened her back as she strode towards them.

Somehow she must get to Chippenham! Give the three of them the slip at the market; then off along the back lanes to the old Saxon fortress town, now home to the Danish King and his whole entourage. Once there and she would be safe.

# Chapter Sixty

Up on the tops Biddestone market was shrouded in mist, even thicker if anything than down below in the deep valleys. No sunshine at all. Colours muted, flags and signs limp, as there was little breeze to move things along, people draped in long capes with hats and hoods on their heads, everything wet and dank. Even the pie sellers were lacklustre; their wares damp, despite wide linen covers over them. And on that chill morning nothing stayed hot for long, going from just warm to cold and soggy quite quickly. Even their hand bells lacked the bright sound of a few weeks ago.

In the beast lines there were fewer animals on show as the Danes had done so much damage to the local markets. Sheep and cattle were in smaller stalls; geese and chickens in short supply, most animals being taken to Chippenham where the Danes had need of them to feed their men. And with the horse fair due to be staged at Chippenham in just a week's time, there were few beasts for sale, more donkeys and mules, and not many of them either.

And there were fewer stalls that morning. No armourer offering weapons and coats of war; no potter with his glazed bowls and dishes, oil lamps and tableware, and no exotic draper offering silks and satins, sendal, damask or fine linens.

They left their horses on a hitching rail put there for the purpose, watched over by a couple of urchins for a silver penny that Brioni bestowed on them with a brilliant smile - a gift astonishing them into a stunned silence that made Jaenberht laugh. They hitched up their hoods and walked through the market, suddenly anxious that the big cobbler should be there, so few were the visiting merchants' stands that day.

But Godric's big tent and sprawling stall were right where they had hoped they would be. Fine leathers and suedes were set out under cover of his wide tarpaulin that reached out from the broad entrance to his tent, its fringe dripping with soft water all along its edge. Oscar, lounging on a thick fleece in his large wicker basket just inside the tent itself, his long chain pegged out as usual, roused himself to greet his master's visitors with a great playful *wooof!*

"So, two lovely ladies to visit me today," the big cobbler said, coming forward from inside, his eyebrows arched in surprise. "And on such a miserable day, too. Surely you bring brightness and light into my life. Your beauty is such that I am dazzled by it," he said with a smile, looking both girls over carefully, especially admiring Gytha's lovely white deerskin cape. "Surely you outshine the sun, which given the day, does not say much after all!" and they all laughed. Even Jaenberht joined in, who had been taciturn the whole of their journey up from the forge, constantly looking around him with his hand on his sword as if a whole bunch of the Heathen were about to rush out upon them.

Offering them mulled wine instead of ale was a treat he had been saving for a while as wine was expensive and not so easily come by in those troubled times, the merchants being so wary of travelling. Nevertheless, he had his own charcoal burner for such a luxury, and the spices to give the wine its full flavour, so it was not long before they were all settled around the big trestle table he always used.

"You have come for Cuthbert's boots, I suppose, young Gytha?" he asked the girl, looking her squarely in the eye.

"Yes," she replied precisely, without a quiver in her voice, while her heart beat wildly and her feet jumped; the others watching her avidly. "His mother has sent me with the money to pay for them. I had hoped to find you here, but with so many troubles around I was not sure."

"Oh, the troubles are not a bother for me. Guthrum's men serve my needs well..."

"After all," Brioni interrupted him with a wry smile, "you are the best this side of the River Thames. Correct?"

"So I have been informed," he replied with a studied shrug of his shoulders, and an incline of his head towards her. "All sorts of people come to me for a fitting, and well-made shoes. Even the hand maid of the Queen herself," he said, his sleepy eyes fixed on hers with a smile.

"Just so, Godric, only this time it is a pair of fleece-lined boots that I need, not stylish palace shoes. I will come in to your tent presently for you to take my measurements after you have dealt first with young Gytha," she said clearly as she looked him full in the face, her eyes unblinking as she sipped spiced wine from her own horn, beautifully polished and limmed with gold.

"So, let me get these boots for Cuthbert that his mother has so generously paid for," he said, sorting through the coins that he had tipped into his palm from the scarlet bag that Gytha had handed to him. "There are too many here," he said, pushing six of the silver coins to one side. "I do not say one price and then charge another. So you take these back and do what you will with them, as I am sure Mistress Aelfrid will have already determined." And with a warm smile he gave them back into Gytha's hand, which swiftly closed around them.

"Thank you, Godric. She thought there might be too many coins, and has bid me spend the remainder freely where I will. So, if Cadoc will come with me," she said calmly, rising from her place, her heart beating a desperate tatoo in her chest as she put down the ceramic drinking bowl that Godric had given her, "I will go amongst the stalls and see what I can find while you deal with the Lady Brioni, and fetch Cuthbert's boots." And with a nod of her head towards the tall cobbler, she looked around them all briefly and without another word flicked her deep fur-lined hood over her head and turned away, Cadoc following close behind her after a deep look at Brioni, his hand on his seaxe, his bow and quiver still over his shoulder.

*

"So, the two of you together," Godric said as Gytha swept out into the misted market place. "That was a surprise. Does she know?"

"Too damned much!" Jaenberht growled nastily. "I would have had her hog-tied by now and her blood on the ground, the treacherous little bitch! How you can stomach her lies, my Lady," he snarled at Brioni, "is beyond me!"

"Because to have such a brou-ha-ha as her disclosure, and that of her husband, would make on the very eve of setting out tomorrow would be a real disaster. Noah's flood would be small beer in comparison!" she replied to Godric's astonishment.

"Setting out?" he queried anxiously.

"Yes! But not out here!" she replied tersely. "In your tent where you can also take my measurements for those boots you promised me."

"So, follow me my Lady," he said grimly, getting up swiftly and moving to the big tent behind him, Jaenberht following close behind. "And you can tell me all the rest." Pausing to put Oscar on guard outside beneath the wide awning, he pulled the tent flaps closed and brought them both to the table within, on which his wine warmer was standing on its small charcoal burner.

"That is in part what we have come to do today," Brioni said quietly once she was seated, Jaenberht standing just behind her. "To tell you that Bath will be Leofric's last raid, and both settlements are pulling out before dawn tomorrow."

"Where to?"

"To Battlesbury hillfort above Warminster."

"*Everyone?*"

"Yes, Godric, everyone! But the message for Guthrum is all about assaulting Swindon, not Bath. The Danes must believe that Swindon is the Iron Hand's target. We need Oscytel to pull all his men out of Chippenham, leaving Bath isolated with no more men than it has already. And at the same time we are telling Guthrum that Ford is where his enemies lie hidden, so he will take his forces and assault it. It is all in this message," and she pulled it out of her jerkin pocket and slid it across the table towards him.

"This it?"

"Yes. It must reach Guthrum tomorrow, in time for him to make a raid at first light on Friday...but there is a serious problem."

"What is that?"

"We think the girl knows that the attack is really to be on Bath. Worse, she also knows that someone close to Guthrum is a traitor. She has no name to spill," she said swiftly, "but even what little she knows is a deadly danger. "

"Grimnir!"

"Exactly! So tell him, and tell him that it is time to tell Guthrum about Ford; that way he may be able to convince the Danes of his faithfulness.

"For Alfred's sake we need to do all we can to keep him in place. His information about the enemy must have helped the King hugely, and Alfred will want to keep that flowing. But if he must get out, then he is to get to Warminster; to the hillfort on Battlesbury hill above the river Wylie. You too, Godric. If you feel in danger, then get out fast."

"And the girl?" Godric asked dangerously.

"She goes with us. Her husband is with Leofric. He goes on the raid tomorrow and is in terror of it, and desperate to have his new boots. Is that them?" she asked pointing to a handsome pair of dark brown leather boots standing in a corner in a wicker basket of their own.

"Yes," he said with enormous pride. "Steel toes and curved steel over the instep beneath the laces, and up the shin. They are heavy, but will withstand stabbing and cutting blades. He may lose his life on Saturday, but he will not lose his feet!" And they all chuckled.

"I must have a pair like that," she said, as Godric went to pick them up. "They're lovely. And some for Leofric; they are just what every good war-leader needs," she said, running her hands over them. "And made to fit, wonderful!"

"Now, my Lady," Jaenberht growled, tapping his feet. "Let's find our little 'pigeon' and get back. Every moment she is out there makes me nervous. As I said, she knows too much...and may yet guess the rest. Unlike her stupid husband, that one is as sharp as any knife in the box, and I will not feel happy until we have her safely back at Ford."

\*

466

The moment Gytha was outside, her mind was alert for any chance she might have of escaping, and with Cadoc beside her, she set out across the wide market, her white cape drawn close around her, its hood pulled well over her face.

Everywhere there were people looking and buying despite the weather, some of necessity, others for the fun of it, and often items were exchanged for barter as coins were hard to come by: so many chickens for a good copper bottomed skillet with a turned wooden handle; or a prime goose for a donkey colt or a set of leathers, embroidered jacket and tough trousers. And everywhere there was noise: stall holders calling out their wares, buyers dickering over their purchases, women in groups chattering about their problems, fingering goods, exclaiming at prices and children skittering amongst them all with shrieks of laughter or shouts of rage and temper.

Through all of this Gytha made her way, noting where her horse was at all times and what stalls lay between them, stopping at some and moving on to others, but always coming back to the donkey stalls where half a dozen dejected-looking beasts were standing heads down to the hazel hurdles that penned them in, where there was a bucket of water and another of broken cabbage ends.

Right beside the donkeys was a deep stall for baskets and woven rush works, some large for clothes and linens, others smaller for eggs, pegs and fallen fruits. And just beyond was a wide covered stall for iron skillets, pans and tripods, with deep pots and cauldrons and the chains from which to hang them, even a magnificent copper pot and cover that had many admirers. And not twenty paces from there were their horses, and the two youngsters who were watching over them, together with a motley collection of scruffs all desperate to see the amazing silver coin that Brioni had given to their friends.

Cadoc, who by now was thoroughly bored by the whole procedure, stopped beside the donkeys for the third time. He liked donkeys, with their neat little feet, dark crossed backs, big eyes and doleful faces, and while the girl stopped by the basket stall, and chatted to the skillet man next door about his large copper pot…"Four silver pennies, Mistress. And none finer this side of Winchester"…he sighed and leaned over the pen to fondle the nearest pair of long grey ears.

"And what about this skillet?" she asked the wizened stallholder, lifting one off the wooden stand to feel its weight, looking round as she did so to where the nearest basket was amongst a pile of others on a large square of canvas on the ground.

"A fine piece, Mistress," the trader said, squinting his eyes at her, noting the fine clothes she was wearing, the quality of the material and the smart half boots on her feet in scarlet leather to match her kirtle. "Copper bottomed, as you can see. Two silver pennies for it…and a half," he added, looking at her sideways from the corner of his face. "Just feel the weight of it," and he moved away from his stall to give her more room, while others clustered round him to see what was going on, and join in the fun; all knowing that two and a half silver pennies was an outrageous charge, even for a copper bottomed skillet!

And with that Gytha took her chance. Calling Cadoc's name she stepped forwards, swung the heavy skillet round and as he turned towards her she brought it down on his forehead with a *thump!* that knocked him to the ground, leaving him slumped, almost unconscious, against the hurdles that kept the donkeys penned.

Dropping the heavy pan, while everyone shrieked and scrambled out of her way, she rushed into the basket stall and seizing the nearest large basket, tipped it over his head where an impressive 'egg' was already forming. Pushing over a hurdle she drove the donkeys out, who fled with wild *hee-haws* and kicking heels away from her as she ran to where her horse was hitched to the rail. Scattering small boys in all directions, she unhitched Gemma and leapt onto the mare's back, pulling her head round to face towards St Nicholas' church at the far end of the market, almost opposite the main trackway that led directly to Chippenham five miles away.

And digging in her heels she drove the startled mare through the market, leaning forward against Gemma's withers as she fled, knocking stalls over as she raced by, with goods and chattels tumbling everywhere and people leaping out of her way with shouts and cries. Past the church she went at a wild pace, her white cloak fanning from her shoulders like wings, and turning left-handed onto the trackway beyond she rushed towards Guthrum's Danes, and freedom.

Behind her was turmoil, anger and distress as donkeys were chased, market stalls were restored, small boys collected and Cadoc rescued from his plight. The basket taken from his head and pulled to his feet, he was appalled by the manner in which he had been felled, and in moments he had reached for his bow. But by then it was far too late. He was still muzzy from the blow he had taken, his head throbbing wildly, the 'egg' on his forehead of frightening goose-like proportions, and it was in that state that he lurched back to the cobbler's stall, ignoring the massive dog who leapt towards him with a deep woofing bark, and almost fell inside to deliver his message: " She's escaped!"

## Sixty One

*F*earful for her life, Gytha pushed the mare through the heavy mist as fast as she dared, galloping the first miles in a wild spray of mud and slush from her flying hooves, before slowing to a fast canter as she raced through the thick mist. But soon she was forced to pull up to a swift trot as she had to thread her way through scattered groups of people leaving the market, as well as those wending their way there, it being still some time before midday.

Constantly she looked behind her, terrified that her pursuers should catch up with her before she reached the town. She had no knowledge of weapons, indeed she had no weapon on her, and would be no match for the Lady Brioni whom she knew to be a doughty fighter, and one whom the men respected, and she put her hand up to her neck and shivered. One slash across her throat with the girl's seaxe and it would be all over for her.

Sweating despite the chill, she kicked her tired mare on again along the narrow trackway as it wound through great stands of timber and across bleak open countryside. Past burned out buildings and rows of graves by the wayside, she pushed on towards Chippenham and the Danish King's hall where once King Alfred and his family had stayed in happier times.

\*

*B*ehind her in the cobbler's tent all was wild consternation, with everyone blaming everyone else for what had happened, while Cadoc sat slumped under the awning, his head swimming and feeling sick, a bowl of hot spiced wine under his hand, his bow dropped in a corner with Oscar guarding it.

"We must get after her," Brioni said briskly through tight lips. "And as soon as possible. Jaenberht, you come with me. Cadoc must bide here with Godric until he is better. Then he must go back down to Ford and tell Leofric what has happened. This is all an absolute disaster. The very worst imaginable," and she sat forward at the table, her head in her hands and felt like weeping. Leofric had trusted her and now this! It was almost more than a girl could bear.

"Do not despair, my Lady," Godric said quietly. "All may not be lost. You may yet get her back before she can do any harm."

"*How?*" she snarled, turning on him with a swift flash of rage. "Even if we leave immediately she will still be in Chippenham before us. I know the town well. Once through those gates and she will be lost to us. The place is not big and the King's hall is just at the top of the hill above the river. Through the gates, up the hill and she is right there at the front of Guthrum's hall. Nothing could be easier!" and she flung herself off her stool and went and leaned against one of the tent poles, glowering out across the market, her eyes going to the horses on the rail and to the gap where Gemma had been tied up just a few minutes before.

"You are forgetting something in all this, my Lady," Godric said calmly, drinking from his glazed bowl.

"*What?*" she snapped, turning baleful eyes towards him.

"The Danes! The Danes themselves," he answered her calmly. "Chippenham is not run as it was when Alfred was at home. There are guards everywhere, and anyone wishing to enter, or leave the place, must have a pass. Even more so to get anywhere near the King. Blue to enter the town, or leave it, and red to enter the King's hall. Guthrum knows how easily he gulled Alfred into allowing his army to get into the best defended fortress in all Wiltshire, and he is not about to suffer the same plight!

"She may get to Chippenham, my Lady...but she will not get inside it. *Not today!* He emphasised strongly. "She may plead she has a message for Guthrum of burning importance all she likes. But she still will not get inside until all she says has been checked out. Especially as she is a girl on her own with no man to speak for her. The Danes are very tight on things like that. Guthrum likes things done properly, and he is not there today."

"What?" she asked amazed, her heart beginning to beat more steadily. "Where is he?"

"He has gone to see what is happening near Cricklade, where the ships come up from London. Remember he is a Viking at heart, and Vikings like ships. So she may rail at them as much as she pleases, but without the King's say so she will not get in tonight."

"What about the Lord Oscytel? Surely he will see her if not the King?"

"Oscytel's star is not so high these days, thanks to your man and his war group. Too many good men have died. It is Guthrum's word that is law in the Great Army. After all, he is still their King, not the Black Jarl, for all he would like to be."

"So where will she stay?" Jaenberht growled at him

"Where she can find a place. Has she any money?"

"A little. That which was left from paying you," Brioni replied more calmly, coming across from where she had been brooding.

"So…half a dozen silver pennies! That is a small fortune these days, and will buy her accommodation and a good supper, especially at the 'Stag', the only inn worthy of the name in Chippenham beyond the walls. Even a bath, if she is lucky, and still have plenty left over for another day."

"We don't have time for another day, Cobbler," Jaenberht snarled, banging on the table. "*Everyone leaves tomorrow!* We need the Lady Brioni to lead us, and Leofric leaves to assault Bath. Grimnir needs our message, and to know about the danger he stands in if this little bitch gets through the Danes' cordon. We need her back tonight. So let's mount up now and get after the little cow."

"Right!" Brioni said sharply. "We have talked enough. We leave now, Godric, and will take my message with us. Hugo the Bearmaster has his tents and equipment parked outside the town. And his daughter is a great friend of mine, as I said when I first met you. We will go there and see what can be done. He will know all the places that a girl might stay, including the 'Stag', and will know just where to find Grimnir Grimmersson. Then I can give it to him."

"*Don't do that, my Lady!*" he urged her vehemently. "If the Danes stop you, and they may, and search you, and find that message on you, then your life will be forfeit for certain. And don't think your sex will save you. These are men of the Great Army, and they will spare you nothing. Leave the message with me and I will see it safely on its way as usual. I shall be in to Chippenham tomorrow, and can have it before Guthrum in plenty of time for it to do its work. Of course, if you should see Grimnir then you can tell him all, but the message will still travel in the usual way. Just don't get caught with it on you!"

Brioni looked at him steadily and nodded, her face grim.

"That is good advice. I thank you, Godric, with all my heart. I shall do as you say," pausing just to hand it over swiftly, before turning to where Cadoc was still sitting looking dazed and ill.

"Now, my friend, when you are feeling stronger, you must go from here to Ford, and tell Leofric all that has happened. He will not blame you, any more than I do. These things happen and you should not have left here without Jaenberht to back you up. That is my fault. I did not stick to my orders, so he cannot blame you for that. I blame myself. But tell him that he is not to come looking for me. He is to ready himself to leave tomorrow morning as arranged. Nothing must stop that. If I need help I will get all I need from Hugo the Bearmaster. You understand, Cadoc?" she repeated tersely, her face creased with worry at the way the little Welsh archer was looking, and his lack of ready response.

"I understand, my Lady Brioni," he said eventually. "I will tell Lord Leofric all that you have said, and will be on my way presently. But my head hurts and is very buzzy. If I try to ride Charlie now I will just fall off, but after I have had the rest of this mulled wine I will leave, I promise you."

"You're a good man for a Welshman," Jaenberht said then, with a pat to his shoulder. "I should have been with you. We all underestimated the girl. She caught us all on the hop. Stop blaming yourself, and take the weight of it off your back, just get to Ford as soon as you can. God willing we will be back with you before nightfall."

And with that, thanking Godric for all he had done – and for all his advice - they left without another backward glance, striding to where their horses were still under their scruffy guard, and unhitching them they rode off swiftly through the market and along the same road that Gytha had taken not half an hour before.

*

Ahead of them the Saxon girl rode as swiftly as she could towards the town that she could now dimly see through the persistent fog that still shrouded everything, nestled in a tight bend of the river Avon that flowed round three sides of it, and across which there was just the one bridge, built of massive timbers round which the Avon rushed in a swift flow, bubbling white and busy as it raced through them.

Steep earthen ramparts ran all round the town, with tall towers at either entrance, both front and back, crowned with a great palisade of huge logs behind which armoured men were walking, their spears and helmets clearly visible as they moved.

But it was not the town itself that caught her eye so much as the ramshackle shanties that had sprung up all around it outside: shacks, barns, bothies of every sort, cruck houses, chicken sheds and goose shelters, byres and stables, a two storey inn with side buildings attached and a little warren of lanes and alleys that ran all through them. And off to one side, in a pasture of its own, a massive tent of brightly striped cloth, like the sails of several dragon boats, with more tents clustered around it, horse lines, stables, carts and wagons of every sort, including one great wagon with bars all round it, part covered with its own canvas roof, round which a host of people had gathered with trumpets blowing nearby. And she pulled Gemma off the trackway to consider her next move.

Where to now?

She knew no-one in the town, though she had been there before when Alfred was still King of Wessex, not 'King of the Marshes' as so many referred to him now. Then she had either been with her father, or with Eadwine and his family, and always been protected and honoured, a young girl of good family with prospects and all the trappings of wealth. Now she was on her own, with no man to speak for her, and expecting the Danes to let her in to see their King. And on whose say so? A young girl on a grey mare with a fancy cape across her shoulders? She felt suddenly daunted, and slumped in her saddle, head between her hands as the true awfulness of what she was attempting struck home for the first time.

Treachery to her true King and to her family.

Surely if this failed she would be slain; the hand of all good Saxons would be against her. But she was not on her own in believing the Saxon King to be doomed, and the Danes the ones to deal with. Why should she be any different from those Thanes who had already abandoned their duty and either fled abroad or paid tribute? The fact that her treachery, if successful, would result in the death of all those around her, including her husband, did not move her.

*She hated them all!*

And straightening her back she kicked on towards the town, upright in her saddle, but moving towards the town beyond the walls and not the great tented area that lay to one side. She knew about those tents. That Saxon bitch had told her all about them. About Hugo the Bearmaster, his daughter Maritia, her friend Julio the acrobat and of Oswald the bear. They might not know her...but she knew of them and had no wish to meet up with any of them for fear they would seize hold of her until Brioni could get there, and then all would over. And she put her hand to her neck again and shivered.

Minutes later she was deep amidst the narrow ginnels and alleys that separated the houses from one another, and led to a wide open area before the bridge itself, where there was a communal well with stone water troughs around it. This area was heavily guarded with a ring of hard-faced warriors before the bridge itself, in black steel byrnies and nut-shaped nasal helmets, armed with swords, spears and axes, each man with his shield on his back, the ragged knife in gold, rimmed with scarlet, boldly painted on each great plate of thick linden and leather.

*Jomsvikings!*

She shuddered. She knew about these men, the Lord Oscytel's personal warriors, ruthless when fighting, who were closely examining every person who wished to enter the town. Checking passes, which she did not have and

473

had no idea where to get hold of...and a lone female would get nowhere without a man to speak for her.

She remembered that now and suddenly despaired.

How could she get near them to give her message? She suddenly felt defeated and sat her horse like a half-filled sack of meal, while Gemma dipped her head into a stone trough and slaked her thirst.

But if she had eyes only for the armed Danes before her, and for the whole ramshackle collection of houses, bothies, inns and assorted buildings that made up Chippenham beyond the walls, there were others who had eyes on her, including very sharp eyes that viewed her white, deerskin cape with astonishment on that dank, grey day with the mist still heavy on everything, shrouding man and beast alike, all walking like wraiths.

Eyes that having looked, and recognised with surprise, now moved towards her on neat, purposeful steps.

*

Grimnir Grimmersson had been walking towards the gateway when his senses had been caught by the sudden movement of a horse and rider coming into town from the Biddestone trackway, and with Brioni very much on his mind he had stopped to watch...and been astonished.

This was no everyday Saxon churl on the usual nag, which was commonplace. This was an attractive woman, beautifully dressed in the most exotic cape he had seen in many months, with scarlet underdress and half boots of finest leather in the same colour, and looking more out of place than if a peacock had landed, with tail spread, in a dirty barnyard. And he stopped in his tracks as did several others, equally astonished at so much easy largesse so suddenly placed before them.

But there was something else...*he knew who this girl was!* He had seen her before, and with that knowledge came action of both body and mind. For she was plainly unescorted. The Lady Brioni was nowhere in sight and no others appeared to be guarding her, and in this town, at that time, that was essential.

No one dressed as she was would escape attention, and attention of the most unwanted kind, as he could already see several men nudging each other in preparation to making a move towards her, for not only was she plainly worth good money...but so was her horse, a beautiful dappled grey with a fine head and neck, lustrous eyes and strong quarters. And stepping forward he came up to her and put his hand on her horse's neck.

474

"A fine beast, Mistress, if I may say so," he said in his precise voice, every word beautifully modulated. "I have not seen so lovely a mare in many months. Are you new in town today?"

Gytha, astonished to be so addressed, looked down and saw a small man with silver hair and beard, neatly dressed in dark green leather trousers, cross gartered with blue linen strips, a blue tunic top in fine suede with red fastenings under a long plaid cape, with green harp bag on his back and scarlet boots on his feet. A man who spoke beautifully and smiled up at her with real warmth and kindness.

"Yes!" she exclaimed, eagerly wanting his friendship, indeed as he had intended she should do. "I..I have come ahead of my party," she said hesitating briefly, inventing swiftly as she went along, suddenly realising how strange it must be for a well-dressed girl of good family to be on her own in a strange place. "I was too excited to wait, my servant's horse threw a shoe and I came on alone. I need to get into the town. We are staying with Godric the cobbler. He is well known here. My family have known him for years." That at least was true, as Grimnir knew, but not the rest.

"Did he not tell you that you cannot just enter the town as one used to do when the King was here? You will need a pass, and that you cannot easily get without a man to speak for you, or you being known by the guard."

"Then what can I do?" she asked then, a note of panic in her voice.

"Come with me to the inn over there," he pointed to a large stoutly built house of two storeys across from the well, on the other side of the wide open space before the bridge. "Beorhtwulf, the innkeeper, is known to me of old, and his wife the redoubtable Thelflaeda. You can take shelter there until your party come through. And then we can see about a pass into the town. I am well recognised by the guard and so is Godric. He makes shoes for the Danish King, Guthrum. Did you know? With us to speak for you, you will not have a problem. I know the commander of the King's guard well, Bjorn Eriksson, he will be sure to help us."

And helping the girl down from her horse, he took Gemma by the bridle and without leaving Gytha the chance to object, he led them both towards the large inn he had pointed out, while others who had thought to accost her slunk away into the mists that filled the streets and disappeared.

"You are very good to me, sir," she said shyly, looking at him from beneath her wide fur-lined hood. "Who are you?"

"I am Grimnir Grimmersson the Skald, harper and glee man to the King. I told you I was well known to the guard."

"King Guthrum?"

"Is there any other king in Chippenham today?" he replied, looking at her deeply, his mind a kaleidoscope of thoughts.

"Are you a friend to the King, Sir?" she asked breathlessly, almost unable to believe her good fortune. "To Guthrum? Would he trust you?"

"Why? Mistress…?"

"Gytha of Ford," she answered him with a bright smile. "Please Sir Skald…would he trust you?"

"The King? Yes, he trusts me in many things. Why does that matter to you?"

"I carry an urgent message for him," she said then, stopping to face him, her eyes fixed on his. "A message that only I can give to him. Please will you help me? You are close to him, and can get me before him. There is not a moment to lose."

"But the King is not here, my dear," he said quietly.

"*What?*" she exclaimed appalled, panic in her voice. "*Not here?*"

"No…but calm yourself, child. There is another to whom you could speak with if it is a matter of life and death that you carry with you."

"Who?"

"The Lord Oscytel. It is his men who guard the King, and the town; whom you saw checking everyone who leaves or enters the place. The King guards his security closely."

"The Black Jarl of Helsing?" she asked, terrified, almost shrinking from his grasp.

"You have heard of him?"

"All men have heard of the Lord Oscytel. He is a dread lord with magic powers," she whispered, looking all round her as if he would appear at any moment before her, and she swallowed hard. "But if King Guthrum cannot be reached, then bring me before the Jarl himself. Once he knows the news I carry, he will reward you well, I assure you," she said more firmly, clutching his arm. "And me also for all the risks I have taken in your cause!"

"Very well. If it means so much to you," Grimnir replied, patting her hand as she spoke, and smiling warmly at her on his arm. "I will see what I can do. But first let me get you safely settled here. I will tell Beorhtwulf that you are only waiting for your family to arrive, he will be satisfied with that. Then you can tell me all you know before I go in search of the Black Jarl, for he is not easily reached," he lied, knowing that the Lord Oscytel was lounging in the King's Hall at that very moment. "It may take even me some time to find him, and persuade him. So, bide you well here," he said as they reached the Inn's deep entrance, an ostler running out to take her horse, "and all will be well.

476

Now, come and I will introduce you to your host, and his lady, and they will make you comfortable."

# Chapter Sixty Two

*M*eanwhile, Brioni and Jaenberht had also reached the outskirts of the town in a spray of mud and torn grasses, their horses steaming in the chilly air, and had reined in to look around them.

This was the first time that she had been near the place since leaving for her home just after Christmas, and despite all that had happened since then it looked just the same! The river sliding by in its usual rush, the ramparts, the palisade and bridge…and the huddle of roofs within the walls, all the same; and the same with Chippenham beyond the walls. More troops perhaps; it was hard to see in all the mist that stubbornly persisted, and now a huge raven banner flew from each of the entrance towers that guarded the gateway. But the biggest difference was still beyond the walls, where a monstrous tent of faded blue and scarlet stripes had been thrown up in the paddock where Alfred's cattle had formerly been pastured, together with a host of other tents and wagons, and Brioni leaned forward in her saddle and smiled, pointing to where it lay.

"Come on, Jaenberht, that's Hugo's encampment. We'll go there first. If all that Godric said is true, then either he, or Maritia, will know where we must look to see if we can find her. God knows, in that mess of pottage down there, there cannot be many places where a young girl could stay…or would take her in with no baggage and no servants to support her. I wonder if she thought of that when she took off this morning?" And jagging in her heels she kicked on, Rollo following with a snort and side swipe of his tail, as their riders picked their way through people, carts and driven beasts towards where Hugo's stables had been thrown up, not far from Oswald's great travelling wagon.

Around it there was already a sizeable crowd, many watching open-mouthed as a young woman, with long black hair and in black leathers and scarlet boots, fed the great bear by hand and cuddled up to his massive shoulders. Plodding by, Brioni paused to watch, and applaud, throwing her hood back off her head and laughing, her short blonde hair flying up as she did so. Many eyes caught that movement, some startled by the unusual beauty of such a sight, some stirred by the grace with which this strange girl sat her horse, but not all were friendly. There were those that watched her with slitted eagerness, as she and her escort pushed on to the stable area, recognising her as someone their master had long looked for, and who eeled silently away through the crowd to tell him that his patience had finally been rewarded.

*

*M*oments later, as she strode through the deep flaps of the tent's entrance, there was a roar from within as Hugo the Bearmaster caught sight of his new visitors, striding forward to sweep Brioni up in his arms as if she were a baby, batting Jaenberht with his hands as he did so, a buffet that almost made the big huscarle stumble, while a dozen faces came popping up to see what all the fuss was about, and swiftly joined in the homecoming.

"*Well!*" the big man exclaimed, putting her down at last. "This is a joyous occasion, and here we were thinking you had forgotten us all!"

"No such thing, Hugo," Brioni panted, checking to see she had no cracked ribs, so warm had been the giant's welcome; as Maritia came rushing in just moments later, her face flushed with pleasure, to sweep Brioni up in a deep hug of her own, and many kisses.

"I knew it was you when I hear your laughter. Where have you been? What have you been up to? How is Leofric?" Maritia asked in a rush of words. "We have heard bits and pieces, of course, from Grimnir and Godric…"

"You know Godric?" Brioni asked her, astonished.

"Everyone knows Godric who wants good footwear. He is the finest…"

"…This side of the Thames River!" Brioni finished for her, laughing. "Yes I have heard his boast before. But listen, sweetheart. I do not have time for chatter. Not now. I have a desperate problem that I hope you will be able to help me with…" And with no further ado, she brought Maritia and her father to the table on the dais, and while Hugo shouted for mulled wine and fresh bannocks from the long-suffering Gilbert, she told them both all she knew.

*

"*S*o…" the huge Bearmaster said, sitting back in his great armed chair as Brioni and Jaenberht stopped talking, "the little traitor has fled here and hopes to speak with Bjorn Eriksson, or even with the King himself. But she has no pass and no-one to speak for her, until Godric himself gets here, and that will not be until tomorrow. And Guthrum is not here."

"No, so Godric told us. He has gone to Cricklade, something to do with boats up from London," Brioni acknowledged with a wave of her hand. "But we need to find her today!" she said urgently. "Leofric leaves tomorrow to assault Bath, and I leave to lead the settlement travellers to Battlesbury at first light. We cannot afford to have her loose in the town a moment longer than is necessary. The knowledge she carries is deadly! What can we do?"

"Julio and I will go round the town presently, starting with 'The Stag' opposite the bridge. There are very few other places that she could stay, but we will search them all."

"That was a favourite of Alfred's when he went hunting," Brioni chipped in. "They always came running out with mulled ale and Easter biscuits, hounds and children everywhere and half the town to see the King and his companions off; the shouting, hallooing and barking, and the lovely costumes, especially the Queen and her ladies," she said wistfully.

"Well, not any more since the Danes came," Maritia said, with a bite in her voice. "They do not hunt as Alfred used to do...at least not the deer and the wild boar. Just Saxons!"

"So, you will start with Beorhtwulf and Thelflaeda at the 'Stag'," Hugo said in his deep voice, "and work outwards. There are only two other places, but I would not recommend either of them, they are little better than stews. Pigswill would have more nourishment in it than the food they serve! But they might take her in for the money she has with her. Poor child, she will be lucky to last the night!"

"'Poor child' indeed!" Jaenberht growled, banging the table. "Nasty little traitor who would have us all dead! Her whole family as well. Eight inches of sharp steel would sort her out nicely!" he snarled, drawing his seaxe and banging its hilt on the table.

"Well, well," a man's clipped, precise voice called out from the edge of the dais, making everyone swing towards him with astonishment. "Are we talking of the lovely Gytha, fresh from her escapade at the market? Or is there another traitor that I need to know of who walks abroad in Chippenham this day?" And onto the raised dais, with a horn of mulled wine that Gilbert had given him just minutes before, stepped the neatly dressed Norse Skald, Grimnir Grimmersson. Silver hair and beard neatly brushed, scarlet boots on his feet, and plaid cape flowing from his shoulders, his arrival was quite unexpected, and they all gaped at him.

"I see you are amazed?" he queried them cheerfully. "Come, drink with me, for I have your little pigeon safe, and know all her secrets." And lifting his horn, he drank to them all...and they in stunned silence repeated the honour.

"You have her?" Hugo boomed a moment later.

479

"Yes! Safely in the 'Stag' across the way with Thelflaeda clucking over her, and Paega their ostler looking after her horse, which is a real beauty."

"Not her horse, her mother-in-law's horse," Brioni said with a grin. "And she wants it back! So hands off the horse, Skald."

"Pity," he replied with a smile and nod of his head, "because the horse is so much nicer than the rider who is as nasty a piece of work as I have come across in some time. Not only is she quite willing to sell your lives to the Danes anyway, but quite happy for that to be in the person of Oscytel as of Guthrum…and is cheerfully willing to unmask me as well, I understand?" he added grimly.

"She does not have your name," Brioni said soothingly.

"No…but Guthrum is not stupid, and Oscytel even less so. It would not take a man of his ability long to work it all out very quickly. And I rather like my body in one piece, not spread about in bits beneath the greenwood trees!" he said succinctly. "After all there is no-one closer to the King, and the Black Jarl, than I!"

"Yes," Brioni said wincing. "I had rather Leofric had not said what he did. But there really was no other way at the time. But with God's will, Grimnir, you have found her for which Leofric will reward you well, or I will from my father's hoard which Hugo has been holding safe for me since I left him nearly two months ago."

"And that is a fine thing, my Lady Brioni, and I will be pleased to accept your largesse. But immediate action would not be wise. She is safely cooped up, and like to be eating her head off as I left sharp instructions that she was to be fed…and I have advised her, most strongly, that if she wishes to meet with Oscytel she should keep to her room and not mingle with the common herd below in the great room.

"So she is quite safe where she is," the little harper went on. "But it grows darker outside and that always makes the Danes jumpy. They patrol the perimeter of their defences at dusk. It is a bad time of day for them, evil spirits walking abroad and such like. They are even more superstitious than we are, and they are likely to seize hold of anyone moving around before they close the gates for the night. That will be the time to go and 'liberate' your pigeon. It may make your journey home more difficult in the dark, but at least you will not be bumping into any Danes!

"Just bide your time with our host's excellent mulled wine, which grows better the more I drink of it," he added with a broad smile, "and tell me all I, or the King of the Marshes, need to know that the Lord Leofric Iron Hand has been up to. Our Lord King has been active too and will shortly be stirring the thanes and fyrdsmen of Wessex into action."

"The muster at Ecberht's stone, Grimnir?" Brioni asked eagerly, her eyes shining.

"Yes…but you will not be here by then."

"No, and that is why it is so important to be away from here, with that wretched girl, as soon as possible!" And reaching for a bannock, a dish of which with honey and butter Gilbert had placed on the table, she reminded Grimnir of all that was about to happen, filling in whatever gaps that Gytha had left in her story; telling him that the right message for Guthrum was coming with Godric the following day and to reinforce Leofric's advice to get out to Battlesbury at once if he should feel his life seriously threatened. The same advice as was given to Hugo and the *Circus Maximus*, the big Frank nodding his head in understanding, while they all settled to a cheerful exchange of news and information that Brioni particularly enjoyed, feeling safe and cosseted by Hugo and his daughter whose company she had sorely missed.

*

While all this was taking place, Gytha, in the 'Stag', was resting having been nobly fed by Beorhtwulf and Thelflaeda in her room, one of just half-a-dozen off a narrow gallery along the side of the main house. This was reached by a steep staircase that led down into the great room of the inn, where there was a central fire; from where blue wood smoke spiralled upwards to a wide smoke-hole high in the roof space.

This room was very simple with a box bed, canvas covered mattress of straw and lavender, with coarse linen sheets and heavy woollen covers and hand stitched counterpane. There was a low wooden chest against the wall, with a simple oil lamp on it, and a table on which a glazed bowl of slow-cooked belly pork with onions and mashed turnip, flavoured with sage and garlic, had been placed with fresh white bread, and she had also been given hot water and potash soap with which to clean herself.

By the time she had washed and eaten, and used the covered bucket in her room, it was getting dark and cold, and she was very glad of her fur-lined cape with which she lay back on the bed, a woollen blanket pulled over her, while she prepared herself for the meeting to come with the Lord Oscytel. So it was not surprising that in the end she fell asleep.

Outside the mist still lingered as the late February daylight faded, and lights came on in the houses round about, every window like a small haloed moon in the murky darkness. Below in the inn people gathered slowly; the fire in the centre of the great room built up so that the flames writhed and twisted and drove the darkness away into the far corners of the building. The enormous wood box in a corner of the room was filled, simple oil and tallow lamps were lit, and men gathered round the row of barrels on rough cradles that lined one side of the room, from which Beorhtwulf in his leather apron and his assistants, men and women both, would tap the beer into big jugs ready to pour it into the drinking bowls and horns that every man brought with him.

Beyond the inn the town was settling for the night, as with horns booming the great gates of the fortress town were hauled close and fastened, and the guard was doubled. Flambeaux were lit above the battlements, while behind the palisade that ringed the town armoured men moved steadily around. In the King's Great Hall, with the Lord Oscytel in command, his friends and companions flooded in for food, drink and wassail, in all their finery, their weapons left outside...strong beer and sharpened steel not being an easy mix where boastful warriors were concerned! So only his personal guard was allowed to go fully armed. With Guthrum absent, the Black Jarl occupied his seat of power, with only the harper's chair empty, the famous Norse Skald out about the town that night, and not within the hall as many had hoped, as there was no-one who could tell a tale, or harp a tune as he could.

*

O ne by one Brioni, Maritia, Jaenberht and Grimnir slipped out of the huge tent like drifting shadows and disappeared amongst the mist-shrouded, ramshackle buildings that made up Chippenham beyond the walls. Sliding along the narrow alleys and ginnels that ran amongst the bothies and mean houses, they made their way towards the Stag.

Leading the way with a faultless sense of direction and skill, were Grimnir and Maritia, deeply cloaked but not carrying weapons; while Brioni and Jaenberht, went armed and similarly cloaked, their hoods up and their faces hidden as they rushed from alley way to alleyway, pausing and running, pausing and running. The stench of rotting food and dung was rich in all their nostrils, mixed with the heavy, earthy scent of the river itself as the Avon flowed heavily round the ramparts on its long journey to the sea.

With the town closed up there was little danger of coming across Danish warriors in the darkness, but the enemy were not the only danger abroad in the thick murk of that February night, for robbers, masterless men and hired killers also lurked amongst the noxious lanes and pathways between the houses, always ready for a chance to thieve and murder in the dark passages of the night. The bodies left to be found in the morning, no questions asked, and then tipped into the river, or buried in a common pit with no-one to raise a prayer for their souls. For these were perilous times, and all men who stirred about

Chippenham beyond the walls after dark went in armed groups, or stayed at home.

Yet despite all their care there were other, secret, hungry eyes that watched them from the darkest places that murky night, marked where they went and knew the paths they travelled...and lurking in the deep shadows were content to bide their time.

Then, quite suddenly, Grimnir's hand flew up and they were there, right beside the ancient Stag inn that had stood before the river since the days of Brioni's grandfather. Outside its iron-studded oaken door two flambeaux flared and flickered, the flames wavering in a light wind that had sprung up from the east, the mist making them strange and unworldly as they twisted in their iron holders, the scent of hot tar and resin heavy in the smoky air.

"Right! Here we are," Grimnir muttered quietly. "Once inside, busy or not, we go straight round the walls to the staircase opposite. Just slip in and follow me. Beorhtwulf knows we are coming so you will not be hailed. Keep your hoods up, especially you, my Lady with your short hair. You do not want a hue and cry after you. I will go first. Gytha has been told to wait for my voice. She will not answer to anyone else and we do not want screams this night. So, swiftly in and bind her mouth. She will be shocked rigid to see you, my Lady, so do not miss the moment. Now, come on!"

And with his own hood up, he turned the handle and opened the door...and a wave of noise and heat rushed out upon them from within, which was packed with people, almost all men, some with their dogs at heel or sprawled across the floor, some slumped in corners, others standing and laughing, the only women those who worked in the great room, and in the kitchens with Thelflaeda, while Beorhtwulf rushed with jugs of ale and beer for his army of drinkers, almost as much spilt on the floor as was inside them. The noise was tremendous, as was the heat from the fire, leaping and crackling in its long stone-edged trough down the centre of the room.

Pushing their way swiftly amongst the great throng of folk who had gathered at the inn that night, they reached the staircase at the far side of the great room in moments, none speaking, while Grimnir raised his hand in silent salutation to their host who briefly nodded his head before turning away to deal with yet another customer.

Then they were mounting the stairs, their cloaks flowing around them, their hoods pulled well over their faces, Jaenberht's tall figure bringing up the rear.

Paused beside a door at the end of the narrow gallery, Grimnir knocked sharply on its scarred surface and called through the woodwork in his neat precise voice: "Come, open the door Mistress Gytha. It's time for your meeting. The Black Jarl waits for no man, so open swiftly." And with a rattle of metal the lock turned, the door swung open and they were in.

The moment she saw who had come to greet her the colour rushed out of the girl's face and she almost fainted with sheer fright, as Brioni strode swiftly forward and grabbed her by her arms. Giving a pitiful squeak, she held her hands out and cried: "No! No!" while Jaenberht expertly thrust a cotton square into her open mouth, and then bound it in with a short length of linen strip that he had brought with him.

Petrified with fear, unable to move as much because Brioni had her arms pinioned behind her as from panting, palpating terror, Gytha's eyes rolled up in her head and she collapsed onto the floor in a dead faint.

"Quick, search her, Maritia," Brioni ordered tersely. "She has a message on her somewhere, and we must find it!"

So, while Brioni turfed the girl onto the bed on her back, Maritia tore open her tunic and her chemise, and rummaged between her breasts until, with a sharp cry of success, she seized hold of a folded square of cheap parchment and held it up for all to see. "Got it! Now, let's see what the little bitch has to say for herself," and turning away from the collapsed girl on the bed, her clothes torn awry, her breasts spilled out of them, pale and pink tipped in the lamplight, they all clustered around the large lamp on the chest by the wall to read what had been written:

'*Warning. Urgent. The Fox leaves for Swindon on Thursday. Come quickly and tear them apart. This is the third time of writing. Beware. There is a traitor close to the King and the Black Jarl. I have no name, but he is close to both and knows them well. He is Alfred's man in your midst. Kill all, but save the land for me. Cuthbert of Ford.*'

Grimnir snorted in disgust, and crumpled the parchment between his hands before Brioni snatched it back, smoothed it out and re-read it, mouthing the words as if they were too soiled actually to be spoken.

"And you want to take this piece of human debris back to Ford?" Jaenberht snarled, indicating where Gytha still lay spread out and unconscious on the bed. "I would cut her throat here and now and be done with it. She is not worth the trouble and danger to us one moment longer. You have told Grimnir all he needs to know and Godric will be in tomorrow, so all can go forward as planned. Rhonwen can find another message amongst her yeast and barley, and Grimnir can tell those bastards up there whatever he likes because none of us will be there come tomorrow's sunset."

"*No!*" Brioni said, swiftly. "I cannot kill her in cold blood. That would be murder. That would make us no better than the Danes whom we despise so much for what they do. No, we will bind her and carry her back with us to

Hugo. Tie her to a horse and get her back to Ford. We cannot take her own beast, that will take too long. Looks as if you may get that horse after all, Skald," she said grimly. "The Council must decide her fate, and that of her husband," she added, thrusting the still crumpled message into Jaenberht's hands. "They may choose to hang her if they please, but I do not want her blood on my hands today. Now, come on," she said to the room at large. "We have lingered long enough, and must be gone from here before Beorhtwulf or his lady come to see what we are about. The right message will come in with Godric tomorrow, and as Grimnir said earlier, we do not want the hue and cry after us tonight!"

*

*G*ytha, terrified out of her senses, in fact came to quite swiftly and lay there on the rumpled bed in desperate, panting silence, pretending unconsciousness, while they read out what she had written, her heart hammering in her chest, swiftly aware that Jaenberht had not tied the gag into her mouth securely, nor tied her up in any other way either.

And then, eyes opened as narrow slits, she watched them clustered round the lamp at the other side of the room, her mouth clemmed with the cotton cloth that she tried desperately to expel with her tongue, twisting her head from side to side to remove the linen strip that Jaenberht had used to tie it in, unwilling to make too much movement with her hands for fear of attracting their attention.

She heard Jaenberht say that he wished her dead, but that Brioni would not allow it, and with that the strip fell off her face, she drove the gag out of her mouth and in the same instant she shot off the bed, legs pumping, a scarlet streak already beginning to shriek like a banshee as she raced for the door, still open after everyone had rushed inside.

*

*A*t the first sound everyone turned and shouted, or tried to get in her way to seize her, but only Jaenberht moved like lightning, turning, lifting and hurling a heavy throwing knife from behind his head in one smooth movement, flashing it across the distance to slam into the back of the fleeing girl's neck, at the very base of her skull. With frightening power it cut off the sound in an instant and flung Gytha stone dead upon the floor, spread-eagled, hands and feet splayed apart, her spinal cord shattered, her neck broken apart and her heart stopped before any blood could flow spurting onto the dirty floorboards of the room.

And there was stunned silence, then a rush of relief, while Jaenberht strode forward and plucked his knife out of Gytha's neck, wiped it on his trousers and put it back in its sheath.

"So, that's that then!" he said a moment later, looking calmly round at their shocked faces. "And don't expect me to show any sorrow. She was as nasty a little traitor as I have come across in years. She needed putting down, and now I have done it…before she put us all down as she intended. Now what do we do?"

"Pick her up as if nothing has happened," Grimnir said in his precise voice, shutting the door as he spoke, "and carry her out, wrapped up in her deerskin cloak, as if she were asleep. That's your job, Berti," he said colloquially, with a grim smile. "You put the little bitch down, so you can carry her off. And please remind me to be very careful around you in future. I have never seen anything like that before. Astounding! Someday, I will have to put it all in a song!"

"And I remember what you said about Oscar that day we first met with Godric," Brioni chipped in quietly, as the big man bent to pick the dead girl off the floor. "I asked Eadberht later if you had meant it, as I didn't believe it possible…but I certainly do now!"

*

*M*oments later they were all packed up and leaving; Gytha's body cradled against Jaenberht's shoulder as if she was asleep, her eyes closed, her small body still supple enough to be so held, her white deerskin cape covering all of her, especially her neck from where a small seepage of blood had leaked out of the wound.

Blowing all the lights out and closing the door behind them they went down the stairs in the same order they had come up, Grimnir leaving them briefly to give Beorhtwulf some money and to thank Thelflaeda for her kindness, explaining that the young lady's people had come in at last; that he was returning her to their care and would come back for the horse in the morning.

Then they were outside in the night, the sky clearing at last before the east wind that had blown up as they had left Hugo's tent, so that now there was a glimmer of moonlight that would see them all safely home, and a hint of stars in the sky, wracks of cloud skimming the moon's face from time to time, casting black shadows over everything.

486

Briefly they paused together for a final whispered talk, to say 'good luck', 'farewell', and 'see you soon'...Brioni lingering to have a last word with Grimnir who then bustled off back to his own lodgings in Chippenham itself. Knowing that he had arranged with the guard to let him in through the sally port, within the great left hand valve of the gates themselves, he had no concerns. Meanwhile Jaenberht marched on ahead, with Maritia close by his side and Brioni some way behind and hurrying to catch them up.

Round the edge of the square they went, back the way they had come, Maritia now leading the way, hurrying through the ginnels and alleyways, the moon's light going black-white, black-white as the clouds fleered across its face, looking forward, looking backward, always trying to see where the next turn would be. So when the attack came Brioni was completely unprepared for it.

One moment she was following in her friends' footsteps...the next she was fighting for her life, hampered by her skirts and by her cloak which she could not fling off her shoulders, so she took two sharp blows on her arm before she knew what was happening. Not sword cuts, cudgel blows from men not out to slay her...but to seize her! And with that realisation she finally shrugged off her cape and drew Blood Drinker, swinging round to confront her enemies while calling out desperately: "*To me! To me!*"

Four of them there were, maybe five, shadowy, snarling creatures of the night, hulking figures who threatened her on every side, and she taunted them to bring them closer in, wishing she had her shield and long sword to give her greater reach.

Then they were rushing in on her, cudgels swishing hand over hand, jabbing and striking at her like snakes, calling to each other in Norse. But she had not worked her heart out on the practice ground for nothing, and twisting her body backwards and sideways she lashed out with her long-bladed scramaseaxe and felt its edge bite deep and heard the great yowl of pain as one of her attackers lost all interest in the fight, his hand lopped from his wrist to lie like a discarded glove in a fountain of blood, making all the others draw back with hisses and growls of hatred.

"*To me! To me!*" she cried out again, and at last heard Jaenberht's shout from a distance as he dropped his burden and came running back to find her in the darkness.

But already her enemies were closing in again, growling like beasts and grunting with the efforts they were making to overwhelm her. Again she took a sharp blow on her shoulder, but turning she drove her blade up and over the clumsy weapon her enemy was using and felt her blade sink into the man's belly with a whoosh of foetid air and rush of blood over her wrist, and heard the howl of pain as his bowels were ripped out of him, and still they came after her, this time without hesitation. More oaths and cries in Norse, so no common thieves then, these fighters. Common thieves would have given up long ago and run off into the night. These were professionals, mercenary Danes hired for the job, Vikings, and she gritted her teeth with determination. They would not take her easily.

"Hang on, my Lady!  *Hang on!*" she heard Jaenberht's desperate cry as he searched in the shadowed darkness for where she was fighting.  "*I am coming!*"

But next moment they were on to her again even more fiercely than before, one man teasing her to step forward and fight him, the other two angling to take her from the side. Difficult...so she slipped away until she could put her back up against a wall they could not get round, and now she began to fight back, dashing forward and lunging and cutting at her foes, taking their blows on her blade and parrying with swift turns of her wrists, like steel springs after the weight of a lead-covered practice blade with Trausti shouting out behind her!

Again she disabled another of her attackers, brushing his cudgel away with her shoulder and slicing into his leg with her sharpened steel so that he fell crippled and writhing on the ground, his blood spraying black in the stippled moonlight..

And then there were two.

One man rushing in on her from the front to engage her fully, a great bear of a man with Danish on his lips, words she knew from Beornred and Finnar, with a longer reach than his fellows and not afraid to hazard himself against her long-bladed scramaseaxe, a proven fighter almost as fast as she was, who used his long cudgel like a sword, *Stab! Stab! Stab!*...while she parried furiously and longed for Jaenberht to come and rescue her.

And while the one man attacked her front, leaping in on her with his swordlike cudgel, so his companion attacked furiously from the side, batting at her sword arm, not daring to come in closer like his fellow, but continuously hampering her until suddenly one sharp reverse blow just caught her on the point of her elbow, a sizzling shock of stunning agony shot up her arm and into her hand...and she dropped her sword.

The next moment they were on her like tigers on a goat. And while the smaller man knocked her silly with his cudgel, the larger grabbed her arm and, sliding his other through her legs, threw her over his shoulders and rushed off with her into the stinking darkness of the night.

Just moments later Jaenberht arrived gasping, to find only the remnants of the fight:  one man dead; one handless and dying, and another with his leg almost ripped down to his ankle who would never walk again. But of the Lady Brioni of Foxley there was no sign, just her cape in a distant corner and her fallen sword.

She was gone...and leaning against the wall where she had fought so bravely he lifted his face and shouted his rage and despair to the stars.

# BOOK TWO

## The Ravens Fall

*Athelney, the Somerset marshes: March 878.*

### Chapter One

Athelney on a wet day, Heardred thought, gazing morosely out across the dreich, windswept marshlands that surrounded him, was probably the most gloomy, lonely, and miserable place in all Wessex. God knows they were safe enough from prowling Danes, but the emptiness, the constant sighing swish and rustle of reeds; the rippling chuckle of water, and the endless keening bird calls were sometimes enough to make a man doubt his sanity.

Surrounded by the miry boglands, reeded waterways and rhynes of the River Tone and its fens, the high ground of Athelney, and nearby Lyng, raised themselves out of the ooze and drowned wetlands like floating islands in a swampy sea. A vast watery desert made tidal by the rise and fall of the River Parrett where it flowed into the sea. The water extended for miles, almost as far as the eye could see, with the huge hill of Burrow Mump towering up in the distance. To those who knew its secrets there were many paths and hidden trackways that led to every 'island' heart, but to strangers it was an eery, misted place of intimate danger that could swallow men and horses without a trace, sucking them down to a desperate death, their last despairing cries echoed by the curlews across the waving reed beds.

Eight weeks or more since they had first arrived there, saddle sore and weary…and still he could not forget her, his Brioni. She had become an even more important part of his life than he had realised. And now that he had lost her, he felt as though only a part of him still lived. Even her name, *Brioni*, still conjured a picture of such sweetness and flowering beauty that it made him want to cry out, a pain so deep it was embedded in his very soul.

He sighed, and turned to look around him at the dozen or so horses busily cropping at the tough sward left over from the winter, and the new grass just beginning to spring into life, and at the remains of his battered command. Those that remained to him from the constant warfare to which he had committed them all in defence of Alfred's lost kingdom. The desperate raids, the fierce cut and thrust with sword and spear at a brutal enemy, the howling rage and spitting fury of every fight, the blood and stench of close combat, the agony of wounds and the loss of good men who could not easily be replaced.

Dear God, but they were a sorry lot from those who had set out from his home at the cusp of the New Year, before Guthrum had burst out of Gloucester and raced across Wessex to seize Chippenham and destroy the king.

A dozen men less.

Some killed, some wounded and left behind in Athelney, and the remainder now stood in little armoured groups quietly discussing the day's activities, their shields on their backs, swords by their sides and long spears grounded at their feet. Their armour no longer shone, but was dull with usage, helmets dented and tough leather hose scuffed and streaked with mud.

And how much he missed the companionship of his friends, of Edwin and Harold...and how he wished they could all have come south together instead of having to split up after the horrors of Foxley.

He coughed in the fire smoke and smacked his big hands together as he turned to crouch down over the flames that Baldred had finally managed to coax into sulky life after the heavy overnight rain, and warmed his hands. The man was a miracle worker. He knew of no-one who could get wet wood to burn the way he could. No matter how terrible the conditions her had never failed them yet, never setting out anywhere without his fire-pouch well stuffed with dry grasses and fine chippings, neatly chopped kindling and a fat pair of flints.

Now he looked at the flames flittering and sparkling around the crude pyramid of sticks and twiglets that Baldred had built in the great hollow beneath a huge fallen tree, its twisted roots making a fine over-hanging shelter, and shivered as he cracked his knuckles over the flames.

The journey down to Athelney had been a nightmare.

Mercifully the days had been too crowded with the simple problems of staying alive and free from the Danes for his mind to dwell on the misery and shock of finding Brioni's body so brutally hacked and mangled. So unrecognisable.

For two days they had pushed south-west as hard as their beasts could carry them, and in some of the bitterest weather that anybody could remember. A real wolf-winter, when the stars were brittle-edged with diamonds and the

491

frost-rime lay finger deep each frigid morning, the raw breath freezing on the beards and whiskers of man and beast alike. Nights when the grey brothers howled to each other from the forests and deserted uplands, the *woo-ooo-ooo* of their calls making the hair stand on end of every man who stood guard; and days of hard riding, sometimes on proven trackways, and always with the threat of pursuit to spur them on.

Changing horses whenever possible, even at sword point on occasions, they had pressed on relentlessly. Sometimes they had found willing shelter in some loyal hall, but more often they had been forced to spend the night huddled round a great fire in some wretched clearing in the bleak woodlands that lay all round them, or in some burned out, half-ruined hall, watching the hungry eyes of prowling beasts beyond the leaping firelight, flicker and blink out...only to reappear balefully somewhere else.

And all the time they had been aware the Danes would follow them hard, knowing that they must keep constantly on the move, even doubling back on their tracks to throw Guthrum's flying raiders off the scent of their desperate quarry. Truly all Wessex seemed in turmoil, whole villages fleeing into the woods at their approach, terrified they were heathen outriders of the Danish host that had burst like a steel wave across the land, carrying death and destruction in their raven wings.

Nor had they escaped unscathed.

Just past Chippenham, on the long road to Bath and Taunton, they had been forced to fight off a band of Guthrum's marauders. Mounted Vikings who had been driving hard to seize Bath, both sides coming together in a violent blood and steel hell in a white-washed world. Horses twisting and biting in a spray of snow and torn ground, the savage thrust and hack of spears and swords, the screech and spark of blades and the roar of men fighting for their lives; the screams of the wounded, blood spewing from heads and arms; entrails torn out in obscene loops and spirals, hands lopped and the bang and smash of shields.

It had been a furious skirmish at the back-end of a long day as the sun had tilted in a scarlet ball towards the misted hills. A fierce struggle that had left eight of the enemy spread-eagled on the torn ground along with two of his own men, with others wounded, bruised and battered by the fight; while the survivors of Guthrum's war-band had fled, their blood flying in scarlet splashes as they went, the horses of their dead racing away with them in snorting terror.

Finally at Glastonbury they had drawn breath, pausing at the old abbey to take stock of their situation, to gather news of the King, for fresh food for man and beast, and a last night's rest in peace and comfort before the final stage of their long journey into the desolate miry wastelands that surrounded

Athelney. And it had been there, amidst the quiet of the ancient building, with its pattering monks, hushed chanting and deserted grounds that he had at last come to terms with his bitter loss. There was something timeless and ethereal about the place that had drawn his heart and mind into more peaceful waters than at any time since he had left Foxley.

Though her memory would live with him always, there were others now to whom he was responsible, who looked to him for leadership and a safe passage through the harshly troubled times in which they found themselves. He would still grieve for her, for her beauty, her loving warmth and gentleness, her sparkling spirit and her laughter. His body would still yearn for her, and he would still hear her voice whispering to him on the wind, and turn and call her name.

But there, in the faded ruins of the abbot's garden into which he had wandered unawares, in the thin sunlight of that bleak January day, he had finally said goodbye to her, folding their love into his heart like a precious flower whose summer glory would never die.

For one moment he had stood there wrapped in thought amongst the tangled weeds that filled the abbot's herb beds, the piercing sweetness of a robin's song the only sound to break the silence. His heart suffused with longing and sadness as the myriad pictures of her ran through the dark recesses of his mind like a sun-drenched river, he stared unseeing into the chill, misted distance. Then, with a sigh, he smiled and kissed the wind, his eyes suddenly filled with tears. She was gone, and life must go on...and yet he felt her close, as if he only had to turn quickly round and she would be there, arms outstretched to hold him, lips already parting for a kiss.

He shook his head and smiled at his foolishness. It was only an illusion, and turning his back on the solitude he had so badly needed he had gathered his cloak around him and quietly walked away, committed to wreaking a terrible revenge upon his enemies that would not end until he had seen Guthrum cast down, Oscytel slain and Alfred returned to his rightful place as the true King of Wessex.

*

Since then he had filled his days with fighting and constant warfare. The Heathen had taken her from him, and they should pay full score in blood and gristle for his loss. No task that Alfred gave him was too difficult or dangerous for him and his men to attempt. They had become the shock troops of the royal warband, and wherever he led, his command always followed, crupper to crupper, there was no separating them.

They killed the most Danes and took the most booty as a result, stripping the dead of armbands, coins and armour wherever they killed them, terrifying friends and foes alike with the ferocity of their attacks and their single minded determination to wipe the Viking pirates from the face of God's earth. And it was in pursuit of just that need that they had left the King a few days since to follow up a loose report that had come in from one of the more remote villages on their northern flank.

A small group of outlanders had been spotted quartering the marshes in that area. It could have meant anything. In those parts the word 'outlander' covered anyone who wasn't a fen dweller. On the other hand it could have been a sign that the Danes were on the move against them. It had happened before – after all they had been raiding and killing out of Athelney for nigh on two moons now – it couldn't just be left unexplored. So he and his men had left to enquire into it. But that had been days ago, since when they had found nothing. It was very frustrating…and the foul weather did not help!

He sighed and poked the fire with a stick, and huddled deeper into his cloak. If only it would stop raining and they could get a sight and feel of the sun. Then this bloody mist haze would lift clear of the drenched land and they might really see something worthwhile. If nothing else they would all feel a deal more cheerful. Much more of this and their clothes would rot and they might even take root and become one with the countryside. One more day of this and he would lead them back to Athelney, and good riddance!

"So, what's new in the world this bright and sunny morning?" a harsh voice broke in on him suddenly. "You're looking more clenched than a fist full of nails!"

"Oh, it's you old friend," he replied, twisting round to look up at the tall warrior who now loomed over him. "I thought I recognised your dulcet tones. Come and warm your hands, this filthy weather is enough to make anyone's muscles creak…is there any further news of our missing quarry?" he continued as the well armoured man he had been addressing chinked down beside him. "Dear God, but I wish these blasted peasants would get their information correct. Not hide nor hair have we seen of any enemy since we arrived here. Whoever it was must be long gone by now!" And he poked the fire morosely.

The man Siward was a hard-faced, rangy looking warrior with a shambling gait that belied his speed. His grey eyes missed little and his thick wrists and powerful forearms proclaimed the well-practised swordsman that indeed he was. A dangerous opponent at any time, he was a fury on the battlefield as many an incautious Danish carl had discovered as he breathed his last, his body shattered by the Saxon swordsman's brutal attack. He was a

494

loyal friend to those he took to, and after Foxley he had become Heardred's right-hand man.

"Nothing, lord, bar an old campsite or two, and they looked long abandoned. If there were Danes around here there can't have been many of them, or we must have come across their tracks by now. The Saints only know what those fools saw...but it certainly wasn't a war band of Guthrum's heroes."

"I agree. But you know what the King's like for information. So, we'll make one more sweep to the north-east, then call it a day and turn back.

"Aller and Stathe? Beyond Borrow Mump?"

"Why not? It may add a day to our journey, but it will be wonderful to ride dry ground once more before plunging back into that bloody mire around Athelney. And the people around there won't have seen any of the King's men for a moon's length. I could do with a good meal in my belly after the rubbish we have been eating. And a good night's rest under a proper roof would be a blessing."

"How long?"

"As soon as possible. We broke camp at dawn anyway, so it shouldn't take long, Tell the men to check all equipment and horses. Feet particularly. We cannot afford a lame beast today. And the sooner we are on our way the better. The weather's foul, and we have a long way to go."

*

*A*nd so it was done. Within a candle-bar's length they were all re-mounted and on their way again: peering through the cloying mists of rain, pleased to be on the move, but too collectively damp and low to make any but the briefest of conversations. Then, quite suddenly, not a mile from where they had set out, they came upon fresh tracks, three sets altogether, showing one man mounted and two on foot...and all making for Athelney.

Heardred, who was in the lead, flung up his hand and the whole troop came to a bouncing halt, their breath hanging in the chill, damp air, the steam rising in thin tendrils from the heaving flanks of their horses.

"So, there is strange life in these parts after all," he said briefly, turning to Siward as he did so. "I thought you said this section had been checked out already?

"It was, Lord, at first light. These tracks are very fresh."

"How long since?"

"Half an hour, may be more. These hoof prints are still quite clear...and two men in clogs. See, the rain has not had a chance to decay them yet. Trouble?"

"Most unlikely. Least of all not for us, and not a trap either. This pathway is obviously little used and no others have passed along it save those three and ourselves. If it were the enemy, they would be in far greater numbers."

"What now then, my Lord?" Baldred asked, coming up beside him.

"We'll take them; but no killing if we can avoid it. I doubt they'll show fight anyway, whoever they are. Well, would you when confronted by these ruffians?" he asked with a smile, looking round at his command, sitting glowering in the pouring rain. "I would sooner run than fight any day. So, come on. Let's find out who it is that dares to brave the wrath of the King on such a lovely day as this!"

And, with that, they dug in their heels and flew along the narrow miry path, the shaggy hooves of their beasts lost in a welter of dark spray and far flung oozy filth.

It was a wild ride that made each man want to shout and shake his spear arm in the air, despite the rain; the sudden release after days of painful, sludging progress a swift tonic that forced the blood through their bodies in a surging torrent. The sheer exhilaration of the ride driving each man to be the first to spot their quarry and reap the quiet praise of their leader.

Along the track they went at breakneck speed, their horses' heads stretched out in their efforts, powerful muscles bunched and pounding, nostrils thrown wide and eyes staring, while the foam from their snorting mouths flecked their riders like the salt spume from a curling roller on a storm wracked shore, and their tails streamed out behind them.

Careering round first one corner and then another they covered a half hours' journey in the length of time it takes to boil a white goose egg, and burst upon their startled prey like eagles, with talons stretched and curved beaks ready to rip and tear.

There were three of them. One mounted on a powerful bay in riveted mail byrnie, shield and spear across his back, and nut-shaped helm on his head, with face plates hanging open. Cloaked and spurred he forced his horse backwards, making no move to draw his sword, while the two men with him on foot, with wooden staves and mud stained woollens, threw themselves face down on the path with cries of terror.

Wrenching his mount's head up, Heardred brought his whole column to a rearing, plunging halt, then sat his steaming horse with hands crossed upon his pommel while Siward and two others leapt on the mounted warrior and

496

dragged him from his prancing steed, taking his helm from his head as they did so, and gripping him firmly by arm and shoulder so that he could in no way reach his weapons.

"And who are you to come so boldly into Saxon lands?" Heardred growled down at him, as his men held their captive motionless before him, hard eyes staring into hard eyes, with not a flicker of anxiety or fear to betray the stray warrior's thoughts. "A warrior by all you carry with you," he added, pointing to the man's sword and waving his helmet at him, that Siward had handed over. "Come now, your name and whom you seek, and I warn you to be careful how you answer. We have learned not to be too particular with prisoners for whom we have no care.

"Tell your guards to leave me be," the man replied smoothly, shrugging his wide shoulders in their grip. "I am a freeborn Saxon, as you seem to be yourself. And who are you to lay hold of peaceful travellers? Is it forbidden for a man to ride through Wessex that he needs must be arrested and questioned by any who may seek to say him nay?"

"Release him, Siward," Heardred gestured as he spoke, leaning back in his saddle, his eyes still fixed on the armoured man before him. "But watch him like a hawk! Now, friend, see, my men have stood you clear. They have even left you your sword and seaxe in your belt..."

"Still I have not your name," the tall Saxon warrior interrupted grimly, gesturing with his hands. "Nor your business in these parts, where Danes ride free and many Saxon lords support them!"

"I am the Lord Heardred of the Sommerseatas, and I ride for the King."

"Which King?" the man replied swiftly with a barking laugh. "There are two kings in Wessex now so I hear!"

"For the true King," Heardred snarled back, his hand flashing to his sword hilt, "for Alfred of the right line of Cerdic. Seize him, Siward!" he ordered sharply, waving his men back towards the big Saxon standing stiffly before him. "You are too bold and peremptory for my liking, Saxon. Watch your tongue or I may order it plucked out before it wearies me completely!"..............................................................................................................